MY STRUGGLE: BOOK 5

SOME RAIN MUST FALL

Also by Karl Ove Knausgaard

SOME RAIN MUST FALL

MY STRUGGLE: BOOK 5

KARL OVE KNAUSGAARD

Translated from the Norwegian by Don Bartlett

Alfred A. Knopf Canada

PUBLISHED BY ALFRED A. KNOPF CANADA

www.penguinrandomhouse.ca

Alfred A. Knopf Canada and colophon are registered trademarks.

'Death Fugue' by Paul Celan, translated by Michael Hamburger, from *Poems
of Paul Celan*, published by Anvil, 2007. Copyright © 1972, 1980, 1988, 1995
by Michael Hamburger. Reprinted with the permission of the publishers Carcanet
Press (Manchester, UK) and Persea Books, Inc. (New York, USA, www.perseabooks.
com), with thanks to the Estate of Paul Celan and Deutsche Verlags Anstalt, Random
House Germany.

Library and Archives Canada Cataloguing in Publication

Knausgård, Karl Ove, 1968–
[Min kamp femte bok. English]
Some rain must fall / Karl Ove Knausgaard ; translated from the Norwegian by
Don Bartlett

(My struggle ; 5)
First published with the title: Min kamp femte bok, in 2010.
Issued in print and electronic formats

ISBN 978-0-345-81554-5
eBook ISBN 978-0-345-81556-9

1. Knausgård, Karl Ove, 1968– —Fiction. I. Bartlett, Don, translator. II. Title.
III. Title: Min kamp femte bok. English. IV. Series: Knausgård, Karl Ove, 1968– . Min
kamp. English ; 5

PT8951.21.N38M5613 2016   839.82'374   C2015-907006-6

Cover photograph © Linn Heidi Stokkedal/Millennium Images, UK
Typeset in India by Thomson Digital Pvt Ltd, Noida, Delhi

The *My Struggle* cycle is published with the support of NORLA

Printed and bound in the United States of America

2 4 6 8 9 7 5 3 1

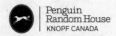

Penguin
Random House
KNOPF CANADA

SOME RAIN MUST FALL

The fourteen years I lived in Bergen, from 1988 to 2002, are long gone, no traces of them are left other than as incidents a few people might remember, a flash of recollection here, a flash of recollection there, and of course whatever exists in my own memory of that time. But there is surprisingly little. All that is left of the thousands of days I spent in that small, narrow-streeted, rain-shimmering Vestland town is a few events and lots of sentiments. I kept a diary, which I have since burned. I took some photos, of which twelve remain; they are in a little pile on the floor beside the desk with all the letters I received during those days. I have flicked through them, read bits and pieces, and this has always depressed me, it was such a terrible time. I knew so little, had such ambitions and achieved nothing. But what spirits I was in before I went! I had hitchhiked to Florence with Lars that summer, we stayed there for a few days, caught the train down to Brindisi, the weather was so hot it felt as though your head was on fire when you poked it through the open train window. Night in Brindisi, dark sky, white houses, heat as in a dream, big crowds in the parks, young people on mopeds everywhere, shouting and noise. We queued by the gangway for the big ship going to Piraeus with lots of others, almost all young and carrying rucksacks like us. It was forty-nine degrees in Rhodes. One day in Athens, the most chaotic place I have ever been and so insanely hot, then the boat to Paros and Antiparos, where we lay on the beach every day and got drunk every night. One evening we met some Norwegian girls, and while I was in the toilet Lars told them he was a writer and had been accepted to start at the Writing Academy in the autumn. They were discussing this when I returned. Lars just smiled at me. What was he up to? I knew he was prone to telling little fibs, but while I was standing there? I said nothing, decided to give him a wide berth in the future. We went to Athens together, I had run out of money, Lars was still rolling in it, he decided to fly back home the day after. We were sitting in a terrace restaurant, he was eating chicken, his chin glistening with fat, I was drinking a glass of water. The last thing I wanted to do was ask him for money, the only way I could get any out of him was if he asked me whether I wanted to borrow some. But he didn't, so I went hungry. The next day he left for the airport, and I took a bus to the suburbs, got off near a motorway slip road and started hitchhiking. After no more than a few minutes a police car stopped, the officers couldn't speak a word of English, but I got the message that hitchhiking wasn't allowed there, so I caught a bus back to the city centre, and with the last of my money bought a train ticket to Vienna, a loaf of bread, a big bottle of Coke and a carton of cigarettes.

I thought the trip would take a few hours and was shocked to learn it would be more like two full days. In the compartment were a Swedish boy of my age and two English girls who turned out to be a couple of years older. We were well into Yugoslavia before they twigged that I had no money, nor any food, and they offered to share theirs with me. The countryside outside the window was so beautiful it hurt. Valleys and rivers, farms and villages, people dressed in ways I associated with the nineteenth century and obviously worked the land the way they did then, with horses and hay carts, scythes and ploughs. Part of the train was Russian, I walked through the carriages in the evening, spellbound by the foreign letters, the foreign smells, the foreign interior, the foreign faces. When we arrived in Vienna one of the two girls, Maria, wanted to exchange addresses, she was attractive and normally it would have gone through my mind that I could visit her in Norfolk some day, perhaps start a relationship and live there, but on this day, wandering through the streets on the outskirts of Vienna, the idea meant nothing to me, I was still consumed by Ingvild, whom I had met only once, at Easter that year, but to whom I later wrote. Everyone else paled into insignificance compared with her. I got a lift with a stern-looking blonde woman in her thirties to a petrol station on the motorway, where I asked some lorry drivers if they had any room for me, one of them nodded, he must have been in his late forties, dark-complexioned and thin with deeply glowing eyes, first though he had to have something to eat.

I waited outside in the warm dusk smoking and watching the lights along the road, which were beginning to become more and more distinct as evening fell, surrounded by the drone of traffic, occasionally interrupted by the brief but heavy slamming of doors, the sudden voices of people crossing the car park on their way to or from the service station. Inside, people sat silently eating on their own except for a few families who swamped the tables they sat around. I was filled with an inner exultation, this was precisely what I loved best, the familiar, the known – the motorway, the petrol station, the cafeteria, which weren't familiar at all actually, everywhere I looked details differed from the places I knew. The driver came out, nodded to me, I followed him, clambered up into the enormous vehicle, put my rucksack in the back and settled in. He started the engine, everything rumbled and shook, lights were switched on, we set off slowly, gradually speeded up, but were still lumbering until we were safely coasting on the inside lane of the motorway, at which point he glanced at me for the first time. Schweden? he said. Norwegen, I said. Ah, Norwegen! he said.

Throughout the night and well into the next day I sat at his side. We had exchanged the names of some football players – Rune

Bratseth in particular had excited him – but since he couldn't speak a word of English that was as far as we got.

I was in Germany, and I was very hungry, but without a krone in my pockets all I could do was smoke and hitch and hope for the best. A young man in a red Golf stopped, his name was Björn, he said, and he was going a long way, he was affable, and in the evening when he had gone as far as he was going to go, he invited me into his house and gave me some muesli and milk, I ate three portions, he showed me some pictures of his holidays with his brother in Norway and Sweden when he was young, their father was crazy about Scandinavia, he told me, hence the name Björn. His brother's name was Tor, he said, shaking his head. He drove me to the motorway, I gave him my cassette of The Clash's triple album, he shook my hand, we wished each other good luck, and I took up a position on one of the slip roads again. After three hours a tousled bearded man in a red 2CV stopped, he was going to Denmark, I could have a lift all the way. He asked me questions, was interested when I said that I wrote, I wondered if he might have been a professor of some kind, he bought me food at a cafeteria, I slept for a few hours, we reached Denmark, he bought me more food, and when I finally left him I was in the middle of Jutland, only a few hours away from Hirtshals, so I would soon be home. But the last part of the journey was more difficult, I got lifts of thirty-odd kilometres at a time, by eleven in the evening I had advanced no further than Løkken, and I decided to sleep on the beach. I wandered along a narrow road through a low forest, here and there the tarmac was covered with sand, and soon dunes rose before me, I walked up them, cast my eyes over the shiny grey sea lying in front of me in the light of the Scandinavian summer night. From a campsite or a cluster of seaside cabins a few hundred metres away came the sound of voices and car engines.

It was good being by the sea. Breathing in the faint aroma of salt and the raw breeze off the water. This was my sea. I was nearly home.

I found a dip in the sand and unrolled my sleeping bag, crept inside, pulled up the zip and closed my eyes. It was unpleasant, anyone could stumble across me out here, that was how it felt, but I was so tired after the last few days that in an instant I was gone, as if someone had blown out a candle.

I woke to rain. Cold and stiff, I struggled out of the sleeping bag, pulled on my trousers, packed everything and set off for the town. It was six o'clock. The sky was grey, there was a light, almost imperceptible drizzle, I was freezing cold and walked fast to generate some heat. I'd had a dream and the images were still tormenting me. Dad's brother Gunnar had been in it, or his anger, that was because I had drunk so much and done so many bad things, I realised now as I hurried through the same low forest I had walked through the previous evening. All the trees were motionless, leaden, beneath the dense cloud cover, more dead than alive. The sand lay in mounds between them, swept up in their changing and unpredictable yet always distinctive patterns, like a river of fine sand grains traversing the coarser tarmac.

I came onto a bigger road, continued along it for some distance, put down my rucksack by a crossing and started thumbing. It wasn't many kilometres to Hirtshals. Though what would happen there, I had no idea. I had no money so it wouldn't be that easy to get onto the Kristiansand ferry. Perhaps I could arrange to have a bill sent on to me? If I came across a kindly soul who appreciated the predicament I was in?

Oh no. Now the raindrops were getting bigger as well.

Fortunately it wasn't cold though.

I lit a cigarette, ran a hand through my hair. The rain had made my hair gel sticky, I dried my hand on my thigh, leaned forward and took the Walkman from my rucksack, rummaged through the few cassettes I had with me, chose *Skylarking* by XTC, put it in and straightened up.

Had there been an amputated leg in the dream as well? Yes. It had been sawn off just below the knee.

I smiled, and then, when the music began to flow out of the tiny speakers I was taken back to the time the record came out. It would have been the second class at *gymnas*. Mostly, though, I was filled with recollections of the house in Tveit: sitting in a wicker chair drinking tea and smoking and listening to *Skylarking*, head over heels in love with Hanne; Yngve, who was there with Kristin; all the conversations with mum.

A vehicle came down the road. It was a pickup truck with a company name on the bonnet in red, probably a builder on his way to work, as he raced past he didn't even look at me, and then the second song seemed to rise out of the first, I loved this segue, something rose in me as well, and I punched the air several times as I slowly danced round and round.

Another vehicle hove into view. I stretched out my thumb. Once again the driver was sleepy and didn't acknowledge my presence with so much as a glance. I was obviously hitching on a road with a lot of local traffic. But couldn't they stop anyway? Take me to a main road?

Only after a couple of hours did someone take pity on me. A German in his mid-twenties with round glasses and a severe expression pulled over in a tiny Opel, I ran towards him, threw my rucksack onto the back seat, which was already full of baggage, and got in beside him. He had come from Norway, he said, and was on his way south, could drop me off by the motorway, it wasn't far, but it might help. I said, yes, yes, very good. The windows misted up badly, he leaned forward as he drove and wiped the windscreen with a rag. Maybe that's my fault, I said. What? he said. The mist on the window, I said. Of course it is, he hissed. OK, I thought, if that's how you want it, and leaned back in my seat.

He dropped me off twenty minutes later, by a big petrol station, I walked back and forth outside asking everyone I saw if they were going to Hirtshals and whether they would take me with them. I was wet and hungry, my appearance was a mess after all the days on the road, and everyone shook their heads until, a long time later, a man driving a van I could see was full of bread and bakery products smiled and said, come on, jump in, I'm going to Hirtshals. The whole way I kept thinking I should ask him if I could have something to eat, but I didn't dare, the closest I came was to say that I was hungry, but he didn't take the hint.

As I was saying goodbye to him in Hirtshals a ferry was just about to leave. I ran over to the ticket office with my rucksack heavy on my back, breathlessly explained my situation to the clerk, I had no money, would it be possible to have a ticket anyway and have the bill sent on to me? I had a passport, so could produce ID and I was a reliable payer. She smiled nicely and shook her head, she was unable to help, I had to pay cash. But I *have* to get across! I said. I *live* there! And I haven't got any money! She shook her head again. Sorry, she said, and turned away.

I sat down on a kerb in the harbour area with my rucksack between my legs and watched the big ferry slip its moorings, glide away and vanish from view.

What was I going to do?

One possibility was to hitchhike south again, to Sweden and then go up that way. But wasn't there some water that had to be crossed as well?

I tried to visualise the map, wondering if there was a land connection between Denmark and Sweden somewhere, I didn't think there was, was there? So you would have to go right down to Poland and then up through Russia to Finland and from there into Norway, was that right? A couple of weeks' hitchhiking then. And you would probably need a visa or something for the Eastern Bloc countries. Of course I could go to Copenhagen, that was only a few hours away, and then do whatever it took to get some money for the ferry to Sweden. Beg on the streets if necessary.

Another way would be to get mum to transfer some money to a bank here. That wouldn't be a problem, but it might take a couple of days. And I didn't have any coins to phone home.

I opened another packet of Camels and looked across at the vehicles that were quietly rolling in and joining the new queue as I smoked three cigarettes, one after the other. Lots of Norwegian families who had been to Legoland or the beach in Løkken. Some Germans heading north. Lots of camper vans, lots of motorbikes and, furthest away, the juggernauts.

With a dry mouth I took out my Walkman again. This time I inserted a Roxy Music cassette. But after only the second song the sound became distorted and the battery light came on. I put the Walkman away and stood up, swung my rucksack over my shoulder and set off for the town centre, through the few dreary Hirtshals streets. Now and then hunger gnawed at my guts. I considered going to the bakery and asking if they could spare me some bread, but of course they wouldn't give me any. I couldn't bear the thought of such a humiliating rejection and decided to save my efforts until I was in serious discomfort, and wandered back towards the harbour. I stopped in front of a kind of café-cum-snack-bar, where it would surely be possible to get a glass of water at least.

The girl nodded and filled a glass from the tap behind her. I sat down by the window. The place was nearly full. Outside, it had started raining again. I drank the water and smoked. After a while two boys of my age came in the door, wearing full rain gear. They undid their hoods and looked around. One of them came over to me. Were the seats free? Of course, I said. We got into conversation, it turned out they were from Holland, on their way to Norway and they had cycled up. They laughed in disbelief when I told them I had hitchhiked from Vienna without any money and now I was trying to get on the ferry. Is that why you're drinking water? one asked, I nodded, he asked if I would like a cup of coffee, that would be nice, I answered, he stood up and went off to get me one.

I left with them, they said they hoped we would meet again on board, took their bikes and were gone, I plodded over to the lorry queue and began to ask the drivers if they would take me along, I had no money for the boat. No, no one was interested, needless to say. One by one they started their engines and trundled on board while I walked back to the café and sat watching the ferry, which, once again, glided slowly away from the quay and became smaller and smaller until, half an hour later, it had disappeared.

The last ferry left in the evening. If I didn't get on it I would have to hitch down to Copenhagen. That would have to be the plan. While waiting I took the manuscript from my rucksack and read. I had written a whole chapter in Greece, on two mornings I had waded out to a little island and from there to another island with my shoes, T-shirt, writing pad, pen, cigarettes and a paperback copy of *Jack* in Swedish in a little bundle on my head. There, in a hollow in the mountainside I had sat all on my own writing. It felt as if I had arrived at where I wanted to go. I was sitting on a Greek island in the middle of the Mediterranean writing my first novel. At the same time I was restless, there was *nothing* there, only me, and it wasn't until that was all there was that I experienced the emptiness it entailed. That was how it was there, my own emptiness was everything, and even when I became immersed in *Jack* or was bent over my pad writing about Gabriel, my protagonist, what I noticed was the emptiness.

Sometimes I dived into the water, dark azure and wonderful, but I had hardly swum a few strokes before it occurred to me there might be sharks around. I knew there were no sharks in the Mediterranean, but I still had these thoughts as I scrambled up onto the shore dripping wet and cursing myself, it was idiotic, scared of sharks *here*, what was this, was I seven years old? But I was alone beneath the sun, alone by the sea and utterly empty. It felt as if I was the last human on earth. It rendered both my reading and writing meaningless.

Yet when I read the chapter about what I thought was a seamen's pub in the harbour quarter of Hirtshals I thought it was good. The fact that I had been accepted at the Writing Academy proved I had talent. Now all I had to do was demonstrate it on paper. My plan was to write a novel during the coming year, and then have it published next autumn, depending on how long it took to print and that kind of thing.

Water Above/Water Below it was called.

A few hours later, in the falling dusk, I walked along the queue of lorries again. Some of the drivers were dozing in their cabs, I knocked on the side windows and saw them give a jolt, then either open the door or roll down the window to hear what I wanted. No, I couldn't have a lift. No, that wasn't on. No, of course not, were they supposed to pay for my ticket or what?

The ferry was moored at the quayside with its lights blazing. Everywhere around me people began to start up their engines. One line of cars moved slowly forward, the first ones disappeared through the open jaws into the bowels of the ship. I was desperate but told myself everything would be fine in the end. Had there ever been any stories of young Norwegians starving to death on their holidays or being stranded in Denmark, unable to get home?

Outside one of the last lorries, three men stood chatting. I walked over to them.

'Hi,' I said. 'Could any of you take me on board? I haven't got any money for the ticket, you see. And I have to get home. I haven't eaten for two days, either.'

'Where are you from?' one asked in a broad Arendal dialect.

'Arendal,' I said, in as thick an accent as I could muster. 'Or, to be precise, Tromøya.'

'You don't say!' he said. 'That's where I'm from!'

'Which town?'

'Færvik,' he said. 'And you?'

'Tybakken,' I said. 'Could you take me then?'

He nodded.

'Jump in. Squat down as we drive on board. It'll be a cinch.'

And that was what I did. As we drove on board I sat huddled up on the floor with my back to the windscreen. He parked, switched off the ignition, I grabbed my rucksack and jumped down to the deck. My eyes were moist as I thanked him. He shouted after me as I left, hey, hang about! I turned, he handed me a Danish fifty-krone note, said he didn't need it, perhaps I did?

I sat down in the cafeteria and ate a large portion of meatballs. The boat began to move off. The air around me was full of animated conversation, it was evening, we were under way. I thought about my driver. Usually I had no time for his type, they had wasted their lives sitting behind a wheel, they had no education, were fat and full of prejudices about all manner of things, and he was no different, I saw that straight away, but what the hell, he had got me on board!

After the cars, lorries and motorbikes had – amid much revving and banging – driven off the ferry and onto the roads in Kristiansand next morning, the town lay still behind them. I sat on the steps of the bus station. The sun was shining, the sky was high, the air already warm. I had saved some of the money I had been given by the lorry driver so I could ring dad and say I was coming. His pet hate was surprise visitors. They had bought a house thirty kilometres or so away, which they rented out in the winter and lived in themselves throughout the summer until they had to start back at work in northern Norway. My plan was to stay there a few days and then borrow some money for a ticket to Bergen, perhaps catch a train there, whatever was cheapest.

But it was too early to ring.

I took out the small travel diary I had been keeping for the last month and entered everything that had happened from Austria onwards. I spent a few pages on the dream I had in Løkken, it had made such an impression on me, it was deeply entrenched in my body, like a barrier or a boundary I mustn't cross, it seemed important.

Around me the frequency of the buses began to increase, until at one point barely a minute passed without a bus stopping and disgorging its passengers. They were going to work, I could see it in their eyes, they had that vacant wage-earner look.

I stood up and went for a walk around town. The pedestrian street, Markens, was almost completely deserted, only a lone figure dashing up or down. Seagulls were pecking and snatching at the rubbish under a litter bin with no bottom. I ended up at the library. It was habit that drove me there, some of the same sensation of panic I'd had when I walked around there during my years at *gymnas* had me in its grip now, I had nowhere to go and everyone could see that, I had always solved this by seeking refuge there, the place where you could hang about without anyone questioning what you were doing.

Before me lay the market square and the grey stone church with the verdigris roof. Everything was small and dismal, Kristiansand was a minor town, I could see that very clearly now after having been in southern Europe and experiencing how things were there.

Against the wall on the other side of the street sat a tramp, asleep. With his long beard and hair and his ragged clothes he looked like a wild man.

I sat down on a bench and lit a cigarette. Just suppose he was the one who had the best life! He was doing exactly what he liked.

If he wanted to break in somewhere, he did. If he wanted to drink himself senseless, he did. If he wanted to hassle passers-by, he did. If he was hungry he stole some food. Fine, people treated him like shit or as though he didn't exist. But as long as he didn't care about anyone else, it was water off a duck's back.

This must have been how the first humans lived before they established communities and started farming, when they just wandered around eating whatever they could find, sleeping wherever seemed appropriate, and every day was like the first or the last. The tramp had no house to return to, no house to tie him down, he had no job to attend to, no schedules to keep, if he was tired, well, then he lay down wherever he was. The town was his forest. He was outdoors all the time, his skin was tanned and wrinkled, his hair and clothes filthy.

Even if I wanted to, I could never end up the way he was, I knew that. I could never go mad and become a tramp, it was inconceivable.

An old VW camper van stopped by the market square. A plump, lightly clad man jumped out on one side, a plump, lightly clad woman jumped out on the other. They opened the rear door and started unloading boxes of flowers. I threw my cigarette down on the dry tarmac, slipped on my rucksack and walked back to the bus station, where I rang dad. He was bad-tempered and annoyed and told me I had arrived at an inconvenient time, they had a little child now, they couldn't receive visitors at such short notice. I should have rung before, that would have been OK. As it was now, grandma was coming, and a colleague too. I said I understood, apologised for not calling before and rang off.

I stood with the receiver in my hand for a while thinking, and then I dialled Hilde's number. She said I could stay there and she would come and pick me up now.

Half an hour later I was sitting beside her in her old Golf, on our way out of town, with the window open and the sun in my eyes.

She laughed and said I smelled terrible, I would have to have a bath when we arrived. Then we could sit in the garden behind the house, in the shade, and she could serve me breakfast, I looked like I needed it.

I stayed at Hilde's for three days, long enough for mum to transfer some money into my account, and then I caught the train to Bergen. I left in the afternoon, the sun flooded the heavily forested countryside in Indre Agder, which received it in its manifold ways: the water in the lakes and rivers glittered, the dense conifers shone, the forest floor blushed, the leaves on the deciduous trees flashed on the few occasions a gust of wind caught them. Amid this interplay of light and colour the shadows slowly lengthened and thickened. I stood by the window in the last carriage for a long time watching features of the countryside that kept disappearing, cast aside as it were, to be replaced by new ones, which always made their appearance in quick succession, a river of stumps and roots, cliffs and uprooted trees, streams and fences, unexpected cultivated hillsides with farmhouses and tractors. The only features that didn't change were the rails we followed and two shimmering dots on which the sun was reflected all the way. It was a strange phenomenon. They looked like two balls of light, which seemed to be standing still while the train was travelling at more than a hundred kilometres an hour, and the balls of light remained at the same distance from me.

Several times during the journey I went back to see the balls of light again. They lifted my spirits, made me somehow happy, as though there was hope in them.

Otherwise I sat in my seat smoking and drinking coffee, reading newspapers but no books, on the basis that it might affect my prose, that I might lose whatever it was that had got me into the Writing Academy. After a while I took out the letters from

Ingvild. I had carried them with me all summer, the folds were wearing thin and I knew them nearly off by heart, but a radiance emanated from them, something good, something pleasurable, which touched me whenever I read them. It was her, both what I remembered of her the one time we had met and the her that arose from what she wrote, but it was also the her of the future, the unknown her that awaited me. She was different, something else, and the odd thing was that I also became different and something else when thinking about her. I liked myself better when I thought about her. It was as though thinking about her erased something in me, and that gave me a fresh start or moved me on.

I knew she was the right one, I had seen that straight away, but perhaps I hadn't thought, only felt, that what she had in her and what she was, and which in glimpses her eyes revealed, was something I wanted to be close to or embrace.

What was it?

Oh, her self-awareness and insight into the situation, which laughter suspended for an instant, but which returned the very next second. Something evaluative and sceptical even, in her nature, that wanted to be won over but was afraid of being duped. In it resided vulnerability but not weakness.

I had enjoyed talking to her so much, and I had liked writing to her so much. The fact that she was the first thought in my mind the day after we had met didn't necessarily mean anything, it was often like that, but it hadn't stopped there, I had thought about her every day since, and now four months had passed.

I didn't know if she felt the same way about me. Presumably she didn't, but something in the tone of her writing told me there was some excitement and appeal in this for her too.

Mum had moved from a flat with a terrace to a basement in a house in Angedalen, in Førde municipality, ten minutes from the centre. It was a wonderful location with a forest on one side, a field ending in a river on the other, but the flat was small and studenty – one big room with a kitchen and bathroom, that was it. She was planning to stay there until she found something better to rent or perhaps even buy. I had intended to do some writing while I stayed with her, during the two weeks before I would finally move to Bergen, and she suggested I use Uncle Steinar's cabin, which was up by the old house in the forest pasture above the farm grandma came from. She drove me there, we had a coffee outside the house, then she made her way back and I went into the cabin. Pine walls, pine floor, pine ceiling and pine furniture. A woven rug here and there, a few plain paintings. A pile of magazines in a basket, a fireplace, a kitchenette.

I placed the dining table by a wall without a window, put my pile of papers on one side, a pile of cassettes on the other, and sat down. But I couldn't write. The emptiness I had first felt on the island off Antiparos returned, I could feel it again, exactly as it had been before. The world was empty, or nothing, an image, and I was empty.

I went to bed and slept for two hours. When I woke dusk was falling. The bluish-grey twilight lay like a veil over the forest. The thought of writing still repelled me, so instead I put on my shoes and went outside.

I could hear the roar of the waterfall in the forest above, otherwise everything was still.

No, it wasn't, I could hear bells ringing somewhere.

I walked down to the path by the stream and followed it up into the forest. The spruces were tall and dark, the rock face beneath was covered in moss, here and there roots lay bare on the surface. In places small thin deciduous trees tried to force their way up into the light, elsewhere little clearings had formed around fallen trees. And alongside the stream the forest was open, of course, where it swirled and crashed, threw itself over rock and stone on its way down. Otherwise everything was dense and dark green from the spruce needles. I could hear my own breathing, could feel my pulse beating in my chest, throat and temples as I walked up. The noise from the waterfall became louder, and soon I was standing on a crag above a deep pool, looking at the steep bare rock face where the water plummeted downwards.

It was beautiful, but it was of no use to me, and I walked up through the trees beside the waterfall, climbed to the exposed rock, which I wanted to follow right to the top, a few hundred metres above me.

The sky was grey, the water that cascaded down beside me shiny and clear, like glass. The moss I was walking on was drenched and often gave way; my foot slipped and the dark rock beneath was revealed.

Suddenly something jumped out just in front of my feet.

Paralysed by fear, I stood stock still. My heart seemed to have stopped too.

A small grey creature darted off. It was a mouse or a small rat.

I laughed nervously to myself. Continued upwards, but the little scare had a hold on me. Now I peered into the dark forest with a sense of unease, and the constant blanket of sound from the waterfall which I had hitherto regarded as agreeable became threatening, prevented me from hearing anything else except my own breathing, so a few minutes later I about-turned and made my way back down.

I sat by the brick grill outside the farmhouse and lit a cigarette. It might have been eleven o'clock or maybe half past. The farmhouse looked the way it must have done when grandma worked here, in the 1920s and 30s. Yes, everything looked more or less the same as it did then. Yet everything was different. It was August 1988, I was an 80s person, contemporaneous with Duran Duran and The Cure, not that fiddle and accordion music grandad listened to in the days when he trudged up the hill in the dusk with a friend to court grandma and her sisters. I didn't belong here, with all of my heart I felt that. It didn't help that I knew the forest was actually an 80s forest and the mountains actually 80s mountains.

So what was I doing here?

My plan had been to write. But I couldn't, I was all on my own and lonely to the depths of my soul.

When the week was over and mum drove up the narrow gravel road, I was sitting on the steps waiting with my rucksack packed and ready between my legs, not having written a single word.

'Have you had a nice time?' she said.

'Yes, great,' I said. 'I didn't get much done though.'

'Oh yes,' she said, looking at me. 'But perhaps the rest did you good.'

'Yes, I'm sure it did,' I said, buckling my seat belt, and then we drove back to Førde, where we parked and had lunch at Sunnfjord Hotel. We chose a window table, mum hung her bag over her chair, then we went over to the buffet in the middle of the dining room to serve ourselves. The place was quite empty. When we sat down, each with a plate, a waiter came over, I asked for a Coke, mum wanted a Farris mineral water, and after he had gone she began to talk about her plans – which now looked as if they were going to materialise – to establish a further training course in psychiatric patient care at the school. She had located some suitable premises herself, a wonderful old school, according to her, which wasn't that far from the School of Nursing. It had soul, she said, it was an old timber building, with big rooms, high ceilings, quite different from the cramped brick bunker she was teaching in now.

'That sounds good,' I said, my gaze wandering to the car park, where a handful of vehicles glinted in the sunlight. The mountainside across the river was completely green apart from one plot that had been blasted out with dynamite, where a house had been built which vibrated with all of its many different colours.

The waiter returned and I drank the glass of Coke in one long draught. Mum began to talk about my relationship with Gunnar. She said I seemed to have internalised him and turned him into my super-ego, the one that told me what I could and couldn't do, what was wrong and what wasn't.

I put down my knife and fork and looked at her.

'Have you been reading my diary?' I said.

'No, not your diary,' she said. 'But you left a book you'd been writing in on your holiday. You're usually so open and tell me everything.'

'But, Mum, that was a diary,' I said. 'You don't read other people's diaries.'

'No, of course not,' she said. 'I know that. But if you leave it on the sitting-room table there's hardly anything secret about it, is there?'

'But you could see it was a diary, couldn't you?'

'No,' she said. 'It was a travelogue.'

'OK, OK,' I said. 'That was my mistake. I shouldn't have left it lying around. But what was it you said about Gunnar? That I'd internalised him? What did you mean by that?'

'That's how it seemed from the dream you described and your subsequent thoughts.'

'Really?'

'Your father was very strict with you when you were growing up, as you know. But then he was suddenly gone, and perhaps you had a sense that you could do whatever you liked. So you've got two sets of norms, but both derive from the outside. What's important is that you set your own limits. That has to come from the inside, from you yourself. Your father didn't do that, and that's maybe why he was so confused.'

'Is,' I said. 'He's still alive to my knowledge. At any rate, I spoke to him on the phone a week ago.'

'But now it appears you've installed Gunnar in your father's place,' she continued, flashing me a look. 'This has nothing to do with Gunnar. We're talking about setting your limits. But you're old enough now. You'll have to work it out for yourself.'

'That's what I'm trying to do in my diary,' I said. 'Then all sorts of people read it, and it becomes impossible to work it out for myself.'

'I apologise,' mum said. 'I really didn't think you regarded it as a diary. If I'd known, I wouldn't have read it.'

'I've told you it's not a problem,' I said. 'Shall we have a sweet as well?'

We sat in her flat chatting until late, then I went into the hall, closed the door behind me, fetched the lilo, which was leaning against the wall in the little bathroom, laid it on the floor, covered it with a sheet, undressed, switched off the light and lay down. Faintly, I could hear her moving about and the occasional car passing outside. The smell of plastic from the lilo reminded me of my childhood, camping trips and the open countryside. Times were different now, but the feeling of anticipation was the same. The next day I was off to Bergen, the big university town, I would be living in my own digs and attending the Writing Academy. In the evenings and at night I would sit in Café Opera or go to gigs with great bands at Hulen. It was fantastic. But the most fantastic thing of all was that Ingvild would be moving to the same town. We had arranged to meet, I had her phone number, I would ring her when I arrived.

It was too good to be true, I thought, lying there on the airbed, filled with a restlessness and a joy that this was about to begin. I lay on one side, then on the other, listening to mum talking in her sleep in the sitting room. Yes, she said. Then there was a long pause. Yes, she said again. That's true. Long pause. Yes. Yes. Mhm. Yes.

The following day mum took me to Handelshuset, where she wanted to buy me a jacket and some trousers. I chose a fur-lined denim jacket, which looked pretty cool, and a pair of green military-style trousers, as well as some black shoes. Then she drove me to the bus station, gave me the money for the ticket, stood by the car waving as the bus moved off and into the road.

After a few hours of forests, lakes, vertiginously steep mountains and narrow fjords, farms and fields, a ferry and a long valley where the bus was high up a mountainside one minute and right down by the water's edge the next, and an endless succession of tunnels, the frequency of houses and signs began to increase, there were more and more populated areas, industrial buildings appeared, fences, petrol stations, shopping centres and estates on both sides of the road. I saw a sign for the Business School and it struck me, that was where Agnar Mykle went forty years ago. On one side I saw Sandviken Psychiatric Hospital rise like a fortress at the foot of the mountains, while on the other the water glittered in the afternoon sun, with yachts and boats whose outlines seemed to blur in the haze against a backdrop of islands and mountains and the low sky over Bergen.

I jumped off the bus at the far end of Bryggen, the old wharf. Yngve was working the evening shift at the Orion Hotel and I had arranged to pick up the key to his flat there. The town around me was sunk in the stupor that only late-summer afternoons can evoke. Now and then a figure sauntered past in shorts and a T-shirt, followed by a long flickering shadow. House walls shimmering in the sun, motionless leaves on trees, a yacht chugging out of the harbour, masts bare.

The reception area at the hotel was packed with people. Yngve, busy behind his desk, looked up at me and said a coachload of Americans had just arrived, look, here's the key, see you later, OK?

I caught the bus to Danmarksplass and walked the three hundred metres up to his flat, unlocked the door, put down my rucksack in the hall, stood still for a while and wondered what to do. The windows faced north and the sun was in the west, setting over the sea, so the rooms were dark and chilly. They smelled of Yngve. I went into the sitting room and looked around, then into the bedroom. There was a new poster on the wall, an eerie photograph of a naked woman with *Munch og fotografi* written at the bottom. Photos he had taken himself were there too, a selection from Tibet, the ground was a gleaming red, a group of ragged boys and girls posing for him, their eyes dark and foreign. In one corner, beside the sliding door, his guitar was leaning against an amplifier. On top of it a large echo box. A plain white Ikea blanket and two cushions converted the bed into a sofa.

I had visited Yngve several times while I was at *gymnas*, and to me there was something almost sacred about his rooms, they represented who he was and who I wanted to become. Something that existed outside my life and something that one day I would move into.

Now I was here, I thought, and went into the kitchen to make some sandwiches, which I ate standing in front of the window, with a view of the terraces of old workers' houses going down to Fjøsangerveien at the bottom. On the other side, the mast on Mount Ulrich flashed in the sunshine.

It occurred to me that I had been on my own a lot recently. Apart from the few days with first Hilde and then mum, I hadn't spent time with anyone since I said goodbye to Lars in Athens. I could hardly wait for Yngve to come home.

I put on a Stranglers' record and settled down on the sofa with one of Yngve's photo albums. My stomach ached and I didn't know why. It felt like hunger, not for food but for everything else.

Perhaps Ingvild was also in town? Perhaps she was sitting in one of the hundred thousand bedsits around me?

One of the first questions Yngve asked me when he arrived was how it was going with Ingvild. I hadn't told him much, a few words when we were sitting on the steps earlier that summer, that was all, but it had been enough for him to realise it was serious. Maybe also that it had huge significance for me.

I told him she was coming to Bergen around now and would live in Fantoft, and I would be ringing her to arrange the first meeting.

'Might turn out to be your year,' he said. 'New girlfriend, Writing Academy . . .'

'We're not there yet.'

'No, but from what you've said, she's interested, isn't she?'

'A little maybe. But I doubt it means as much to her as it does to me.'

'But it could do. If you play your cards right.'

'For once, you mean?'

'I didn't say that,' he said, eyeing me. 'Fancy some wine?'

'Certainly do.'

He got up and disappeared into the kitchen, reappeared with a carafe in his hand and went to the bathroom. I heard some snorting and gurgling noises, then a steady glug until he emerged holding a full carafe.

'Vintage 1988,' he said. 'But it's pretty good. And there's quite a lot of it as well.'

I took a swig. It was so sour it made me wince.

Yngve smiled.

'Pretty good?' I said.

'Taste is relative, as you know,' he said. 'You have to compare it with other home-made wine.'

We drank for a while without speaking. Yngve stood up and went towards the guitar and amplifier.

'I've written a couple of songs since you were last here,' he said. 'Want to hear them?'

'Yes, love to,' I said.

'Well, they're not really songs,' he said, fastening the strap over his shoulder. 'Just a few riffs really.'

I felt a sudden tenderness as I watched him.

He switched on the amplifier, stood with his back to me and tuned the guitar, adjusted the echo box and began to play.

The tenderness vanished, this was good, what he was playing, the guitar sound was big and majestic, the riffs melodious and catchy, it sounded like a cross between the Smiths and the Chameleons. I couldn't understand where he had got it from. Both his musicality and the dexterity were way beyond my capacities. He simply had the gift, from the moment he started, as though it had always been there.

He turned towards me only after he had finished and put down the guitar.

'That was really good,' I said.

'Do you think so?' he said, sitting down on the sofa. 'It's just a couple of little ideas. I could do with some lyrics so that I could finish them off.'

'I don't understand why you don't play in a band.'

'Well,' he said. 'I jam a little with Pål now and then. Otherwise I don't know anyone who plays. You're here now though.'

'I can't play.'

'You can start by writing a few lyrics, can't you? And you can play the drums as well.'

'No, I can't,' I said. 'I'm not good enough. But perhaps I could write something. That'd be fun.'

'You do that,' he said.

Autumn was on its way, I thought, as we stood in the road outside the long line of low brick terraced houses waiting for the taxi. There was a kind of heaviness in the light summer night, impossible to localise yet unmistakable. An augury of something damp and dark and gloomy.

The taxi arrived a few minutes later, we got in, it raced recklessly down to Danmarksplass, past the big cinema and over a bridge, along Nygårds Park and into the centre, where I lost my bearings, streets were just streets, houses just houses, I disappeared into the large town, was swallowed up by it, and I liked that because I became visible to myself, the young man on his way into a metropolis filled with glass and concrete and tarmac and strangers caught in the light from street lamps and windows and signs. A shiver ran down my spine as we drove into the centre. The engine hummed, the traffic lights changed from green to red, we stopped outside what must have been the bus station.

'Isn't that where we went that time?' I said, nodding towards the building across the road.

'That's right,' Yngve said.

I had been sixteen, visiting him for the first time; I had held the hand of one of the girls we were with in order to get in. I had borrowed Yngve's deodorant, and in the minutes before we left his place he had stood in front of me, rolled up the sleeves of my shirt, passed me his hair gel, watched me rubbing it in and said, good, now let's go.

Now I was nineteen and all this was mine.

I caught a glimpse of the lake in the middle of the town, and then we turned left, past a large concrete building.

'That's the Grieg Hall,' Yngve said.

'So that's where it is,' I said.

'And there's Mekka,' he said straight afterwards, nodding towards a supermarket. 'That's the cheapest in town.'

'Is that where you shop?' I said.

'If I've got any money,' he said. 'Anyway, this is Nygårdsgaten. Do you remember The Aller Værste! song? "We ran down Nygårdsgata as though we were in the Wild West."'

'Yes,' I said. 'What about "Disken" then? "I went into Disken and the place was bloody heaving"?'

'That was the disco in Hotel Norge. Right behind that building there. But it's called something else now.'

The taxi pulled into the kerb and stopped.

'Here we are,' the driver said. Yngve passed him a hundred-krone note, I got out, looked up at the sign on the building where we we had stopped. CAFÉ OPERA it said in pink and black letters on a white background. Inside the big windows the place was full of people, shadowy figures among the small clear flames of candles. Yngve got out on the other side of the taxi, said goodbye to the driver and slammed the door shut. 'Right, in we go,' he said.

He stopped inside the entrance and scanned the crowd. Looked at me.

'No one I know. Let's go upstairs.'

I followed him up, past some tables, which were laid out in exactly the same pattern as downstairs, and over to the bar. I had been there before, but only fleetingly and in the daytime; this was different. Everywhere people were drinking beer. The room looked a lot like an apartment, I reflected, with chairs and tables and a curved bar in the middle.

'There's Ola!' Yngve exclaimed. I followed the direction of his nod. Ola, whom I had met once earlier this summer, was sitting at a table with three others. He smiled and waved. We walked over.

'Find yourself a chair and let's sit here, Karl Ove,' Yngve said.

There was a chair beside a piano by the other wall, I went and took it, feeling quite naked as I lifted it into the air, was that how I should do it? Could I carry it through the room like this? People looked at me, the place was full of students, regulars who were on their home ground, and I blushed, but saw no alternative and carried the chair to the table where Yngve was already sitting.

'This is my little brother, Karl Ove,' Yngve said. 'He's about to start at the Writing Academy.'

He smiled as he said that. I briefly met the eyes of the three people I hadn't seen before: two girls and a boy.

'So you're the famous little brother,' said one of the girls. She had fair hair and narrow eyes, which almost vanished when she smiled.

'Kjersti,' she said.

'Karl Ove,' I said.

The other girl had black hair in a page-boy cut, bright red lipstick and a black outfit, she told me her name, and the boy next to her, a shy figure with reddish-blond hair and pale skin, followed suit with a broad smile. I forgot their names the very next second.

'Do you want a beer?' Yngve said.

Was he going to leave me here, all on my own?

'Please,' I said.

He stood. I looked down at the table. Suddenly remembered I could smoke here, took out my tobacco pouch and began to make a roll-up.

'Were you at R-Roskilde?' Ola said.

He was the first person I had met since junior school who stammered. You wouldn't believe it to look at him. He had Buddy Holly glasses, dark hair, regular facial features and even though he didn't dress flashily at all there was still something about him that had made me think he was in a band the first time I saw him. Nothing had changed. He was wearing a white shirt, black jeans and a pair of black pointed shoes.

'Yes, I was,' I said. 'But I didn't get to see many bands.'

'Why n-not?'

'There was so much else going on,' I said.

'Yes, I c-can imagine.' He smiled.

You didn't have to be with him for long to know that he had a warm heart. I was glad he was Yngve's friend, and the stammering, which had made me ill at ease the previous time – did Yngve have friends who stammered? – didn't feel as disconcerting now that I could see that at least he had three more friends. None of them reacted to the stammer, either with forbearance or condescension, and what I myself felt when he said anything – that the situation I found myself in, he is stammering now and I mustn't show that I've noticed, was so obvious and awkward, because couldn't he see that was what I was thinking while he was talking? – wasn't apparent on their faces.

Yngve placed the beer on the table in front of me and sat down.

'What do you write then?' said the dark-haired girl, looking at me. 'Poetry or prose?' Her eyes were also dark. There was something unmistakably aloof about her manner.

I took a long swig of beer.

'I'm writing a novel at the moment,' I said. 'But I'm sure we'll be doing some poetry as well. I haven't done much of that, but perhaps I'll have to . . . heh heh!'

'Wasn't it you who had your own radio programme and stuff?' Kjersti said.

'Plus a review column in the local paper,' Yngve added.

'Yes,' I said. 'But that's a while ago now.'

'What's your novel about then?' said the dark-haired girl.

I shrugged.

'Variety of things. It's a mixture between Hamsun and Bukowski, I suppose. Have you read any Bukowski?'

She nodded and slowly turned her head to watch the people coming up the stairs.

Kjersti laughed.

'You'll have Hovland as your teacher, did Yngve tell you? He's fantastic!'

'Right,' I said.

There was a little pause, the focus of conversation moved away from me, and I leaned back as the others chatted. They knew one another as they were in the same department, Media Studies, and that was what they were talking about. Names of lecturers and theorists, titles of books, records and films ping-ponged across the table. While they were talking Yngve took out a cigarette holder, stuck a cigarette in it and started smoking with gestures that the holder made seem affected. I tried not to look at him, not to show I had noticed, which is what the others did too.

'Another beer?' I said as a distraction, he nodded and I walked over to the bar. One of the barmen was standing by the beer taps on the opposite side while the other was putting a tray of glasses through a hatch which turned out to be a dumb waiter.

How wonderful, a little lift going up and down between floors with food and drink!

The barman by the taps turned lethargically, I raised two fingers in the air, but he said nothing and turned back. The second barman faced me, and I leaned over the bar to signal that I wanted to order.

'Yes?' he said.

He had a white towel slung over his shoulder, a black apron over a white shirt and long mutton chops, and what looked like a tattoo was visible on his neck. Even the barmen looked cool in this town.

'Two beers,' I said.

He held the glasses in one hand under the two taps while scanning the room.

A familiar face appeared at the back, it was Yngve's friend Arvid, he was with two others, they made a beeline for the table where Yngve was sitting.

The first barman put two half-litre glasses on the bar.

'Seventy-four kroner,' he said.

'But I've just ordered them from the other barman!' I said, nodding towards the second man.

'You just ordered two from me. If you've ordered two from him as well, you'll have to pay for four.'

'But I haven't got enough money.'

'Are you expecting me to tip the beer away? You have to be clearer with your orders. One hundred and forty-eight kroner, please.'

'Just a moment,' I said, and went over to Yngve.

'Have you got any money?' I said. 'You'll get it back when I have my study loan.'

'Weren't you supposed to be paying for this round?'

'Yes . . .'

'Here you are,' he said, handing me a hundred-krone note.

Arvid looked at me.

'Ah, it's you, is it?'

'Yes,' I said with a quick smile, not knowing quite what to do, and ended up pointing towards the bar and saying, 'Just gotta . . .' and going to pay.

When I returned they had sat down at another table.

'Did you get *four* beers?' Yngve said. 'Why?'

'Just the way it went,' I said. 'Some mix-up with the order.'

The following morning it was raining, and I stayed in the flat all day while Yngve was at work. Perhaps it was meeting his friends that had done it, perhaps it was just term fast approaching, at any rate I suddenly panicked: I was no good and soon I would be sitting alongside the other students, who were probably much more experienced and gifted than me, writing texts, reading them out and being judged.

I took an umbrella from the hat shelf, opened it and trotted down the hill in the rain. There was a bookshop in Danmarksplass, as far as I remembered. Yes, there it was. I opened the door and went in, it was completely empty and sold predominantly office equipment, it seemed, but they had some shelves of books, which I ran my eye along with the dripping umbrella in my hand. I had very little money, so I decided to buy a paperback. *Hunger* by Hamsun. It cost 39.50, which left me with twelve kroner – I spent it on a nice loaf at the baker's in the little market square just behind. I plodded back uphill in the pouring rain which, along with the dark heavy clouds, cast a thick shroud over the landscape and changed its whole appearance. The water ran down windows and over car bonnets, trickled out of gutters and down the hills, where it made plough-shaped wavelets. The water gushed past me as I trudged upwards, rain beating down on my umbrella and the bag containing the loaf and the book slapping against my thigh with every step I took.

I let myself into the flat. The inside was dimly lit, in the corners furthest from the windows it was dark, but all the furniture and objects in it quietly made their presence felt. It was impossible to be there without sensing Yngve, his personality seemed to permeate the rooms, and while I was slicing the fresh bread on the worktop and taking out margarine and brown cheese, I wondered what atmosphere my place would exude and whether there was anyone in existence who would care. Yngve had organised a bedsit for me, he knew a girl who was going to Latin America for a year, she lived up on the Sandviken side of Bergen, in Absalon Beyers gate, and I could have it until next summer. I was lucky, most new students lived in one of the halls of residence at first, either Fantoft, where dad had rented a room during his studies when I was small, or Alrek, where Yngve had stayed for his first six months. Living in a student hall had low status, I knew that, the cool option was to live in the centre, preferably near Torgalmenningen, but Sandviken was good too.

I ate, cleared away the food and settled down to read in the sitting room with a cigarette and a cup of coffee. Usually I read quickly, raced through the pages without taking much notice of how it was written, what devices or style of language the writer used, all I was interested in was the plot, which sucked me in. This time I tried to read slowly, take it sentence by sentence, notice what went on in them, and if a passage seemed significant to me, to underline it with the pen I held at the ready.

I discovered something on the very first page. There was a tense shift. First of all Hamsun wrote in the past, then he suddenly switched to the present, and then back again. I underlined it, put the book down and fetched a sheet of paper from the desk in my bedroom. Back on the sofa, I wrote:

Hamsun, Hunger. Notes, 14/8/1988

Starts in general terms, about the town. Perspective from a distance. Then main protagonist wakes up. Switches from past to present. Why? To create more intensity, presumably.

Outside, the rain was tipping down. The roar of the traffic in Fjøsangerveien sounded like an ocean. I carried on reading. It was striking how simple the storyline was. He wakes up in his room, walks noiselessly downstairs as he hasn't paid his rent for a while and then into the town. Nothing particular happens there, he just walks around and is hungry and thinks about it. I could write about exactly the same topic. Someone waking up in their bedsit and going outside. But he had to have something about him, something special, like being hungry for example. That was what it was all about. But what could it be?

Writing wasn't black magic. You just had to come up with an idea, as Hamsun had done.

Some of my fears and anxieties subsided after I had formulated that thought.

When Yngve came home I was asleep on the sofa. I got up the moment I heard the door go, rubbed my face a couple of times, for some reason not wishing to show that I had been sleeping in the middle of the day.

I heard him put his rucksack down on the floor in the hall, he hung his jacket on the hook and said a brief hi to me on his way to the kitchen.

I recognised the closed face. He didn't want to have anything to do with anyone, least of all me.

'Karl Ove?' he shouted after a while.

'Yes?' I said.

'Come here.'

I did as he said and stopped in the doorway.

'Just look at the brown cheese? You mustn't cut such thick slices. Shall I show you how to do it?'

He placed the slicer on the cheese and shaved off a sliver.

'Like this,' he said. 'Do you see how easy it is to cut a thin slice?'

'Yes,' I said and turned away.

'And another thing,' he said.

I turned back.

'If you eat here clear away the crumbs. I don't want to have to go round cleaning up after you.'

'Right,' I said and went into the bathroom. There were tears in my eyes, and I rinsed my face a couple of times with cold water, dried it, went into the sitting room, sat down, started reading *Hunger* while listening to him eat in the kitchen, clean up and go into the bedroom. Soon there was total silence and I realised he must have fallen asleep.

A similar incident took place the next day, this time what annoyed him was that I hadn't dried the bathroom floor after having a shower. He ordered me about this time as well, as though he were on a higher level than me. I said nothing, bowed my head, did as he commanded, but inside I was furious. Later that day, as we were returning from a shopping trip, I closed the car door in a way which he considered was too hard – do you have to slam the door so bloody hard, can't you just be a little bit careful, this is not my car – and I exploded.

'Stop telling me what to do, all right!' I yelled. 'I can't take any more of this! You treat me like a bloody kid! Always telling me off!'

He looked at me for a moment with the car key in his hand.

'Have you got that?' I said, my eyes shiny.

'I'll never do it again,' he said.

And he never did, either.

We went out often that week, and every time the same thing happened, Yngve met people he knew, introduced me to them, said I was his brother and I was about to start at the Writing Academy. That gave me an advantage, I was somebody already, didn't have to prove myself, although it also made things more difficult since I had to live up to the billing. Had to say something a writer-to-be might conceivably say which they hadn't considered before. It didn't work like that though. They had considered everything, they all knew more than me, indeed to such a degree that I gradually realised that what I said and thought was what they had said and thought a good while ago and had now put behind them.

But it was good drinking with Yngve. Our spirits rose after a few beers, all that lay between us during the day – the silences that could develop from nowhere, the irritation that could set in, the sudden inability to find areas of common interest even though there were so many – all of that vanished as our spirits soared and we felt the concomitant warmth: we looked at each other and knew who we were. Walked through the town half-drunk and uphill to the flat without a care in the world, not even the silences troubled us, street lights shone on the smooth tarmac, taxis raced past in dark haste, lonely men or women came towards us, or other young people who had been out on the town, and I could look at Yngve, who was walking bent double, just as I was, and ask: how is it with Kristin, have you got over her? And he could look at me and answer no, I'll never get over her. No one is a patch on her.

The drizzle, the clouds above scurrying past, illuminated from below by the lights, Yngve's serious face. The strong odour of car fumes, which I had realised always hung over Danmarksplass. The moped carrying two teenagers, which stopped at the traffic lights:

the boy at the front who put his feet down on the road, the girl at the back with her arms wrapped tightly around him.

'Do you remember when Stina finished with me?' I said.

'Vaguely,' he said.

'You played The Aller Værste! for me. "All things pass, all things must decay."'

He looked at me and smiled.

'Did I?'

I nodded.

'The same holds true for you now. It'll pass. Then you'll fall for another girl just the same.'

'How old were you then? Twelve? It's not quite the same. Kristin was the love of my *life*. And I only have one.'

I said nothing in response. We walked up the hill on the other side of Verftet, the old docklands complex, turned left beneath the massive red-brick building I knew was a school.

'But one good thing has come out of it,' he said. 'Showing no interest in other girls has meant they've suddenly started taking an interest in me. I don't give a damn, and *as a result* I can have them.'

'I know that's how it works,' I said. 'My problem is that I can't not give a damn. Take Ingvild, for example. I get so bloody nervous before we meet that I can't say a word. So she thinks that's the way I *am*, and then it's no good.'

'Don't worry,' Yngve said. 'It'll be fine. She knows who you are. You've been writing to each other all spring and summer after all.'

'But that's the point, then I'm *writing*,' I said. 'Then I can be anyone I want to be. I can take my time, right, think things through. But I can't when I meet her face to face.'

Yngve snorted.

'Don't think about it so much and it'll be fine. She'll be feeling the same as you.'

'Do you think so?'

'Yes, of course! Have a few beers with her and relax. It'll be fine.'

He took the key from his pocket, lowered his umbrella and went in through the gate, up the little steps, which were dark and slippery from the rain. I stood behind him waiting for him to open the door.

'Do you want a glass of wine before going to bed?' he said.

I nodded.

My impatience grew throughout the week, I became more and more restless, a feeling I had otherwise never experienced. It must have been because I wanted life to get moving, to turn serious. And to do my own thing, not to be dependent on Yngve for whatever I did. I had already borrowed a couple of hundred kroner from him and probably needed a couple more to tide me over until my student loan arrived. When I moved from Håfjord I had been stupid enough to tell the Post Office that I was changing address to c/o Yngve, so when I arrived, a debt recovery letter from the northern Norwegian electricity company and the shop where I had bought the stereo were waiting for me. The latter was the more serious: if I didn't pay this time they would take legal action to recover the money.

If it had been a good sound system I wouldn't have minded so much. But what I had bought was such crap. Yngve had a NAD amplifier and two small but good JBL speakers, and Ola also had a good system made up of components he had bought individually – that was what you should have, not a fucking Hitachi rack system.

Soon I would receive twenty thousand kroner.

I was also wondering whether to buy myself a porn magazine. I was living in a big town now, I knew no one, all I had to do was take one down from the shelf, place it on the counter, pay, put it in a bag and go home. But I couldn't bring myself to do it, I was in a nearby tobacconist's a couple of times, and my eyes roamed down to the women's blonde hair and their big breasts, and the mere sight of their skin, printed on glossy paper, made my throat tighten. But it was always a newspaper that I placed on the counter, and a pouch of tobacco, never any of the magazines. Mostly because I was living with Yngve, it didn't feel right to have to hide things in his place, but also because I didn't have the courage to meet the assistant's eyes as I laid the magazine on the counter.

I would have to wait.

The day of the move came, with Yngve I carried my Håfjord possessions up from the cellar into the car, there were eight boxes in all and they completely blocked the rear view when Yngve, more cautiously than usual, pulled away from the kerb and set off down into Bergen.

'If you brake sharply now my neck's a goner,' I said because the boxes reached right up to the car roof.

'I'll try not to,' he said. 'But I can't promise anything.'

For the first time in several days it was nice weather. The dense cloud cover over the town was greyish-white, and the light in the streets around us was gentle, though not such that it veiled or enhanced, it was more that it allowed whatever there was to appear in its own right. Tarmac grey and speckled black, walls green and yellow, dulled by car fumes and street dust, trees grey and green, the water in the bay by Verftet grey and shiny. The colours became more vivid as we began to climb the hills on the Sandviken side of town, most of the houses there were timber constructions, and the shiny paint shimmered through the neutral light.

Yngve pulled into the kerb by a little park, in front of a telephone box. On the wall across the road there was a sign saying Absalon Beyers gate.

'Is it here?' I asked.

'It's the corner house,' Yngve said, getting out. He raised his hand in a brief greeting, I followed his gaze, there was a girl with a cloth in her hand watching us from behind the window in the ground-floor bedsit.

We crossed the street, she came to the door, I shook her hand. She said it was good timing, she had just finished cleaning the place up.

'Come on in!'

The bedsit consisted of a small room furnished in the simplest fashion: beneath the window there was a sofa, in front of it a coffee table, and against the wall on the opposite side a desk. There was also a sofa that could be turned into a bed. Adjoining the little room, separated by a door, was a tiny kitchenette. That was all. The walls were a dark, brownish colour, and would have been drab but for the fire wall beside the kitchen door, on which a landscape had been painted: a tree on a cliff above the sea, not dissimilar to the picture on the front of matchboxes, the one Kjartan Fløgstad had used as the cover for *Fire and Flame*.

She noticed me staring at it and smiled.

'Yes, isn't it nice!' she said.

I nodded.

'Here are the keys,' she said, passing me a little bunch of them. 'This one's for the front door, this is for this door and that's for a storage room in the loft.'

'Where's the toilet?' I said.

'Downstairs. There's a shared shower and toilet. It's a bit impractical, but it reduces the rent by quite a bit. Shall we go down and have a look?'

The staircase was steep, the corridor downstairs narrow, with a small basement bedsit on one side, where someone called Morten lived, a shower and a toilet on the other. I liked the unrefinedness of it and the old walls that vaguely smelled of mould, it had a Dostoevsky feel, the impoverished young student in the metropolis.

Back upstairs, she gave me a wad of rental forms, already filled in, grabbed her empty bucket in one hand, the broom in the other and turned to us in the doorway.

'I hope you'll have a nice time here! I've spent some happy hours here anyway.'

'Thank you,' I said. 'Have a good trip and see you next summer!'

She disappeared round the corner with the broom slung over her shoulder and we set about bringing in the boxes. When that was done, Yngve got in his car and drove down to the hotel, where he had an afternoon shift, while I put my feet on the table and smoked a cigarette before starting to unpack.

The bedsit was at street level, the pavement went by the windows, and if there wasn't a constant stream of people passing there was a regular bobbing of heads, and so enticing was the sight of a curtainless bedsit that almost everyone succumbed to the temptation to peer in. I was bending over my record collection when I turned and met the gaze of a woman in her forties, who despite immediately looking away still left an impression on me. I hung up my poster of John Lennon, turned and met the eyes of two twelve-year-old boys. I assembled the coffee machine, inserted the plug in the socket beside the cupboard, turned and found myself looking straight into the eyes of a bearded man in his late twenties. To put an end to this, I pinned a bedsheet over one window, a tablecloth over the other, and then I sat down on the sofa, strangely restless, it was as though the tempo inside me was greater than that outside.

I played a few records, brewed some tea and read some pages of *Hunger*. Outside, it was beginning to rain. In the short pauses between the LP tracks I heard raindrops pitter-pattering against the window just behind my head. Now and then I heard noises from the floor above as dusk fell and the room slowly darkened. The stairs creaked, loud voices came from above, music was turned on, it was a pre-loading session.

I wondered whether to ring Ingvild, she was the only person I knew in town, but dismissed the idea, I couldn't meet her unprepared, I had only one chance and I mustn't waste it.

Strange what an impression she had made. I had sat at the same table as her for half an hour.

Could you fall in love within half an hour?

Oh yes, you certainly could.

Could someone you didn't know, you barely knew about, captivate your senses entirely?

Oh yes.

I got up to find her letters. The longest one had arrived in the middle of the summer, she told me she was on her way across America with her ex-host family, they stopped at all the sights worthy of the name, there were many, according to her, nearly every single town had something it prided itself on and was famous for. She used the stops to sneak off and have a quiet cigarette, she wrote, otherwise she lay on her bed in the mobile home staring out at the countryside, which at times was sensationally beautiful and dramatic, at others monotonous and boring, though always exotic.

I could visualise her, but it was more than that, I also identified with her, that is, I knew exactly what she thought, how she felt, there was something about the tone in which she wrote, or the glimpses she gave of herself, which I recognised from myself, and I hadn't experienced that before, another person reaching the point where I was. Light, happiness, ease, excitement, somehow balancing on the edge of nausea, constantly on the verge of despair, because I wanted it so much, it was all I wanted, but what if it didn't work out? What if she didn't want me? What if I wasn't good enough?

I put down the letters, slipped on my jacket and shoes and went out, considered walking down to see Yngve, he didn't finish his shift until eleven, but if I was lucky he wouldn't have much to do, so we could exchange a few words or have a smoke or something.

First I crossed the street to have a look up at the floor above mine, but all I could see were the backs of some heads in the window. It was raining quite heavily, I didn't have an umbrella and I didn't want to wear my raincoat, so even though it was unpleasant and hair gel was beginning to run down my forehead, I hunched my shoulders and began to tramp downhill.

In the district closest to me, the houses were white and made of wood, all the angles skew-whiff, the roofs of varying heights, some had stone steps down to the pavement, others none. In the district below, the buildings were made of brick, long relatively tall blocks of flats that might have been built at the beginning of the twentieth century, probably for workers, judging by their plain unadorned walls.

Rising above the town, visible from even the deepest and darkest alleyway, were the mountains. And below, in glimpses between houses and trees, was the sea. The mountains here were higher than those in Håfjord, and the sea was just as deep, but they didn't affect your consciousness to the same degree; the main weight here lay in the town, in the cobblestones, the tarmac, the solid blocks of flats and timbered houses, in the windows and lights, cars and buses, the mass of faces and bodies in the streets, against which the sea and mountains were insubstantial, almost weightless, something that merely caught your eye, a backdrop.

If I had lived here all on my own, I thought, in a little cabin in the mountains, for example, without a house nearby, but set in exactly the same landscape, then I would have felt the weight of the mountains and the depth of the sea, then I would have heard the winds sweeping across the peaks, the waves beating against the shore, and although I would hardly have been afraid I would definitely have been vigilant. I would have taken my leave of the landscape every night and woken up to it every morning. Now that wasn't the case, I could feel it with every fibre of my being, now it was faces that counted.

I walked by the long red timber shed where the rope makers used to ply their trade, up the road on the other side, past the supermarket, down to the wider main road and turned right at the bottom, past quiet grey St Mary's Church, which I had noticed when I visited Yngve and mum here three years ago, as it was so unpretentious and merged so unobtrusively into its surroundings, it had stood there since the twelfth century, past it and down to Bryggen.

Cars drove by with their lights on. The water, gently billowing in the harbour, was pitch black. A few yachts were moored to the quay, their shiny hulls dully reflecting the light from the street lamps along the road. On board one of them some people sat drinking under a canopy, voices low, faces barely illuminated. From over in Vågsbunnen came the strident sounds of cars, music, shouting, which had already become distant.

Yngve was standing behind the reception desk next to a colleague. He turned his head towards me as I entered.

'Are you bored already?' he said. Glanced at his colleague. 'This is my brother, Karl Ove. He moved here a week ago.'

'Hi,' said the other person.

'Hi,' I said.

He went into the back room. Yngve tapped a pen on the desk in front of him.

'Just had to get a breath of air,' I said. 'I thought I would pop by so my walk had some purpose.'

'Well, there's nothing going on here,' he said.

'So I see,' I said. 'Are you going home afterwards?'

He nodded.

'But Asbjørn's in town. Perhaps we can drop in on you tomorrow and see how you're getting on?'

'Yes, you do that,' I said. 'Could you bring an umbrella with you? You've got two, haven't you? Then I can borrow it until I get my study loan.'

'I'll try and remember.'

'See you then.'

He nodded, and I went back out. I still didn't want to sit around in my bedsit, so I went for a walk through the rain-wet streets, up past Café Opera, which as predicted was packed with people, but I didn't dare venture in alone, down to the sea on the northern side of Vågen, past some run-down warehouse buildings, up a hill, on the crest of which I stopped because now, lo and behold, Bryggen and Sandviken were below me, on the far side of the bay, glittering in the damp grey-black air.

I strolled down to the broad open square on the southern side, passed a hotel of brick and glass called Neptun, an apt name, it struck me, in this town where water was constantly trickling and dripping, and then I thought I had better remember it so that I could write it down when I got home, looked behind me and saw a large stone gatehouse at the end of a pedestrian street, and knew this was one of the old town gates because mum had shown me an identical one at the other end of the city centre. I crossed the street, passed a large office block that towered up from the water like a rock face, rounded the corner and in front of me stood Strandkai Terminal, where the Sognefjord ferry departed, and behind it, once again, Vågsbunnen.

A rush of happiness surged through me. It was the rain, it was the lights, it was the city. It was me, I was going to be a writer, a star, a beacon for others.

I ran a hand through my hair, greasy with gel, wiped it on my trouser leg and stepped up my pace in the hope that this feeling of happiness would last all the way home and deep into the time awaiting me in the bedsit until I felt able to go to bed.

While asleep that night I imagined my bed was in the street. That wasn't so strange, I thought as I woke up, presumably because of the distant pealing of church bells – the bed was against the wall under the windows, and not only could you clearly hear every footfall on the pavement outside, but the house was also situated next to a junction where people going in their various directions stopped to have a chat on their way home from town, and across the street was a telephone box, which it turned out was in constant use, also at night, people trying to book taxis, crowds of them, people wanting to deliver a few home truths to a partner or a friend or whoever it was they imagined had let them down and now needed to be put in their place or begged for forgiveness.

I lay still for a while to gather my thoughts, then dressed and went down to the basement with a towel in one hand and shampoo in the other. The corridor was full of steam, I placed my hand on the shower door, it was locked, a girl's voice from inside shouted, I won't be long! OK, I said, and leaned against the wall to await my turn.

The door beside me opened and a boy of my age with tousled hair stuck his head out.

'Hi,' he said. 'Thought I heard someone. My name's Morten. Have you moved into the bedsit on the ground floor?'

'Yes,' I said, shaking hands.

He chuckled. He was standing there in no more than his underpants.

'What do you do?' he said. 'Are you a student?'

'I've just come to town,' I said. 'I'm about to start a kind of writing course.'

'Interesting!' he said.

At that moment the shower door opened. A girl I reckoned was in her mid-twenties came out. She had a large towel wrapped around her body and a smaller one around her head. A cloud of steam followed.

'Hi,' she said with a smile. 'We'd better do proper introductions later. Anyway, the shower's free now!'

She went down the corridor.

Heh heh heh, Morten chuckled.

'And what about you?' I said. 'Are you a student?'

'Let's save that for later! You have a shower, and we'll come back to it!'

The shower-room floor was made of concrete and freezing cold where the hot water hadn't been. The drain was full of tangled hair which glistened in the foam from her shampoo. The foot of one wall panel was warped, and the otherwise white door was black and discoloured at the bottom and a good way up. But the water was hot, and soon I was massaging shampoo into my hair and for some strange reason humming 'Ghostbusters'.

Returning upstairs, I didn't dare go out as Yngve hadn't said when they would come, but that didn't matter, my body felt much calmer than the day before, and I spent my time putting the kitchen utensils in their places, arranging clothes in the wardrobe, hanging up the last posters, making a list of what I needed to buy when the study loan arrived. That done, I stood by the door and tried to see the room through Yngve's and Asbjørn's eyes. The typewriter on the desk, that looked good. The poster of the barn and bright yellow corn under the dramatic black American sky, that was good, a source of inspiration. The poster of John Lennon, the most rebellious of the four Beatles, that was also good. And my record collection on the floor against the wall, it was large and impressive, even for Asbjørn, who I was told knew what he was talking about. On the downside, the book collection was limited, comprising only seventeen volumes, and I didn't have enough experience of other collections to determine what impression the various titles made. *Beatles* and *The Snails* by Saabye Christensen couldn't be too far wide of the mark though. The same was true for Ingvar Ambjørnsen. I had three of his books: *The 23rd Row*, *The Last Fox Hunt* and *White Niggers*.

I left *Novel with Cocaine* open on the table and placed a couple of issues of *Vinduet* next to it, one open, one closed. Three books open seemed a bit much, it looked arranged, but no one would be suspicious of two open and one closed, that was perfect.

An hour later, while I was trying to write at the desk, there was a ring at the door. Yngve and Asbjørn were standing on the steps.

There was a restlessness about them, I felt, they couldn't wait to move on.

'Bit of a turn-up you coming to Bergen, Karl Ove,' Asbjørn said with a smile.

'Yes,' I said. 'Come in!'

I closed the door behind us. They stood in the middle of the floor looking around.

'You've done a nice job here,' Yngve said.

'Mm,' Asbjørn said. 'Great place to have a bedsit. Hang on though.'

'Yes?' I said.

'The Lennon poster has to come down. That's no good.'

'Oh?' I said.

'That's what you have at *gymnas*. John Lennon. Bloody hell.'

He smiled as he spoke.

'Do you agree?' I said, looking at Yngve.

'Of course,' he said.

'What should I put up instead?'

'Anything,' Asbjørn said. 'Norwegian C & W would be better. Bjøro Håland.'

'Actually I like the Beatles,' I said.

'You don't say,' Asbjørn said. 'Not the Beatles surely.'

He turned to Yngve and smiled again.

'I thought you said your brother had great taste in music. And his own radio programme.'

'No one's perfect,' Yngve said.

'Take a seat,' I said. Even though I had been wrong-footed by the Lennon-poster discussion, and my head was still buzzing, since I had understood exactly why it was wrong the moment Asbjørn said – it was schoolboy-ish of course – I was still proud to have them both here, in my bedsit, surrounded by my possessions.

'We were thinking of going into town and having a café au lait or something,' Yngve said. 'Are you coming?'

'Can't we have a coffee here?' I said.

'It's better in Café Opera, isn't it?' Yngve said.

'Right,' I said. 'Just a moment. I'll put on some clothes.'

When we emerged onto the steps, both Yngve and Asbjørn donned shades. Mine were indoors, but it would have been too embarrassing to go back to fetch them, so I rejected the idea, set off down the hill with them, along the wet streets gleaming with the reflected sunbeams breaking through the holes in the clouds above us.

I had met Asbjørn only a couple of times, had never chatted with him at any length, but I knew he was important to Yngve, so he was important to me too. He laughed a lot and always went very quiet afterwards, I had noticed. He had short hair, a hint of sideburns, a slightly plump face and warm observant eyes. With a not infrequent glint in them. Today, like Yngve, he was dressed all in black. Black Levi's, black leather jacket, black Doc Martens with yellow seams.

'Getting into the Writing Academy is pretty cool,' he said. 'And of course Ragnar Hovland's bloody great. Have you read anything by him?'

'No, actually I haven't,' I said.

'You must do. *Sveve over Vatna*, that's the definitive Norwegian student novel.'

'Really?'

'Yes. Or the definitive Bergen novel. It's completely over the top. Oh yes, he's good, he is. He likes the Cramps. Enough said!'

Over the top was an expression they used a lot, I had noticed.

'Yes,' I said.

'You've heard of the Cramps, I take it.'

'Yes, of course.'

'You're starting tomorrow, aren't you?' Yngve said.

I nodded.

'I'm a bit nervous, I must admit.'

'You got in,' Yngve said. 'They know what they're doing.'

'Let's hope so,' I said.

Café Opera during the day was quite different from Café Opera in
the evening. Now it was no longer packed with students drinking
beer, now there were all sorts of people, even ladies in their fifties, each with a cup of coffee and a piece of cake in front of them.
We found a window table on the ground floor, hung our jackets
over the backs of our chairs and went to order. I was flat broke, so
Yngve bought me a café au lait while Asbjørn ordered an espresso.
When I saw him being handed a little cup I recognised it, it was
like the ones Lars and I had been served at the first motorway café
after the Italian border, we had asked for coffee and were given
those tiny cups with coffee that was so concentrated and strong
it was completely undrinkable. I had spat it back into the cup and
looked at the waiter, who ignored me, nothing wrong with this
coffee, *ragazzi*.

But Asbjørn seemed to like it. He blew on the black-brown surface and took a sip, put the cup down on the saucer and looked
out of the window.

'Have you read anything by Jon Fosse?' I said, looking at him.

'No, is he good?'

'No idea. He's one of the teachers too.'

'He writes novels, I know,' Asbjørn said. 'He's a modernist. A
Vestland modernist.'

'Why don't you ask me if I've read anything by Jon Fosse?' Yngve
said. 'I read books too, you know.'

'I haven't heard you mention him, so I concluded you hadn't,' I
said. 'But you have?'

'No,' Yngve said. 'But I might have done.'

Asbjørn laughed.

'You two are brothers and no mistake!'

Yngve took out his cigarette holder and lit up.

'You haven't given up on the David Sylvian poses yet, I see,' Asbjørn said.

Yngve just shook his head and slowly blew smoke across the table.

'I was looking for some Sylvian glasses, but my *frame* of mind changed when I heard the price.'

'Dear God, Yngve,' Asbjørn said. 'That's the worst joke yet. And that's saying something.'

'Yes, I hold up my hands.' Yngve laughed. 'But out of ten puns maybe one or two work well. The problem is you have to go through all the bad ones to get to the really good ones.'

Asbjørn turned to me.

'You should've seen Yngve when he joked the tiny rural airstrip in Jølster would have to be called Astrup International Airport. After our famous local artist. He laughed so much he had to leave the room!'

'Well, it was a good 'un,' Yngve said, starting to laugh. Asbjørn laughed as well. Then, as if a switch had been thrown, he stopped and for a moment sat completely still. Took out his pack of cigarettes, he smoked Winston, I noticed, lit one and emptied his cup of espresso with his second sip.

'Is Ola in town, do you know?' he said.

'Yes, he's been here some time,' Yngve said.

They began to talk shop. I had never heard of most of the names they mentioned, I knew nothing about media studies, so I couldn't join in, not even when they touched on films and bands I knew. It almost developed into an argument. Yngve thought there was nothing that was genuine per se, everything was in some way a pose, even Bruce Springsteen's image, which he used as an example. His naturalness was as affected and carefully studied as the eccentricity and posturing of David Sylvian or David Bowie. Of course, Asbjørn said, you're absolutely right, but that doesn't necessarily mean there can be no genuine expression, does it?

Who then? Give me an example, Yngve said. Hank Williams, Asbjørn suggested. Hank Williams! Yngve snorted. He's surrounded
by myths, that's all there is to him. What sort of myths? Country
music myths, Yngve protested. Oh my God, Yngve, Asbjørn said.

Yngve glanced over at me.

'It's the same in literature. There's no difference between pulp
fiction and highbrow fiction, one is as good as the other, the only
difference is the aura they have, and that's determined by the
people who read the stuff, not by the book itself. There's no such
thing as "the book itself".'

I hadn't thought about any of this before, and I said nothing.

'What about comic books then?' Asbjørn said. 'Is Donald Duck
just as good as James Joyce?'

'In principle, yes.'

Asbjørn laughed and Yngve smiled.

'But in all honesty,' Yngve said 'it's the reception that defines
a work or an artist, and that's what artists play on of course. Irrespective of whether they enjoy high or low status, everything is
a pose.'

'You work as a *receptionist*, so you ought to know about *reception*,'
Asbjørn said.

'And the seams on your Doc Martens, by the way, they aren't
real, they just *seem* to be,' Yngve said.

They laughed again, and then there was silence. Yngve got up
for a newspaper, I did the same, and while we flicked through the
pages I was so exhilarated by this scenario, by me sitting with two
worldly-wise students in a café in Bergen on a Sunday afternoon
and the fact that this wasn't an exception, wasn't a visit, I was
part of this scenario and belonged here, that I could hardly take
in what I was reading.

Half an hour later we left, they were going to see Ola, he lived
in one of the streets behind the Grieg Hall, and Yngve asked me if
I wanted to string along, but I said no, I had to try and prepare for

the following day, while the real reason was that I was so happy it was too much for me and I had to be on my own.

We parted at the end of Torgalmenningen, outside a restaurant called Dickens, they wished me luck, Yngve told me to ring and say how everything had gone, I asked if he could lend me some money, the very last time, he nodded and dug up a fifty-krone note, and then I hurried across the large open square in the middle of the town as the rain gusted down, for even though the sun was still shining on the houses along the mountainside, the sky directly above me was heavy and black.

Back home in my bedsit, I didn't just take down the poster of John Lennon, I tore it into small pieces and threw them into the waste-paper basket. Then I decided to ring Ingvild and ask if we could meet at the weekend, it was a good opportunity, I was in such a cheerful mood, and it was as though my cheerfulness opened a path to her, because it was her I had been thinking about all the way up the long hills, as though my inner being knew no better way to cope with the excitement after the hour with Yngve and Asbjørn than to counter it with more excitement, of a very different kind it was true, for while the unbearable excitement generated by Yngve and Asbjørn resided in the moment itself, what was happening there and then, the tension and excitement I felt with regard to Ingvild was about what was going to happen at some point in the future, when the tension could actually be released and she would be mine.

Her and me.

The thought that this was indeed a possibility, and not just an illusory dream, exploded inside me.

Outside, the sky was clouding over, the sun could no longer be glimpsed, rain spattered on the road. I ran over to the telephone kiosk, placed the slip of paper with the Fantoft number on top of the coin box, inserted a five-krone piece in the slot, dialled the number and waited. A young man's voice answered, I asked to speak to Ingvild, he said no one by that name lived there, I said she was moving in soon, maybe she hadn't done so yet, he said, oh yes, that's right, one of the rooms is still unoccupied, I apologised for the disturbance, he said it was no problem, and I cradled the receiver.

At around seven the doorbell rang. I went out into the hallway and opened up; it was Jon Olav.

'Hi!' I said. 'How did you know I was here?'

'I rang Yngve. Can I come in?'

'Yes, yes, of course.'

I hadn't seen him since Easter when we had been out in Førde and met Ingvild. He was studying law in Bergen, but I understood from what he said over the next half an hour that he spent most of his time and energy on Young Friends of the Earth. He was the idealistic type, always had been: one summer when we had been staying with grandma and grandad in Sørbøvåg, twelve or thirteen we must have been at the time, I had been leaning over the handlebars of a bike and talking about various girls who lived nearby, one of whom I had described as yukky, quick as a flash he had riposted, think you're a great catch, do you, eh?

I had cycled back and forth in my embarrassment, and I have always remembered that moment, his consideration for others and willingness to spring to their defence.

We chatted and drank a cup of tea, he asked if I wanted to see his bedsit, it was nearby, of course I did, and off we went, down the hills.

'Have you seen anything of Ingvild this summer?' I said.

'Yes, a bit, a couple of times. How's it going with her? You were writing letters, weren't you?'

'Yes, we've been writing ever since. She's coming to Bergen now, so I was thinking of meeting her.'

'Are you interested?'

'That's an understatement,' I said. 'I've never felt so strongly about anyone.'

'Wow,' he said with a laugh. 'Here we are, by the way.'

He stopped by one of the doors to a long tall brick building opposite the rope makers' shed. The hall and stairs were made of wood, making it seem bare, almost primitive. The bedsit consisted of two small rooms with a toilet in the corridor, no shower. His record collection, which I flicked through while he was in the loo, was small and random, there were as many good records as there were bad, some everyone bought when they came out, a couple of really good ones, like the Waterboys, a couple of less good ones like The Alarm. It was the kind of collection that belonged to someone who wasn't particularly interested in records and who mostly followed the herd. But he had been in a band once, he could play the saxophone and he had taught me the basic beat on the drums when we were young, and how to coordinate the hi-hat, the snare and the bass drum.

'We'll have to go out one evening,' he said when he returned. 'Then you can meet my friends.'

'Are they the same ones as before?'

'Yes. They always will be, I hope. Idar and Terje, they're the two I see most.'

I got up.

'Let's talk about it. I'd better be off. First day of the course tomorrow.'

'Congratulations on getting in, by the way!' he said.

'Thank you, it's a nice feeling,' I said. 'But I'm a bit nervous too. I've got no idea what the level is.'

'Just do your thing. What I read was good anyway.'

'Let's hope it goes all right,' I said. 'Catch you later!'

I came in the middle of the night, it woke me up and I lay for a few seconds in the darkness wondering whether to get up and put on clean underpants, but fell asleep immediately afterwards. At ten to six I opened my eyes again. As soon as I became conscious and knew where I was, my stomach churned with nerves. I closed my eyes in an attempt to go back to sleep, but the tension inside me was too strong, so I got up, wrapped a towel around my waist, walked down the cold stairs, along the cold corridor and into the equally cold shower room. After half an hour under the boiling-hot water I went back upstairs and dressed, carefully and methodically. A black shirt and the black waistcoat with the grey back. The black Levi's, the studded belt, the black shoes. Not a drop of gel spared to make my hair stand up as it should. I had also saved a plastic bag Yngve had given me, from Virgin, and in it I put my notebook and a pen, as well as *Hunger*, to give it a bit more weight.

I tidied the bed to make it into a sofa again, had a cup of tea with a generous helping of sugar as I didn't feel like any breakfast, sat looking out of the window at the shiny telephone box sparkling in the sunshine, the sunless grass in the park behind, the trees at the back and then the mountain that rose steeply, with the row of brick houses above, also in shadow, then got up and put on a record, flicked through a few issues of *Vinduet*, all to pass the time until it was nine and I could leave. Lessons didn't start until eleven, but I had planned to walk around town first, perhaps find a café and read a little.

A chimney sweep came down the street with his long brush wound into a circle over one shoulder. A cat strolled across the grass. An ambulance drove down the road along the mountainside, behind the brick houses, visible between them as it passed, it moved slowly, no siren blaring, no lights flashing.

Right there, at that precise moment, I felt as if I would be able to meet whatever challenges came my way, as if there were no limits to what I could do. This wasn't about writing, this was something else, a boundlessness, as if I could get up and go now, this very minute, and then just walk and walk to the end of the earth.

This feeling lasted for thirty seconds perhaps. Then it was gone, and even though I tried to summon it back it refused to return, a bit like a dream that goes, slips from your grasp as you struggle to recall it after waking.

When, a couple of hours later, I wandered down to the centre it was with a gentle, not unpleasant, nervousness in my body, indeed I felt light and at ease as I walked, there was something about the sun shining and the life in the streets around me. On my way up the hill to the square known as Klosteret I saw that long stalks of grass were growing through the tarmac and that in some places there were small bare boulders between the houses, they linked the town to the wild mountains around, and to the sea below, everything that had not been wrought by human hand, and the fact that the town was part of the landscape, not separate, somehow closed in around itself, as I had felt during the first two days there, sent a fresh wave of good feeling through me. Rain fell everywhere, the sun shone everywhere, everything was connected with everything.

Yngve had explained the route to me in detail and I had no problem finding my way, I walked down a narrow path, passed some strange crooked cottages and there, at the bottom of a hill, lay Verftet at the water's edge. Made of brick, and built in the nineteenth century, it even had a tall factory chimney. I walked round to the entrance, touched the door, it was open, went in. An empty corridor with some doors, no signs. I continued along it. A man came out of one door, in his thirties or thereabouts, wearing big black glasses, a stained T-shirt, an artist.

'I'm looking for the Writing Academy,' I said. 'Do you know where it is?'

'No idea,' he said. 'It's not here anyway.'

'Are you sure?'

'Of course I'm sure,' he said. 'If I wasn't I wouldn't have said what I did.'

'No, right,' I said.

'But try upstairs on the other side. There are some offices and stuff there.'

I did as he said. Went upstairs and through the door. A corridor with some pictures of Verftet in its heyday on the walls, a spiral staircase at the end.

I opened a door and walked along a corridor, one of the many doors was ajar and I peeped in, a workshop, I turned round and went back, stopped at the entrance hall, where a woman, probably in her early thirties with a light blue coat and a plump face, big eyes and slightly crooked teeth, was just coming in.

'Do you know where the Writing Academy is?' I said.

'I think it's up there,' she said. 'Are you on the course?'

I nodded.

'Me too,' she said, laughing. 'I'm Nina.'

'Karl Ove.'

I followed her up the stairs. She carried a big bag over her shoulder, and the conventionality of her appearance, which resided not just in her coat, bag and the small lady-like boots she wore but also in the way her hair was pinned up, how little girls used to have it in the nineteenth century, disappointed me, I had expected something rougher, wilder, darker. Not the norm at any rate. If they let in the norm, maybe I was also there because I was the norm.

She opened the door at the top of the stairs, and we stepped into a large room with slanting walls and three big windows on one side, two doors with a bookshelf between them on the other. In the middle were some desks arranged in a horseshoe shape. Three people sat there. Two men were standing in front of them. One, tall and slim, wearing a suit jacket with the sleeves rolled up, looked straight at us and smiled. He wore a gold chain around his neck, I noticed, and had several rings on his fingers. The other man, shorter in stature, also wearing a suit jacket, with a slight paunch which the much-too-tight jacket emphasised, sent us a hasty glance and looked down. Both had moustaches. The former may have been pushing thirty-five; the latter, who stood with his arms crossed, was around thirty.

They appeared nervous in the sense that they both radiated a feeling that they would rather not be right here, right now. But in diametrically opposed ways.

'Welcome to the Writing Academy,' the tall one said. 'Ragnar Hovland.'

I shook his hand, said my name.

'Jon Fosse,' said the other one, and he said it quickly, in fact, he almost spat it out.

'Take a seat while we're waiting,' Ragnar Hovland said. 'There's coffee in the pot, and water in there, if you want it.'

As he said this he alternated his gaze between Nina and me, but once he had finished he looked away. His voice trembled slightly as though he really had to make an effort to say what he did. At the same time he gave an impression of wiliness, as though he knew something no one else knew and then looked away to laugh at us inside.

'I haven't read any of your books yet,' I said, looking at him. 'But I've just been working as a teacher and at the school we used one of your textbooks.'

'Well, that's strange,' he said. 'I've never published any text-books.'

'But I saw your name on it,' I said. 'I'm absolutely certain. Rag-nar Hovland, isn't it?'

'Yes, it is. But, as I said, I haven't written any textbooks.'

'But I saw it,' I said.

He smiled.

'You can't have done. Unless of course I have a doppelgänger somewhere.'

'I'm absolutely positive,' I said, but realised I wouldn't get any further with this and put my bag down on a chair, went to the coffee machine, pulled a plastic cup off the low stack and filled it with coffee. I had seen his name, I was pretty sure. Why wouldn't he admit it? Surely there was no shame in publishing a textbook for schoolchildren? Or was that precisely what it was?

I took a seat, lit a cigarette and pulled over an ashtray. Across the table a dark-haired middle-aged woman sat looking at me. She smiled when I met her eyes.

'Else Karin,' she said.

'Karl Ove,' I said.

Beside her a girl was reading. She was probably about twenty-five, had long fair hair in a ponytail, it seemed to tauten her face and along with her small straight lips gave her a stern appearance, which the fleeting glance she sent me – in which I sensed a good deal of scepticism – reinforced.

On her other side there was a man of the same age, tall and thin, he had a small head and a big Adam's apple, and a conspicu-ously drooping mouth, there was something distinctly formal about him, and conventional.

'I'm Knut,' he said. 'Nice to meet you.'

At the door two more appeared, one had a beard and glasses, a red lumberjack shirt, a light blue windcheater and a pair of brown corduroy trousers. He reminded me of the kind of temp who worked in shops selling second-hand comics or something like that. The other was a girl, quite short, wearing a large black leather jacket, black trousers and a pair of robust black shoes. Her hair was also black, and she tossed her head and stroked back her fringe twice in the short time I was watching them. But her mouth was sensitive, and her eyes were as black as two lumps of coal.

'Petra,' she said and pulled a chair back.

'And my name's Kjetil,' he said, and smiled slyly down at the desk.

She blinked twice in quick succession, and her lips drew back over her teeth as though she were snarling.

I didn't want to gape, so I stared through the large roof windows onto the fjord, there was a dock on the other side containing a great rusting hull of a boat.

The door opened again, a woman of thirty to thirty-five came in, thin with a grey dull appearance, apart from her eyes, which were happy and alive.

I took a sip of coffee and glanced at the dark-haired girl again.

Her face was so attractive, but her aura was hard, almost brutal.

She looked at me, I smiled, she didn't smile back, and I blushed, stubbed my cigarette out firmly in the ashtray, took my pad and placed it on the desk in front of me.

'I imagine that's everyone,' Ragnar Hovland said, walking to the other end of the room with Jon Fosse, where there was a board on the wall. They sat down.

'Shall we wait for Sagen?' Fosse said.

'We'll give him a few more minutes,' Hovland said.

I was definitely the youngest person there, by a fair margin. The average debut age for writers in Norway was a little over thirty, I had read somewhere. I would be a little over twenty. But several of the others were also younger than the average. Petra, the stern girl, Knut, Kjetil. They were all around twenty-five. The dark-haired one might be forty. She dressed like a forty-year-old anyway, wide sleeves and big earrings. But tight trousers. Meticulously drawn eyebrows. And thick lipstick on her narrow lips. What the hell could she write?

And then there was the other one: Nina. There was something nebulous about her face, pale, a lot of skin, dark shadows under her eyes, cascading fair hair. She was probably better at writing; however, how good could she be?

In through the door came a short man who must have been Sagen. He was wearing a blue fur trapper hat, a brown leather jacket, blue shirt and dark brown corduroy trousers. Dark curly hair, a slight paunch.

'Sorry I'm late,' he said, opened the door to the right, rummaged around in the room there, re-emerged minus his jacket and hat. Sat down. A little bald patch.

'Shall we start then?' he said, looking at the other two. Hovland holding the edge of the chair, Fosse sitting with his arms crossed and looking down with his head turned to the side. Both nodded, and Sagen welcomed us to the course. He told us a little about how the school had come about, it had been his idea, how it had been established, this was the second year, and how it was a privilege to be here, we had been selected from more than seventy applicants, and the lecturers were among the best writers in the country. He handed over to Fosse and Hovland, who told us a bit about the teaching programme. This week we would go through the texts that we had sent in with our applications. Then there would be a section devoted to poetry, followed by one on prose, drama and essays. In between there would be writing periods and guest lecturers. One of them would be here for several of the periods, his name was Øystein Lønn and he would be a kind of main teacher, as well as Hovland and Fosse, that is. In spring there would be a longish period for writing, after which we would submit an extended piece before the end and we would be assessed on that. As regards teaching, the two lecturers would deal with the theory first, and this would be followed by written activities and textual analysis. There would be no history of literature, Jon Fosse said, this was the first time he had spoken, the texts they would go through and discuss would be predominantly recent ones, therefore modernist and postmodernist.

Øystein Lønn, another unknown writer.

I put up my hand.

'Yes?' Hovland said.

'Do you know anything about who the other guest lecturers are?'

'Yes. Not all the names have been confirmed yet. But Jan Kjærstad and Kjartan Fløgstad are two definites.'

'Great!' I said.

'No women?' Else Karin said.

'Yes, of course,' Hovland said.

'Perhaps we should do a round of introductions?' Sagen said. 'If you say who you are, how old you are and what you write, that sort of thing.'

Else Karin, who started, took her time and looked at everyone around her individually as she spoke. She was thirty-eight, she said, and had published two novels, but she had never had any form of training, this year she hoped to take a step forward. Bjørg, as the dull woman with the lively eyes was called, had also published a novel. None of the others had made their debut yet.

When it came to my turn, I said who I was, told them I was nineteen and wrote prose, somewhere between Hamsun and Bukowski, and was working on a novel at the moment.

'Petra, twenty-four, prose,' Petra said.

We were given a syllabus, and then Sagen fetched a pile of books, they were for us, a gift from a publishing house, we could choose: either *Gravgaver* by Tor Ulven or *Fra* by Merete Morken Andersen. I hadn't heard of either of them, but chose Ulven because of his name, the wolf.

Everyone drifted out of the rooms at the same time, and up the hill above Verftet I found myself walking alongside Petra.

'What do you reckon?' I said.

'About what?'

'The course!'

She shrugged.

'The lecturers were full of themselves and vain. But they might be able to teach us something all the same.'

'They weren't vain, were they?'

She snorted and tossed her head, ran her hand over her fringe, looked at me and a little smile flitted across her lips.

'Did you see all the jewellery on Hovland? He was wearing a necklace and rings and even a bracelet. Looked like some kind of pimp!'

I didn't say anything, although I thought she was being hard.

'And Fosse was so nervous he didn't even dare look at us.'

'They're writers, aren't they,' I said.

'So? Is that supposed to give them a dispensation? They only sit somewhere and write. That's all there is to it.'

Kjetil sidled up alongside us.

'I wasn't actually accepted,' he said. 'I was on the waiting list and someone cried off at the last minute.'

'That was lucky for you,' Petra said.

'Yes, it wasn't a big issue. I already live here, so all I had to do was turn up.'

He spoke the Bergen dialect. Petra spoke the Oslo dialect, the others did too, apart from Nina, who came from Bergen, and Else Karin, who came from somewhere in southern Vestland. I was the only Sørlander, and now I thought about it, had there been any writers from Sørland at all? Vilhelm Krag, yes, but that was around the turn of the last century. Gabriel Scott? Same. Bjørne-boe, of course, but then he had almost tried to erase all traces of his origins from his personality, at least that was how it seemed, judging by the TV interviews I had seen, in which he had spoken a refined form of *riksmål*, and, as far as the books he wrote were concerned, there weren't many characteristic Sørland features such as sea-smoothed rocks or double-ended boats in them.

Else Karin came up behind us all in a flurry. She seemed to be one of those women who surrounded themselves with a cloud of gestures and objects, bags and clothes and cigarettes and arms.

'Hi,' she said, planting her eyes on me. 'I've worked out that I'm exactly twice your age. You're nineteen and I'm thirty-eight. You're really young!'

'Yes,' I said.

'Fantastic that you got on the course.'

'Yes,' I said.

Petra turned away, Kjetil watched us with his good-natured eyes. Then we caught up with the others, they were standing at a junction and waiting for the lights to go green. The houses opposite were run-down, the walls grey with traffic fumes and dust from the road, the windows completely opaque. The sun was still shining, but over the mountains to the north the sky was very black.

We crossed the road, walked up a gentle hill, past a second-hand bookshop of the grubby kind, from what I could see in the windows: various comics were hanging at the back and some cheap paperbacks were laid out on a green felt cloth, all badly faded by the sun, which shone on the shopfront during the afternoon. A bit further, on the other side of the road, was the indoor swimming pool. I decided I would go there some day soon.

Up at Café Opera, we dispersed, I said goodbye and hurried homewards. I would have liked to buy some books, preferably a couple of collections of poetry because I had barely read a poem, except for those we'd had at school, which had mostly been by Wergeland and Wildenvey, and the stuff I encountered during the weeks when we put on a kind of cabaret in Norwegian at *gymnas*, with Lars and me reading texts by Jim Morrison, Bob Dylan and Sylvia Plath on stage. Those six poems were the only real poems I had read in my life, and firstly I didn't remember any of them and secondly I had an inkling the kind of poems we would be analysing at the Writing Academy would be different. However, books would have to wait until my loan arrived.

In the post box at home there were nothing but advertising leaflets, but among them was a little catalogue for an English book club based in Grimstad, of all places, which I perused carefully as you didn't need to have cash to get books there. I put a cross by *Shakespeare's Collected Works*, *Oscar Wilde's Collected Works*, *T.S. Eliot's Collected Poems and Plays*, all in English, and on one of the last pages there was a photography book, which I ordered, with pictures of scantily clad and naked women, it wasn't porn though, it was art, or at least serious photography, but for me it was all the same, and pins and needles ran down my spine at the thought that I could soon be sitting here and poring over them and . . . yes, wanking. I still hadn't done it, but now I sensed that it would be unnatural not to do it, everyone probably did it, and then up came this opportunity, this book, and I put a cross next to it, wrote the number and title on the back, my name and address underneath, and tore out the order form. It was free, the receiver also paid the postage.

While I was posting it I could send some change-of-address cards, I thought, and strolled off to the Post Office with the form and my little red and black address book in hand.

On the way back it began to rain. And it wasn't just the odd drop or two gradually increasing in intensity, which I was used to, no, here it went from zero to a hundred in one second flat: one moment it wasn't raining, the next, billions of drops were falling to the ground at once, and from the road around me came a spattering, almost a clattering sound. I jogged downhill, laughing inside, what a fantastic town this was! And as always when I saw or experienced something wonderful I thought of Ingvild. She was a living person who existed in the world with her own way of perceiving it, her own memories and experiences, she had her mother and father, her sister and her friends, the countryside she had grown up and walked in, all this resided within her, this immense complexity that is another person and of which we see so little when we are with them, yet it is enough to like them, to love them, for it takes nothing for this to happen, two serious eyes that suddenly beam with happiness, two playful teasing eyes that suddenly become unsure or introspective, that falter, a person faltering, is there anything more beautiful than that? With all their inner richness, yet faltering all the same? You see it, you fall in love with it, and it is not much, perhaps you will say it is not much, but the heart is always right. It never errs.

The heart never errs.

The heart never ever errs.

For the next few hours it was all pounding rain, bobbing umbrellas, furious windscreen wipers, car headlights piercing the rain and murk. I sat on the sofa occasionally looking out to see what was happening, occasionally looking down at my book, Ulven's *Gravgaver*, of which I understood not one word. Even when I really concentrated and read as slowly as I could, several pages at a time, I didn't understand. I understood as good as all the words, that wasn't the problem, and I also understood the sentences, as such, but I didn't understand what they meant. I had no idea. And that took the wind out of my sails because I knew of course that there was a reason we had been given these two particular books. They were regarded as good literature, as having importance, and I didn't understand them.

I didn't have a clue. There was something about someone coughing on an old gramophone recording, then there was a man who drove an unbelievably overheated car to a funeral, and then there was a couple who were at some kind of holiday resort. I understood that, but firstly there was no plot, and secondly there was no sequence of events, and no coherence, everything came at you higgledy-piggledy, and that was fine per se, but *what* was it that was higgledy-piggledy? It wasn't thoughts, there was no one in particular thinking this. There were no lines of argument either, or descriptions, it was just a bit of everything all at the same time, but it was no use trying to understand this, as I couldn't make sense of the bigger picture, what did it *mean*?

I hoped this was what we were going to learn.

I would have to follow closely, note down everything that was said, not waste a moment.

Modernism and postmodernism Fosse had said, that sounded good, it meant us and our time.

While I was eating lunch – because of my impecunious state, five slices of bread, butter and three soft-boiled eggs – there was a knock at the door. It was my neighbour from down below, Morten, holding a long black umbrella with a walking-stick handle and wearing a red leather jacket, blue Levi's and boat shoes with white socks, and even though his hair wasn't a mess this time, there was still something wild about him, perhaps especially the look he was giving me, but it was in his body language too, as if something powerful was stirring inside him and he was expending all his energy on that. And then there was his laughter, which burst forth in the strangest of places.

'Hi again!' he said. 'Can I come in? For a chat? Bit brief last time, you might say, heh heh.'

'Come in,' I said.

He stopped inside the door and looked around.

'Take a seat,' I said, kneeling down by the stereo to put on a record.

'*Betty Blue*, yep,' he said. 'I've actually seen that one.'

'It's a good film,' I said and turned to face him. He hitched his trousers up over his knees before he sat down. There was something formal about him, which, along with the vague yet intense impression of wildness, filled the whole room.

'Yes,' he said. 'Nice, she is. Especially when she went nuts!'

'Yes, she did go nuts,' I said, sitting down on the chair across the table from him.

'Have you lived here long?' I said.

He shook his head.

'No, sir! I moved in two weeks ago.'

'And you're studying law?'

'Exactly. Clauses and paragraphs. And you're going to be a writer, didn't you say?'

'Yes. Started today.'

'Shit, I wouldn't mind doing that. Articulating everything you feel inside,' he said, thumping his chest. 'I get so sad sometimes. Maybe you do too?'

'Yes, it happens.'

'Great to get it out, is it?'

'Yes. But that's not why, you know.'

'Why what?'

'Why I write.'

He looked at me with a self-assured smile, slapped both palms against his thighs and prepared to stand up, or so it seemed, but he didn't, instead he leaned back in the sofa.

'Are you in love? Right now, I mean,' he said.

I looked at him.

'Are *you*? Since you're the one asking.'

'I'm fascinated by a girl. If I can put it like that. Fascinated.'

'I am too,' I said. 'Incredibly so.'

'What's her name?'

'Ingvild.'

'Ingvild!' he said.

'Don't tell me you know her,' I said.

'No, no. Is she a student?'

'Yes.'

'Are you a couple?'

'No.'

'Same age as you?'

'Yes.'

'Monica's two years older than me. That's perhaps not so good.'

He fiddled with the ribs of the umbrella, which was propped up against the sofa next to his calf. I took out my tobacco pouch and began to make a roll-up.

'Have you met the others in the house yet?' he said.

'No,' I said. 'Only you. And I caught a glimpse of the girl who was having a shower.'

'Lillian,' he said. 'She lives behind the staircase on the same floor as you. An old lady lives above her. She sticks her nose into everything, but she's not dangerous. Above you is Rune. A nice fellow from Sogndal. That's it.'

'I'll get to know them in time,' I said.

He nodded.

'But now I won't take any more of your time,' he said, getting up. 'See you. I have the feeling I'll be hearing more about Ingvild soon enough.'

He went out, his steps grew fainter as he went downstairs, I continued eating.

The next morning I walked up to the university to find out whether my loan had come through, it hadn't, and I went down a street alongside Høyden, as the university area was called, at the end was Mount Dragefjell, where the law students' building was, there I turned right down one of the narrow alleyways and emerged unexpectedly by the swimming pool. As I passed I drew the air deep into my lungs because from a grille set in the pavement came the smell of chlorine, and with it all the pleasant memories of my childhood unfolded like flowers in the first rays of sun after a night of slumber.

Where I walked, however, there wasn't much sun to speak of, the rain was pouring down, hard and unremitting, and between the buildings the water in the fjord was heavy and grey, beneath a sky that was so low and so full of moisture that the dividing line between it and the fjord appeared to have been erased. I had admitted defeat and put on a raincoat, a light, green affair that made me look like a bumpkin or a hick from the hills or something, but in this weather there was nothing else you could do, these weren't showers over in half an hour; the cloud cover above me was thick and grey, bordering on black, and hung over the town like a tarpaulin bulging with water.

It affected the atmosphere in the classroom because with all the boots and umbrellas and wet coats, as well as the grey light outside, which caused the room to be reflected in the windows, it was vaguely reminiscent of how it had been in all the various classrooms I had sat in over the years, including those in northern Norway, which had already joined all the other good memories I had of rooms.

I sat down, took out my notebook, grabbed one of the stapled photocopies from a pile and started to read, as that was what all the others were doing. Under the blackboard sat Fosse and Hovland, doing the same. We were going through Trude's – she was the stern one – texts first. They were poems, and they were beautiful, I could see that right away. There were dreamy landscapes, horses, wind and light, all concentrated into a few lines. I read them, but I didn't know what I was supposed to be looking for, had no idea what was good or not, or what might make them better. And as I read the fear grew in my breast, for this was immeasurably better than what I had written, there was no comparison, this was art, that at least I did understand. And what would I say if Fosse or Hovland asked me to comment on them? Some horses standing under a tree and, in the next line, a knife sliding across skin – what did it mean? Horses galloping across a field with thundering hooves and an eye hanging above the horizon?

Minutes later, work started in earnest. Fosse asked Trude to read. She sat still for a few moments, concentrating, then she began. Her voice seemed to tone into her poems, it wasn't as if the poems came out of her mouth, I felt rather that they were already there in advance and she used her voice to access them. At the same time there was no room for anything else, her voice could only contain the poems, the few words that made up a rounded whole, with nothing of her in it.

I liked her writing but also felt uncomfortable because it meant nothing to me, I didn't know what she was trying to say or what the poems were about.

After she had finished Hovland took over. Now we had to comment on the texts, and we would do it in sequence so that everyone spoke and had a chance to say something. What we had to remember, he said, was that none of the texts we discussed in class was necessarily finished or complete, and we learned through criticism. But it wasn't only criticism of our own texts that was important to us, it was equally important to be involved and discuss others' texts, for what this course was based on primarily was reading, learning to read, improving our ability to read. For a writer it was perhaps most important not to write, but to read. Read as much as you can because in so doing you won't lose yourselves, become unoriginal, what happens is the opposite, by doing this you'll find yourselves. The more you read, the better.

The round of comments began. There was a lot of hesitation and groping for words, most people confined themselves to saying they liked this image or that sentence, but amid all this some concepts emerged which were carried on and slowly became the standard currency for everyone, such as 'rhythm', the rhythm was 'good' or 'didn't quite flow', and then there was mention of 'tone' and 'the opening' and 'the ending' and 'deleting' and 'cutting'. That was a nice opening, and the rhythm's spot on, there's something a little unclear in the middle section, I'm not quite sure what it is, but something jars there, well, maybe you could shorten it a bit, I don't know, but then there's that strong image at the end which elevates the whole poem. That was how it began to sound when poetry was under discussion. I liked this way of talking because it didn't exclude me, I could understand openings and endings, I became particularly good at endings, the idea that something had to rise and resonate after the last line. I always looked for that, and if I found it I piped up. If I didn't, I said so too. You sort of shut off the poem here, I would say then. Can you see? The last line? It's a conclusion, it shuts itself off. Can't you delete it? Then you open everything up. Do you see? Also the question of line breaks came up in these readings. It soon transpired that chopped-up prose, as it was called, whereby standard prose was divided up as if it were a poem, was the enemy, the nightmare in person. It looked like a poem, but it wasn't, and this was the 1970s, something they did back then. In addition, we discussed all the literary devices, such as metaphors and alliteration, but not often because Fosse and the students who wrote poetry had an aversion to metaphors, I noticed, there was almost something ugly about metaphors, or old-fashioned, in the sense of passé or antiquated and useless for our purposes. It was bad taste, quite simply, naff. Alliteration was even worse. What was important was mostly rhythm, tone, line breaks, openings and endings. Jon Fosse, I noticed, when he made any comments, was always looking for whatever was unusual, different, out of the ordinary, as well.

This first session, however, was almost completely terminology-free, only Knut had a vocabulary fit to talk about poems, and his words also had the greatest impact. Trude sat in deep concentration, listening the whole of the time, making occasional notes and also asking direct questions, why this, why not that. I could see she was a writer and a poet, and she not only wanted to go far, she was already well ahead.

When my turn came I said the poems were full of atmosphere and they were profound but a bit difficult to talk about. In some places I didn't quite understand what she was trying to achieve. I said I agreed with a lot of what Knut had said, I particularly liked *this* line while she might consider leaving out *that* line.

While I was speaking I could see she didn't care. She didn't take any notes, she wasn't concentrated, and she watched me with a little smile at the corners of her mouth. I was upset and angry, but there was nothing I could do, other than sit back, push my papers away, say I had nothing more to add and sip my coffee.

After that Jon Fosse held forth. While both the way he moved his head – in jerks, like a bird, sometimes as if he had been startled by or remembered something – and the way he spoke – hesitantly, full of pauses, stutters, coughs, snorts, an unexpected deep breath here and there – suggested nervousness and unease, what he said was, by contrast, completely assured. He was utterly sure of himself, there was no room for doubt: what he was saying was right.

He went through all the poems, commented on their strengths and weaknesses and said that horses were a fine ancient motif in poetry and art. He cited the horses in the *Iliad* and the horses in the Parthenon Frieze, he cited the horses in Claude Simon, but these, he said, were more a kind of archetype, I don't know, have you read Ellen Einan? Something here is reminiscent of her. Dream language.

I wrote everything down.

The *Iliad*, the Parthenon, Claude Simon, archetype, Ellen Einan, dream language.

On my way home that afternoon I nipped up the alleyway to the left after the hill by Verftet to avoid having to walk with the others. It was still raining, as persistently and heavily as when I arrived, and all the walls, all the roofs, all the lawns and all the cars were wet and shiny. I was elated, it had been a good day, and Trude's total disregard for what I had to say, indeed her demonstration of this to the others, didn't bother me at all any more because in the break, when we had been in the café opposite Klosteret, I had spoken to Ragnar Hovland and exchanged opinions about Jan Kjærstad. In fact, it had been me who brought up his name. Else Karin had asked me what I liked reading, apart from Hamsun and Bukowski, I had said my favourite author was Kjærstad, especially his last book *The Big Adventure*, but also *Mirrors* and *Homo Falsus*, yes, and also *The Earth Turns Quietly* was good. She said his books were a little cold and contrived. I said that was exactly the point, Kjærstad wanted to describe humanity in a different way, not from within but from without, and the notion that characters in books were warm was a delusion, that was a construct too, of course, we had just got used to it and thought of this mode as genuine or warm while other ways of writing were equally genuine. She said yes, I understand that, but I still think his characters are cold. And this 'I think' was a victory for me, it wasn't an argument, just a feeling, empty words.

After the break it was Kjetil's turn, and his texts, which were prose and bordered on fantasy and the grotesque, were talked about in quite a different way. This wasn't about openings and endings or tone, we dealt more with the plot and individual sentences, and when someone said it was too exaggerated I said I had perceived this to be the whole point, that it was 'over the top'. The discussion was much livelier, this was easier to talk about, and it was a relief, this was material I could get my head round.

Tomorrow my texts would be read and discussed. I was terrified yet looking forward to it too as I walked up Strandgaten, in some way what I had written had to be good, otherwise I wouldn't have been accepted on the course.

Up the mountainside, from the station with the gleaming cobblestones, the bright red Fløybane glided smoothly into the green. FUNICULAR, it said in neon lights, and there was something alpine about this short ascent, a funicular railway rising from a town centre, a stone's throw from the old German wooden houses.

If you took away the water you could well imagine yourself in the German-Austrian Alps.

And oh the darkness that was a constant in Bergen! Not linked to night in any way, nor to shadow, nevertheless it was almost always here, this muted darkness suffused with falling rain. Objects and events became so concentrated when it was like this because the sun opened up airspace, and everything that was in it: a father putting shopping bags in a car boot outside Støletorget while the mother bundled their children onto the back seat, got in at the front, drew the safety belt across her chest and buckled it into place, watching this when the sun was shining and the sky was light and open was one thing, then all their movements seemed to flutter past and vanish the moment they were carried out; however, it was a very different matter watching the same family if it was raining, enveloped by the muted darkness, for then there was a leadenness about their movements, it was as if they were statues, these people, transfixed in this moment – which, the very next, they had left anyway. The dustbins outside the stairs, seeing them in strong sunlight was one thing, they were hardly there, as almost nothing was, but it was quite a different matter in rain-darkened daylight, then they stood like shining pillars of silver, some of them magnificent, others sadder and more wretched, but all there, just then, at that moment.

Yes, Bergen. The *incredible* power that lay in all the various house fronts squeezed together everywhere. The head rush you had as you slogged your way uphill and saw this, at your feet, could be wonderful.

But it was also good to lock yourself in your room after a walk through the town, it was like being in the eye of a storm, sheltered from prying eyes, the only place where I was totally at peace. This afternoon I had run out of tobacco, but I had known it would happen and had saved all my dog-ends from recent days. After putting on the coffee machine, I took the scissors from the drawer and set about snipping the ash off the stubs. When I had done that I opened them up and sprinkled the bone-dry tobacco into my pouch, which in the end was half full. My fingertips were black and reeked of smoke, I rinsed them under the tap, and then I cut a slice of raw potato and put it into the pouch; soon the tobacco would have absorbed the moisture and be like new again.

In the evening I went to the telephone box and rang Ingvild. Once again a man answered. Ingvild, yes, hold on a moment and I'll see if she's at home.

I was trembling as I waited.

Footsteps approached. I heard someone take the receiver.

'Hello?' she said.

Her voice was darker than I remembered.

'Hello,' I said. 'Karl Ove here.'

'Hi!' she said.

'Hi,' I said. 'How's it going? Have you been in town long?'

'No, I arrived on Monday.'

'I've been here a couple of weeks already,' I said.

Silence.

'We were talking about meeting if you remember,' I said. 'I don't know if you still want to, but what about Saturday?'

'Yes, I've got nothing on the calendar then, no.' She chuckled.

'Café Opera maybe? Then we can go to Hulen afterwards. What about that?'

'Just like real students do, you mean?'

'Yes.'

'Sounds fine. But I warn you: I'll be a bundle of nerves.'

'Why?'

'I haven't been a student before, that's for starters. And second, I don't know you.'

'I'll be a bundle of nerves too,' I said.

'Good,' she said. 'So perhaps it doesn't really matter if we don't say much.'

'No,' I said. 'Quite the contrary. That sounds great.'

'Now don't exaggerate.'

'It's true!' I said.

She chuckled again.

'This is my first student date,' she said. 'Café Opera on Saturday. Shall we say . . . well, when do students actually go out?'

'Your guess is as good as mine. Seven?'

'That sounds about right. Let's say seven then.'

My stomach constricted as I crossed the street and went back into my bedsit. I felt as if I could throw up at any time. And that was after everything had gone well. However, a few words on the phone was not the same as sitting face to face with nothing to say and your guts on fire.

There were two things that particularly bothered me in those days. One was that I came too fast, often before anything had happened at all, and the other was that I never laughed. That is, it did happen once in a while, maybe once every six months, when I would be overcome by the hilarity of something and just laugh and laugh, but that was always unpleasant because then I completely lost control, I was unable to regain my composure, and I didn't like showing that side of myself to others. So basically I was able to laugh, I had the capacity, but in my everyday life, in social situations, when I was with people around a table chatting, I never laughed. I had lost that ability. To make up for this, I smiled a lot, I might also emit some laughter-like sounds, so I don't think anyone noticed or found it conspicuous. But I knew: I never laughed. As a result, I became especially conscious of laughter as such, as a phenomenon – I noticed how it occurred, how it sounded, what it was. People laughed almost all the time, they said something, laughed, others said something, everyone laughed. It lubricated conversations or gave them a shot of something else which didn't have so much to do with what was being said as with being together with others. People meeting. In this situation everyone laughed, each in their own way, of course, and sometimes because of something genuinely funny, in which case the laughter lasted longer and could at times completely take over, but also for no apparent reason at all, just as a token of friendliness or openness. It could conceal insecurity, I knew that well, but it could also be strong and generous, a helping hand. When I was small I laughed a lot, but at some point it stopped, perhaps as early as the age of twelve, at any rate I remember there was a film with Rolv Wesenlund that filled me with horror, it was called *The Man Who Could Not Laugh*, and it was probably when I heard about it that I realised actually I didn't laugh. From then on, all social situations were something I took part in and watched from the outside as I lacked what they were full of, the interpersonal link: laughter.

I wasn't glum though. I wasn't a wet blanket! I was no introverted brooder! I wasn't even shy or diffident!

I just seemed to be.

Even though it was only the third time I had attended the Writing Academy it already felt familiar, almost homely, both the way there, first the steep hills down to Vågsbunnen, then along the row of office blocks and shops in Strandgaten, then up the hills by Klosteret and down the narrow alleyway opposite, all woven into the veil of rain that fell from the low sky, and even the room we occupied, with the bookshelf on one side, the board on another and the slanting wall with the windows on a third. I entered the room, said hi to those already present, took off my wet coat, retrieved my papers and book from my wet plastic bag, placed them on the table, poured myself some coffee and lit a cigarette.

'What weather,' I said, shaking my head.

'Welcome to Bergen,' Kjetil said, looking up from a book.

'What are you reading?' I said.

'*All Fires the Fire*. Short stories by Julio Cortázar.'

'Are they good?'

'Yes. But they're perhaps a bit cold,' he said, smiling. I smiled back. In the middle of the table was a pile of photocopies, I recognised them as mine from the typeface, the typewriter symbols and the few corrections I had made with a black felt pen, and took one.

Else Karin caught my eye.

She was sitting with one leg tucked underneath her on the chair, her left arm wrapped around her knee, her right hand holding a cigarette and my manuscript.

'Are you nervous?' she said.

'Yes and no,' I said. 'Bit maybe. Did you like it?'

'You'll have to wait and see!' she said.

Bjørg, who was sitting next to her, glanced at us and smiled.

Through the door at the other end came Petra – with neither an umbrella nor rain gear – her black leather jacket glistening and her wet hair hanging over her forehead. Right behind her came Trude, wearing green waterproof trousers and jacket, the hood laced up tightly around her neck, on her feet high wellies, on her back a leather rucksack. I stood up, went to the kitchenette and poured myself another cup of coffee.

'Anyone else want any?' I said.

Petra shook her head, no one else looked in my direction. Trude was standing under the slanting window and pulling off her trousers, and even though she had jeans on underneath, just the movements, wriggling and squirming, gave me a hard-on. I put my hand in my pocket as I walked back to my place as nonchalantly as possible.

'Is everyone here?' Hovland said from his chair under the board. Fosse was sitting beside him with his arms crossed and his eyes downcast, as on the first two days.

'We're going to spend the first part of today on Karl Ove's texts. Then we'll go through Nina's after the break. If you're ready, Karl Ove, you can start reading yours.'

I read, the others followed attentively in their copies. When I had finished, the commentary round began. I jotted down key words. Else Karin thought the language fresh and alive, but the plot somewhat predictable, Kjetil said it was credible but slightly tedious, Knut thought it was reminiscent of Saaby Christensen, not that there was anything wrong with that per se, as he put it. Petra considered the names stupid. Come on, she said, Gabriel and Gordon and Billy. That's intended to be cool, but it's just childish and silly. Bjørg thought it was interesting, but she would like to know more about the relationship between the two boys. Trude said the writing had oomph, but there were many clichés and stereotypes, in fact, as far as she was concerned there were so many it bordered on being unreadable. Nina liked the radical use of 'a' endings in the Norwegian and the descriptions of nature.

Finally, Hovland gave his opinion. He said this was realistic prose, it was recognisable and good, in some places he had been reminded of Saaby Christensen as well, and of course there were some linguistic shortcomings here and there, but the writing had great power, and it was a story, which was an artistic achievement in itself.

He looked at me and asked if I wanted to add anything or if I had any questions. I said I was happy with the way we had gone through the text and I had got a lot out of it, but I was wondering what the clichés and stereotypes were, could Trude give me some examples?

'Yes, of course,' she said, and picked up her text. '"Land where no white man has set foot" for example.'

'But that's supposed to be a cliché,' I said. 'That's the whole point. That's how they see the world.'

'But even *that's* a cliché, you know. And then you've got "the sun peeped through the foliage" and "the ominous black clouds that betokened thunder" – betokened, right? Then you have "the Colt nestling warmly in his hand" – nestling warmly. I ask you. And it's like that throughout.'

'It's also quite affected and pseudo,' Petra said. 'When "Gordon",' she said, making finger quotes and smiling, 'says "*gir deg five seconds*", that's so stupid because we understand the writer wants us to understand the characters have seen it on TV and, like, use English.'

'Now I think you're being unfair,' Else Karin said. 'This is not poetry we're talking about. We can't make such high demands of single sentences; it's the totality that counts. And as Ragnar said, this is a story, and making it work is an art.'

'Just keep at it,' Bjørg said. 'I think it's interesting! And I'm sure there will be a lot of changes along the way.'

'I agree,' Petra said. 'Just change the stupid names and I'm happy.'

After this discussion I was angry and ashamed, but also confused because although I assumed the positive words had been said to reassure me the fact still remained that I had been accepted on the course, which, for example, Kjetil had not, so there must have been something good in what I had written. Clichés though were the problem, and according to Trude my texts consisted of nothing else. Or was it just that she was so snobbish she thought she *was* someone, a poet, in some way better than everyone else? Else Karin had said that I wasn't writing poetry, and Hovland had also emphasised that this was realistic prose.

This was how my mind was working as the others unpacked their lunches and Else Karin put on a new pot of coffee. But I realised I couldn't turn introspective now, that would give the impression it had upset me, that they had scored a hit, which would be the same as admitting that what I wrote wasn't as good as what they wrote.

'That book you were reading, could I have a look at it?' I said to Kjetil.

'Of course,' he said, and passed it to me. I skimmed through it.

'Where's he from?'

'Argentina, I think. But he lived in Paris for a very long time.'

'Is it magic realism?' I said.

'Yes, you might call it that.'

'I really like Márquez,' I said. 'Have you read him?'

Kjetil smiled.

'Yes, but he's not quite my style. It's a bit too high-flown for me.'

'Mhm,' I said, handing the book back and writing Julio Cortázar in my notebook.

After lessons I went to Høyden to pick up my student loan. I joined the queue at the Natural History Museum, it wasn't very long, the day was almost over, I showed my ID, signed and was given an envelope with my name on, I shoved it into my plastic bag and set off towards the Student Centre, where among many other things there was a little bank. The grey concrete building on a gentle slope shimmered in the rain. Through the doors, one at the front and two at the sides, students came and went, individuals hurrying, groups walking slowly, some familiar with this world, others new like me – they weren't difficult to spot, at least if my theory was correct: that those who seemed flustered and confused, with all their senses open, could not have been there more than a few days.

I went in the door, up the long stairs and entered the large open concourse full of columns and staircases, people at stands everywhere, there was Student Radio, Student Newspaper, Student Sports Association, Student Kayak Club, Student Christian Association, but I had been here before and headed at a determined pace towards the bank at the end, where once again I joined a queue, and after a few minutes I had transferred the money into my account and taken out three thousand kroner, which I stuffed into

my trouser pocket before going down to Studia, the student bookshop, where I wandered among the shelves for the next half-hour,
at first disorientated and irresolute, there were so many subjects
that were interesting and I thought I might need when I was writing, such as psychology, philosophy, sociology or art history, but I
concentrated on literature, that was the most important, I wanted
something about how to read poetry, and perhaps a book about
modernism, as well as some collections of poetry and novels. First
I found a novel by Fosse called *Blood. The Stone is*, the cover was black
with a picture of a semi-illuminated face, I turned the book over,
on the back it said 'Jon Fosse, 27 years old, cand. Philol. and lecturer at the Writing Academy in Hordaland, has this year published
his fourth book', and I was proud because I studied at the Writing
Academy, it was almost as though this was about me. I had to have
that one. In addition, there were several books by James Joyce, I
chose the one with the most appealing title, *Stephen Hero*, and then
I found one on textual analysis, it was Swedish and called *From
Text to Plot*, I had a flick through, the chapters were entitled 'What
is a Text?', 'Explain or Understand?', 'The Text', 'The Plot', 'The
Story', and might have been a bit basic, I thought, yet there were
terms in it I didn't understand, such as 'Towards Critical Herme-
neutics' or 'Historical Time and Phenomenological Time's Aporia',
but that just whetted my appetite, I wanted to learn, and I took
the book with me. I found a collection of poems by Charles Olson,
I knew nothing about him, but as I leafed through it I saw the
same kind of poetry as Trude had written, and I took that as well.
It was called *Archeologist of the Morning*. I added two books by Isaac
Asimov to the pile, I had to have something light to read as well.
Beside them was a novel, *G*, by someone called John Berger, on the
flap inside it said it was an intellectual novel, and I took that too.
I couldn't find any Cortázar, but I did find a paperback entitled
The Thief's Journal by Jean Genet, which I couldn't resist either, and
finally I decided I should have some philosophy as well and was

lucky enough to lay my hand immediately on a book about philosophy and art: *Introduction to Aesthetics*, Hegel.

After paying for all these books I went up the stairs to the canteen. I had been there once before, with Yngve, but then I hadn't
needed to think, he had taken care of everything, now I was on
my own, and my brain reeled at the sight of all the students sitting
in the enormous room eating.

.At one end was the counter, where you were either served
lunch or you helped yourself to what there was in a glass cabinet,
and then you paid at one of three cash desks and went to find
somewhere to sit. The windows at the opposite end were misted
up, the air, through which the buzz of voices rose and sank, was
damp and clammy.

I looked across all the tables, but needless to say didn't see anyone I knew. The thought of sitting there all alone was terrible,
so I turned and went the other way, for there, on the side facing
Nygård Park, was the grill where they served hot dishes and beer, a
bit more expensive than the canteen, but what did that matter, my
pockets were full of money and I didn't need to scrimp and save.

I ordered a hamburger, chips and a large beer and carried it to
an unoccupied window table. The students sitting here seemed
older and more experienced than those in the canteen, and there
were also some old men and women who, I guessed, were lecturers, unless they belonged to the group of eternal students I had
heard about, men in their forties with tousled hair and beards and
jumpers, who in the fifteenth year of their studies were still working on their majors in an attic somewhere as the world raced past.

As I ate I flicked through the books I had bought. On the inside
flap of the Fosse book there was a 1986 quote from Kjærstad: 'Why
isn't *Bergens Tidende* full of feature articles about Jon Fosse?'

So Fosse *was* a good writer, and not just that, he was one of
the leading lights in the country, I thought, raising my gaze as
I chewed the bread and meat into a tasty pulp. The bushes in

Nygård Park stood like a green wall against the narrow wrought-iron fence, and in the grey air above them the rain angled down, caught by a sudden gust of wind which whistled along the street beneath me that very next moment and flapped at the umbrellas of two women who had just walked down the stairs.

In the evening I called Yngve and asked where he had been hiding recently. He said he had been working and he had been out the night the loan arrived and I had to get a phone so that he didn't have to walk all the way up to my digs every time he wanted something from me. I said I'd got my loan now and I would think about buying a phone.

'Did you have a good time?' I persisted.

'It was good. I came home with a girl.'

'Who was she?' I said.

'No one you know,' he said. 'We've seen each other at Høyden, that's all.'

'Are you going out with her now?'

'No, no, no. It's not like that. What about you? How's it going?'

'Fine. But there's quite a bit to read.'

'Read? I thought you were supposed to be writing.'

'Ha ha. I've just bought a Jon Fosse. Looks good.'

'Oh yes,' he said.

There was a silence.

'But if you haven't started writing yet, perhaps you can write some lyrics for me? Or preferably several. So that I can finish the songs.'

'I'll try.'

'You do that.'

I sat over Yngve's songs all evening and into the night, with music on my stereo, drinking coffee and smoking. When I went to bed at three, I had two semi-finished, well on the way, and one completely finished.

You Sway So Sweetly

Give me a smile
don't be unfair
just want to undress you
layer by layer

Dance, dance, dance
In a mindless trance
Don't ever stop
Keep on dancing
Until you drop

You sway so sweetly
You sway so sweetly

Give me a smile
don't try to fight
just wanna love you
all day and night

Dance, dance, dance
In a mindless trance
Don't ever stop
Keep on dancing
Until you drop

You sway so sweetly
You sway so sweetly
You sway so sweetly
You move so well

After lessons on Friday we went out. Hovland and Fosse took us
on their obviously well-worn path to Wesselstuen. It was a great

place, the tables were covered with white cloths, and as soon as
we sat down a waiter in a white shirt and black apron came over
to take our orders. I hadn't experienced that before. Our mood
was nice and relaxed, the week was over, I was happy, there were
eight of us carefully selected students sitting round the table with
Ragnar Hovland, already a legend in student circles, at least in
Bergen, and Jon Fosse, one of the most important young postmod-
ern writers in the country, who had also received good reviews
in Sweden. I hadn't spoken to them privately yet, but now I was
sitting next to Hovland, and when the beer arrived, and I'd had a
swig, I seized the opportunity.

'I've heard you like the Cramps.'

'Oh?' he said. 'Where have you heard such malicious gossip?'

'A friend told me. Is it right? Are you interested in music?'

'Yes, I am,' he said. 'And I do like the Cramps. So, yes . . . Say hi
to your friend and tell him he's right.'

He smiled, but there was no eye contact.

'Did he mention any other bands I liked?'

'No, just the Cramps.'

'Do you like the Cramps then?'

'Ye-es. They're pretty good,' I said. 'But the music I listen to most
at the moment is Prefab Sprout. Have you heard their latest? *From
Langley Park to Memphis*?'

'Certainly have, although *Steve McQueen* is still my favourite.'

Bjørg said something to him from across the table, and he
leaned over to her with a polite expression on his face. Jon Fosse
was sitting beside her and chatting to Knut. His texts had been the
last ones we went through, and he was still full of it, I could see
that. He wrote poems, and they were remarkably short, often only
two or three lines, sometimes only two words beside each other.
I didn't grasp what they were about, but there was something
brutal about them, and you wouldn't believe that when you saw
him sitting there smiling and laughing, his presence was almost

as friendly as his poems were short. He was garrulous as well. So personality wasn't the reason.

I put my empty beer glass down on the table in front of me and wanted another, but I didn't dare beckon to the waiter, so I had to wait until someone else ordered.

Petra and Trude sat beside me chatting. It was as if they knew each other from before. Petra suddenly seemed very open while Trude had completely lost her stern concentrated demeanour, now she had a girlish air, as though a burden had been lifted from her shoulders.

Although I couldn't really claim to know any of the other students, I had seen enough of them to form an impression of their characters, and even though these didn't necessarily coincide with their texts, except in the case of Bjørg and Else Karin, who both wrote the way they looked, I felt pretty sure I knew who they were. The exception was Petra. She was a mystery. Sometimes she would sit quietly staring down at the desk, with no presence in the room at all, it was like she was gnawing at her insides, I thought then, for despite not moving and despite her eyes being fixed on the same point, there was still an aggression about her. She was gnawing at herself, that was the feeling I had. When she eventually looked up there was always an ironic smile playing on her lips. Her comments were usually ironic, and not infrequently merciless, though somehow correct, albeit exaggerated. When she was enthusiastic this could vanish, her laughter might then become heartfelt, childish even, and her eyes, which so often smouldered, sparkled. Her texts were like her, I thought, as she read them, just as spiky and grudging as she was herself, at times clumsy and inelegant, but always full of bite and force, invariably ironic, though not without passion even so.

Trude got up and walked across the room. Petra turned to me.

'Aren't you going to ask me what bands I like?' she said with a smile, but the eyes she fixed on me were dark and mocking.

'I can do,' I said. 'What bands do you like?'

'Do you imagine I care about boys' room banter?' she said.

'How should I know?' I said.

'Do I look like that type of girl?'

'In fact, you do,' I said. 'The leather jacket and so on.'

She laughed.

'Apart from the stupid names, and all the clichés, and the lack of psychological insight, I quite liked what you wrote,' she said.

'There's nothing left to like,' I said.

'Yes, there is,' she said. 'Don't let what others say upset you. It's nothing, just words. Look at those two,' she said, motioning towards our teachers. 'They're wallowing in our admiration. Look at Jon now. And look at Knut lapping it up.'

'First of all, I'm not upset. Second of all, Jon Fosse is a good writer.'

'Oh yes? Have you read any of his stuff?'

'A bit. I bought his latest novel on Wednesday.'

'*Blood. The Stone is*,' she said in a deep Vestland voice, fixing me with her eyes. Then she laughed that heartfelt bubbling laugh of hers, which was abruptly cut short. 'Ay yay yay, there's so much posturing!' she said.

'But not in the stuff *you* write?' I said.

'I've come here to learn,' she said. 'I have to suck as much out of them as I can.'

The waiter came over to our table; I raised my finger. Petra did the same, at first I thought she was taking the mickey out of me, but then realised she wanted a beer too. Trude came back, Petra turned to her and I leaned across the table to catch Jon Fosse's attention.

'Do you know Jan Kjærstad?' I said.

'Yes, a bit. We're colleagues.'

'Do you consider yourself a postmodernist as well?'

'No, I'm probably more of a modernist. At least compared with Jan.'

'Yes,' I said.

He looked down at the table, seemed to discover his beer and took a long draught.

'What do you think of the course so far?' he said.

Was he asking me?

I flushed.

'It's been good,' I said. 'I feel I've learned a lot in a short time.'

'Nice to hear,' he said. 'We haven't done much teaching, Ragnar and I. It's almost as new to us as it is to you.'

'Yes,' I said.

I knew I ought to say something, for I suddenly found myself at the beginning of a conversation, but I didn't know what to say, and after the silence between us had lasted several seconds, he looked away, his attention was caught by someone else, whereupon I got up and went to the toilets, which were behind a door at the other end of the room. There was a man peeing in the urinal, I knew I wouldn't be able to perform with him standing there, so waited for the cubicle to become vacant, which happened the very next moment. There was some toilet paper on the floor tiles, wet with urine or water. The smell was rank and I breathed through my nose as I peed. Outside the cubicle I heard water rush into the sinks. Immediately afterwards, the hand drier roared. I flushed and went out just as the two men left through the door, while another older man with a huge gut and a ruddy Bergen face came in. Although the toilet was a mess, with the floor wet and dirty and the smell vile, it still had the same solemnity as the restaurant outside with its white tablecloths and aproned waiters. No doubt it had something to do with its age: both the tiles and the urinals came from a different era. I rinsed my hands under the tap and looked at my reflection in the mirror, which bore no resemblance to the inferiority I felt inside. The man positioned himself, legs apart, by the urinal, I thrust my hands under the current of hot air, turned them over a few times and went back to the table, where there was another beer waiting for me.

When it was finished and I had started on the next, slowly my timidity began to ease, in its place came something soft and gentle and I no longer felt I was on the margins of the conversation, on the margins of the group, but in the centre, I sat chatting first with one person, then with another, and when I went to the loo now it was as though I took the whole table there with me, they existed in my head, a whirl of faces and voices, opinions and attitudes, laughter and giggles, and when some began to pack up and go home I didn't notice at first, it happened on the extreme periphery and didn't matter, the chatting and drinking carried on, but then Jon Fosse got up, followed by Ragnar Hovland, and it was terrible, we were nothing without them.

'Have another one!' I said. 'It's not so late. And it's Saturday tomorrow.'

But they were adamant, they were going home, and after they had gone the urge to leave spread, and even though I asked each and every one of them to stay a bit longer the table was soon empty, apart from Petra and me.

'You're not going to go as well, are you?' I said.

'Soon,' she said. 'I live quite a way out of town, so I have to catch the bus.'

'You can doss at my place,' I said. 'I live up in Sandviken. There's a sofa you can sleep on.'

'Are you that keen to keep drinking?' she laughed. 'Where shall we go then? We can't stay here any longer.'

'Café Opera?' I suggested.

'Sounds good,' she said.

Outside, it was lighter than I had expected, the remnants of the summer night's lustre had blanched the sky above us as we ascended the hill towards the theatre, past the row of taxis, the ochre glow from the street lamps as if drawn across the wet cobblestones, the rain pelting down. Petra was carrying her black leather bag and although I didn't look at her I knew her expression was serious and dogged, her movements rigid and awkward. She was like a polecat: she bit the hands of those who helped her.

At Café Opera there were many vacant tables, we went up to the first floor, beside a window. I got us two beers, she drank almost half hers in one swig, wiped her lips with the back of her hand. I searched my brain for something to say, but found nothing, and drank almost half mine in one swig too.

Five minutes passed.

'What did you actually do in northern Norway?' she said out of the blue but in a matter-of-fact way as though we had been chatting for ages, while staring into the nearly empty beer glass she was nursing in front of her.

'I was a teacher,' I said.

'I know that,' she said. 'But what made you decide to do that? What did you hope to achieve?'

'I don't know,' I said. 'It just happened. The idea was to do some writing up there, I suppose.'

'It's a strange notion, looking for work in northern Norway so you can write.'

'Yes, maybe it is.'

She went to get some beer. I looked around me; soon the place would be full. She had rested her elbow on the bar, held up a hundred-krone note, in front of her one of the barmen was pouring a beer. Her lips slid over her teeth as she knitted her brow. On one of the first days she told me she had changed her name. Her surname, I assumed, but no, she had changed her Christian name. It had been something like Anne or Hilde, one of the most common girl's names, and I had thought a lot about Petra rejecting her first name because personally I was so attached to mine, changing it was inconceivable, in a way everything would change if I did. But she had done it.

Mum had changed her name, but that was to dad's surname, it was a convention, and when she changed it again, it was back to her maiden name. Dad had also changed his name, that was more unusual, but he had changed his surname, not his Christian name, which was him.

She walked across the floor, half a litre in each hand, and sat down.

'Who do you reckon will make it?' she said.

'What do you mean?'

'In class, at school.'

I didn't care much for her choice of word – I preferred academy – but I said nothing.

'I don't know,' I said.

'I said *reckon*. Of course you don't know.'

'I liked what you wrote.'

'Flattery will get you nowhere.'

'It's true.'

'Knut: nothing to say. Trude: posturing. Else Karin: housewife's prose. Kjetil: childish. Bjørg: boring. Nina: good. She's repressed, but she writes well.'

She laughed and slyly glanced up at me.

'What about me?' I said.

'You,' she snorted. 'You understand nothing about yourself and you have no idea what you're doing.'

'Do you know what you're doing?'

'No, but at least I know I don't know,' she said and laughed again. 'And you're a bit of a jessie. But you've got big strong hands, so that makes up for it.'

I looked away, my insides on fire.

'I've always had a wicked tongue on me,' she said.

I took some long swigs of the beer and scanned the room.

'You weren't offended by that little gibe, were you?' she said with a giggle. 'I could say far worse things about you if I wanted.'

'Please don't,' I said.

'You take yourself too seriously as well. But that's your age. It's not your fault.'

And what about you then! I felt like saying. What makes you think you're so bloody good? And if I'm a jessie, you're butch. You look like a man when you walk!

I said nothing though, and slowly but surely the fire subsided, not least because I was beginning to get seriously drunk and approaching the point where nothing meant anything any longer, or to be more accurate, when everything meant the same.

A couple more beers and I would be there.

Into the room, between all the occupied tables, strode a familiar figure. It was Morten, wearing his red leather jacket and carrying a light brown rucksack on his back and a folded umbrella in his hand, the long one I had seen before. When he spotted me his face lit up and he rushed at full speed across to our table, tall and lanky, his hair spiky and glistening with gel.

'Hi there!' he grinned. 'Out drinking, are you?'

'Yes,' I said. 'This is Petra. Petra, this is Morten.'

'Hi,' Morten said.

Petra gave him the once-over and nodded, then turned and looked the other way.

'We've been out with the Academy,' I said. 'The others went home early.'

'Thought writers were on the booze 24/7,' he said. 'I've been in the reading room until now. I don't know how this is going to work out. I don't understand a thing! Not a thing!'

He laughed and looked around.

'Actually I'm on my way home. Just popped by to see if there was anyone I knew. But I'll tell you one thing: I admire you writers-to-be.'

He looked at me seriously for a moment.

'Well, I'm off,' he said. 'See you!'

When he had rounded the corner by the bar I told Petra he was my neighbour. She nodded casually, drank the rest of her beer and got up.

'I'll be off now,' she said. 'There's a bus in fifteen minutes.'

She lifted her jacket from the back of the chair, clenched her fist and put it in the sleeve.

'Weren't you going to sleep at my place? It's not a problem, you know.'

'No, I'm going home. But I might take you up on your offer another time,' she said. 'Bye.'

So, with her hand round her bag and a steadfast gaze ahead she walked towards the staircase. I didn't know anyone else there but sat for a little longer in case someone turned up, but then being on my own began to prey on my mind and I put on my raincoat, grabbed my bag and went out into the blustery night.

I woke up at around eleven to rattling and banging inside the wall. I sat up and looked around. What was that noise? Then I realised and slumped back down. The post boxes were on the other side of the wall, but so far I hadn't slept long enough to know what it sounded like when the postman came.

Above me someone was walking around singing.

But the room, wasn't it remarkably light?

I got up and lifted the curtain.

The sun was shining.

I got dressed, went over to the shop and bought some milk, rolls and the daily papers. When I returned I opened my post box. Apart from two bills that had been sent on to me there were two parcel-delivery cards. I hurried to the Post Office and was given two fat parcels, which I opened with the scissors in the kitchen. *Shakespeare's Collected Works*, *T.S. Eliot's Collected Poems and Plays*, *Oscar Wilde's Collected Works* and a book with photos of naked women.

I sat down on my bed to flick through it, trembling with excitement. No, they weren't completely naked, many of them were wearing high heels and one had a blouse hanging open around her slim tanned upper body.

I put down the book and had breakfast while reading the three papers I had bought. The main news in *Bergens Tidende* was a murder that had taken place yesterday morning. There was a picture of the crime scene, which I thought I recognised, and I had my suspicions confirmed when I read the text underneath: the murder had been committed only a couple of blocks from where I was sitting now. And as if that wasn't enough the suspected murderer was still at large. He was eighteen years old and attended Technical School, it said. For some reason, this made quite an impression on me. I pictured him at this moment in a basement bedsit, in my imagination, alone behind drawn curtains which every so often he parted to see what was going on in the street, he viewed it from ankle height, his heart pounding and despair tearing at his insides because of what he had done. He punched the wall, paced the room, considering whether to hand himself in or wait for a few days and then try to get away, on board one of the boats perhaps, to Denmark or England, and then hitchhike his way down through Europe. But he had no money and no possessions, only what he stood up in.

I peered out of the window to see if anything unusual was happening, uniformed officers gathering, for example, or some parked police cars, but everything was as normal – except for the sunshine, that is, which hung like a veil of light over everything.

I could talk to Ingvild about the murder, it was a good topic of conversation, his presence here, in my part of town, right now, while virtually the whole of the police force was out looking for him.

Perhaps I could write about that too? A boy who kills an old man and goes into hiding while the police slowly close in on him?

I would never ever be able to do that.

A wave of disappointment washed over me and I got up, took the plate and glass, put them in the kitchen sink, together with all the other dirty crockery I had used during the week. Petra was wrong about one thing, and that was that I didn't understand myself, I thought, looking across the resplendent green park as a woman crossed with a child in each hand. Self-knowledge was the one quality I did have. I knew exactly who I was. Not many of my acquaintances knew as much about themselves.

I went back into the sitting room, was about to bend down to browse through my records when it was as if my eye was *dragged* towards the new book. A stab of joy and fear went through me. It might as well be now, I was alone, I had nothing in particular to do, there was no reason to defer it, I thought, and picked the book up, looked over my shoulder, how could I take it down to the toilet unnoticed? A plastic bag? No, who on earth takes a plastic bag with them to the toilet?

I opened the button of my jeans and unzipped, pushed the book down inside, covered it with my shirt, leaned forward as far as I could to see what it looked like, whether anyone would realise I had a book there.

Maybe.

What about taking a towel with me? If anyone came I could casually hold it over my stomach for the few seconds the encounter lasted. Then I could have a shower afterwards. Nothing suspicious about that surely, going to the toilet and then having a shower.

And that was what I did. With the book stuffed down my trousers and clasping the biggest towel I had I went out of the door, crossed the landing, down the stairs, along the corridor, into the toilet, where I locked the door, pulled out the book and began to leaf through.

Even though I had never masturbated before and wasn't exactly sure how to do it, I still knew more or less, the expressions 'jerk

off' and 'beat the meat' had been ever-present in all the wanking jokes I had ever heard over the years, not least in football
changing rooms, and so with the blood throbbing in my member
I took it out of the little pouch formed by my underpants, and as
I ogled the long-legged red-lipped woman standing outside a kind
of holiday bungalow in the Mediterranean somewhere, judging by
the white walls and the gnarled trees, beneath a line of washing,
with a plastic bowl in her hand, although otherwise completely
naked, while I looked and looked and looked at her, all the beautiful erotic lines of her body, I wrapped my fingers around my dick
and jerked it up and down. At first the whole shaft, but then after
a few times only the tip, while still staring at the woman with the
bowl, and then as a wave of pleasure rose in me, I thought I should
look at another woman too, to make maximum use of the book,
as it were, and turned over the page, and there was a woman sitting on a swing, wearing only red shoes with straps up her ankles,
and then a spasm went through me and I tried to bend my dick
down to ejaculate into the toilet, but I couldn't, it was too stiff, so
instead the first load of sperm hit the seat and slowly oozed down
while later blobs were pumped out, further down, after I had the
great idea of leaning forward to improve the angle.

Oh.

I had done it.

I had finally done it.

There was nothing mysterious about it after all. On the contrary, it was incredibly easy and quite remarkable that I hadn't
done it before.

I closed the book, wiped the seat, washed myself, stood stock
still to hear if, contrary to expectation, anyone was outside, shoved
the book back down my trousers, grabbed my towel and left.

It was only then that I wondered if I had done it right. Should
you shoot into the toilet? Or maybe the sink? Or a wad of rolled-up
toilet paper in your hand? Or did you usually do it in bed? On the

other hand, this was an extremely secretive business, so it probably didn't matter if my method deviated from the norm.

Just as I had put the book down on the desk, folded the unused
towel and placed it in the cupboard there was a ring at the door.

I went out to answer it.

It was Yngve and Asbjørn. Both were wearing sunglasses, and as
on the previous occasion there was something restless about them,
something about Yngve's thumb in his belt loop and Asbjørn's fist
in his trouser pocket or them both standing half-turned away until I opened the door. Or perhaps it was the sunglasses they didn't
take off.

'Hi,' I said. 'Come in!'

They followed me into my room.

'We were wondering if you fancied coming with us into town,'
Yngve said. 'We're going to some record shops.'

'Great,' I said. 'I've got nothing to do anyway. Right now?'

'Yes,' Yngve said, picking up the book with the naked women.
'I see you've bought a photography book.'

'Yes,' I said.

'It's not hard to guess what you're going to use that for.' Yngve
laughed. Asbjørn chuckled too, but in a way that suggested he
wanted this aspect of the visit over as quickly as possible.

'These are serious pictures, you know,' I said as I put on my
jacket, bent over and tied my shoes. 'It's a kind of art book.'

'Oh yes,' Yngve said, putting it down. 'And the Lennon poster
has gone?'

'Yes,' I said.

Asbjørn lit a cigarette, turned to the window and looked out.

Ten minutes later, side by side, all wearing sunglasses, we were
crossing Torget. The wind was blowing off the fjord, flags were
fluttering and cracking on masts, and the sun, which was shining
from a clear blue sky, glittered and shimmered on every surface.

Cars tore down the street from Torgalmenningen like a pack of hounds whenever the traffic lights changed to green. The market was packed with people, and in the fish tanks in the middle, caught in their few cubic metres of greenish and probably freezing-cold water, cod swam around with their mouths agape, crabs crawled on top of one other and lobsters lay still, their claws bound with white elastic.

'Shall we eat at Yang Tse Kiang afterwards?' Yngve suggested.

'Can do,' Asbjørn said. 'If you promise not to say Chinese food in China tastes quite different.'

Yngve didn't answer, took a packet of cigarettes from his pocket and stopped by the traffic crossing. I looked to the right where there was a vegetable stall. The sight of the orange carrots lying in bunches in a big heap made me think of the two seasons I had worked at the market gardener's on Tromøya, when we pulled up the carrots, washed them and packed them, and I was always so near to the earth, rich and black, under the late August and early September evening sky, the darkness and the ground so close together, and the rustle of the bushes and trees at the end of the field sent small shivers of happiness through me. Why? I thought now. Why had I been so happy then?

The lights changed to green and we crossed the street surrounded by a crowd of people, passed a watchmaker's shop, continued to a large square which opened up between the buildings like a clearing in a forest, I asked where we were going actually, Yngve said *actually* we were going to Apollon, and afterwards we were planning to visit some second-hand record shops.

Flicking through records in music shops was something I was good at, I knew most of the bands in the racks, I picked them up and looked to see who the producer was, who played what on the various tracks, which studio was used. I was a connoisseur, yet still I glanced over at Yngve and Asbjørn as we flicked through the LPs, and if either of them lifted a record out I tried to see what it was, what passed muster here, and in Asbjørn's case I could see it was partly old stuff, and curiosities such as George Jones or Buck Owens. What particularly caught my eye was a Christmas record he held up to show Yngve, they laughed, Asbjørn said it was really over the top, and Yngve said yes, it was really camp. But he kept to the same categories that I liked, British post-punk, American indie rock, the odd Australian band perhaps and of course a couple of Norwegian bands, but nothing beyond that as far as I could see.

I bought twelve records, most by bands I already had and one on Yngve's recommendation: Guadalcanal Diary. An hour later, sitting in a Chinese restaurant, they laughed at me for having bought so many records, but I sensed there was some respect in their laughter, it didn't just say I was a new student who had never had so much money in his hands before but that I was dedicated. A huge dish of steaming rice was set on the table, it stuck to the big accompanying porcelain spoon, we dug in and each transferred a heap onto our plates, Yngve and Asbjørn poured the brown sauce onto the rice and I did the same. It almost completely disappeared between the grains, and what had been at first thick and black was brown the very next moment, and the grains of rice visible through it. It tasted a little sharp, I felt, but the next mouthful, of beef chop suey, more than compensated for that. Yngve ate with chopsticks, manipulating them with his fingers like a native. Afterwards we had fried banana with ice cream, and then we had a cup of coffee with a small After Eight mint in the saucer.

During the whole meal I had tried to suss out what exactly the chemistry was between two such good friends when they got together. How long they looked into each other's eyes when they said anything before breaking off and looking down. What they talked about, how long for and why they had chosen that particular subject. Reminiscing: do you remember the time . . .? Other friends: did he say this or that? Music: have you heard this or that song, this or that record? Studies? Politics? Something that had just happened, yesterday, last week? When a new topic was broached was it linked to the previous one, did it peel off, so to speak, or was it just plucked out of the air?

But this didn't mean that I sat silently observing them, I was actively involved throughout, I smiled and made comments, the only thing I didn't do was embark on long monologues off my own bat, out of the blue, which both Yngve and Asbjørn did.

So what was going on? What was it all about?

First of all, they asked each other almost no questions, which I usually did. Secondly, to a large extent everything was connected, very little came up that was unrelated to what went before. Thirdly, most of it was aimed at making them laugh. Yngve told a story, they laughed at it, Asbjørn picked up the baton and moved the story into hypothetical mode, and if that worked, Yngve built on it until it became wilder and wilder. Their laughter ebbed away, a few seconds passed, Asbjørn recounted something that was closely related, also with the intention of making them laugh, and then it was more or less the same routine. Now and again they did touch on serious matters, in the same way, then they tossed a subject to and fro, sometimes in the form of a debate, all right, yes, but, you may say that, however, no, I'm not with you there, and there might be a pause, which made me fear there was bad blood between them, until a new story, anecdote or piece of banter emerged.

I was always especially vigilant with regard to Yngve, it was important for me that he didn't say anything stupid or display any form of ignorance, thus appearing inferior to Asbjørn, but that wasn't the case, they were on a level footing, and that pleased me.

Both replete and content, I walked uphill from the centre with a bag of records dangling from each hand, and it was only when I was almost home and saw a police car slowly driving past that I remembered the young murderer. If the police were still looking for him, well, he would be in hiding somewhere in the town. Imagine how frightened he must be. Imagine how insanely frightened he must be. And horrified by what he had done. He had killed another human being, stabbed a knife into another person's body, who fell to the ground dead. For what? a voice must be shouting in his head. For what? For what? A wallet, a few hundred-krone notes, nothing. Oh, how terrible he must feel.

When I had got myself ready to meet Ingvild it was only a few minutes past five, and so to kill the remaining time I went down to Morten's and knocked on his door.

'Come in!' he yelled from inside.

I opened the door. Dressed in a T-shirt and shorts, he turned down the stereo.

'Hello, sir,' he said.

'Hello,' I said. 'Can I come in?'

'Why of course, grab a seat.'

The white brick walls were high with two narrow rectangular almost opaque skylights as windows at the top. The room was spartanly furnished, if not bare: a box bed, also white, with a brown mattress upholstered in a kind of corduroy and large brown cushions made of the same material. A table in front and a chair on the other side, both the sort you find at flea markets and in second-hand shops, 1950s style. A stereo, some books, of which the fat red *Norwegian Law* was the most prominent.

He sat down on the bed with two of the large cushions behind him and appeared more relaxed than I had seen him before.

'One week at bloody Høyden behind me,' he said. 'Out of how many? Three hundred and fifty?'

'It's better to count days in that case,' I said. 'Then you've already done five.'

'Ha ha ha! That's the daftest thing I've ever heard! In which case, there are two and a half thousand to go!'

'That's true,' I said. 'If you think in years, you've only got seven left. On the other hand, you haven't done a thousandth yet.'

'Or a millionth, as someone in my class once said,' he said. 'Sit down, monsieur! Are you going out tonight or what?'

'How do you mean?' I said, sitting down.

'You look like you are. So well groomed, sort of.'

'Yes, but I have to be. I'm meeting Ingvild. In fact, it's the first time.'

'First time. Did you find her in a lonely-heart ad, eh? Ha ha ha!'

'I met her once this spring, in Førde, for half an hour or so. I was completely sold on her. Since then I've hardly thought about anything else. But we've been writing to each other.'

'I see,' he said, and leaned across the table, knocked a cigarette packet back towards him, opened it and tapped out a cigarette.

'Want one?'

'Why not? My tobacco's upstairs. But you can have a roll-up from me some other time.'

'I moved here to get away from people who smoke rollies,' he said, throwing me the packet.

'Where are you from?' I said.

'Sigdal. A little dump in Østland. All forest and misery. That's where they make the kitchens, you know. Sigdal Kitchens. We're proud of that, we are.'

He lit up and ran his hand quickly through his hair.

'Is it good or bad to look well groomed?' I said.

'It's good, of course,' he said. 'You're going on a date. You have to doll yourself up a bit.'

'Yes,' I said.

'And you're from Sørland?' he said.

'Yes. I come from a little dump down there. Or rather a shithole.'

'If you come from Shithole, I come from Shiteham.'

'Shit and shite are quite alike, if you don't like shit you won't like shite,' I said.

'Ha ha! What was that again?'

'Dunno,' I said. 'I just made it up.'

'Oh yes, you're a writer,' he said as he leaned back against the cushions on the bed, put one foot on the mattress and blew smoke up to the ceiling.

'What was your childhood like?' he said.

'My childhood?'

'Yes, when you were a young boy. What was it like?'

I shrugged. 'Don't know. I howled a lot, I remember.'

'Howled a lot?' he said, and then had a fit of hysterics. It was contagious, I laughed too, although I didn't really know what he was laughing at.

'Ha ha ha! Howled?'

'What's wrong with that?' I said. 'I did.'

'How?' he said, sitting up. 'OOOOOOUUUU! Like that, was it?'

'No, howled as in blubbered. Or cried, if you want it in plain language.'

'Oh, you cried a lot as a child! I thought you howled and yelled!'

'Ha ha ha!'

'Ha ha ha!'

After we had finished laughing there was a pause. I stubbed out the cigarette in the ashtray, crossed my legs.

'I went around on my own a lot when I was a kid,' he said. 'And I longed to get away from *ungdomskole* and *gymnas*. So it's fantastic to be here, basically, in my own bedsit, even though it looks terrible.'

'Right,' I said.

'But I'm nervous about studying law. I'm not sure it's really up my street.'

'You only started on Monday, didn't you? Isn't it a bit early to say?'

'Maybe.'

A door slammed outside.

'That's Rune,' Morten said. 'He's always taking showers. An un-believably hygienic person, you have to say.'

He laughed again.

I got up.

'I'm meeting her at seven,' I said. 'And I've got a few things to do first. Are you going out this evening?'

He shook his head.

'I was going to read.'

'Law?' I said.

He nodded.

'Good luck with Ingvild!'

'Thanks,' I said, and went back up to my place. Outside, the evening was exceptionally light; the sky in the west, which I could barely see from the window, rising from the trees and rooftops, had a reddish glow. Some black clouds hung like discs in the distance. I put on an old Big Country maxi single, ate a bread roll, put on my black suit jacket, moved my keys, lighter and coins from my trouser pocket to a jacket pocket to avoid the inelegant bulge on my thigh, put the tobacco pouch in an inside pocket and went out.

Ingvild didn't see me at first when she entered Café Opera. She wandered around shyly, looking from side to side, dressed in a white pullover with blue stripes, a beige jacket and blue jeans. Her hair was longer than when I last saw her. My heart was pounding so much I could barely breathe.

Our eyes met, but hers didn't light up as I had hoped. A little smile on her lips, that was all.

'Hi,' she said. 'You're here already, are you?'

'Yes,' I said, half-getting up. But we didn't know each other, a hug was perhaps too much, yet I couldn't just sit down again like some jack-in-the-box, so I followed through and offered my cheek, which luckily she brushed with hers.

'I'd hoped I would arrive first,' she said, hanging first her bag, then her coat over the back of the chair. 'So that I would have home advantage.'

She smiled again and sat down.

'Would you like a beer?'

'Ah, good idea,' she said. 'We have to drink. Could you buy this round and I'll buy the next?'

I nodded and went over to the bar. The room had begun to fill up, there were a couple of people ahead of me in the queue, and I studiously avoided looking straight at her, but from the corner of my eye I could see that she was staring out of the window. She had her hands in her lap. I was glad of the break, glad not to be sitting there, but then it was my turn, then I was given the two beers, then I had to go back.

'How's it going?' I said.

'With my driving? Or are we past that stage?'

'I don't know,' I said.

'There's so much that's new,' she said. 'New room, new subject, new books, new people. Well, not that I've studied any other subject before,' she added with a giggle.

Our eyes met, and I recognised that happy-go-lucky expression in her eyes that I had fallen for the first time I saw it.

'I said I'd be a bundle of nerves!' she said.

'I am too,' I said.

'*Skål*,' she said, and we clinked glasses.

She leaned to the side and took a packet of cigarettes from her bag.

'Well, how are we going to do this?' she said. 'Shall we start again? I come in, you're sitting here, we give each other a hug, you ask how it's going, I answer and then I ask you how it's going. Much better start!'

'I feel a bit the same,' I said. 'A lot of new things. Especially at the Academy. But my brother is studying here, so I've been hanging on his coat-tails.'

'And your cheeky cousin's?'

'Jon Olav, yes!'

'We've got a cabin where his grandparents live. There's a 50 per cent chance they're yours too.'

'In Sørbøvåg?'

'Yes, we've got a cabin on the other side of the water, at the foot of Lihesten.'

'Have you? I've been there every summer since I was a kid.'

'You'll have to row over and visit me one day then.'

There was nothing I would rather do, I thought, a weekend alone with her in a cabin beneath the mighty Lihesten, what on this earth could be better than that?

'That'd be fun,' I said.

There was a pause.

I tried to keep my eyes off her but couldn't stop myself, she was so beautiful sitting there looking down at the table with the lit cigarette in her hand.

She glanced up and met my gaze. We smiled.

The warmth in her eyes.

The light around her.

At the same time there was that slightly gauche insecurity that came over her when the moment was past and she watched her hand flicking the ash from her cigarette into the ashtray. I knew where the feeling came from, I recognised it in myself, she was wary of herself and the position she was in.

We stayed there for almost an hour, it was torture, neither of us managed to get a grip on the situation, it was as if it existed independently of us, something much bigger and heavier than we could handle. When I said anything it was tentative, and every time it was the tentativeness, not what was said, that prevailed. She kept looking out of the window, not wanting to be where she was, either. But, I sometimes thought, perhaps she too is struck by sudden intense waves of happiness at just sitting there with me, as I was at sitting with her. I couldn't begin to guess, I didn't know her, didn't have a clue what she was like normally. But when I suggested leaving it was relief she felt, I could see that. The streets had grown dark, apart from the heavy rain clouds there was something summery about the dusk, it was more open, lighter, filled with promise.

We walked up a hill towards Høyden, along a road cut into the mountain, a high wall on one side, railings on the other, and a row of tall brick houses beneath. The rooms inside the lit windows looked like aquariums. People were out in the streets, footsteps resounded in front and behind us. We said nothing. All I thought about was that she was only a few centimetres from me. Her footsteps, her breathing.

When I woke up next morning it was raining, the steady precipitation that was so typical of this town, distinguishable neither by its force nor its ferocity but still dominating everything. Even though you wore waterproofs and wellies when you went out you were still wet when you got back home. The rain crept up your sleeves, soaked into your collar, and the clothes under your rain gear steamed with humidity, not to mention what the rain did to all the walls and roofs, all the lawns and trees, all the roads and gateways as it relentlessly bucketed down onto the town. Everything was wet, everything had a membrane of dampness over it, and if you walked along the quay it felt as though what was above water was closely related to what was below it, in this town the borders between the two worlds were fluid, not to say floating.

It even affected your mind. I stayed at home all Sunday, yet still the weather impacted on my thoughts and feelings, which were somehow enveloped in something grey and unvarying and vague, reinforced by the Sunday atmosphere – empty streets, everything closed – which compounded with all the countless other Sundays I had known.

Apathy.

After a late breakfast I went out and called Yngve. Fortunately he was in. I told him about my date with Ingvild, how I was unable to say anything or be myself, he said she probably felt exactly the same, that was his experience, they were just as nervous and self-critical. Ring her and thank her for the evening, he said, then suggest meeting again. Not perhaps for a whole evening but a coffee. Then I would know how the land lay. I said we had already arranged to meet again. He asked who suggested it. Ingvild, I said. Well, that's all sorted then, he said. Of course she's interested!

I was happy to hear he was so sure. If he was sure, I was too.

Before we rang off he told me he was going to have a party at his place on Saturday, I could come and bring someone with me. As I ran across the street in the rain, I wondered who it should be, who I could take with me.

Oh, Ingvild of course!

Back home again, I thought about Anne who had been the technician for me when I was working for local radio in Kristiansand, she was in Bergen and would no doubt like to come along. Jon Olav and his friends. And maybe Morten?

Three times during the following hours I went down to the basement with the book stuffed down my trousers. I spent the rest of the day writing, and when evening came I sat on the sofa with the collection of poetry and the text analysis book I had bought to prepare for the poetry course which began the next day.

The first poem was short.

Nowadays

Whatever you say, let
the roots follow, let them
dangle

With all the dirt

just to make it absolutely clear
where they came from

Make it absolutely clear where *who* came from?

I read it again, and then I realised it was referring to the roots of words. That is, you should display the roots of words and the dirt around them to make it clear to those listening where the words came from. So, talk coarsely, or at least don't be frightened to.

Was that all there was to it?

No, surely it couldn't be. The words were probably a symbol of *something else*. Perhaps of us. In other words, *we* mustn't hide our origins. *We* mustn't forget who we once were. Even if this was nothing to be proud of. The poem wasn't at all difficult, you just had to read carefully and think about every word. But this didn't work with all the poems, some of them I couldn't crack however many times I read them and however much I thought about what they might mean. One poem in particular irritated me.

He who walks with a house on
his head is heaven he
who walks with a house
on his head is heaven he who walks
with a house on his head

This was pure surrealism. Was it the man who had the house on his head – and what did that mean by the way? – who was like a heaven or was it the house that was his heaven? OK, let's say the house was a symbol of a head and his thoughts were various rooms in the house and this arrangement was heaven. So? Where was he going with this? And why repeat *exactly* the same words two and a half times? This was just pretension, he had nothing to say, he put a few words together and hoped for the best.

For the next two days we were bombarded with poems and names of poets, schools and movements. There were Charles Baudelaire and Arthur Rimbaud, Guillaume Apollinaire and Paul Eluard,

Rainer Maria Rilke and Georg Trakl, Gottfried Benn and Paul Celan, Ingeborg Bachmann and Nelly Sachs, Gunnar Ekelöf and Tor Ulven, there were poems about cannons and corpses, angels and whores, gatewomen and turtles, coachmen and soil, nights and days, all thrown together in incongruous assortments, it seemed to me as I sat there taking notes because, since I had never heard of any of these names before, apart from Charles Baudelaire and Tor Ulven, it was impossible to establish any kind of chronology in my mind, they all became part of the same morass, modern poems from modern Europe, which clearly wasn't so modern after all, it was quite a long time since the First World War had raged, and I talked a bit about that in one of the breaks, the paradox of the poems being modernist while being so old-fashioned, at least as regards the content. Jon Fosse said that was an interesting point, but they were modern primarily as regards form and the radical thinking they expressed. This was still radical, he said. Paul Celan, no one had gone further than he had. And that made me realise that everything I didn't understand, everything I couldn't get my head round, everything in these poems that appeared closed or intro-spective to me, *this* was precisely what was radical about them and made them modern, also to us.

Jon Fosse read a poem by Paul Celan called 'Death Fugue', and it was dark and hypnotic and eerie, and I read it again at home in the evening, and heard in my inner ear the way Fosse had recited it, and I found it just as hypnotic and eerie then, surrounded by my own familiar things, which merely by virtue of these words going through my head lost their familiarity, they too were woven into the poem, and darkness swept through the poem, for the chair was only a chair, dead; the table was only a table, dead; and the street outside, it lay empty and still and dead in the darkness which emanated not only from the sky but also from the poem.

Although the poem touched a nerve in me, I didn't understand how it did or why.

Black milk of daybreak we drink it at sundown
we drink it at noon in the morning we drink it at night
we drink it and drink it
we dig a grave in the breezes there one lies unconfined

One thing was the fathomless darkness that existed in this poem, quite another was what it meant. What thoughts lay behind it? If I were ever to write like this I would have to know where it originated, be conversant with its starting point, the philosophy it expressed. I couldn't just write something similar. I had to understand it.

What would I write if I were to write a poem now?

It would have to be about what was most important.

And what was most important?

Ingvild was.

So, love. Or falling in love. The lightness of spirit that flooded through me whenever she was on my mind, the surge of happiness at the thought that she existed, she was here now, in the same town and we would meet again.

That was what was most important.

What would a poem about that be like?

Immediately, after two lines, it would be traditional. There was no way I could rip it into pieces, so to speak, and fling it over the pages the way modernists did. And the images that came to mind when I was thinking about it were also traditional. A mountain stream, cold mountain water glittering in the sun, the high mountains with white glaciers down the sides of the valley. That was the only image of happiness I could conjure up. Her face maybe? Zoom in on her eyes, the iris, the pupil?

Why?

The way she smiled?

OK, that's fine, but I was already light years away from the starting point, the dark hypnotic and bewitching allure of Paul Celan.

I got up from the bed and switched on the light, sat down at the desk and began to write. Half an hour later I had finished a poem.

Eye, I'm calling you, come
Face, my beloved, sorrow
And life that plays
a black melody
Eye, I'm calling you, come

That was the first decent poem I had written, and when I switched off the light and settled back in bed I had a better feeling about the Writing Academy than I'd had since I started. I had made huge progress.

The next day we were given our first written assignment, by Jon Fosse. Write a poem based on a picture, he said, any picture at all, and after lunch I was on my way to the art museum by Lille Lungegård Lake to look for a picture I could write about. The sun had come out in the morning, and there was a vibrancy about all the colours in town, everything was wet and gleamed with rare intensity, dazzling beneath the verdant mountain slopes and the azure sky.

Once inside, I took my notebook and a pen from my rucksack, then deposited it in a cloakroom, paid and went into the quiet, almost deserted gallery. The first picture that caught my eye was a simple landscape painting, depicting a village by a fjord, everything was clear and tangible, the sort of scene you could imagine seeing anywhere along the coast, yet there was something dream-like about it, not in a fairy-tale way as with Theodor Kittelsen, this was a different dream, harder to grasp but even more compelling.

Had I seen this landscape in real life I would never have dreamed of staying there. But when I saw it here, hanging in the white room, I wanted to go there, I longed to go there.

My eyes moistened. I liked the picture, which had been painted by someone called Lars Hertervig, it was so intense, and in a way it turned the whole situation on its head, I wasn't just a Writing Academy student without a notion in his head about art who had to write a poem about a picture, a pretender, but rather someone who felt so passionate about it that it brought tears to his eyes.

Happy about this, I went on. The museum had a large collection of Astrup paintings, I knew, that was one of the reasons I had come here. Astrup came from Jølster, grandma's home village, where his father had been the priest. During the whole of my childhood we'd had an Astrup painting on the wall above the staircase. It portrayed a meadow stretching up to an old farmyard, beneath some mighty, towering, though not unfriendly, mountains, and it was a midsummer night, the light floated gently across the meadow, which was full of buttercups. I had seen this picture so many times it was part of me. Outside the wall it hung on was the road and a housing estate, a quite different, sharper and more concrete world with manhole covers and bicycle handlebars, post boxes and caravans, home-made carts with pram wheels and kids with moonboots, nevertheless the nocturnal world in the picture was not a dream, not a fairy tale, it also existed in reality, near the farm grandma came from, where many of her siblings still lived and whom occasionally we visited in the summer. Grandma could remember Astrup, mum said, he was someone people talked about in the village, and at grandma and grandad's house there was another picture he had painted, which I had also seen all my life. It depicted a birch forest, thick with black and white tree trunks and children walking between them picking something or other, the picture was eerie and almost completely without a sky, but it hung there in the midst of their everyday life, above their sideboard, and merged into the sense of security there.

By and large all the pictures by Astrup had motifs from Jølster, they portrayed places I knew in real life, and were recognisable, yet they weren't. This duality, scenes that were both known and unknown, wasn't something I thought about or reflected on, but I was still familiar with it in much the same way that I never reflected on the room I went into to read, although I was familiar with it: the way I left the reality surrounding me and went into another from one moment to the next, and invariably longed to be where I wasn't.

The Astrup painting was part of me, and when Jon Fosse asked us to write a poem based on a picture that was the first one that occurred to me. I walked around the museum, keeping my senses open, if anything loomed up and inspired me I would write about it, but if not, I would write about an Astrup painting that was already in my head.

I wandered around for half an hour, stood taking notes in front of the picture by Lars Hertervig and the Astrup paintings, described the details so that I could remember them later, when I got home and had to write the poem. Afterwards I walked around the lake and into Marken, an area of town I had hardly ever been in before. It was packed, the sunshine had brought people outside. I had a coffee and wrote a few lines at Café Galleri, continued towards Torgalmenningen, and there, seeing the church towering over the town, it struck me that I could pop up and see whether Ingvild was in the reading room. The mere thought made me tremble. But there was nothing to fear, I told myself, she was only a human being like everyone else, the same age as me, what was more, and it wasn't just me who had found it difficult to talk and behave naturally last time, she had probably felt the same, and the very idea that she might be full of trepidation but wanted this as much as me was such a good uplifting thought that I scampered up the steps to Høyden.

Besides, I thought, when I arrived at the top and started walking in the direction she had indicated, I did also have a reason to see her, I was going to invite her to Yngve's party. If the meeting went well, I could wait until later, then I would have a reason to ring her again, but if it didn't I could use the invitation as a trump card.

After the bright sunshine the entrance to the Psychology Building was so dark that at first I couldn't read the letters on the sign there. And when they became clearer I was so distracted by nerves that for a few seconds I could hardly concentrate. My throat dry, my head burning, I finally managed to locate the reading room, and when I got there, so obviously flustered compared with the students I had met on the way, and scanned the rows of desks, there was someone standing at the far end and waving, it was her, she cleared her desk at a rate of knots, put on her denim jacket and came over to me with a smile on her lips.

'Great to see you!' she said. 'Shall we go for a coffee?'

I nodded.

'You'll have to lead. I don't know my way around here at all.'

There were lots of students outside today, on benches and kerbs and steps, and in the canteen at Sydneshaugen School, where we sat down with a cup of coffee, there was plenty of room between the tables. The atmosphere between us this time was much more relaxed, first we chatted a little about her studies and the people she shared her kitchen with in Fantoft, I told her about Morten, mentioned Yngve, how fantastic it had been to visit him in Bergen when I was at *gymnas*, she started to tell me about her childhood, she said she had been a typical tomboy playing football and scrumping apples, I commented there couldn't be much left of that in her now, she laughed and said she hadn't been planning to play football in Bergen, but that she would be going to the stadium the next time Sogndal came and she had also been thinking of taking in some of the home games at Fosshaugane. I talked a bit about IK Start and said that Yngve and I had been at the stadium when they beat Rosenborg 4–3 in the last match of the season in 1980 and became league champions, I described how we had stormed onto the pitch and stood outside the dressing room cheering the players, and how they had tossed their shirts out, and unbelievably I had caught Svein Mathisen's, the most valuable of all, the number 9, but a man had ripped it out of my hands and gone off with it. I said it was great being able to talk with a girl like her about football, she said she might have a few more surprises up her sleeve. She started to talk about her sister again, and then about all her inferiority complexes, there wasn't one thing she was good at, or so it seemed, but what she said was constantly contradicted by her laughter, and by her eyes, which not only belied her tale of wretchedness but also turned it onto its head. For some reason I told her about an incident in my childhood: I had got hold of some slalom goggles, I could only have been eight or nine, they were so cool, but there was one snag, they didn't have any glass in. Despite that I put them on the next time we went mini-skiing on the slopes down from our house. It was snowing, the snow blew into my eyes making it almost impossible to see but I kept on going all the same, and everything was fine until some bigger boys turned up. They thought my goggles were as cool as I did, and said so, at which my chest burst with pride, and then of course they asked if they could borrow them, I said no, no way, but in the end I allowed myself to be persuaded, and one of them donned the goggles and was about to set off when he turned to me and said, there's no glass in them! He didn't make fun of me or anything, he was just genuinely surprised, why would anyone ski with slalom goggles if there was no glass in them?

We sat there for half an hour until I accompanied her back to the reading room. We stopped outside and continued chatting, then Morten came up the hill, it was impossible to mistake him, even at a distance, there weren't many young men who wore red leather jackets, and of those only Morten could stride along the way he did, his limbs as rigid as a doll's, yet energetic and full of power. But now his head wasn't held high, as it had been the other times I had seen him, it was bowed, and as he approached

and I waved a hand in greeting I could see his face was racked
with anguish.

He stopped, I introduced Ingvild and Morten, he smiled fleetingly, then trained his eyes on mine. There were tears in them.

'I'm so desperate,' he said. 'I'm so bloody desperate.'

He looked at Ingvild.

'Excuse my language, fair maid.'

He turned back to me.

'I don't know what to do. I can't stand it. I have to get hold of a
psychiatrist. I *have* to talk to someone. I rang one, and do you know
what they said? They only take acute cases, I said I *was* an acute
case, I can't stand it any longer, I said, and they asked whether I
had suicidal thoughts. Of course I've got suicidal thoughts! I've got
a broken heart and everything's going to pot. But apparently that
wasn't acute *enough*.'

He fixed his eyes on me. I didn't know what to say.

'You study psychology, Ingvild, don't you?'

She glanced at me before answering.

'I started a week ago.'

'Do you know where I can turn in such circumstances?'

She shook her head.

He looked at me again.

'I may come up and see you tonight. Is that all right?'

'Yes, of course, come whenever you like,' I said.

He nodded.

'See you,' he said, and strode off again.

'Is he a close friend?' Ingvild said when he was out of earshot.

'Can't say he is, no,' I said. 'He's the neighbour I was telling you
about. I've only spoken to him three or four times. He wears his
heart on his sleeve. Never seen anything like it.'

'You can say that again,' she said. 'I'll be off then. Can you call
me?'

What a shock. For a brief moment, no more than a second or
two, I was unable to breathe.

'Yes,' I said. 'I can.'

When, shortly afterwards, I stopped at the top of the hill and saw the town beneath me, my feeling of happiness was so ecstatic that I didn't know how I would be able to make it home, sit there and write, eat or sleep. But the world is constructed in such a way that it meets you halfway in moments precisely like these, your inner joy seeks an outer counterpart and finds it, it always does, even in the bleakest regions of the world, for nothing is as relative as beauty. Had the world been different, in my opinion, without mountains and oceans, plains and seas, deserts and forests, and consisted of something quite different, inconceivable to us, as we don't know anything other than this, we would also have found it beautiful. A world with gloes and raies, evanbillits and conulames, for example, or ibitera, proluffs and lopsits, whatever they might be, we would have sung their praises because that is the way we are, we extol the world and love it although this is not necessary, the world is the world, it is all we have.

So as I walked down the steps towards the town centre on this Wednesday at the end of August I had a place in my heart for everything I beheld. A slab of stone worn smooth in a flight of steps: fantastic. A sway-backed roof side by side with an austere perpendicular brick building: so beautiful. A limp hot-dog wrapper on a drain grille, which the wind lifts a couple of metres and then drops again, this time onto the pavement flecked with white trodden-in chewing gum: incredible. A lean old man hobbling along in a shabby suit carrying a bag bulging with bottles in one hand: what a sight.

The world proffered its hand, and I took it. All the way through the town centre and up the hills on the other side, straight into my bedsit, where I immediately sat down to write my poem.

At the beginning of the first lesson on the following day we handed in our pieces of work. As we sat chatting and drinking coffee they were being copied, we could hear the drone of the photocopier and, as the door was open, see the flashes in the room whenever the machine illuminated the sheet of paper. The pile was ready, Fosse distributed the poems, for the next few minutes we read in silence. Then he threw out his arm and checked his watch, time for the analysis.

There was already a routine: one student read, the others commented in turn, and when the round was over, the teacher gave his analysis. The latter carried the most weight, especially when the teacher was Fosse, because even though he was nervous and never seemed to be at ease, there was a gravitas and a conviction in what he said that made everyone listen whenever he spoke.

He spent a long time on each poem, went through them line by line, sometimes word by word, praised what was good, rejected what wasn't, highlighted what was promising and could be developed in other directions, concentrated throughout, his gaze fixed on the text, hardly ever on us, making notes on what he said.

My poem, which was the last one we analysed, was about nature. I had tried to describe the beauty and openness of the countryside, and the poem closed with the grass whispering *come*, as though it were talking to the reader, and expressed the feeling I'd had when I saw the painting. As it was a landscape painting there was nothing modern about the poem, and I had sat over it for a while trying various techniques to make it feel more contemporary and had suddenly thought of a word, *widescreen*, which I put to use in *widescreen-sky*, it made the same kind of impression I had created in my prose, the boys' reality was coloured by what they had seen on TV and read, but mostly TV. This produced the same effect, indirectly. It represented a break with the lyrical and poetic description of nature, I had thought, and when I read the poem aloud to the others it seemed to have that function.

Fosse, wearing a white shirt with rolled-up sleeves and blue jeans, stubble on his chin and dark bags under his eyes, didn't study the poem immediately after I had read it out, as he had done with some of the others, but went straight to the point.

He said he liked Astrup, and I wasn't the first to choose a painting by him, Olav H. Hauge had done so too. Then he started on the poem. The first line, he said, is a cliché, you can cross that out. The second line is also a cliché. And the third and fourth. The sole value of this poem, he said after rejecting every single line, is the word *widescreen-sky*. I've never seen that before. You can keep that. The rest you can scrub.

'But then there's nothing left of the poem,' I said.

'No,' he said. 'But the description of nature and your enthusiasm for it are clichés. There's nothing of Astrup's mystique in your poem. You've completely trivialised it. But *widecreen-sky*. As I said, that's not bad.'

He looked up.

'That's it then. Anyone want to come for a beer at Henrik's?'

Everyone did. We walked together through the drizzle up to the café across the street from Café Opera. I was on the verge of tears and said nothing, knowing full well I could only get away with this while we were walking, you could be silent now but as soon as we sat down I would have to say something and seem happy, or at least interested, so that they wouldn't realise how much Fosse's words had hurt me.

However, I thought, as I slumped down on the sofa with a beer on the table in front of me, I mustn't appear too enthusiastic either, then it would be obvious that I was fighting too hard to act nonchalant.

Petra sat down beside me.

'Nice poem you wrote.' She giggled.

I didn't answer.

'It's what I told you, you take yourself too seriously. It's just a *poem*,' she said. 'Come on now.'

'Easy for you to say,' I said.

She looked at me with those ironic eyes of hers and smiled her ironic smile.

Jon Fosse eyed me.

'It's difficult to write good poems,' he said. 'Not many people can. You found a great word there, and that's good, you know.'

'Yes. Yes, I know,' I said.

He looked as if he wanted to say more, but instead he sat back and averted his gaze. His attempt to console me was even more humiliating than his analysis. It meant he perceived me as someone who needed consoling. He talked literature with the others, but he consoled me.

I couldn't be the first to leave, everyone would think it was because I was upset and couldn't take criticism. Nor the second, nor the third. They would think the same. If I was the fourth, though, no one would think that, at least not with any reasonable justification.

Fortunately this didn't look as though it was going to be a long evening, we had come here for a beer following the day's work, and after an hour I was able to get up and go without losing face. It was raining harder now, the wind was gusting through the streets, which in the centre were empty now that the shops were closed. I didn't give a damn about the rain, I didn't give a damn about people, I didn't give a damn about all the rows of crooked wooden terraced houses on the sloping mountainside I was walking up as fast as I could. I just wanted to get home, lock the door and be on my own.

Once indoors, I took off my shoes, hung my dripping raincoat in the wardrobe and placed the bag with my texts and notebook on the top shelf because one glance at that and my mortification would return.

To my dismay, we had been given another writing assignment. Another poem had to be written this evening and read and assessed the following day. I wasn't going to give a damn about that either, was I?

At any rate I can't be bothered with it now, I thought and lay down on my bed. The rain beat against the window above my head. There was a faint whoosh as the wind swept across the grass and pressed against the walls of the houses. The woodwork creaked. I was reminded of the wind outside the house where I grew up, its whoosh was so much stronger and more powerful because of the trees it moved. What a sound it had been. It soared into the air, moved off, disappeared, soared again, sigh after sigh went through the forest and the trees threw themselves forwards and backwards, as though trying to escape.

The trees I had liked best were the pines which stood on the vacant plots in the housing estate. They had been part of a forest, but then it had been cut down, the rocks had been blasted and lawns had been laid and houses built, which they stood beside. Tall and slim, many of them with branches only towards the top. Reddish, almost flame-like, when the sun shone on them. They resembled masts, I thought whenever I was standing by the window in my bedroom and looking up at the neighbouring plot, where they swayed to and fro and creaked, the plots of land were ships, the fences railings, the houses cabins, the estate an armada.

I got up and went into the kitchen. The night before I had put all the dirty crockery and cutlery in the sink, filled it with hot water, squirted a bit of washing-up liquid in it and left it to soak; now all I had to do was rinse everything in cold water and it would be spotlessly clean. I was pleased at having discovered this method, thereby avoiding all the hassle.

Once this was done, I sat down at my typewriter, switched it on, rolled in a sheet of paper and stared at it for a while. Then I began to write a new poem.

CUNT. CUNT.

CUNT. CUNT. CUNT. CUNT. CUNT. CUNT. CUNT. CUNT.
CUNT. CUNT. CUNT. CUNT. CUNT. CUNT. CUNT. CUNT.
CUNT. CUNT. CUNT. CUNT. CUNT. CUNT. CUNT. CUNT.
CUNT. CUNT. CUNT. CUNT. CUNT. CUNT. CUNT. CUNT.
CUNT. CUNT. CUNT. CUNT. CUNT. CUNT. CUNT. CUNT.
CUNT. CUNT. CUNT. CUNT. CUNT. CUNT. CUNT. CUNT.
CUNT. CUNT. CUNT. CUNT. CUNT. CUNT. CUNT. CUNT.
CUNT. CUNT. CUNT. CUNT. CUNT. CUNT. CUNT. CUNT.
CUNT. CUNT. CUNT. CUNT. CUNT. CUNT. CUNT. CUNT.
CUNT. CUNT. CUNT. CUNT. CUNT. CUNT. CUNT. CUNT.
CUNT. CUNT. CUNT. CUNT. CUNT. CUNT. CUNT. CUNT.
CUNT. CUNT. CUNT. CUNT. CUNT. CUNT. CUNT. CUNT.
CUNT. CUNT. CUNT. CUNT. CUNT. CUNT. CUNT. CUNT.
CUNT. CUNT. CUNT. CUNT. CUNT. CUNT. CUNT. CUNT.
CUNT. CUNT. CUNT. CUNT. CUNT. CUNT. CUNT. CUNT.
CUNT. CUNT. CUNT. CUNT. CUNT. CUNT. CUNT. CUNT.
CUNT. CUNT. CUNT. CUNT. CUNT. CUNT. CUNT. CUNT.
CUNT. CUNT. CUNT. CUNT. CUNT. CUNT. CUNT. CUNT.
CUNT. CUNT. CUNT. CUNT. CUNT. CUNT. CUNT. CUNT.
CUNT. CUNT. CUNT. CUNT. CUNT. CUNT. CUNT. CUNT.
CUNT. CUNT. CUNT. CUNT. CUNT. CUNT. CUNT. CUNT.
CUNT. CUNT. CUNT. CUNT. CUNT. CUNT. CUNT. CUNT.
CUNT. CUNT. CUNT. CUNT. CUNT. CUNT. CUNT. CUNT.
CUNT. CUNT. CUNT. CUNT. CUNT. CUNT. CUNT. CUNT.
CUNT. CUNT. CUNT. CUNT. CUNT. CUNT. CUNT. CUNT.
CUNT. CUNT. CUNT. CUNT. CUNT. CUNT. CUNT. CUNT.
CUNT. CUNT. CUNT. CUNT. CUNT. CUNT. CUNT. CUNT.
CUNT. CUNT. CUNT. CUNT. CUNT. CUNT. CUNT. CUNT.
CUNT. CUNT. CUNT. CUNT. CUNT. CUNT. CUNT. CUNT.
CUNT. CUNT. CUNT. CUNT. CUNT. CUNT. CUNT. CUNT.
CUNT. CUNT. CUNT. CUNT. CUNT. CUNT. CUNT. CUNT.
CUNT. CUNT. CUNT. CUNT. CUNT. CUNT. CUNT. CUNT.
CUNT. CUNT. CUNT. CUNT. CUNT. CUNT. CUNT. CUNT.
CUNT. CUNT. CUNT. CUNT. CUNT. CUNT. CUNT. CUNT.
CUNT. CUNT. CUNT. CUNT. CUNT. CUNT. CUNT. CUNT.
CUNT. CUNT. CUNT. CUNT. CUNT. CUNT. CUNT. CUNT.

CUNT. CUNT. CUNT. CUNT. CUNT. CUNT. CUNT. CUNT.
CUNT. CUNT. CUNT. CUNT. CUNT. CUNT. CUNT. CUNT.
CUNT. CUNT. CUNT. CUNT. CUNT. CUNT. CUNT. CUNT.
CUNT. CUNT. CUNT. CUNT. CUNT. CUNT. CUNT. CUNT.
CUNT. CUNT. CUNT. CUNT. CUNT. CUNT. CUNT. CUNT.
CUNT. CUNT. CUNT. CUNT. CUNT. CUNT. CUNT. CUNT.

I took out the sheet of paper and looked at it.

The thought of reading this at the Academy filled me with glee, I purred with delight as I imagined what it would be like, how they would react, what they would say. The text consisted of nothing more than clichés and I would have to cross everything out, except for one word?

Ha ha ha!

I poured a cup of coffee and lit a cigarette. The delight was not undiluted, I would be taking a big risk if I read it aloud, it was a provocation, a slap in the face, and if there was one thing I didn't want it was to fall out with anyone. My fear of this was so strong that it made the thought of doing it even more enticing. It was the attraction of the forbidden that I could feel, that I could actually do it, a dizzying sensation, like the fear of heights.

At around eight there was a ring at the door, I thought it would be Morten, but it was Jon Olav, he stood there in an open jacket and trainers in the rain, as though he had only crossed the yard, and in a way this was true, it wasn't far from his bedsit to mine.

'Are you working?' he said.

'No, I've finished,' I said. 'Come in!'

He flopped down on the sofa, I made two cups of coffee and sat on the bed.

'How's it going at the Academy?' he said.

'Well enough, I suppose,' I said. 'But it's tough. They don't mince their words when we discuss texts.'

'Really?' he said.

'Now we're writing poetry.'

'Can you do that?'

'I've never done it before. But that's the whole point of being there. You have to try new things.'

'Yes,' he said. 'I haven't really got going yet. And there's so much to read that I already feel left behind. It's not like arts subjects, where you can get by with what you already know or use your common sense . . . Well, of course you have to use your common sense as well.' He laughed. 'But there's so much you have to *know*. There's quite a different degree of precision involved. So the only thing that counts is reading. And everyone's so disciplined. They're in the reading room from the crack of dawn to late at night.'

'But not you?'

'I'll have to at some point,' he smiled. 'I just haven't started yet.'

'I think the Writing Academy's just as tough, only in a different way. We don't have to *know* the way you do. You can't read your way to becoming a writer.'

'That's clear,' he said.

'You've either got it in you or you haven't, I reckon. But it's important to read too, of course. But that's not the decisive factor.'

'No, right,' he said, taking a sip and glancing at the desk and the meagre selection of books on the shelf.

'I've been thinking of writing about ugliness and trying to find the beauty in it, if you see what I mean. It's not true that a thing of beauty is exclusively beautiful or ugly things are only ugly. It's a lot more relative than that. Have you heard the latest by Propaganda?'

I looked at him. He shook his head. I went over and put the record on the stereo.

'This bit is nice and dark and beautiful, and then all of a sudden we're in an atonal ugly bit and it destroys the beauty, but it's still good, do you understand?'

He nodded.

'Listen. This is where the ugly bit starts.'

We both sat listening in silence. Then it finished and I went over and turned down the volume.

'What you said about ugliness was really good. But it wasn't quite how I'd imagined it,' he said. 'It wasn't *that* ugly.'

'Perhaps not,' I said. 'But writing's different anyway.'

'Yes,' he said.

'I wrote a poem last night. I'm going to read it out at the Academy tomorrow. Well, I'm not sure. It's pretty radical. Do you want to see it?'

He nodded.

I went to the desk, picked up the poem and passed it to him.

He took it unsuspectingly, read with concentration, then I saw a pink flush spread across his cheeks and he suddenly turned round and burst into loud laughter.

'You're not going to read this, are you?' he said.

'Yes, I am,' I said. 'That was the idea.'

'Don't even think about it, Karl Ove. You'll make a fool of yourself.'

'It's a provocation,' I said.

He laughed again.

'It certainly is,' he said. 'But don't read it out. You said you weren't sure. Don't do it.'

'I'll see,' I said, took the piece of paper he handed me and placed it on the desk. 'Would you like some more coffee?'

'I have to be getting back soon.'

'By the way, Yngve's having a party on Saturday. Do you fancy coming? He asked me to ask you.'

'Yes, that would be fun.'

'I was thinking of having pre-drinks here. Then we can take a taxi up there afterwards.'

'Great!'

'I'm sure you can bring along some friends if you like,' I said.

He got up.

'What time shall I come?'

'I don't know. Seven?'

'See you then,' he said, slipped his feet into his shoes, shrugged on his jacket and went out. I accompanied him to the steps. He turned to me.

'Don't read it out!' he said. Then he disappeared round the corner into the darkness and rain.

Straight after I had gone to bed, at around two, I heard someone stop outside the front door, unlock it and then slam it shut. From the footsteps that went along the hall and down the stairs I guessed it was Morten. Some music was put on, louder than he had ever played it before, it lasted for maybe five minutes, then suddenly everything went quiet.

Waking up next day, I still hadn't decided what to do and I took the poem with me so that I could make a last-minute decision. It wasn't difficult. As I went into the seminar room and saw the others sitting in their places, relaxing with a cup of tea or coffee on the desk in front of them – a handbag, rucksack or plastic bag resting against the desk leg unless they were lying against the wall behind them with the wet umbrellas, which were sometimes left open on the floor in the photocopy room or between the table and the kitchenette, so that they could dry, ready for use again – as I saw all this and absorbed the friendly atmosphere this created, I realised I couldn't read out the poem. It was full of hatred, it belonged in my room, where I was all alone, not here where I was with other people. Of course I could break down the partition between these two worlds, but there was something very strong holding them apart, which told me they shouldn't be mixed.

Having to admit I hadn't written a poem was humiliating. Everyone realised I hadn't written one because of Fosse's analysis the previous day, and that was tantamount to saying I had no spine, no stamina, was hypersensitive, a child, I lacked independence and strength of mind.

To rectify this impression I tried to appear attentive, interested and enthusiastic as the others' poems were analysed. And it went quite well, I had already begun to grasp the technique of how to comment on poems, I knew what to look for, what was considered good or not good, and also succeeded in articulating this in a concise comprehensible manner, which not everyone could do. For people who were supposed to have language at their fingertips there was a conspicuous amount of fumbling and hesitation, around the table there were evasive looks and arguments that were retracted the moment they were presented, some almost unbearably flimsy and lame, and sometimes when I spoke up it was simply to bring clarity and order into the discussion.

On my way home I popped into Mekka and spent more than seven hundred kroner on food, I came out with six full carrier bags, and the prospect of schlepping them all the way home was so demoralising that I hailed a taxi, which pulled into the kerb and came to a halt, I put the bags into the boot and got into the back to be transported through the wet streets like royalty, elevated from the daily slog that was evident all around me, and even though it was expensive and I knew I was spending the money I had saved by shopping at Mekka it was worth it.

At home I put away my purchases, took a little trip down to the basement with the photography book, had lunch and tried to do some writing, not poems this time, I had finished with poems, I was a prose writer, and when I noticed that the sentences were coming as easily as before, all I had to do was write, I was relieved because somehow I had feared that Fosse's analysis of the catastrophic poem would affect my confidence with regard to prose too, but such was not the case, everything flowed as before, and I wrote four pages without a pause before going to phone Ingvild.

This time I wasn't so nervous, firstly she had asked me to ring, secondly I was only going to invite her to the party, and if she said no, it wasn't the same as her saying no to me.

Under the little dome of transparent plastic I stood with the receiver pressed to my ear waiting for someone to pick up at the other end. Raindrops sailed across the plastic, gathered in large clusters beneath and let go at regular intervals and fell with little plops onto the tarmac. In the light from the street lamp above me the air was striped with rain.

'Hello?'

'Hi, I'd like to talk to Ingvild . . .'

'Hi, it's me!'

'Hi. How's it going?'

'Well, I think. Yes, it's going pretty well. I'm sitting alone in my room reading.'

'Sounds nice.'

'Yes, and what about you?'

'It's going well. I was wondering whether you fancied going to a party on Saturday? Tomorrow, that is. My brother's having a party at his place.'

'Sounds like fun.'

'I'm having a pre first. Then we're taking a taxi. He lives in Solheimsviken. Would seven-ish be OK?'

'Yes.'

'Jon Olav's coming anyway, so there's someone you know.'

'Is he everywhere, that cousin of yours?'

'Yes, you could say that . . .'

She chuckled, and then there was a silence.

'Shall we say that then?' I said. 'Seven tomorrow at my place?'

'Yes. I'll bring along my usual cheery good humour and positive approach to life!'

'Great,' I said. 'See you then. Bye.'

'Bye.'

The next morning I cleaned my room, changed the bedding, washed my clothes and hung them on the stand in the basement, I wanted everything to be perfect in case she came home with me after the party. Something had to happen anyway, that much was obvious. My passivity and awkwardness the first time were understandable but not crucial; our second meeting had been different, it took place in the middle of the day and was a chance for us to get to know each other better, but now, the third time we were meeting in Bergen I would have to make my intentions known, make a move, otherwise she would slip through my fingers. I couldn't talk my way into a relationship with her, some action was required, a kiss, a hug, and then, perhaps later that night when we were walking in the streets outside Yngve's flat, a question, would you like to come home with me?

It was an intimidating thought, but I had to, there was no way out, otherwise nothing would happen. And it wasn't that I had to follow this plan slavishly, I would have to improvise as I went along, read the situation, try to see what she wanted, where she was, but I couldn't not act, I had to act and then she could reject me if she wasn't willing or felt it was too soon.

But if she wanted to come home with me I would *have* to tell her about my physical problem. I *couldn't* go through the humiliation of trying to hide the fact that I came so quickly, as I had done so many times, I just had to *tell* her, treat it as a minor matter, no big deal, a manageable problem. The only time I had really made love to a girl, in a tent at Roskilde Festival that summer, it had got better and better the more times we did it, so at least I knew I *could*. I hadn't liked her much though, not as a person, she didn't mean anything to me beyond the sex, but Ingvild did, everything was at stake with her, I only wanted to be together with her, and I *couldn't* allow myself to fail because of that.

I also knew it helped to drink, but I shouldn't get *too* drunk, then she might think I was after only one thing with her. And I wasn't! Nothing could be further from the truth.

Jon Olav and his two friends, Idar and Terje, were the first to arrive. I'd had three beers beforehand and was feeling confident in everything I said and did. I put out a dish of crisps and a bowl of peanuts, and told them about the Writing Academy. They had read books by Ragnar Hovland, knew about Jan Kjærstad and Kjartan Fløgstad, of course, and I suspected they were impressed when I told them they were going to come and teach us.

'I imagine they'll tell us a bit about their writing,' I said. 'But the main thing is they're going to read our texts and talk about them. Do you like Kjærstad?'

At that moment the bell rang and I went to answer the door. It was Anne. She was dressed in black, had a little hat on her head and a long lock of hair hanging down over her face. I leaned forward to give her a hug, she placed a hand on my back, held it there for a moment after I had straightened up.

'Great to see you,' she said with a little laugh.

'Great to see you too,' I said. 'Come in!'

She put down a small rucksack on the floor inside the door and said hello to the others as she took off her coat. Her bubbly personality had once struck me as incompatible with the black gothic element of her interests and approach to life. It was The Cult and The Cure, the Jesus and Mary Chain and the Belgian Crammed Discs bands, This Mortal Coil and the Cocteau Twins with Anne, fog and darkness and death romance, but with a smile on her lips and excited little jumps wherever she went. She was older than me, but when we had worked together, she behind the knobs and switches in the control room on the other side of the window, me behind the microphone, I once had the sense she might be interested in me, without being able to say for certain – such matters were impossible to know with certainty – anyway nothing happened, we were friends, both music fans, me slightly more interested in pop than her. Now she was a student, alone in Bergen like me, but she already had a host of friends as far as I could glean from what she said in the chair, reclining over the armrests, chatting with the others. No surprises there, she was outgoing and soon became the focal point of the little student gathering in my room that evening.

I drank steadily to reach a level where I no longer considered what I said or did, I just *was*, free and easy, so when the bell rang at a little before eight and I went out to open the door, I wasn't in the slightest bit nervous or tense, just happy to see her, Ingvild, standing on the steps in the rain with a bag over her shoulder and a smile on her face.

I gave her a hug, she followed me in, said hello to the others, a touch shy, possibly also nervous, and took a bottle of wine from her bag. I hurried into the kitchen to fetch a corkscrew and a glass. She sat down between Jon Olav and Idar on the sofa, inserted the corkscrew, placed the bottle between her knees and pulled out the cork with a pop.

'So this is where you live,' she said, filling her glass with white wine.

'Yes,' I said. 'I've been cleaning all day ready for you all.'

'I can imagine,' she said.

Her eyes narrowed and seemed to fill with laughter.

'*Skål*,' she said.

'*Skål*,' said the others, and we clinked bottles and glasses.

'What are you writing at the moment?' Idar said.

'A novel,' I said. 'A contemporary novel. I'm trying to make it entertaining but profound too. It's not so easy. I'm fascinated by paradoxes. By whatever is both ugly *and* beautiful, both high *and* low. A bit like Fløgstad actually.'

I glanced at Ingvild, who looked at me. I couldn't show the others how ridiculously in love I was, that all I really wanted to do was sit and stare at her, and I couldn't show her either, so I tried to pay her as little attention as possible.

'But now I want to be published,' I said. 'I don't want what I write to be read by only a few people. There's no point in that. I might just as well do something else. Do you know what I mean?'

'Yes,' Idar said.

'Did you read out your poem then?' Jon Olav laughed.

'No,' I said, glaring at him. I didn't like him laughing. It was as though he was trying to tell the others something.

'What kind of poem?' Anne said.

'It was just something I wrote for the Academy. A practice activity,' I said and got up, went over to the record player and put on *The Joshua Tree*.

'It wouldn't be hard to recite from memory,' Jon Olav said, and laughed again.

I spun round.

'If you want to play tough, that's fine by me,' I said.

He stopped laughing, as I thought he would, and at first looked surprised.

'What's the matter?' he said.

'I'm serious about what I do,' I said and sat down.

'*Skål!*' Jon Olav said.

We *skål*-ed, the brief flash of ill will was gone, the conversation flowed again. Ingvild didn't say much, interjected with the odd ironic comment, livened up when the conversation turned to sport, and I liked that so much, while at the same time it struck me that I didn't know her at all, so how could I have fallen so much in love with her, I wondered, sitting on the stool across the table from her, a bottle of cold Hansa beer held to my mouth and a lit cigarette in my hand, but I knew the answer with the whole of my being, there was no arguing with feelings, and nor should you, they always knew best. I saw her, she was here, and what she radiated, which was her, lived its life irrespective of what she said or didn't say.

Now and then I was struck by the enriching thought that here I was, in *my* bedsit, surrounded by *my* friends and, only a metre away, was the girl I loved more than all else.

Life can't get better than that.

'Anyone want another beer?' I asked, rising to my feet. Idar and Terje and Anne nodded, I fetched four beers from the fridge, handed them round, saw there was a space between Jon Olav and Ingvild on the sofa if they budged up, and sat down there. When I opened the beer it foamed over, I held it away from me, the froth landed on the table, oh shit, I said, put down the bottle, went for a cloth from the kitchen and wiped it up. On the wall between the windows, just behind the sofa, there was a nail, and for some reason I hung the cloth there.

'A wet cloth has come between us,' I said to Ingvild, and plumped down on the sofa. She looked at me in bemusement, and I guffawed from the pit of my stomach, haw, haw, haw.

I rang for two taxis from the telephone box opposite. The others stood on the steps drinking and chatting. I watched them, thinking once again, they've come for a pre to *my* place. The rain had eased, but the sky was still overcast. A pale darkness hovered in the streets, through which we passed shortly afterwards, it suddenly became lighter as we emerged by Puddefjorden and the high open sky there, then it became darker again as we climbed the hills in Solheimsviken between the rows of workers' houses.

It was already half past nine. We were more than slightly late. Yngve had said eight or half past when I asked him when we should turn up, however this was worse for us, not for them, not for all Yngve's friends and acquaintances, our presence didn't mean anything to them.

I paid one taxi driver, Jon Olav paid the other, and then I walked up the short drive with the others close on my heels, and rang the bell.

Yngve opened the door. He was wearing a white shirt with grey stripes and black trousers, his hair was combed back except for a strand hanging over one side of his forehead.

'We're a bit late,' I said. 'Hope you don't mind.'

'Not at all,' he said. 'The party's a flop anyway. No one's turned up.'

I looked at him. What did he mean?

He said hi to the others, didn't make any fuss about Ingvild, fortunately, I didn't want her to realise how much I had talked about her to Yngve. We took off our shoes and coats in the entrance hall and went into the sitting room. It was empty apart from Ola, who was watching TV.

I couldn't believe my eyes.

'Are you watching *TV*?' I said.

'Yes? No point starting a party if there are no people.'

'Where are they then?'

Yngve shrugged and forced a weak smile.

'I didn't give much advance warning. But there are lots of you!'

'Yes,' I said, sitting down on the sofa under the *Once Upon a Time in America* poster. I was shaken, this was a bolt out of the blue, I had imagined the rooms would be packed with people, sophisticated young men and women, a buzz of conversation, laughter, the air dense with smoke, and then this! Yngve and Ola watching the Saturday film on NRK? And it would have to be when I brought Ingvild! I wanted her to see Yngve and his friends, students who had been here several years and knew the town, knew the university, knew the world, so that I could share the limelight with them, he was my brother, I was invited to his parties. But what did she see? Two guys watching TV, no guests, they hadn't come, they had other, better, things to do on a Saturday evening than go to a party at Yngve's.

Was he a loser? Was Yngve a sad loser?

He switched off the TV, moved the two chairs to the table with Ola, fetched some beers and sat down, started talking to the others, a bit of polite small talk to make them feel at home, Anne and Ingvild and Idar and Terje, what they studied, where they lived, and the atmosphere, which at first had been somewhat hesitant, despite the fact that we had been drinking together for more than two hours, soon began to lift. The conversation went from involving the whole table to breaking up into smaller groups, I chatted with Anne, she was unstoppable, suddenly there was so much she had to tell me, I felt claustrophobic and said I had to go to the toilet. From there I went into the kitchen, where Terje was chatting to Ingvild, smiled at them, went over to Ola and Yngve, there was a ring at the door, Asbjørn walked in, followed closely by Arvid, and now the flat was full, there were people everywhere, or so it felt, faces and voices and bodies in motion everywhere, and I mingled among them, to and fro, drank and chatted, chatted and drank, getting drunker and drunker. The sense of time vanished, everything was open, I was no longer inhibited by my own shortcomings, I walked around happy and free without a thought for anything except the moment and Ingvild, whom I loved. I kept my distance, if there was one thing I knew about girls it was that they didn't want someone who was easy to get, someone who followed them round, slack-jawed, so instead I chatted with the others, who, in intoxication's shining light, were drawn from the darkness as if by a torch. Everyone was interesting, everyone had something to say that I could listen to and be moved by until I left and they were reclaimed by the darkness.

I sat between Ola and Asbjørn on the sofa. On the other side of the table sat Anne, she asked if she could bum a fag off me, I nodded, the next moment her head was down and she was concentrating on making a roll-up.

'I th-thought of something,' Ola said. 'George V. Higgins, have you r-read anything by him?'

'No,' I said.

'You sh-should do. It's good. Really good. Almost only dialogue. Very Am-m-merican. Hard-boiled. *The Friends of Eddie Coyle.*'

'Then there's Bret Easton Ellis,' Asbjørn said. '*Less Than Zero*. Have you read that one?'

I shook my head.

'An American in his twenties. It's about a gang of kids in Los Angeles. They've got rich parents and do what they like. It's all boozing and dope and parties. But everything's utterly cold and stripped back. It's a very good novel. Kind of hyper-realistic.'

'That sounds good,' I said. 'What was his name again?'

'Bret Easton Ellis. Remember you heard it here first!'

He laughed and looked away. I glanced at Yngve, who was talking to Jon Olav and Ingvild, he had that excited flush he sometimes had when he was trying to make a point.

'And the latest John Irving is also very good,' Asbjørn said.

'Are you kidding?' I said. 'John Irving's a bloody pulp fiction author.'

'He can still be good,' Asbjørn said.

'Can he hell,' I said.

'But you haven't read it!'

'No, but I know it's poor.'

'Ha ha ha! You *can't* say that.'

'I write myself, for Christ's sake. And I've read John Irving. His latest novel is poor, I *know* it is.'

'For Christ's sake, Karl Ove,' Asbjørn said.

'Imagine us sitting here, Anne!' I said. 'So far from shitty Kristiansand!'

'Yes,' she said. 'But I don't know what I'm doing here. You know what you're doing. You're going to be a writer. But there's nothing I want to be.'

'I *am* a writer,' I said.

'Know what?' she said.

'No?' I said.

'The only thing I want to be is a legend. A real legend. I've always thought that. And I've never doubted that that's how it will be.'

Asbjørn and Ola exchanged glances and laughed.

'Do you understand? I've always been sure of it.'

'What kind of legend?' Asbjørn said.

'Any kind,' Anne said.

'What can you do then? Sing? Write?'

'No,' she said. Tears began to run down her cheeks. I looked at her at a loss to understand. Was she crying?

'I'm never going to be a legend!' she wailed.

Everyone was staring at her now.

'It's too late!' she exclaimed, and put her face in her hands. Her shoulders shook. Ola and Asbjørn burst into laughter, Yngve and Jon Olav and Ingvild sent us enquiring looks.

'I'm never going to be a legend,' she repeated. 'I'm never going to be anything!'

'You're only twenty,' I said. 'It's not too late.'

'Yes, it is!' Anne said.

'So?' Jon Olav said. 'What do you want to be a legend for? What's the point?'

She got up and went towards the front door.

'Where are you going?' Yngve said. 'You're not going, are you?'

'Yes,' she said.

'Come on, stay a bit longer,' he said. 'You definitely won't be a legend if you leave at midnight. Come on. I've got a whole demi-john of wine. Would you like a glass? It's a legendary vintage.'

She smiled.

'Perhaps one glass then,' she said.

Yngve got her one and the party continued. Ingvild stood by the wall with a glass in her hand, a tingle ran through me, she was so beautiful. I must go and talk to her, I thought, and went over.

'Proper student party, eh!' I said.

'Yes,' she said.

'Have you read anything by Ragnar Hovland by the way? He writes a lot about this sort of thing, I believe.'

She shook her head.

'He's one of the teachers at the Academy. From Vestland, like you. In fact, I've got a bit of Vestland in me too. I mean, my mum comes from Sørbøvåg after all. So I'm half a Vestlander anyway!'

She looked at me and smiled. I clinked glasses with her.

'*Skål*,' I said.

'*Skål*,' she said.

From the sofa I met Anne's eyes. I raised my glass to her too, and she raised hers. Jon Olav stood in the middle of the floor swaying to and fro, searching with his hand for something to lean on, found nothing and staggered a few steps to the side.

'He can't take his drink!' I laughed.

He regained his balance and, with a rigid expressionless face, walked through the room and into the adjacent bedroom.

Where were Idar and Terje?

I went for a walk to find out. They were sitting in the kitchen and chatting, their heads bowed over the table and their hands wrapped around a bottle of beer. When I returned, Ingvild was sitting beside Anne on the sofa. Anne's eyes were glazed and somehow completely disconnected with her smile.

She turned to Ingvild and said something. Ingvild took a deep breath and sat up straight, from which I concluded that what Anne had said shocked her. She replied, Anne just laughed and shook her head. I went over to them.

'I know your sort,' Anne said, getting up.

'I'm not standing for that,' Ingvild said. 'You don't know me.'

'Yes, I do,' Anne said.

Ingvild laughed scornfully. Anne walked past me, I sat down where she had been sitting.

'What did she say?' I asked.

'She said I was the sort who took other women's men.'

'Did she say that?'

'Did you two ever go out together?' she asked.

'Us? No. Are you crazy?'

'I'm not standing for that,' Ingvild repeated and got up.

'Of course not,' I said. 'But please don't go because of Anne. It's not very late! And it is a good party, isn't it?'

She smiled.

'I'm not going,' she said. 'Only to the loo.'

I went into the bedroom. Jon Olav was lying on the bed, on his stomach with his head burrowed into the blanket and one hand hanging limply over the side. He was snoring. Arvid stood in the hall doorway.

'Hi, Knausgård Junior,' he said.

'Are you going?' I said, suddenly afraid, I wanted everyone to stay and the party never to end.

'No, no,' he said. 'I'm going for a little walk to clear my head.'

'Good!' I said, and went back into the sitting room. Ingvild wasn't there. Had she gone after all? Or was she still in the toilet?

'Won't be long now before Yngve puts on Queen,' Asbjørn said to me, getting up from the stereo. 'This moment always comes. When he's so drunk that the evening is as good as over. At least for him.'

'I like Queen too,' I said.

'What is it with you two?' he said with a laugh. 'Is it genetic or was there something in the air on Tromøya? Queen! Why not Genesis? Pink Floyd? Or Rush!'

'Rush are quite good,' Yngve said from behind us. 'In fact, I've got a record by them.'

'What about Bob Dylan then? He's got such good lyrics! Ha ha ha! Yes, how he didn't get the Nobel Prize is a scandal.'

'The only thing Rush and Dylan have in common is that you don't like them,' Yngve said. 'Rush are good in lots of ways. The guitar playing, for example. But *you* can't hear that.'

'Now you disappoint me, Yngve,' Asbjørn said. 'Falling so low that you defend Rush. I'd come to terms with you liking Queen, but Rush ... What about ELO? Jeff Lynne? Nice arrangements, eh?'

'Ha ha,' Yngve said.

I went into the kitchen. Ingvild was sitting with Idar and Terje. Darkness hung over the valley below. The rain was illuminated in the light from the street lamps. She looked up at me and smiled, a touch quizzically, what now?

I smiled back, but had nothing to say, and she turned to the other two. In the sitting room the music was taken off and the murmur of voices rose for some seconds until the scratch of the stylus on a new record came through the speakers. It was the first notes of a-ha's *Scoundrel Days*. I liked the record, it was full of memories, and I went into the sitting room.

At that moment Asbjørn came out of the adjacent room. He strode determinedly across the floor towards the stereo, leaned over, lifted the stylus and took off the record. Clearly, his movements were for show, almost didactic.

He held up the record and started to bend it.

The room went quiet.

Slowly he bent the record further and further until at last it cracked.

Arvid laughed out loud.

Yngve had been watching Asbjørn. Now Yngve turned to Arvid, poured his wine onto his hair and walked out.

'What the f . . .?' Arvid said, getting up. 'I didn't do anything, did I.'

'Aren't you g-going to b-burn some b-books too?' Ola said to Asbjørn. 'Make a l-little b-bonfire?'

'Why did you do that?' I said.

'Jesus,' Asbjørn said. 'You boys don't have to make such a fuss. I was just doing him a favour. Yngve knows me. He knows I'll buy him a new record. Perhaps not by a-ha, but a new record anyway. He's playing to the gallery.'

'It might not be the material value of the record on his mind,' Anne said. 'You might have hurt his feelings.'

'Feelings? Feelings?' Asbjørn laughed. 'He's playing to the gallery!'

He sat down on the sofa and lit up. He acted as if nothing had happened, or was so drunk he didn't care, yet at the same time something came over him, either his facial expression or body language, which suggested a guilty conscience, and then it took over, then it was obvious to everyone that he was sorry for what he had done. The music came back on, the party continued; after half an hour Yngve returned, Asbjørn said he would replace the record and soon everything was fine between them again.

After the beer ran out I had started necking wine. It was like fruit juice, and the source was inexhaustible. Now it wasn't only time that was dislocated, it was also place, I no longer knew where I was, it was as though darkness had descended between the various faces I spoke to. And how they shone. I was very close to my emotions in that I talked completely without inhibitions, said things I never usually said and didn't know I had even thought, such as when I joined Yngve and Asbjørn and said I was so happy they were such good friends or when I went over to Ola and tried to explain how I had felt about his stammer the first time I had heard it, all while the wave which was connected with the thought of Ingvild rose within me more and more often. It was like a feeling of triumph, and while I was in the bathroom, looking at myself in the mirror, washing my hands and moistening my hair to make it stand up, smiling all the time, my thoughts coming in short jerky phrases, *fucking great, this, oh fucking bliss on earth, oh so bloody brilliant, so bloody brilliant!* I decided to make a move on her, kiss her, seduce her. I wasn't planning to invite her back to my place any more, no, there was a room upstairs on the second floor I had discovered, an old maidservant's room, no one was sleeping there now, it was probably used as a guest room, it was perfect.

I went into the sitting room, she was standing and talking to Ola, the music was loud, on the verge of distortion, around them some people were dancing, I watched them until she looked at me. Then I smiled, and she smiled back.

'Can I talk to you?' I said.

'Yes,' she said.

'The music's so loud here,' I said. 'Shall we go into the hall or something?'

She nodded. We went into the hall.

'You're so beautiful,' I said.

'Was that what you wanted to say?' She laughed.

'There's a room upstairs, on the second floor. Shall we go up there? It's an old servant's room, I think.'

I set off up the stairs and a moment later heard her following me. I waited on the first floor, took her hand and led her up to the room, which was exactly as I remembered it.

I put my arms around her and kissed her. She stepped back and sat down on the edge of the bed.

'There's something I have to tell you,' I said. 'I'm . . . well, a kind of monster when it comes to sex. It's a bit difficult to explain, but . . . oh, to hell with it, it doesn't matter.'

I sat down beside her, put my arm around her and kissed her and laid her down and kissed her again, she was bashful and reserved, I kissed her neck, caressed her hair, slowly pulled up her jumper, kissed one breast, and she sat up and pulled down her jumper and looked at me.

'This doesn't feel right, Karl Ove,' she said. 'You're moving too fast.'

'Yes,' I said, and sat up as well. 'You're right. I apologise.'

'Don't apologise,' she said. 'Never apologise. There's nothing I hate more.'

She got up.

'Are we still friends?' she said. 'I like you very much, you see.'

'And I like you,' I said. 'Shall we join the others downstairs?'

We joined the others, and perhaps because her rejection had sobered me up I suddenly saw everything very clearly.

There were very few people there. Eight, apart from us – that was the extent of the party. What for several hours had appeared to be a grand decadent human spectacle, the great student party with quarrels and friendship, love and confidences, dancing and drinking, all borne aloft on a wave of happiness, collapsed in an instant and revealed itself for what it was: Idar, Terje, Jon Olav, Anne, Asbjørn, Ola, Arvid and Yngve. All with small glazed eyes and ungainly movements.

I wanted the party back, I wanted to be in the centre again so I poured some wine and drank two glasses quickly, one after the other, and then one more, and that helped: slowly the thought of the meagre turnout relaxed its grip and I sat down beside Asbjørn on the sofa.

Jon Olav came in from the bedroom. He stopped in the doorway. People clapped.

'Wahey!' Ola shouted. 'Back from the dead!'

Jon Olav smiled and sat down on the chair beside me. I continued talking with Asbjørn, trying to explain to him that I also wrote about young people who drank and took dope in as cold and stripped-back a style as that American writer Asbjørn had mentioned earlier. Jon Olav looked at us and grabbed one of the half-full bottles of beer on the table.

'*Skål* to Karl Ove and the Writing Academy!' he shouted. Then he laughed and took a swig of the beer. I was so angry that I stood up and leaned towards him.

'What the FUCK do you mean?' I yelled. 'What the FUCK do you know about anything? I'm SERIOUS about what I do, do you understand? Do you know what that is? Don't you bloody come here and be ironic with me! You think you're so damned clever! But you study law! Remember that! Law!'

He looked up at me, surprised and maybe a bit frightened too.

'Don't you bloody come here!' I yelled and left the room, put on my shoes, opened the door and went outside. My heart was beating fast, my legs were shaking. I lit a cigarette and sat down on the wet brick step. The rain was percolating down through the darkness above and landing in the small front garden with a quiet pitter-patter.

If only Ingvild would come now.

I inhaled deeply in order to do something at a slow deliberate pace. I let the smoke settle deep into my lungs before gently exhaling it again. I felt an urge to smash something. To take one of the kerbstones and hurl it through the window in the door. That would give them something to think about. Bloody twats. Fucking shitheads.

Why didn't she come?

Come on, Ingvild, come on!

Getting steadily wetter in the rain, I finally decided to stand up, threw the cigarette end into the garden and went to join the others. Ingvild was in the doorway talking to Yngve, they didn't see me and I stopped and tried to catch what they were saying, perhaps she was asking him questions about me, but no, they were talking about the best way home. Yngve said he would call a taxi for her if she wanted, she did, and when he turned down the music and lifted the receiver I went into the bedroom to keep out of her way, mostly so as not to remind her of what had happened. She started to put on her coat and hat, I went into the sitting room and sat down on the sofa, and waved to her when she poked her head round to say goodbye. And that was fine, I was one of them, and not the person who had tried to sleep with her in the loft.

Shortly afterwards Yngve ordered two more taxis, and then there were only Ola, Asbjørn, Yngve and me left. We played records and chatted about them, stared for long spells into the air until someone made a move and put on another good song. In the end, Ola got up, he was going to take a taxi, Asbjørn went with him, and I asked Yngve if it was OK if I slept on his sofa, and it was, of course.

*

On waking, my first thought was the scene in the maidservant's room on the second floor.

Was it real? Had I dragged her there, pushed her down on the bed and pulled her jumper up over her breasts?

Ingvild? Who was so fragile and apprehensive and shy? Whom I loved with all of my heart?

How could I have done that? What was I thinking?

What a stupid idiot I was.

I had ruined everything.

Everything.

I sat up, pulled the blanket to the side, ran my hand through my hair.

Jesus Christ.

For once none of the details of the night's events had disappeared, I remembered everything, and not only that, the images of Ingvild, the way she looked at me, which I hadn't taken in at the time, but which I grasped the full significance of now, were ever-present, they quivered in my consciousness, especially when I pulled up her jumper, the look she gave me, because she didn't want it, yet she let me do it anyway, it was only when I closed my lips around her nipples that she sat up and said no.

What must she have thought? I don't want this, but he wants it so much, shall I let him?

I got up and went to the window. Yngve must have been asleep, at any rate it was silent in the flat. My head was heavy, but it wasn't bad considering how much I had drunk. What was it again? Beer on wine, not so fine. Wine on beer, never fear? I had drunk beer first, then wine, that was why.

Oh hell!

Hell, hell, hell.

What a bloody fool I was.

She was so lovely and so alive.

I went into the kitchen and drank a glass of water. The clouds over the town were dense and greyish-white, the light between the houses was like milk.

From the bedroom came the sound of footsteps. I turned, Yngve appeared in just his underpants, he went into the bathroom without looking at me. He looked pale and groggy. I brewed coffee, found some ham and cheese and salad, sliced the loaf and listened to him showering.

'So,' he said as he emerged, wearing a light blue shirt and jeans. 'Was it a good party?'

'It was,' I said. 'But I made a terrible blunder with Ingvild, that was the only downside.'

'Really?' he said. 'I didn't notice. What happened?'

He poured coffee into a cup, added a drop of milk and sat down. I blushed and looked out of the window.

'I took her up to the room on the second floor and tried it on with her.'

'And?'

'She didn't want it.'

'That can happen,' he said, stretched for another slice of bread and buttered it. 'It doesn't necessarily mean anything. Except that she didn't want it then. You were probably a lot drunker than she was, that could be the reason. It could have been too early. You don't know each other that well, do you?'

'No.'

'If she's serious, and by that I mean really serious, she might not want it to happen like that, at a party.'

'I don't know,' I said. 'All I know is that I made a big, big blunder. Now I've scared her off. I'm sure of that.'

Yngve placed a piece of ham on the bread, sliced a bit of cucumber and raised the sandwich to his mouth. I poured coffee into a cup and took some sips.

'What are you going to do about it then?'

I shrugged. 'There's nothing I can do.'

'What's done is dung and cannot be undung,' he said. 'Yes, a poor one, I'll admit that. Sorry. But I had a good one this summer, we ordered some shrimps, they came in a bowl and went in a flash.'

'Ha ha,' I said.

'You have to meet her again, as soon as possible, and then you have to apologise to her, it's as simple as that. You're sorry and it wasn't like you.'

'Yes.'

'Can't you invite her down here? Ola and Kjersti are coming at two. I'm going to make waffles. That would be the perfect setting.'

'Do you think she'd come here again after last night? I don't think so.'

'We can drive up and collect her. You knock on the door and invite her, say I'm waiting in the car outside. If she says no, well, that's not the end of the world.'

'Are you up for it?'

'Absolutely.'

An hour later we got into the car and drove downhill to Danmarksplass, turned right at the crossing and headed for Fantoft. It was a Sunday, the traffic was minimal, there were already little patches of yellow in the green mountains on both sides of the valley. Autumn was here, I thought, tapping my fingers on my thigh to the music.

'I've written some lyrics for you, by the way,' I said.

'Oh, fantastic!'

'Yes, but I don't think the lyrics are that fantastic. That's why I haven't shown them to you. I wrote them more than a week ago.'

'What's the title?'

'"You Sway So Sweetly."'

He laughed.

'Sounds like good pop lyrics, if you ask me.'

'Mm, maybe,' I said. 'And now I've told you they're done, you'll have to see them too.'

'If they're no good you'll have to write some more, won't you.'

'Easier said than done.'

'Are you a writer or aren't you? I only need a few verses and a chorus, then I can finish the songs. Easy enough for a man like you.'

'I'll do it then.'

He indicated left, we entered a large square in front of some high-rise buildings.

'Is it here?' I said.

'Haven't you been here before?'

'No.'

'Dad lived here for a year, did you know that?'

'Yes, I did. Leave the car here and I'll pop up to her place.'

I knew the address off by heart, so after a bit of confusion I found the right block, took the lift up to her floor, went down the corridor until I saw the right number on the door, concentrated for a few seconds, then rang the bell.

I heard her footsteps inside. She opened the door, and when she saw me she almost jumped backwards with the shock.

'You?' she said.

'I'd like to apologise for last night,' I said. 'I don't usually behave like that. I'm really sorry.'

'Don't apologise,' she said, and suddenly I remembered that was exactly what she had said the previous night.

'Would you like to come with me to Yngve's? He's going to make waffles. Ola and Kjersti, they were at the party last night, do you remember, they'll be there too.'

'I don't know . . .' she said.

'Come on. It'll be nice. Yngve's outside now. He'll drive you back afterwards as well.'

She looked at me.

'OK then,' she said. 'I'll just change into something more suitable. Hang on a minute.'

Yngve was waiting outside, leaning against his car smoking.

'Nice to see you again,' he said with a smile.

'You too,' she said.

'I'll sit in the back,' I said. 'You go in front.'

She did, pulled the safety belt across her chest, clicked the buckle into place, I looked at her hands, they were so attractive.

Not much was said on the way to town. Yngve asked Ingvild about her studies and about Kaupanger, she answered, asked him about his studies and about Arendal, I slumped back against the seat, glad to avoid responsibility for the conversation.

Every Tuesday evening, right through our childhood, Yngve or I made waffles. It was something we were good at, it was in our blood, so for me that afternoon, eating waffles in the sitting room and drinking coffee, was not as strange and un-studenty as it was for the others, quite the contrary, the waffle iron was one of the few objects I had brought with me from home when I moved a year ago.

As in the car, I let the conversation flow without me. Sitting at the table with Yngve, Ola, Kjersti and Ingvild, after what had happened the night before, I had everything to lose. The other three were more experienced; if I said anything it might be stupid and my inexperience would appear in flashing lights before Ingvild's eyes. No, I said as little as possible, mumbled *I agree* once or twice, nodded now and then, and I smiled. I interspersed the conversation with the odd question to Ingvild, mostly just to show I was thinking about her and it was important to me that she was there.

'Put on a record, will you?' Yngve said. 'And I'll make some more waffles.'

I nodded, and while he went into the kitchen I knelt down by his record collection. I saw it as a test, it was decisive which music I chose, and in the end I plumped for R.E.M.'s *Document*. By mistake I put on the second side and realised what a terrible mistake I had made just as I sat down, next to Ingvild.

Oh, no, what was that he sang, to the one he loved?

I blushed.

She would think I had chosen this song to tell her. Face to face. This is for the girl I love.

She must think I'm an absolute prat, I thought, looking out of the window so that she couldn't see how red-faced I was.

And on it went, to the one he's left behind.

No, no, no. Oh, how embarrassing!

I glanced at her, to see whether she had noticed.

She hadn't, but if she had and thought I was sending her a secret message, would she show it in any obvious way?

No.

I took a sip of coffee, wiped up the small dark seeds of the raspberry jam with the last piece of waffle on the plate, put it in my mouth, chewed and swallowed.

'Excellent waffles,' I said to Yngve, who had come into the room at that very moment.

'Yes, I used lots of eggs this time.'

'The way you t-talk!' Ola said. 'Anyone would think you were a c-couple of old b-biddies.'

I got up and went to the bathroom, rinsed my face with cold water, avoided looking at myself, dried my hands and face on the towel hanging there, which smelled faintly of Yngve.

When I went back in, the song had finished. We sat for another half an hour, and when Ola and Kjersti were about to go I said that maybe it wouldn't a bad idea if we went too, in fact I had a lot on tomorrow, and Ingvild said, yes, she had too, and five minutes later we were in Yngve's car again, heading at full speed for Fantoft.

Ingvild got out, waved to us, Yngve turned the car and started to drive back to town.

'That went well, didn't it,' he said.

'Do you think so?' I said. 'Did she enjoy herself?'

'Ye-es. I'm sure she did.'

'The waffles were good anyway.'

'Yes, they were.'

Not a lot more was said before he dropped me outside my bedsit. I jumped out, thanked him for the lift, closed the door and ran up the three steps to the door as he drove round the corner.

I had imagined it would be good to get home, but the smell of the freshly cleaned floor and bed linen, which still hung in the air, reminded me of the plans I'd had before the evening started, imagining I would wake up here with Ingvild this morning, and a new wave of despair and anger at myself washed over me, as well as all my feelings about the Academy, which launched themselves at me from all sides. The typewriter, the books, the plastic bag with my notebook, the pens, yes, even the sight of the clothes I had worn there depressed me and filled me with a sense of hope-lessness.

Bonfire of books, Ola had said, and I understood the need for it very well, just chuck everything you don't like and don't want, all life's detritus, on the flames and start afresh.

What a fantastic thought. Lug all my clothes, all my books and all my records into the park, pile them up on the grass, plus my bed and desk, typewriter, diaries and all the damned letters I had received, in fact everything that carried the tiniest hint of a memory: onto the fire with it! Oh, the flames licking up at the dark night sky, all the neighbours flocking to their windows, what's going on, well, it's just our young neighbour purging his life, he wants to make a new start, and he's right, I'd like to do that too.

And then all of a sudden bonfire after bonfire, the whole of Bergen aflame at night, helicopters with TV cameras hovering above, reporters in dramatic mode, saying Bergen is ablaze tonight, what is happening, they appear to be setting light to the fires *themselves*.

I sat down on the chair by my desk, the sofa and the bed were too soft and giving, I wanted something harder. I rolled a cigarette and lit it, but the roll-up was too crooked and saggy, I stubbed it out after a few puffs, there was a packet of cigarettes in my jacket pocket, wasn't there, yes, much better, and then, staring down at the table I tried to do a reality check, look at the situation as rationally and objectively as I could. The Writing Academy, it had been a defeat, but first of all was it such a problem that I couldn't write poems? No. Secondly, was this always going to be the case? Couldn't I teach myself, couldn't I develop over the year? Yes, of course. And if I was going to develop I would have to be open and, importantly, unafraid to make mistakes. Ingvild, with her I had made a fool of myself, once by being boring and reticent, once by coming on to her much too quickly and with force. In other words, I had been insensitive. I hadn't taken her wishes into account sufficiently. That was the point. I hadn't considered her feelings, only my own. But, firstly, I had been drunk, that did happen now and then, it happened to everyone. And, secondly, if she had any feelings for me, surely that wouldn't ruin everything? If she had any feelings for me surely she would be able to put herself in my shoes too and understand how things turned out the way they had? Fortunately, we had two previous meetings to build on, one in Førde, when everything had gone like a dream, and the other in the canteen, when at least we had chatted normally. Furthermore, there were the letters. They were funny, I knew that, or at least they weren't boring. Moreover, I was attending the Writing Academy, so I wasn't like all the other students, I was going to be a writer, people found that interesting and exciting, perhaps Ingvild did too, although she hadn't said as much. And then there was the waffle session at Yngve's that we'd just had – that did a little to remedy the impression I had made the previous night – now at any rate she could see how nice Yngve was, and as we were brothers, the notion that I was nice as well might not be too distant.

At around seven I went down and rang the bell at Jon Olav's.

'Good to see you!' he said with a smile. 'Come in. We've got a little debriefing to do.'

'Good to see you too,' I said, and followed him in. He brewed some tea and we sat down.

'I'm sorry I shouted at you,' I said. 'But I don't want to apologise.'

He laughed.

'Why not? Are you too proud?'

'I was angry when you said what you said. I can't apologise for that.'

'No,' he said. 'I went too far there. But you were too much. You were almost manic.'

'I was just drunk.'

'I was also drunk.'

'No hard feelings?' I said.

'No hard feelings. But did you mean what you said? That law is nothing?'

'Of course not. I had to say something.'

'I don't have much time for the legal milieu myself,' he said. 'I see law primarily as a tool.'

He looked at me.

'Now you have to say that you see writing as a tool!'

'Are you at it again?' I said.

He laughed.

When I returned I lay down on the bed and stared at the ceiling. I could still be friends with Jon Olav. That was no problem. But not with Ingvild, that was quite a different matter and much more complicated. The question was basically what to do. What had happened had happened and couldn't be undone. For the future, though, what could I do? What would be best?

I had taken the initiative twice now, invited her out today and yesterday. If she was interested she would contact me, drop by – she knew where I lived – or write a letter. It was up to her. I couldn't invite her out again, that would be, firstly, too pushy and, secondly, I had no idea if she was really interested in me, and I needed a sign.

The sign would be her coming here.

That was how it would have to be.

I didn't expect any move on the Monday after Yngve's party, it was too early, Ingvild wouldn't contact me that evening, I knew that, yet still I sat waiting and hoping; whenever I heard footsteps in the street I leaned forward and peeped out of the window. If someone stopped on the steps, I froze. But of course it wasn't her, I went to bed, another day dawned, more rain and mist, another evening spent waiting and hoping. Tuesday was a more realistic bet, she would have had time to think, distanced herself from what had happened and her real feelings would have had time to develop. Someone walking in the street: over to the window. Someone on the steps: I froze. But no, it was too early, tomorrow maybe?

No.

Thursday then?

No.

Friday, would she come with a bottle of wine we could share?

No.

On Saturday I wrote her a letter, even though I knew I wouldn't post it, she was the one who had to take the initiative, she was the one who had to make an approach.

In the evening I heard music coming from Morten's room in the basement, we hadn't spoken since the last time at Høyden when he was so desperate, I thought I could join him for a little while, I hadn't spoken to a living soul all day and was hungry for company. I went downstairs and knocked on his door, no one answered, but I knew he was there, so I opened it.

Morten was kneeling on the floor, his hands folded and outstretched in supplication. On a chair in front of him sat a girl. She was leaning back with her legs crossed. Morten turned to me, his eyes crazed, I closed the door and hurried back to my room.

He came up next morning, said he had made a last-ditch attempt, but it had led nowhere, it had failed, she didn't want him. Nevertheless he was in fine fettle, it shone through his stiff body language and formality of expression, what radiated from him was not despair but warmth.

To me he was like a character from one of the many Stompa books I had read when I was smaller, a young Norwegian boy at a boarding school in the 1950s.

I told him about Ingvild, he advised me to go and see her, sit down with her and tell her everything.

'Tell it as it is!' he said. 'What have you got to lose? If she loves you she'll obviously be happy to hear it.'

'But I have done,' I said.

'When you were drunk, yes! Do it now you're sober. It requires courage, my boy. And that'll impress her.'

'The blind leading the blind,' I said. 'I saw you in action downstairs, didn't I.'

He laughed.

'But I'm not you. What works for one person doesn't necessarily work for another. I think we two should pay a visit to Christian one evening. We can take Rune along. All of us boys. What do you say?'

'I haven't got a phone,' I said. 'So if Ingvild wants to get hold of me she would have to walk up here. And I would have to be at home.'

Morten got up.

'Naturally. But I don't think staying *on the premises* is the be-all and end-all.'

'I don't either. But I'd like to be here anyway.'

'OK, we'll wait then. Goodnight, my son.'

'Goodnight.'

I went out and rang Yngve, he wasn't at home, I remembered it was Sunday and he was probably working at the hotel. I rang mum. We first went through the events in my life, that is, at the Academy, then through the events in hers. She was looking for somewhere new to live, and she was working hard on plans to introduce an FE course at her school.

'We must try to meet soon,' she said. 'Perhaps you and Yngve could come to Sørbøvåg one weekend? It's a long time since you've been there. We could all meet up.'

'Good idea,' I said.

'I'm busy next weekend. What about the weekend after?'

'I'll see what I can do. Yngve has to be free too.'

'Let's start there then. And we'll see what happens.'

It really was a good idea. Grandma and grandad's smallholding was a completely different world because it was rife with child-hood memories, untouched somehow, as I was there so seldom and because of its location, on a little hill with a view of the fjord and the mountain behind, so close to the sea, far away from every-thing. It would be wonderful to spend a few days there, where no one cared about what I was or what I wasn't, I had always been enough for them.

This week we were going through short prose at the Academy. The pointillist novel was all the rage, a form whose Norwegian history began with Paal-Helge Haugen's *Anne*, from what we were told, this and other pointillist novels were situated somewhere between prose – the line, that is – and poetry – the point. I read

it, and it was fantastic, permeated with darkness much like Paul
Celan's *Death Fugue*, but I couldn't write like that, there was no
chance, I didn't know what created this permeation of darkness.
Even though I went through it sentence by sentence, it was impossible to say, it wasn't in any defined place, wasn't conjured
up by any particular words, it was immanent everywhere in the
same way that a mood is immanent in a mind. Mood isn't in a
particular thought or a particular part of the brain, nor in a particular part of the body, such as a foot or an ear, it is everywhere,
but nothing in itself, more like a colour in which thoughts are
thought, a colour through which the world is seen. There was
no such colour in what I wrote, no such hypnotic or evocative
mood, in fact there was no mood at all, and that was the heart
of the problem, I assumed, the very reason I wrote so badly and
immaturely. The question was whether you could *acquire* such a
colour or mood. Whether I could fight my way there or whether
it was something you either had or you didn't have. At home, writing, I thought what I did was good, and then came the round of
critique at the Academy, where the same was said every time, a
bit of polite praise for appearance's sake, such as, there is a lively
narrative style, before they weighed in with clichéd, stereotyped,
perhaps even tedious. But what hurt me most was that my writing was immature. When the prose course began we were given
a simple task, we had to write about one day or the start of a day,
and I wrote about a young man waking up in his bedsit to the
sound of the post, he slept on the other side of the wall to the post
box, and it made a racket. After breakfast he went out, on the way
he saw a girl, whom I described, and whom he decided to follow.
When I read this out the atmosphere became rather uncomfortable. They came up with the usual vague praise, said it was good,
said it was easy to visualise, suggested I deleted this and that . . .
It was only when it came to Trude's turn that what I had sensed
in the air was articulated. It's so immature! she protested. Listen:

'. . . he looked at her well-formed 501 bottom'. I mean, honestly, a well-formed 501 bottom?! She's just an object, and, not only that, he follows her as well! Had this been an exploration of immaturity and the objectivisation of women I wouldn't have said anything, but there's nothing in the text that suggests it is. In short, it's a bit creepy to read, she concluded. I tried to defend myself, conceded she had made some good points, but insisted my text *dealt with* exactly what she had said and there *was* a distance in the writing. I could of course have added a meta-level in the text, I said, as Kundera does, but I didn't want to, I tried to stay on the same level as the character.

'That isn't apparent from what I read anyway,' Trude said.

'No,' I said. 'Maybe it isn't visible enough.'

'I thought it was fun!' said Petra, who for some reason often defended me during these critique sessions. Presumably because she also wrote prose. Whenever we discussed our texts feelings became heated and more and more often the group tended to divide into two camps: on the one side were those of us who wrote mainly prose and, on the other, those who wrote poetry, with Nina, who wrote equally brilliantly in both genres, in the middle. Not that she said that much, she was perhaps the one student who found it hardest to formulate her views orally, it was almost impossible to grasp what her opinion was, if she had an opinion at all, that is. Judging by what she said, it didn't seem so, it was all vague, completely directionless, she might just as well have been presenting arguments about coats as about literature, but what she wrote was crystal clear, not in the sense that her opinions became coherent there, no, it was the language, her sentences, they were as clear and exquisite as glass. She was the best, Trude was the next best, Knut the third best. Petra, whose sentences resembled beetles at the bottom of a bucket, wasn't in the competition, I reckoned, she wasn't the finished article in the way that the other three were, but one day she would utterly outshine them, her talent was so obvious and it lay in her unpredictability: anything could happen in her texts, it was impossible to predict from the person she was or what she wrote, with the others you often could, but not with Petra, something unusual or unexpected was always on the cards. I was at the bottom, with Kjetil. The last two students, Else Karin and Bjørg, were above us, they had both had novels published, in a way they were fully fledged writers, and what they handed in during the course was also always accomplished and reliable. But sparks never flew in their writing in the way that they did in Nina's and Petra's, they were more like two horses hauling logs through the forest in the winter, it was heavy work, they made slow progress, their eyes were firmly set on the path ahead.

If I was at the bottom I had to rise. If I accepted that I belonged down there, in the terrible abyss of immaturity and ineptitude, I had failed. I couldn't fail. After a stint at the Academy I often weakened and told myself it was right, I wasn't a writer, I had no business being there, but never for long, maximum one evening, then my mind rose in opposition, it wasn't right, I might not be a writer now, but this was a temporary state that had to be, and would be, overcome, and when I woke in the morning, showered and packed my things to go to the Academy it was with a new-found self-confidence.

Rounding off the week at either Wesselstuen or Henrik had started to become a habit. I hadn't gone along the first two Fridays, but that afternoon I decided I couldn't sit at home waiting every single weekend and, if Ingvild were to come this evening of all evenings, she would probably leave a note to say she had been.

During the month we had been at the Academy we had got to know the teachers better and better, they weren't stiff and un-comfortable any more even though I had a suspicion the awk-wardness would never quite go, it was in their characters and nature, especially in Fosse, who had less of the outgoing spirit that Hovland revealed with his repartee and the constant, though slightly evasive, glint in his eye. No such repartee with Fosse, no such glint. But he still got close to us, expressed his opinions about what we were discussing, at first in a serious tone, but that often dissipated into laughter, in his rather sniffling, semi-giggling way, and sometimes he told us anecdotes about experiences he'd had, which, taken as a whole, gave us a picture of who he was. Not a complete one though because he was a very private person, like Hovland, who hardly ever spoke about anything to do with his private life, but with what they revealed of themselves in class there was enough for me to have a sense of who they were. Fosse was shy but also self-assured, to a very high degree he knew who he was and what he was good at, the shyness was more like a cloak he had wrapped around himself. With Hovland it was the opposite, I established: with him the shyness was protected by his quick tongue and ironic sense of humour. It was obvious that Hovland and Fosse liked and respected each other, although what they wrote was like night and day. Twice they had sung a children's song – '*Blåmann, blåmann bukken min*' – at the end of the evening.

We walked up the gentle slope from Nøstet, put down our umbrellas, shook them and closed them, went up to the first floor at Henrik, found a table, ordered beers and chatted. It was several days since the immaturity comment had been made, and I had come up with a new idea for a novel, inspired somewhat by the handful of novels I had read by Borges and Cortázar that week, also any thoughts about Ingvild had been entirely lost in all the tensions at the Academy so I was in a relatively good mood. After maybe an hour most of us had drunk enough for the limits on what could be said and what could not, which everyone felt to varying degrees, started to loosen. Jon Fosse was describing his childhood and he said that at a certain point he could have ended up on the streets. Petra laughed in derision. You could not, she declared. You're just mythologising your own past. On the streets indeed! Ha ha ha. No, no, Fosse insisted in his quiet way, looking down at the table, that was precisely how it had been. He could have been on the streets. Who's ever heard of a street urchin in a village? Petra countered. No, this was Bergen, Fosse replied. Everyone listening to this exchange was ill at ease. Fortunately Petra dropped the topic. The evening continued, more beer was drunk, the atmosphere was good until Jon Fosse got up to go to the bar. The street urchin wants some beer, Petra said. Jon Fosse didn't respond, got his beer, came back, sat down. Petra taunted him with another gibe a little later, in the same way, calling him a street urchin. In the end he rose to his feet.

'Well, I can't be bothered with this,' he said, put on his jacket and went down the stairs.

Petra laughed as she looked down at the table.

'Why did you do that? You made him leave,' Trude said.

'Argh, he's so pompous and self-important. On the streets . . .'

'But you didn't have to bully him. What good could that do?' I said. '*We* wanted him here. *We* thought it was fun drinking with him.'

'Since when have you been our rep?'

'Come on. You behaved very badly,' Knut said.

'Jon's a nice friendly man. There's no reason to treat him like that,' Else Karin said.

'Now all of you just pack it in,' Petra said. 'You're a bunch of hypocrites. Everyone thought what he said about ending up on the streets was ridiculous.'

'I didn't,' I said.

'No, because you're another one who'd like to be a street urchin. Street urchin! Have you ever heard anything so stupid!'

'Now let's drop this,' Knut said. 'You apologise on Monday if you dare.'

'I certainly will not,' Petra said. 'But we can drop it. I agree. It's a trivial matter.'

Everything was different after Fosse had gone, people packed up and left one by one soon after, apart from Petra and me, and we went to Café Opera. She asked if she could doss at my place, I said, of course, and we found ourselves a table and carried on drinking. I told her about my new idea for a novel. Firstly, it would consist of a variety of dialogues, people talking in various contexts, in cafés, on buses, in parks and so on, all the conversations would be about central themes in these people's lives, so they spoke about something important, one said he had just been told he had cancer, for example, or a son had been sent to prison, perhaps for a murder, but then, I told Petra – who was listening, though not looking at me apart from the odd fleeting glance followed by one of her equally fleeting smiles – but then, the context for these conversations is slowly revealed. There was a man recording them on tape. Why did he do that? I said to Petra, well, come on, tell me, she answered, I smiled, she smiled, well, that's what I'm working on, I said. He belongs to, or is employed by, an organisation, you see. In all towns of a certain size there are people who work for this organisation, they all go round recording conversations, which are written down and filed away somewhere, and this isn't something that started this year, it's been going on since time immemorial. I think there are conversations in existence from the Middle Ages, and from antiquity, thousands upon thousands of them, all in some way important to the respective individuals.

'And?' Petra said.

'And? Nothing else. That's it. Do you believe it?'

'I think it's a fun idea. But why?'

'Why what?'

'Why do they collect conversations? What do they do with them?'

'I'm not quite sure. I suppose they just document them.'

'Now I've remembered what this reminds me of. Wim Wenders' *Wings of Desire*. Have you seen it? There are some angels going round and listening to people's thoughts.'

'But this is conversations. And they're not angels.'

'Yes, yes, but have you seen it?'

'A long time ago. But that wasn't what I was thinking of. Not at all, in fact.'

And it was true, I hadn't had that film in my mind for one second, although I understood what she meant, there was a similarity.

'Do you want another beer?' I said, getting up.

'Please,' she said.

In the queue I scanned the room to see if Ingvild might have come, which I had been doing ever since I set foot in Café Opera, but she was nowhere to be seen. I raised two fingers in the air and, not without a mild sense of pride, saw the almost imperceptible twitch in the barman's eye that told me he had registered the order, I was a dab hand at this game now.

What if they *were* angels?'

That would solve everything! They were collecting material for a Bible in reverse, one about humans they couldn't understand. For them humanity was incomprehensible! So they analysed these conversations!

I placed the two large beers on the table and sat down.

'I've heard you shouldn't talk about what you're planning to write,' I said.

'Why not?' Petra said, not that interested, she was staring into the distance and her lips slid over her teeth the way they did when she was thinking about something else or when I imagined she was thinking about something else.

'You should keep your powder dry, in a way,' I said. 'Save it.'

'Ach, that's just what people say. You do as you like. If you want to talk about it, you just talk away to your heart's content.'

'Maybe you're right,' I said.

I always felt so pure and innocent when I was with her, like a squeaky-clean middle-class son, the teacher's pet, good at school but zero at life. She told me that in recent weeks she had gone out nearly every night, on her own to the bar at Wesselstuen, and men always came up and bought her a drink, she didn't spend a single krone all night, she said, and did nothing in return, except listen to them, not even that sometimes. It amused her, these men were entertaining, she said, and she would never have met them otherwise. I didn't understand what pleasure she could derive from that, but I respected her, admired her even, for it, I had read Bukowski and Kerouac of course and all the other books about people hanging out in bars drinking, and I had been drawn to life in the glittering shadows ever since *gymnas*, but I didn't know it, didn't go there myself, to sit alone in a bar chatting with strangers would have been inconceivable for me, it was closer to my nature to make waffles alone in my bedsit, I reflected, that at least was the feeling Petra evoked in me, I was that type, a shallow happy-go-lucky chap who was always ringing mum and was a bit afraid of dad. She got off her high horse when she sat with me, and I didn't understand why, but I was happy she did and so I just had to put up with her laughing at me and making derogatory comments. She did that to everyone anyway.

I looked behind me at all the small knolls, the heads.

Ingvild?

No.

Anyone else I knew?

No.

I looked at my watch. Half past eleven.

Angels studying the Bible in reverse!

Could I pull that one off?

'I'm writing a short story about a hairdresser's,' Petra said. 'There are two dogs lying in a basket. This is my idea!'

'I'm sure it'll be really good,' I said.

'Talking about it isn't a problem anyway,' she said, and smiled as her eyes narrowed into a sudden sneer.

'Hello,' said a familiar voice behind me.

It was Yngve.

'Hello!' I said. 'I was hoping you would be out tonight.'

'I'm just nosing around. I've come from work, thought I'd see if there was anyone here I knew.'

'Get yourself a beer and sit down! This is Petra, by the way, from the Academy. This is my brother Yngve.'

'Guessed as much,' Petra said.

When he sat down a few minutes later I was a bit concerned that Petra would have a go at him, in her eyes he would seem really straight-laced, but that didn't happen at all, on the contrary, they chatted while I leaned back and drank beer and relaxed and listened with half an ear. Petra asked Yngve what he was studying, and that alone was unexpected. Perhaps it was the Fosse incident that had forced her to pull herself together. Yngve started telling Petra about a book by Baudrillard on America, she was interested and I was happy. She got up to go to the toilet, Yngve said he liked her, she was nice, I said yes, but she's got a terrible tongue on her when the mood takes her.

We stood in the taxi queue outside Wesselstuen, we waited twenty minutes, then we were in the back seat of an elegant low-slung Mercedes gliding through the rain-gleaming streets up to my place. I paid, checked there wasn't a message by the front door or the door to my room, unlocked it, not caring what Petra might think about what she saw, which I would have done with almost anyone else, made some tea, put on some Velvet Underground, who for some reason I associated with her, perhaps it was her cynicism and urbanity that did it, she said Yngve had been pleasant and asked how we got on, I answered that we had a good relationship, but I might be too dependent on him in Bergen, at least that thought had gone through my head, I didn't have any of my own friends, except for those at the Academy, so I had to rely on Yngve. Once a younger brother, always a younger brother, she commented. We smoked our cigarettes, I said I didn't have a spare duvet, but she could have mine, she snorted and said the bedspread was enough, she would sleep in her clothes, that wasn't a problem, she often did that. OK, I replied, but what about a sheet? She snorted again, as you wish, I said and stood up.

Should I get undressed in front of her? Or sleep with my clothes on as well?

No, to hell with it, I lived here, I thought, and started getting undressed. She turned away and fidgeted with something or other until I was in bed, supporting myself on one elbow. She looked at me.

'What's that there? Ugh, how revolting!' she said. 'Have you got *three* nipples?'

What on earth was she blathering about?

I looked down at my nipples.

She was right. An extra nipple had grown next to one of the original two, equally as big.

Horrified, I held it between thumb and forefinger.

Could it be cancer?

'Yuk!' she said. 'If I'd known you were a freak I wouldn't have stayed here.'

'Relax,' I said. 'It's just a pimple. It's grown in a pore or whatever you call them. Look now!'

I squeezed the new nipple and a yellow blob squirted onto my chest.

'Ugh! Ugh! What are you doing!' she said.

I got up, took a towel from the cupboard and wiped the pus, looked down at my chest, which was back to normal now, and got into bed.

'Will you turn off the light?' I said.

She nodded, went over to the switch and pressed it, sat down on the sofa, swung her legs up and pulled the white bedspread over her.

'Goodnight,' I said.

'Goodnight,' she said.

*

I woke to her walking through the room and sat up.

'Are you going?' I said.

'Reckon so,' she said. 'It's nine. Sorry to wake you up.'

'No problem,' I said. 'Don't you want any breakfast?'

She shook her head.

'What a racket you made last night. Do you remember?'

'No.'

'You stood up, threw the duvet on the floor and stamped on it, really hard again and again. "What are you doing?" I said. "There's a mink in the duvet!" you shouted. I almost died laughing. What a sight that was.'

'Is that true? I don't remember anything.'

'It's true. Thanks for the use of the sofa. See you!'

I heard her walk through the hall, heard the front door open and shut, her footsteps round the corner and fade as she went down the hill. A vague image of an animal appeared, it was between the duvet cover and the duvet, I remembered it and remembered throwing down my duvet in fear and disgust. I had no memory of stamping on it at all. How spooky. For all I knew, there might have been scenes like that here every night.

Two evenings later there was a ring at the door, I jumped up, absolutely convinced it was Ingvild, who else would ring?

Jon Olav.

He wondered what had happened to me, was I writing twenty-four hours a day or what?

Yes, it was a bit like that.

He asked me if I fancied going out for a beer, Sunday was a good day for it, everything was so still and peaceful.

I said probably not, I had a lot to do.

'OK,' he said, getting up and putting on his jacket. 'Thanks for the chat.'

'Thank *you*. Are you going out anyway?'

'I'll see. Incidentally, I met Ingvild yesterday.'

'Oh yes? Where?'

'There was a party in Møhlenpris. Loads of people.'

'What did she say?'

'Nothing special. Actually I didn't talk to her that much.'

'Anyone else I knew there?'

'Yes, lots. Several of those at Yngve's party. Asbjørn and Ola, was that his name? Very nice guy anyway.'

'Yes, he is,' I said. 'Whose party was it?'

'I don't know. I went with some friends of friends. It was a big do. Half of Høyden was there.'

'I was at home,' I said.

'So you said. You could catch up now.'

'I fancy a drink, but no.'

'OK. I respect a man who has self-discipline!'

He left, and I sat down to write. I had three complete conversations now and was going to try to finish a fourth before I went to bed. This one takes place in a café, the two participants are criminals and they become edgy and evasive when they catch sight of the microphone the collator positions on the table, they soon leave.

I went to bed early and fell asleep at once as usual. At seven I was woken by a dream, which was a very rare occurrence.

I had been dreaming about a party with Yngve and Ingvild. I went into the hall, stopped by the sitting-room door, they were standing at the far end, by a window. Ingvild looked at me, then she tilted her head and Yngve kissed her.

I lay back in bed.

Ingvild was going out with Yngve.

That was why she hadn't come.

I brooded over it all morning. I believed in dreams, I believed they told you something about life and at a deeper level were always true. If so, the image had been unmistakable. They were standing together, Ingvild saw me and then she kissed Yngve.

Surely that couldn't be true?

Dear God, tell me it isn't so!

But I knew it was, and the truth burned inside me all day. The whole of my body ached, my stomach churned, at times I could barely breathe, my heart was beating so fast.

Oh God, tell me it isn't true.

Suddenly it all changed. A dream? Was I a complete moron? Who believed in dreams?

It was only a dream.

I fetched my trainers and the old tracksuit I had once been given by Yngve, which I regarded as a good omen, he had never wished me any ill, and then I went into the street and began to run. I hadn't run since I lived in northern Norway, I was gasping for breath after only a few hundred metres. But I had to smash this ridiculous idea, crush it and my method was to wear myself out, run and run until there was nothing left to run with, and then take a hot shower and sit reading a neutral novel of some kind which dealt with anything other than love, and then, as tired as a child after a long day, go to bed, hopefully to wake up refreshed the next morning, free of jealousy and unfounded suspicions.

It didn't quite go according to plan, the image stayed with me all week, but it didn't torture me in the same way, there was a lot to think about in connection with classes, and when I rang Yngve to arrange the details for the trip to Sørbøvåg I noticed nothing unusual about him.

It had just been a dream.

We had Friday free, and I planned to catch the boat north on Thursday afternoon, although Yngve couldn't come until the day after. Mum was taking the Friday off and would pick me up from the quay at Rysjedalsvika.

The rain was teeming down as I jumped off the bus by Fisketorget and walked over to Strandkai Terminal, where the boat was moored with the engines running, waiting for passengers. The water level in Vågen was high, the bluish-grey sea bobbed up and down, a very different density from the angry raindrops lashing the surface. I bought a return ticket from the office window, crossed the quay, went up the gangway, found myself a seat at the very front so that I could see the countryside through the large sloping front windows while it was still light.

Hydrofoil had been one of the magic words in my childhood, along with catamaran and hovercraft. I didn't know for sure, but I assumed this boat with its split hull was a hydrofoil. I still liked the word.

Through the side windows I saw passengers arriving with suitcases and bags, heads tucked into their coats beneath the rain, moments later they sat down around me, all performing the same series of movements. Waterproofs had to be removed, umbrellas closed and placed on the racks above the seats, bags placed on the floor under the back of the chair, tray tables raised and vacant seats pulled down before they could slump into their own seat with a sigh. The snack bar at the back of the boat, where you could get newspapers and coffee, hot dogs and chocolate, was open. Most of the passengers appeared to be from the rural areas of Sogn og Fjordane, there was something about the way they dressed that you rarely saw in Bergen, but also about the way they behaved, as though the thought that someone could see them had never occurred to them, and maybe also about their physiognomy, that is, their facial features and body types. In the weeks I had lived here I had started to recognise certain Bergen faces, there were similarities, whether they were boys, elderly women or middle-aged men they had some common features I hadn't seen elsewhere. Among these faces there were hundreds, indeed probably thousands, which were not similar. They disappeared, dissolved the moment they had passed, while the Bergen faces returned, oh, there was that type! Bergen had been a town ever since the early Middle Ages, and I liked the idea that Håkon's Hall and St Mary's Church weren't the only remnants of those times, as well as the countryside of course, and that the crooked trading houses in Bryggen weren't the only remnants of the fifteenth century, but also the various facial features, appearing and reappearing in new generations, still visible around town. I saw elements of the same faces in the people around me on the boat, except that I associated them with the farms and villages of the fjord landscapes to the north. Mum told me that in her grandparents' time they used to attribute specific characteristics to people from the various farms. This family was like this, that family was like that, and the idea was passed down through the generations. That mode of thinking belonged to a completely different era and was basically incomprehensible to me, who hadn't come from any of the places I had grown up in, unlike all the others there. Everything was first generation with me, everything was happening as if for the first time, nothing, neither bodies, faces, customs nor language, originated in that place or had been bound up with it for a longer period, and so couldn't be viewed in that way.

Actually there were only two forms of existence, I reflected: one that was tied to a place and one that wasn't. Both had always existed. Neither could be chosen.

I got up and went aft to the snack bar, bought a coffee and a chocolate Daim, and as I folded down the table and put the cup in the tiny round hollow, the mooring ropes were thrown on board, the gangway was lifted and the engine revs increased. The hull trembled and shook. Slowly the boat moved forward as it swung to the left and soon the bows were facing the islands off Bergen. I closed my eyes, enjoyed the throb of the boat, the regular hum that rose and sank, and fell asleep.

When I opened my eyes I saw the contours of an enormous forest stretching back and, behind it, in the distance, a range of mountains.

So, not far to go.

I got to my feet and walked to the stern, up the stairs and onto the deck. It was empty and as I approached the railings, no longer sheltered by the superstructure, the wind was so strong that it almost upended me. I held on tight and was laughing inside with joy because not only was the wind full of raindrops, which beat against my face, but darkness had fallen and the immense wake behind us was a luminous white.

Only when the lights of the ferry terminal became visible, just a few small twinkling dots in the dense darkness, still far off, although because of the boat's great speed we would soon be gliding alongside, illuminating the waiting room, the ticket office window, the two buses, some cars and a crowd of people either about to embark or meet someone, only then did I go back in.

Mum was one of those waiting with their arms down by their sides and heads bowed in the rain and wind, she waved to me, I went over and gave her a hug, and as we walked towards the car the express ferry was already roaring into the distance.

'Great to see you,' she said.

'Ditto,' I said and got in. 'How are things?'

'Good, I think,' she said. 'There's a lot to do, but it's interesting work, so I'm not grumbling.'

We drove through the forest and came out by the bay on the other side, by the shipyard where Kjartan worked. There was an enormous hull visible in a shipbuilding hall or a dock. Kjartan crawled through shafts and small passages fitting pipes, and when he talked about his work it was not without a certain pride in his voice, although he did admit he was a mediocre, if not poor, pipe-fitter, it lay so far from who he was, it was an occupation poorly suited to him and had been ever since he joined the proletariat at the end of the 1970s. He was also the safety rep at the shipyard, which occupied a lot of his time, from what I gathered.

A steep climb up a forest-clad mountain, over the summit and down the other side to Hyllestad, the municipal centre at the end of Åfjord, along the fjord to Salbu, where grandma and grandad's and Kjartan's houses stood on top of a little hill.

Rain fell across the cones of light as mum parked in the yard, and when she switched off the headlamps it was as if for a moment the deluge had stopped until the engine died and the rat-a-tat-tat on the roof and bonnet took over.

I got out, took my bag, walked across the soft gravel and opened the front door.

Oh, that smell.

I hung my jacket on the hook above grandad's overalls, moved back a couple of steps to make room for mum, who hung up her coat, put her bag at the foot of the stairs and went into the sitting room.

Grandma was in the chair beside the window at the back, grandad on the sofa beneath the window in the long wall, both watching TV with the volume deafeningly loud.

'Well, look who it is,' grandma said.

'Hi,' I said.

'Yes, the Norwegian population is growing!' he said.

'Think I've stopped growing now,' I said, and turned to grandma, wanting in some way or other to greet her with more warmth, but I couldn't exactly give her a hug where she was sitting, I had never done that and I never would. She held one arm across her chest, as if in a sling, it trembled and shook. Her head shook too and her feet were stretched out on a stool. Everything all right, Grandma? No, I couldn't say that.

I walked towards her and smiled.

She looked at me and her mouth moved.

I went up to her and lowered my head to hers.

She had almost no voice left, all I heard was a breathy whisper.

What did she say?

Hi.

Her eyes smiled.

'I came by boat,' I said. 'The rain's terrible, I must say.'

Yes.

I straightened up and looked at the door as mum came in.

'Shall we make some supper?' she said.

The next morning I slept until twelve and went down in time for lunch, which they always had at this time here. Mum had made potato dumplings, we ate them in the kitchen, the mist hung heavy in the air and the leaves on the tall birch outside the window were yellow and glistened with moisture.

After lunch, while they rested, I went for a stroll around the two-hectare property. Beyond the little mere, which was black and covered with water-lily leaves alongside the banks, rose the spruce-clad hillside, silent and sombre against the low sky. I wandered over to the barn, even more sunken and run-down than I remembered, opened the door to the animals on the ground floor, the three cows shifted in their stalls, the one furthest away turned its head and watched me with its gentle eyes. I walked past them and through the low door leading to the barn. It was half-full of hay, I climbed to the edge of the loft and swung myself up, poked my head into what had once been a hen house, and where there were still feathers on the floor, even though it must have been ten years since a hen had roosted on a perch here.

I would have to bring Ingvild here one day.

This was such a happy thought, that she might sit on the sofa and chat to grandad, chat to mum and see this world here, which was so magical for me. At the same time there was something almost criminal about the idea, something transgressive and forbidden, of bringing two completely different worlds together in this way: if I saw her on the sofa I would immediately realise that she didn't belong there.

I went onto the barn bridge and lit a cigarette, shielding it with my hand against the drizzle, which was turning into rain. Mum appeared outside the house, she opened the car door and got in, drove towards me so that she could turn. I went down to find out where she was going.

'I'm off down to the shop. Want to come with me?'

'No, I think I'll do a bit of writing.'

'OK. Is there anything you want?'

'Some newspapers would be nice.'

She nodded, turned and drove back down. Soon afterwards her car passed me on the road below.

I tossed my cigarette where they usually burned paper and went indoors. Both of them had got up, they were in the kitchen. I quietly closed the door behind me, thought of going up to my room and trying to write a bit, but then I saw something through the open door and stopped. Grandma lifted her trembling hand and took a swipe at grandad, which with some doddery footwork he managed to sidestep. She sat down in her wheelchair, paddled it with her feet and took another swipe. He stepped to the side again. All this went on in eerie slow motion and without a sound. Grandad went out the other door, into the sitting room, and grandma manoeuvred her chair back to the table with tiny foot movements.

Upstairs in my room, I lay on the bed. My heart was pounding with agitation at what I had just witnessed. It had been like a dance, the grisly dance of the aged.

I had never considered what the relationship between my grandmother and grandfather was like, in fact, I had never thought they even *had* a relationship. But they had been married for what would soon be fifty years, they had lived on this smallholding, brought up four children, struggled and toiled to make ends meet. Once they had been young, as I was now, with their lives ahead of them, as I had mine. I had never considered that either, not *seriously*.

Why did she try to hit him?

She was heavily medicated, which made her paranoid, gave her delusions, that was why.

I knew that, but it didn't help, the image of the two of them was stronger.

Through the floor I could hear the radio, the weather forecast and the news. I could imagine him sitting right next to it with one hand under his ear, staring straight ahead, unless his eyes were closed in concentration.

Grandma trembling in the kitchen.

The impact of what I had seen was so overwhelming that I got up and went downstairs in an attempt to smooth things over, my presence might re-establish a kind of normality, I thought vaguely, as the steps creaked beneath me and the sight of the grey telephone on the table under the mirror reminded me of the old telephone they'd had, the one hanging on the wall, consisting of a mouthpiece and an earpiece, all in black Bakelite.

But could that be right? Could there have been such an old nineteenth-century-style contraption here when I was young? Or had I seen it in a film and imagined there was one here and it had stuck in my memory?

I opened the sitting-room door, grandad instantly got up in the awkward way he did and straightened as he watched me.

'It's good you came,' he said. 'I've been thinking we should put up a new fence below the barn, and now you're here perhaps you could help me?'

'Be happy to,' I said. 'Right away?'

'Yes,' he said.

In silence we put on our outdoor gear, I followed him down to the cellar, where he had some green impregnated fence posts and a roll of wire netting. I carried everything down to the end of the property, to the top of the little mound where the neighbour's land started, and went back to fetch the sledgehammer grandad had just pointed to.

Manual work was not my strong suit, to put it mildly, so I was a bit nervous as I walked towards him with the sledgehammer in my hand, I wasn't sure I could do this or do it in a way that would satisfy him.

Grandad took some wire cutters from an overall pocket and snipped off the old netting, then wriggled the first post to and fro until it was loose enough for him to pull up. I did the same on the other side, according to his instructions. When we had done that he put one of the new fence posts in position and asked me to knock it in the ground with the sledgehammer. My first blows were circumspect and probing, but he didn't say anything and soon I had built up enough courage to hit it harder and with more assured swings.

The black peaked cap he always wore was dotted with droplets of rain. The blue material of his overalls had darkened. He gazed across the fjord and told me the story about the plane crash on Mount Lihesten in the 1950s, I had heard it many times, it was the mist and the drizzle that had reminded him, I supposed. But I liked hearing him tell stories, and when he had finished and hadn't said anything for a few minutes, he just stood there with his head bowed next to the fence post, which was now firmly bedded in, I asked him about the war. How had it been here during the war, had anyone offered any resistance and had there been any Germans stationed here? We moved towards where the next post would be and he started telling me about those days in April 1940. When the invasion was announced he and a pal went to Voss, where they were mobilising for war. They went on foot, borrowed a boat and rowed across Sognefjord, crossed the mountain, it was April, crusty snow and moonlit nights, he said, descended to Voss, to the military camp there, where everyone from Vestland was supposed to meet. He shook his head and laughed. They were all drunk when he arrived and there were hardly any weapons. Nor any uniforms. The officers were in Fleischer's Hotel drinking.

When they ran out of booze, he told me, they requisitioned the bar on the cruise ship *Stella Polaris*. It was moored in Bergen and the alcohol was sent up by train.

'So what did you do?' I said.

'At first we tried to get hold of weapons and uniforms. We walked around Voss and asked all the uniformed soldiers we met if they could help us. No one could. My friend said to a guard, you know we're soldiers even though we're not in uniform. Can you ring someone? No, answered the guard, and then he showed us the telephone cable. It had been cut. So we went back home. When we rowed across Sognefjord we took boats with us and left them on the northern side so the Germans would find it harder if they followed us. But of course when we arrived, the country had been occupied.'

It took him an age to tell the story, no detail was too trivial, right down to the dogs barking as he approached the farms at night, and by the time he had finished there was only one post left. I hammered it in, he fetched the roll of wire netting, we started to attach it to the posts, he held it while I banged in fence staples.

'There were Germans stationed here, yes,' he said. 'I got to know one of them well. He was an Austrian and had been to northern Norway when he was growing up, they sent poor kids up here in the summer in the 30s, and he had been one of them. A nice fellow. He had a lot of interesting things to say.'

Grandad told me there had been a prison camp in the district, mostly Yugoslavs and Russians working on a road scheme. Grandad had a lorry, it had been requisitioned by the Germans, and he often used to drive to the camp, which was in Fure. He took food with him for the prisoners, he said, grandma made packed lunches and he hid them under rocks in the surrounding terrain. He said he reckoned the guards knew, but they turned a blind eye. Once he had seen one of the prisoners being shot.

'He was standing in front of the German soldiers screaming *Schiesst! Schiesst!* And that was when one of them shot him. But the officers were furious. Discipline was strict, you know. So the soldier who fired his gun was sent to the Eastern Front. For German soldiers Norway was a dream posting compared with all the other places they could have been stationed. Towards the end of the war they mostly sent old men and young boys here. I remember I saw a new contingent arriving, and one of the officers said to them, *Was wollen Sie hier, alte Leute?'*

He laughed. I hammered in the staples and unrolled the wire as far as the next post. He carried on telling me stories. The Austrian, who seemed to have been a friend from what he said, decided to make his escape in the days before the German capitulation, he boarded a boat with a woman from the village and her two sons and vanished. Later the two sons were found floating in the water on the other side of the fjord, presumably killed with a rock.

I looked at him. What on earth was he telling me?

'Not so long ago a book came out about it. I've got it in the house. It's very interesting. Who could have guessed he would be capable of something so awful? But he must have killed them. There is quite simply no other explanation. And then he disappeared. Into thin air. He may still be alive.'

I straightened up and helped grandad to roll out the wire to the next post, where I pulled it as tightly as I could and secured it at the top and bottom so that it would retain the tension, then I banged in more staples.

'What was he like?' I said, and looked up at grandad, who was gazing into the mist above the fjord.

'He was a nice man, you know,' he said. 'Polite and cultivated and friendly. I haven't got a bad word to say about him. But there must have been something else inside him,' he said.

'Yes,' I said. 'Did he get away, do you think, or did he die?'

'It's hard to say,' he said. 'He probably died trying to escape.'

That was the last post, grandad snipped off the ends of the wire and I carried the roll and the sledgehammer to the cellar while he walked beside me. As we entered the sitting room, both red in the face after the rain, mum was making pancakes in the kitchen.

Grandma was sitting in her chair, and when she saw me she said something. I went up close and lowered my head.

The clock, I thought she said. He's taken the clock.

'Who has?' I said.

Him, she said, looking at grandad, who sat down on the sofa.

'He's taken the clock?' I whispered as softly as I could so that he wouldn't hear.

Yes, she whispered.

'I doubt that,' I said. 'Why would he?'

I stood up, my stomach hurt, I went to join mum, half-closing the door behind me so that they wouldn't hear us in the kitchen.

Mum was holding a ladle over the big hotplate and carefully pouring the mixture, which immediately began to solidify with a sizzle.

'Grandma says grandad took her clock,' I said. 'Stole it, from what I could hear.'

'Yes, I heard her say that too,' mum said. 'It's the medication. It might be making her paranoid and causing her to imagine things. She's pretty bad at the moment. But she'll come out of it. Do you understand?'

'Yes,' I said.

For some reason I was close to tears and went into the hall, put on my boots and stood under the overhang by the front door to have a smoke.

A bus stopped down by the road outside the school. A few minutes later Kjartan walked up over the hill, dark-eyed and white-skinned, carrying a bag in one hand, some letters and a newspaper in the other. It was *Klassekampen*. He had read it for as long as I could remember.

'Hello there,' he said.

'Hi, Kjartan,' I said.

'Did you arrive yesterday?'

'Yes,' I said.

'We'll have a chat later,' he said.

'Yes,' I said. 'Mum's making pancakes. They'll probably be ready in a quarter of an hour or so.'

He continued towards his door, stopped and looked across.

'There's that one-legged crow!' he said.

I took a few steps towards him and stared in the direction he was pointing, up to the pole carrying the electricity cable to the barn. Sure enough, on the top, there was a crow with one leg.

'Johannes shot its other leg off. It's stayed here ever since.'

He chuckled and closed the door behind him, I stubbed out my cigarette in the soft gravel and took it with me to put in the waste bin under the sink.

'Yngve rang, by the way,' mum said. 'He had to do an extra shift this evening and won't be here until tomorrow morning. He's driving up, he said.'

'What a shame,' I said. 'Shall I set the table?'

'That'd be nice, she said.'

After we had eaten at the table in the TV lounge, since grandma and grandad had moved their bedroom to the sitting room because of the trouble grandma had with stairs now, Kjartan looked at me and asked if I felt like a chat at his place. I nodded, we went up to the large, open and light top floor where he lived, he put on some coffee, I settled down on the sofa and flicked through the pile of books on the table.

Bobrowski. Hölderlin. Finn Alnæs, *Musica*, the first volume in his major oeuvre *Ildfesten*, which, according to mum, he had broken the back of now, only two of the promised five novels had come out anyway. Kjartan had been passionate about these books for several years, there was something about the presence of the cosmos that appealed to him, I inferred from the way he talked about them.

'Are you learning anything at the Writing Academy?' he said from the kitchen.

'Yes, I am,' I said.

'I've met Sagen,' he said. 'He's run lots of the writing courses for Sogn Skrivarlag.'

'We haven't met him yet,' I said. 'We've only met Fosse and Hovland.'

'I don't know them,' he said, and came in with two cups. They were wet, he had just rinsed them, in mine there were still coffee grains at the bottom, half-dissolved in the water.

'We've finished the poetry course now,' I said.

'So you've been writing poems?'

'Yes, we had to. But it didn't go well.'

'Don't say that,' he said. 'You're only nineteen. When I was nineteen I barely knew what a poem was. You're lucky to be there.'

'Yes,' I said. 'Have you written anything recently?'

'A couple of poems.'

He got up and went over to the dining-room table where his typewriter was, grabbed a pile of sheets, flipped through them, came back and handed them to me.

'You can have a browse if you like.'

'Yes, I'd love to!' I said, suddenly touched that he regarded me as his peer.

dwindling beck

skegges nibble
at the green rock
weave through the swaying grass
the shade cools

a brother of the sun
lashes its tail

'What's a skegge?' I said, looking up at him.

'Skegge? A trout. What do you think?'

'It's very good,' I said. 'I particularly like the start. It seems to elevate it somehow.'

'Yes,' he said. 'It's the trout in the mere, you know.'

I read on.

with a mouth of lush church grass
I stand at the crossroads
drinking the light of faith
on the shores of eternity
I lead my body, on
like a dun horse in the dusk
towards the forest somewhere

I had tears in my eyes again, this time because of the poem, the image of the body which he leads towards the forest like a horse in the dusk.

I seemed to be full of tears, they had accumulated inside me, waiting for an opportunity to be released.

'This poem is fantastic,' I said.

'Do you think so?' he said. 'Which one is it?'

I passed it to him.

He skimmed through it for a few seconds and snorted.

'"On the shores of eternity",' he recited. 'I was being a bit ironic there, you know.'

'Yes,' I said. 'Nevertheless.'

He got up and fetched the jug of coffee, poured and placed it on a newspaper.

A door went downstairs; from the way it was closed I realised it was mum.

'So this is where you are!' she said.

'We're reading some poems,' Kjartan said. 'Have a look if you like.'

'I'd love to,' she said.

I got up and walked with the cup in my hand to the other end of the room, where there were bookshelves, an armchair and a stereo. I took out a few books and thumbed through them.

When they started talking I stood by the window and gazed out at Mount Lihesten, which had just become visible through the mist, a black wall rising where the sea began and falling at the end where the fjord finished.

Was that where Ingvild's family cabin was?

When I entered the sitting room, grandma was asleep in her chair, her head lolled back, her mouth wide open. She'd had Parkinson's disease for as long as I could remember, I had barely a memory in which she wasn't shaking. But when I was a boy the illness wasn't as far advanced, it didn't prevent her from working on the smallholding she had moved to at the end of the 1930s, when she married grandad and where she had lived ever since. According to Borghild, she had been surprised how small it was and how small people were out here. It might have been simply that conditions were tougher here than in the inland region she came from, there was less food and therefore the people were also smaller. Mum told me she had always emphasised that they should be impeccable in the clothing they wore and the way they behaved and for that reason grandma had the reputation of wanting to be better than others. Grandad worked as a driver, he drove buses; grandma was in charge of nearly everything that was done on the farm. This was the 1950s, but from what mum had told me about her childhood it sounded more like tales from the previous century. A man came here in the autumn and did their slaughtering for them, she told me, grandad never did it himself. Nearly every single part of the animal found a use. Grandma rinsed the intestines in the stream to use them for sausages. The blood was boiled in big pots in the kitchen. I had no idea what else she did, apart from what mum told me. There were only two generations between us, yet I knew nothing of how she had spent her life, not really, not essentially, I knew nothing of her relationship with objects and animals, life and death. When grandma and I looked at each other it was from either side of a chasm. For her, family was the central point in her life, in other words, her family, the one that came from the farm where she grew up, and then her children. I had the impression that grandad's family, which had moved inland from the islands a generation earlier, was not important. Her family was the centre of her existence, and the soil. Kjartan would sometimes say that the soil was her religion, that they were soil-worshippers in Jølster, where she came from, a kind of ancient heathendom they had clad in the language and rites of Christianity. Look at Astrup's pictures, he would say, all the fires they lit on Midsummer Eve, that's Jølster folk for you, they dance around the flames as though they were their gods. Kjartan would laugh when he said such things, and it was not without disdain, yet there was always some ambivalence because Kjartan had a lot of her in him: the serious attitude to life and the deep sense of duty were in Kjartan too, and if she worshipped and cultivated the soil, Kjartan worshipped and cultivated nature, the presence of the universe in the form of birds and animals, mountains and skies. He would deny that any such connection existed between him and his mother, after all he was a communist, an atheist, a ship's pipefitter. However, all you had to do was look them in the eye to banish any lingering doubts. They had the same brown eyes, the same wary gaze.

Now there was nothing left of her life, disease had consumed her, eaten up her body, leaving only shaking and fits. It was hard to believe when I saw her sitting there asleep with her mouth agape that her strong will, which couldn't even rule her body now, and her strict morality, which she was no longer able to express, could have left such a deep mark on her children. But it had.

*

Mum helped grandma into bed, undressed her, brushed her hair and helped her on with her nightdress, all while I read *Ceremonies*, my latest favourite book, trying not to look. Not because grandma was being undressed necessarily, but because it was mum doing it, and it seemed so intimate and private, the daughter caring for her old mother, this wasn't meant for my eyes, so I sat with my eyes trained on my book, attempting to let it absorb me.

It wasn't difficult, all the spaces in it were so open and still connected with one another in quite sensational ways. Not just the spaces, incidentally, also the characters, which were usually closed off, could suddenly open and simply merge into one another. A man staring at an axolotl in an aquarium is mysteriously transformed into an axolotl staring out from an aquarium at a man. A fire in antiquity becomes a fire in the modern age. Then there were all the other peculiar things that went on. A man suddenly starts regurgitating rabbits, it becomes a problem, a minor catastrophe, the whole of the flat he has rented is full of small white rabbits.

Mum said goodnight to her parents, came out and closed the sliding door.

'Would you like some coffee? Or is it too late for you?' she said.

'I wouldn't mind a cup,' I said.

I liked these short stories so much, but I couldn't write like this, I didn't have the imagination. I didn't have any imagination at all. Everything I wrote was connected to reality and my own experiences.

Yes, but not the new novel.

A wave of pleasure surged through me.

It was really fantastic. Some mysterious men, maybe angels, who collect people's conversations and reflect on them.

But this pleasure didn't come alone, it also brought with it some despair, for I knew I would never be able to carry this off. I couldn't write the story, it would never work.

Mum came in with a pot of coffee and two cups, put them down and went to fetch a dish of thin squares of potato pancake.

'Borghild made them,' she said. 'Do you want to try a bit?'

'Please.'

Borghild was mum's sister, a strong vivacious woman who lived alone in a little house above the farm where they grew up. She usually cooked for the weddings in the district, she knew all the old recipes and she knew everything about the family, those who had died and those who were still alive. Mum was close to her, even more now, as they didn't live far from each other.

'How are you, Karl Ove?' mum said. 'You've said so little since we've been here. That's not like you.'

'Maybe not,' I said. 'But I'm fine. The Writing Academy's pretty hard going, that's all.'

'What's hard going about it?'

'It feels as if I'm not good enough to be there. I don't write well enough, as simple as that.'

'Remember you're only twenty,' mum said.

I took a whole pancake and ate it in two bites.

'Nineteen,' I said. 'But I'm at the Academy now, you know. It doesn't help me to think it might be better when I'm twenty-five.'

Mum poured coffee into the two cups.

'And I'm in love,' I said. 'That might be why I don't say much.'

'Someone you've met this autumn?' she said, and lifted her cup to her lips and drank while watching me.

'I met her at Easter, when I was staying with you. Just once. Then we wrote to each other, and then we met in Bergen. She's studying psychology. Comes from Kaupanger. Same age as me.'

'But you're not going steady?'

I shook my head.

'That's the point. I don't know if she wants me. I made a fool of myself and then . . . well, nothing.'

A snore that sounded like a snarl came from the other room. Then someone coughing.

'I'm sure it'll be fine,' mum said.

'Maybe,' I said. 'We'll see. Otherwise I'm OK. I love being in the bedsit and Bergen generally.'

'I might come and see you both in a couple of weeks,' mum said. 'There are also a couple of student friends I'd like to visit. Gerd, do you remember her?'

'Yes, of course.'

'I've been wondering whether to do another course, you know. I'd like to do a degree as well. But it's a question of finance and I would also have to apply for a leave of absence.'

'Yes,' I said, taking another pancake.

Upstairs in the bedroom I lay in the darkness for ages before I fell asleep. The darkness linked the little space inside with the enormous space outside. The old wooden bed was like a little boat, or that was how it felt. Now and then a tree whooshed and the rain on the leaves pitter-pattered against the window. When it stopped, there would be a whoosh somewhere else, from some other trees nearby, as though tonight the wind had strategically deployed its energies and was riding across the countryside in several units.

The feeling I had when I arrived here was that life was over. Not in the sense that the house stood under the sign of death, more that what was going to happen had happened.

I lay on my other side, my head on my arm. The sound of my pulse beating reminded me of something grandad had once said, that you shouldn't lie listening to your heartbeat if you wanted to sleep. It was an odd thing to say, I couldn't remember what had occasioned the comment, but whenever I lay like this and my pulse beat against my ear I was reminded of it.

Only a few months ago mum had told me that grandad had suffered from anxiety for a long period at the beginning of the 1960s, it had been so bad that he didn't go to work, he didn't move from the sofa, so terrified was he of dying. Kjartan was the last child at home then, he had been young and wouldn't have understood anything.

This information was unsettling, in a way, most of all because I hadn't known anything about it and would never have guessed. Were there more such pockets of drama in the lives of my closest family? But the information in itself, what it said about grandad, I couldn't get it to tally because if there was one characteristic I associated with grandad it was his *joie de vivre*. Then again I had never thought of him as an independent person with an independent life, he had always been simply 'grandad', in the same way that grandma had always been 'grandma'.

A whoosh went through the old birch again, and a little cascade of droplets hit the wall as though the tree were a dog shaking off the rain.

Darkness. Silence. The beat of my pulse. Da-dum. Da-dum. Da-dum.

Unlike grandad it wasn't death I heard but life. My heart was young and strong, it would beat away through my twenties, it would beat away through my thirties, it would beat away through my forties, it would beat away through my fifties. If I got to grandad's age, and he was eighty, I had used only a quarter of my life so far. Almost everything lay before me, bathed in the hopeful light of uncertainty and opportunity, and my heart, this loyal muscle, would take me through it whole and unscathed, ever stronger, ever wiser, ever richer in life lived.

Da-dum. Da-dum. Da-dum.

Da-dum. Da-dum. Da-dum.

I saw Yngve's car from the sitting-room window, the windscreen wipers sweeping from side to side, the dark shadow in the driver's seat that was him, and told mum, who was massaging grandma's feet on her lap, that Yngve had arrived. She gently lifted grandma's feet to the floor and got up. Grandma and grandad had eaten lunch at twelve, we had waited, now she went into the kitchen to prepare the meal.

The car stopped outside. Straight afterwards the door went, I heard him in the hall and turned to him as he came in.

'Hi,' he said.

'The Norwegian population is growing, I can see,' grandad said.

Yngve smiled. His eyes brushed mine.

'Hi,' I said. 'Good trip?'

'Absolutely fine,' he said and passed me a pile of newspapers. 'Brought these along for you.'

Mum came in.

'There's some food ready if you're hungry.'

We went into the kitchen and sat down. Mum had made a big pot of stew. I guessed the plan was to freeze it so that grandad only had to heat it when they were alone again.

'Was the drive OK?' mum said, placing the pot on the table, where there were already crispbreads and butter and a jug of water.

'Yep,' Yngve said.

It was as though he had a membrane around him which prevented me from getting into proper contact. But that didn't have to mean anything, sometimes that was how it was, and he had been driving for several hours, sitting alone in the car and thinking his own thoughts, it was a change coming here, where we had been all day and a very different atmosphere of familiarity and naturalness had been established.

Yngve filled his deep dish with stew, positioned the ladle on my side of the pot, I helped myself. Steam rose from the dish, I took a crispbread and bit off a piece, poured water into a glass, raised a spoonful of stew to my mouth, blew on it.

'Ann Kristin says hello, by the way,' Yngve said. 'I met her yesterday and said I was coming up here.'

'Thanks,' mum said.

'Where did you meet her?' I asked as casually as I could. He had said he was staying in town to work, not to go out, and if he had gone out and met Ann Kristin, then he was lying and why would he lie?

'In the canteen at Sydneshaugen,' he said.

'Oh, right,' I said.

After the meal we drank coffee in the sitting room, grandad chatted, we listened. Kjartan came in wearing the same clothes he had worn for the last two days, his hair a mess, eyes flashing behind his glasses. Yngve didn't respond to Kjartan's monologic conversation as he usually did, there was something submissive and withdrawn about him, as though he were looking inwards and not outwards. Could be anything, I thought, he was just a bit reticent.

Outside, the rain was tipping down.

Kjartan went back to his flat, I read the newspapers, mum washed up in the kitchen, Yngve took his bags up to his room and was gone for a while. When he returned he sat in the chair by the fireplace with a book.

I lowered the newspaper and stared out of the window. Dusk was falling. The light from the lamp outside the neighbours' house, a stone's throw below us, was striped with rain.

Grandma was asleep in her chair. Grandad had also fallen asleep. Mum, on the sofa beside him, was reading. Yngve was reading too. I watched him and knew he had noticed, because you do when someone watches you in a silent room, you notice. Nevertheless, he didn't look up, he kept his eyes firmly on the book.

There *was* something wrong.

Or was I being paranoid?

He was reading, for Christ's sake, I couldn't make *that* into a sign something was wrong.

I lifted the newspaper and continued reading. Then it was his turn to watch me. I concentrated on not looking up.

Why was he watching me?

He got up and went out. Grandad woke as the door was closed, blinked a few times, struggled to his feet and wandered over to the wood burner, opened it and threw in two logs. The wooden floor above creaked.

Then it went quiet.

Had he gone to bed?

Now?

Because he had been out last night? And hadn't been working at the hotel as he said?

I took my cup to the kitchen and poured myself a refill. The fjord lay a somewhat lighter shade of dark in the growing murk. The rain drummed on the roof and walls. I went back to the sitting room, grabbed my pouch of tobacco and made myself a roll-up. Grandad was cleaning his pipe, he tapped it on the glass ashtray a few times, poked at some black clumps and flakes with a white pipe cleaner. Grandma had woken up, she tried to sit upright, leaned forward but fell back again. Then she moved her hand to the two buttons on the armrest, succeeded in pressing one, and the chair began to rise with a low hum as she was lifted up, or pushed forward, and a moment later was able to grasp her walking frame. But her back was too bent for her to walk, and mum got up and asked where she wanted to go. I couldn't hear the answer that issued from her trembling lips, but it must have been the kitchen, because that was where mum steered her steps. While all this was going on, grandad was engrossed in his pipe activities.

The floorboards above creaked, and then the staircase. The door opened and Yngve fixed me with a look.

'Coming for a walk, Karl Ove?' he said. 'There's something we have to discuss.'

The hope that had held me aloft melted and my insides crumbled. Everything collapsed.

Yngve was going out with Ingvild.

I got to my feet and went into the hall. He had his back to me as he donned his waterproof jacket. He said nothing. I slipped my feet into my shoes, bent over and tied them, then rose and put on my jacket. He stood still, waiting. After I had zipped up, he opened the door. Fresh air streamed into the house. I pulled the hood over my head and tied it under my chin, Yngve walked over to the car, opened the door and took out his umbrella. The rain was a regular drumbeat on the gravel and the house, more of a soft patter beyond in the vast darkness, where it fell on grass and moss, trees and bushes.

Yngve opened the umbrella, I closed the door behind me, we set off down the hill. I stared at him, he had his eyes on the path ahead. My legs were trembling jelly, my insides in disarray, but there was also something hard in the centre. I wasn't going to give him anything. He would get nothing from me.

We walked through the gate, past the neighbours' house and down onto the tarmac road.

'Shall we walk down?' Yngve said.

'OK,' I said.

The junction, where three roads met, was illuminated by street lamps, but as soon as we had passed it and reached the road leading into the valley the night was all around us. Trees stood like a wall on either side. There was a faint rushing sound from the river and the rain falling in the forest. Otherwise all we heard was our own footsteps. I stared at him. He glanced at me.

'There's something I have to tell you,' he said.

'Yes, so you mentioned,' I replied. 'What do you have to tell me?'

He looked straight ahead again.

'Ingvild and I are going out together,' he said.

I said nothing, just glared at him.

'It's only—' he began.

'I don't want to hear any more,' I said.

He went quiet, we carried on walking.

The falling rain, our footsteps, the wall of trees in the darkness. The smell of wet spruce, the smell of wet moss, the smell of wet tarmac.

'I have to explain what happened,' he said.

'No, you don't.'

'But, Karl Ove—'

'I don't want to hear about it, I told you.'

We reached the firing range, a shed in front of a long narrow piece of open ground to the right of the road.

In the distance was the drone of traffic. It came down the slope from the mountain at the end of the valley.

'It wasn't something I planned,' he said.

'I DON'T want to hear!' I said. 'Don't you understand? I don't want to hear anything!'

We walked on in silence. He glanced at me once, was about to say something, changed his mind, looked down, stopped.

'I'm going back then,' he said.

'You do that,' I said and carried on walking, listening to the sound of his fading footsteps behind me. The next moment a car came round the bend and transformed the darkness into an inferno of light, which lingered on the retina for several seconds after the car had passed, and I walked on blindly until my eyes had got used to the night again, and the road and the trees reappeared.

I would never talk to him again. I couldn't leave until tomorrow morning, so I would see him, and I would see him in Bergen, that was inevitable, sooner or later I would bump into him, the town wasn't that big, but I wouldn't say anything then, nor here, I wouldn't say a word to him ever again.

I walked to the end of the valley, to where the waterfall plunged down the mountainside and the river flowed beneath the road, saw the faint glint of water as it hit the rocks and the pool at the bottom, it seemed almost obscene, water in the water, in the pouring rain, what was more, and then I made my way back. My trousers were wet and I was frozen, and there was nothing good waiting for me in the house.

Had they slept together?

Everything in me seized up. I stopped.

Yngve had slept with her.

When he left here he would go home and sleep with her again.

Stroke her breasts, kiss her on the mouth, pull down her panties, penetrate her.

My heart was pounding wildly, as though I'd been running.

She called his name, whispered his name, kissed him, spread her legs for him.

I started off again.

She would ask how it had gone, what I had said. He would tell her. I was the 'him' they talked about. The little brother. The naïve little brother who sat in his room waiting for her, who thought she wanted him while she was out partying with Yngve, fucking at Yngve's place. Just that, the fact that she spent the night at his place and in the morning showered in the bathroom there, sat down and had breakfast there, with a growing sense that it was normal and her due.

She caressed him, she must have done that, she looked into his eyes, she must have done that, she said she loved him, she must have done that, this wasn't me being paranoid, this is what happened. It happened every day.

The little house on the hill shone before me, the darkness profound, almost impenetrable on all sides.

I would never be a part of his life again. I would never visit him wherever he lived. I wouldn't give a damn about him in a way that I had never done with anyone else before. If he thought everything would be as it was between us, that I would ever tolerate this, then he had another think coming.

Now it was all about getting through the evening. He was here, I couldn't avoid him, but it didn't matter, I would ignore him, and

that was good because then he would believe it was just something I was doing now and eventually everything would go back
to normal, only later would he realise that in fact I would never
speak to him again.

I opened the front door and went into the hallway, hung up my
jacket, darted up to my room and changed my trousers, dried my
face on a towel in the bathroom, then went down to the ground
floor and into the sitting room, where they were watching TV.

Yngve wasn't there. I looked at mum.

'Where's Yngve?' I said.

'He's gone to see Kjartan,' mum said.

I sat down.

'What's going on?' mum said.

'Nothing,' I said.

'Something is going on, I can see,' mum said.

'Do you remember me saying I was in love?' I said.

'Yes, of course,' mum said.

'Yngve's going out with her,' I said. 'He's just told me.'

Mum took a deep breath and sighed as she looked at me.

'Well, it's not *my* doing,' I said.

'You mustn't fall out,' she said. 'It'll pass, Karl Ove. It's bad now
but it'll pass.'

'Yes, it might,' I said. 'But that doesn't mean I ever want anything to do with him again.'

She got up.

'I've made some supper,' she said. 'Can you set the table?'

'All right.'

I carried in cups and plates, bread and butter, salmon and
scrambled eggs, a selection of meats and cheese, a pot of tea and
milk. Once I had finished mum asked me if I could fetch Yngve. I
looked at her.

'OK,' I said. I slipped on my shoes and walked the few metres
down the yard to the other door. Perhaps he would think every-

thing was as it was when I arrived and he was welcome to think that.

I opened the door, entered the hall, went over to the stairs. Music was on loud upstairs. I took a few steps up, enough to see the sitting room. Yngve was sitting in a chair staring into the air. He hadn't heard me. I could have shouted, but I didn't because, to my horror, I saw tears running down his cheeks.

Was he crying?

I quietly went back down, out of sight. Stood for a moment in the hall, silent. That was the first time I had seen him crying since he was a little boy.

But why was he crying?

I stuffed my feet into my shoes, closed the door carefully behind me and shuffled across the yard.

'He's coming,' I said as I went into the sitting room. 'He said we should start away.'

Early the next morning mum drove me to the ferry in Rysje-dalsvika. The boat was fairly empty when it arrived, I sat down in the same seat I'd had on the way over. The weather had eased a little during the night, the sky was still overcast, but the cloud cover was lighter and it wasn't raining any more. The boat sliced through the heavy grey water at a strangely fast pace beneath the tall motionless overarching mountains between which the fjord lay.

I had gone to bed before Yngve returned in the evening and was up before he woke in the morning, so I hadn't seen him since briefly catching sight of him in the chair at Kjartan's, but I had heard him, his voice from the floor below as I was trying to sleep and his footsteps up the stairs to his room on his way to bed. Being under the same roof as him was unbearable, I seemed to burn inside, all I could think of was that he would regret what he had done.

Now, surrounded by light in a boat in the middle of the fjord, on my way home, everything seemed different. Now it was her I thought about. She had allowed herself to be taken in by him, to be blinded by his surface charm and had said yes. She didn't realise I was better than him. She had no idea. But she would find out. And what then? Would I be there for her? Or would I let her go her own way?

Could I go out with her after she had been with Yngve?

Oh yes.

If she wanted to be with me, I would.

There was nothing to say I had to remain in Bergen after this year and nothing to say she had to, if they broke up.

I went to the back, to the snack bar, and ordered a coffee, took it with me up onto the deck and sat down on a bench under the roof from where I could see the forest, which on the way had just been a large deep shadow beneath the mountains, but was now clearly defined beneath the white sky. Dark green, almost black, spruces packed into a dense jagged area with the odd deciduous tree luminous in its autumn-yellow colours.

I caught a taxi home from the ferry quay, after all that had happened I deserved that. However, being back in my bedsit, surrounded by all my possessions, didn't feel as good as I had imagined because this was where I had waited for her, day in, day out, and now, knowing what I did, that she had never been on the point of coming up to see me but had been with Yngve, I could see with total clarity how foolish I had been. All the fine thoughts I'd had about her, the whole dream I had built up around her appeared immeasurably naïve now that I knew how the land actually lay, what had actually gone on.

Yngve knew how I had felt, he knew that I was waiting at home, hoping, while he was meeting her and going out with her. Was that part of the thrill? I wondered. Having me sitting here like an idiot and looking out of the window?

I couldn't stay in my room, so I put on my jacket and went out, but where could I go? It was Sunday, all the shops were closed and I didn't want to sit on my own in the cafés that were open.

I stopped outside the block of flats where Jon Olav lived and rang the bell. No one answered, I walked on, up the hill and down past Støletorget, and soon I was crossing Torgalmenningen, burning inside the whole time, I was a fool, I had nowhere to go, no one to visit, I just walked, burning with shame about everything. I walked along Nygårdsgaten, cut up by the Science Building and went into the park, the plan was to sit down and have a smoke, it was Sunday, I was out for a Sunday walk, but in the park, look, that was where I held Ingvild's hand and I didn't want to think about that, even then she must have known she didn't want me, that I was no good for her, and I didn't want to go to Danmarksplass, Yngve lived there, and for all I knew she had his keys for the weekend and was in his flat now. I didn't want to walk the other way either, Sydneshaugen School was there, where we had drunk coffee, the gate where we had stood talking when Morten appeared. Instead I walked down the first hill and came out by the Grieg Hall, followed the road past the library and the station, turned right where the old town gate once stood, and then continued uphill, back along the roads at the top of Fjellsiden.

Yngve was probably on his way home now. If Ingvild wasn't in his flat he would drive straight up to Fantoft, where she would be expecting him.

She opens the door and gazes at him with tenderness and affection.

They embrace.

They kiss and kiss with mounting passion.

Glance at the room, then they undress each other at top speed.

A cigarette afterwards.

What did your little brother say?

He got angry. But it'll pass. You should have seen him. Ha ha ha! Ha ha ha.

Wave upon wave of heat rose to my head, which I lowered, and into my face. I walked past an old fire station, it was made of wood and painted white, beneath it the town's myriad colours vibrated, I walked along the very highest line of houses until I slowly began to descend and was back outside my bedsit.

That is where he lives, I thought. The brother who believes he is a writer. And when I opened the door and went into my room it was as though I was still in the street looking at myself, the conceited idiot who closed the curtains and kept out the world.

Rolf Sagen was going to teach us for the next two weeks. His course didn't deal with genres, neither prose, nor poetry, nor drama, nor essays, but writing itself, the process of writing and a variety of relevant strategies. He gave us a number of practical tips, such as how it could be useful for prose writers and dramatists to make what he called a hinterland, you wrote down everything about the characters and their relationships and in so doing knew much more about why they acted as they did than was apparent from the finished text – a hinterland was the complete world of which the narrative revealed only glimpses – and also he talked about the underlying motives or premises of writing. Sagen was a trained psychologist, and he spoke a lot about how important it was to penetrate down into the deeper layers of consciousness when you wrote. He had a few activities for us to do. One of them was about emptying our minds of thoughts, it was like meditation, we should try to be ahead of our thoughts, deny them space, just forge on into the unthought, and then, at his command, write down the first things that occurred to us.

'Let's start now,' he said, and so we sat around the table, all of us with our heads bowed and eyes closed. I couldn't do it, I was just thinking about this situation, about having to empty my mind, but it was beyond me. Two minutes passed, three, maybe four.

'Now write,' he said.

The first thing that occurred to me was the name of a town: Darmstadt. I wrote a little story about it. When everyone had finished we had a break and when we resumed we had to read out what we had written.

Sagen held his beard between thumb and forefinger in concentration, nodded and said this was interesting, unusual, remarkable, fruitful. When it was my turn the string of superlatives came to an end. He listened to what I read out, then eyed me.

'You're using only the surface of your mind when you write,' he said. 'And if you do that there won't be any depth in the text. What was the first word that occurred to you?'

'Darmstadt.'

'Hm, a German town,' he said. 'Have you been there?'

'No.'

'Well,' he said. 'I'm afraid there isn't very much more to say about the text. You'll have to try and penetrate deeper into your consciousness.'

'Yes,' I said.

What he was actually saying was that my writing was superficial. He was right, I had realised that, there was a chasm between what the others wrote and what I wrote. I described a young man walking the streets of Kristiansand. I hadn't drawn either him or the streets he walked from the depths of my consciousness. Sagen confirmed what I had suspected, he articulated it in words, I had to descend into the depths of my own consciousness, into the darkness of my soul, but how the hell was I supposed to do that? This was not something I found easy! I had read *Death Fugue*, no writer had ever delved further into their consciousness than Celan when he wrote that, but what use was this insight to me?

The next day we had another activity. This time we were given a few nonsense words to keep repeating in our heads until Sagen told us to write the first thing that occurred to us.

Once again all eight of us sat around the table with bowed heads and closed eyes. Now you can write, Sagen said, and I scribbled the first words that came into my mind.

> Two leather chairs
> in the wind

That was all.

Sagen scratched his chin.

'That's interesting,' he said. 'Two chairs in the wind. They're outside, I take it. Yes, they must be.'

'That's an exciting intro,' Knut said.

'You'll have to work on it a bit more, Karl Ove,' Trude said. 'It might turn into a poem.'

'It's an image that doesn't immediately make itself apparent,' Sagen said. 'There's a tension, there's nothing contrived about it. Yes, that *is* interesting. You're on the right path, I think.'

I had been thinking about the two leather chairs we had at home when I was growing up. They stood on a green hill and the wind blew in from the sea. But this was just nonsense, I realised that, although I found myself unable to dismiss the others' comments that it might be the beginning of something, a poem.

I carried on when I got home.

> Two leather chairs
> in the wind
> a yellow bulldozer – that was the next bit that occurred to
> me –
> noise from a town
> you have already left

As soon as I had written that I knew the sort of comments I would get. Delete the yellow bulldozer. Remove the 'already' from the last line, it's redundant. So I did that and the poem was finished.

> Two leather chairs
> in the wind
> noise from a town
> you have left

At any rate it looked like a poem. I knew where the image of the leather chairs originated, ever since I was small I had been fascinated by the relationship between inside and outside, when what was supposed to be inside was outside, and vice versa. One of the most hypnotic memories I had was the time Geir and I had stumbled over a cellar full of water in a half-finished house. Not only that, there was no floor, so we stood on a little rock surrounded by water, *indoors*! The episode on the refuse site, which featured in one of the texts that got me accepted on the course, also dealt with this idea, the way Gordon and Gabriel set out chairs, a table and lamps in the forest. *Two leather chairs in the wind* had its roots there, the magic of childhood in six words. *noise from a town/ you have left* was different, I had seen many instances of it in the poems I had read, something is stated and revoked at the same time. Also the converse, where the same merges into the same, such as, *the hare snows into the hare*, but so far I hadn't come up with any such images myself.

Up until now!

Oh!

In a trice I added two more lines.

> Two leather chairs
> in the wind
> noise from a town
> you have left.

The girl disappears
into the girl.

That was it. A fully fledged poem.

To celebrate I stuffed the photography book down my trousers, left my shirt hanging outside them and went down to the basement to have a wank. With the book, which I could now hold and leaf through simultaneously, open in my left hand, and my right hand around my dick, I stared at one photo after another. The girl with the basket of laundry was still my favourite, but there was no longer anything pure about it, every situation I imagined myself in with her was permeated by the thought of Yngve and Ingvild and the fact that I had lost Ingvild, the only girl who meant anything to me. I flicked to and fro to escape the thought – more or less as Sagen had advised us, it struck me – and I finally succeeded in concentrating long enough on one of the girls' wonderful bodies for me to come.

That was at least something.

Back upstairs, I killed time until I could go to bed. Fortunately I had no problem sleeping twelve hours at a stretch. I couldn't say I looked forward to going to the Writing Academy, not a day passed without something disparaging being said about me, or rather something disparaging about my writing. No one meant it as such, it was called critique and supposed to be constructive, but in my case it was so useless because there was nothing *else* in my texts to compensate for the criticism. It *was* immature, it *was* clichéd, it *was* superficial and I *was* truly incapable of penetrating deeper into my own consciousness, where the essence of a writer was to be found. In all the discussions we had I was reminded of this, it was my role, and if I wrote something good, such as the poem about the two leather chairs, it would still be seen in the light of the person I had shown myself to be, as a sort of fluke, the anthropoid who writes *Hamlet*.

The only benefit of the Academy during those days was that so much happened, there was so much to react to while I was there, that the thought of Yngve and Ingvild was pushed into the background. For the same reason, my room was unbearable, there were no distractions, so if we didn't have any writing assignments I went out just for a walk – one night to Jon Olav's, where I could have a cup of coffee, but then couldn't visit again until a certain number of days had elapsed so that my lack of friends wouldn't become a burden to him, I had placed myself in a kind of quarantine – the next night to Anne's, for her the same rules applied, after a cup of tea and an hour-long chat I couldn't show my face there until after four or five days, preferably more – and there was no one else to visit. I couldn't go to the cinema alone, that carried too much of a stigma, and Café Opera was out of the question. To stand alone in the bar, ashamed not to know anyone, that wasn't a situation I wanted to expose myself to. Besides, the chance that I would bump into Yngve and Ingvild, or their friends, was too great. Just the thought of being in the same room as them, of being present as they gazed at each other or even touched each other, made my flesh run cold. Morten was a saviour: even though we had nothing in common we could always chat for an hour about something, and he didn't find it strange that I popped by, after all we were 'neighbours'.

One evening there was a ring at the door. I thought it was Jon Olav and went to open up.

Ingvild stood on the steps.

'Hi,' she said, sending me a hurried glance.

At that second, as I met her eyes, it was as though nothing had happened. My heart was pumping as if I were in love.

'*You?*' I said.

'Yes, I thought we should talk.'

She looked down as she said that, pushed a strand of hair away from her forehead.

'Come in,' I said.

She followed me in and sat down on the sofa.

'Would you like some tea?' I said.

She shook her head.

'I won't be long.'

'I'll put some on anyway,' I said.

I went into the kitchen and put a pan of water on the stove. Her coming to see me was the last thing I had expected and the place was neither tidy nor clean. I sprinkled tea leaves over the bottom of the tea pot and went back to her. She had lit a cigarette. The ashtray was half-full, I took it and emptied it in the kitchen waste bin.

'You don't need to tidy up for me,' she said. 'I'll be off in a couple of minutes. There was just something I had to say to you.'

She laughed as she said it. She glanced down, she glanced up.

'The tea will be ready soon,' I said. 'We're doing poetry at the Academy and we've been given some fantastic poems. Especially one. Would you like to hear it?'

She shook her head.

'Not now, Karl Ove,' she said, squirming on the sofa.

'But it's not very long,' I said. 'Hang on a minute. I'll find it.'

'No, please don't. It's not the right moment.'

'It'll be fine,' I said, rummaging through the pile of photocopied poems, found what I was after and turned to her.

'Here it is. It won't take long.'

I stood in the middle of the floor with the piece of paper in my hand and started to read.

Death Fugue

Black milk of daybreak we drink it at sundown
we drink it at noon in the morning we drink it at night
we drink it and drink it
we dig a grave in the breezes there one lies unconfined

A man lives in the house he plays with the serpents
he writes
he writes when dusk falls to Germany your golden
hair Margarete
he writes it and steps out of doors and the stars are
flashing he whistles his pack out
he whistles his Jews out in earth has them dig for a
grave
he commands us strike up for the dance

Black milk of daybreak we drink you at night
we drink you in the morning at noon we drink you at
sundown
we drink and we drink you
A man lives in the house he plays with the serpents
he writes
he writes when dusk falls to Germany your golden hair
Margarete
your ashen hair Sulamith we dig a grave in the breezes
there one lies unconfined

He calls out jab deeper into the earth you lot you
others sing now and play
he grabs at the iron in his belt he waves it his
eyes are blue
jab deeper you lot with your spades you others play
on for the dance

Black milk of daybreak we drink you at night
we drink you at noon in the morning we drink you
at sundown
we drink and we drink you
a man lives in the house your golden hair Margarete

your ashen hair Sulamith he plays with the serpents
He calls out more sweetly play death death is a master
from Germany
he calls out more darkly now stroke your strings then
as smoke you will rise into air
then a grave you will have in the clouds there one
lies unconfined

Black milk of daybreak we drink you at night
we drink you at noon death is a master from Germany
we drink you at sundown and in the morning we drink
and we drink you
death is a master from Germany his eyes are blue
he strikes you with leaden bullets his aim is true
a man lives in the house your golden hair Margarete
he sets his pack on to us he grants us a grave in
the air
He plays with the serpents and daydreams death is
a master from Germany

your golden hair Margarete
your ashen hair Shulamith[1]

I read it as I had been taught, with a regular rhythm, not stressing individual words, not stressing anything because it carried
meaning, rhythm was paramount, rhythm was everything.

While I was reading, Ingvild smoked and studied the floor in
front of her.

'Isn't that good?' I said.

'Yes,' she said.

[1]Translated by Michael Hamburger.

'I think it's fantastic. Absolutely brilliant. I've never read any-thing like it.'

I sat down at the other end of the sofa.

'Yngve told you what happened, didn't he?' she said.

'The tea,' I said and got up. 'Just a minute.'

I went to the kitchen, poured the boiling water over the dry tea leaves, which would swell up and become soft and supple within seconds, the biggest would go clumpy, while all the properties in them would be released and infuse the water and colour it, golden at first, then darker and darker.

I brought out the teapot with two cups, put them on the table.

'It has to stew a bit first,' I said.

'I have to go soon,' she said. 'I only wanted to talk to you about what has happened.'

'Can't you have a cup of tea anyway?' I said.

I filled her cup, the tea was too weak, and I poured it back into the pot, and then I poured again. This time it was darker, if not perfect, at least drinkable.

'Do you take milk?'

She shook her head and grabbed the cup with both hands, took a sip and put the cup back on the table.

'It had nothing to do with you,' she said. 'What happened.'

'Right,' I said, filling my own cup.

'I hope we can be friends despite everything. I'd like to be friends with you.'

'Of course we can be friends,' I said. 'Why shouldn't we be able to?'

She smiled, no eye contact, took another sip.

'How are things then?' I said.

'They're fine,' she said.

'Course going well?'

She shook her head.

'I'm not sure,' she said.

'Same here,' I said. 'But the Academy course only lasts a year, not six like in psychology. I'll have to see what I do afterwards. Maybe lit. But I'm planning to keep writing.'

Silence.

It was painful with her there.

'Do you still live in Fantoft?' I said.

She shook her head.

'I'm moving into a collective.'

'Are you?'

'Yes. I think I'll have to go,' she said and stood up. 'Thank you for the tea. See you.'

I accompanied her to the hall, smiled at her and said bye, watched her disappear round the corner, went back in, washed the two cups, emptied the ashtray so that I wouldn't be reminded of her visit, lay back on my bed and stared at the ceiling. It was eight o'clock. Two hours until I could sleep.

For as long as there were classes at the Academy I coped very well during the day. I trudged through the rain in the morning and, if nothing else, appreciated meeting the other students – we saw so much of one another that I was relatively natural with them – and then I trudged home through the rain in the afternoon beneath the fast-darkening sky. I made myself something to eat, I sat and read until my restlessness became too much and drove me out, mostly into the great nothing, in other words, I met no one. I had nowhere to go, and I couldn't stay in my room, what was I supposed to do? Ten wild horses couldn't drag me into a cinema on my own or into Café Opera. Living like this was fine for a while, there was nothing wrong with it as such, the situation was explicable, I was attending a course on which there were very few students, and those there were, were older than me, none would have been a friend of mine under normal circumstances, which contrasted sharply with the situation for the average student, who was surrounded by hundreds, if not thousands, of other like-minded people. Yes, there was a rational explanation: I was at the Writing Academy, and when I finished there I would take out a student loan and go to Istanbul to write, a town where no one expected me to know anyone, which furthermore was exotic and foreign, an adventure, by Christ, a room of my own in Istanbul!

I wrote letters and described my plans. I read novels I had heard about at the Academy, by Øystein Lønn, Ole Robert Sunde, Claude Simon, Alain Robbe-Grillet, Nathalie Sarraute. Although they were difficult for me I ploughed through them in the hope that something would stick. I walked down into the town centre and bought records, drank coffee in the cake shops old people frequented, where I didn't care how I looked or what impression I made or if people wondered why I was on my own. I didn't give a shit about old people and I didn't give a shit about myself either. I sat there studying the records, reading books, drinking coffee and smoking. Then I walked home, killed time, went to bed, another day dawned. The weekdays were no problem, the weekends were more difficult, at two or three in the afternoon the urge to go out and have fun, like other students, slowly made itself felt, at six or seven it became acute, they were pre-loading all around me while I sat alone. At eight or nine it felt better, soon I would be able to go to bed. And occasionally something would hold my attention, a book or my writing, to make me forget time and the situation, and when I next checked my watch it could be twelve, one or even two. That was good, for then I would sleep in longer the following morning, thereby shortening the day. Some Saturdays I went out in the evening, I was sick of my room and my footsteps were drawn to the town centre, past Café Opera perhaps, where the windows were full of laughing chatting people and golden beers, and although all I had to do was open the door and go in, it wasn't locked of course, I *couldn't* do it, in some way or other this was how life had become. Once I did anyway, and it was as I had imagined, a nightmare, I burned inside as I stood in the bar drinking, my chest burned and my head burned, I knew no one, I had no friends, and everyone could see that, I was alone in the bar acting as if it were the most natural thing in the world, I drank and calmly surveyed the room, is there anyone I know here tonight? . . . No, indeed, how strange, not one! Never mind, it's nice anyway to have a beer before I go home to bed . . . busy day tomorrow, might as well take it easy now . . . As I hurried home afterwards I was furious at myself and my own stupidity, I shouldn't have gone there, it was ridiculous, why did I have to display my failings in that way?

The following weekend I rang Yngve. He had a TV, I would ask him if he was planning to watch the Saturday match and, if so, could I pop up? I hadn't forgotten the business with Ingvild, I would never forgive him for it, but we had been brothers for much longer than I had been in love with Ingvild, and it ought to be feasible to separate the two relationships from one another, to have two thoughts in your head at once.

'Hello,' he said.

'Hi, this is Karl Ove.'

'Long time, no hear,' he said. 'How's it going?'

'Fine. I was wondering, actually, if you were going to watch the football this afternoon?'

'I was, yes.'

'Would it be OK if I came up to see it?'

'Yes, of course. It would be great.'

'Will Ingvild be there? If so, I won't come.'

'No, she's at home this weekend. Just come on up.'

'Right, see you then. Bye.'

'Bye.'

'By the way, have you done the pools?'

'Yes.'

'How many lines?'

'Thirty-four.'

'OK. See you.'

I bought a bag of beers in the nearby shop, showered and changed my clothes, trotted up the hill in the rain, went into the kiosk and did the pools, waited for a bus, jumped on, sat looking at all the lights and movement that abounded in this town, the many dislocations of colour and form that occurred, all the light that glittered in the water, floated in the water, all the umbrellas and swishing windscreen wipers, all the lowered heads and laced-up hoods, all the rubber boots and waterproof jackets, all the water running down the gutters, by the kerbsides and on the roof, the gulls circling above and settling on the top of a flagpole, bedraggled, or on the ridiculously high statue in Festplassen, a man of normal dimensions standing on a pillar, how high was it, twenty metres? Thirty? Christian Michelsen, what had he done to deserve such a fate?

Bergen, the town of swishing windscreen wipers.

Bergen, the town of draughty toiletless bedsits.

Bergen, the town of human fish. See their gaping mouths.

This is where grandad came after selling books in the outlying districts, going from door to door, offering his little library, and with the money he bought himself a new suit. This is where he bought the ring to marry grandma. Bergen, this was *the* town for them. He dressed up when he came here, put on his best clothes and his finest hat, presumably he had always done that.

Across Danmarksplass, to the right under the signs by the little wooden shed where they sold tyres, to the left again straight afterwards, and uphill between the workers' houses.

Everything was normal, I thought as I rang the bell and waited for him to open up. Everything was as it had been.

And it was.

Yngve had bought chocolate toffees, just like those dad used to give us while we watched the televised English football matches on a Saturday afternoon when we were growing up, he had brewed up a pot of coffee, which we drank before moving on to beer and crisps at the start of the second half. We kept track of the scores in the other eleven matches, he had ten right so far, but it all went haywire towards the end, I had seven correct results, which was more or less what I got whenever I did the pools.

After the match Asbjørn and Ola came up, we sat drinking and chatting for a while, then we caught a taxi into town and went to Café Opera. Ingvild's name wasn't mentioned once. I kept a fairly low profile for the first few hours, I had nothing to say, nothing to contribute, but I got drunker and drunker and then there I was, aglow at the centre of the world, babbling away about anything that came into my head. I told them I was going to move to Istanbul to write next year, I said I wrote better than Brett Easton Ellis, he had a cold heart and I didn't, I said that Jan Kjærstad had read what I had written and liked it. We can't go home now, I groaned, when they flashed the lights and fortunately no one had any plans to, almost everyone who had been in Café Opera was now in the streets chatting and waiting to hear about a party. Erling and Arvid were there, they lived in a big house up in Vil-laveien, right behind the Student Centre, in a collective, we could go there, apparently there wasn't that much to drink, but that wasn't a problem because someone immediately jumped into a taxi to get what booze they had from home while we slowly made our way uphill, Erling and Arvid first, then the rest of us dragging behind like the tail of a comet.

Both Erling and Arvid came from Tromøya. I remembered Erling as the goalkeeper in the team above us when I was growing up. He was always gentle, he always smiled, but he was not averse to making the odd acerbic comment. Although he was not especially tall there was something ungainly and sometimes almost limp about him, I had noticed that even in the days when he kept goal. Arvid was big and sturdy and always occupied a lot of space wherever he was. The two of them formed a focal point. If they gave a thumbs up or a thumbs down it was significant. But I was safe, apparently, as I was Yngve's brother. At any rate, I had been when I arrived in Bergen.

The rooms in the old wooden house were spacious and almost entirely unfurnished, I wandered around, the booze came, I drank, someone was staring at me, I went over to him, asked him what he was staring at, he said he hadn't seen me before and was just wondering who I was, I shook his hand and then I bent his fingers back until he screamed and I let go. What are you doing?! he hissed, Something wrong with you, is there? I left him and went into the adjacent room, where there was a whole crowd sitting on the floor, among them one of Yngve's fellow students, the one who had been sitting at the table the first time we went to Café Opera. You're the spitting image of Jan Kjærstad! I shouted, pointing at him. You look just the same! I do not, he said, I don't look anything like him. He doesn't, Karl Ove, said Asbjørn, who was also there. And you look like Tarjei Vesaas! I said, pointing at Arvid. Is that a compliment or what? He laughed. No, in fact it isn't, I said, and turned away because Yngve was standing behind me. Just take it easy, will you, he said. I heard you almost broke someone's fingers in there. That's not on. You can't do that here. Everyone knows everyone, right? Take it easy. I am taking it easy, I said. I'm having a good time. We're talking about literature. Kjærstad and Vesaas. I left him and went into the kitchen, opened the fridge, the alcohol had made me so damned hungry, and I saw half a chicken, which I grabbed and sank my teeth into, sitting on the worktop and occasionally washing it down with whisky. That moment, which was wonderful, sitting on the worktop in a student flat eating chicken and drinking whisky was the last I remembered. Afterwards everything was black, apart from an image of me hauling rocks into the sitting room and putting them on the floor, running in and out and continuing until someone stopped me and then everything disappeared again.

This was the pattern for the end of autumn, I tagged along with Yngve and his friends, was silent and shy but polite and affable for the first few hours until alcohol had me in its grip and then anything could pass my lips, anything could happen with my hands, until I woke up in an internal darkness the next day, when image after image of what I had done and said was hurled back at me, and I could only get myself going with a huge effort of will, drag myself back to normality, which then slowly took over. Normality was where I belonged, I realised that more and more, the longer the semester went on, I didn't have the depth or the originality you needed to become a writer, on the other hand I didn't want to sit there with the others without saying a word, inhibited and silent, because that wasn't me either, and so the only thing that helped, the only thing that could raise and transport me into something else, something freer, much closer to myself was: drinking. Sometimes it went well, sometimes the evening finished at the right moment, before anything of consequence had happened, except that I had been happy, but then there were the times it didn't go well and I went off my head, the way I had gone off my head in northern Norway the year before, I was completely out of control. One habit I had developed was to feel car door handles as I walked past, if one was open I would get into the driver's seat and try to start the engine, I knew you had to connect some wires but I wasn't sure which, and I never succeeded in starting a car, but the following day just the fact that I had tried was terrible. I released the handbrake inside a car which was open and parked on the hill near where I lived, causing it to roll back down a metre or two and hit the car behind. I ran off chortling inside with amusement. Not only that, I also tried to make off with lots of bikes, I entered backyards and searched for ones that were unlocked, if I found one, well, then I would cycle home on it. Once there was a bike beside the bed in my room when I woke up. I had to wait until it was dark before I could take it out and leave it in a neighbouring street, scared all the while that someone would see me and the police would come. Another time I saw some people sitting behind a window on the second floor somewhere, I went up the stairs, knocked on the door and went in, they shook their heads, I turned round and went back out. There was no evil in me, I just wanted to destroy things, not people, but as long as my sense of judgement was so clouded anything at all could happen, I realised that, and presumably that was why my fears grew so inordinately in the days afterwards. Yngve, with whom I was now spending as much time as I had done before, told me I shouldn't drink and suggested I smoke hash instead, maybe that would be better. He said I had begun to acquire a bad reputation and it was affecting him too. But he didn't stop inviting me out, probably because he saw more of the person I was normally than the person I could become when we were on the town.

In the middle of November I was broke, but basically that suited me fine, we had a month-long writing period and so I went to mum's, stayed in her tiny bedsit and wrote at night while she lay asleep at the far end of the same room, then slept in the hall during the day while she was at work. In the evenings we ate together, chatted or watched TV until she went to bed and my night shift started. After two weeks she drove me to Sørbøvåg, where there was more space, and I immersed myself in the life that went on there, so infinitely far from the life I lived in Bergen, but I was not without a guilty conscience, for what I was doing, the abjectness of it, became so clear when I was surrounded by frailty and disease, but also vitality and warmth.

After Christmas Yngve moved into a collective in Fjellsiden, the flat he had occupied until then was due to be sold. The collective was in a splendid large detached house, I often went there, it was one of the few places I could go. He lived with three others, one of whom, Per Roger, I talked to, he was interested in literature and was a writer himself, but as he was in Yngve's circle I felt so inferior to him that I barely answered when he asked me something and nothing came of the relationship.

An essay course started at the Academy, I wrote about Tolkien's *Lord of the Rings*, one of the books I was really passionate about, alongside Bram Stoker's *Dracula*, and even though they didn't fall into the category of literature the teachers favoured and taught, I still received some praise from Fosse, he said my language was tight and precise, my arguments solid and interesting and that I obviously had a talent for non-fiction. The praise was two-edged: did it mean that my future lay in literature about literature and not in literature itself?

Øystein Lønn dropped by on various occasions, the idea being that we should hand in our texts to him, but I didn't want to, I couldn't face any more humiliation in the classroom, and instead went to see him privately, at his hotel, with my text in my hand. At the beginning of the course he had said he was at our disposal from dawn till dusk, and all we had to do was go and see him if there was anything we wanted to discuss. So, one evening at seven, I trudged down the hills below my bedsit, the street lamps above me swinging in the wind, the rain beating on the walls and roofs. The heavens were inexhaustible, it had rained every day since the beginning of September and except for a couple of hours I hadn't seen the sun for what would soon be eight months. The streets were deserted apart from a few people who rushed past hugging the walls, in Bergen it was vital to get from A to B as fast as you could. The water in Vågen glittered in the reflection from the buildings along the quay, an express ferry drifted in and docked. As I passed the terminal it lowered its gangplank and passengers began disembarking, mostly into waiting taxis.

Lønn was staying at Hotel Neptun around the corner, I went in, was given his room number at reception, went up and knocked on the door.

Lønn, a sturdy fellow with big hands and a broad face, stared at me in surprise.

'You said we could come and see you if we had something to discuss,' I said. 'So I brought a text with me. I wonder if you would mind having a look at it.'

'Not at all,' he said. 'Come in!'

The room was dark, he had only the two bedside lamps switched on, and the carpet, which was red and stretched from wall to wall, seemed to absorb all the light.

'Sit down,' he said. 'What was it you wanted me to look at? I can do it for tomorrow if you like.'

'It's short,' I said. 'Just over a page.'

'I'd better have a look at it then,' he said. I passed him the text, he perched a pair of glasses on his nose and began to read.

I glanced around cautiously. It was a story about some young boys who had climbed up the steel cables of a bridge, it was snowing hard, they disappeared in the whirl of falling snow, one of them jumped. It transpired that this happened regularly, that a boy jumped to his death. The novella, or short prose text, was inspired by Julio Cortázar.

'Ye-es,' Lønn said, removed his glasses, folded them and put them in his shirt pocket. 'A nice little story. Concise and pithily told. There's not much more to say about it, is there?'

'No,' I said. 'Did you like it?'

'Yes, I liked it a lot.'

He got up. I got up too. He handed me the text.

'Good luck,' he said.

'Thank you,' I said.

He closed the door behind me, I walked down the corridor and felt like screaming at my stupidity. What had I been trying to achieve? What had I expected? That he would say actually I was brilliant? That he would tip the wink to his publisher about me?

No, not that I was brilliant, I didn't believe that, but that he would take an interest in me and perhaps tell someone at his publishing house, that would have been a possibility, I had thought. Publishing houses did sometimes take an interest in Writing Academy students, that was well known. So why not in me?

When Lønn finished his course he did it with a few well-chosen sentences about each and every student and the various literary projects that he had been allowed to share. Praise for everyone apart from me, whom he failed to mention.

I left, furious and bitter.

It was true I hadn't handed in any work to him like the others, but he *had* read one of my texts. Why would he make a secret of that? If he thought it was so awful, surely he could at least have said?

After that I stayed away from the Academy for several weeks. I had already done some skiving in the autumn, and I stepped it up after Christmas, there was no obligation to attend classes, we were free to decide, and for as long as it felt as if I was having my head shoved down the toilet whenever I was there, I had no reason to attend everything, I argued, it was better to sit at home and write, after all that was what I had said when I applied, that the course would give me the opportunity to write full time for a year.

So during the spring I was more often at home than at the Academy, and after the Lønn business I almost gave up attending classes. I didn't write either, everything felt meaningless apart from going out, which had continued, I did everything I wanted to do, the decadent bohemian city lifestyle, the writer going to rack and ruin with his eyes open wide and a bottle on the table. I broke one of my rules, I went out drinking on my own one evening, I sat

in Fekterloftet with a carafe of white wine. Fekterloftet's special-
ity was that all the girls who worked there were stunning. That
was why I had chosen this particular place to go, thinking I might
be able to start a conversation with one of them, but it didn't happen, they were interested in serving and little else, so once I had
finished the second carafe I got up and went to Café Opera, where
I hung out in the bar until they closed without seeing one familiar face, then I walked home. I woke up to someone shaking me,
opened my eyes, I was lying in the hall, on the floor, sat up, it was
Jon Olav. I had crashed out next to his door. The pockets in my waterproof bulged with small stones. I realised I must have collected
them to throw at his window. Then someone living there must
have come along and I followed them in. Jon Olav laughed at me,
and I went back home, my body aching for more sleep. A couple
of days later I went to Café Opera in the morning, I couldn't be
bothered to go to the Academy and didn't fancy sitting at home,
so I decided to wander down and buy myself a bottle of wine and
see what happened. Getting drunk in the middle of the day was
a good feeling, there was a lot of freedom in it, suddenly the day
opened and offered quite different opportunities now that I didn't
care about anything. Just walking down the street to buy some
newspapers at a kiosk was an experience when you were drunk.
It was as though a hole into the world had been opened, all the
usual stuff – shelves of chewing gum, pastilles, chocolate – had
an unpleasant air when you saw it through drunken eyes in the
middle of the day. Not to mention the newspaper articles I read,
back at a window table a few minutes later. Something raw and
terrible attached itself to them while I viewed them with vivid,
almost triumphant, feelings. Jesus, man, I was somebody, I could
see something no one else could see, I could see into the depths
of the world.

I drank all day, at around five I ate there, then I went down to a
bookshop and bought a novel by Jayne Anne Phillips, which I tried

to read for the next few hours with limited success, I could no longer concentrate for more than a few minutes at a time, every sentence I read made me swell with emotion. I can do that too, I thought. No, I can do better than that. Much, much better.

I started to doze off, closed my eyes and went absent for odd moments, came to with a jerk, how long had I been gone? Around me Café Opera was slowly filling up. Suddenly Per Roger was standing in front of me.

'Hi, Karl Ove,' he said. 'Are you out on your own?'

I saw no point in denying it and nodded.

'Come over and join us then!' he said. 'We're sitting over there.'

I stared at him. What was that he said?

'How much have you actually had to drink?' Per laughed. 'Are you coming? We've got girls there too!'

I stood up and followed him to his table, sat down on one of the chairs, nodded to the others. There were five of them. The nearest one had shoulder-length fair hair and glasses, sideburns and a T-shirt with a skull, a snake and a dagger on underneath a greyish-white goatskin jacket. The guy beside him had long dark hair and sluggish eyes. Then there was a girl, perhaps a couple of years older than me, whom the last member of the group, a short-haired dark handsome guy with a crafty expression, clearly fancied.

'This is Karl Ove,' Per Roger said.

'I've seen you before,' said the fair-haired guy. 'You a student?'

'I'm at the Writing Academy,' I said.

'You don't say,' he said. 'You're talking to the wrong man then. If there's one thing I haven't got, it's culture! My name's Gaute by the way.'

He was from Bergen, his pal was from Bergen too, while the sly dark-haired guy was from Odda. The girl was an Østlander. Gaute and Per Roger talked and laughed a lot, the others didn't say that much, laughed now and then at what Gaute said, but seemed to be somewhere else. I drank and looked out of the window, at the dry tarmac reflecting the street lamps. A little guy, around twenty-five, wearing a white shirt, sat down at the table. His eyes were blue, cold and bored.

Gaute looked at me.

'Do you know what the skin round a cunt is called?' he said.

'No.'

'A woman.'

He laughed, I did too, and then we *skål*-ed. Slowly I entered a new phase of intoxication, I rose higher and higher, it was wonderful, I didn't care about anything any more. Laughed a bit, made the odd comment, went to the bar and got more beer as the glasses emptied.

You didn't have to be with Gaute for long to know that he disliked everything that smacked of power and the Establishment with the whole of his heart, in fact he hated it. I had met a lot of people with anti-bourgeois attitudes, but they were students and a part of the system, this guy seemed to have acted on his convictions, he was completely on the outside, joking and laughing at everything, quips about Jews and blacks came thick and fast, and I laughed at them so much I could hardly stop. When Café Opera closed he suggested we go back to his place and play a few records and smoke a bit, we shambled out, flagged down a taxi and went to his flat, which it turned out was on the Nordnes peninsula.

When we got out of the taxi and into the stairwell Per Roger said they had been drinking for six months now and were planning to continue. I said I could imagine doing that. Just stick with us, he said, and then we went into Gaute's flat.

'It's my mother's,' he said. 'That's why it's so nice here. Sorry. Ha ha ha! But I don't want any shouting, OK. There are neighbours here too.'

'Come on, Gaute,' Per Roger said. 'If I want to shout I will.'

Gaute didn't answer, took out a record, I sat down at the table. The music he played was sombre and loud. The other long-haired guy, whose name I couldn't remember, got an enormous carrot from the fridge and started carving it, sitting on the floor with his back to the wall, engrossed in his task.

'What are you doing?' I said.

He didn't answer.

'He's making a pipe,' Gaute said. 'He comes from Åsane. Full of tossers there, and that's what they do. But you're not a Lords of the New Church man, are you.'

I shook my head.

'Pop and indie,' I said.

'Pop and indie,' he said, shaking his head. 'Can we be bothered to wait for the pipe? You've got tobacco, haven't you?'

'Yes.'

'What would you say if I put a bit of horse on the table?' he said, with his cold eyes.

'A horse on the table?' Gaute said, laughing. 'What the hell are we going to do with that?'

'Have you got anything to drink?' I said.

'There might be a drop left somewhere. I don't know. You'd better have a look. If you want,' he said, nodding towards the kitchen. 'I fancy a smoke myself.'

He looked at the guy from Odda.

'Did you say you had some on you?' he said.

The Odda guy nodded, took out a clump of hash wrapped in silver paper and a packet of large Rizla papers and passed them to Gaute. He heated up the clump, I put the tobacco in the paper, picked out the longest threads and ran the lighter over it a few times, the way I had seen others do, gave it to him, he mixed the hash into the tobacco, rolled up the cigarette, licked it and passed the whole salami to me.

We smoked half of it, I got up and went to the toilet, I felt as though my head had been blitzed, all my thoughts were scattered, one bit here, one bit there, mumbling to myself as I peed.

When I went back in, Gaute and Per Roger were talking loudly, almost shouting, a wild hotchpotch of Jew jokes, wordplay and brutality. The guy with the eyes wasn't to be seen anywhere. The guy from Odda was sitting with the girl on his lap and snogging. The long-haired tosser was filling the carrot pipe with tobacco. I slid down the wall to the floor. Across the table they began to discuss the most brutal ways you could kill yourself. Gaute leaned forward and passed me the joint. I took a deep drag.

'Give it here,' Gaute said with a snigger. I passed him the joint, he took a drag and his cheeks were hollow for ages before he exhaled the smoke and passed the joint on to Per Roger.

'You've landed in a suicidal viper's nest,' he said and laughed. 'We'll drink for as long as we can, and then we'll kill ourselves. That's the plan. And you're in, Per Roger says.'

'Yes,' I said. 'For the drinking bit at any rate.'

'Can't have one without the other,' Gaute said and laughed again. 'But we have to do it in turn. So those who are left can sell the hair and the gold teeth and keep going for a few more days. Ha ha ha!'

Per Roger laughed as he stared at me.

Then he said:

wriggle with the snake
slither and slide
whither the viper wills

'What was that?' I said. 'Hávamál or what?'

'No, it's a poem I wrote.'

'Did you? That's fantastic.'

'We all know which snake you're thinking about!' Gaute said. 'We also know where it's going! "Slither and slide", that's you!'

Per Roger laughed at what Gaute said, but he stared at me with serious wide-open eyes. I looked down.

The Odda guy and the girl got up and were gone. I couldn't be bothered to look where. I disappeared, when I opened my eyes again the room was empty apart from the guy with the carrot, who was sleeping on the floor. I stood up and went out. The darkness was dense, the streets were deserted. I had no idea what the time was, just walked towards town, barely present inside myself. A car raced up behind me, it was a taxi, I raised my hand in the air, it stopped, I got in, mumbled my address and when it accelerated down the cobbled street it was as though I was taking off, I was floating on the back seat, like a balloon under the car roof. Oh, I had to control this feeling, I couldn't fly inside the taxi, but it was no good, I couldn't hold myself down, I floated like a balloon under the roof the whole way home. Once there, I undressed, went to bed and slept like a log. When I woke it was pitch black outside. I looked at my watch. It was five o'clock.

Five o'clock in the afternoon or the morning?

Surely it had to be the afternoon?

I leaned forward and peered through the window. Two kids in waterproofs were kicking a ball to each other in the park on the other side of the street. Afternoon then. I went down to the basement and had a shower, and then, absolutely ravenous, I fried all the eggs I had and put them on six slices of bread, which I bolted down. Followed by a litre of milk with Nesquik.

It felt as though I had seen hell's gates open.

I wrote all night with the rain beating against the window and drunken night-owls sporadically walking past in the otherwise empty street. In the morning the house filled with the noise of people starting the day, I went back to bed, and when I woke, at around one, it was from a dream in which I had died. I was doing this more and more often, and I was more frightened in these dreams than I had ever been awake. Usually I fell from a great height, but sometimes I drowned. It was as if I was absolutely clear-headed and conscious, as if what happened was real. Now I am going to die, I thought.

I got dressed, ate a few slices of bread and butter and went to Yngve's.

I rang the bell. One of the girls opened the door.

'Hi,' she said. 'Yngve's out. Would you like to come in and wait?

'Could do,' I said. 'Is Per Roger in?'

'No. He's been away for several days. Think he's on a binge.'

I said nothing about having been drinking with him that night, I didn't want any conversation.

'You'll be all right, won't you?' she said, and when I nodded she disappeared into her room. I slumped on the sofa, took one of the magazines on the table and flicked through.

After a while I went over to the window and looked out at the grey ocean that was the sky and the red rooftops and white walls that ran down cheek by jowl towards the town centre. For all I knew he might be out until the following day.

The girl came back, she slipped into the kitchen, poked her head out and asked if I wanted a cup of tea.

'No, thanks,' I said. 'Incidentally, you don't know where Yngve is, do you?'

'No idea. I think he was going to see Ingvild.'

'Oh yes. Well, that might be a while then,' I said. The natural consequence of what she said was that I should go. But I didn't want to. I'll give him another half an hour, I thought, and went into his room. It was a part of the collective and not as private as it would have been had it been his bedroom in a normal flat, but I still felt a little uneasy at being there. It smelled the same as the flat in Solheimsviken, and the possessions were the same, right down to the white Ikea bedspread. I flicked through his record collection, wondering if I should play some music while I was waiting, but decided that would be taking a liberty, sitting in his room and playing his records when he came home, that wouldn't look good.

Perhaps it would be best to go home.

I got up and went into the hall. As I bent down to tie my shoe-laces the door opened and Yngve stood in front of me with a dripping umbrella in one hand and a Mekka bag in the other.

'Are you off?' he said.

'No, not now,' I said. 'Didn't think you'd be here for a bit.'

He took his purchases into the kitchen, I sat down in the sitting room.

'I'm going to make an omelette,' he shouted from inside. 'Want one?'

'OK,' I shouted back.

We ate without speaking, he sat with the remote control in front of him zapping through the sports pages on teletext. After-wards he made some coffee, the girl came down, Yngve cracked a joke, she laughed, I lit a cigarette and thought I'd better go now, however it was still better sitting here than at home.

'I've finished the music for your lyrics by the way,' he said. 'Would you like to hear it?'

I followed him into his room. He hung the guitar strap over his shoulder, switched on the amplifier, adjusted the echo box and strummed a few chords.

'Ready?' he said.

I nodded and he began to play, slightly embarrassed. He didn't sing very well, but that wasn't the point, I only had to hear how the tune went, nevertheless I still couldn't watch him as he stood there with his head lowered and the guitar hanging over his hips, singing. But it was catchy, a nice simple pop song.

I told him. He lifted the guitar over his head and put it on the stand.

'I need some more songs,' he said. 'Couldn't you just dash off a few?'

'I'll try.'

We went back into the sitting room. He said he was going to a party tomorrow, someone in his department was giving it, a little out of town.

'Do you feel like coming?'
'Could do,' I said. 'Will Ingvild be going?'
'Think so, yes.'

I had met them together two or three times. It had been strange, but it had gone well, all three of us pretended nothing had happened, and now that I no longer believed there was a chance of going out with her, I didn't have any problem talking to her either. Once we had been alone at the same table in Café Opera, the conversation had flowed easily and naturally, she talked about her father and her relationship with him, I listened, she talked about her time at *gymnas*, and I told her a little about mine, she laughed in the fantastic way she did, when her eyes seemed to burst into laughter. All my feelings for her were intact, she was still the one I wanted, still the one I yearned for, but now that it was impossible, now that there was a definitive obstacle in the way, I was no longer afraid of talking to her. And while at the beginning of their relationship I had avoided them like the plague, I hadn't wanted to see them at all, yet had started meeting Yngve, though still not her, everything had been turned on its head: now I wanted her to be there or come along when I was with Yngve. I just wanted to see her, just be in the same room as her, be filled with her presence.

I sat up all night penning lyrics for Yngve. It was fun, it was quite different from writing texts to read out at the Academy, this was about thinking up some phrases that sounded good and then finding something that would rhyme. This wasn't about anything in particular, didn't have a theme, didn't go anywhere and it was liberating. It was like doing a crossword.

By three in the morning I had one song ready.

Over My Head

I die in dreams
Nights in blue

Cannot forget
Know we're through

Howl at the moon
There we lie
Know no bounds
Off we fly

Know it's all right
Take it as read
Know you can do it
Tho' it's over my head

You're moving on
Why, oh why
You know no bounds
Off you fly

I die in dreams
Nights in blue
No way, it seems
Gone like the dew

Know it's all right
Take it as read
Know you can do it
Tho' it's over my head

When I went to see Yngve the next evening Ingvild was there and I left the lyrics in my jacket pocket, sat down with a beer in my hand instead and casually asked how she was doing. She was wearing the white jumper with the blue stripes and blue jeans. She was both at home and not at home with her surroundings, and I wondered whether she was always like that, split somehow, always with one eye on herself, or was it just here at Yngve's? They sat beside each other on the sofa but apart. They hadn't touched each other since I arrived either. Was that because of me? Were they being considerate to me? Or was that how they behaved with each other?

She said everything was going well and she loved being in the collective in Nygårdsgaten. The history of the collective went back to the 1960s, she said, actually Kjartan Fløgstad had lived there once. Now some of Yngve's friends lived there: Frank from Arendal, an odd character, according to her, and Atle from Kristiansand, as well as two other girls.

After a while she got up to go for a shower, and after she had gone I took out the song I had written for Yngve. He cast a quick eye over it. It's great, he said and stuffed it in his back pocket.

Ingvild walked through the room wrapped in a large towel.

I looked away.

'We have to go soon,' Yngve said. 'You'll have to hurry.'

'Yes, yes,' Ingvild said.

We had another beer, then he stood up and started to get dressed. Opened the door to the room where Ingvild was standing and drying her hair.

'Let's go. Come on,' he said.

'I just have to finish drying my hair,' she said from inside the room.

'Couldn't you have done it a bit earlier?' Yngve said. 'You knew we had to go soon, didn't you.'

He closed the door.

'Good job I didn't book a taxi anyway,' he said without looking at me.

'Yes,' I said.

There was a silence. The girl who lived there went into the sitting room and switched on the television.

At the party, which consisted mainly of media students plus a crowd of music types, I was as usual the younger brother of Yngve and nothing else. Girls thought it amusing that we were so alike, I said next to nothing, apart from when someone put on a classical record and asked what it was and none of the media students could answer, and I said, my face half-averted and embarrassed at myself, that it was Tchaikovsky. It was. Yngve eyed me with surprise. How did *you* know? he said. Lucky break, I said, and it was too, I had one record by Tchaikovsky and that was the one.

Ingvild took an early taxi home, Yngve stayed and it was painful to see that he didn't appreciate her more, that he was happy to see her go. If it had been me I would have flung my arms around her. I had worshipped her. I had given her everything I had. Yngve didn't do that. Did he care about her at all?

He must do. But he was older, more experienced, a different light burned in him to my stupid naïve one. And what I also saw was that he gave Ingvild space, a larger space than she occupied, which I couldn't have done, never in this world, because we were in the same space, she and I, the space of uncertainty and hesitation, half-groping and half-clutching. She needed him as much as I did.

After we had run through various dramatists and various drama traditions at the Academy, the idea was that we should write something in the genre ourselves, as usual. I put off doing this until the evening before it was due, then I plodded off to Verftet to sit there all night. We had a standing offer of a desk there if we needed an undisturbed place to write in the afternoon and evening, I had borrowed the keys and done it a couple of times, there was something about being alone in a common room that I liked, perhaps because there was nothing in it that reminded me of myself, I wasn't quite sure why, that was just how it was, this evening too, when I let myself in and walked through the empty hallway, up the empty stairs and into the empty rooms at the top.

The others had already handed in their contributions, photocopies of their work lay in piles on the table in the adjacent room.
I fetched a typewriter, put on some coffee, stared at the reflection
of the room in the black windows, looking as though it had been
pulled out of the drifting waters of Vågen. It was nine o'clock, I
had decided I would sit here until I had finished, even if it took
all night.

I had no idea what to write.

The coffee was ready, I drank a cup, smoked a cigarette, stared
at the image of myself in the window. Turned and looked at the
bookshelves. They wouldn't have a photography book of scantily
clad or naked women here, would . . .?

But they did have a book about the history of art. I reached it
down and leafed through. Some of the sixteenth- and seventeenth-
century paintings were of naked women. Perhaps there was something I could use there?

It was too big for me to fit into my trousers. And I didn't want to
carry it under my arm because even though the chance of someone appearing at this time was minimal it wasn't impossible, and
how would I explain lugging an art book down to the toilet?

I put it in a plastic bag and went down the spiral staircase and
into the toilet. A picture by Rafael stood out at once, two women
in front of a well, one naked, the other dressed, the naked one was
strikingly beautiful, she was looking enigmatically to the side, her
small breasts were pert, a strip of cloth covered her nether regions, but her thighs were visible and I got a hard-on, I flicked
through, stared at a picture by Rubens, *The Rape of the Daughters of
Leucippus* (1618), one of the two naked women was the red-haired
pale freckly type with a small chin and a full body, then there was
Botticelli's *The Birth of Venus* (1485), where one breast was bared,
and Titian's *Venus of Urbino* (1538), in which the woman in the foreground had one hand resting between her legs while she gazed
straight at the observer with a provocative self-assured expression

on her face. I studied her naked breasts for a long time, her broad hips and small feet, but there was more to see of course, and I went on to Bartholomeus Spranger's *Vulcan and Maia* (1590), in which the woman, with her hands on a strong bearded man, thrusts her hips forward with a lustful glint in her eye. Her breasts were supple, her skin was all white, her face almost childish. She was good. The next was Delacroix's *The Death of Sardanapalus* (1827), the woman in the foreground had her back to us, one breast was revealed, thrust right forward, because she had a sword to her throat, and the whole of her bottom was visible, perfectly formed. During this time, as I flicked backwards and forwards, trying to decide which picture to go for, I wanked slowly, holding myself back. Maybe Delacroix? No, it had to be Ingres! *Odalisque with Slave* (1842). She's lying full length with her arms behind her head and is all wonderful curves, or, oh, of course *The Turkish Bath* (1862). Only women in this one and they were all naked. They sat and stood in every conceivable pose and every possible type was rep-resented: cool, passionate, half-concealed, fully exposed. All skin and flesh and female forms as far as the eye could see. But which one, oh, which one? The one with the chubby face and the open lips? I loved faces in which the mouths were slightly open and the teeth always visible. Or the blonde just behind with the haughty gaze? The one with the small breasts staring at her hand? Or the one, oh yes, sitting behind her, leaning back, arms outstretched, eyes closed in ecstasy, it had to be her!

Afterwards I stood still for a moment to make sure there was no one in the corridor outside, then I went back up, returned the book to its place on the shelf, poured myself a cup of coffee, lit a cigarette and sat staring at the blank page.

Nothing. I had no idea what to write.

I went for a little walk, browsed through the books, went into the photocopy room, skimmed through the others' work. They were what you would expect, each and every one of them had written in complete keeping with their own particular style. Most I just cast a quick glance at, but I took Petra's into the classroom and read it carefully. It was a kind of absurd, almost surreal, comedy where people did totally unmotivated and pretty crazy things, it was high tempo, devoid of meaning, my main impression was: chaos and randomness.

Surely I could do that too?

I began to write, and I wrote quickly, one scene after the other appeared on the paper as a kind of extension of what I had read. There might have been some slight similarities in the characterisation, what they got up to was also unmotivated and unexpected, but it was not a carbon copy of Petra's, ultimately the characters did do *different* things, and I was very pleased when I had a first draft at around three. I touched it up, went through the whole drama one more time and by eight in the morning I had got so far that I was able to photocopy the text ten times and put the copies in a pile beside the others. When the first student arrived, at a quarter to ten, I was asleep in my chair.

The whole day was spent analysing the texts. I was praised for mine, although Hovland had some criticisms regarding its dramatic quality, in other words the link between the characters and the scenes, I defended myself by saying there wasn't supposed to be a link, that was the whole point, and he nodded and said yes, but even incoherence requires coherence; the rule of thumb for all writing is that you can write about boredom, but it mustn't be boring.

Petra had watched me during the analysis, but she said nothing, even when Hovland asked her directly for her opinion she said she had no comment to make. It was only when the lesson was over and people were tidying up and putting on coats that it came.

'You copied my text,' she said.

'I did not,' I said.

'You were here last night, you read my text and then you wrote yours. That's copying pure and simple.'

'No,' I said. 'I didn't read yours at all. How can I copy it if I haven't read it?'

'Do you think I'm stupid or what? You sat here, read it and wrote a variation on a theme. You might as well admit it.'

'Well, I would admit it if there was anything in your claim,' I said. 'But there isn't. I *didn't* read your text. And I didn't copy it. If there's any similarity at all it's pure chance.'

'Ha!' she said, and got up, put her papers and books in her black bag. 'It makes no difference to me, it's all right if you copy what I do, but lying about it is not bloody all right.'

'I'm not lying,' I said. 'I knew nothing until you read it out.'

She rolled her eyes, put on her jacket and walked towards the exit. I waited a few minutes for my head to cool down and for Petra to be so far away that I couldn't catch her up, then I made my way home. I recognised this situation, it was the same as the one I had been in at school when I had voted for myself as class rep and received only one vote, and someone found out by asking everyone in the class who they had voted for. I denied it, they couldn't prove anything, I just said no, it wasn't true. In this case, it *wasn't* possible to prove anything, no one else but me knew that I had read her piece, I just had to keep denying it, she was the one making a fool of herself. But I had no great desire to show my face there again, for if no one else knew for certain, *I* did. The night before it had seemed natural, a matter of course, I had only borrowed a little from her, surely that was justified, but during the analysis and in our subsequent exchange it took on a different aspect, I had plagiarised her work and what did that make me? How had I become so desperate that I not only plagiarised a fellow student's work but on top of that deluded myself into thinking I had made up everything myself?

Once I had copied a poem into my diary and pretended it was me who had written it. I had been twelve at the time, and strange as it might seem that I could so openly dupe myself, you wrote this Karl Ove, you did, while I had copied it from a book, age was a mitigating circumstance. Now I was twenty though, an adult man, how could I have knowingly done anything so base?

For the next few weeks I stayed at home. I wrote my novel, it was hopeless, but I was nearing the end, and it was important I had something concrete and tangible to show for my work this year.

I had sent a text, the one Øystein Lønn had read, to the Cappelen magazine *Signaler*, and one day it came back. I nurtured wild hopes of an acceptance as I opened the envelope, but guessed which way the wind was blowing, so it was no surprise when I read:

Dear Karl Ove Knausgård,
Thank you for sending me your contribution. I read it with interest, but I am afraid I cannot use it in *SIGNALER 89*.
Best regards,
Lars Saabye Christensen

It gave me a little frisson of excitement to see Saabye Christensen's signature, it meant he had read what I had written. For a few minutes at any rate I had filled his mind with what existed in mine!

XTC brought out *Oranges and Lemons*, I played it again and again, right until deLillos released their *Hjernen er alene, The Brain Is Alone*, then that was what was on my stereo day and night. Outside, the skies were lighter and the rain fell less often. The feelings of spring, which had been so strong when I was a boy, which had filled all my senses and somehow raised body and soul after the winter's heaviness and darkness, overcame me again. I stuck at my novel, I wouldn't finish it until the semester was over, but I planned to hand in what I had done as my final assignment at the Academy. It was the same novel that I had been accepted on the

course for, and there was no development evident in it, I wrote
in exactly the same style now as I had done then, the whole year
had been wasted, the sole difference was that when they accepted
me I thought I was a writer, while now, on the verge of finishing,
I knew I wasn't.

One evening Yngve and Asbjørn appeared on the steps.

'Are you coming out?' Asbjørn said.

'I'd love to,' I said. 'But I don't have any money.'

'You can borrow some if you want,' Asbjørn said. 'Yngve has a
broken heart, so we have to drink him through it.'

'It's over with Ingvild,' Yngve said and smiled.

'OK,' I said. 'Count me in. Hang on a moment.'

I fetched my jacket and tobacco and walked to town with them.
The next three days were a blur, we drank day and night, slept
at Asbjørn's, got drunk in the morning, ate in town, continued
drinking in his bedsit, went out in the evening to all sorts of weird
places such as Uglen or the bar at Rica, and it was wonderful, nothing could beat the feeling of walking across Torgalmenningen and
Fisketorget in the middle of the day, drunk, it was as though I
was right and everyone else was wrong, as though I was free and
everyone else tied and bound to everyday life, and with Yngve and
Asbjørn it didn't seem wrong or excessive, just fun. On the last
night – we didn't know it would be the last – we took cans of spray
paint with us. At Hulen, where we ended up, the place wasn't
very full, when I went to the toilet I spray-painted a slogan inside
the cubicle, soon afterwards a member of the staff came with a
cloth and bucket to clean it off, once he had left I did it again,
we laughed and decided to go the whole hog, spray-paint some
buildings in town, and we went to Møhlenpris, I wrote U2 STOPS
ROCK 'N' ROLL along a big brick wall in letters as high as myself,
they had just played on a rooftop, it hadn't been good, and Bono
had formulated the slogan U2 Stops Traffic, which was even less
good, while Asbjørn wrote RICKY NELSON RULES OK over the tram depot

wall, and Yngve wrote CAT, WE NEED YOU TO RAP on another wall, we continued like this towards his collective, where we stopped to have more to drink. An hour later we had all crashed out. When we woke up it was to the fear of what we had done, because the trail led to us: the graffiti started outside Hulen and continued all the way here, to the wall beside the door, where you could read YNGVE IS A BLOODY . . . It wouldn't take much of an investigation to work out where the vandals who had spray-painted the whole of Møhlenpris lived. Asbjørn was especially jittery, but I wasn't immune, and that was strange because all I wanted to do was to keep on drinking, live life, not give a toss, yet I hit a wall whenever I did that, a wall of petite bourgeoisie and middle-class manners, which could not be broken down without enormous anguish and fear. I wanted to, but I couldn't. Deep down I was decent and proper, a goody-goody, and, I thought, perhaps that was also why I couldn't write. I wasn't wild enough, not artistic enough, in short, much too normal for my writing to take off. What had made me believe anything else? Oh, but this was the life-lie.

What I had learned over the course of the year at the Writing Academy was that there was a literature that was real literature, the true lofty variety, which stretched from Homer's epics and the Greek dramas through the course of history up to the present day with writers such as Ole Robert Sunde, Tor Ulven, Eldrid Lunden, Kjartan Fløgstad, Georg Johannesen, Liv Lundberg, Anne Bøe, Ellen Einan, Steinar Løding, Jon Fosse, Terje Dragseth, Hans Herbjørnsrud, Jan Kjærstad, Øystein Lønn, Svein Jarvoll, Finn Øgeland, the Danes Søren Ulrik Thomsen and Michael Strunge, the Swedes Katarina Frostenson and Stig Larsson. I knew that the great Scandinavian poet of this century was Gunnar Ekelöf, and the great Finnish–Swedish modernist Gunnar Björling, I knew that our own Rolf Jacobsen wasn't fit to tie their shoelaces and Olav H. Hauge was rooted in tradition to a far greater degree than they were. I knew the last great innovation in the novel took place in France

in the 1960s, and that it was ongoing, especially in the novels of
Claude Simon. I also knew that I couldn't reinvent the novel, I
couldn't even copy those who were being innovative as I didn't
understand where the novel's *essence* lay. I was blind, I couldn't
read; if I read Stig Larsson's *Introduction*, for example, I couldn't say
what was new about it or what the essence was, I read all novels
the way I had once read crime fiction and thrillers, the endless
series of books I had read as a thirteen- or fourteen-year-old, about
the Black September group and the Jackal, about spies during the
Second World War and randy elephant-hunters in Africa. What had
changed during this year was that now I definitely knew that there
were differences. But this hadn't had any impact on my own writing.
To solve this problem, I had made a sub-genre of the modern novel
my own, this was the one I marketed as my ideal, American novels
and short stories written by Bret Easton Ellis, Jayne Anne Phillips,
Jay McInerny, Barry Gifford. This was how I excused what I wrote.

I had gained an insight. At great expense, but it was real and
important: I was not a writer. What writers had, I did not have.
I fought against this insight, I told myself I *might* be able to have
what writers had, it might be attainable provided I persisted for
long enough, while knowing in fact this was only a consolation.
Probably Jon Fosse had been right: probably my talent did consist
in writing about literature and not writing literature itself.

This was my final assessment, some days after going on a bender
with Yngve and Asbjørn, walking home from the Academy after
handing in my manuscript. The novel wasn't finished, and I had
decided to spend the rest of the spring and summer on it. When
it was completed I would send it to a publisher. I had decided on
Cappelen, to whom I felt some loyalty after the personal rejection
by Lars Saabye Christensen. I assumed I would get another rejection, but I wasn't entirely sure, they might see something in my
writing that Jon Fosse and Ragnar Hovland hadn't, after all they
too had seen something inasmuch as they had accepted me onto

the course – this was a small hope, but it was there and would be there right until a letter from Cappelen landed in my post box. It wasn't over until then.

The light in the town had been changing character during the spring. The dampness and the gloom of the autumn and winter hues were gone. Now the colours were dry and light and, with the white houses reflecting the light, even the indirect light when the sun was behind the clouds, shimmering and bright, it was as though the whole town had risen. In the autumn and winter Bergen was like a bowl, it lay still and took whatever came its way; in the spring and summer it was as though the mountains folded back like the petals of a flower, and the town burst forth in its own right, humming and quivering.

You couldn't sit inside in the evenings then.

I knocked on Morten's door, asked if he wanted to go with me to Christian and if so could he lend me some money, he could, and we perched at a table staring at all the beautiful girls out walking, not the black-clad, intellectual kind, but the nicely dressed blonde conventional kind, while we discussed how difficult everything was and we slowly got drunk and the evening dissolved into the usual darkness. I woke up under a bush by Lille Lungegård Lake with someone tugging at me, it was a policeman, he said I couldn't sleep there, I got up sleepily and went home.

I knocked on Ingvild's door in her new collective, she was surprised to see me but also happy, I sensed, and I was happy too. It was a big collective with a corner window facing Nygårdsgaten and the Grieg Hall, I said hello to the others living there, faces I had seen but not spoken to, all in some way or other connected with Yngve. Ingvild was fully integrated into student life, that was good to see, at the same time it made her harder to reach, I was on the outside, she said twice she wanted me as a friend and I assumed that probably meant she didn't want me as a boyfriend.

We sat there on the big sofa, she had made some tea, seemed happy, I looked at her, tried not to show how depressed I was, how sorry I was that we weren't together and never would be, then I smiled and talked about more pleasurable matters, and when I left she must have thought it was all over as far as I was concerned and now we were actually only friends.

Before leaving I asked her if she could lend me a hundred kroner or two. I was flat broke, didn't even have enough money for a smoke.

'Yes, of course,' she said. 'But I want it back!'

'Goes without saying,' I said. 'Have you got two hundred?'

I owed both Yngve and Asbjørn so much that I couldn't borrow any more. I also owed Morten quite a bit, and Jon Olav and Anne. I had also begged a hundred here and a hundred there when I had been out, off Yngve's friends, no one was that careful when they were out drinking, and I didn't have to pay everyone back.

Ingvild had two hundred. I stuffed the money in my pocket and went downstairs as she returned to her room.

Strange, I thought as I emerged and felt the warm air on my face and saw the row of trees that had begun to burst into leaf behind the Grieg Hall. The moment she was out of sight, I missed her. I had seen her only a few minutes earlier, she had been sitting a metre away from me, her knees together and her upper body leaning over the table, and now I was both excited and sad at the thought that she might be sitting alone in her room at this minute, at the mere knowledge that she existed.

At the end of May Yngve had exams and I joined him and his friends in the evenings when they were out celebrating. The town was awash with people, they were everywhere, the air was warm, the trees were an explosion of green, and as I walked around in the evening beneath the light sky, in the dusk-grey streets that never really became dark, all of this gave me strength, all of this lifted my mood, I had such a strong feeling of being alive and, not least, that I wanted to live more.

The year was over, the next day we would be having the end-of-year meal at the Academy and be given a certificate, or whatever it was, to prove we had attended the course. I would go, say goodbye to everyone and then I would turn my back. Never think about it again.

Among Yngve's student friends spirits were high, beer after beer was brought to our table, and even though I didn't say that much, even though I was temporarily my silent self, I was still there, I drank and smiled and looked at the others, who babbled away about this and that, Ola was the only person I knew, the others I had only seen, so I sat down beside him, he had always taken me under his wing in the sense that he took me seriously and listened to what I said, as though there was something sensible or interesting in it, although he himself was light years above it. He even laughed at my jokes. But I didn't want to impose on him, or Yngve, who sat there with his head raised, clinking glasses and talking.

By the time the lights flashed and we drank up, then went downstairs to hang around outside until we were all gathered in a group as always, I was so drunk that I felt as if I were in a tunnel, the sides were all dark, the light was only ahead, wherever I was looking or thinking. I was free.

'There's our Kjærstad!' I said.

'Pack it in,' he said. 'It's not funny, even if you think it is.'

'It is *quite* funny,' I said. 'Shall we go now? What are we waiting for?'

Yngve came over to me.

'Easy now,' he said.

'OK,' I said. 'But let's go, shall we?'

'We're waiting for someone.'

'Aren't you pleased it went well?'

'Of course.'

He turned to the others. I rummaged through my pockets for cigarettes, couldn't make my lighter work and threw it to the ground.

'Got a light?'

I asked the guy who resembled Kjærstad, and he nodded, took out a lighter and lit my cigarette, cupping his hand to shield the flame.

I spat and took a drag, looking around me. The girls with us were four, five years older than me, but I was good-looking, surely this wasn't the first time a twenty-year-old had fucked a twenty-five-year-old?

But I had nothing to say to them, even when I was as drunk as I was now, so there was no hope there. You had to say something first, that much I had learned.

Suddenly they started walking. I followed them, always staying in the middle of the crowd, I saw Yngve's head bobbing up and down a few metres ahead of me, and the luminous May night with all the smells, the animated voices, all the other people on the streets, my brain was whirring with thoughts of how good this was. I was a student in Bergen, surrounded by other students, we were off to a party, walking through the streets of Høyden towards Nygård Park, which lay still, breathing quietly, in the darkness between all the roads and buildings, it was 1989, I was twenty years old, full of life and energy. And, watching the others walking with me, I thought they weren't like that, only I was, I rose higher and higher, further and further, while they stayed where they were. Bloody media students. Bloody media twats. Bloody media theorists. What did they know about life? What did they know about what was really important?

Listen to my heart beating.

Listen to my heart beating, you dozy fucking little imbeciles. Listen to it beating!

Look at me. Look at the strength I've got!

I could crush every bloody one of them. And it wouldn't be a problem either. I could just go on and on and on. They could belittle me, they could humiliate me, they always had, but I would never give up, it wasn't in my make-up, while all the other idiots, who thought they were so bloody clever, they had nothing inside them, they were completely hollow.

The park.

Oh Jesus, the entrance to the park! Oh shit, how beautiful. The dense green foliage, nearly black in the gathering dusk, and the pond. The gravel and the benches.

I took it all in. It became me. I carried it within me.

They stopped, one of them pulled out a bunch of keys from a trouser pocket and opened a door to a detached house on the opposite side of the street from the park.

We went up an old battered staircase, entered an old battered flat. There was a high ceiling, a fireplace in one corner, rag rugs on the wooden floor, 50s furniture bought at the flea market or at Fretex, the Salvation Army shop, a poster of Madonna, a poster of Elvis with a gun that Warhol had done and a poster of the first Godfather film.

We sat down. Spirits and glasses appeared on the table. Yngve sat at the head of the table, I sat at the opposite end, I didn't like having anyone close to me, as you had if you sat on the sofa.

I drank. More darkness. They discussed, I threw in comments, Yngve sent me occasional glances and I could see he didn't like what I said or the way I said it. He thought I was showing him up. Let him think that, it wasn't my problem.

I got up and went to the toilet. I pissed in the sink and laughed at the idea of them putting in the plug, filling the sink with water and washing their faces the following morning.

I went back, poured more whisky, almost everything was dark now.

'Look at the park!' I said.

'What about it?' someone said.

'Easy now, Psycho,' Yngve said.

I dragged myself to my feet, grabbed my glass and hurled it at him as hard as I could. It hit him in the face. He fell forward. Everyone got up screaming, rushed to his side. I stood still for a moment and watched the scene unfolding. Then I went into the hall, put on my shoes and jacket and staggered down the stairs, onto the street and into the park. The feeling of finally having acted was strong. I looked up at the sky, which was light and bright and wonderful, and stared into the green darkness of the park, and then I was gone, it was as though I had been switched off.

I woke up on a corridor floor.

It was light, the sun was streaming in through the windows.

I sat up. There were several doors along the corridor. An old lady stood eyeing me, behind her a younger woman, perhaps forty, she was eyeing me too. They didn't say anything but they looked scared.

I struggled to my feet. I was still drunk, my body leaden. I understood nothing, it was like being in a dream, but I knew that I was conscious and staggered off down the corridor, a hand against the wall every now and then.

There was something about a fire engine. A fire and a fire engine. Wasn't there?

At the end of the corridor there was a staircase, at the bottom a door with frosted glass in the top part. I went down the stairs, pushed open the door, stopped outside and squinted into the sun.

In front of me was the end wall of the Science Building. To the left was Lille Lungegård Lake.

I turned and looked at the building where I had slept. It was white and made of brick.

A big police car came down the road and turned into the gravel area in front of me as two women came out of the door behind me.

Two officers walked towards me and stopped.

'I think there's a fire,' I said. 'A fire engine went that way,' I said, pointing across. 'It's not here. It's further away. It must be.'

'That's him,' said the woman behind me.

'What are you doing here?' one policeman said.

'I don't know,' I said. 'I woke up here. But I think you should hurry.'

'What's your name?'

I looked at him. I teetered to the side, he put his hand on my shoulder to steady me.

'What difference does it make what my name is?' I said. 'What's a name?'

'You'd better come with us,' he said.

'In the car?'

'Yes, come now.'

He put his hand on my arm and led me to the car, pushed open the door, and I got in the back, a large space which I had all to myself.

Now I had experienced this as well. Being driven through the streets of Bergen in a police car.

Had they arrested me?

But it was the end-of-year meal today!

There were no sirens wailing or anything, they drove sedately and stopped at all the traffic lights. They arrived at the police station, grabbed my arm again and led me into the building.

'I need to make a telephone call,' I said. 'It's important. I should be at a meeting. They have to know I won't be coming. I have the right to make a call, I know that.'

I was laughing inside, this was just like a film, me, flanked by two policemen, asking to make a telephone call!

And I got my way. They stopped by a phone at the end of the corridor.

I didn't know the number of the Writing Academy. There was a telephone directory underneath, I tried to look it up and failed.

I turned to them.

'I give up,' I said.

'OK,' they said, and led me to a hatch where I had to empty my pockets and hand over my belt, and then they steered me down to the cellar, or whatever it was, at any rate there were iron doors on either side of the corridor and I had to go through one of them. The cell was completely bare except for a big blue mattress.

'Sleep it off here. Someone will collect you for questioning when you wake up.'

'Yes, sir!' I said in English, standing in the middle of the cell until they had closed the door behind them, then I lay down on the blue mattress and laughed to myself for a long time before falling asleep.

The next time I woke up I was still drunk and everything that had happened out there and on the way here had something dream-like about it. But the iron door and the concrete floor were tangible enough.

I knocked on the door.

I ought to have shouted, but I didn't know quite what. Guard? Yes.

'Guard, I've woken up!' I shouted. 'Guard! Guard!'

'Shut up!' someone shouted.

That frightened me a bit and I sat down on the mattress. Some time later the door was unlocked and a policeman stared in at me.

'Are you sober now?' he said.

'Yes, I think so,' I said. 'Perhaps not completely though. Better than before anyway.'

'Come with me,' he said.

We went up from the cellar, him first, me next, into a lift and through the floors. He knocked on a door, we went into an office, an older man, maybe fifty, maybe fifty-five, plain clothes, looked at me.

'Sit down,' he said.

I sat down on the chair in front of his desk.

'You were found in Florida,' he said. 'You'd fallen asleep in the corridor of a nursing home. What were you doing there?'

'I don't know,' I said. 'I was so drunk. I don't remember a thing. Just that I woke up there.'

'Do you live in Bergen?'

'Yes.'

'What's your name?'

'Karl Ove Knausgård.'

'Have you any convictions?'

'Convictions?'

'Have you ever been convicted of anything? Drugs, breaking and entering?'

'No, no, no.'

He looked over at a man standing in the doorway.

'Will you check that?'

The man went into the office next door. While he was there the man who was questioning me sat, head down, filling in a form without saying a word. Blinds covered the windows; outside, between the slats, the sky was blue.

The second man came back.

'Nothing,' he said.

'You don't remember anything?' said the man questioning me. 'Earlier in the evening, you don't remember anything? Where did you go?'

'I was at a party. By the park.'

'Who were you with?'

'My brother, among others. And some of his friends.'

He looked at me.

'We'd better call him in then.'

'Who?'

'Your brother.'

'What's he got to do with this? And what's all this about? I slept in the corridor of a nursing home, that's not good, I know, and you might consider it breaking and entering, but that's all I did.'

'You don't remember anything?' he said. 'The home was burgled last night and in the immediate vicinity there was a car crash. So things were happening. Then we find you in the corridor of the same home. That's what this is about. What's your brother's name?'

'Yngve Knausgård.'

'His address? And yours?'

I told him.

'You'll be hearing from us. You can go now.'

I was escorted down to the ground floor, given my few possessions and I went into the car park outside. I was so tired I could barely walk. I stopped several times to catch my breath, and before Steinkjellergaten I had to sit down on a step, I simply had no energy left. Up the hill, would I make it? But ten minutes later, after passers-by had stared at me, every single one, I got to my feet and lurched up the hill. The walk home from the police station took me close to an hour. In my room I lay down on the bed and fell asleep for the third time within twenty-four hours. Not for long. When I opened my eyes again it was still early afternoon. The heaviness had left my body, it felt normal now apart from a terrible hunger. I ate ten slices of bread and cheese, drank a litre of milk with Nesquik and went to the phone box to call the Academy. Fortunately Sagen was there. I told him I had been arrested and hadn't been able to go to the dinner. Arrested? he said. Are you joking? No, I said, I spent the night in a cell. I'm still in a bad way, I'm afraid to say.

Could you send me the certificate, do you think? Certainly, he said. Shame you weren't here for the meal. Arrested, you say? Yes, I said. Thank you for everything this year anyway. I'm sure we'll meet again.

I rang off and, with my last coins, caught the bus into town. The sky was dark blue, the sun red and above Askøy the clouds in the east looked as if they were on fire. I walked past the Student Centre and down to Møhlenpris, intending to visit Yngve, perhaps he could clarify what had happened.

The door was open, and I went up the stairs to the floor where the collective was and rang the bell.

Line, a nice blonde girl from Østland, a few years older than me, opened the door.

She looked at me with something akin to fear in her eyes.

'Is Yngve in?' I said.

She nodded.

'Come in,' she said. 'He's in his room.'

I went in, took off my shoes, kept my jacket on, knocked softly on Yngve's door and opened it.

He was standing by the stereo and turned when he heard me.

I stared at him in amazement.

Half of his face was covered with a bandage.

Suddenly it all came back to me.

I had hurled a glass at him with all the strength I possessed.

I had thrown it at his eye.

He didn't say anything, just looked at me.

'Did I do that?' I said.

'Yes,' he said. 'Don't you remember?'

'Yes, now I do,' I said. 'Did I hit you in the eye? Are you blind?'

He sat down on the chair.

'No, the eye is intact. You hit me just next to it. I had to have stitches. There'll be a permanent scar.'

I began to cry.

'I didn't mean it,' I said. 'I didn't mean it. I don't know why I did it. I didn't mean it. Can you forgive me? Oh Yngve, can you forgive me?'

He sat like an emperor on the chair in the room, his back erect, legs apart, one hand on his knee, looking at me.

I couldn't meet his gaze, I couldn't look at him.

I lowered my head and sobbed aloud.

PART SEVEN

PART SEVEN

Three and a half years later, between Christmas and New Year 1992, I stood at the far end of the Student Centre by the stairs up to the concourse where the student organisations had their stands, waiting for the Student Radio programme manager. I was going to do my civilian service there and had just come down from a couple of months at a camp in Hustad, on the coast outside Molde, where I had been with other Vestland conscripts to learn various aspects of peace work and conscientious objection to military service. It had been a joke; hardly anyone cared about the idealistic side of civilian service. The majority were undoubtedly against war, but their principles didn't leave any deeper marks on them, and I felt I had been transported back to my confirmation camp in the eighth class, where everyone thought it was fun being alone and away from home but no one had any time for the reason, our relationship with God and Jesus Christ, and consequently every opportunity to sabotage the teaching and exploit the freedoms we had for our own purposes was taken. The only real differences were age – most people in Hustad were in their early or mid-twenties – the length of the course – not two days but two months – and the facilities. They had a well-equipped music room, a well-stocked library, they had a dark room and video equipment, they had kayaks and diving gear, and we could take a diving certificate. Tours to the district were arranged, a bus came and picked us up; one evening we were driven to Kristiansund, where we were allowed to go out and get drunk. But the most important part was the courses. Someone had worked hard for conscientious objectors to be taken seriously back when young people were passionate about such matters and full of idealism. We didn't give a shit. Attendance was obligatory, but those who didn't feel well or had a headache could barely follow what the teacher was saying, and the mismatch between the teachers' idealism and passion for conscientious objection and our ignorance was occasionally painful to behold.

Beside the common-core subjects we also had some electives, such as film or music or advanced courses on a variety of theoretical areas, and when we were offered the chance to make suggestions I put up my hand and asked if they could arrange a writing course for us. A literary writing course? The proposal was received with enthusiasm; if there was any interest they would certainly arrange it. I became a kind of leader of the little writing group, and the first thing I said was that we couldn't get up at seven like the others, because if you were writing you might have sat up all night, that was often when the inspiration came, and the crazy thing was that the teacher responsible for our group bought that lock, stock and barrel, no, of course you can't get up at seven then, I'll see what I can do. He arranged it, the writing group could sleep in. I felt guilty, he was nice and well meaning and allowed himself to be used, but on the other hand I hadn't asked to come up here and it wasn't my fault they were so hugely well disposed towards us.

He even organised a writer's visit for us. Arild Nyquist was flown up from Oslo to teach us for a day. He sat there with his sorrowful eyes and asked how many of us wrote seriously, who wanted to become a writer. No one raised a hand. We're doing this to make life easier for ourselves here, someone said. I see, said Nyquist, that may not be the soundest criterion, but we'll have to make the best of it. I felt even guiltier then, for all I knew he had left his family to come up here and teach the ardent young conscientious object-ors at Hustad Camp, he had once been ardent himself, and then he came face to face with us. But they probably paid him well, so it didn't matter.

One day we had a role-play session in the gym. We were given different world identities: someone represented America, some-one Russia, someone China, someone India, someone the EU, someone the Scandinavian countries, someone Africa, and then we were handed booklets describing our roles. The teacher in charge suggested I should be the general secretary of the UN and lead the international conference. Why her choice fell on me I had no idea, but such things happened, people did sometimes pick me out and credit me with certain qualities. When I was a literature student one of the lecturers had made a mental note of me and in his lessons he would suddenly point to me and say, what does Karl Ove think about this?

So there I sat in the gymnasium trying to prevent a world war from breaking out, organising meetings with various parties, mediating and suggesting compromises. The only person I knew in Hustad from before, Johs, represented Russia. Johs was what grandad would have called a wizard, he had studied sociology and got the best grades they had given for many years, well, perhaps ever, it was said; he had studied in Paris and was at a level other students could only dream about. However, he carried this talent very lightly, he was a modest man, sometimes bordering on self-effacing, he was genuinely good and friendly, no one had a bad word to say about him, considerate and empathetic, and therefore also vulnerable, it had struck me many times. He also had good friends, they seemed to form a protective ring around him, they were his guardians. His parents were farmers in Jølster, only a few kilometres down from where mum lived. He was strong, but strength was in a way secondary with him, something you hardly noticed. What you did notice was his sensitivity. In his own eyes he was perhaps a very ordinary guy – what did I know – but he wasn't, I had never met anyone with precisely the mix of qualities he had.

He represented Russia in our role play, and he outmanoeuvred everyone, not least me, so that he, that is Russia, by the end of the day had made huge territorial gains in Europe and Asia and become the dominant major power, on the brink of total world control.

He had a good laugh at that.

In the evening, in the homely lounge where music blared and people sat around playing games or reading magazines, smoking and drinking beer, one of the semi-criminal layabouts from Bergen came over to me, I was leaning against the banister to the floor below and he stood so close it felt threatening.

'You think you're someone, don't you,' he said. 'Like the UN general secretary. Sitting there with your books. But you're nothing.'

'I've never said I'm someone,' I said.

'Shut your mouth,' he said and left.

Stories about him were circulating, one was that he had shouted *Fuck you and your family!* in the camp director's office, and the way he had added the family was funny. There were two or three of his kind there, they were hard nuts and could easily have beaten me to pulp if they'd had a mind to, but they were also completely off their trolleys and ignorant, an immense ignorance that could have quite bizarre effects on the teaching when they attended classes, which was seldom.

It was of course ironic that such violent types should be here of all places, in a camp where the peace and pacifist flag flew aloft, but it was also typical because in some way or other they were the 'alternatives', they lived half inside, half outside the bounds of society, and it was there that the most important part of the 70s alternative movement could be found. If you took away their ideology, all that was left was their outsider status and drugs.

There was another gang from Bergen and they were musicians. They came from Loddefjord, Fyllingsdalen and Åsane, and hung around together all the time, slumped on the sofas reading comics or watching TV, but when they jammed together they went through a total transformation, they stood there like demons and conjured up complex soundscapes from nothing, they had mastered their instruments to perfection, but then, after these explosions, they reverted to type, chewing the cud, slumped somewhere. The exception was Calle, one of Bergen's stars, his band had released records, gone on tour and now he was playing with Lasse Myrvold, the legend from The Aller Værste!, in a band he called Kong Klang. He was different from the other musicians, his curiosity stretched beyond the sphere of music, he was open, very much so, and basically brilliant, but when he touched on areas I knew something about, such as literature, he was also naïve, and I found that moving somehow, as I did all chinks in the armour of others.

As far as possible I stayed in the background in Hustad, spent all of the time on my own, did some reading, importantly *The Magic Mountain* by Thomas Mann, which I had bought in Danish as the Norwegian edition was abridged. It was the best novel I had read in many years, there was something about the relationship between sickness and health that was appealing. It made its first appearance when Hans Castorp left the sanatorium to go for a walk up the beautiful mountainsides, and suddenly his nose began to bleed uncontrollably, and he continued his infatuations with women, in whom it is the illness Mann focuses on, the feverishness, the shining eyes, the coughing, the bent backs and poor physiques, all framed by green valleys and gleaming alpine peaks. The long ensuing discussions between the Jesuit and the humanist, which could almost be considered life-and-death duels, where everything really was at stake, were also captivating. They were bound up with descriptions of life at the sanatorium, I assumed, it was part of the same, although I couldn't explain it, I was unfamiliar with the frames of reference within which the discussions unfolded.

I had read *Doctor Faustus* when I was eighteen. All I could remember from it was Adrian Leverkühn's breakdown, when his greatest achievements in art coincided with his reduction to an infantile state, and the magnificent opening, when Zeitblom and Leverkühn are children and the composer's father performs simple experiments for them, he manipulates dead material in such a way that it behaves as if it were alive. And then I had read *Death in Venice*, the old man at death's door who makes himself up and dyes his hair to impress the beautiful youth.

Everything took place in the proximity of death in these books, which were otherwise full of thoughts and theories about art and philosophy, they were at the heart of the great European tradition, but they weren't experimental like Joyce's or Musil's novels, they lacked a certain independence of form, and I wondered why they did, couldn't he do that? Mann wrote *about* the avant-garde, but allowed it to be written by a traditionalist like Zeitblom. Espen, my best friend, had no time for Thomas Mann, presumably because of the traditional and bourgeois character of his novels, this lay outside his sphere of interests. Espen was a poet and omnivorous as regards literature, irredeemably curious and thirsty for knowledge, but more often than not with an eye for the most progressive literature, and that did not include the predominantly realistic novel. Espen kept his French and American poets to himself, I kept my mainstream novels to myself, and then we met in the middle, with authors such as Thomas Bernhard, Tor Ulven, Claude Simon, Walter Benjamin, Gilles Deleuze, James Joyce, Samuel Beckett, Marguerite Duras, Stig Larsson, Tomas Tranströmer. I could talk about Thomas Mann and Espen would listen, but I could never get him to spend time reading him, nor did I dare try, in case he thought it was poor literature, which would definitely have rebounded on me and my taste. I saw our relationship as parallel to the one between Leverkühn and Zeitblom in *Doctor Faustus* – Espen was the artist, bent over his apocryphal books in his study, the poet, the genius, I was the plain, ordinary man, by chance his friend, who watched him at work and knew enough about it to understand he was unique, but not enough, never enough, to produce the same himself. I could write about literature, as Zeitblom wrote about music, I couldn't create it. If I had said something of this kind to Espen he would have objected violently, he didn't see himself like that, I knew, but there *was* an enormous difference between us: he could read Ekelöf, Celan, Akhmatova, Montale, Ashbury, Mandelstam, poets I had barely heard about, as the most natural thing in the world and there was no posturing about his reading, as unfortunately there was about mine, I brandished authors' names the way medieval knights brandished flags and banners, but not him, not Espen, he was genuine.

We had both taken the lit. course in the autumn of 1989 and the spring of 1990. At first I knew no one there and made no attempt at contact either, so it was the *gymnas* all over again, sitting alone in the canteen and drinking coffee and pretending I was reading, standing outside the lecture room in the breaks smoking, sitting in the reading room in the afternoons and evenings, all the while with a slow panic in my body, my mouth open in my consciousness, as I wandered around acting as if everything was as it should be. When I closed my books for the evening I sometimes went down to see Yngve, he had moved in with Asbjørn in Hans Tanks gate just below the Science Building, watched TV with them or just drank coffee in their sitting room. I had taken a bedsit in the same property as Yngve's previous collective, it was big and cost much more than I could afford, but I had gone for it anyway, I could always earn some money when the semester was drawing to an end and my study loan was all gone. When I had been broke the spring before and was still at the Writing Academy, I had moved up to Sørbøvåg and worked for a few weeks with Kjartan. I painted one barn wall, he stood under the ladder watching me and said there was nothing better than watching others work for you. He collected manure from the muck cellar with his tractor, dumped it in great heaps around the farm, which I then spread with a fork. The job was hard work, my arms and upper body ached when I went to bed at night, but it was also satisfying, the physicality of the work, sticking the three prongs into the muck, which was partly caked, partly still wet, grabbing a chunk of it and scattering it, it gave me a good feeling, I could see I was making progress, pile after pile disappeared, and it was wonderful to put the fork down in the afternoon and go in and have a snack with grandma and grandad. I got up at seven, had breakfast, worked till twelve, had lunch, worked till four, it was a purge, a penance, none of my terrible life in Bergen existed here, I was a different person here, someone who could not be criticised. I cooked, I walked grandma across the floor, sometimes I massaged her legs as well, as I had seen mum and Kjartan do, I kept grandad company, and Kjartan, who came home from work at about five, presumably had a little more time for himself than he usually did. Grandma was poorly, and when I left them to work it was as if her shaking and convulsions lived on in me outside, something that had to be subdued and suppressed but lay beyond my control. It was barely possible to speak to her, her voice was so weak, just a whisper, it was difficult to distinguish words. One afternoon grandad was talking about Hamsun, whom he had read with such pleasure, and grandma whispered something from her chair, I leaned forward to listen, couldn't understand until the coin finally dropped: Duun! Olav Duun, the writer. Another afternoon I could see she was upset, she was trying to catch my attention, I went over and bent down, she pointed to grandad and whispered something I didn't understand, say it again, Grandma, I can't hear what you're saying, one more time, just . . .

I thought she said that grandad had killed someone.

'Has grandad killed someone?' I said.

Then she laughed! A quiet, breathy, barely audible laugh, but her chest shook and her eyes gleamed.

So that wasn't what she had said, I thought, and laughed as well. But it wasn't so strange that I had heard it, a paranoid shadow sometimes lay between her and the world, if she could say grandad was a thief in her deepest confusion, couldn't she say that he had killed someone as well?

It was fantastic to see her laugh. Normally her days were so humdrum and full of suffering that it was painful to witness. One night I woke up to grandad calling for Kjartan, I hurried downstairs, both of them were waiting for me in the double bed in the dining room, grandma shaking, eyes wide open, grandad sitting on the edge of the bed.

'Kjartan has to help her go to the bathroom,' he said. 'Go and get him.'

'I can do it,' I said.

She wore nappies at night, I understood, but I kept away from this part of the nursing, anything to do with intimate areas, dressing and undressing, it wasn't right, I was her grandchild, mum or Kjartan had to do that. But in this situation I would have to do whatever was required.

I put one hand behind her back, the other under her arm and began to lift. She was so stiff that it took a long time, but eventually she was sitting on the edge of the bed. She whispered something. Her jaws trembled, but she looked straight at me with her clear blue eyes. I leaned forward.

'Kjartan,' she said.

'I can take you,' I said. 'Then we won't have to wake him. I'm already awake.'

I took her arm and raised her into a standing position. But it was too quick, she was too stiff and fell back. I did it again, more slowly, and pulled the walking frame over with one hand, placed it in front of her, watched her gently, almost imperceptibly, move her hands down to the handles.

Finally she was holding it with both hands and her balance was good enough for her to be able to walk. She was wearing only a thin white nightdress, her lower arms and legs were bare, her grey and white hair was loose, and I did not like what I had walked into, I was much too close to her, in the wrong way. When we were in the bathroom I would have to help her to sit down on the toilet seat and undress her. No, no, no. No, no, no. But we were on the way, tiny step by tiny step she shuffled across the floor, first the dining room, where they slept, then the sitting room, where the TV was. Her hands shook, her head shook, slowly and laboriously she put one foot in front of the other, they too shook. A lamp shone in the corner, otherwise everything was dark inside. I strode forward and opened the door to the hall. Beyond it was the bathroom.

'Soon be there,' I said.

She moved a trembling foot forward. And then pee began to run down her thigh, and then it came in a stream and splashed on the floor. She stood perfectly still as it happened. Leaning forward, stock still, the pee splashing down, she looked like an animal, I thought. Standing in front of her, I met her eyes and they were anguished.

'It doesn't matter, Grandma,' I said. 'It happens. It doesn't matter. Just stay here and I'll get Kjartan.'

I ran out, rang the bell twice in quick succession, opened the door and shouted up. He came steaming downstairs a few seconds later, prepared for the worst.

'You've got to help grandma,' I said. 'It's nothing serious. She only wants to go to the loo.'

He said nothing, went with me, took grandma and led her into the bathroom with firm resolute movements and closed the door behind them. I filled a bucket with water, wetted the cloth and wiped the floor.

I went back to Bergen with enough money to manage for the rest of the semester. I didn't tell anyone about what I had experienced, but slipped into depressing Bergen life leaving Sørbøvåg as a closed room, a sealed experience, alongside all the other experiences I'd had that were incompatible with my life now or irrelevant to it. Especially after I had thrown the glass at Yngve's head it seemed like that: it was impossible to reconcile the person I was then, someone trying to inflict damage, destroy, preferably blind his brother, with the person when I was with them or with mum, who knew nothing of all this. This was all I thought about, and the power in it was immense, it dragged me down to a place inside myself I hadn't been and hadn't known existed. If I could throw a glass at Yngve's face what else was I capable of? There was something in me I couldn't control, and it was terrible: if I couldn't trust myself who could I trust?

This wasn't a matter I could discuss with anyone else either. That afternoon in Yngve's collective when I understood what I had done, I sat crying and begging for forgiveness, so upset that I couldn't go home, I slept there, on the sofa in the collective, surrounded by other students who didn't quite know where to look or what to do when I was there. One of them I hadn't seen before, he came in when I was on the sofa with my head bowed, so you're Karl Ove, he said, you live in the bedsit above Morten, don't you? Yes, I said. I'll pop by to see you one day, he said. I live in a flat just opposite you two. I raised my eyes and looked at him. He was smiling so much his face seemed to split into two. My name's Geir, he said.

Two days later he knocked at my door. I was writing, shouted come in, thinking it was Morten as the front doorbell hadn't rung.

'Are you writing?' he said. 'I don't want to disturb you.'

'No, no, come in. You're not disturbing me,' I said.

He sat down, we chatted tentatively about common acquaintances, it transpired we were the same age and that he came from Hisøya and had gone to *gymnas* with several of the children I had been at school with and hadn't seen since then. He had gone to a military academy, dropped out, moved to Bergen and started studying social anthropology. At first he wanted to talk about how happy he was and how good it was being in Bergen. He had his own money, his own flat and the university was overflowing with girls, could life be any better?

No, perhaps it couldn't, I said.

He laughed and said he had never met such a gloomy individual as me. Anyone would think Job had taken up lodgings in Bergen! Come on, let's go for a walk to put you in a better frame of mind!

Why not! I said, and we headed downhill to the town centre. We stood at the bar in Fekterloftet, ordered a carafe of white wine, and the embarrassment I always felt with people I didn't know, the thought that I was boring and of no interest and that actually they didn't want to be here, was completely absent. There was something about him I trusted. What I discussed with Geir that evening I couldn't have discussed with anyone else I had met in Bergen, not even Yngve. You carried your inner thoughts and passions within you, and perhaps shared with a partner – what did I know about such matters – at any rate it wasn't something you brought up one night you were on the town, it would have killed everything, caused others to shy away. Because it was all about having a good time, laughing, telling stories or arguing till the sparks flew, but about matters that were outside your inner life, about what was between people, about what they shared. Bands, films, books, other students, lecturers, girls, various experiences remodelled as entertaining anecdotes or jokes.

There was nothing of that this evening.

I talked about my year in northern Norway, how I had been slightly in love with a thirteen-year-old and I had kissed another,

how I had been completely crazy about a sixteen-year-old and
had almost gone out with her, how I had drifted round and got
drunk, been out of control, and it had continued down here,
and I was scared of myself, not in some make-believe way, not
to make myself interesting, but in reality, scared of what I might
do. If I could try to destroy my brother anything was possible. If
I'd had a knife would I have stabbed him? I also talked about my
grandmother, the dignity she possessed in all the misery in which
she was trapped. But most of all I talked about Ingvild. I told him
about all our meetings, I held forth on how fantastic she was but
admitted I had done everything wrong from the very beginning.
I said I was like Lieutenant Glahn, I could also shoot myself in the
foot to make her look at me and perhaps think about me. Yes, I
have got a scar on my foot, I said, and put my leg on a rung on the
bar stool, look here, I got that trying to kick away a rocket on the
ground near Hanne. Who on earth is Hanne? he said, someone I
was in love with, I said, another one, he said and laughed. What he
told me about himself was not only different, it was diametrically
opposite.

He was actually a militarist, he said, he had loved life at the
Military Academy, the sound of reveille in the morning, the smell
of leather and weapon grease, the uniforms, the guns and the
discipline, he had dreamed about it all his life, he had joined the
Cadet Force at home in Arendal and had never been in any doubt
about his career path after finishing *gymnas*.

'Why did you leave then? If you liked it so much?'

'I don't know. It might have been because I discovered that I
could do it, I knew it, and I wanted to do something I couldn't do.
And then there was the lack of individuality. I spoke to the com-
mander about that, I said I didn't want to be some sheep with a
bell round its neck, he said that being led wasn't the problem,
but where you were led. Basically he was right. But the moment
of truth was when I saw the regulations. Then I realised that

someone would always know where I was. And that was no good. So I stopped and became a conscientious objector.'

'Are you a *conscientious objector*?'

'Yes. Nevertheless I still love the sound of marching boots.'

I hadn't even considered the possibility of liking the military; it stood for everything I was against. War, violence, authority, power. I was a pacifist but unhappy, he was a militarist and happy. It wasn't easy to say who was right. He also told me about one morning he had walked home with a girl he had been interested in for a long time, the sun was up, the town was deserted, they strolled hand in hand through the park and were heading for his bedsit and the huge waterbed he had there, how perfect the moment had been in every respect. He told me about everything he was learning in social anthropology and laughed at some of the bizarre rituals people had. He also laughed at me, but not in a way that annoyed me, quite the contrary, suddenly I could laugh at myself too. I thought, I've got a new friend here. I had as well, but not for long because soon afterwards he said he was moving to Uppsala after the summer. I was sorry but said nothing. Fekterloftet closed its doors, we were drunk and did the rounds of the nightclubs, ending up in Slakteriet, as always Bergen's last late-night stop, and stirred by the light sky and all the happy people on the street at the beginning of June I suggested dropping in on Ingvild so that he could see her with his own eyes and so that I could say some of the many things that I had thought about her. He was up for this, we made our way towards Nygårdsgaten, I remembered that as visitors we ought to have something to take with us, ran over to the flower beds by the Grieg Hall, tugged at a rhododendron bush, it had just blossomed and was beautiful, pulled it free and stood there with it in one hand while Geir struggled with his. Then we crossed the street, I found some pebbles and started throwing them at her window. It must have been around four or half past. She opened the window, at first she didn't want to let us in, but I begged, she said OK, I'll be right down. As she opened the front door a police car came down the street and stopped next to us. A policeman stepped out, Ingvild closed the door and disappeared, the officer asked us what we were doing, I said we were going to give the young lady some flowers, I realised this was wrong, we had taken them from in front of the Grieg Hall, but, look, the roots are intact, we can run back now and replant them, it'll be fine. OK, said the policeman, and when we went to put the bushes back the car followed us and waited in the middle of the road until we had finished before driving on.

'That was lucky,' I said.

'Lucky? The police came.'

'Yes, but they could have fined us or thrown us into the drunks' cells. Come on.'

'I'm beginning to get the idea,' Geir said. 'You want to go back to Ingvild, don't you.'

'Yes, come on.'

He shook his head but came along. I threw pebbles at the window, this time she didn't open it, and Geir tugged at me, he wanted to go home, I told him he could go, I didn't feel like going to bed yet. When he left I went over Høyden and down to Møhlenpris, felt some car door handles, sneaked into some backyards looking for unlocked bikes, sat down on a step and smoked, it would soon be morning, the sun was already shining at the edge of the sky. I went to the telephone box behind the football pitch and rang Ingvild's collective. One of the men answered the phone, I said I wanted to speak to Ingvild, he said, do you know what time it is, she's asleep, everyone's asleep, you can't call in the middle of the night, now I'm ringing off. I smacked the receiver a few times against the top of the coin box, but it didn't break and I opened the door and kicked the glass panel.

Then another bloody police car came!

It stopped in front of me, a policeman rolled down the window and asked me what I was doing. I said I was fed up, my girlfriend had finished with me that evening, and so I had kicked the telephone box, I'm sorry, I said, I won't do it again.

'OK, you'd better go home to bed.'

'Right,' I said.

'Yes, and now. Let's see you on your way!'

And so I walked up towards Hulen while they sat in the car watching me. As I rounded the bend they followed me and only left when I turned up towards the park.

The fear and shame when I woke were so great that I felt I was going to split open. I could have stood up and screamed, I hadn't learned anything, I had been there again, where there was no control and there were no limits, where anything could happen. Something shrieked inside me, but it would pass. Either simply by gritting my teeth or talking to others. That had a mitigating and deadening effect. I went downstairs to Morten, he leaned back against the sofa and listened, his appearance had changed completely, he no longer wore deck shoes and red leather jackets, and he no longer studied law, he had done a volte-face and was now an arts student, with all that that implied in terms of black trousers, black T-shirts, black shoes, a ring in one ear and Raga Rockers on the stereo. He was already well versed and often finished his arguments with we're machines in Nirvana, Karl Ove, we're machines in Nirvana.

The next day a letter arrived from Cappelen. At first I didn't do anything, thinking it was like Schrödinger's cat: until the moment the envelope was open and I had read what was in the letter it could equally well have been an acceptance as a rejection. It lay on the table all morning, I gazed at it every now and then, when I was shopping I thought of nothing else, and in the end, at around four, I could stand it no longer and opened it.

Yes, indeed. It was a rejection.

It was as expected, but I was still disappointed, so deeply in fact that I couldn't bear to be alone. I went downstairs to see Morten, he wasn't at home. I thought of Jon Olav, but didn't want to flag up my defeat to him. Nor Yngve. Remembered Geir, he lived only a few minutes away, and I went up to see him. He had already packed, some removal chests were still on the floor, but he magicked up two cups of instant coffee, we sat down on the floor and I recited my rejection to him.

'"We have read your novel with interest, but I am sorry to say we cannot undertake to publish it. It is at times both entertaining and engagingly written, but as a whole we consider you have too little to say and it lacks pace. Accordingly, we would like to thank you for allowing us to read the manuscript, which you will find enclosed,"' I said.

Geir laughed.

'First of all, I'm impressed that you can already reel it off by heart,' he said. 'Secondly, that you've written a novel at all. I don't know anyone who would even entertain the idea.'

'That's small comfort,' I said.

He snorted.

'Write another one!'

'Easy for you to say,' I said.

'I suppose so. I'm basically dyslexic. I'd hardly read a novel before I came here. What would you recommend, by the way, if I were to get the idea in my head?'

'*Dead Heat* by Erling Gjelsvik perhaps?'

'Is that the best novel you've ever read?'

'No, no. I thought it would be a good start for you.'

'Now don't you underestimate me. Come on. What's the best novel you've read?'

'*Lasso Round Mrs Luna* by Mykle maybe? Or *Pan* by Hamsun. Or *Novel with Cocaine* by Ageyev.'

'Then I'll read Mykle as he was the first one you said. You've already told me the whole plot of *Pan*.'

'Yes, except for the fact that he takes his own life at the end. I didn't say that.'

'Ha ha.'

'He does!'

'Are you going to spoil all my reading pleasure?' he said.

'Everyone knows he does,' I said.

'I didn't.'

'You do now.'

'Is there anything else you think I should know, Mr Literature?'

'In fact, there is,' I said. 'I discovered it a couple of weeks ago. I was lying in bed and glanced at the bookshelf. And I read some of the writers' names backwards.'

'Oh yes?'

'Yes. Do you know what T.Eliot becomes?'

'No.'

'Toilet. Such a shame about the S though. If it had been before the T it would have been Toilets.'

'And you're about to start a lit. course, did you say?'

'Yes?'

There was a pause.

'What a pity you're going to move,' I said.

'I've done Bergen. I know what it's like here. Now I have to try something else.'

'I was thinking of going to Istanbul this autumn,' I said. 'Just renting a room and writing for a year.'

'Why don't you?'

I shrugged.

'It feels as if I've got stuff to sort out here. And I have nothing to write about. Or everything to do with writing is just depressing. I have to learn. And I might just as well do that here.'

'Come to Uppsala then!'

'No. What the hell would I do there?'

'What the hell am I going to do? That's the whole point of it. Go somewhere you know nothing about and see what happens.'

'But I don't want anything to happen,' I said. 'Seriously. I don't.'

I put my coffee cup down on one of the chests and got to my feet. There was a view of the park and the road down to the house where I lived from his window, and the fjord and the islands beyond. The sun was out now, dark orange against the deep blue sky, and the trees in the park cast long narrow shadows.

'I wish you all the best then. You write first and I'll answer, OK?'
'OK.'

We shook hands and I walked back downhill to my bedsit. Of course I didn't know as I was unlocking my door that fourteen years would pass before I saw him again, the memory of him was only a few minutes old, and I assumed he would return to Bergen after a year in Uppsala; the thought that it was possible to leave everything for good was one I toyed with now and then, I didn't consider it a real possibility. For my part, I had decided to commit to another year in Bergen and then *do* something else, move elsewhere.

I reread the rejection letter. Then I sat down in front of the fire, scrunched up a few sheets, lit them and started to place sheet after sheet in the flames. I had three copies of the novel and burned two. I would give the third to Ingvild. That would be my last act with her. No more visits, no more telephone conversations, no more nonsense, nothing. The novel would be a final farewell.

I burned my diaries while I was at it, and then I put the manuscript in a bag and walked downhill towards the town.

The bottom door was open, I went up to the first floor and rang, she answered.

'Hi,' she said. 'Nice to see you.'

'Likewise,' I said.

'We're having dinner,' she said. 'I don't know. Would you like to come in anyway?'

'Yes. Thank you,' I said.

I went in, took off my shoes, put the bag in the corridor and followed her into the sitting room. Eight people were sitting around the table. Residents in the collective and some of their friends. I knew who everyone was. But they had been invited, I had only dropped by, and as they looked at me there was a strained atmosphere.

'Would you like to eat with us?' Ingvild said.

I shook my head.

It was humiliating, getting an extra little plate on the corner, the unbidden guest's extra little plate.

'No, I only wanted a few words with you, but we can do that another time.'

'We can,' she said.

My face was red, everything was wrong. I had come, made an entrance, now I would go again without anything happening.

'Bye,' I said, and could hear how stupid that must have sounded.

'Bye,' they said.

Ingvild accompanied me out.

'I just need the loo,' I said and made for the toilet. She went into the kitchen, I nipped out, grabbed the plastic bag containing the manuscript, dashed into her room, placed it on her bed, went back out and was putting on my shoes when she reappeared.

Now it definitely would be a surprise, I thought as I ran down the stairs and emerged into the warm summer evening, the streets suffused with sunlight, and that was actually the whole point.

The university was a new start. And, not least, it was something to hold on to. The lectures were a fixed point, the reading room was a fixed point, the books were a fixed point. Irrespective of what happened, irrespective of how dreadful I felt, I could always go up to the reading room and find myself a seat and sit there and read for as long as I wanted, no one could object to that, no one could say there was anything odd about it, it was the very essence of university life. I bought a two-volume encyclopedia of world literature and ploughed my way through, writer by writer, from Homer to the 1960s, tried to remember a line or two about each one, about what they did. I went to the lectures, Kittang on classical poetry, Buvik on classical epics, Linneberg on classical drama. Among all the names and figures were some great emotional insights. Odysseus, who tricked the Cyclops by saying his name was 'No one'. He was lost, but he gained life. The song of the Sirens. Those who heard it were also lost, felt themselves being drawn to them, did everything in their power to get close and perished. The Sirens were both Eros and Thanatos, desire and death, the most desirable and the most dangerous. Orpheus, who sang so beautifully that everyone who heard him became spellbound and was lost, descended into the underworld to retrieve Eurydice and this was within his power as long as he didn't turn and look at her, but he did, and so she was lost for ever. A French philosopher by the name of Blanchot had written about this, and I read his essay about Orpheus in which he wrote that art was the force that caused the night to open, but that it is Eurydice he wants and she was the utmost that art could attain. Eurydice was the second night, Blanchot wrote.

These ideas were too grandiose for me, but I was attracted by them and tried to get my head around them, to capture them, to assimilate them, but unsuccessfully, I saw them from the outside, knowing that their full meaning escaped me. Give the sacred back to the sacred? The night of the night? I recognised the main figure, that which appears and disappears at the same moment or the simultaneous presence of the one and the other which cancels out the one, this was a figure I had seen in many poems from that period, and I also felt a particular attraction to the ideas about the night, the second night and death, but as soon as I attempted to think independently about it, in other words beyond the form in which the ideas were presented, it became banal and stupid. It was the same as mountaineering, you had to place your foot exactly there or there, your hand had to grip exactly there or there, if not, you were left standing still or you lost your grip and fell.

The utmost is that which disappears when it is seen or recognised. It was the core of the Orpheus myth. But what is *that*?

When I sat in the reading room, which was old and had a kind of sombre atmosphere, and read Blanchot in the afternoon, a completely new feeling arose in me, something I had never felt before, a sort of extreme excitement, as though I found myself in the proximity of something unique, mixed with an equally extreme impatience, I *had* to go there, and these two feelings were so incompatible that I wanted to jump up and run and shout and sit perfectly still and read on all at the same time. What was strange was that the restlessness began to course through me at the moment when I read something good which I had understood and absorbed, it was as though it was simply impossible to bear. Often I stood up and took a break then, and while I walked along the corridors and up the stairs to the first floor of the canteen, the excitement and the impatience mingled with the dropped jaw of my consciousness, which was to do with my pursuing these paths alone, and that kind of thing, my soul in an inexplicable turmoil, I bought myself a coffee and sat down at a table and tried to appear as calm as possible.

There was also something panicked about my desire to acquire knowledge, in sudden terrible insights I saw that actually I didn't know anything and it was urgent, I didn't have a second to lose. It was almost impossible to adapt this urgency to the slowness that reading required.

In the middle of September I went to Florence with Yngve, we took the train down and spent four days at Pensione Palmer not so far from the cathedral, where I had stayed the previous summer during the hitchhiking trip with Lars. We didn't talk about what had happened between us, we simply skipped over it, we were brothers, this bond was stronger than everything else, yet something had changed, perhaps most of all in me, where the final remnants of naturalness had disappeared, I was conscious of

everything that was said and done when we were together. The silences that sprang up were painful, we were brothers after all, we
ought to be able to chat in a light-hearted unforced way, but then
there was a silence and I sat thinking about something natural I
could say to break it. About a band? About Asbjørn or some of his
other friends? About football? About what was around us, a town
the train passed through, an incident outside the window on the
street, a beautiful woman entering the bar where we were? Sometimes this worked well – for example, we could discuss the difference between the girls at home and the ones we saw here, the
incredible elegance they had, not just the dresses with their tight
jackets and narrow coats, their long boots and small neat scarves,
but also the way they walked, studied and genteel, so glaringly
different from our girls' homely Fjällräven gait, which suggested
nothing other than forward motion, slightly bent over, eternally
prepared for a cloudburst, jogging, strolling, no more, no less,
we're on the go! Yet the sight of the Italian women – girls would
be the wrong word for them – was also depressing, they were in
a different league, out of reach for us, who were of course of the
same unsophisticated material as Norwegian girls, you just had to
cast a glance at young Italian men, who were as sharply dressed
and elegant as their female counterparts, who knew all the tricks
in the book and who, what was more, courted them with an urbanity we could not have achieved if we had practised every day
for the next year, in fact, if we had studied elegance and manners
at university for six years we wouldn't have got near them.

'I was twenty-two when I ate a steak for the first time,' Yngve
said as we sat on a *terrazza*, each with an espresso, which we knew
we should drink standing, but drank sitting anyway. Being Norwegian, we might just as well have drunk it standing on our heads as
standing at the bar.

'I thought steaks and chops were the same thing,' he said.

'Aren't they?' I said.

He laughed, thinking I was jesting.

'In which case I've never eaten a steak,' I said. 'But then I'm only twenty.'

'Is that right?' he said. 'We'll definitely have a steak tonight then.'

While autumn had arrived in Bergen it was still hot and summery in Florence. In the middle of the day the sun was boiling even when it was behind a veil of clouds, and the only yellow in the vegetation was caused by the aridity. We went to the Uffizi Gallery, wandered through the endless corridors looking at the paintings, all identical, we saw Michelangelo's statue of David and some of his unfinished works, the figures looked as if they were trying to break out of the marble blocks that entombed them. We strolled around the large cathedral, went up the stairs and stood right under the roof, continued along a narrow corridor and emerged at the top with the whole of Florence beneath us, we drank coffee in small cafés, ate ice cream and took pictures of each other, Yngve was especially keen, I posed in front of every conceivable kind of wall in my black Ray-Bans, wearing black baggy pants and shirts with a variety of patterns. Now it was all happening in Manchester, and if this had gone unremarked in Italy, it hadn't in Bergen. First of all I had read about the Stone Roses, then I had gone to listen to them in a record shop, but the sound had been a bit weird, I had thought, I wasn't sure it was good, but Yngve had bought it, he said it was great, and I bought it too and agreed. It grew and grew on you. The strange thing was that exactly the same had happened with the Smiths, I had heard their debut record in Kristiansand after reading about them in the *NME*, thought it was too odd, but then the hype reached Norway and it no longer sounded odd but right.

And so we wandered around the town, as beautiful as it was lively, full of people and small scenes, mopeds and palaces; in the evening we walked home and got dressed and went to a restaurant.

It was a more refined eatery, I was ill at ease, didn't like to talk to the waiters, didn't like being served, didn't like being seen, didn't know what to do in the situations that arose, from how to taste wine to what to do with the serviette on the plate, but fortunately Yngve handled everything and soon we were eating our steaks and drinking red wine.

Afterwards we smoked, drank grappa, which tasted like poor-quality moonshine, and talked about dad. We often did this, told each other about minor incidents we remembered with him and discussed recent events, his life in northern Norway, which wasn't distant to us even though we met him only a couple of times a year and perhaps talked to him on the phone once a month, because he loomed large in our consciousnesses. Yngve hated him or at least was completely unreconciled, didn't want to hear about how he had changed and wanted a different relationship with us, that wasn't true, he was the same person, he didn't lift a finger for us, he wasn't in the slightest bit interested in us, if he showed a different face it was because he had convinced himself that was how it should be, not that it actually was. I agreed with Yngve, but I was much weaker; if I spoke to dad on the phone I ingratiated myself with him and I had sent him a letter with photos of the Writing Academy although *really* I wished he didn't exist, indeed that he was dead.

Weak, that was the word.

I was also weak with respect to Yngve. If there was a silence it was my fault and my responsibility. I knew Yngve didn't think like that, didn't care about silences, didn't feel the need to fill them at all costs, he was sure of himself. This was for the same reason that he had friends and I didn't. He was relaxed, didn't give any importance to what he said or did, went out with Asbjørn one Saturday morning, for example, and just mooched around town, perhaps sitting in a café for a few hours, it was no big deal, whereas if I did the same the whole time was so enormously significant that any jarring tone, any discordance, was potentially fatal, and therefore I was forced into, or I forced myself into, a kind of unnatural silence. So was it *that* silence that distinguished this situation and who would want it around them? Who could stand such stiff and forced behaviour? And I didn't mean any harm to anyone, so it was better to keep my distance or stay under Yngve's wing, under his cloak of affability.

The same lack of ease characterised my behaviour with him, but here there was a decisive difference, to wit, the link between us was not dependent on fluctuating situations; however stupidly I behaved I was his brother, he could never get past that and might never want to. The glass-throwing incident gave him a hold over me, it meant that I would always be beneath him, which I basic-ally considered reasonable and felt I deserved.

We paid and went out into the Italian night, I was a bit merry, we looked for a suitable bar, found one, it was new and completely empty, but they played good music and we didn't know a soul in Florence anyway. We had envisaged having one drink there, but the bar staff were effusive, wanted to talk and hear about Norway and Bergen, asked what kind of music we liked and im-mediately afterwards the Stone Roses was throbbing through the building. We sat there, getting more and more drunk, and all my inhibitions, all the ties, all the silence and all the forcedness in me dissolved, I was sitting with my brother and we talked about whatever occurred to us and laughed and were happy.

'None of the people you know do anything *themselves*,' I said. 'But *you* can. You can play the guitar and write music. I don't under-stand why you don't start a band and play seriously. You make great songs.'

'Do you think so?' he said.

'Of course,' I said. 'The others *talk* about music and bands. Sure-ly that's not enough for you?'

'No, I want to play of course. But you have to find people to play with.'

'Pål's good, isn't he?'

'Yes, he is. That's two. If you play the drums, that's three. Then we need a vocalist.'

'There are twenty thousand students in Bergen. One of them must be able to sing.'

'I'll see what I can come up with.'

We didn't need to go to the bar any more to order, they came to us with more drinks the moment we had finished the last, joked with us and asked what other records they should play. When we got up to go it was with a lurch. But we managed to get out and home, talked more about the new band, switched off the light and slept through till late the next day.

In the evening we went back to this fantastic bar. But this time it was crowded and the staff didn't recognise us. It was impossible to believe that they actually didn't remember us because no one else had been there and it was only the previous night, so they must have been putting on an act. But why? We ordered a beer each, drank up and left, headed for a discotheque recommended in a travel guide, it was by the river, which we followed, along a broad avenue, with less and less traffic the further we went. It started raining, the streets shone in the light, beside us the river flowed slowly in the darkness, not a soul in sight. We should have seen it ages ago, Yngve said. Perhaps we've walked past it, I said. We must have been walking for three-quarters of an hour, and so we turned back. The effect of the beer was long gone. The rain was falling thick and fast. The lights from the hills across the river seemed to be hovering in the air. We didn't talk any more, walking was enough. After half an hour Yngve stopped. Below us lay a kind of wooden platform, above it hung cables bedecked with light bulbs, unlit, chairs stacked around the edge. Is it here? Yngve said. Here? I repeated. Well, we have come in the off season. Come on, let's go back and go to bed.

*

Two days later we got out of the train at the station in Bergen, this funnel of a town, and it was good to step into it, everything seemed homely and familiar, my place on earth. It was early evening, I knew being alone in my room after a week with company would be an anticlimax, so I went to Yngve and Asbjørn's, where we cracked open the bottle of whisky we had brought with us and started drinking. Asbjørn said that unfortunately he had some bad news for us. Oh? we said, looking at him. Yes, your grandmother has died. Has she? Died? Yes, your mother phoned when you were on your way down to Italy. Did she say when the funeral was? Yes, it's been and gone. She said it had been impossible to get hold of you.

We got drunk and went to Hulen, it was a weekday and not very full, we hung around the bar drinking, when they closed we went home and carried on. There was a good atmosphere, I felt as though I was in the eye of a storm of people and action. At some point I put on a Superman outfit, sat drinking whisky in the red cape and the rest of the outfit or bopped around to the music. It was a party, it felt as if the flat was packed, I swung round, banged into the fridge, drank, changed the music, sang along, chatted to Yngve and Asbjørn, all while in this fantastic Superman costume, until suddenly everything receded, like powerful tidal waters and the bare facts were revealed: only Yngve, Asbjørn and I were there. We were alone. The party was in my mind. And grandma, grandma was dead.

Even though the music was still playing it was as though there was silence.

I put my face in my hands.

Oh, oh, oh, oh, oh, oh.

'What is it, Karl Ove?'

'Nothing,' I said, but my shoulders were shaking and tears were running down my face, wetting my fingers.

They turned off the music.

'What is it?' they said again.

'I don't know,' I said, looking at them. A sob escaped me, I couldn't stop it. 'It's nothing.'

'Do you want to sleep here? Maybe that's best,' Asbjørn said.

I nodded.

'Lie on the sofa. It's late anyway.'

I did as they said, lay down on the sofa and closed my eyes. One of them covered me with a blanket and I fell asleep.

The next morning everything was fine again, apart from my embarrassment at what had happened, crying in front of them. It didn't matter too much about Yngve, even though that wasn't good either, but Asbjørn?!

And the idiotic Superman outfit!

I took it off, had a cup of coffee with them in the sitting room, where Asbjørn told Yngve off for never putting the milk back in the fridge, it was just fantastic looking forward to a glass of milk and coming home and finding out it was piss-warm.

I smiled and said they were like a married couple. They didn't like hearing that. I went down to Møhlenpris with my old suitcase, let myself in and had a shower. With my hair wet, my shirt sticking to my shoulders and chest I sat down to read. I had got to the end of the eighteenth century, which was bursting with English poets and novelists, and French dramatists, of whom I knew Racine was the most important, and some philosophers and letter-writers. I closed my eyes and tried to remember the names and one work by each of them, continued into the nineteenth century, put down the book, took out the sheets showing the lecture programme, there was one in the afternoon, I decided to go. It was about modern literary theory and I found the selection of texts for it and browsed through them before leaving. Stanley Fish. What a name. And Harold Bloom. My name's Fish. You don't say. Mine's Bloom. And over there's Paul de Man. Do you know him? Yes, I'm a fan of Paul the Man.

That was a text!

I'm a fan of Paul the Man.

When I had finished the text, I put a few books and a writing pad in a bag and walked up to the university. The grass in the park was dry, the sky grey, the leaves on the trees were pale green and yellow. A group of druggies sat under a tree, I took a detour so as not to see them or be accosted, everything about them filled me with unease, from their loud voices and aggressive actions when they weren't doped up to total apathy, which was inhuman, sitting or lying there disconnected from the world, yet with their eyes open, eyes in which you could read nothing. Then there were the syringes, the leather straps, the cartons of milkshake or chocolate milk, the food containers and plastic bags strewn around them, and their clothes, filthy, ragged, as if they hadn't been in contact with humans for several years but had spent the winter in the middle of a forest, after a plane crash maybe, with only one set of clothes. They drifted, they didn't live. And that was what they wanted to do, drift not live.

Past them and out through the gate, past the Student Centre, up the hill and onto the gravel path alongside the Botanical Garden, over to the passage between the Maritime Museum and the university library, past the Faculty of Arts and through the gates of Sydneshaugen School, where I stopped, put the bag on the ground between my feet and lit a cigarette.

Further ahead, beside the steps, someone from my department was standing and smoking. He looked up at me at that moment, then shifted his gaze elsewhere. His name was Espen, I knew, fresh from *gymnas*, and although he hadn't said much when I had been with him I knew he was frighteningly well read. He had spoken about Beckett once with Ole, another student in our department, and I had been deeply impressed despite being two years older than him. He had long dark hair, sometimes collected in a ponytail, brown eyes, glasses, he was thin, wore a brown leather jacket, often with a woollen jumper underneath, would come to lectures on his bike and often sat for hours in the reading room. He seemed shy, on his guard though not suspicious, more like a wary animal.

I picked up the bag and walked towards him.

'Are you going to the lecture?' I said.

He smiled as if to himself.

'Reckon so,' he said. 'Are you?'

'That was the plan. But as I was coming here I lost interest. Think I might go and read instead.'

'What are you reading then?'

'Odds and sods. Nothing special. Stanley Fish.'

'Oh.'

'And you?'

'Dante at the moment. Have you read any Dante?'

'Not yet. But I will. Is it good?'

'It's very good,' he said.

'OK.'

'Mandelstam's written a really great essay about *The Divine Comedy*.'

'Really?'

'Yes.'

'Well, perhaps I should give it a go. Mandelstam?'

'Yes. You do that. It might be tricky to get hold of, but I can copy it for you if you'd like?'

'Yes, I would,' I said. 'That'd be great!'

I smiled, tossed my cigarette to the ground and trod on it.

'See you,' I said and went into the old school building.

On my way home I rang mum. Fortunately she was at home. I asked her how she was, she said fine, but it was incomprehensible that grandma had gone. It had been quick. She had caught a lung infection and only a few days later she had breathed her last.

It happened at the care home where she had been moved at the end of the summer when she could no longer live on the farm, her condition required more nursing and supervision than she could get there. Perhaps that was the reason she went so quickly, there was nothing to hold her back, like her intimate surroundings at home, where she had lived for more than forty years. But Kjartan had been present when she died and she hadn't been afraid.

I could hear that mum was upset, but I didn't know how to react. She wanted to talk about how it had been in Italy, I said only that it had been good, I couldn't go into detail, after all we had been drinking and staggering around while grandma was dying, that in itself was unseemly and nothing mum needed to know. We arranged that I would travel up in a few weeks, go and see her grave, she was in the old cemetery across the fjord, it was nice there, mum said, that was a nice thought.

We rang off, I walked home in the gathering dusk, lay on my bed reading Mark Twain, whom Ragnar Hovland had talked about, fell back into reality now and again, into the darkness surrounding the meagre light from the reading lamp, the material of the light blue pillow, the thought of grandma, the first person close to me who had died. It was impossible to understand. But she was at peace now. She had been tormented, now she had peace. I read on, the thought of her lay constantly in the shadows of my consciousness, now and then it stepped out, she was dead, she was no more, grandma, dear grandma. I hadn't known her, but what is there to know? I had known who she was, who she was to me, ever since I had been a small boy. And that was what filled my mind now, her gentle presence, her eyes. How heart-breaking it must have been for her to depart this world, solely because her body no longer obeyed her, it refused her the most elementary support.

I had to write about this, had to write about her.

I got up, sat at my desk in just my underpants and wrote a poem:

Growing Wild

Your eyes are gone from the day
you're gently faded out
My thoughts like mirrors
I lose control
Feel you within

Soft nights fall over me
My eyes are plunged in darkness
I want to fly
Want to believe in miracles
Feel you within

I shy from light and darkness
Who knows what you see
Who knows what will happen
Silence, silence
growing wild

The days crumble, disappear
Leaving no trace
I am always awake, waiting
Feel you within
feel you within

I shy from light and darkness
Who knows what you see

Who knows what will happen
Silence, silence
growing wild

The following day Espen came over to me in the reading room and gave me the Mandelstam essay. We went for a coffee, chatted about our course, some writing that had impressed us, I asked him a few questions about himself, where he came from, what he did and I told him I had attended the Writing Academy. He knew, he said. He held the cup with both hands, but not in an embracing kind of way, more a confirmation by his hands, here we have a cup, while he held his head slightly lowered, staring straight down at the table. Sitting like this, it was as though he was negating the situation, as though it didn't exist. There was great strength in him, it gripped my insides, have I said something tedious? Something boring? Something stupid?

Then he cast a glance up at the clock, smiled and said he hoped I would enjoy the essay and he was looking forward to discussing it with me.

We went back to the reading room, I started Olof Lagercrantz's book about Dante and sat over it until the afternoon, when I went to the canteen to eat. It was Friday and they always had rice pudding.

Ann Kristin was sitting at a table on the first floor. She smiled when she saw me and I went over holding a tray of rice pudding, juice and coffee.

'Hi, Karl Ove,' she said. 'It's been a long time. Take a seat. This is Rolf, by the way.'

She nodded towards a man on the other side of the table.

'So you're Karl Ove,' he said. 'I had your father at *gymnas*. He's the best teacher I've ever had. He was fantastic.'

'Really?' I said. 'Where was that?'

'Vennesla.'

'Right,' I said and sat down, took the bowl of rice pudding, the cup of coffee and the glass of juice off the tray, pushed it away and started to eat.

'What's he doing now?'

'He's working in northern Norway. He's remarried and has a child.'

'Classic midlife crisis,' Ann Kristin said. 'Heard by the way that you went to Italy with Yngve.'

I nodded and swallowed.

'Florence.'

'Shame you couldn't be at the funeral.'

'Yes. How was it?'

'It was dignified and lovely.'

Ann Kristin was the eldest daughter of my mother's sister Kjellaug and Jon Olav's sister. In our childhood it had always been her and Yngve and Jon Olav and me, and that had continued during our studies, at least at first when Yngve and Ann Kristin had spent a lot of time together. But they had drifted apart, unless it had been prompted by a particular event, I wasn't aware of anything, I only knew they didn't meet outside family commitments any more.

She was a strong character and could appear a little brusque, especially with Jon Olav, but she didn't hold back with me either, not that I was afraid of her, it was just surface, underneath it all she was nice and more than usually considerate. I liked her, I always had done.

This Rolf, was he her boyfriend?

'Do you study Russian too?' I said.

He nodded.

'That was where we met,' he said.

'Rolf's the department's wunderkind,' Ann Kristin said.

'You weren't the boy who always got the top grade at *gymnas*, were you? Dad talked about it for a while.'

'I'm afraid so.' He smiled.

'You really were his favourite pupil,' I said.

'Yes, what do you expect?' said Ann Kristin. 'Of course the teacher likes someone who only gets top grades.'

'Not dad,' I said, to flatter him.

'Give him my best regards,' Rolf said.

'Will do,' I said.

'How's Yngve getting on?' Ann Kristin said. 'I haven't seen him for ages. Is he still with . . . what's her name . . .?'

'Ingvild?'

'Yes.'

'No, they finished this spring,' I said.

'She was so like your mother.'

'Was she?'

'Didn't you notice?'

'No. Where was the resemblance?' I said.

'The eyes, Karl Ove. They had the same eyes.'

She smiled and turned to Rolf, who raised his eyebrows and grabbed his jacket from the back of the chair.

'Can you manage on your own?' Ann Kristin said to me. 'Or should we stay and keep an eye on you?'

'Think I'll manage,' I said. 'Nice to see you both. Bye!'

They left by the door on the first floor, where corridors branched off to various other parts of the building, and I ate the rice pudding alone.

The following Sunday I met Gunvor. It was a coincidence, I had gone out with Yngve for a beer, he had been working, he met some people he knew, one of them invited us to his place, candles were lit, tea was served, quiet records were played. I sat on some kind of pouffe and was itching to leave when a girl sat down beside me. She was small, fair-haired with a small retroussé nose and beautiful gentle eyes. Her energy levels were high, her personality was winning.

'Who are you?' she said.

'I'm Yngve's brother,' I said.

'Well, that leaves me none the wiser. Who's Yngve?'

'The guy standing over there and flirting.'

'Oh. I haven't seen him before either. But, at any rate, it's not hard to see you're brothers!'

'No,' I said.

'What are you doing in Bergen then?'

'Lit.'

'Do you like Ragnar Hovland? He's my all-time favourite. *Suicide in Turtle Café*, just the title.'

'Yes, he's funny. What are you studying?'

'Admin and organisation theory. But I'm going to start history after Christmas.'

'History? I fancy doing that as well.'

She was open, but not in a naïve way, she wasn't the type to burst out with something she didn't understand, she was just very self-confident.

The others left one by one, we sat chatting, it was the kind of night when you could tell each other everything about yourself, and it is meaningful because there is also a common willingness to listen. She was from a farm in Vestland, she had two brothers and a sister, she loved riding, particularly Icelandic horses, she had worked for a year on an Icelandic farm and spoke Icelandic fluently. I asked her to say something in Icelandic, she said *Thad er ekki gott ad vita hver Karl Ove er!* It's not easy to know who Karl Ove is. I laughed, I had understood. She said Icelandic horses had two additional gaits, and I laughed again, I found it difficult to understand how you could be so passionate about animals. Try riding one yourself some time and you'll understand, she said.

We sat there until the guy whose flat it was wanted to go to bed. Then she accompanied me home, we talked the whole way, outside my front door for maybe half an hour, then she asked if we could see each other again, and I said yes, I would like that.

'Tomorrow?'

'Yes, great.'

'Shall we go to the cinema?'

'Yes, let's.'

She left, I went to bed, strangely light-headed.

Two weeks later she turned round on the steps going up to her place.

'We're going out together now, aren't we, Karl Ove?'

'Yes,' I said. 'I am anyway!'

By then we had spent almost every evening since we met with each other. Her place, my place, Café Opera, Fekterloftet, long walks through Bergen's streets. We talked and talked, one night we kissed, and then we spent the night together, but nothing happened, she wanted to wait, wanted to be certain about me. You can be certain about me, I said, because I was aching with desire, all the time, I was walking beside her doubled up, but no, time was on our side, time was a friend. An evil friend, I said, come on, how dangerous can it be? No, it wasn't dangerous, but she wanted to wait, she didn't know me. But I've shown you everything! There's nothing left to see! I'm so small! She laughed, shook her head, I would have to wait. Lying next to her hot naked body!

These were hard conditions, but everything else was like a fever, like a dream, she came and went, the rest was like dozing, unimportant, she gave the world shape and gravity, she, Gunvor, my girlfriend.

Jon Olav had moved into a big flat down by the cinema, I had introduced her to him long ago, now he was going to be away for a few days, we could use his flat if we wanted? Oh yes. We were there for two days and nights, we only went out for food, we couldn't be without each other, but still she wouldn't, she still didn't know me well enough.

Her youngest sister and boyfriend invited us to visit them in Hardanger, where they lived in a big old house. We caught the bus there, it was dark, the countryside was white with snow lit up by the moon, and above us, glittering in the sky, myriad stars. It was twenty degrees below zero, the snow creaked as we walked up the hills, the cold air burned in our lungs, the skin on our faces was rigid, and around us there was silence.

They had lit the fire, made dinner, we sat chatting and eating and drinking red wine, I was happy. We had a room up in the loft, it was freezing cold, even under the duvet, and my desire was so great that I didn't know what to do, I snuggled up to her, kissed her beautiful breasts, her beautiful stomach, her beautiful feet, but no, I had to wait, she didn't know me well enough, still didn't know who I was.

'I'm Karl Ove Knausgård and I want you!' I said then.

She laughed and she hugged me, she was so soft and supple, and her eyes were gentle, and she was mine.

But not completely, not fully, it was still just her and me, and not us.

I didn't read much during those weeks. It felt unimportant, but she went up to university every day, and so I did too, though mostly for appearance's sake, the sentences didn't make much sense to me, for everything was churning around, everything was open and undefined, until I saw her come and make the world secure and clear again. Her, Gunvor, my girlfriend.

Espen came over during a break, he asked if I had read the Mandelstam essay yet, I hadn't, I was thinking of reading *The Divine Comedy* first, he thought that wise.

'Which edition are you reading? The Nynorsk one? I started it, but it's so archaic it's pretty impossible. So I bought the Swedish version. It's very good.'

'I bought the Nynorsk edition,' I said. 'I'll have to see how I get on.'

His gaze, which had been open and innocent, suddenly turned stern and introspective and he directed it at the field down in front of us.

I hurriedly revisited what had just been said. After a while, with neither of us saying anything, he glanced up at me.

'Would you like to come to Alrek one afternoon? Then we can play chess or something. Do you play chess?'

'I know the rules,' I said. 'But I can't exactly say I play.'

'You can have a refresher,' he said.

'Yes, of course,' I said. 'But I'd like a trip over anyway.'

We arranged to meet the following afternoon. In the reading room I took out the translation of *Divina Commedia*, started reading without taking notes, whatever stuck would stick of its own accord. I knew a little of what it was about, I had read a third of Lagercrantz's Dante book and formed a clear impression of what it was like. Still, however, I wasn't prepared for the feeling of time I got from the first pages, for the book not being *about* the four-teenth century but actually *dating* from that century, it was a *part* of that century, and I was able to experience it *now*.

Lasciate ogni speranza, voi ch'entrate.

The gates of hell, Easter 1300. Dante, who has lost his way, in midlife, and who will find redemption by seeing all there is to see.

He will see everything and he will be redeemed.

But at the beginning of the first canto it wasn't in life where he had lost his way but in a forest, and the animals that attacked him were not sins or treachery, they were beasts of flesh and blood, baring their teeth and snarling. Hell wasn't an internal state, the entrance to it lay there, in the middle of the world, at the bottom of a precipice, surrounded by forest and wilderness on all sides.

I understood of course that the contents of the explanatory foot-notes, about what the individual animals and places and occur-rences represented, were real enough, but what was exceptional about the opening, which I felt in every cell of my body like a gnaw-ing hunger, was the concrete physical and material nature of it, not the shadows cast into the world of ideas. Something was com-pared with the building of a ship in a yard in Venice, and suddenly, with immense force, I realised that Dante must have been sitting somewhere and writing this, perhaps peering into the air and pondering what comparison he could draw, and then he remembered a shipyard he had seen once, in Venice, *which was still there as he wrote*.

I was supposed to meet Gunvor in the afternoon, I packed up my things and walked through the corridors dangling a plastic bag from my hand and into the courtyard between the buildings, I had stopped to have a smoke when I saw her coming towards me. She smiled with her whole body, she stretched up onto her toes and kissed me on the lips. We walked hand in hand, down the hills and over to Nøstet, where her bedsit was. She shared it with a girlfriend called Arnhild. Her best friend was Karoline, and on paper, with their ponderous unfashionable names, they were an intimidating trio – Gunvor, Arnhild and Karoline – but in reality they were happy and cheerful and wonderfully normal. Arnhild was at the Business School and wore lambswool sweaters and a pearl necklace, Karoline studied at university and was a few notches tougher, she was closer to Gunvor, they had the same sense of humour, they followed in each other's footsteps in the way that I gathered girlfriends did. Once she told us about the time a boy had tried to chat her up, he had come up to her and asked her if she wanted to go back to his place, she had asked why, he had said so that he could fuck her senseless. They laughed at that! They were dutiful and sensible, would never fritter away their lives, and the security of that meant that everything else around us had no effect on them. Going out on the town for them, for example, was enjoyable and there was absolutely nothing demonic about it.

Even though I lived alone in a relatively spacious bedsit we preferred to be at Gunvor's; my place was dark and gloomy and there was almost no furniture, hers was light, it was in good condition and moreover there was something girly and feminine about the furnishings, all their soft frilly unfamiliarity that I liked to be surrounded by, it was so clear that she was my girlfriend then. Waking up there, more often than not with the rain pelting down in the street, so early that it was still dark, having breakfast with them and going off to the reading room with her, was something I hadn't experienced before and I loved it with the whole of my black heart.

I introduced Gunvor to Yngve and Asbjørn and his other friends, who in a way had become mine too, or not friends exactly but at any rate people I was often with, by dint of being Yngve's younger brother, my safeguard in Bergen, and she was a great hit with them. That wasn't so strange, it was impossible not to like Gunvor, she always laughed at what others said, was sociable and affable, didn't take herself seriously, but nor was she frivolous, she worked hard at what she did and was no stranger to high seriousness, she also had a pietistic side to her, you had to work, you had to go to lectures, you had to read, only then did you deserve time off. But this sense of moral duty, which I also knew and regarded as an enemy, something I had to oppose, something that stood for the opposite of what I wanted to be, this sense of moral duty didn't weigh heavy on her, it didn't affect her personality, it was more like a kind of guiding line, thin and straight and strong, a sinew in her soul, not visible but important, it gave her strength and security, meant that she never doubted that where she was and what she was doing were right.

When I was with her it was as though something was being drawn out of me. The darkness became lighter, the crippled straighter, and the strange thing was that it didn't come from outside, it wasn't that she lit the darkness, no, it was something that happened inside me because I saw myself with her eyes, and not just my own, and in her eyes there was nothing wrong with me, quite the contrary. In this way the balance shifted. When I was with Gunvor I no longer wished to do myself any harm.

As arranged I hoofed over to Espen's the day after, up the hills behind the railway station, over the long flat stretch there, to Alrek, where I had been only once before, when as a sixteen-year-old I had visited Yngve four years ago.

Espen was cooking in the shared kitchen when I arrived. Chicken casserole with tomato, he said, want some?

It was heavily seasoned but good, he lit up when I said that.

Afterwards he made coffee in a strange shiny, almost sculpted, jug, it was shaped like a little man with a hat on, and Espen dismantled it first, poured water into one part, then poured fine-grained specialist coffee of some kind into a funnel-like contraption which he dropped into the water part, before screwing on the top half, which had a lid with a black ball in the centre, and put it on the hotplate. I had no intention of asking what kind of coffee it made, I would accept everything he served with a worldly air.

Each carrying a cup, we went to his room.

Oh, how strong it was, it tasted a bit like espresso.

Espen flicked through his records.

'Do you like jazz?' he said.

'Ye-es,' I said. 'I don't listen to so much, but it's OK.'

'Let's take a classic then, eh? *Kind of Blue*?'

'Fine by me,' I said, trying to read the cover to see who had made the recording. Miles Davis.

Espen sat down on the bed.

'I went to see him at a concert in Oslo. I didn't have a ticket, so I sneaked in.'

'You sneaked in? How did you manage that?'

'I went into the building next door, down to the cellar, where I found some chairs. I carried them to make it look as if I was working there. Then I opened a door, and there I was, in the middle of the auditorium.'

He laughed.

'Is that true?'

'Yes. It was a fantastic concert.'

Pale melancholic music began to float through the room. Espen took out his chess set, placed the board between us, grasped one

black and one white pawn in each hand, swapped them about
behind his back and then held his fists in front of me.

'That one,' I said.

He opened his fist. Black.

'I'm not quite sure how to set out the pieces,' I said. 'It's pawns
first, isn't it?'

'Yes,' he said, laying out his pieces in an instant. I copied him.

I hated chess, losing at chess felt to me much more significant
and revealing and humiliating than a game of tennis, for example.
I wasn't so intelligent, wasn't so smart, even if I strained my brain
so much smoke came out of my ears, I could never work it out,
could never plan more than two moves ahead, at least not when I
was small and played with dad or Yngve, who beat me every time.
I hadn't played since then, however, I was an adult now, I thought.
Maybe the experience I had acquired would benefit me in some
way or other. It was only problem-solving really.

'No stopwatch?' he said.

'No,' I said.

We started and three minutes later I was in checkmate.

'Do you want a return game?'

'OK.'

Three minutes later I was in checkmate again.

'Best of three. Then you've got a chance of turning things
round.'

'Can do.'

He crushed me for the third time. But I couldn't see a hint of
gloating in him as he packed away the set and silently set about
rolling a cigarette.

'Are you an active player then?' I said.

'Me? No. No, no. I just like it.'

'Do you read chess columns in the paper?'

'Sometimes, yes. It can be incredibly interesting to follow the
moves in old games between the masters.'

'Oh yes,' I said.

'But there are some standard moves you can learn. Openings and so on. I can show you if you'd like.'

I nodded.

'Shall we do it next time?'

'Yes.'

Outside, the sun was shining through the clouds. The light that fell diagonally through the air made the colours in the country-side beneath seem shrill in comparison with the matt-grey surroundings.

'What books do you actually like reading? In modern Norwegian literature?' he said.

'Bit of everything,' I said. 'Kjærstad, Fløgstad, Jon Fosse. All sorts of books really. What about you?'

'A broad range too. But Øyvind Berg is good. Tor Ulven is fantastically good. Ole Robert Sunde, have you read anything by him? A whole novel about the main character, who walks to a kiosk and back. *Odyssey*, right? His language goes in all directions. It's enormously digressive, almost essayistic. You should read it.'

'I've heard about it,' I said. 'Think there was something in *Vinduet* once.'

'Then there's Ekelöf of course. And Jan Erik Vold! *Enthusiastic Essays*. I think that's my favourite book. It's so unbelievably rich. Have you seen it?'

I shook my head. He jumped up and went through one of the piles of books on his desk, passed me a fat blue book with a picture on the cover of Vold swimming.

'There,' he said. 'He writes about all sorts. Not just literature. Loads about jazz and . . . well.'

'Great,' I said, leafing through it.

The music had stopped, he took the record off the deck.

'What shall we play now?' he said.

'I don't know,' I said.

'Flick through and see if there's anything you like.'

'OK,' I said, kneeling down.

Would you believe it, he had *Heaven Up Here*!

'Do you like Echo and the Bunnymen?' I said.

'Yes, certainly do. Ian McCulloch has a wonderful voice. And he's so fantastically arrogant.'

'Can we play that one? Perhaps it's a bit pathetic. After all I've got it myself, but it's so good.'

'Yes, go on. It's a long time since I've listened to it.'

When I left an hour later, down the hills shining in the wan November light, I was full of tensions. Espen was the kind of person you noticed. He had a strong presence, and as I was so weak I picked up all the different moods he radiated and probably didn't register himself. There was also something introspective about him, sometimes it was as if his gaze didn't leave his eyes, it stayed where it was, inside, making it seem hard and irreconcilable, but when it let go he was openness in person, friendliness itself, in a way that I wasn't sure he registered either, because his enthusiasm seemed to take over and actually he was just following the currents inside him.

I was impressed by him, not least because he was two years younger than me. What I couldn't work out though, as I walked along, was why he had invited me of all people to his place. Our department was full of interesting and well-read students and he had turned to the one person who had no depth and no insight into literature.

But I was glad he had. If I couldn't live up to expectations right now I might be able to do so eventually.

At home there was a letter protruding from the crack between the door and the frame. I opened it. It was a notice to move. Owing to renovation work I would have to be out before the middle of December.

Was that legal?

Oh shit. I was living way beyond my means anyway. It was just as well. But I would have to get out and look for new accommodation.

I went to bed early, but woke to the sound of someone banging on the window. I got up and went over. It was Gunvor. She smiled and pointed to the door, I nodded and went to open up.

Five minutes later she crawled into the narrow bed beside me and the fullness of her breasts against my hands made my body explode with desire.

'Not yet,' she said. 'But soon.'

I was more than lucky with the accommodation problem. It turned out that Jon Olav's friend Ben had just moved out of a large four-room flat by Danmarksplass and no one had moved in yet. It had formerly belonged to the shipyard in Solheimsviken, it was an extension of the office buildings there and was now owned by a bank. I rang them, yes, the flat was free, I could move in, but I ought to know that the whole building was due to be demolished soon and I would have to be able to move out at a month's notice. When would that be? Well, she didn't know, not in the immediate future at any rate. I accepted, and one evening Gunvor and I went there, we were met by Ben and he showed us around the four rooms. There had been a whole gang of them living there, but the rent was so low that two could easily make ends meet. Originally there had been two flats: one with two rooms behind the kitchen and one with two rooms behind the bathroom. There were wall-to-wall carpets on the floors, they could be removed, apparently there were attractive wooden boards underneath, the windows were single-glazed, filthy from car fumes and the traffic noise from the flyover was tangible, but according to Ben you got used to it. The general condition of the place wasn't good, the kitchen was old, the stove looked to be from the early 1960s, but there was a shower cabinet in the bathroom and the rent, as Ben reminded me, was low.

I was given the keys and he left.

Together with Gunvor I walked around the rooms once more. We hugged in the middle of the floor of what I had just decided would be the sitting room in my part.

'Don't you want to move in with me then?' I said.

'No,' she said. 'Absolutely not! But perhaps one day. Who knows what might happen!'

'Then I'll have to get hold of someone to live here. Do you know anyone who needs somewhere to live?'

'No. But I can keep my ear to the ground. No girls, that's all. I daren't take any risks.'

'You? You've got nothing to fear. Is that how you think? Is that true?'

She went over to the window. I followed her, stood behind her, kissed her neck and gently fondled her breasts.

'What's your favourite?' she said.

'Eh?'

'Food. What's your favourite food?'

'Shrimps, I think. Why?'

'I was just wondering.'

I pulled up the carpet in one room, cleaned away all the remnants of glue, levelled any uneven bits and painted it green like a ship's deck. The few pieces of furniture I possessed Yngve brought in a van we hired, I would buy anything else I needed from Ikea when my study loan came in. He told me he had organised a rehearsal room, it was at Verftet, we could use it two nights a week. Fired up with enthusiasm, we talked about songs, lyrics and getting hold of a vocalist. The following day we met in a café at Verftet. Me with two pairs of drumsticks, him with a guitar case, Pål with a bass gig bag. I was nervous, I hadn't played the drums since the early days at *gymnas*, and I couldn't do much except for the absolute basics. Yngve was aware of this, it was less easy with Pål, who was probably expecting a proper jam session with three musicians.

'Actually, I can't play,' I said. 'Did Yngve tell you? I only fiddled around on the drums when I was at *gymnas*. Absolutely hopeless I am. But I can learn.'

'Relax, Yngve Junior,' Pål said. 'It'll be fine.'

Pål was tall and thin and pale with dark hair and a slightly childish attitude to life. He wasn't exactly afraid to show his little quirks, it was more like he cultivated them. He was an eccentric and in Bergen was famous for having read poems during the student demos with bells in his hair. He read a little, shook his head to make the bells ring, then read a bit more. Explosion of cheering. He played in an experimental band that emerged from the Shit Tape cassette label in Arendal, they were called the Coalmine Five after the politician Kullmann Five presumably, he loved everything that was odd, weird, way out. Yngve and he had been in the same class at their first school, I had heard his name all my life, but I had only met him in the last year. He had published two collections of poetry through his own publishing house and was studying marine biology. In his early youth he had played with the Salvation Army, and as a bass player, Yngve said, he wasn't your steady plodder but melodious, inventive, an improviser. It was obvious from the very first moment we started to play that he knew his stuff. That is, from the first moment they started to play. I was fazed. I sat on the chair with the drumsticks in my hand, behind the kit, all the drums and cymbals, the two of them standing on either side playing, and I didn't dare make a move, I was too afraid of messing up.

They played 'You Sway So Sweetly'. Pål tried various fingerings, he was searching for something, and once he had it, it stayed while he went off on other forays, came back with new lines and then he was off again until he was happy and the song was in place.

Yngve stopped and looked at me.

'Come on then,' he said.

'Play yourselves in,' I said. 'Then I can hear how it goes.'

They did. When they were about halfway I tentatively started to play. I should be able to keep the beat anyway, even if not much else was right.

'That was good, Karl Ove,' Pål said. 'But try to get the bass drum to fall in with the bass. I can mark it for you. DUM dum DUM DUM dum. OK?'

'And play a bit louder,' Yngve said. 'We can hardly hear you.'

I blushed and played and hoped this would soon be over. Pål looked at me and his whole upper body rose whenever the beat on the bass drum was imminent. After a while he turned away and just played, but then there was eye contact and raised shoulders again.

We continued for two hours with the same song, over and over again. It was all about getting me on board, of course they had it off pat. After we had finished for the day and they were starting to roll up the cables and pack the boxes and straps, my shirt was drenched.

'You'd better find someone else,' I said.

'Not at all,' said Yngve. 'It'll be great.'

'That went really well,' Pål said. 'I don't know what you're talking about. All we need now is a vocalist and a name for the band. I suggest Misc M. Then we'll always have our own section in record shops.'

'I was thinking of Odd & Bent,' Yngve said. 'That works in both English and Norwegian.'

'Sounds like a description of a dick,' I said.

'Speak for yourself,' Yngve said.

'He is. He's talking about his own syphilitic dick.' Pål laughed.

'What about Mao?' I said. 'I was toying with that. Short and sweet.'

'Troubled Waters,' Pål said. 'That's good too. Now we have to pour oil on troubled waters! Either of you know what troubled waters are actually?'

'No,' I said. 'Beside me in the reading room is someone with a great name. I wondered about this. He's called Finn Iunker. We could just use the name of someone we don't know, couldn't we?

Finn Iunker and something or other. Finn Iunker and the Sea-
planes, for example?'

'Not bad,' Yngve said. 'I wondered about Smith and the
Smudgers.'

'Or what about Ethnic Cleansing Cream?' said Pål.

Yngve laughed so much he had to walk around the room to
recover.

'Or Holocaustic Soda?' I said.

'Kafkatrakterne?' Pål said, wriggling his shoulders to get the
bass strap to sit better. 'Kafkatrakterne!'

'Mm,' Yngve said. 'Not Coffee Machines but Kafka Machines.
Yes, I like it.'

'Kafkatrakterne it is,' I said. 'It's great!'

The last two bedsits I'd had were at street level and all I had seen
from them was passing heads and umbrellas. The new flat was
quite different. It was at the top of an old brick building, and from
the sitting room there was a view of the big flyover in Danmarksplass, the offices behind, the big old cinema, the new REMA 1000
supermarket and on the opposite side of the road the bookshop
where I had in my, now incomprehensible, naïvety and immaturity bought *Hunger*. A crowd of alkies used to sit on the benches
by the little car park outside the supermarket, there was a taxi
rank – it took me a couple of nights to realise that was where the
low ringing sound I heard came from, the phone was going almost
all the time – and the road was one everyone used to get in and
out of the town centre, so there was always something happening. In addition, the hospital was close by, and a regular stream
of ambulances, with and without sirens and blue lights, weaved
through the traffic day and night. For me this was a rewarding
sight, I often stood looking out of the windows, like a cow out of
a stall, because I was empty inside then, I registered movements
and followed what was happening, that was all. Look, a pickup

carrying a long plank on the back with a white neckerchief tied around the end! A lorry full of braying sheep, what on earth was this, was I in Yugoslavia all of a sudden? A lady with a fox stole around her neck, the kind where the head is intact, obviously insane, her stiff, rigid movements were unmistakable, she strode first down one side of the street, then back up the other. A group of at first three, then four and five, men gathering by the end of the hill up from the subway at half past three in the morning, what skulduggery were they up to? Woman gives man an earbashing, man gives woman an earbashing, countless variations on that theme. I also saw quite a number of swaying figures, sometimes in such a dire state that I couldn't believe my own eyes, people staggering along the middle of the three-lane motorway, people losing their balance and running to one side, stopping when they regained it, running to the other side, just like we had done when we were children pretending to be drunks, copying what we had seen in silent films we were shown at parties.

Another improvement on my previous accommodation was the telephone that had been installed. I had the line connected and now had my very own number.

Gunvor was the first to ring.

'Will you be at home tomorrow?' she asked after we had been chatting for a while.

'If you come I will be.'

We agreed she would come at twelve-ish. At twelve sharp she rang the bell. She had a carrier bag in her hand.

'I've bought some shrimps,' she said. 'They didn't have any fresh ones, I'm afraid, so these are frozen.'

She took them out, a plastic bag of frozen Greenland shrimps, which I put on a dish so that they would thaw faster. She had also bought some butter, mayonnaise, a loaf and a lemon.

'Is this a special day or what?' I said.

She smiled and looked down, and I suddenly twigged. Today was the day. We hugged, went into the bedroom, I slowly undressed her, we lay down on the mattress by the wall. One leg kept trembling. The light from the overcast sky filled the room, fell over our white bodies, her face, her eyes constantly watching me.

Afterwards we showered together and then we went to see how the shrimps were doing, we were strangely shy with each other, as though we had suddenly become two strangers. But this didn't last long, the gap closed, soon we were chatting as if nothing had happened, until our eyes met and once again the atmosphere became charged with seriousness. It was as though we were seeing each other for the first time. We were the same, but the non-committal nature of our relationship had become committal in a way that changed everything. We gazed at each other in an intense serious way, then her face dissolved into a smile, shall we eat your shrimps now?

This was the first time a glimpse of the future had shown itself in our relationship. Now it really was us, and what did that mean?

I was twenty years old, she was twenty-two, of course we would just continue as before. There was nothing to plan, everything came of its own accord. So far we had spent almost all of our time together, we were discovering each other, there was so much we had to tell each other about our lives, as well as everything else going on around us, while also doing things. We weren't conscious of what we were doing or why, at least I wasn't, hardly any of the others I knew were either. Everyone went to the cinema now and then, and to the Film Club, everyone went to Café Opera or Hulen, everyone went around visiting everyone else, everyone bought records and everyone went to the odd gig. Everyone slept with everyone else, or wanted to, either casually after a night out or on a regular basis, like those in a relationship. Occasionally a child was born, but that was an absolute rarity, a peculiarity, becoming a parent in our twenties as so many of our parents' generation had done was a no-no. Many students went up Mount Fløyen or Mount Ulriken at the weekend, I didn't, I drew the line there, I would never be one for the outdoor life, and Gunvor wasn't either, or at least she restricted that part of her life to a minimum. Not much more than that happened, yet I experienced it as rich and meaningful in the sense that I never questioned it, there were no alternatives, in more or less the same way that people never questioned a horse and cart in the centuries before the car was invented. And somehow it was rich too, and full of significance, because every one of the tiny arenas of interest contained an unending wealth of nuances and distinctions, a band was not just a band, for example, it carried with it a multitude of other details, and there were thousands of them. A literature student was not only a literature student, although it probably looked like that from a distance, once you got closer to one, as I did with Espen, each and every one of them was their own complete world, there were hundreds of them, and of students, thousands. Then there were all the books that existed and all the knowledge they contained, as well as their interconnections. There were millions of them. Bergen was a tract of land and it wasn't just rain that fell onto it, there was also everything that was thought and done throughout the world that found its way here, to the foundations of this town in whose streets we walked. 808 State released *808:90*, the Pixies *Doolittle*, Neneh Cherry *Raw Like Sushi*, the Golden Palominos *A Dead Horse*, Raga Rockers *Blaff*. People were beginning to buy their own computers. There was talk of a new Norwegian commercial TV channel which might be based in Bergen. Raga Rockers played at Maxine, Arvid shouted 'Hey, that's Yngve' as a guy ran onto the stage and threw himself into the audience. It was so unlike him and everyone laughed. I read *The Divine Comedy* in the Nynorsk translation, wrote an assignment on it, which I presented on Buvik's course, gave a forty-five-minute talk, which I had been dreading for several weeks, but it went well, at least according to Espen. Buvik said that I used Lagercrantz as a crutch, but that was allowed, and after that he would sometimes pick on me during lectures, apparently keen to hear my opinion on

this or that. I blushed and mumbled and was so uncomfortable
it must have been glaringly obvious, but I was also proud it was
me he had asked. I liked Buvik, I liked his style, the easily kin-
dled enthusiasm, despite the fact that he had been a lecturer for
many years and we were on the bottom rung of the hierarchy. He
had short fair hair, round glasses, always dressed elegantly, was a
good-looking man with a tinge of effeminacy about his gestures
and body language, but he had obtained his doctorate in France, as
far as I was led to believe, and I suspected it was predominantly an
expression of his refinement, manners that were so perfect they
were reflected in his body language. Linneberg was his opposite in
so many ways: he spoke a kind of self-constructed working-class
Oslo dialect, made a great point of it, had a ring in his ear, a great
big head, his smile was often sardonic, and he liked to wear guises,
such as the time he gave a lecture wearing a clown's red nose
or when he held forth wearing a monkey mask. If he had to talk
about Brecht he did it puffing on a huge cigar. Both of them had
immense power over us, they were important figures and if they
went to one of the first-year parties they could pick up any girl
they wanted, I often thought about that, there was always an energy in the room when they lectured and it wasn't just intellectual
curiosity and a thirst for knowledge from the students' side. They
had such high status it was as if the gods had descended from
Mount Olympus to sit among us in the canteen. Which, of course,
they never did. That Buvik had asked me a question twice during a
lecture was a sign of favour from the Sun God in my eyes. I didn't
know what the others thought, with them I exchanged very few
words, apart from Espen and Ole. But I was beginning to get a
hold on the subject, I wrote another assignment, about Fløgstad's
aesthetics, and reckoned in fact I had cracked the code. Academic
writing was actually about hiding what you didn't know. There
was a language, a technique, and I had mastered it. In everything
there were gaps which language could cover over as long as you

had acquired the know-how. I had, for instance, never read Adorno, knew practically nothing about the Frankfurt School, just the snippets I had picked up here and there, but in an assignment I could manoeuvre the little knowledge I actually had in such a way as to make it appear greater and more comprehensive. Another technique that was held in high regard was the ability to transfer knowledge from one field to another, preferably in a surprising way, this too was simple, all you had to do was build a bridge between them and then your work seemed to have a new original element, even though actually there was nothing new or original in it. It didn't have to be brilliant, nor even particularly good, because all it was intended to do was provide evidence that you thought for yourself, had your own opinions, besides of course showing that you had knowledge of the topic.

These practice assignments on Dante and Fløgstad I called essays when I talked about them. I've just written an essay about Fløgstad, by the way. In the essay about Dante, you know, I wrote about . . .

One day I was standing smoking under the Arts Block roof with Espen as the rain poured down from the leaden sky, there was something about him, a kind of heightened wariness, and it was on the tip of my tongue to ask him directly what it was when he suddenly glanced at me.

'I was thinking of applying to the Writing Academy,' he said.

'Oh?' I said. 'That's great! I didn't even know you wrote. Though I did have a suspicion. Heh heh.'

'I was wondering if you would mind casting an eye over something I've written. I'm not quite sure what I should send in. Or if there's any point.'

'Not at all,' I said.

'I've got some texts with me today actually. You can have them afterwards if you want.'

When he gave me the texts later that day it was with the utmost discretion. We were like spies and the texts were secret documents concerning not only the security of our own country but all the countries in the NATO pact. A plastic folder came out of his bag, it was passed behind our backs, half hidden, we were standing next to each other, then popped into my carrier bag with the same fleetness of hand. Once the transfer was complete we talked about something else.

Being a writer was no great disgrace, quite the opposite, in literature it represented the supreme, the highest pinnacle of achievement, but it was shameful to boast about it because almost everyone wrote and until your writing had appeared in a journal or, oh bliss, had been published, it was basically nothing, non-existent, and if you needlessly revealed this fact you lost face, you showed you didn't want to be here but somewhere else, that you had a dream which, and this was the crux of the matter, probably wouldn't come to fruition. Until there was any evidence to the contrary, what literature students wrote was for the desk drawer. The situation was a little different for me, I had been to the Writing Academy and had a 'right to write', but if I displayed my work, and it was poor, I would immediately lose all credibility.

So it was important to be cautious. What Espen gave me in deepest secrecy was, on the one hand, 'nothing', that is, invisible and had to be treated as such; on the other hand, for Espen it was probably more important, indeed, *much* more important than a document regarding the security of NATO pact countries.

I treated it with the respect and dignity it warranted. I didn't open the folder until I got home and was completely alone. After I had read the texts, which were poems, I regretted not having said to Espen that I was no good even if I had attended the Writing Academy course, actually I was a fraud because I could immediately see that the poems were good, I recognised the mark of quality from the first line, but I was incapable of saying a word about them. About why they were good, about how they could be better. I could only say they were good.

But he didn't notice, didn't ask for further comment, he was happy I had liked them.

One weekend I took Gunvor home to meet mum, who had moved to a house in Jølster, fifteen kilometres outside Førde. It was old and nice, situated on a small plain below some big farms on slopes leading up to high mountains. On the other side of the road was the River Jølstra. We caught a bus which stopped only a hundred metres from mum's house, freezing mist hung over the river as we walked up, mum was waiting with a hot meal, she came into the hall as we tramped in, they shook hands and smiled, I was a little tense but not as tense as Gunvor, she had been dreading this meeting for ages and talked a lot about it on the journey there. She was the first girlfriend I had brought home since I was sixteen, the first real girlfriend since I had grown up and, for all we knew, the last. It was important that mum liked her for both Gunvor and me.

She did, of course. There were no signs of tension or nervousness to be seen in Gunvor, she was herself, as always, and they soon warmed to each other. I noticed their mutual regard and was happy about that and about being able to show Gunvor the easy relationship mum and I had, and always had had. Gunvor witnessed me having long conversations, and in this way, in this context – in which I was also somehow closer to Gunvor – she saw the person I was when mum and I were together, more real, less ambivalent.

The fire crackled, we sat around the table chatting. Outside, in the freezing-cold river landscape, cars rushed past in the distance.

'What a fantastic mother you have,' she said when we went to bed.

'She likes you,' I said.

'Do you think so?'

'Yes, it's easy to see.'

The following day we all went up to see Borghild, grandma's sister. She had curly white hair, a plump body with big upper arms and wore thick glasses which made her eyes look frighteningly large. A long-time widow, she had a mind as sharp as a razor, latched onto the most surprising stories from all over the world and was always quick to condemn whatever she didn't like.

She stared shamelessly at Gunvor for a few seconds when they met.

'So this is a visit from the young students!' she said. We sat down in her little sitting room, there were piles of magazines on the table with a large magnifying glass on top, she went into the kitchen and saw to some pancakes and coffee, which were served five minutes later with a long list of apologies for the paucity of the offering.

'Borghild's responsible for the catering at weddings in this district,' mum told Gunvor.

'Well, I was once,' she said.

'The last time was no more than six months ago, wasn't it?' mum said with a smile.

'Yes, but that was nothing,' she said. 'Weddings now are not what they used to be. They used to last three days!'

Mum asked about various relatives and Borghild replied.

'Grandma came from the farm down there,' I said to Gunvor, and she stood up to see. I stood behind her. I controlled the impulse to cup my hands around her breasts, which always announced itself when I was standing behind her, and placed my hand on her shoulder instead.

'When I was growing up we still had sixteenth-century buildings there,' Borghild said.

I glanced at her and my spine froze.

The sixteenth century, that wasn't long after Dante.

'But they were demolished, all of them.'

'Has the same family lived there all that time?' I said.

'Yes, I rather think they have,' she said.

I hadn't been there often and I didn't even know the names of all grandma's sisters, knew nothing about their parents except that he, my great-grandfather that is, had been an avid Bible reader and had not only worked long hard hours but also enjoyed toil more than anything else. My great-grandmother, Borghild's mother and mum's grandmother, I knew nothing about. She had given birth to eleven children, she had lived down below, that was the extent of my knowledge. I had a bad conscience about knowing so little, it felt as if it was my responsibility, if I was so ignorant I didn't deserve to be called a relative.

I determined that one day I would go up to see Borghild on my own and write down whatever she told me, not just for my sake, to get to know more about my family, but because all the knowledge she possessed was interesting in itself.

We drove home alongside the big silent deep lake where Borghild told us fishermen used to sweep the waters with cocks; wherever the cocks crowed they got out their fishing tackle. Outside, it was pitch black. Apart from the road and the trees or the water beside them, which all lay beneath the yellow light of the street lamps, only the snow-clad mountain peaks were visible. It was a starry sky, everything felt open and spacious.

The bus back to Bergen left at four in the morning, we stayed awake till then and were waiting at the stop, stamping our feet to keep warm, when it arrived, thundering around the bends above us. We slept leaning against each other for the four and a half hours the journey lasted, surrounded by the thrum of the heater, the drone of the engine, the occasional cough from other passengers, the door opening and closing, all in a distant dream, the characteristic sounds of vehicles boarding ferries, the silence afterwards, when the monotony of the road takes over.

We walked straight up to the university from the bus station, said bye, I read for a few hours, then Yngve came and asked me to join him in the canteen, he had good news. At the weekend he had been staying in a cabin in the mountains with some people from Student Radio, one of them had sung and played the guitar, Yngve said he had such a good voice that he had asked him straight out if he wanted to be in a band. He did. We would go out one night, all four of us, and get to know one another, they had agreed. His name was Hans and he came from Geiranger, studied history and liked Neil Young, that was all Yngve knew.

We met him at Garage, the new rock scene which consisted of a small room and a long bar on the ground floor and a big dark basement beneath with a stage. They had started booking a number of good English and American bands as well as many from Bergen, where bands were springing up everywhere, Mona Lisa Overdrive were indisputably the best, Pogo Pops came a good second.

From Yngve's brief description I had expected a rough-looking guy with a lumberjack shirt, torn jeans, sturdy boots, tousled hair and wild eyes, it was the Neil Young reference that did it, but the young man who came in through the door holding a dripping closed umbrella in one hand and whose eyes immediately sought Yngve's had nothing in common with the phantom I had conjured up, and it disappeared the instant he came over to our table.

'Hans,' he said, proffering his hand. 'You must be Yngve's younger brother and the drummer.'

'That's me,' I said.

He removed his glasses and wiped off the moisture.

'We're waiting for Pål,' Yngve said.

'I'll get myself a beer in the meantime,' he said, and went towards the bar. Someone put The Clash's 'London Calling' on the jukebox and my spine tingled, that was a good sign.

'This has all the potential for being a legendary moment,' Yngve said when he returned. 'The night the vocalist met the rest of Kafkatrakterne for the first time.'

'We'd seen one another at art school but didn't like what we saw,' Hans said. 'Perhaps we even got into a fight. But then the guitarist heard me sing and had a vision that would redefine the course of rock history.'

'While the drummer said nothing and the bassist arrived late,' Yngve said.

'Drummers don't have to say anything,' Hans said. 'Theirs is the most important function in the band. They're supposed to be silent and tough. To drink a lot, say little and fuck loads.'

'Actually I'm silent and soft,' I said. 'Hope you can still use me.'

'You don't look soft,' Hans said. 'But if you insist, OK. It's good to have variations on this theme. Tiny unexpected details which make it that bit more exciting. On the other hand, there is the Charlie Watts type. The gentleman who stays with his wife and plays jazz in his spare time. Spot of gardening and so on.'

'I can't play, either,' I said. 'Yngve probably didn't tell you, but I'm afraid it's true.'

'This could be interesting,' Hans said.

'*Skål*,' Yngve said. 'To Kafkatrakterne!'

We raised our glasses, drank up, went downstairs and watched the band playing for a while, Pål eventually turned up and we hung around the bar chatting. I said nothing, it was the others who did the chatting, but I was still part of it, I didn't feel I was on the outside.

Hans had played in bands all his life, from what I could understand. He wrote in the student newspaper *Studvest*, made programmes for Student Radio, was interested in politics, against the EU, wrote in Nynorsk, was confident but not in the least bit boastful, that lay as far from his character as it was possible to be. He had a strong sense of irony, liked to make jokes, often with a dangerous sting in the tail, but his presence was usually so friendly that the danger was somehow neutralised. I really liked him, he was a good person. Whether he liked me or not was a different matter. The little I said came from the bottom of a deep well, dark and somehow quaking.

When Garage closed and the evening was over I didn't go home but to Gunvor's. She had moved to one of the apartment blocks near Bystasjonen and rented a room in the loft. I let myself in with the key I had been given, she lifted her head a fraction and smiled through the hair covering half her face and asked if I'd had a good time. Yes, I said, and lay down beside her. She went back to sleep at once, I lay awake studying the ceiling and listening to the occasional traffic in the streets, the rain falling on the roof and the skylights. There was little I enjoyed more than coming here after I had been out on the town, having a place that wasn't mine but where I was welcome, where I could cuddle up to her and feel her bare skin against mine. Now and then I wondered if she felt the same, if she lay awake feeling my bare skin against hers with her soul at peace. The notion was alien, almost scary, because then I was viewing myself with her eyes while knowing who I was myself.

The clock radio came on, I opened my eyes drowsily, Gunvor got up and went to the bathroom in the hall, I closed my eyes, heard the faint hiss of the shower, the rumble of the traffic on the road past Bystasjonen, fell asleep, woke up to her standing there putting on first her bra, then a blouse and a pair of trousers.

'Are you going to have breakfast?' she said.

'No,' I said. 'I'm going to sleep a bit more.'

Then, apparently the next moment, she leaned over and kissed me on the cheek in her waterproof trousers and jacket.

'I'm off. See you this afternoon?'

'OK,' I said. 'Can you come to my place?'

'Yes. Bye!'

She vanished as if in a dream, into the wet streets of Bergen, beneath its grey sky, while I stayed in bed until eleven. Instead of going to the reading room I spent the day in town. Went into all the second-hand shops and bookstores, bought some records and some old paperbacks as well as a brand new novel that Else Karin from the Academy had just brought out. It was called *Out*, the cover was white with a picture of a woman kneeling, half of her was naked and the other dressed in a harlequin costume. I had no expectations, I only bought it because I knew the author and was curious to see how her style compared with what I had written.

On the back, it said JEALOUSY – ILLNESS – INSANITY?

My goodness.

I went into the café with all the old people and sat down to read. On the second page, no less, came the bombshell. It was about me!

You never came near, Karl Ove.
The jury agrees with me.
Your fingers were absent, just ask us.
You didn't get my juices on you
unless you lied.

I read on, ploughed through the pages scanning for my name. Ay, yay, yay.

Karl Ove, you'll have to come and love me.

Karl Ove, you didn't come near me.

You were a disaster, Karl Ove –
and I was already so thin.

Lots about dicks and wombs, I noticed. Screams and ovaries being injected. Whipping and burning. Nothing short of a cabinet of horrors. *One day you might understand, Karl Ove,* I read. *Hell, Karl Ove,* I read. Then suddenly in lower case, *why, karl ove, why did you have to love me.*

I put the book to the side and gazed down at Torgalmenningen. I realised of course this wasn't about me, yet I was shaken, it was impossible to read my name with complete neutrality, and it certainly wasn't neutral either, because she had chosen it, the name of someone she had attended a course with last year, and not another name, one that wouldn't have been a problem, there was no shortage of names.

On the other hand, I thought, this was a good story, one I could tell people. I went to the Writing Academy and although I might not have made my debut afterwards at least I became a character in a book. *Karl Ove has tossed and turned and been afraid. It's beautiful outside – Karl Ove knows – and he grabs the pole and closes the blinds tight, so tight, and the sun and the spruce trees are gone. Today he won't touch a drop of alcohol.*

That evening we practised with Hans. The first thing he did was to translate my lyrics into Nynorsk. They sounded good, better than before. He also had a couple of songs with him, we began to work on one of them, 'Home Father Nation'. Afterwards we went into the hall at the back of the factory where there was a stage and a couple of local bands were going to play. As the lights were lowered and the first band was about to start, to my astonishment, I saw Morten walk across the stage and take the mike.

Morten!

Thin and dressed in black, he stood there holding the microphone stand with both hands as he sang. I couldn't believe my eyes. The last time I saw him, when we were living in the same house only six months ago, he had been a conventional, though unusually open and sensitive, Østlander; now there he was singing on the stage, his body language not unlike Michael Krohn's, full of devil-may-care assurance. He sang like Michael Krohn as well, and the band played like the Raga Rockers, so that wasn't good, they had no originality of their own, but from where I was standing that wasn't the point, it was the metamorphosis Morten had undergone.

He was studying history, he said when I met him afterwards. Though mostly he was playing with his band. And you? he said. Have you made your debut yet? No, I said, I can't say I have, everything went to pot. But now I'm playing in a band too. Kafkatrakterne.

He laughed at that and disappeared into the enormous space that had arisen between us now that we were no longer neighbours.

At the beginning of January I finally managed to find someone to move into the second bedsit which I had been paying for until then. His name was Jone, he came from Stavanger and was the ex of Kari, Asbjørn's new girlfriend. He worked for an oil company, had his own little record enterprise on the side, organised record fairs, now he had been given a leave of absence to study at the Business School and was more than happy to live with me. I was pleased about that, didn't give the poor state of the flat a thought until the evening when he parked a white van outside and I went down to help him carry up the furniture.

'Hi, Karl Ove!' he said, although we had never seen each other before, and I realised he was the extrovert type.

Red hair, pale skin, somewhat torpid movements.

'Hi,' I mumbled back. I wouldn't have dreamed of using his first name until I knew him properly.

'What sort of a hovel is this?' he said, looking up at the filthy decaying brick facade.

'Cheap,' I said.

'I'm only teasing,' he laughed. 'Come on. Can you give me a hand with the heavier stuff?'

He opened the doors, put on some gloves and climbed into the back of the van. Everything was top quality, I could see. A decent waterbed, a decent sitting-room table, a decent sofa, a large TV and a fantastic stereo. We started with the bed. After we had man-oeuvred it upstairs and into his room I had such a bad conscience I could barely look him in the eye. The two draughty rooms with the old kitchen and the old bathroom would be no good for him, I should have spelled out what sort of flat it was he was moving into, but now it was too late, now he was here and looking around. But he said nothing, we carried up one piece of furniture after the other, one box after the other, he joked and laughed, which it soon became clear was how he was, and he didn't appear to be bothered by the poor standard of the accommodation, which was all I could think about. By the next day he had unpacked and organised everything, and what his part of the flat said was, there is something out of kilter here: an elderly man in a spanking new discotheque, an old biddy dressed and made up like a young woman, a rotten tooth with a new white cap.

But he liked where he was. And I liked him, knowing he was there on the other side of the hall was good, and bumping into him in the morning and evening was good too, I was never alone somehow, although we had little to do with each other beyond that.

A few weeks later I discovered that the flat beneath mine was free. I told Espen, with whom I had spent more and more time that winter, and suggested he ring the landlord, the bank, that is, and ask them if he could move in. They said yes and only a few days later we were neighbours. He was the frugal type, he wan-dered around town searching for skips full of old furniture, used whatever he found to furnish his whole flat, which was identical to mine except that it was totally separate from the adjacent one and his toilet was in the hall and as cold and draughty as all the oth-er student toilets in this town, where not one flat or bedsit could have been done up since the early 1940s. His coffee table consisted of aircrete blocks with a board across, the rest of the furniture was old but fully functional, and the overall impression when you entered was brilliant, what with all the books he had accumulated.

This was my life now. I was twenty-one years old, doing the first year of a literature course, I had a stranger living next door to me, I had a friend I still didn't really know on the floor beneath and a girlfriend. I knew nothing, but I was getting better and better at pretending I did. I had a brother who allowed me into his world. In addition, there were Jon Olav and Ann Kristin, whom I met occasionally, and Kjartan, who had moved to Bergen and started studying when grandma died. I saw him now and then in the canteen at the Student Centre, where he stuck out, forty years old and grey-haired as he was, alone at a table, surrounded by youth on all sides. I also saw him in the canteen at Sydneshaugen, he was often sitting with others from his course, all young, and the glint he'd had in his eyes when he pontificated on all his philosophers at home in Sørbøvåg was gone. It was still Heidegger and Nietzsche, the Pre-Socratics and Hölderlin, at least when he talked to me, but for him they were no longer the future, as they had been when everything in his life gathered around this burning point.

I had no future either, not because it existed somewhere else but because I couldn't imagine it. That I might control my future and try to make it turn out the way I wanted was completely beyond my horizon. Everything was of the moment, I took everything as it came and acted on the basis of premises I didn't even know myself, without realising this is what I did. I tried to write, but it was no good, everything went to pieces after a few sentences, I didn't have it in me. Espen, however, was a poet to the very core of his soul. There was no doubt that he would be accepted onto the course at the Writing Academy, and rightly so, there was nothing false about what he did, I saw nothing other than entirely pure and genuine motives as far as literature was concerned.

After he moved in below we spent a lot of time together. If he wanted company or if he had made something he considered I ought to taste, which he often did, he was as experimental and ingredient-conscious in the kitchen as he was in poetry, he banged a broomstick on the ceiling and I went down. We played chess, listened sometimes to jazz and sometimes to bands I introduced him to because, as regards pop and rock, our preferences were relatively similar, both influenced by having lived our early teenage years in the mid-1980s, which included a lot of post-punk but also more rhythmical stuff like Happy Mondays, Talking Heads, Beastie Boys. He liked dancing, which was not entirely apparent at first glance, however there was little that excited him as much as driving music, and most of all, and above all else, we talked. We both read a lot, each in our own area, and that was what we discussed or took as a springboard for discussion because our own experiences were also woven into the conversations, which were endless, we could sit late into the night and continue in the afternoon of the next day, there was nothing forced or constrained about it, both he and I were hungry for knowledge, beating in our hearts we both had a desire to learn, we both felt the pleasure of moving forward, for this was what was happening, we were pushing each other forward, one leading the other, suddenly I could hear myself talking about something I had never thought of before, and where did that come from?

We were nobodies, two young lit. students chatting away in a rickety old house in a small town at the edge of the world, a place where nothing of any significance had ever happened and presumably never would, we had barely started out on our lives and knew nothing about anything, but what we read was not nothing, it concerned matters of the utmost significance and was written by the greatest thinkers and writers in Western culture, and that was basically a miracle, all you had to do was fill in a library lending slip and you had access to what Plato, Sappho or Aristophanes had written in the incomprehensibly distant mists of time, or Homer,

Sophocles, Ovid, Lucullus, Lucretius or Dante, Vasari, da Vinci, Montaigne, Shakespeare, Cervantes or Kant, Hegel, Kierkegaard, Nietzsche, Heidegger, Lukács, Arendt or those who wrote in the modern day, Foucault, Barthes, Lévi-Strauss, Deleuze, Serres. Not to mention the millions of novels, plays and collections of poetry which were available. All one lending slip and a few days away. We didn't read any of these to be able to summarise the contents, as we did with the literature on the syllabus, but because they could give us something.

What was this 'something'?

For my part, it was something being opened up. My whole world consisted of entities I took for granted and which were unshakeable, like rocks and mountains of the mind. The Holocaust was one such entity, the Age of Enlightenment another. I could account for them, I had a clear image of them, as everyone did, but I had never *thought* about them, never asked myself what circumstances had made them possible, why they happened when they did, and definitely not whether there was any connection between them. As soon as I started to read Horkheimer and Adorno's book *Dialectic of Enlightenment*, of which I understood very little, something opened, in that things which could be viewed in one way could also be viewed in another, words lost their force, there was no such thing as the Holocaust, for what the term indicated was so incredibly complicated, right down to the comb in the pocket of the jacket in the pile of jackets in the warehouse, it had belonged to a little girl, the whole of her life exists in the term 'the Holocaust', and up again to the big concepts like evil, indifference, guilt, collective guilt, individual responsibility, mass man, mass production, mass extinction. In this way the world was relativised but also more real: lies or misunderstandings or deceit were inherent in notions of reality, not in reality, which was inaccessible to language.

Espen could read a passage aloud that Leonardo da Vinci had written about the movement of a hand, and the simplest of the simple, the most obvious of the obvious, was no longer simple and obvious, it appeared as the mystery it really was.

Yes, we read to each other. Mostly Espen, he could jump up in the middle of a conversation, return with a book and start reading from it, and me too, on rare occasions I found something I considered had value for him too. There was an imbalance in our relationship, Espen led, he was the dominant partner, I followed and was always happy when his face lit up at something I had said or he found interesting, that spurred me on, the ensuing conversation was always good because I was freer, but if he didn't respond, which also happened, I retreated, held back, forever controlled by his moods, while he, for his part, never placed much weight on what I thought or felt; if he didn't agree he said so at once, took it as a challenge, but he didn't draw any link with his own capacities, he never doubted his own abilities as I did.

This was the only thing we couldn't discuss, what went on between us. He never heard me say that I couldn't say any more about this matter, as his lack of response had made me too unsure about myself, that I was a mere Zeitblom while he was a Leverkühn, that I was doomed to becoming a literary critic or a cultural correspondent, he to becoming what he was: a poet, a writer, an author.

No two people in Bergen were further apart than Espen and Gunvor. At any rate I couldn't think of any. Having them in the same room was an exercise in futility, they never got beyond hi, how are you, they had nothing to say to each other, weren't the slightest bit interested in each other. So I lived two completely separate lives, one with Gunvor, which was all about closeness, being and doing things together, such as making love, having breakfast, visiting her friends, watching films, going for a walk, chatting about whatever entered our heads, everything closely related to our bodies, the smell of her hair, for example, the taste of her skin, the feeling of lying hip to hip in bed and smoking, in other words, sharing life. We talked about brothers and sisters, parents and friends, never about theoreticians or theories, and if we moved on to the university in our conversations it would be to talk about the guy who fell asleep in the reading room, which Gunvor also did once, he had woken up with a start and when he had stood up to leave he had collapsed in a heap. I'm paralysed! I'm paralysed! he had shouted, but then the feeling in his legs returned, they had gone to sleep too, and he got to his feet with a sheepish ashamed expression while everyone around him laughed, not least Gunvor, judging by her mirth as she told me the story.

Yngve and Espen had nothing to say to each other either, they weren't types I wanted to bring together, and this rift was harder to reconcile myself to because while the differences between Espen and Gunvor also had something to do with them being man and woman, friend and girlfriend, and were therefore quite natural and acceptable, the differences between Yngve and Espen were based on something else. Sometimes I saw what Espen and I did through Yngve's eyes, then we were transformed into two nerds sitting alone and reading aloud and playing chess and listening to jazz, as far from the social, sociable world of bands and girls and nights out as it was possible to be. Yngve saw that it wasn't me, and I carried that view with me, I was the guy in the street who liked football and pop music, what was I doing with all this modernist elitist literature? However, it worked the other way too because what Yngve said didn't always sound so convincing in my ears any more, but this was such a painful thought that I suppressed it the instant it appeared.

I met Kjartan a couple of times that spring, and something had happened to him, I could see that. Although he spoke as he always had, the fire was gone and in his eyes there was a dejection I hadn't seen in him before. One evening mum phoned to say he had been admitted to the psychiatric ward at the hospital. He had become psychotic, it was serious, he had wrecked the whole of his bedsit, smashed everything in it, thrown the TV out of the window and then he had been taken away. Now he was in Førde, at the hospital there, where mum, Ingunn and Kjellaug, his three sisters, were moving heaven and earth for him to be given the best possible treatment. Mum was beside herself with worry. A psychosis could last a long time and he was still unapproachable.

In the May exam we got Dante. Several students turned and looked at me as the papers were being distributed, I had marketed myself as a Dante fan, I had become a little Dante expert and you could hardly get luckier than this.

But I hadn't read anything about the canto in the question, so instead of writing about that specific passage, which was about two lovers moving back and forth in the mass of sinners drifting like a flock of birds in the wind who can never come close to each other, I reconstructed the essay I had written about Dante as well as I could, almost verbatim, and referred vaguely to the passage at the start and the end. Espen had also chosen Dante, didn't think it went particularly well, but it hadn't been a catastrophe either.

When the results were pinned up on the board outside the institute it turned out I had got only a 2.4. It was a cum laude and perfectly acceptable, but a far cry from what I had hoped for and expected. I wanted to be at least the best in the year. Espen, however, got a 2.2, one of the best grades that had been given this semester. I understood why: he had written about that particular canto, read it and extracted something from it on the spot, while I had sewn a finished product onto the text and rendered it invisible.

I got what I deserved, but it was hard to swallow; the sole reason for taking this subject, in my view, was to be the best. What was the point of being a mediocre lit. student? It was absolutely meaningless.

I decided to drop philosophy and concentrate on literature to make up for lost ground at once. Espen was going to start at the Writing Academy and wouldn't be a threat to me there, which pleased me. He wasn't competitive, but he won anyway and there was no safeguard against that.

The summer lay before me and as usual I didn't know what to do or where to go. The only certainty was that I had to earn some money. Gunvor, who was working at an old people's home all summer, suggested I apply for a job at a mental health institution situated between Haugesund and her home known to students as a place where they always needed people. Two colleagues from her department would be working there all summer, she knew, and they weren't from the district either, they would be staying in some rooms the local council used in a school.

I rang up, said I had worked at a similar institution before, I had also taught in a school for a year, and the woman I spoke to said I could have a temporary post for six weeks. So in the middle of June I packed a bag and took a bus south. Gunvor was leaning against her father's car and smiling as, a few hours later, I alighted in the town centre. She took off her sunglasses and we hugged.

'I've missed you so much,' she said in her local dialect, stretching up to kiss me.

'I've missed you too,' I said.

The houses around us were white, the sea behind us was blue, the forest on all sides green and bathed in sun. We got into the car, it was the first time she had driven me and for a moment I felt the subordination which that entailed, she had the skills, I didn't. I was the eternal passenger. Now I was also the passenger in my girlfriend's car.

'Is it far?' I said, pushing the seat back to make room for my legs.

'Three kilometres,' she said. 'They're waiting for you with dinner. Are you nervous?'

'No,' I said. 'It'll be fine, I'm sure.'

She sent me a smile before looking straight ahead again. She had so much happiness in her, expressed not only by her lips and eyes but her whole body. Even when she was concentrating on her driving, it radiated off her.

On the way she described what we could see around us. There was the school, that was where her best friend lived, there was a ski slope over there, that was where she had her first kiss . . . After some minutes she slowed down and turned into a gravel road, we drove past some fields, some big old white houses, and at the bottom of a gentle slope, by the forest, with the fjord beneath, was their house.

'Here it is!' she said. 'Isn't it lovely?'

'Beautiful,' I said.

She parked, we got out, I followed her to the door, which was instantly opened by a woman who must have been her mother.

'Hi, and welcome to our house,' she said with a smile. I shook her outstretched hand.

'Thank you,' I said.

'How nice to have you here at last!'

'It's nice to be invited,' I said. 'I've heard so much about this place.'

'Is dad out?' Gunvor said.

'Yes,' she said. 'I was thinking we'd eat when he gets back.'

'Then I'll show you where you'll be sleeping,' Gunvor said and grabbed my hand. 'Come on!'

We went into the hall and through the house, dark and cool, to the furthest room, where I put down my bag and looked at her. She sat on the tightly made bed and dragged me towards her. Before coming here she had warned me there would be no chance of us sharing a room.

'Can't you come to my room during the night?' I said. 'Just sneak in?'

She shook her head. 'Not when they're in the house. But they're going early tomorrow morning. I'll come then.'

*

When we sat down at the table her father folded his hands and said a short prayer. Gunvor and her mother did the same. Ill at ease, I laid my hands on my lap so that no one could see whether they were folded or not and lowered my eyes as they had done.

'Amen,' they said, and as if with the wave of a magic wand we were somewhere else, hands helping themselves, questions being asked and answered, food being chewed and swallowed, laughter and merriment. As always when I was with people I didn't know, I was completely open to them. The mother, who was jolly but still scrutinising me, the father, who was more serious and sombre, clean-cut and solid, Gunvor, halfway between them and me, as uneasy about what I might be thinking about them as what they might be thinking about me. I answered the questions they asked, tried to appear polite and friendly, to give them what I imagined they wanted. If the atmosphere flagged, with a sudden lull in the conversation or a facial expression I interpreted as disapproval, for instance, I gave them an extra helping.

After the meal we walked down to the fjord for a swim.

'Well?' Gunvor said, grabbing my hand. 'Did it give you a shock when grace was said?'

'Not at all,' I said. 'But it was a bit unexpected. I had the feeling they belong to an earlier generation than my parents.'

'They probably do too,' she said. 'What do you think of them then?'

'They're nice,' I said. 'They have very different temperaments, it seems, but they seem to be on the same wavelength, if you know what I mean.'

'I think so,' she said, looking at me. 'It's strange having you here.'

'It's strange being here, too,' I said.

We cleaned our teeth together in the bathroom, kissed each other goodnight and went to our separate rooms. Outside, it had begun to rain. I lay listening to the light pitter-patter, which ceased whenever the wind gusted through the forest. From inside the sitting room a clock ticked, every hour a mechanism was activated and its delicate chime sounded. This was a house where, from my perspective, everything functioned as it should and where lives were lived in an orderly manner. I understood more about Gunvor when I saw her at home. She was a student, lived her life in Bergen, but was also a part of this, she was loyal to her parents, to whom she was both close and distant. I assumed the feeling I had while I was there, that I was false and bad, that I was duping them, was alien to her nature.

The clock chimed twelve. Someone was up and in the corridor, a door was opened and closed, the toilet flushed. I liked being in other people's homes so much, I thought, I always had done, although what I saw there could seem unbearable to me, perhaps because I saw things I wasn't intended to see. The personal life that was peculiar to them. The love, the helplessness that resided in that, which was usually hidden from others' eyes. Oh, trifles, trivialities, a family's habits, their exchanged glances. The vulnerability in this was so immense. Not for them, they lived inside it, and then there was no vulnerability, but when it was seen by someone who didn't live there. When I saw it I felt like an intruder, I had no right to be there. At the same time I was filled with tenderness for them.

The clock readied itself to chime again. I opened my eyes, there was no question of me being able to sleep straight away. The trees outside the window were black, the darkness between them pale. It wasn't raining any more, but the wind was still rising and falling in the forest like billowing breakers of the air.

One o'clock.

I thought about the one time I had been to hospital in my childhood. I had broken my collarbone, it hurt so much I was crying but didn't realise anything was wrong until I complained to mum in the evening and she drove me to see the doctor in

Kokkeplassen, where she worked, a red-haired freckled young man, who said the bone was probably broken and we would have to go to hospital to have an X-ray. After it had been done the doctor there said I could sleep in the hospital that night. There was nothing I would rather have done, it was an adventure, something to tell the others, but if I said yes perhaps mum might think I preferred to sleep in the hospital than at home, she would be sad about that, and so I shook my head to the doctor's suggestion, said I wanted to sleep at home if that was all right. Yes, of course, he understood, wound a bandage tightly around my shoulders in a figure of eight and wished me all the best as we left.

Even then I had felt I was being false, someone who carried thoughts no one else had and which no one must ever know. What emerged from this was *myself*. *This* was what was *me*. In other words, that which in me that knew something the others didn't, that which in me I could never share with anyone else. And the loneliness, which I still felt, was something I had clung to ever since, as it was all I had. As long as I had that no one could harm me, for what they harmed then was something else. No one could take loneliness away from me. The world was a space I moved in, where anything could happen, but in the space I had inside me, which was me, everything was always the same. All my strength lay there. The only person who could find his way in was dad, and he did too, when I was dreaming and he seemed to be in my soul and shouting at me.

For everyone else I was unreachable. Well, in my thoughts they could reach me, anyone at all could stir them up, but what were thoughts worth? What was consciousness other than the surface of the soul's ocean? Other than small gaily coloured boats, floating plastic bottles and driftwood, waves and currents, whatever the day might bring, over a depth of several thousand metres.

Or depth was the wrong word.

What was consciousness other than the cone of light from a torch in the middle of a dark forest?

I closed my eyes and rolled over onto my side. In six or seven hours she would come to me and I longed to feel her body against mine after holding her in my arms. It was so long since we had been together I was aching for this. If only I could sleep now, I thought, then when I woke she would be here. But I couldn't. I slipped into a kind of semi-conscious state of desire and expectation, it was absolutely unbearable, I wanted her, and I slept registering the chimes of the clock, oh, it is only two, only three, only four . . . When the door finally did open and she crawled over to me, in the enthusiastic-tentative way that was so typical of her, the sleep I rose from was so deep that everything that happened was in a dream.

We had breakfast, she behaved like her mother, washed up when the meal was over, I stood in the yard smoking with a cup of coffee in my hand, she came out, sat down on the step, squinted into the sun, which was already high.

'You haven't seen me ride yet,' she said. 'That's a scandal, if you ask me.'

'I think I just did, didn't I?' I said.

She blushed and looked down. Then she eyed me and smiled.

'That was a cheap shot, Karl Ove,' she said.

'Couldn't resist it,' I said.

'In fact I was serious,' she said. 'Come up with me now. You can even have a ride yourself if you want.'

'Not on your life. But I'm happy to watch.'

Half an hour later we walked up the hill, Gunvor carrying a saddle. We stopped in front of an enclosure, a Fjord pony trotted down to us, she stretched out a hand and said something, it lowered its muzzle to her hand, she patted it, fitted the saddle, swung herself up and soon she was riding to and fro across the green pasture in the full sunshine while I watched and took pictures. Sometimes I clapped to make her laugh, there was something forced about the situation, she actually wanted to show me this, her riding a horse, but at the same time she was uncomfortable, she wasn't the type to show off, but it went well, it was a happy moment, she was beaming when she had finished and jumped down in front of me.

'You should join a circus,' I said and took a picture of her with the reins in one hand and a carrot in the other.

'You should come with me to a gymkhana one day,' she said. 'With Icelandic ponies. Preferably in Iceland.'

'Don't let it go to your head,' I said. 'Be happy I came here.'

'It's just a start,' she said. 'When I've finished with you you'll be a real *hestamadur*!'

'What's that? A horseman?'

'Yes, more or less. It's a term of distinction in Iceland.'

'I don't doubt it.'

'I had an idea some time ago,' she said. 'I was thinking of doing my subsid. at the university in Rekyavik. If I did would you come with me?'

'Yes.'

'Would you? Seriously?'

'Yes.'

In the evening she drove me to the town where I would be living for the next six weeks. We went first to the institution, which was situated just outside the town centre, and collected the key for my room, then we drove down to the hall of residence, if that was what it was, which stood on a slope a few hundred metres from the quay. A room with bare plaster, a shiny lino floor, a bed, a cupboard and a pine table, a kitchenette, a small toilet with a shower.

'I think I'd better be getting back now,' Gunvor said, standing in the doorway with the car keys in her hand.

'You do that,' I said. 'See you next weekend.'

We kissed fleetingly, her car started up soon afterwards, the sound reverberated against the wall, disappeared down the hill and was gone.

After I had slipped the cover onto the duvet I had borrowed from them, put the sheet on the bed, my clothes in the cupboard and books on the desk, I went out for a walk, drifted down to the quay area, which apart from some youths' cars parked by a snack bar and a little crowd sitting around the wooden tables was empty. They had long hair, denim jackets and denim waistcoats, one of them even wore wooden clogs, and they stared at me as I walked by. I stopped at the edge of the quay and looked down into the water, which, close to the harbour wall, was cold and black. Music blared from one of the cars, a door was open, I saw. 'Forever Young'. I walked past them again, strolled to the little town centre, which apart from a large cooperative store and a Narvesen kiosk also had a small mall, a Chinese restaurant and a handful of shops along the main street. There wasn't a soul around, but that wasn't so surprising, it was Sunday, ten o'clock in the evening.

On the hill up to the building where I was staying I turned and stared across at my workplace-to-be, which from here was visible as dots of light in the forest beneath a steep mountainside. I could feel I was dreading starting, not so much because of the job itself as all the people I would meet, all the situations where the counter was on zero and I would have to make a good impression.

Freshly showered, I went out of the door next morning, down the hill, through the town centre, out the other side, across a river and up towards the forest, where there were around ten buildings among the trees. The sky was overcast, the air warm and still. A bus passed me and stopped by the turnaround at the end of the road, a line of people got off and made for the buildings. I followed them. Two of the patients, clearly with disabilities, stood watching us, which I could imagine them doing every morning. No one spoke; the sound of footsteps and people on the move, slowly making their way forward, surrounded by the stillness of the forest on both sides.

A large brick building came first, this was the administration block where I had picked up my key the previous evening. No one went there. We fanned out, heading for the other blocks in a circle around it. Lawns, dry and discoloured, had been laid between narrow tarmac paths. A tarmac handball court nestled in a hollow surrounded by embankments. Scattered here and there were islets of trees, once part of the forest around them, which now began a few metres behind the various buildings.

I had no idea what lay in store for me and was nervous as I entered. I had to report to Department E, the block to the left, and it was, I soon established, like the other constructions, long, made of brick and painted white, two storeys. I would be working on the top one. The entrance was at the back, by a small semi-full car park. I opened the door and went down a corridor with stairs at the end. I recognised the smell, it was the same as at Eg Hospital, where I had worked three years before, and the same as at the school I had attended in the 1970s, a mixture of green soap and a faint odour reminiscent of cellars and sewage, something dark and damp and subterranean in all the assiduously maintained hygiene.

There was a bench by the wall, above it a line of hooks from which hung jackets and overall trousers. Two wheelchairs stood by the wall opposite, beneath small narrow windows that had been positioned at the top of the wall, 1950s-like.

I went up the stairs, opened the door and came into a long corridor with doors either side. By the wall sat a man in a chair staring at me with fierce eyes. His legs were stumps, cut off at the knee, from what I could see. Otherwise he looked normal. High forehead, red hair, white freckled skin, powerful upper body. He was wearing red jogging trousers and a white T-shirt with a Dole bananas logo.

'Hi!' I said.

The look he sent me was full of contempt. He put his hands on the floor, swung his lower body down between them, fell forward with his hands, swung his lower body between them again and in this unusual but deft way moved off down the corridor.

A woman stuck her head out of the nearest door. She was probably in her mid-thirties, had dark curly hair and a slight overbite.

'Karl Ove?' she said.

'Yes. Hello,' I said.

'Marianne,' she said. 'Come in here. This is where we hang out!'

I went into the little room, where a man with a moustache, a perm, colourful baggy pants and a singlet was sitting with a cup of coffee in front of him, next to a slumped podgy woman with glasses and slightly messy blonde hair, wearing jeans and a denim jacket, twenty-five, more or less, also with a cup of coffee in front of her.

'Hi,' said the man. 'My name's Ove. This is Ellen, and that's Marianne. Marianne's finished her shift now, so it'll be us three today.'

The woman called Ellen lit a cigarette.

I took off my jacket, rummaged for my tobacco pouch and sat down.

'Have you worked here before?' Ove said.

I shook my head.

'Just copy what we do and you won't go far wrong,' he said. 'Isn't that right, Marianne?'

He looked up at her – she was putting on her jacket – and winked. She smiled.

'Have a nice day,' she said and went out of the door.

'When you've had a smoke we'll start,' Ove said.

The man without any legs came into the room, sat up at the table like a dog and stared at Ove.

'This is Ørnulf,' he told me. 'Would you like a cup of coffee, Ørnulf?'

Ørnulf didn't answer; he sucked in air through clenched teeth. His eyes glowed. He smelled awful. I lit a cigarette and leaned back against the sofa. Ove placed a cup under the Thermos spout and filled it in two pumps, added milk and set the cup in front of Ørnulf, who grabbed it with both hands and drained it in three long gulps. He then put it down on the table, gave a wheezy belch, picked it up again and held it in front of Ove imploringly.

'No, no, you've already had two,' Ove said. 'Now you'll have to wait for breakfast.'

Ørnulf put down the cup and swung out of the room to the wall on the opposite side of the corridor, where he sat with his hands under his stumps, staring in at us.

Couldn't he talk? Or didn't he want to?

'Breakfast's at eight,' Ove said. 'Then four of the residents go to the workshop. Three are left here. One of them, Are, needs care. The other two manage fine, but you have to keep an eye on them. The crew in the workshop come back here for lunch. Anything else you need to know we'll deal with as it crops up. OK?'

'Sounds good,' I said.

He took a green book from the table beside him, opened it, and from the lined pages and compact writing I assumed this was where they logged their reports.

'You can have a flip through this later,' he said, looking at me.

I nodded.

He didn't like me, I had realised at once. What he said was well-meaning enough, but the friendliness in his voice was somehow forced, and something about his attitude – I didn't know whether it was his eyes or his body language – told me he had already formed an opinion about me and it didn't do me any favours.

Ellen, for her part, was indifferent.

Could she be a lesbian?

'Well,' Ove said, getting to his feet. 'We'd better go and wake them up. Come along so that you can meet the residents.'

I followed him along the corridor. At the end on the left was the kitchen, on the right a little dining room, and inside it a door to an office where half the wall was glass.

Ørnulf, who had followed us, stopped outside the swing doors to the kitchen.

'He always sits there until the food comes,' Ove said. 'Don't you, Ørnulf?'

Ørnulf grimaced, bared his teeth and sucked in deeply, and a kind of eerie hissing sound issued.

Was that a yes?

'Ørnulf sits in his wheelchair when we go out. But inside he can move around really well. Can't you, Ørnulf?' Ove said, without looking at him. 'You see the swing door to the kitchen? It's important we keep it closed when we're not in there ourselves. Have you got that?'

'Right,' I said.

'So let's start with Hans Olav. He's got his own little ward to himself in here,' he said, opening the door at the end of the corridor. 'He can be a bit unruly at times, if I can put it like that, that's why he lives on his own. See? But he's a good boy.'

Inside there was a little hall with a dining table, and in the continuing corridor three doors. The closest was open, and at the back of the room there was a man, in his forties maybe, lying in bed and wanking. His dick was fat and limp. Ove stopped in the doorway.

'Hi, Hans Olav,' he said.

'Wan!' Hans Olav said.

'No, no wanking now,' Ove said. 'You have to get up and put on your clothes for breakfast.'

'Wan, wan,' said Hans Olav. He had a big flattish nose, deep furrows down his cheeks and he was almost completely bald. His head was round, his eyes were brown, and I gave a start when I saw him, he was the spitting image of pictures I had seen of Picasso in his later years.

'This is Karl Ove,' Ove said. 'He's going to be working here this summer.'

'Hi,' I said.

'Shall I help you up?' Ove said.

Without waiting for an answer, he went over to Hans Ove, grasped one arm with both hands and hauled him into a sitting position. Annoyed, Hans Olav hit out, not aggressively, more the way you swat a fly, slowly struggled to his feet, grabbed his trousers and pulled them on. He was taller than me, almost two metres, but seemed weak and unable to stand.

'Hans Olav has breakfast here with a member of the staff,' Ove said. 'I'll do it today, but tomorrow it's your turn.'

'That's fine,' I said.

We went back into the main ward, Hans Olav moving quickly, stooped and with a swaying gait, his fingers constantly fidgeting beneath his chin, and three times I saw one arm shoot out and hit the wall as he laughed his low chuckle. He walked past Ørnulf, keeping well clear of him, and disappeared into the ward.

Ove opened the next door, inside was an elderly man sitting on his bed and getting dressed. He wore glasses, had a gentle face and full lips, a bald pate with hair growing all the way round, and from his appearance and style of clothing might have been a mid-range accountant or perhaps a storeman in a building warehouse or, why not, a woodwork teacher.

'You're up already!' Ove said. 'Well done, Håkon!'

The man called Håkon looked down like a bashful girl. A fine blush spread across his ageing cheeks.

'Thank you,' he mumbled.

In the next room sat an elderly man on the edge of his bed, maybe sixty, sixty-five, with white hair in a wreath around his otherwise bald head, tearing out pictures from a pile of magazines. On his back he had a large hump, broad and so flat at the top you could have rested a tray on it.

'How's it going, Kåre?' Ove said.

'Hoo, hoo,' Kåre said, pointing out of the room.

'Yes, the food will soon be here. I'll shout when it arrives.'

The rooms looked more or less like those in old people's homes, a few things belonging to the institution such as blankets and tablecloths, Ikea pictures on the walls, some personal possessions such as framed photographs on the tables, the occasional orna- ment, maybe a plastic flower in a vase on the windowsill.

We walked down the corridor until everyone was woken up. Some of them were still asleep, others were awake, one, Egil, gave us an earful because we woke him. They were all men aged between forty and sixty apart from one needing special care whom Ellen looked after, he couldn't have been more than twenty-five. He stood out in other ways too, he was completely paralysed, lay back in an enormous wheelchair, used nappies and was fed, and his eyes were utterly vacant, no personal- ity resided in them, they were only eyes. I froze with unease when I saw that. His facial features were clean-cut and would have been handsome had it not been for his permanently open mouth and the saliva running down from the corners. Some- times hollow grunts came from him, but as far as I could see these had no particular meaning, at any rate I didn't discover one or a system.

The last room was Ørnulf's. Even though he was awake and sitting in the corridor Ove showed me in. The room was smaller than the others. Apart from a blue mattress, not dissimilar to the one we had in gym at school, the room was completely empty. No furniture, no ornaments, no pictures, nothing. Not even bed linen or a duvet.

'Why is there no furniture in *his* room?' I said.

Ove looked at me as if I were stupid.

'Well, what do you imagine? He smashes everything in his path, if he's in the mood, or else he tears it into pieces. Do you understand? He might not do anything for a few days but then it all wells up.'

'OK,' I said.

'One rule: we never talk about the residents when they're around. However little we think they understand. We have to be like their pals. Do you understand? Of course, we're the ones who are in charge but we have to be open and chummy with them.'

'I see,' I said, following him back into the corridor.

'I'll help them to shower and get dressed,' he said. 'In the meantime could you make breakfast?'

'Right,' I said. 'What do they have?'

'Bread and stuff, that's all. And coffee. They love coffee, as you might have worked out.'

'OK,' I said and went into the kitchen. It was a relief to do something specific and mechanical which didn't involve the residents. Everything I had seen of them filled me with disgust.

I opened the fridge and took out anything you could put on bread. Cut up a few tomatoes, some slices of cucumber and strips of a pepper, and laid it all out on a dish, spread some salami and ham on another, put a mild white cheese and a brown cheese on a third. I kept myself busy, wanting to make a good impression on the others who worked there. Switched on the coffee machine, took out milk and juice, set the two tables. One of the residents came out of his room in just his underpants, he was athletic and had a serious masculine face, at first glance he appeared to be a magnificent human specimen, but then there was something about the way he walked, balancing on the outer edge of the balls of his feet somehow, and you realised everything was not quite as it should be. He stopped by the threshold to the bathroom, stepped over, stepped back, stepped over, stepped back, and I had a feeling he would have kept going all day if Ove hadn't come, put an arm around his shoulders and taken him in. Håkon, the bashful one, waddled down the corridor, his back was crooked. Egil came with his head bent right back and his gaze directed at the ceiling the whole way to the table. Hans Olav stood still by the wall with his fingers formed into a quivering ball beneath his chin. Ørnulf sat as he had sat for the last half an hour, with his hands under his stumps. He kept drawing in air sharply between his teeth. Perhaps hyperventilating gave him a kick.

I poured coffee into a pump-action jug and stood it on the table. Sliced a loaf, searched for a toaster, but they didn't appear to have one. Cast a glance through the window, a group of residents was coming across the grey tarmac, most seemed to be in their forties, and among them were two carers in conversation, one with a lit cigarette in his hand. The sky above them was light but sunless.

Ove took a tray of food into Hans Olav's room, Ellen shouted that breakfast was ready, we sat down at our respective tables and the residents made their way along the corridor. The athletic man, whose name was Alf, was now walking with some strange robotic jerks. Right behind him came Håkon, the girlish-looking older man, with an apologetic nervous smile on his lips. Kåre, the hair-wreath man with the magazines, walked bent forward with the hump on his shoulders like a sack, and he kept shaking one hand to and fro in the air just under his face.

'Where are you from then?' Egil said, leaning forward and staring right into my face.

'Arendal,' I said.

'How old are you then?'

'Twenty-one.'

'What kind of car have you got then?'

'I'm afraid I haven't got a car.'

'Why not then? Why haven't you got a car? Eh?'

'Now don't pester him, Egil,' Ellen said.

Egil sat back instantly.

'No,' he said. 'No, I won't. No, no, no.'

He looked up at the ceiling for a while, then began to eat. The whole time he was breathing heavily, and when he had food in his mouth it was like sitting next to a small steam engine. His shirt hung outside his trousers, on top he wore a red pullover, slightly stained, and his hair, which was thick and curly, stood up at the back. His cheeks were reddish, perhaps because of burst blood vessels, and his eyes were bloodshot too. He made a confused absent-minded impression and reminded me of a scientist or a *gymnas* teacher who had lived alone for too long and perhaps thought he hadn't had all the success he felt was his due but actually enjoyed teaching and therefore didn't give a damn about his appearance. Egil was like that. But added to this were the sudden lunges he made, a hand shot into the air and waved as though he had suddenly caught sight of a colleague down the corridor or he might jerk forward so abruptly that everyone around him recoiled. Then there was the staring at the ceiling.

He could also burst into laughter for no apparent reason.

'Ha, ha, ha, ha!' he might go, as if he had heard a joke and wanted to reward whoever had told it.

'Have you got a girlfriend then?' he said.

'Yes,' I said.

'What's her name then?'

'Gunvor.'

'Is she nice then?'

'Egil,' Ellen said.

'Are you going for a swim today then?' he said, looking at her.

'No,' she said.

'Why not?' he said.

'The weather's not so good today,' she said.

'Why?' he said with a heavy sigh and sank back into his chair. All his questions had been mechanical, without a trace of any curiosity in his voice. He was like a child who has learned something off by heart but without understanding what it meant.

'Was that good, Håkon?' Ellen said.

'Yes,' Håkon mumbled from a lowered chin. 'Thank you very much. Thank you very much.'

Ellen was sitting beside Are and feeding him. He half-lay in his chair with his mouth open. Porridge trickled down from the corners. Kåre often emitted tiny sounds, he obviously couldn't speak, but he communicated with sounds, gestures and looks. Ørnulf sat rocking in his chair baring his teeth and staring at me.

'Are we friends?' Egil said. 'Us two. Are we friends?'

What was I supposed to say to that? We obviously weren't friends. But to say no might create a terrible agitation in him.

'Yes, we are, aren't we?' I said.

'Then you can come and see my pictures of the king,' he said.

'OK, I'd like that,' I said.

'Good,' he said. 'That's a deal.'

The door to the corridor opened and Hans Olav ran out. He looked behind him with a laugh, his hands under his chin, his mouth in constant motion, and set off at full speed down the corridor, staggering beneath his heavy body. Ove started after him with a tray in his hands. The similarity with Picasso was disturbing, it upset the whole balance of the world, I thought. But the others didn't seem bothered and I supposed I would probably get used to it, given time.

'If you clear up after us, Karl Ove, I'll take the boys to the workshop.'

I nodded.

The four who were going to work got up and went to their rooms. Ørnulf swung down from his chair and occupied his customary position in the corridor. Ellen wiped Are's mouth and trundled him into his room. I put the food into the fridge, the plates and glasses into the dishwasher, wiped the tables clean with a cloth and swept the floor with a dustpan and brush.

After finishing I went to see Ellen. She was washing Are, he was lying naked on the bed, rigid and white, she ran the cloth over him while making small talk. There we are, she said, it's important to wash down here, you know. Now I'll pour a bit more water on, it's nice and warm.

He stared at the ceiling with vacant eyes.

'Is there anything I can do?' I said.

She peered at me through her thick lenses.

'Nope,' she said. 'Sit down and have a cup of coffee while you're waiting. He's had constipation for a few days now, so I was thinking of administering an enema later. You could give me a hand with that.'

'OK,' I said.

'Otherwise you could go for a walk with Ørnulf this morning. Just round and about.'

I nodded, she wrung the cloth and continued washing Are.

On one thigh and buttock he had a large scarred area.

'What's that?' I said. 'Is it a birthmark or what?'

She shook her head.

'It's a burn. Someone left him in front of a fan heater. Happened many years ago now.'

'Is that true?'

'Unfortunately. He can't move, you know. And he never says anything. So he just lies there.'

'How awful,' I said.

'Yes,' she said. 'But it's a long time ago. His unit is closed down now. He's got his own flat – the new reform, you know. But until it's fully finished he's here with us. Aren't you, Are?'

Not a single expression crossed his face as she talked. I hung around so as not to seem unsympathetic, then I went into the duty room and poured myself a coffee. From the corridor I heard the sound of hands smacking and clothes rubbing against the floor. It was Ørnulf, he stopped by the table and sent me an imploring look. It must have been the sound of the coffee jug that had spurred him into action.

'Do you want some coffee?' I said.

Without batting an eyelid, he took a cup and raised it towards me.

'You had a cup for breakfast,' I said. 'That'll have to do.'

I started rolling a cigarette. For a long time he sat in exactly the same position with his cup held out. Then, as if a spell had been broken, as though the hundred-year sleep was over, he suddenly put it down and began to hyperventilate.

'I think it's best if you sit in the corridor,' I said. 'Then we two can go for a walk afterwards.'

Was that *contempt* in his eyes?

At any rate he didn't budge.

I ran my tongue over the glue, stuck the edge to the paper, put the cigarette in my mouth and lit up. A protruding flake of tobacco burned up at once and fell glowing to the floor, the rest caught the next moment and I inhaled a cloud of smoke into my lungs as I looked out of the window in the balcony door. A group of three carers, each pushing a wheelchair, was coming towards us. A car parked in front of the admin block at the other end. From the floor beneath came a protracted roar, a sound that was hard to associate with anything human, while Ørnulf sucked and hissed only half a metre away from me.

I turned back towards him.

He immediately took the cup and held it up to me, begging.

'No,' I said.

He continued to hold it outstretched, this was another hundred-year sleep.

'Do you want some coffee, Ørnulf?' Ellen said as she came in the door. 'Here, I'll give you some.'

She took his cup, filled it with equal parts of coffee and milk, he gulped it down and then dragged himself out of the room and across the corridor. Ellen sighed and sat down on the sofa on the other side of the table, lit a cigarette and closed her eyes.

I sorted through the residents in my head. There were seven in the ward. Four of them looked more or less normal, and of them two could speak. Two were badly deformed but could move, one was a vegetable. By mentally handicapped I had imagined some Down's syndrome residents and some vegetables. I hadn't known that every shade in between existed, but of course it was obvious and was no surprise to me once I had seen them.

Outside Hans Olav and Ove came walking along the road.

'Where's Are now?' I said.

'He's in bed in his room,' Ellen said. 'I'll get him up soon and we'll go for a walk.'

'Is he asleep?'

'No, no. He just lounges around in bed.'

The roars from the ground floor resounded again. From the corridor I could hear Ørnulf's hissing. Otherwise there was silence. I was dreading the walk with Ørnulf. It would be the first time I had been alone with one of them and I knew nothing about how to behave, what I would say to him, what might happen. What would I do if he wanted to go to the loo? Could he go himself or did he need help? Should I lift him into his wheelchair or could he manage by himself? Could he get dressed? Should I push the wheelchair? Where would we go? He couldn't talk, what if I didn't understand what he wanted?

On top of all that, I was afraid. The look he had sent me was filled with hatred, and his room had no furniture or objects, only a mattress, because he either smashed everything that came into his path or tore it to pieces, so Ove had said.

What would I do if he had a similar fit when we were outside? Would I be able to stop him? And what if he attacked me? Of course he didn't have any legs, but his biceps were strong.

The door in the corridor from the stairs banged open. The next moment Hans Olav trotted past, bent forward, his hands fidgeting under his chin. Ove, who was following, stopped in the doorway.

'I'll stay with him for a while,' he said. 'Then perhaps he'll sleep.'

I got up, it was probably best to see to Ørnulf. I watched Ove walking down the corridor, quite small but so powerful that his arms didn't quite rest against his body, they always stuck out, which meant he walked with a little wiggle. He must spend a lot of time training, I thought.

Ørnulf was squatting in his room, facing the wall.

'Hi, Ørnulf,' I said. 'Fancy a walk?'

Without looking at me he turned and shot out to the door to the stairs, which he opened with a stretch. The steps he took one arm at a time, like a kind of large insect, also deftly and at speed. By the time I reached the end of the corridor he was sitting with his arms around his legs beside a wheelchair.

I hated this.

I looked for his name above the hooks, found it, took a jacket.

'You'll have to wear a jacket,' I said. 'Shall I help you?'

He didn't react, his face was blank, there was nothing to tell me what he was thinking.

I leaned down and carefully took his arm to insert it in the sleeve. He yanked it away.

'If we're going for a walk you'll have to wear a jacket,' I said. 'Otherwise there's no walk.'

He didn't move.

'OK,' I said. 'Let's go back up.'

I started back. I turned, he was sitting in the same position. Went up the stairs, stopped to listen whether he was following, nothing.

Ellen looked up at me from the sofa.

'I can't put his jacket on,' I said. 'He doesn't want it.'

'Does he need to wear a jacket? It's quite warm outside.'

'OK,' I said. 'Is there anything else I ought to know?'

She shook her head, I hurried back down, for all I knew he could have taken advantage of the short time I had left him alone to escape.

But he was sitting beside the wheelchair, arms around his short legs and chin resting on his chest.

'Shall we go then?' I said.

He clambered up onto the chair, turned the wheels with seasoned dexterity, rolled down to the door and glanced up at me.

The moment I opened the door he set off at a furious pace. I had to walk as fast as I could to keep up with him. He had found a rhythm, moving along with quick regular thrusts, hands on the wheels, off, on, off. We passed the admin block. Further ahead, a group was walking towards us, I saw at once it was two carers and four residents, their body movements were unmistakable.

The two carers looked at me.

'Hi,' I said.

'Hi,' they said. 'Hi, Ørnulf.'

He ignored them, and soon we had put them and all the buildings far behind us. His face had stiffened into a sort of grimace with bared teeth. It was red with exertion. Deciduous trees lined the road, dense and green, occasional spruces towered up, heavier and darker. Ahead of us was the main road, alongside it ran a cycle path, which I had decided we would follow.

Ørnulf didn't want to. He pointed to the left, where the road looped around a little housing estate. I couldn't let him rule me totally, I thought, and grabbed the handles of the wheelchair and began to push. He tried to brake me with his hands. His eyes were panic-stricken. What an idiot he was.

'It's no good protesting,' I said. 'We're going *this* way.'

He jumped out and headed up towards the end of the road under his own steam. This was very dangerous, he was crossing the main road, not much taller than a dog, if a car came this could end really badly, I ran after him with the wheelchair, shouting for him to get back in.

He stopped on the other side and stared at me. Dragging his legs over tarmac didn't seem to affect him.

I placed the wheelchair in front of him. He swung himself up. I wasn't going to give in and pushed him down the slope. He jumped out again and went the other way, his palms on the tarmac, his lower torso swinging between his arms. I followed, but now he wouldn't get back into the chair, now he was moving on his own, and that was how we entered the housing estate, him on the tarmac, which was dry and covered with sand and gravel, staring straight ahead, me walking behind pushing the wheelchair. This was no good, if anyone met us now I would be given the boot, but I was fuming with anger, couldn't he just sit in the chair and do as I wanted? What was it about this estate that was so incredibly important to him? It was just stupid, I was his carer, we were out on a morning walk, one route was as good as another, and if it wasn't, it definitely wasn't worth sacrificing the comfortable wheelchair for.

I ran a few steps, overtook him and placed the chair in his path. He turned and tried to get past, I moved, he grabbed a wheel and tried to shove it away.

'We're going *this* way,' I said. 'I'm telling you. *This* way. Sit up on your wheelchair and then we can go.'

He dragged himself up, and when he was in position his hands began to turn the wheels at a furious pace again. I walked beside him through the estate, which consisted of relatively new houses with gardens that were not yet established. A bus stopped in the road, a couple of passengers got out and started walking. We reached the crossroads and Ørnulf, who had been frenetically pumping his arms, suddenly stopped.

'Shall I push you?' I said.

He didn't react to my question, so it was impossible to read an answer from his face, but when I grabbed the handles and pushed he didn't object. I walked as quickly as I could and soon we were back near the institution.

As we passed the admin block he suddenly jumped out of the wheelchair and sat on the ground a few metres from the steps to the main entrance.

'You can't sit here,' I said. 'Come on now. The unit's over there!'

He didn't look at me, he ignored me, hyperventilating, his arms firmly planted on the ground.

'Don't you want to go back to the ward, is that it?' I said.

No reaction.

I tried to lift him, but he grasped the chair so firmly that it was impossible.

'Do you want to sit here? While the others are having a nice time drinking coffee?'

No reaction.

'Fine by me,' I said. 'I get paid the same money anyway. I can stand here, no problem.'

I took shelter under the projecting roof and lit a cigarette, but after a couple of minutes I realised this didn't look very good, a resident in the road, his carer ten metres away, smoking, so I stubbed out the cigarette and went back to him.

'Come on now,' I said. 'You've made your point. You don't need to be stroppy any more. Jump up and we'll be off.'

No reaction.

Hands around his knees, a grin on his lips, sucking through his teeth.

'All right, all right,' I said. 'As you wish.'

I folded my arms and scanned the area trying to find a way out of the situation I found myself in. He might be defiant and strong-willed, but he had met his match in me. I could stay there until darkness fell, I could stay there all night and into the next day if I had to. The trick was to think about something else. Not about him or time dragging.

But it was hard, there was something about him, the aggression I could feel in him, his presence cast a shadow over my thoughts. He couldn't have much in his head, almost all his movements were conditioned by reflex, such as when he rushed in after hearing the sound of the pump-action coffee jug and mechanically held out a cup. He didn't enjoy the taste of the coffee, drinking it was just something that had to be done, something that had to be expedited, something that had to happen. If it did, he would want it to happen again. Outside, there was only one route that counted. Not the walk as such, because then he could equally well have taken the other route.

I looked down at him. I disliked him intensely, everything about him, but especially his dog-like traits and his stupidity. *He* was the one losing out, not me. I was paid a wage, it made no difference to me whether we sat here or up a tree, I was ready for anything.

He met my eyes for an instant and when he looked back down he smiled.

It was the first time I had seen him smile.

He really thought he was punishing me. That it was him who had the whip hand.

I walked away and sat down on a kerbstone in the car park. There was something crab-like about the way he moved, the lightning-quick pendulum movement across the ground or floor. What I found confusing was that his face, if you could forget about the rest of him, was completely normal. A red-haired freckled man in his late forties. Had it been the case that he was *only* misshapen, that he was *only* deformed I wouldn't have reacted in the same way. But the fact was his thoughts were obviously also deformed and misshapen. His soul was also crippled. What did that make him?

Oh, sweet Jesus.

Here he was, the lowest of the low, the weakest of the weak, and there was I, filled with contempt for him.

It was me who was the monster. But I couldn't help myself. His stupidity infuriated me, sitting there, not wanting to go any-where, thinking he was punishing me, the sweat running down his forehead and breathing in and out through his clenched yel-low teeth.

The cloud cover had slowly and, almost imperceptibly, cleared. The sun shining on us now came from a pale blue sky. Vehicles in the car park were opened and started, they drove down the road, others arrived, were parked, engines were switched off, doors opened. Everyone saw us sitting there, no one said anything. I had no idea whether this was normal or not, whether it was just me or it happened to Ørnulf's carers every day.

'Up you get now and we'll go,' I said every so often. He didn't react. If I walked towards him he would grab the wheelchair so tightly that I couldn't lift him into it.

He sat there for an hour and a half. Then Ellen came along, pushing Are, she had given him some sunglasses to wear. They stopped beside us.

'It's lunchtime,' she said. 'Come on, Ørnulf, up into your chair!'

Ørnulf jumped up into the chair, sat with his hands in his lap. Was I supposed to push him now?

Yes, apparently I was.

Walking alongside Ellen, I pushed the wheelchair back. The air was warm, the sunshine boiling hot. I hated myself and the whole of my being.

Sleep came that night, empty and meaningless, for a long time I was merely a body with a slow-beating heart and slow respiration, which together with the blood circulating kept it alive, no more than that, until the dreams began to emerge, these flickerings of atmosphere and images that rule the brain when we are asleep and which for me were always the same: I was alone, I had my back to the wall, I was terrified or humiliated. There were people laughing at me, there were people after me, and above them all, in his many and various forms and guises, loomed dad. In my most common nightmares we were still living in Tybakken and he was in the house with me, but in the worst ones of all he came back while I was visiting mum and it turned out he lived there, because at mum's I took liberties, I did as I wanted, and if there was one thing that enraged him it was that.

Every morning a feeling of humiliation sat deep in my body, that was how I started the day, and if it gradually dissolved as routines anchored me in another world, the real world, the feeling of being humiliated and debased was a continuous presence, and it took nothing, nothing, for it to flare up again and burn through me, yes, burn up the whole of my miserable self.

That morning I woke up half an hour before the alarm clock went off, dreaming I was dead, and the relief when I came to and discovered I wasn't was so great that I let slip a chuckle.

I got out of bed, ate a piece of bread, dressed, locked the door and walked towards the institution again.

Ørnulf was sitting by the wall with his arms around his legs rocking to and fro when I opened the door. He sent me a fleeting glance, lowered his eyes again, utterly indifferent. In the duty room Ellen was with another girl of my age. She stood up and shook my hand. Her name was Irene, she said. She was tall and slim, had short blonde hair, blue eyes, high cheekbones. She was beautiful in that cool way I had always found myself drawn towards. Her presence there complicated everything, I knew that as soon as I sat down and poured myself a cup of coffee. I would be aware of her at all times, and therefore of myself, of how I appeared in her eyes.

She suggested that she attend to Ørnulf, Ellen attend to Are and I attend to Hans Olav. That meant I would have breakfast with him, relax a little afterwards, clean his 'flat' and then perhaps be with him in the ward until midday, unless he wanted to sleep instead. He seemed to sleep a lot.

I buttered some slices of bread for him, some for me, poured juice into two glasses and coffee into two cups, one of which was half milk, and carried everything in on a tray, placed it on his dining table, closed the door to the main ward, knocked on his bedroom door and went in.

He was lying in bed and pulling at his dick, which was flaccid.

'Hi, Hans Olav,' I said. 'Time to get up. I've brought you some breakfast!'

He looked at me while continuing to wank.

'I'll wait a bit then,' I said. 'Get up when you're ready!'

I closed the door and sat down on the chair at the table, which was positioned next to the entrance to a little balcony. It was grey and worn and the paint was peeling, and beneath it was the hand-ball court; behind this, beyond the embankment, were several buildings identical to the one I was sitting in. Behind and between them pines and isolated deciduous trees.

Some residents came walking towards us and slightly behind them two women, each pushing a wheelchair. I got up and walked around. In the living room there was a Monet picture, the kind you can buy framed in big chain stores. The furniture was made of pine and consisted of a large red-patterned sofa, a low coffee table with turned feet and a bookcase. The shelves of the bookcase were empty apart from an ornamental dog, a small candlestick and a glass tea light. The room was decorated to look like home, but of course it didn't.

I knocked on the bedroom door and opened it again. He was lying as before.

'You've got to come now,' I said. 'I've got breakfast for you. Your coffee's getting cold!'

I stood beside him.

'Come on now, Hans Olav. You can do that afterwards.'

He waved me away with one hand.

I put a hand on his shoulder.

He screamed, a loud rasping scream, I took fright and stepped back.

But I couldn't give in, I had to show him who was boss, if not I would have problems later, so I took his arm and tried to pull him up. While he tried to get rid of me with one hand he kept wanking with the other.

'OK,' I said. 'Shall I take your breakfast back? Is that what you want?'

He screamed again, an equally hoarse rasping scream, but swung his legs down, supported himself with his hands on the mattress and slowly and stiffly pushed himself into a standing position. As he stood up his trousers fell down. He pulled them up and started to walk out of the room, holding them up with one hand. He sat down on his chair and drank his coffee in one draught. I ate my bread and tried to act as if nothing had happened while my heart hammered behind my ribs and all my senses were focused on him.

With one sweeping movement of his hand he sent the glass of juice, the empty coffee cup and the plate of bread flying to the floor. It was all plastic, Irene had made sure of that, and didn't break.

'What are you doing?' I said. 'You mustn't do that!'

He stood up. Then he grabbed hold of the table, hoisted it onto the two legs furthest from him and pushed it over.

I didn't know what to do. I was terrified of him, perhaps he had noticed. Fortunately he left the room at once, for the adjacent bathroom, and I set the table back and was picking up the food when the ward door opened and Irene poked her head round.

'Having problems?' she said.

'He tipped up the table,' I said.

'Do you want me to take over?'

'No,' I said, although that was exactly what I wanted. 'It'll be fine. We just have to get used to each other. It probably takes a bit of time.'

'OK,' she said. 'If you need anything we're here. He isn't dangerous, you know. Imagine he's really a one-year-old!'

She closed the door, I put the last slice of bread on his plate and went to find something to wipe up the pool of yellow juice.

He was standing by the little window in the bathroom and peering out when I went in.

'I'll just have to get something to wipe up with,' I said. Suddenly he wasn't aware of me, but I didn't care as long as he left me in peace.

I had to wash the floors in the morning anyway, might as well do it now, I thought. I ran water into a red bucket, added a dash of green soap, took a cloth and scrubbing brush, set about cleaning the living room, then the hall, the bedroom and the little kitchenette. While I was busy doing this he approached, stood a few metres away and watched me. After a while he came closer and carefully poked the bucket with his foot, as if to tell me he could kick it over if he wanted.

He laughed his gurgling laugh and was suddenly overcome with a sense of purpose, he quickly left the room laughing out loud as he fidgeted beneath his chin. When I went into his room with the bucket and brush he was lying on his bed and wanking again, with an equally flaccid dick.

'Wan! Wan!' he said.

I ignored him, finished cleaning up, hung the cloth over the rim of the bucket and slumped down in the living room. I was tired and closed my eyes, ready to jump to my feet if a door went or a sound came from him.

I sat there for half an hour and slept. When I woke the food had gone and Hans Olav was back in bed.

I stood in front of the window in the living room looking out. There was a small mountain crag, bare in some places, covered with grass and bushes and thickets in others. The forest stretched up high behind.

From the other room the bed creaked, I heard him mumbling something to himself and I went in. He was on the floor, still holding his trousers up with his hand, as he had done all morning.

'Shall we go for a walk, Hans Olav?' I said. 'A bit of fresh air would be good, wouldn't it?'

He looked at me.

'Shall I do up your trousers?'

No reaction.

I walked over to him, leaned forward and held the waistband of his trousers, he at once poked two fingers at my face, one went in my eye, it swelled with pain.

'Hey! Cut that out!' I shouted.

At first I could see nothing, only darkness filled with luminous dots, but after a few seconds my eye started working again. I stood blinking, he went into the hall and banged on the door to the main ward with both fists.

He obviously didn't like me and now he wanted to be with the others or have me changed. But it takes two to tango.

'Come on,' I said. 'Let's go out. Get your jacket on and we'll go.'

He continued banging. Then he turned to me, but instead of going for me, which I had expected, and perhaps trying to poke out my eyes again, he walked around me and into his bedroom.

'Now you come here!' I shouted. 'Come on. Do you hear me!'

He lay down on the bed, but his eyes seemed nervous and I took his hand and pulled as hard as I could to get him on his feet. Although he didn't offer any resistance, in fact he tried to meet me halfway, he slid off the bed to the floor, slowly, like a boat listing.

This was hell.

He lay on his side with tears in his eyes. He tried to push himself up with one hand, all I could do was watch, hoping no one would choose this precise moment to come in. Once he was in a sitting position I took his hands again and he, no longer struggling, pushed off with his legs and was finally upright.

He looked at me and hissed, not unlike a cat, and then he slunk into the hall. I went and sat down on the chair in the living room. Listened to him shuffling around.

It was ten minutes to nine.

Something fell to the floor, I hurried out, it was the plate and cup. He was standing and pissing in the corner.

I said nothing, fetched the cloth and bucket, put on gloves and wiped it up. He seemed less stressed, walked to and fro around me as I worked.

'Shall we go for a walk?' I said.

He went over and got his jacket, stuffed his feet into his large shoes. He couldn't manage the zip, I moved towards him, he twisted away, opened the door to the corridor and with small cautious tripping movements walked down the steps and waited for me by the front door. I opened it and we were outside. He stayed ten strides ahead of me as we walked. After a few minutes he turned, I tried to make him go on, but he said no! no! and we walked back up to his flat, he lay down on the bed and started wanking. I sat down on the chair. Not even a third of the day had gone.

Life in the institution was not only different from outside, time was too. Standing by the window and looking into the forest, I knew that if I had been there, sitting under a tree and looking over at these buildings, time would have been barely noticeable, I would have drifted as lightly through the day as the clouds across the sky, whereas inside the institution and looking out, time was much heavier, almost clay-like, as though here it met obstacles and was always being forced to take detours, like a river traversing a plain before joining the sea, one might imagine, winding its way in countless labyrinthine meandering bends.

When my shift was finally over it always came as a surprise and was an experience I used to help me endure the strain: everything passes. On the way to work in the morning I dreaded it, but now it was over and I was free again, it was as though the interim didn't exist, had never existed, it was quite palpably gone.

It was no surprise that time went more slowly there, it was a place where nothing was supposed to happen, where no progress was possible, you noticed that as soon as you entered, this was storage, a warehouse for unwanted people, and the notion was so awful that you did whatever was in your power to act as if this were not the case. The residents had their own rooms with their own possessions, which were identical to the rooms and possessions of people outside, they had meals together with their ward colleagues and carers, who were supposed to represent their family, and every day they went to 'work'. What they created there had no intrinsic value, the value lay in the fact that the work gave their lives a semblance of the meaning lives outside had. And it was the same with everything in their world. What they were surrounded by looked like something, and it was in that outward semblance that its value lay. This became clearest to me on the first Friday when I was doing the afternoon shift and the whole ward was going to a 'disco' after dinner. It was to take place in a function hall in the district, a large room with tables and chairs in one half and a dance floor in the other. The lighting was muted, the windows were covered with curtains. Pop music blared out of the speakers, some Down's syndrome residents moved back and forth on the dance floor. The place was full of wheelchairs, gaping mouths, rolling eyes. The residents of my ward sat around a table by the windows, each with a Coke. I sat beside Ellen, who every so often sent me tired looks. Egil was wearing a creased white shirt with ketchup stains on the front. His hair stood on end. He stared up at the ceiling as his mouth moved. Håkon sipped cautiously at his soft drink. Alf stared sombrely down at the table. Next to us a carer stood up and pushed a resident in a wheelchair onto the floor, jiggled him to and fro in time to the music. His mouth hung open and emitted hollow happy noises as he drooled. The other carers at the tables were smoking and chatting about their own lives as far as I could see. Now and then they shouted, no, don't do that, or, sit still, or, you know what we say about that. Hans Olav was standing in the corner with his Picasso face, screwing and unscrewing a wall lamp. This was deeply disturbing. Disturbing because all these misshapen bodies and crippled souls which had been trundled into the discotheque – the most important room for youth culture, created for dreams about romantic love, charged with the future and potential – didn't experience any dreams, any yearnings, any electric charges, all they saw was hot dogs and soft drinks. And the music, which was meant to fill the body with joy and happiness, was only noise. When they danced it was just movements, and when they smiled it was because it was a semblance, now they were doing what normal people did. Everything was like the world as it was, but all the meaning had been stripped from it, and what was left was a parody, a travesty, grotesque and painful.

'They've got coffee over there if you want some,' Ellen said.

'Thanks,' I said and went to the table with the Thermos, pumped myself a cup, watched the happy Down's syndrome patients, who must have been in their forties. It was hard to watch them, their faces were always young, had a youthful shape, didn't seem to get older, except for the wrinkles that spread across them and made them look like children suffering from progeria.

I sat back down with the residents from my ward, lit a cigarette, glanced at Hans Olav, who had now started ripping down the curtains.

Alf looked up and stared into my eyes. My spine froze. It was as though he knew all about me, he knew my innermost thoughts and hated me from the bottom of his heart.

'Hans Olav!' Ellen shouted and stood up. Alf stared back down at the table. Ellen stopped in front of Hans Olav, he lowered his eyes to the floor as she spoke to him. Suddenly he glanced to the side and walked off as though he hadn't noticed Ellen at all or that they were in the middle of a conversation. Kåre, bent beneath his hump, which it was difficult to believe was part of him, moved to another table. The carers there welcomed him, he ignored them, lowered his head and shook his hand close to his ear, the way you do with a tin to hear if there is anything inside.

Irene and Ørnulf came in through the door. I was relieved when I saw her, in some way or other she had an effect on me. We had chatted in the breaks during the last few days, she had asked me what had made me apply for a job here as I neither came from the area nor lived here, I had said my girlfriend lived nearby, she asked what her name was, I told her. Gunvor! she said. We went to *gymnas* together! This information made me feel uncomfortable, I had been looking at her and thinking about her – nothing she noticed, I hoped, but you never knew with such matters. It made me feel I had been unfaithful. I had betrayed Gunvor. I had glanced at her when she was putting on a clean sheet and a duvet cover in one of the rooms, the old ones were in a pile in the corridor, outside each and every door, all the way down. A fleeting glance was no crime, after all we worked on the same ward, but the thoughts were there, I liked her a little too much. Or when she pushed the food trolley to the tables and began to set them and met my gaze and sent me an ingenuous professional smile, absolutely uninterested in me as anything except a colleague. That was also humiliating. So there I was, caught between two minor humiliations: on the one hand, I liked her too much given the fact that I was going out with Gunvor and, on the other, she was completely uninterested in me or who I was. Of course, I kept all this hidden, I did nothing, said nothing, behaved appropriately in all ways, indeed I was discouraging rather than encouraging, whatever took place was unseen to anyone except myself, and so it didn't really exist, did it?

She went to get a soft drink and hot dog for Ørnulf, who immediately leaned over and sucked at the yellow straw. When he thought there wasn't enough coming he pulled it out and threw it on the floor, put the bottle to his mouth and drained it in one long swig.

She looked at me and smiled sweetly.

'What are you doing this weekend?' she said.

'I'm going to Gunvor's, I imagine. She's picking me up after work.'

'Say hi from me.'

'I will. And you?'

'Well, I'll probably go to Stavanger. Or I'll stay here. Depends on the weather.'

'Doesn't look too good,' I said, because it was raining and had been doing so all day.

'No,' she said.

The Beach Boys' 'Good Vibrations' came on. The Down's syndrome residents waggled from side to side, some with a smile on their faces, others in deep concentration. Roars and groans from all sides. Ellen wiped Are's dribble, he sat with his mouth agape staring at the ceiling.

'Lovely summer music,' Irene said.

'Mm,' I said.

The mist hung over the trees, the rain was heavy and pummelled the ground, which glinted in the light from windows and lamps. I stood outside the admin block waiting for Gunvor, who was coming to pick me up. The evening sky was grey and shambling, seeming to sink into the countryside. It was beautiful. The tarmac was damp, the grass was damp, the trees were damp and their greenery muted the grey, but was still strong and bright. The forest of twisted limbs and disordered minds. With the lights from the windows and the silence among the trees it was as disturbing a place as it was appealing. Everything aroused ambivalence, nothing was clear-cut: if all the routines and the slow rhythm in which everything happened occasionally caused me to collapse into a semi-apathetic tedium it was still always mentally agonising to be there as well. It was as though I was running and sitting still at the same time, my breathing was accelerated and my heart hammered wildly while the rest of my body was motionless.

I wanted to be a good person, full of empathy for those worse off than me, but if they came too close, what I felt for them was contempt or anger, as if their deficiencies touched something deeper inside me.

When Gunvor and I stepped out onto the drive in front of their house after the long car journey I still had the institution in my body, standing in me like stagnant marsh water. Any feelings I had were coloured by it, even when I filled my lungs with pure clean air. Her parents had gone to bed, we had supper alone in the kitchen, she made some tea, we sat in the sitting room and chatted for ages, kissed each other goodnight and went to bed in separate rooms, though not without a few quips about it. I felt like I was in a *fin de siècle* novel when I was there, the young couple living in a morality different from their own, surrounded by prohibition, denial, non-living, while we were in the midst of pulsating life, full of repressed desires which occasionally forced their way to the surface. I liked that feeling, it was the most romantic feeling I could imagine.

The next morning I borrowed some boots and waterproofs, went down to the slippery quay with Gunvor and her brother, got into a boat, which measured fourteen, perhaps sixteen, feet and sat on the front thwart while Gunvor's brother pulled the starter rope of the outboard motor and slowly reversed until he could turn and accelerate. The rain was pelting down. The forest on the shore stood like a green wall behind the completely flat light grey surface of the water, the prow ploughed through it, converting it into swirls of white, with some almost transparent, almost glasslike layers below, and I had a distinct sense of depth, of being on the surface of an immense depth, which was reinforced when we stopped by the fishing net and the boat was rolling on its own waves and the net was drawn closer and closer together, then the spine of a fish appeared far below. It swam round and round, came higher and higher, and it was enormous. It was as big as a child and as shiny as silver. It came higher and higher, and when at last it lay in the boat and Gunvor's brother hit it repeatedly on the head with a wooden mallet the resistance it put up was so great he had to sit astride it while we did what we could to hold it down. The power in its slender body was frightening.

On the way home, as it lay still between our feet, with only the occasional twitch running through it, inside my head I had the image of it rising through the water. It was as though it came from an era other than ours, up and up it came from the depths of time, a beast, a monster, an *ur* force, yet there was something so clear and simple about it. Just water, the glint of silver in the depths, the immense power it possessed, surging through it in its dying throes.

The rain beating down now on the dead fish and coursing over its scales and perfectly white belly.

Gunvor was on the evening shift that Sunday, so I caught the bus early in the afternoon and arrived at my accommodation block at about five. I had thought I might be able to do some writing in the hours before I went to bed, but gave up after thirty minutes, nothing new could be activated in such an alien place as this, it seemed to me. Instead I went for a walk down to the town centre, followed a whim and entered a Chinese restaurant, had a meal there, alone in a room full of families eating their Sunday dinner. Afterwards I lay on my bed reading a novel by V.S. Naipaul I had found on offer a few days earlier, it had been in a box outside the bookshop and was called *The Enigma of Arrival*. I liked it even though there was no plot, just a description of a man who has moved to a house in a remote village in England, everything is alien to him, but slowly he conquers the countryside, or the countryside conquers him. It struck me that you could find rest in the prose, the way you can rest under a tree or in a chair in the garden, and that had a value in itself. Why actually should you write about actions? X loves Y, Z kills W, F commits embezzlement and is caught by G . . . His son A is deeply ashamed and moves to another town, where he meets B, they live together have two children, C and D . . . What was the description of a father compared with that of a tree in a meadow? The description of a childhood compared with that of a forest seen from above?

If only I were able to describe a forest seen from above! The openness and freedom of deciduous trees, the way their crowns rippled as one, seen from a distance, green and magnificent and alive, though not alive in our way, no, alive in their own equally simple secretive way. The sheerness and verticality of spruces, the frugality and loftiness of pines, the paleness and greed of birches, and the aspen, the trembling of aspens as the wind whistles up the mountainside!

Green, grey, black. Forest lakes and fields, fallen trees and bogs, clearings and copses, stone walls so old they seem to have grown into the landscape. Meres with water lilies and muddy bottoms full of tree carcasses. Meadows and pastures, crevices and cliffs, pine moors and heaths, rivers and streams, waterfalls and deep pools. Ash, aspen, beech, oak, rowan, birch, willow, alder, elm, pine, spruce. All with their own characteristic individual shapes, yet representative of the same.

But I couldn't write about that, it was completely beyond me, both because my language was insufficient – I didn't know how to approach the subject, how to express it – and because I lacked the knowledge. The last time I found myself in the heart of a forest I was in the ninth class. I couldn't tell the difference between an elder tree and an ash, barely knew the names of any flowers apart from a wood anemone and a blue anemone and what we called a buttercup, but it probably had a completely different name.

I couldn't describe a forest, neither seen from above nor from within.

No, the composure he possessed I didn't have in me, and the self-assurance and serenity, which all great prose writers have, I couldn't even achieve as a pastiche.

Such was my experience of reading Naipaul, like reading almost all other good writers: enjoyment and jealousy, happiness and despair, in equal portions.

But it took my mind off the institution at any rate, and on the eve of a new working week, that was all I really wanted. The thought of the place, all the days that stood before me, was worse and more unbearable than the days themselves, which of course always passed in the end. Tramping around in there, back and forth between the kitchen and the duty room, the washroom and the ward, it was as though nothing else existed, the whole unit with its harsh light and linoleum floor, its rank odours and heaps of frustration and compulsions was an existence all of its own, which I descended into, it engulfed me, crossing the threshold to the corridor was like stepping into a zone. It wasn't without its problems, but the problems were bound to the life there, the people there, both the carers and the residents. It had something to do with the fact that we were locked in, that we moved in such restricted space, where every little displacement in one direction or another had an immeasurable effect, while the slow advance of time and the lack of anything to distract us lulled life there into a kind of calm, a kind of standstill.

Most weekends I was at Gunvor's, we went swimming and relaxed, walked in the forest, watched TV, drove somewhere in the car when she wanted to smoke, as she couldn't do that at home. I loved her, but without life in Bergen, where there was so much happening, it became clear to me that this was not enough, that just her was not enough, and this was a painful thought, not least when we were having lunch with her parents, who loved her so much, or when we were watching TV or playing Trivial Pursuit in the evening, because if Gunvor couldn't or didn't want to see it, her mother did, of that I was very sure. So who was I?

One evening we went for a swim in the sea down by the rocks. The air was warm and full of insects, the blazing sun hung just above the treetops. Afterwards we sat next to each other gazing at the water. Gunvor got up, went behind me and covered my eyes with her hands.

'What colour are my eyes?' she said.

I went cold.

'What is this? Are you testing me?' I said.

'Yes,' she said. 'Tell me. What colour?'

'Stop that,' I said. 'You don't need to test me. Of course I know what colour your eyes are!'

'Tell me then!'

'No. I won't. I don't want to be tested.'

'You don't know.'

'Of course I know.'

'Then tell me. It's simple.'

'No.'

She removed her hands and began to walk back up. I rose and followed her. I said I loved her, she told me to stop saying that, I said it was true, it came from the bottom of my heart. And added that I was self-centred and inattentive, distant and absent, but that had nothing to do with her.

The weekends I spent with her I took lots of photographs, which I had developed in a photo shop on the Mondays. I sent some of them in a letter to dad. Here is my new girlfriend, Gunvor, I wrote, and this is me standing beside her horse on the farm where she lives. As you can see, I haven't changed much. I was thinking of visiting you this summer, if I do, I'll ring first, take care, Karl Ove.

When the six weeks at the institution were over I caught the boat to Stavanger and the train from there to Kristiansand. For the first few days I stayed with Jan Vidar, who had moved into a terraced house on one of the estates outside town with his girlfriend, Ellen. We sat in the garden drinking beer and talking about the old days, about what we were all doing now. He had taken his diving certificate, my old dream, and he did a fair bit of diving, he told me, otherwise it was mostly work. It had always been like that with him, right from his time at vocational school, when he had got up in the middle of the night to start his work as a confectioner and baker. Going with him to the cinema had been hopeless, I remembered, after a couple of minutes in the darkness his eyelids closed irrespective of what was showing on the screen.

The house was on a hill, from his back garden there was a view of the fjord, the sky was blue and the wind whispered through the trees on the slope beneath us, as it always did in the afternoon. They had a cat and he told me about the time it had given birth to kittens. It had been much too small or there was something else wrong, because one afternoon Ellen had come home and the young mother had killed all her young. There had been nothing short of a bloodbath in the house. Jan Vidar laughed as he told me, I was shaken, I imagined how it must have been, all the squeaking and snarling and crawling on the carpet.

The next day I woke to an empty house and caught the bus down to Kristiansand, filled with the old feeling of panic, it was such a fantastic day, not a cloud to be seen anywhere, and I didn't leave town, I stayed in the hot narrow streets sweating while everyone else was sailing their boats around the islands and swimming and drinking beer and having a good time. I had never managed that, I had never been invited, and you don't do that kind of thing on your own. What was a record shop on a baking-hot day in Kristiansand? What was the library, who was that sat there, gawping?

I visited grandma and grandad, they were surprised to see me, I told them a little about life in Bergen, that I had a girlfriend and I saw a lot of Yngve and he was doing very well. Nothing had changed with them, everything was as before, it was as though they had reached their final age, I thought, as I caught the bus back up to Jan Vidar's, and from now on they wouldn't be a day older.

I had no connection with Kristiansand, it was no longer my 'home'. Bergen wasn't either, the thought of returning there and starting a new semester was not a happy one, but what alternative did I have?

On the last day of my short Sørland holiday I visited dad and Unni. I was in a good mood as I left the bus stop on the E18 and walked through the streets of the estate where they lived, although a slight stab of fear of dad always made itself felt as I approached him. He was sitting on the sofa when I came up the stairs and I didn't know where to look, he had become so fat. He sat there like a barrel, staring at me. As brown as a berry, wearing shorts and a voluminous shirt, his eyes black.

'Ah, there you are,' he said. 'It's been a while.'

'Thanks for your letter!' Unni said. 'How exciting to hear about Gunvor. We were kind of hoping you'd bring her with you!'

'But what a name!' dad said.

'She's working all summer,' I said. 'She'd like to meet you though, of course.'

'Was it history she was studying?' Unni said.

'Yes,' I said.

'And she rides horses, does she? Or was that any old horse you took the photo of?'

'No, she's a big horse-riding fan. She went to Iceland for a year just because of the ponies,' I said.

Dad and Unni exchanged long glances.

'Actually, we're thinking of going there for a bit. Next year maybe.'

'That sounds good, Karl Ove,' Unni said.

I sat down on the chair across the table from him. He took a sip of the beer he had in front of him. Unni went into the kitchen. I said nothing, he said nothing.

'How's it going up north then?' I said after a while and started to roll a cigarette.

'It's going pretty well,' he said.

He looked at me.

'Would you like a beer?'

'Yes, maybe,' I said.

'You'll find one in the kitchen.'

I got up, went in, Unni was sitting at the table and reading a newspaper. I opened the fridge and took out a beer. She smiled at me.

'She's attractive, Gunvor is,' she said.

'Yes, she is,' I said, and smiled back, then rejoined dad.

'There you go,' he said.

'*Skål*,' I said.

He didn't answer, though he raised his bottle and drank.

'How's your scribbling going?' he said eventually.

'It's mostly my studies now,' I said.

'You should find yourself a course with better prospects than literature,' he said.

'Yes,' I said. 'I will eventually.'

'What course is Yngve doing?'

'Media studies.'

'Well, that's not such a stupid idea,' he said, looking at me. 'Are you hungry?'

'A bit maybe.'

'I'll make some food soon. But it's so hot. It's not so good to eat now. I don't have much of an appetite in the heat, you know. That's why they eat so late in southern Europe.'

There was a confidentiality in his reasoning that made me happy. I finished the bottle, fetched another, felt the desire to get drunk creep up on me. It had been a long time.

And I did get drunk. Dad fried chops and boiled potatoes, we ate, Unni went to bed early, we sat drinking in the twilight. He couldn't be bothered to turn on any lights and so I didn't either.

He said he and Unni were always together, they couldn't be apart, after only a few hours they began to miss each other. That was what had happened that day he had been an external examiner in Kristiansand and we were supposed to visit him, he hadn't been able to cope with being away from Unni and had drunk on his own and fallen asleep, do you remember that time, Karl Ove? The Hotel Caledonien had burned down two days later, that could have been me, I could have been there. Yes, I did remember, I had thought the same, I said.

He withdrew into himself, I fetched another beer, went for a pee, came back, he got up and went to the toilet, drank more. I told him grandma had died in the autumn, yes, he said, she had been ill. I finished my bottle, he finished his, I fetched two more, thinking this was fine, it was perfectly all right being together with him. I felt strong. If he had a go at me now I would be able to give as good as I got. But he didn't have a go at me, why would he, he was too deep inside himself, and at length he stood up in front of me in the semi-darkness, the fat bearded drunken man who was my father and had once been the very symbol of correctness – well dressed, slim and good-looking, a young respected teacher and politician – and he said well, that's me for tonight, there'll be another day tomorrow, you know.

Unni had made a bed for me in the room downstairs, and with my head buzzing with thoughts and feelings I got into bed and enjoyed the feeling of cool clean linen and lying in an unfamiliar room, one which wasn't mine but where I still belonged, at least in a way. The wind soughed in the trees, the floorboards creaked upstairs and, outside, the flaxen summer darkness became paler and paler as I lay in bed asleep, until the first blue patch in the sky slowly broke through and a new day dawned.

I spent the last weeks of the summer at mum's. It was like my refuge, where everything I usually struggled with did not exist.

Kjartan, whom mum had visited close on every day since he had been admitted, had finally been discharged and I met him at hers. He seemed tired and low on energy, a touch stiffer in his demeanour but otherwise healthy. He showed me some new poems, which were fantastic. He said he was going to move back to Bergen and resume his studies. I didn't ask him any questions about what had happened, that belonged to those topics you couldn't mention directly, but after some time had elapsed he told me unbidden. After he had trashed the flat he had shouted he was forty years old. I'm forty years old, he had shouted, and destroyed everything around him. By the time he arrived at the hospital in Førde he had deluded himself into thinking he was in Japan, that those receiving him were Japanese, and he made a deep bow to them, as was the custom in Japan. When he had psychosis he also heard voices, he received constant directives from a god, and to me it seemed as if there was some good in that, being taken care of by something else, while it was also extremely scary as this something else was him, a part of him.

Back home in Bergen I started a new novel. The plot took place in a fjord landscape, it was the 1920s, the main protagonist in the first chapter was playing cards in a cabin up in the mountains, he was about to get married and didn't want to spend money he had won gambling on the wedding, so he put everything in the pot and leaned back in bed and watched with immense pleasure as the others got very excited about the large sum of money that might come their way. The main protagonist in the second chapter was a young man in Bergen, it was the 1980s, he stood browsing through the titles on his bookshelf waiting for his girlfriend, in the kitchen the espresso maker was chugging away, he thought about his grandparents on the farm by the fjord; they were old, she was ill, their lives would soon be over. That was as far as I got when the semester restarted because every sentence had been written and crossed out and rewritten countless times, everything had been laboriously worked through, it was a time-consuming process, and since I had to hand in an important assignment in only a few months I put it to one side.

'Intertextuality in James Joyce's *Ulysses*' was the working title of the assignment. It was ambitious, I knew that, but I had an aim and an intention with it, I wanted a sensationally good grade and so I had to go for it.

As Julia Kristeva had coined the term intertextuality at first I concentrated on her and read *Revolution in Poetic Language*, but I was unable to understand, it was simply too hard. She wrote a lot about Lacan, I wanted to go to the source and I read a book by him in a Swedish translation, which if this were possible was equally difficult, especially because both his and her ideas originated from a kind of basic structuralist stance, which was new to me. In some ways it made me feel proud, as I was dealing with material at such a high level, in some ways it made me feel desperate and angry, as I could never quite grasp the ideas. Almost but not quite. Furthermore, it was problematic that so many of their references were unfamiliar; if any were familiar at all they were always vague, and that was no good, accuracy was the very premise of this activity at literature's particle level. The novel itself, *Ulysses*, was, however, not difficult to understand, it was about one day in three people's lives, told in chapters with widely varying styles. I got hold of a book that went through all the references to Dante in *Ulysses*, I doubted any of the lecturers had it, so I could use it freely, perhaps let Dante's presence in Joyce be the principal example of the book's intertextuality.

I bought a second-hand computer when my study loan came, an Olivetti, from one of Yngve's friends, Borghild, whom I had met the first time I went to Café Opera, she had become an editor at *Syn og Segn* and hung around with Asbjørn for a short period. She wanted five thousand kroner for it, a quarter of my study loan, but this was my future we were talking about, so I agreed and for the first time in my life wrote letters on a screen and not a sheet of paper. Green luminous futuristic letters, which were stored on one of those tiny floppy disks, as they were called, and could be summoned up whenever I wished. There was also a game of Yatzy on the computer, I could sit throwing dice for hours on end, they were green and luminous as well. Sometimes this was how I started the day, an hour's Yatzy before breakfast. Yngve and Asbjørn did the same, and if I set a new record I always told them when we met.

Gunvor had also bought a computer, occasionally I took my floppy disks with me and wrote on hers, either after she had gone to bed, only a few metres away, and lay asleep, breathing, tossing and turning, the way sleepers do, in a completely different world from the one I was in, or after she had gone to the reading room for the day. I didn't show my face at the university, everything was about the assignment this semester, so I might as well read and write at home, I thought. In practice, I often ended up doing nothing, the days passed doing shopping, having breakfast and reading a newspaper, looking out of the window, perhaps going to some record shops or second-hand bookshops in town, returning home for lunch, spending the evening with Espen or Gunvor, unless I went out drinking with my fast-dwindling money. If I went with Espen or Gunvor and her friends things always turned out fine, I got back home without having lost control, but if it was anyone else, that is, Yngve and his friends, it was a much riskier venture. Once, at five in the morning, I came home without a key and rang the bell, fortunately Gunvor had been sleeping at my place, she opened the door, in her eyes I could read fear, I walked past her, wanting only to sleep, remembered nothing of the way home or any of the night, only the moment I stood at the door unable to find my key remained.

'Whose jacket's this?' Gunvor said.

'It's mine of course,' I said.

'No, it isn't,' she said. 'You've never had a jacket like this. And what's this? There's blood on it! What happened?'

I examined it. It was a blue denim jacket. There was blood on the lapel.

'It's my jacket. I've had it for years. I don't know what you're going on about. I'm off to bed. I've had it.'

When I woke it was one o'clock and the bed was empty, she had gone to her lecture at nine as always.

I remembered nothing from when I was at Garage until I was standing outside the door.

Freezing cold and frightened, I went into the hall and re-examined the jacket hanging there. I had never seen it before.

It didn't have to mean much. I had probably been to a party and picked up the wrong jacket from the heap, I had been drunk and that wasn't so strange.

But the blood?

I went into the bathroom to look at my face. Nothing, not so much as a nosebleed.

So the jacket must have been bloodstained from before.

I rinsed my face in cold water and went into the kitchen. I could hear Jone's radio, I knocked on his door and poked my head in. He was sitting in his armchair with a record cover between his hands.

'Want some coffee? I'm making some now.'

He laughed.

'What a sight! Did you go out last night?'

I nodded.

'Yes, I'd like some coffee,' he said.

'I don't remember a thing,' I said.

'Have you got the shakes?'

'Yes.'

'It'll go. I'm sure nothing happened. Can you smell any perfume?'

'No.'

He laughed.

'That's all right then. I don't suppose you killed anyone, either.'

But that was precisely what was worrying me.

I put on the espresso maker and heated a little saucepan of milk. Jone came in when the pot had finished hissing, took a cup from the cupboard, poured some coffee, placed a foot on a chair and blew at the steam coming from his cup.

'The police were here when I was leaving this morning,' he said.

'Ha ha,' I said.

'It's true! I was on my way downstairs, and there, you know, by the post boxes, were two policemen. They were opening the door with a crowbar. They didn't say anything, they were silent, didn't even look at me. Just yanked open the door. Surreal.'

'Was it a raid or what?'

He shrugged.

Some immigrants lived on the ground floor, it was always packed with people, Espen thought they might have been selling dope, and the fact the police were there suggested he was right. On the other hand, they might not have had residence permits. Jone, who chatted to everyone, had also tried to talk to these neighbours of ours, but without much luck.

'How's it going with the band? Kafkatrakterne?'

He laughed again. The name was too studenty for his taste.

'It's going well,' I said. 'We're playing tonight.'

'By the way, got a few bargains up north,' he said. 'Do you want to see them?'

He had taken the bus all the way up to Trondheim and back again over the weekend just to go to a record fair.

Anything that could make me forget the night was good and I followed him into his room. He dug out a few singles, all in plastic covers, mostly Norwegian punk and new wave.

'Do you remember this one?' he said, passing me Blaupunkt, 'Let Me Be Young'.

'Yes, I do!'

Betong Hysteria, Kjøtt, Wannskrækk, Lumbago, The Cat and some DePress singles followed.

'This is one for you,' he said and took out a completely round XTC cover, it was *The Big Express* in the shape of a train wheel.

'How much do you want for it?'

'Not that much. A hundred and fifty? Two hundred?'

'Why not two hundred and fifty?' I said.

He laughed.

'I'll give it a miss,' I said. 'I've got it.'

I smacked my forehead.

'I *used to have* it.' I had forgotten my stupid stand at the fair.

At the end of last semester I had been so hard up and had borrowed so much money that I had succumbed to the temptation and a bought a few metres of sales space at a record fair Jone was going to in Bergen and I had sold all my records. Every single one. I got a few thousand for them, which I had drunk my way through a week later, that had been when Bergen was really buzzing and everyone was out – and that had been that. Six years' worth of collecting out of the window. My whole soul had been in those records. And that was partly why I had done it, I wanted to purge myself of everything, it was shit, all of it, anyway.

'If you're interested in collecting, it's CDs that count now,' Jone said. 'It was wise to sell up! Don't give it another thought!'

He laughed again.

'There was some blood on my jacket when I came home this morning,' I said. 'It wasn't my jacket either. And I can remember zip all. Nothing.'

'You're as decent as the day is long, Karl Ove. Calm down. You didn't do anything wrong.'

'I feel as if I've killed someone.'

'It's always like that. I'm sure you just went round saying how fantastic everyone was.'

'Yes.'

'I'm off to class. I've got a late lecture today.'

'OK. I have to go too. See you.'

We didn't practise at Verftet any more, Pål had found us a place in the basement of the HIB, the technology centre, which was over the bridge from my flat, a grey building with blue lines and a blue logo, it looked more like a grey plastic bottle of shower gel than anything else, with grooves and a blue cap. Pål's laboratory was in the building, I had been up there once, walked wonderstruck through the small rooms with all the instruments, I loved 'science', or rather the aura that surrounds the work, not science in itself, which I despised, it was technical, instrument-based, non-human, restrictively rational. But 'science', that was everything from Captain Nemo's submarine to Darwin's *Beagle* diary, Bruno, who was burned at the stake, and Galileo, who gave the Church all the concessions they wanted, Marie Curie's in retrospect frightening experiments with radiation, Oppenheimer and his circle's splitting of the atom. There was the man who had an iron rod blown through his head in the 1880s and underwent a complete personality change – before nice, after evil – allowing medical science to take a step forward because now they knew that certain functions were housed in certain parts of the brain and, thanks to this accident, they had localised one of them and could develop theories to make lobotomy possible. Was there anything more desperate or crazier than a lobotomy? If so, it must have come from the same people who strapped down their patients and sent enormous electric shocks through them to shake them out of their depressions. It did help though, they were on the right track, and that was what I liked, that someone had learned how to control, in this case electricity, tame and store it, thus enabling something new to enter the world. At the same time there was something crazy about it, all this speed that was being released or all this light being transmitted everywhere. Human bodies being viewed as an arena, being treated with electric shocks to see how they would react, or cutting into, for instance, connections in the brain to produce a more harmonious type of personality. You wouldn't believe this could be true or you thought it was something they did in pre-biblical times, but it was true, this was what we were doing, and the aura of total insanity existed here too, in these small rooms, with their microscopes and all manner of underwater specimens, collected from the bottom of the sea by their research ship. Not that I understood what they were doing, or that I cared, all I saw was 'science', the romance of blue rubber gloves.

I could never see Pål fitting in there, he was the most unscientific person I had ever met, but that was perhaps exactly why he was so successful at what he was doing.

I met Yngve and Hans down at reception, Pål was late as always, we took the lift up and went to his department, he was standing over his desk, his long hair covering his face like a mini-curtain.

'Oh, that's right!' he said. 'It's music time.'

His bass was in the corner, he grabbed it and we took the lift down to the basement, where Pål unlocked the door and let us in. The room was big, the concrete floor covered with a yellow felt carpet, the drum kit was already there, plus some amplifiers and a sound system.

The mere sight of it, the three musicians immediately unpacking their cases and taking out their instruments, the cables, the straps, the plectrums, the speakers, plugging in and switching on their amps, tuning their guitars, adjusting the sound, excited me, this was what I had always dreamed of, being in a band, doing band things. I gave the snare drum a few exploratory taps and tightened it, although I had no idea how to tune it, I couldn't hear when it sounded good, banged the bass drum, tightened the screw on the crash cymbal and pulled it closer in a – for me – reasonable imitation of a genuine drummer.

'I've spoken to someone planning a big party for New Year's Eve today,' Yngve said.

I looked at him, he was sporting that secretive expression of his, he was holding something back, like a child, and he smiled.

'Someone's been pulling your leg,' Pål said. 'It's not New Year's Eve today.'

'Did they give you some money to stay away?' Hans said.

'Ha ha,' Yngve said. 'They wanted us to play.'

'Are we going to play at a New Year's dance then?' I said.

'Absolutely,' Yngve said. 'It's at Rick's, and there'll be loads of people, so we've got to practise.'

'What shall we play then?' Hans said.

'I don't know,' Yngve said. 'Can't we just do all the songs we've got?'

We had been playing together for almost a year, we were getting better and better, especially me, because although I was still a lousy drummer and always would be, I had with the others' help managed to produce a variety of beats for a variety of songs, a fixed pattern for each which I clung to when we played. At home I went through every single song in meticulous detail several times a day, I knew them inside out, right down to every last touch of the cymbals, I sat drumming on my thighs and tapping my feet on the floor, all to sustain the minimum of rhythm and drive the band needed. Half a rehearsal had been spent getting me to achieve syncopation. A full hour, the same theme again and again, me unable to find the beat in one place, more and more embarrassing, it was eating away at everyone's patience, was I a complete idiot or what, it was so bloody *easy*, until it clicked. The whole time I was scared I would be given the boot because Yngve, Pål and Hans were competent musicians and they would, in one fell swoop, be so much better if they got rid of me, which

I told them often enough, but no, stop talking rubbish, you're the drummer, that's it.

After the rehearsal Yngve, Hans and I went into town while Pål caught the bus home. I was still haunted by that night's drinking, the most terrible thoughts and imaginings constantly lay beneath the surface, and my stomach ached with fear, for which in fact there was only one remedy and cure – Gunvor, an evening with her. But when Yngve suggested going out and celebrating there still wasn't a suggestion of a no on my lips.

'I just have to nip back home first,' Hans said. 'I'll come out later. Are you going to Garage?'

'Yes, aren't we?' Yngve said, looking at me.

'Yes.' I nodded.

It started to rain, not much, just a few drops on my face, but the sky above us darkened quickly, an entire wall of black was on its way across the mountains.

'Well, think I'd better get going,' Hans said. 'See you later.'

He disappeared up the hill to the left and we continued on our way to Garage. Hans lived on the other side of the Dragefjellet district, in a flat he shared with Tone, his girlfriend. Before that he had lived in a little collective in Sandviken with Ingar and Kjetil, two of his best friends, both active in Student Radio and *Studvest*, as he was. I had been there once, to a party with Yngve, that was the night he got together with Gunnhild, with whom he had moved into a flat in Marken only a few weeks ago. She was good-looking in a gentle retiring way, studied biology, came from a farm in Hardanger and was everything Yngve, or for that matter any other young man, could dream about. I was there that night, the place had been packed, and then I was there a few days later, alone, I had been walking around the town not knowing what to do, and I had thought, I'll go and visit Hans. I didn't know him, but we played in a band together, so it wouldn't seem that strange. Uphill from Bryggen, along the main Sandviken road, down the narrow passages to the crooked old house where they rented the first floor. I rang the bell, no one answered. I rang again, but they obviously weren't at home, so I turned and was about to go back up. At the end of the alley I saw Ingar. He had seen me because our eyes met, but he pretended he hadn't and carried on.

Why did he carry on?

Wasn't he going home?

He was probably going shopping, I thought, walking up the hill. At the same time I had a nagging suspicion it was me he was avoiding, me he didn't want to meet, perhaps feel obliged to invite in. So instead of walking down to the town centre I went up the next street and waited for him.

He appeared only a few seconds later, scanned both sides of the street before walking the last bit to the entrance of the house, took out his keys and, after glancing up the hill, unlocked the door.

My heart was heavy as I left, it was me he had been avoiding, there was no doubt about it, but why, what was it about me?

Oh, I knew of course, I felt it all the time, there was something about me people didn't want to know, something they tried to avoid if they could. Something I had, something about the way I behaved.

But what was it?

I didn't know.

I didn't say a lot, of course, I could safely assume that this was noticed and commented on unfavourably. Perhaps also that what I did say tended to be about inappropriate topics. What I said was often heartfelt, at least as soon as I was alone with someone, and people shied away from that like the plague. The alternative was to say nothing at all. These were my only *modi vivendi*, it was my entire register.

Well, not with Gunvor. She knew who I was.

The rain increased as Yngve and I hurried down Nygårdsgaten.

'I'll just have to ring Gunvor,' I said. 'She might be waiting for me at hers.'

'That's OK,' Yngve said. 'I'd better tell Gunnhild.'

'Is there a phone box anywhere near here?'

'There's definitely one in Festplassen. On the corner, down from Garage.'

'Shall we go there first then?'

'Yes.'

'What about swapping?' Yngve said when we stopped by the phone box rummaging through our pockets for coins. 'You ring Gunnhild and I'll ring Gunvor? See if they notice the difference?'

We were alike, Yngve and I, but only at first glance, we shared a kind of general resemblance which meant that I could be mistaken for Yngve by people who didn't know him that well. But our voices were almost identical. Often when I had rung up Yngve's old collective they had thought it was Yngve taking the piss.

'OK,' I said. 'Shall I ring Gunnhild first?'

'Yes, tell her I'm going to Garage with you and I don't know when I'll be back.'

I lifted the receiver and dialled the number.

'Hello?' Gunnhild said at the other end.

'Hi, it's me,' I said.

'Hi!' she said.

'Gunnhild, I'm going to Garage for a bit with Karl Ove,' I said. 'I don't know when I'll be home. But don't wait up anyway!'

'I might still do,' she said. 'But have a good time! And say hello to Karl Ove.'

'Will do,' I said. 'Bye.'

'Bye.'

Yngve laughed.

'You've only been together a few months,' I said. 'Gunvor and I have been together for more than a year. She'll notice.'

'Want a bet?'

'No, I daren't.'

Yngve picked up the receiver, inserted the money and dialled the number.

'Hi, Karl Ove here,' he said.

Silence.

'I'm going out with Yngve and Hans. But I'll come back to yours afterwards, is that all right? I don't know how long we'll be, but . . . Yes . . . Yes . . . I love you too. Bye!'

He rang off and turned to me with a smile.

'Did you say you loved her?' I said.

'Yes? She said she loved me!'

'Shit. You shouldn't have done that,' I said.

He laughed. 'We don't have to say anything. Then she'll never know.'

'But I know.'

He snorted.

'You're so sensitive,' he said. 'It was just a joke!'

'Yeah, yeah,' I said, and set off towards Garage.

Six hours later I was at a party in Fosswinckels gate, thinking how talented I was, writing actually wasn't a problem, I was full of energy, I *really* did own the world. That wasn't how things were, as I would have been the first to admit, but *really* they were. A couple of girls had given me the once-over in the basement of Garage, they had been long hungry looks, but of course I did nothing, I had a girlfriend, didn't I, Gunvor, asleep at home waiting for me. But this felt like a missed opportunity, a regret, and while Bendik, who owned the flat, put on the Happy Mondays and people around me were shouting and laughing excitedly, I sat staring at the ceiling thinking, it was fine, all I had to do was finish the relationship, then I would be free, and there would be nothing to stop me doing anything I wanted.

It was getting on for half past four, people were starting to leave, again there was only the hard core left, Bendik, Arvid, Erling, Atle, and when all hope of any more fun had gone I drained my glass, got up and went downstairs without saying goodbye, made a beeline for the backyard next door, where I went round pulling at the bikes, but they were all locked, I would have to walk, unless there was one left unlocked in the adjacent yard.

No, there wasn't.

The rain was teeming down as I trudged down the hills. In front of Garage, which now lay dark and empty, with raindrops running slowly and ornately down the windows and one taxi after another racing out of the tunnel beneath Høyden, I stood wondering what to do. I didn't want to go home, no question about that. I trotted towards Slakteriet, but that was closed too. I lit a cigarette, cupped my hand over it against the rain, walked up the gentle incline ending at the theatre. What I wanted was to sleep with someone, a girl I hadn't slept with before, one of the two who had been looking at me. Why hadn't I grasped the opportunity, how could I have been so incredibly stupid? Gunvor would never find out, and I wasn't doing it to spite her, I just wanted it so much I hadn't thought about anything else all evening. A woman's soft body, downcast eyes, new breasts, a new backside, she bends forward for me, on all fours for me, doggy position, and I, and I, well, I ram it in. That was basically all I wanted, but it was hopeless here, in a town where the rain fell remorselessly, deserted apart from the occasional darkened taxi, at half past four in the morning, how could it happen?

There was someone in Nøstet, she might have been in love with me once, she would probably receive me with open arms.

I went there. My hair plastered flat against my skull, jacket and trousers soaked, the streets empty, the only sound the squelch of my shoes.

I felt the front door. Locked.

She lived on the first floor, and I knelt down to gather some pebbles, threw them at the three windows of her bedsit.

No reaction.

I stood wondering what to do. Shout? That was no good, the whole neighbourhood would hear.

I grabbed the door frame, got a foot on it and swung myself up. There were narrow ledges and projections at various places on the wall, windows with protruding sills, and it should have been easy to do it, climb up to her floor and knock on the windows, or if I had the unimaginable good luck to find one of them unlocked, simply open it and step inside and give her a real surprise.

I was perhaps three metres up when I lost my grip and slipped down, fortunately in a relatively controlled manner, I didn't hit myself very hard, just a bit on one knee, which throbbed with unabated pain as I began to climb back. But I fell once again, this time badly, I landed on my chest, and the fall knocked all the air out of me. It was as though I was drowning, I couldn't breathe, and the pain radiated up into my brain from a thousand different places. The pain was incandescent, like a star.

OOOOOHHHHH I said.

OOOOOHHHHH

OOOOOHHHH

I lay still, breathing. Feeling the water in the puddle soaking into my clothes. My legs and arms and chest were freezing cold. Nevertheless it struck me that I could close my eyes and sleep there. Just for a moment . . .

The very next, Christ how it hurt!

I struggled into a kneeling position, lifted my head to the sky, from where all the rain was falling. I stood up straight and slowly began to walk, stiffly at first, then more and more easily. For some reason I walked uphill to Klosteret square, and on the way a police car glided alongside and stopped and the window slid down and a policeman asked me what I was doing.

'I've been to a party,' I said. 'And I saw a guy down there as I was passing. He was trying to climb up the front of a house. Don't know what the hell he was after, but it didn't look good.'

I must have appeared lucid enough for them to let me continue, not only that, they turned down the hill to follow up my tip-off.

Ha ha ha, I laughed as I walked down to Torgalmenningen.

Ha ha ha.

Ha ha ha.

I couldn't go to Gunvor's, not in all this mess, so I turned right and walked to the taxi rank instead. Five or six minutes later I got out of the car and went through my entrance, saw that the door to the immigrants' place had been nailed up and sealed with a strip of plastic, rested my shoulder against the line of post boxes, struggled up the next two floors, unlocked the door and stopped.

There was a scratching noise coming from the cabinet in the kitchen.

Was I finally going to see them? I was sick of finding evidence of their activities but not them, and as nimbly as a cat I ran into the kitchen and tore open the cabinet door. Nothing. Empty.

But the plastic rubbish bag had bite marks on it and coffee grains and eggshells had spilled out.

It had to be rats, couldn't be anything else, no mouse would behave like this, would it? The following day I would buy a rat trap or poison, I thought, and pulled off my clothes and a moment later I was asleep in bed.

I woke up to the telephone ringing. It's Gunvor, I thought, I'd better not answer it, I'll have to think of an excuse first, but the ringing wouldn't stop and in the end I answered it, with a pounding heart in an aching body.

'Yngve here.'

'Hi.'

'Heard you ran amok after the party.'

'*Heard?* Who from? Who said that?'

'Bendik. They saw you from the window. You ran into the back-yard looking for a bike. Then you came out and went straight into the next one. "He's a bad 'un, your brother," Bendik said. How was it? Did you do anything else?'

'No. It was fine. I went home. But I'm a little worried.'

'You can't take your drink. That's what's wrong. It's not good for you. You can't take it.'

'No.'

'Well, I don't want to moralise. You have to live your own life.'

'Yes, exactly.'

'You can come here if you like. It's only us. Then we can watch TV or something.'

'No, I don't think so. I have to work. It's only a short semester, isn't it.'

'OK. Talk later then.'

'Yes, all right. Bye.'

'Bye.'

Usually it took a day or so for the fear to subside after a night out; if something special had happened, two, maybe three. But it always did. I didn't understand why it came, why the shame and fear were so great, but they got worse and worse each time, and it wasn't that I had killed someone or hurt anyone. Nor had I been unfaithful. I had felt like sex, and I had done some stupid things to get it, but nothing had happened, I had climbed up a wall, for Christ's sake, should I be afraid for three days because of that? Should I pace the flat and start at every tiny noise, jump every time a siren sounded in the streets, my insides aching all the while with an intensity that was unbearable, except that I did, every time, all the time.

I was a cheat, a traitor, I was a bad person. And I could deal with that, it wasn't a problem as long as it was only me involved. But now I was with Gunvor, and it affected her because she became someone who was going out with a cheat, a traitor, a bad person. She didn't think that; on the contrary, in her eyes I was a lovely person, someone who meant well, who showed her consideration and love, but that was exactly where the pain lay because I *wasn't* like that.

I switched on my computer and while I was waiting for it to warm up skimmed through what I had written so far. I didn't give a shit about the assignment, I couldn't read about proto-language in the state I was in, my priority was the novel, which was now approaching fifty pages and had spread in so many directions, some of them promising at the very least. But I couldn't get a grip on the 1920s, which I wrote a good deal about, there was so much I didn't know about the era, and this ignorance hindered me, I could barely write a sentence for fear it wouldn't be accurate. Furthermore, the 1920s were much too far away for me to pump full with my own life, with what was coursing through my veins now. So the writing became wooden and lifeless, I could see that, but at the same time it was all I had, I was clutching at my last straw.

There was a thump on the sitting-room floor. I saved my work, put on my shoes and went down to Espen. He met me at the door, placed a finger on his lips and beckoned me to follow him into the kitchen. There was a stool in the middle of the floor, he pointed up at the ceiling, where there was a crack he wanted me to look through.

I clambered onto the stool, leaned back and peered in.

A big black rat met my gaze.

'Can you see it? Is it still there?' Espen said in a low voice.

'Ugh, Jesus,' I said, and got down. 'How revolting!'

'Now at least we know what it is,' he said.

'We'll have to buy poison tomorrow then.'

'Or traps. They can lie rotting between the walls, I've heard, impossible to get rid of.'

'What I've heard,' I said, 'is that there's something in the poison that makes them want water and so they run out of the house.' I could hear how odd that sounded and smiled tentatively and shrugged. 'The problem with traps is that the rats lie there and you have to physically throw them away. I don't feel like doing that.'

'Nor me,' Espen said. 'But if we have to, we have to.'

'A rat is a rat is a rat is a rat is a rat,' I said.

'Eh?' Espen said, looking at me. 'A cup of coffee?'

I nodded.

'I can hear you when you're working upstairs. The noise comes right down here. For a while I thought you were drumming your fingers. Then I suddenly twigged, aha, he's writing!'

'I've done fifty pages now,' I said. 'So you'll have to read it soon. If it's dross I don't want to waste a whole year on it.'

'I'd love to read it right away,' Espen said.

'What? Now, do you mean?'

'Why not?'

'A cup of coffee first, then I'll go and print it. OK?'

Espen nodded, and we went in and sat down in the sitting room.

'I was sure it was rats,' Espen said. 'I could hear them scrabbling along the ceiling boards. And then there was your rubbish bag. It couldn't have been anything else.'

'In which case, they're some smart rats. When Gunvor slept here a few days ago she made a packed lunch in the evening to avoid having to do it in the morning. She had to get up early—'

'And?' Espen said.

I looked at him. Was he getting impatient?

Seemed like it.

'Well, she put her lunch in her bag. Then when she was about to eat it later in the day it was empty. But the greaseproof paper was intact. So they'd sneaked into her bag, unpacked the paper, taken the food and scampered off. Well, there were a few bites left, but nevertheless. Sounds to me more like a whole league of them had been at work. It must have required comprehensive planning. Perhaps the one we saw was the brains behind it? In the hole?'

'The demiurge itself?'

'Yes, what do I know? But anyway we've got to flush them out. Gunvor can't stay here if the place is crawling with rats.'

'Is she so pampered?'

'Ha ha.'

'Is that your phone ringing?' he said.

I sat still for a few seconds, listening. Yes, it was.

'I'll run up and get it. And do the printing while I'm at it!' I said, hurrying out and up.

'Hello?'

'Hi, it's me,' Gunvor said. 'You are at home then? I was just about to give up.'

'I was downstairs with Espen.'

'I thought you were coming to my place last night?'

'Yes, I was. But it got late and I was so drunk I thought I would spare you.'

'I like you coming here. It doesn't matter if you're drunk.'

'Sometimes it does,' I said. 'I'm really frightened now. That's two nights in a row. Can't you come here? Then we can make waffles or something? I'm dying for something ordinary and normal.'

'OK. Now or what?'

'Yes, that'd be good. Will you buy some milk on the way?'

'Yes. See you. I'll bring some dirty laundry as well. Is that all right?'

'Of course.'

I attached the holes at the side of the roll of paper to the wheels on the printer, quickly read the last sentences I had written, I knew the first bit almost off by heart, checked the codes on the note I had stuck to the desk and pressed print. Immediately the printer head began to buzz back and forth, and I, still unused to this invention, watched with fascination as my words, sentences and pages appeared as if from a secret source somewhere inside the machine.

What the connection between the floppy disk and the screen was I had no idea; something had to 'tell' the machine that an 'n' on the keyboard would become an 'n' on the screen, but how do you get dead matter to 'tell' anything? Not to mention what went on when the same letters on the screen were saved onto the thin little disk and could be brought back to life with one tap of a finger, like the seeds that had been trapped in ice for hundreds of years and then, under certain conditions, could suddenly reveal what they had contained all this time, and germinate and blossom. Surely the letters I saved would be reawakened as easily in a hundred years' time as they could be now?

I tore off the perforated edges, stacked the sheets in order and went down to Espen.

'Gunvor's coming,' I said. 'So I'll be upstairs tonight. Here's the manuscript. When do you think you can read it by?'

'Day after tomorrow maybe? I'll tell you when I've finished!'

I went back upstairs, and when Gunvor arrived I made the waffle mixture while she sat on the kitchen chair and watched, cooked them in the iron, brewed up some tea and took everything into the sitting room. Perhaps it was the homeliness of the waffle aroma that did it, but at any rate we started talking about having children. It was an outlandish notion for us and everyone we knew, but when I was in Kristiansand Jan Vidar had told me about a couple of the girls from the *ungdomsskole* where we went, they had children now, one didn't even know who the father was.

The idea that we could have children and thus determine the whole of our futures was both a thrilling and a terrible thought.

'It has such enormous repercussions,' I said. 'It moulds the whole of the rest of your life. It's not the same with anything else

we do. For example, whether you study history or social anthropology doesn't really matter.'

'No, that's not true, is it?'

'It is, given a little perspective. Whether we get a cum laude or
not makes little difference. But, by Christ, how we strive for those
little differences. There are so few things that are *truly* all-decisive,
that make a difference.'

'I see what you mean.'

'When I write, you know, for me it has to be life or death. But
of course it isn't! It's just me sitting down and pottering around.'

'Yes,' she said. 'But not everything can be like that. Not everything can be either-or. We've got to have fun as well.'

She laughed.

'Can I quote you on that?' I said.

'Yes, but that's how it is, isn't it? Let's say we had a child now.
That would be a major event. It would determine the rest of our
lives, as you said. But our lives would be much the same nevertheless. We'd have to change nappies and push a baby buggy and so
on, and we'd do that, but that's not exactly momentous, is it?'

'No, you're right there.'

She opened her mouth and bit off a piece of the waffle.

'Is it good?' I said.

She had her mouth full and nodded.

I sprinkled sugar over mine, folded it and took a big bite.

'Yes, they're pretty good,' I said after swallowing.

'Fantastic,' she said. 'Have you made tea as well?'

I poured some in her cup.

'Tell me about yesterday!' she said. 'Who was there?'

I laid my head on her chest. She ran her hand through my hair, I
could hear her heart beating. There was something so girlish about
her, a huge innocence that moved me, while I, from the way I was
lying, was as submissive as a dog, I seemed to be relinquishing

something, not unknowingly, I both liked and disliked being comforted like this, it was nice and degrading at the same time.

After a while we got up and had a smoke in the sitting room, Gunvor with the duvet wrapped around her. We talked about Robert, her sister's husband, he was five or six years older than me and exuded masculinity, at a party where I had met him a few weeks earlier he had told me about an incident when a whole gang of men had been after him. He had grabbed a pole and shouted and gone ballistic, in the end they had cleared off, he had dropped the pole and continued on his way. If you want something, he said, you've just got to go for it. There's nothing to be scared of. You have to cross a kind of threshold where nothing matters, get into a zone where you're not afraid. Then you can do whatever you want. He had been a painter before, but stopped, he said he had been frightened of going mad.

'Did he say that to you?' Gunvor said.

'Yes, those were his precise words. I don't know if I believe him. It sounds a bit arch. I stopped painting because I was scared of going mad. At the same time it didn't seem completely unbelievable when you met him. It's like you know where he's coming from.'

'What do you mean?'

'Well, he's not exactly the student type. University isn't where it starts for him, as it does for us. It's more like the end of something, a place of calm after the storm.'

'It's funny with you and Robert, how we've ended up with you two. You have something in common, don't you?'

'No.'

'No?'

'No. I'm a boy, he's a man.'

'He's older than you, that's all.'

'There's more to it than that.'

Robert was proud of the girl he was with, Gunvor's sister, and he knew what he was doing with her. He was always respectful towards her and seemed to cultivate the differences between them. I wasn't proud of Gunvor, not in that way, I didn't know exactly what I was doing with her, and I didn't always behave respectfully towards her. He was clear in his language, in an un-ambiguous plain masculine way; I was unclear, vague, cowardly in mine. Not when it was just us two, but as soon as others joined us. Then it was a question of listening to where they were going and playing up to their collective will.

We looked at each other and smiled.

'Shall we put the washing machine on?' I said. 'You brought some dirty laundry with you, didn't you?'

She nodded and got up.

'I can do it,' I said.

She shook her head and smiled.

'No way. I have to do it.'

'I see,' I said.

I searched until I found a shop that stocked rat traps. I bought a few, as well as rat poison, and wandered home with everything in a little bag. There was only a couple of hundred kroner in my account, so I worried about it as I walked, the problem returned every autumn and spring, the study loan was spent, it would be several months before the next, in spring sometimes six months. The first spring I worked for Kjartan, the next one I sold all my records while in the autumn I borrowed money from people here and there or went home to mum and lived off her. But in the long term that was no good, it was an endemic problem, ad hoc solutions only postponed finding a real solution. In other words, I had to get a job. Which you did either through contacts or qualifications. I had neither. That is, I had worked for a year as a teacher, which might conceivably make temping at an early-years school a possibility, but not in the town centre, I doubted that very much, applications would be flooding in there, so it would have to be out of town. Another option was the health service. I had no desire to do what I had done before, but if needs must, needs must. There were two big institutions in town, one for the nutters, Sandviken Hospital, and one for the mentally handicapped, Vestlandsheim, and both had a high turnover of un-trained staff, I had heard. If I had to choose it would be Sandviken: better mentally ill than mentally handicapped.

I rang when I got home. I started with the schools, was given some phone numbers by a woman at the local council, most had supply staff already in place, and I was a bit too young, as some-one said, but a couple of them did take my name and telephone number without promising anything, their list of temps was long. At Sandviken they probably needed someone, but they wanted to talk to me first, could I drop by during the week and bring my qualifications with me?

Yes, of course I could.

Was Thursday convenient?

Thursday was fine.

Before I went to bed I put two rat traps in the cabinet under the sink, knocked on Jone's door, he went to bed late, and told him what I had done so that he wouldn't touch anything. He laughed in his cheery way and said he thought the rats were in my head and nowhere else. But he would keep away from the cabinet.

I couldn't take responsibility for the rats on Jone's behalf, I thought, lying in bed trying to sleep, my pulse thumping in my ears, but I did anyway, I thought about them all the time, I couldn't help myself, that was just how I was made.

Rats, we had rats.

I put off checking the traps the following morning, made some coffee first and drank it in the sitting room while smoking a ciga-rette and flicking through a collection of Swedish essays about Jacques Lacan, gazed out of the window, the queue of cars that formed so quickly after the lights had turned red, dwindled and re-formed. The cars were in constant flux, and the people in them, but the patterns they were part of remained the same. Death also made patterns. The raindrops running down windscreens, the sand blown into heaps, the waves beating against the shore and retreating. If you took a closer look, inside a grain of sand for example, patterns were there too. Electrons moving round atomic nuclei. If you went outside there were planets orbiting round suns. Everything was in flux, everything was inside and outside everything. What we didn't know, and never would, was what size really was. Think of the universe, how we considered the universe, infinity, imagine if it were small. Teeny weeny. Imagine if, in fact, it was inside a grain of sand in another world. And that this world was also small and inside another grain of sand.

This was my great idea. And actually it could be right, at least there was nothing to disprove it. But if it was, then everything was meaningless. We were completely dependent on there not being another world, on this being the only one, for what we were doing here to be meaningful. So it was important therefore to keep making literature. But if there was another world, a greater context, literature was simply rubbish, babble in the universe.

I went into the kitchen, put down my cup and opened the cabinet door, crouched and looked straight at a rat caught in one of the traps. The metal bar had hit it in the back. I felt sick. I pulled out the lowest drawer, took a plastic bag and gingerly pulled the trap towards me holding the little wooden base between my thumb and first finger. The plan was to put it in the plastic bag and chuck out the whole lot, rat and trap and everything, instead of fiddling around trying to release the rat.

Its rear part twitched.

I dropped the trap and withdrew my arm like a shot. Stood up.

Was it alive?

No, it had to be a convulsion. A muscle spasm.

I crouched down again, nudged the trap with my finger so that it was facing me.

It was as though the rat was looking at me with its little black eyes.

Another spasm went through one bare leg.

Was it alive?

Oh, no.

It was.

I slammed the door and paced up and down the kitchen floor.

It was important to act quickly, get rid of it, not to think any more about it.

I opened the door, grabbed the trap, slung it into the plastic bag, dashed downstairs, hurried over to the dustbins, opened one and threw the bag in, jogged back up, washed my hands in the bathroom, sat down in the sitting room and smoked a cigarette.

Job done.

At around seven mum phoned, she reminded me that grandad was coming to town on Monday, he was going to hospital and would be there a few weeks. Mum asked if I would mind meeting him off the ferry and taking a taxi up to the hospital with him. I said that was fine. Then we, the grandchildren in Bergen, would have to agree visiting times so that we could spread the load as far as possible. She might come over herself too, in which case it would be the last weekend he was there.

I had hardly got off the phone and turned to go into the sitting room when there was a knock at the door. It was Espen.

'Come in,' I said. 'Like some coffee?'

'Please,' he said. 'If you've got any on the go.'

'Oh yes.'

I fetched cups and we sat down. He wasn't quite himself, perhaps lost in his own thoughts.

'I've read your manuscript,' he said.

'That's good,' I said. 'Have you got time to talk about it now?'

He nodded.

'But perhaps we should go out for a walk? It's easier to talk then. Sitting still soon gets a bit claustrophobic.'

'Yes, I've been indoors all day, so going out is not a bad idea.'

'Shall we go then?' Espen said, getting up.

'And the coffee?'

'We can have it when we're back.'

I put on my raincoat and boots, waited for a moment in the hall below for Espen, who appeared shortly afterwards in his thick old waterproof jacket and locked up.

'The toilet paper disappeared again last night,' he said, turning to me as he stuffed his bunch of keys into his pocket. His toilet was in the hallway. Anyone could use it.

'I know who it is. I heard him and so I looked out of the window afterwards. You know that little Sunnmøre guy who lives across the yard?'

I shook my head, started to walk downstairs.

'Well, anyway, it was him. He ran down the road with a toilet roll in each hand. Imagine sinking so low as to steal toilet paper!'

'Yes,' I said.

'It's very irritating. What do you think I should do? Take the matter up with him? Tell him I know it's him?'

'No, are you out of your mind? Just drop it.'

'But it's so unbelievably cheeky!' Espen said.

'He's a criminal,' I said. 'If you start messing with him you know what can happen.'

'You're probably right,' Espen said. 'But he's so loathsome. I think he's a pervert. He doesn't flush after he's been either, you know. His shit's in the bowl when I go in there.'

'Ooh, bloody hell,' I said.

We arrived at the bottom hallway and emerged onto the worn cracked brick steps. Rain was falling and had been for a long time. Both the building we exited and the one rising before us, three metres away, were dark and gleamed with moisture in the street lighting, and all the protruding sills, ledges and gutters dripped. The narrow passage in front of us was overgrown and full of old refuse; the path between the two buildings was covered over and looked more like a tunnel or a grotto with its green stains and cracks.

When I saw the dustbins I remembered the rat, a memory I had succeeded in repressing, I hadn't thought about it all day.

Perhaps it was still alive. Crawling around and gorging on all the delicious rubbish. What did it matter that it was caught in a trap? If it used its rear feet it could paddle alongside the bulging plastic bags, gnaw at them and they would open and all sorts of splendours would fall out, straight into its mouth. If there was nothing? Well, keep paddling.

We walked up, alongside the other brick buildings, where our sister flats were, all identical, and down the underpass to the left. Water ran and dripped everywhere, graffiti and unintelligible symbols covered the walls, some of the lamps on the ceiling were smashed, and no one ever stopped here unless they wanted something from the Narvesen kiosk, which was in the middle, where I used to buy newspapers every morning. We walked past and up the other side, following the road to town.

'Shall we turn right here and walk to the centre? It's quite a nice area,' Espen said.

'Can do,' I said.

The road came out by the hospital, which now towered over the mist, like a fully illuminated castle, under the mountains. One of the town's big cemeteries lay just below, strategically placed to ensure the sick would not be allowed to forget they wouldn't be living for ever.

We walked side by side into town. Espen said nothing, I said nothing.

'I don't know how to start,' Espen said at length. 'I was wondering at first whether it was a young adult novel you'd written.'

Everything inside me sank.

'A young adult novel?' I said. 'What makes you think that?'

'Something about the tone,' he said. 'The way they speak. Young adult novels are good!'

I said nothing, studied the ground in front of us, the light gleamed on the wet tarmac.

'There's a lot of wonderful material in it, really,' he continued. 'I loved some of the descriptions of nature.'

'But?' I said.

Espen glanced at me.

'In my opinion, it doesn't work as a whole,' he said. 'Somehow, it's not enough. It's difficult to understand why this story of all stories is being told. There's no spark in it, to be blunt.'

'What about the language?' I said.

'Sorry,' he said. 'But it's a bit bland. Bit impersonal. It hurts me to say this. I'd have loved to say something else. But I can't. I have to be honest.'

'I'm really glad you've been honest,' I said. 'Not many people would have been. Most would have played along and said they liked it. You're very brave to say what you think. Thank you.'

'But it isn't *bad*,' Espen said. 'I mean, that's not what we're talking about. I just don't think you make the most of the material you have.'

'Do you think I could? That I could keep working on it and raise it somehow?'

'Maybe,' he said. 'But it'd be a major job. It might be better if you started afresh.'

'That difficult?' I said.

'I'm afraid so,' he said. 'I don't like saying this, believe me. I've been as nervous as a kitten all day.'

'But it's good you did. I'm pleased you did. I know you're right. I've known it deep down the entire time. In fact, it's wonderful to have this feeling confirmed. It doesn't matter.'

'I'm happy you're taking it like this,' he said.

'Not at all. Why shoot the messenger,' I said.

'It's one thing to say that and another to mean it. Most people take it very personally. It's perceived as an insult. Well, you know that, you were at the Academy for a year.'

'Yes,' I said. 'But we're friends. If you can be so sincere I know there's nothing behind it.'

We walked on in silence.

I really meant what I had said. He was courageous and I could trust him. But it didn't prevent me from being upset. That had been my last hope and now it was over. I couldn't write any better than that.

Back home, I threw the copy Espen had read into the waste-paper basket and wiped the document on the disk. Now there was just the assignment left to do. 'The Concept of Intertextuality with Special Reference to James Joyce's *Ulysses*', as it was now called.

Sandviken Hospital wasn't far from the town centre, set back be-neath the mountain. The buildings were massive, like a monu-ment, as all the institutions from that time were. I jumped off the bus and walked up the hill. Above me the windows shone in the mist. After having wandered around for a few minutes between the blocks I eventually found the right one and went in.

The interview consisted largely of a woman entering my details into the system, checking which department was in the most ur-gent need of help, ringing them and giving them my name, put-ting the receiver down and looking at me, could you do a shift tomorrow? Afternoon?

'Yes, I can manage that,' I said.

'If everything goes all right, and I'm sure it will, you'll get more shifts. If you want them, that is.'

'Thank you very much,' I said and stood up.

'Not at all,' she said and turned her attention to the pile of papers she had lying in front of her.

*

Next day, in the afternoon, I got off the bus at the same stop and walked with a palpitating heart up the stairs to the ward I had been allocated. A thin woman with red hair and a slightly child-like expression, thirty-five or so, said hello and shook my hand as I stepped into the duty room. Her name was Eva. Another woman, blonde-haired, blue-eyed, with a Mediterranean complexion and gentle curves, maybe thirty, stood up behind her. Fantastic breasts, as far as I could judge from the corner of my eye. A fresh personality, and presumably fresh in the other sense, for what was she not saying as she regarded me through the narrow glasses on the tip of her nose?

'Goodness me, they've sent us an attractive man this time.'

I blushed and tried to hide it in my subsequent actions: take off my raincoat, put cup under the big Thermos, a couple of creaking pumps, raise it to my mouth, sip the coffee, full of bubbles and froth, sit down, little smile.

'Did I embarrass you?' she said. 'I didn't mean to. It's just the way I am. Straight to the point. My name's Mary, by the way.'

She looked at me without smiling.

'Poor thing. Now he's all flummoxed,' Eva said.

'Not at all,' I said. 'I'm used to a bit of all sorts.'

'That's good,' she said. 'We need all the temps we can get. I'm the ward manager, you see. And we've had quite a turnover here. Well, we have a hard core, but weekend staff have a tendency to be thin on the ground.'

'Really,' I said and took another sip. A bearded man came in, he must have been in his late twenties, thin arms and thin legs, glasses, leftie type. His name was Åge and he sat down next to me.

'Student?' he said.

I nodded.

'What are you studying?'

'Literature,' I said.

'Well, you won't need that here,' Mary said.

'We've had geologists, architects, historians, social scientists, artists, sociologists, social anthropologists here, yep, the whole kit and caboodle. Most stop when they find something better. But some hang around. Isn't that right, Åge?'

'Yes,' Åge said.

'When you've had a smoke come with me and I'll show you round and take you through the routines,' Eva said. 'I'll go and get the medicines ready in the meantime.'

It didn't look good, I supposed, that the first thing I had done was to light up. On the other hand, there were still ten minutes to go before my shift started.

Mary made an entry in the logbook. Åge got up and went out. I followed him, I didn't dare sit on my own with Mary, her presence was electric.

I recognised a great deal in the ward from my summer job, the only real difference was the residents, who were patients here and closer to the carers than they had been there. But the atmosphere was more pressurised, the silence more threatening. People stood rocking backwards and forwards by the windows, sat chain-smoking on the sofas and lay apathetically in their beds. Most had been here a long time. Hardly anyone noticed me or that I was new, they were probably used to change. I kept a low profile, did as many practical jobs as I could, tried to take the initiative but not with the patients, hoping that this would be seen and appreciated, I knew my place. I washed floors, served food, cleared up and put cups and plates in the dishwasher, kept asking the others if there was anything I could do. Time passed infinitely slowly, but it did pass. At the end of the day, when Åge and Eva had gone off duty and the patients were in their rooms, I was alone with Mary in the duty room. She lit a cigarette with little tense movements that I couldn't tally with what she had already revealed of herself, but then, as she inhaled the smoke deep into her lungs and blew it out, waving it away from her eyes, her self-assured expression returned.

I asked her where she lived, she answered that she had a flat not very far away, near the Business School. The flirtatious tone she had used at first was completely gone. But there *was* something about her, the way she didn't look at me, her sudden smiles, which were charged to a much greater degree, presumably because the flirtatious tone had been so open and hence safe, whereas this was no more than evasion and words unsaid.

She told me she was a psychiatric nurse and had worked there for five years. Her words fell like confidences.

'Well,' she said eventually and got up. 'I'll have to do my rounds. You can go if you like.'

'But there's half an hour left.'

'Just go. I can manage on my own. And you'll have some time for your girlfriend this evening.'

I turned and put on my jacket, my cheeks lightly flushed.

'How did you know I had a girlfriend?'

She paused in the doorway.

'Hard to imagine such a handsome man as you being on his own,' she said and continued up the corridor.

I sat at the back of the bus and put on my Walkman, played Sonic Youth, a band I had tried to like for ages without any success, until that autumn when *Goo* came out. One night I had been listening to it downstairs with Espen, we had been smoking hash, and I was lost in the music, literally, I saw it as rooms and corridors, floors and walls, ditches and slopes, small forests between blocks of flats and railway lines, and didn't emerge from it until the song stopped, it was like drawing breath because the next minute a new song started and I was caught again. The exception was the second song, 'Tunic', it just kept moving forward, I sat with my eyes closed and drifted with it. Strange, I thought now as it started in my headset, because the text, or at least the chorus, explicitly stated the opposite. I wasn't going nowhere, I wasn't going nowhere. No, I ain't.

As Gunvor lived so close to the bus station and the next shift started at seven in the morning I slept at hers that night. I told her a little of what it was like up there, but half-heartedly, the essence of the job was atmospheres, the despair locked in these people's bodies, and it was impossible to communicate that. Her eyes suddenly serious, she snuggled up to me, fixed them on me, and then, for a few minutes, it was just us two, there in the room with the sloping windows, the rain running down their length, high above the streets where people walked up and down, but then, as we extricated ourselves and lay on our own sides to sleep, I was alone again until slumber came and released me from everything.

I woke up before the alarm clock, almost ripped asunder by what I had been dreaming, which disappeared the instant I opened my eyes. But the mood lasted. I got up, ate a slice of bread in her cold kitchen, dressed as quietly as I could, closed the door carefully behind me and went out into the darkness and rain.

'Sit yourself down and have a smoke,' Mary said when I arrived. 'Sunday is a long day here. We don't need to exert ourselves before we have to.'

'Sounds good,' I said. 'I was a little lost yesterday. I didn't really know what to do. So could you give me a few tasks, basically?'

She smiled.

'You can always wash some clothes. But first tell me a little about yourself.'

'There's nothing to tell,' I said. 'At least not this early in the morning.'

'Do you know what Eva said about you yesterday?'

'No.'

'"Still waters run deep."'

'That was a charitable interpretation,' I said with a blush.

'If there's one thing we learn here it's to be judges of character.' She winked at me. 'Go and put on the washing machine. Then you can start on the breakfast afterwards.'

I did as she said. The first patients were already up and sitting around the tables in the 'communal area', smoking with nicotine-stained fingers. Some of them were mumbling to themselves. They were the chronically ill, Eva had told me the night before, they had been here for many years and were outwardly calm, but if something were to happen and the alarm went off I had to drop everything and run to the incident. This was the sole instruction I had been given with regard to the patients. No one had said anything at the previous institution either, but here it seemed more striking because it was possible to talk to these patients in a very different way. What should I do if they approached me and wanted to discuss something important? Play along? Say what I thought? Contact someone who had been trained to deal with this?

I emptied the fridge of all the cheese, milk and juice, took out a pile of plates, butter knives, glasses and cups, put everything on the trolley and started to set the tables. As it was Sunday I boiled some eggs and lit a tea light on every table. A lean dark-haired man with trembling hands who resembled Ludwig Wittgenstein had already sat down. He looked straight ahead as though praying.

I put a plate in front of him.

'I'm no bloody homo!' he said.

I put out a cheese board and cartons of milk and juice. He didn't say anything else; he didn't seem to have noticed me at all. Mary came in and gave him a small cylinder of pills, poured juice into his glass, stood there until he had swallowed them, continued through the room. I took out the eggs, rinsed them in cold water, switched on the coffee machine, dampened a cloth and wiped the worktop and bread board. There was an empty car outside in the car park with its lights on. Åge came into the hall, he raised a hand in greeting, I waved back.

'Well?' he said, standing next to me after leaving his jacket and bag in the duty room. 'Did you have a good Saturday night?'

'Yes,' I said. 'Nice and quiet. Went to bed early.'

'You seem like a responsible guy,' he said.

'Maybe,' I said.

'I thought we could take a trip with them this morning,' he said. 'What do you say to that?'

'OK with me,' I said. 'But I haven't got a driving licence. Have you?'

'Yes. Then we can get away from the biddies for a bit.'

This was an idiotic comment, but I didn't want him to know I thought that and feel rejected, so I hung around before I went in to fetch the eggs and egg cups.

He requisitioned a car after breakfast, gathered four of the patients, then we got in and drove off. Through the centre of Bergen and up the other side, where he stopped on a large gravel parking area under the mountain, this was Lake Svartediket, he said, and it lived up to its name, the black dyke, at any rate now in late autumn, because there was barely any colour in the countryside. We piled out of the car and walked up a gentle mountain ridge, he talked non-stop, his voice was a whine and he rolled out a whole litany of complaints about the conditions at Sandviken Hospital. He was particularly dissatisfied with the atmosphere among the nurses on the ward, they were conspiratorial, he said, talked behind one another's backs, he said, and I nodded and nodded while thinking, what an idiot this man is, won't he shut up soon, what the hell has this got to do with me?

We stopped, looked around us, at a lake some distance away, as black as the blackest tarmac, and the mountain that rose almost vertically behind it, and then we walked back to the car. He drove on, turned off by Nesttun and went back. The whole time he played Bob Dylan on the stereo, and I thought, that fits, they're crabby, both of them.

'Ta-dah, three hours gone,' he said as we drove uphill on the Sandviken side of town.

'That's true,' I said.

'It was nice talking to you,' he said. 'I can hear you understand what it's all about.'

'Thanks, and the same to you,' I said.

What a prat.

Mary, on the other hand, I thought, was a different kettle of fish, and a tingle spread through my stomach. Yes, she was thirty years old, yes, she was a nurse, yes, I had only spoken five sentences to her, tops, but none of that was important because nothing else was going to happen. Did it matter that I was full of tension when I was in the same room as her?

As I was about to leave some hours later, Eva asked me if I was interested in any more work. I nodded, she put my name on the internal temporary staff list. At the bus stop, in the pouring rain, I totted up my monthly pay in my head. I went to bed as soon as I got home, slept deeply, was woken by the telephone, everything was pitch black around me and at first I thought I had slept through, but it was no more than half past five. It was Yngve, he was working at the hotel and wondered if I fancied going out when he had finished. I said yes, of course, and we agreed to meet at Café Opera just after ten.

I had promised him a song, I had one started, and after eating I put on the music and got down to work. Jone was in Stavanger and Espen must have been out, judging by the silence from below, so

I ratcheted up the volume and enjoyed myself; when I composed lyrics for Yngve, I felt no restrictions, I just wrote.

An hour later it was done.

I took a shower, and because I was going out I masturbated, it was a way of reducing the risk of being unfaithful, I really didn't want to end up where I had been before, at the mercy of my desires. I couldn't trust myself, I could drink one beer, but if I had two I wanted more and if I had more anything could happen.

Standing there in the shower, dick in hand, the image of Hans Olav sprang to mind at regular intervals, him lying there and wanking in bed, it was as if I had been contaminated, and it removed all my desire. But I managed anyway. I stood in the shower for almost half an hour afterwards. Had the water not been cold I would have been there for another half an hour, there was no energy in me, no willpower, I wanted to stand there with the water pouring down me for all eternity.

I barely had the energy to dry myself, and to get dressed I had to pull myself together and mobilise all the strength I had. After I had finished I felt better. It would be good to have a drink, perhaps get a bit merry, have something quite different to think about.

With the darkness outside the windows like an ocean and the rooms sparsely illuminated I saw them as I had done when I was a small boy. Everything in them was somehow turned away from me, into itself. It was alien, essentially alien. Everything was, I thought, and stood by the window in an attempt to extend this perception and see if everything out there was also essentially alien, turned away from me, from us, the humans who wandered the earth.

Oh this was a scary perception. We were surrounded by death, we wandered in death, but we didn't see it, on the contrary we adapted it to our own advantage and used death for our own purposes. We were islands of life. The trees and the vegetation were related to us, and the animals, but that was all. The rest was, if not hostile, then turned away.

I got dressed and went downstairs, death, out of the door, death, up the hill, death, through the underpass, death, down the road, death, along the fjord, death, and into the park, which wrapped itself around me with its living yet sleeping darkness.

I had a couple of beers on my own while waiting for Yngve, it felt good both because there were so few people around, there was a very special atmosphere with the darkness outside, the light inside and all the space between people, and because the alcohol was slowly having an effect on me, it was promising, I was on the way up and when I reached the top of the arc that was waiting, anything could happen.

Besides I had earned some money recently and my prospects for earning more were good.

'Hello,' said Yngve from behind me.

'Hello,' I said. 'How's it going?'

'Great. Have you been here long?'

'Half an hour. I've been enjoying the feeling of not working.'

'That's the best thing about working,' he said. 'It's brilliant when you stop.'

He stowed his umbrella and small rucksack, went for a beer and sat down.

'How is it? At Sandviken, I mean?'

'Pretty awful really. But it brings in the money.'

'I've worked there,' he said, wiping the froth from his top lip.

'Yes, you have.'

'It's different when you've done a few shifts and you're used to everything.'

'I'm sure it is,' I said.

'Have you thought about Kafkatrakterne at all?'

'Yes, I've written some lyrics.'

'Have you got them with you?'

'As it happens, I have,' I said and took them from my back pocket. Yngve unfolded the sheet and read it.

'Very good,' he said. 'Two more songs and we've got a whole set for New Year's Eve.'

We chatted about it for a while, then there was silence. Yngve glanced around, a few more people had trickled in since he came, but there were still big empty spaces.

'Shall we go to Christian?' he said. 'There might be a few more people there.'

'Can do,' I said.

As we walked he said that Sunday was the day everyone who worked in bars and restaurants hit the town and that Christian was the place where most of them hung out. We paid, sat at a table close to the dance floor, he brought back a couple of gin and tonics, I drank it as if it were juice. One more, and one more.

We got into conversation with two women, one was nice with crooked teeth and reddish hair, maybe thirty, she worked at the Post Office, she told me, and she laughed every time I made a comment to her. I was much too young, she said, besides she had a boyfriend, he was big and strong and jealous, she added, although that didn't frighten me, I was attracted by her laughter. But they eventually got up to go, and Yngve held me back when I wanted to go after them.

Death was in there too, the whole room we were sitting in was dead, and everything in it, apart from those dancing. They were dancing in the realm of death, I thought. They were dancing in the realm of death, they were dancing in the realm of death.

We drank more, we even got on the dance floor for some songs, otherwise we chatted about the band, how exciting it was becoming and what the chances were if we made a go of it. I said I would rather play in a band than write. Yngve sent me a look of surprise, he hadn't expected this. But it was true. Writing was a defeat, it was a humiliation, it was coming face to face with yourself and seeing you weren't good enough. Playing in a band was quite different, that was giving yourself utterly, together with a few other people, and letting things develop from there. I was a lousy drummer, yet despite that something had developed around us a few times, suddenly we were in midstream, it swung, we weren't controlling it, we went with the flow, and that feeling of finding yourself in the middle was enormously pleasurable.

I had a tingling sensation running down my spine and I was smiling. The moment soared and soared, and then it was over. In the next song we were back to where none of the instruments and riffs and drumbeats blended in.

'We've just got to go for it,' I said to Yngve that night. 'That's what we need to do. No safety net. Give up our studies and play music full time. Practise every day for two years. Shit, how great would that be!'

'Yes, but we'll never get Hans and Pål on board.'

'No, but that's what we have to do. That's the only way!'

At that juncture I was seriously drunk, but as always there were few outer signs, I didn't stagger when I walked, I didn't slur my words when I spoke. But inside me there was no doubt, I had started following every impulse I felt and scorned any objections that arose. So when they closed Christian and we went down to Slakteriet to squeeze the last seconds out of the evening there was only one goal I had in mind: a girl I could go home with or who would come home with me.

We sat down at a table, some girls looked at us, I caught sight of them in the corner of my eye and turned, met the gaze of a girl with big lips and shining eyes, she smiled when our eyes met, and I got a hard-on. She was plump and no one would have called her beautiful, but what did it matter, all I wanted was a roll around on a bed with her somewhere.

I looked at her a couple more times, always brief glances, just to check if she was up for it, and she was. After a while she came over and asked if they could sit at our table. I let Yngve answer, he said yes, of course, take a seat. We're on our way home now but . . .

'Are you?' she said.

'Yes, soon,' he said.

She sent me a teasing glance.

'You too?'

'It depends,' I said. My voice was almost choking with excitement.

'Depends on what?' she said.

'Well, if anything special was going to happen.'

'Special?' she said.

My heart was pounding wildly because her eyes were begging me, she wanted it too.

'Yes,' I said.

'What for example?'

'Well, a party for example. Where do you live?'

'In Nøstet. But there's no party.'

'Oh,' I said.

'Where do you live then?'

'In Danmarksplass,' I said, lighting a cigarette.

'Oh, right over there,' she said. 'Do you live alone?'

'Yes.'

'Are you going to have a party there?' she said.

Yngve eyed me.

'No, I don't think so,' I said.

'You've got to take grandad to hospital tomorrow, remember,' Yngve said.

'Of course,' I said. 'I'll be on my way soon.'

Then Yngve got up to go to the toilet.

'Can I have a little chat with you?' I said. 'Outside? I'm going now. I want to say something to you in private.'

'What could that be?' she said and smiled. Looked at her friend, who was chatting to a guy crouching down in front of her chair.

I stood up, she stood up.

'Come home with me,' I said. 'Would you like to?'

'Yes, it might be interesting,' she said.

'Let's take a taxi,' I said. 'Now.'

She nodded, put on her jacket, hung her bag over her shoulder.

'I'm off,' she said to her friend. 'Talk tomorrow, OK?'

Her friend nodded, we left, a taxi came down the cobbled street, I waved a hand and thirty seconds later we were on our way through the town.

'What about your brother?' she said.

'He'll be all right,' I said, putting my hand on her thigh.

Jesus.

I swallowed, ran my hand up her thigh as far as it could go, she smiled, I leaned over and kissed her. She put her arms around me. She smelled of perfume and her body was heavy against mine. I wanted her so much I didn't know what to do in the taxi, minutes away from my flat now, and the bed.

I wriggled my hand in under her jacket, stroked one breast. She kissed my ear. Her breathing was heavy.

Across Danmarksplass.

'Left here,' I said to the driver. 'And then left again. Second door.'

I pulled out a hundred-krone note from my pocket, gave it to him when he stopped, scrambled out, grabbed her hand and dragged her to the front entrance. She laughed. We tumbled up the stairs with our arms around each other, I clung to her as hard as I could, unlocked the door and in the bedroom, where we were only seconds later, I first pulled off her jumper, then undid her bra, unbuttoned her trousers, slipped down the zip and pulled them off. She was wearing black panties, I pressed my face against them as I wrapped my arms around her legs. She fell back, I pulled down her panties as well and pressed my face against her again and then, yes, then we did what I had pictured we would do when our eyes met.

The instant I woke I knew what I had done and was filled with horror.

She was sleeping peacefully at my side.

I had to save whatever could be saved. I couldn't take any account of her.

I woke her up.

'You've got to go,' I said. 'And you mustn't say anything about this to anyone. If I meet you in town you must act as if nothing happened. I have a girlfriend, you see. What happened should never have happened.'

She sat up.

'You said nothing about that,' she said, raising her arms to do her bra up at the back.

'I was drunk,' I said.

'The old, old story,' she said. 'And there was me thinking I had met my knight in shining armour.'

We stood side by side dressing in silence. I said goodbye when she left, she said nothing. But I wasn't bothered about that.

It was ten o'clock, soon grandad would be arriving on the boat. I put the bed linen in the washing machine and showered at full speed. I was still drunk and so drained that I had to summon every ounce of willpower to do what was awaiting me.

As I was about to leave Jone came out of his flat.

'Did you have company last night?' he said.

'No,' I said. 'Why?'

He laughed.

'We heard you, Karl Ove,' he said. 'Your voice and a girl's voice. And it wasn't Gunvor, was it?'

'No, it wasn't. I've been a fool. I don't understand what got into me.'

I met his eyes.

'Please do me a favour and don't mention any of this to Gunvor. Or to anyone.'

'Naturally,' he said. 'I've neither heard nor seen anything. You didn't either, did you, Siren?'

The latter he shouted into his flat.

'Is Siren here too?'

'Yes, but it's OK. This'll stay between us. No worries.'

'Thank you, Jone,' I said. 'Now I've got to be off though.'

I dragged myself down the stairs, speeded up when I was outside, nauseous and with an aching head, but that wasn't a problem, what was a problem was that I was so tired I didn't really have the energy for this. I just caught a bus at the Forum stop, jumped off at Fisketorget ten minutes later as the express boat from Sogn was slowly entering the harbour.

There was radiant sunshine, not a cloud in the sky, all the colours around me shone bright and clear.

I had to act as if nothing had happened. Whenever I thought about it I had to tell myself it hadn't.

That *actually* it hadn't happened.

It hadn't happened.

I stood outside the ferry terminal with a throbbing head and watched the Sogn boat docking, thinking what happened last night hadn't happened.

The gangway was lowered, a few passengers stood in the doorway impatiently waiting for the signal to disembark.

There it was, at the dockside.

They were starting to come ashore.

Nothing had happened.

I was innocent.

I hadn't been unfaithful.

I hadn't.

Passenger after passenger came down the gangway, most carrying a suitcase or two. Grandad was nowhere to be seen.

The wind made the flags flutter, the water ripple. The drone of the engine resounded against the rocks in the harbour, the exhaust fumes fluttered up the length of the white hull.

There he was. Small, wearing a dark suit and a black hat, walking slowly towards the gangway. He was holding a suitcase in one hand. The other was on the railing, and he shuffled ashore. I took a few steps forward.

'Hi, Grandad,' I said.

He stopped and looked up at me.

'There you are,' he said. 'Do you think we can take a taxi?'

'Certainly can,' I said. 'I'll ask them to radio one.'

I walked over to a driver putting some luggage in the boot of his taxi. He said there would be lots of taxis along any minute and closed the boot lid.

'We'll have to wait a bit,' I told grandad. 'There'll be more taxis coming soon.'

'Well, we've got plenty of time,' he said.

Grandad said nothing in the taxi. That was unlike him, but it must have had something to do with the unfamiliar surroundings, I supposed. I didn't say anything either. As we passed Danmarksplass I avoided looking at the flat so as not to be reminded of what had happened, so as not to see how we had run for the door when the taxi stopped. It hadn't happened, it didn't exist, I thought, and we turned left, uphill towards Haukeland Hospital, grandad and me. Slowly he took his wallet out of his inside pocket and began to flick through the notes in it. I ought to have paid for him, but I had very little money and I let him pay.

The sun was reflected in all the windows above us as we got out of the taxi and crossed the area in front of the main entrance. It was dark inside after all the sunshine. We walked to the lift, I pressed a button, we rose up the building. The lift stopped, a woman came in, she had a tube attached to her arm, it led to a bag on a kind of stand with wheels. When she stood still and grabbed the rail with her other hand a cloud of blood appeared in the lower part of the tube.

I felt like vomiting and turned my back. Grandad stared down at the floor.

Was he afraid?

It was impossible to say. But all his authority had ebbed away. I had seen that once before, when he visited us in Tybakken many, many years ago. It must have been something to do with not being on home territory. In his own house he was another man, he radiated calm and security in a very different way.

'Here we are,' I said as the door opened.

We went out, I read the signs, we had to go left. There was a bell, I rang it, a nurse came and opened the door.

I stated his name, she nodded, shook hands with him, I said goodbye to him, promised I would visit him as soon as possible, he answered, good, and then he walked in side by side with her as the door in front of me slid to.

I was deeply ashamed. My life was unworthy, I was unworthy and that became so evident when I met grandad, in his situation, ill, at the hospital, getting towards the end of his life. He was over eighty years old and if he was lucky had ten years left, maybe fifteen, but also maybe only two or three, it was impossible to say.

He had a little tumour in his throat, for the moment it wasn't life-threatening, but it had to be removed, that was why he was here.

Grandma was dead and soon grandad would die. They had toiled and striven all their lives, in the same way that their parents had toiled and striven all their lives. To eat, to keep their heads above water. It was the great struggle, they had fought it and now it was over or approaching the end. What I was doing, what I had done, it was unworthy, an evil deed, abject and utterly wretched. I had a girlfriend, she was wonderful, indeed fantastic, and then I had done this to her.

Why?

Oh, there was no reason. I didn't want to do it. Not now, not when I knew what I was doing, now I didn't want to do it.

I emerged in front of the hospital, stood on the grey tarmac looking around while I smoked. Nothing had happened, that was the point, nothing, absolutely nothing, I had been out with Yngve, gone home alone, slept, picked up grandad.

If I was going to meet Gunvor, if I was going to be able to look her in the eye, I had to stick to this version of events.

Nothing had happened.

An hour later I was sitting in the third-floor café in the Sundt department store drinking coffee while watching the people in Torgalmenningen. This was where I usually sat when I was alone in town, here, surrounded by older Bergen men and women, no one wanted anything from me, I was completely at peace and even though there was a vaguely cloying odour in the air, which the aroma of the cakes and pastries could not dull, in a strange way I liked being there. Sitting and reading, writing in my notebook if I had an idea, every now and then looking down at all the people moving to and fro, the pigeons living their lives in their shadow, with similar movements, just on an enormously smaller scale, always after food that had been dropped or thrown into a refuse bin. An ice cream, a bit of a hot dog, half a roll. Often they were chased by children, then they strutted off in the jerky way they did, in a semicircle, and if that wasn't enough they took to the air and glided for five or six metres before landing and resuming their search for food.

I didn't want to go back to the flat, but I couldn't sit here for ever either, particularly not in my present state of torment. The best option would be to go to the reading room, take the bull by the horns, meet Gunvor and get it over with. If the first few minutes went well, if she didn't notice anything, the rest would go well too, I knew that. I just had to take the plunge.

I went out, put on my sunglasses and set off on the heavy road up to Høyden.

She was reading, one arm resting on the desk by the book, the other supporting her head.

I came to a halt in front of her.

She looked up and smiled, beamed with her whole body.

'Hi!' she said.

'Hi,' I said. 'Coming for a coffee?'

She nodded, stood up and followed me.

'Let's sit outside, shall we?' she said. 'It's such fantastic weather!'

'Can do,' I said. 'I need a coffee anyway. Shall I get you one too? Will you be sitting here?'

'Yes, please,' she said, and sat down on the brick wall, her eyes squinting into the sun.

'I went out last night, you know,' I said when I returned, passed her a coffee and took off my sunglasses so that she wouldn't get the impression I was hiding.

'I can see that,' she said. 'You look a bit the worse for wear.'

'Yes, we stayed out late.'

'Who was we?'

'Yngve and me.'

I sat down beside her. I hated myself for it, but the danger had passed, she didn't suspect anything.

'You don't feel like taking the rest of the day off, do you?' I said. 'We can walk into town. I feel like an ice cream!'

'Yes, what the heck, let's do that.'

Three days later we caught the bus to the hospital together to visit grandad. We got off at the little flower shop, which was in a kind of shack by the road just below the hospital, and was so macabre, it sold funeral wreaths as well as the bunches of flowers many hospital visitors probably bought. It was raining and the wind was blowing, we walked up the hill hand in hand, I was black inside, the thought of my hypocrisy was like an abyss, but I had no choice, she mustn't find out, and sooner or later the memory of the dreadful deed I had committed would pale and become like all other memories, something that had happened in another world.

Grandad was in the TV lounge when we arrived. He brightened up, struggled to his feet and shook hands with Gunvor, said we could go to his room, where he had chairs and a table. He sat up on his bed. In the bed beside him lay an emaciated sallow old man with his eyes closed.

Grandad stared at us.

'You two should be in a movie,' he said. 'You're so attractive you should be in a film. That's where your future lies.'

Gunvor smiled and looked at me. Her eyes were gleaming.

'It was nice of you to come all this way to visit me,' he said.

'Our pleasure,' I said.

In the nearby bed the thin man sat up and coughed, at first a bark, then a clearing of the throat, finally a rattle.

He can't have long left, I thought.

Against the darkness and the window he looked like someone from a horror film. At length he lay down and closed his eyes.

'He keeps me awake at night,' grandad said in a low voice. 'He wants to talk. He's sure he's going to die. But I don't want to be drawn in.'

He chuckled. Then he told us a string of stories. One after the other, and both Gunvor and I were spellbound, there was something about the surroundings that endowed what he said with a special intensity or else it was just that his storytelling was better than it used to be. But it was hypnotic. He talked about pioneers in the USA who had been close to Indians and had also lived through a raid by them. He talked about his youth, when he had travelled around to dances in the district and when he had met grandma, on a farm in Dike, not far from Sørbøvåg, where she worked with her sister Johanna. He went there with a friend one night. Grandma and Johanna slept in a loft, grandad climbed up the ladder, felt

something pulling at his trousers, it was his friend, he had got the
heebie-jeebies and wanted to go home. The following night he had
gone on his own and climbed to the top. His friend had become an
organist, he told us. He wasn't too good at playing, to put it mildly,
and remained a bachelor. Grandad laughed at the memory, tears
rolled down his cheeks. But it was also as though he had forgotten
his own situation, as though he no longer knew where he was or
who he was talking to but had disappeared into his stories, because out of the blue he said he didn't get her at first, then it had
just been a no, but the second time he had got her, he said, and
can't have realised he was telling this to their grandchild and his
girlfriend. Or perhaps he did. At any rate, I didn't want to know
about any of this and asked him a question about something quite
different to get his mind on another track. He listened to what I
said and answered with a new story. And it wasn't just him who
was forgetting his present situation, I was too, everything was beginning to merge, what I had done a few nights ago unknown to
Gunvor, her sitting there now, attentive, rapt, there was the darkness and the wind, there was the thin man with the wild eyes and
his death-rattle coughs, there was grandad telling us about house-
building in the 1920s when he travelled around with his father
erecting houses for people, about the time he wandered around
with a rucksack full of books which he sold in the district, about
herring fishing in the 1930s, when they had lain off the Bulandet
archipelago the whole winter, about building roads in the mountains in the 1940s, when he had been a blaster, about the war,
about the plane crash on Mount Lihesten, about his brother's life
in America. Back and forth in his life, he went, and it felt like an
event, as if we were listening to something unique. Happy and
excited, we left the hospital, passed the cemetery and through the
residential area, down to Danmarksplass, into the house and up
to my flat, where all the horrors returned, but I didn't let them affect me, nothing had happened that evening, I had been out with

Yngve and caught a taxi home, alone, if anyone said anything to the contrary they were a liar.

When I woke up next morning Gunvor had gone to her lectures. I started work on my assignment, there were just a few weeks left to the deadline and I had only written a couple of pages. What was worse was that I had no idea how to do it. Everything grew and expanded but not in a coherent way, the threads ran in all directions and the certain knowledge that I not only had to keep a perspective on them but also gather them into one single strand panicked me. At twelve the phone rang, it was Sandviken, they wondered whether I could do an extra shift that night. I said yes, I needed the money and getting away from everything to do with intertextuality seemed like a good idea. I had a nap in the early evening and caught the bus there at half past ten. The shift was in a different ward from the one I had worked on at the weekend, but although the building may have been different, the atmosphere was the same. A man of around fifty received me and told me what I had to do. It was simple, I was to 'mark' (in football parlance) a patient, he was suicidal and had to be kept under surveillance twenty-four hours a day. Now he was asleep, heavily medicated, and would probably continue sleeping all night.

He was lying on his back in bed, by the wall. The only light came from a wall lamp at the other end of the room. The carer closed the door behind him and I sat down on a chair a couple of metres from the bed. The patient was young, perhaps eighteen or nineteen. He lay there motionless and it was impossible to see from his face that he was so tormented he wanted to take his own life. His complexion was wan, his features delicate. There was a little stubble on his chin.

I knew nothing about him, not even his name.

But there I sat and I was his guard.

*

At long last that night passed too and I was able to walk downhill to the bus in the black morning murk, sit with all the others going to work in town, get off at Danmarksplass, trudge through the dripping underpass, down past the dilapidated brick houses, in through the crooked grotto-like passage and up to the flat. It felt wrong to go to bed now the darkness was lifting and the day beginning, but I slept like a log and didn't wake until four in the afternoon, when the light had almost gone.

I fried some fishcakes and ate them with onions and slices of bread. Studied the assignment, decided to open with a description of *Ulysses* and then introduce the concept of intertextuality and discuss that, and not vice versa, which had been my plan. Pleased that I was beginning to shape my material, I got dressed and went up to the hospital again. Grandad was all alone there and, being the sociable person he was, he would probably welcome a little visit.

As I approached the brow of the hill and could see the hospital ahead of me, a helicopter slowly descended and landed on one of the roofs. I saw a team standing at the ready, waiting, perhaps for an organ in a box, a heart that had just been removed from a body in another town, perhaps someone who'd had a stroke or been seriously injured in a car accident, and it would now be inserted into a waiting chest.

In the spacious entrance, where there was a Narvesen kiosk as well as a bank and a hairdresser's, the reception area had none of the frenetic activity on the roof or in the garage, where ambulances were continually arriving with the sick, open to all to see, nor any of the activity there had to be in the large operating theatres on the floors above, but the knowledge of it left its mark on these spaces nevertheless. The atmosphere in them was curiously sombre.

I took the lift up to the floor where his ward was, walked through the gleaming corridor, past metal beds where patients, half-hidden behind temporary screens, still subject to prying gazes, lay staring at the ceiling and at the door, where I stopped and rang the bell. A nurse opened, I said who I was visiting, she said this wasn't visiting time but I could have a word anyway now that I had made it this far.

He was sitting in the TV lounge.

'Hi, Grandad,' I said.

The state of mind he had been in was still on his face a moment after he turned to me, and what I saw then, a hard, almost hostile, expression, made me think he actually despised me. Then he brightened up and I dismissed the thought.

'We can go into my room,' he said. 'Feel like a cup of coffee? I can order it, you know. They're nice to me here.'

'No, thanks,' I said and followed him in.

The thin man was lying in bed as on the previous occasion, darkness pressed against the windows as on the previous occasion, and grandad's face was as rosy and childlike as it had been when Gunvor and I were here two days ago, but the atmosphere had changed: I was alone, I felt uncomfortable, I asked a few mechanical questions and actually just wanted to get out.

I stayed for half an hour before leaving. He spoke about the millennium, and from the way he was talking I had the impression he thought there would come a time when humans would live for a thousand years. Medical science was advancing so fast, people were living for longer, nearly all the illnesses people died from when he was young there were cures for now. His optimism about progress was immense, but not without reason; once I had gone with mum and him up to Ålesund to visit Ingunn, his youngest daughter, and he had told us what it had been like when he was young. There had been enormous poverty, living conditions were tough, but look now, he said, extending his arms, it's incomprehensible how affluence has spread. Then I saw it through his eyes, everyone had a car, a big showy house, a nice garden, and the shopping centres outside the towns and villages we passed were crammed to bursting with goods and wealth.

With his talk of people living for a thousand years, it was hard to imagine anything else than that he was afraid to die. I decided to visit him again in the not too distant future, it was important he had something else to think about. He thanked me for coming, struggled up and shuffled into the TV lounge while I took the lift back down. I bought some Stimorol gum at the kiosk, glanced at the headlines in *Verdens Gang* and *Dagbladet*, stopped in the middle of the floor to open the packet of chewing gum, put two pieces into my mouth, and the sharp fresh taste gave me a sort of relief.

Some men in taxi-driver uniforms were sitting in chairs below the line of windows at the other end. TV monitors behind the reception desk flickered. Beside it there was a stand with a sign. CLINICAL BIOCHEMISTRY LABORATORY, NEUROSURGERY WARD, PATHOLOGY WARD, I read. The words filled me with unease, there was something unpleasant about all of this. Everything I saw reminded me of one thing, my own body and how little power I had over it. Perhaps it was as simple as that. The network of veins spread so delicately across my body, those tiny vessels, if the pressure of the blood surging through them became too high one day, would a wall burst and blood seep into the brain fluid? The beating heart, would it just stop?

I left the car park. Exhaust fumes floated on the air under the protruding roof. Heavy rain was falling in the glow of the street lamps, like tiny flashes of light. The black trees beyond extended like fingers, the darkness above them was dense. I walked down the hill, crossed the heavy traffic, passed the cemetery and came into the residential area, the rain a constant patter on the hood of my raincoat.

Hospitals were strange. It was first and foremost a strange idea: why collect all physical suffering in one place? Not just for a few years, as an experiment, no, here there were no time limits, the gathering of the sick and ill was a continuous process. If someone was cured and discharged, or they died and were buried, the ambulance was sent out to bring in another patient. They had called grandad right from the mouth of the fjord, and it was like that throughout the region, patients were brought in from islands and small communities, from towns and villages, as part of a system that had already lasted three generations. Hospitals existed to make us well, that was how it seemed from an individual's standpoint, but if you flipped the coin and looked at it from the hospital's angle, it was as though they were feeding on us. Take, for example, the idea that they had allocated the floors according to organs. Lungs on the sixth, hearts on the fifth, heads on the fourth, legs and arms on the third, ears, nose and throat on the second. There was some criticism of this, those who said that specialisation meant that the whole person was forgotten and it was only as a whole person that we could be cured. They hadn't understood that hospitals were organised on the same principle as a body. Did the kidney know its neighbour, the spleen? Did the heart know in whose chest it was beating? Did the blood know in whose veins it flowed? Oh, no, no. For the blood we were just a system of channels. And for us blood was just something that appeared the few times there was an accident and the body was cut open. The call goes out, a helicopter takes off and thwumps above the town to pick you up, it lands like a bird of prey on the road by the scene of the accident, you are taken on board and whisked away, placed on an operating table and anaesthetised, to wake up several hours later to the thought that those gloved fingers have been inside you, those eyes have shamelessly stared at your naked organs glittering under the surgical lights without once thinking they belonged to you.

For hospitals all hearts are the same.

Towards the end of grandad's time in hospital mum came to Bergen. She stayed one night with me, one night with Yngve, and the day after she had left, Gunvor came to the flat. We were sitting on the sofa, chatting about everything under the sun, when she suddenly got up and walked across the floor.

'What's this?' she said.

'What's what?' I said.

'There's a hair on the floor.'

She took it and lifted it up. I watched her, my cheeks getting warm.

'This isn't yours,' she said. 'And it's definitely not mine.'

She eyed me.

'Whose is it? Has anyone been here?'

'I have no idea,' I said. 'Are you insinuating I've been unfaithful or something?'

She didn't say a word, just stared at me.

'Let me have a look,' I said, unusually conscious of my own movements.

She passed me the hair. It was grey. Of course. Oh, thank God!

'That's mum's,' I said as calmly as I could. 'She was brushing her hair here. It's grey, see.'

'Sorry,' Gunvor said. 'I thought it was someone else's. I promise I won't be so suspicious in future.'

'OK,' I said. 'That's the second time. You opened my letter in the autumn as well.'

'I did apologise,' she said.

She had come by one evening and confessed she had read a letter I received from Cecilie, my girlfriend in the second class at *gymnas*. She was so jealous, she had said.

Now she suspected that something had been going on, that was certain. If not, it wouldn't have occurred to her that there could be anything suspicious about the hair. Mum had been here, that would have been her first reaction. But it wasn't.

'I'm sorry, Karl Ove,' she repeated and put her arms around me. 'Can you forgive me? I don't mean to be so suspicious.'

'That's all right,' I said. 'Just remember for another time.'

The night before the assignment was due to be handed in I was only halfway through. I had worked the entire weekend at

Sandviken Hospital and when I sat down at my desk to start on it I was tempted to give up. Go to bed and sleep, not give a damn. But then I noticed how easily it flowed, it was as if the pressure was sharpening my focus, all I had to do was write, and I did, all night and into the morning, but then I touched a key by mistake and everything I had written was gone. I ran up to the university, explained my plight to Buvik, who accompanied me to a special computer data section, they took the diskette and would see if they could retrieve what I had lost. They asked me for the password, I hesitated, for some reason it was pineapple, and I found it unbearably embarrassing to have a smidgen of my private life revealed here, in front of what was presumably one of the country's foremost computer experts, with one of the country's leading literary academics at my side.

'Pineapple,' I said, feeling my cheeks flush.

'Pineapple?' he said.

I nodded, he opened the document but failed to find the missing pages, and I, weary with despair, this had been my last chance, now the whole semester had been spoiled, walked beside Buvik into the institute, where he asked me to take a seat, he would just have to discuss the matter with some colleagues. On his return he informed me I had been granted a twenty-four-hour extension. I thanked him with shiny eyes, hurried home, slept for a couple of hours and embarked on another hellish night with Joyce and intertextuality. Morning dawned, I hadn't finished, everything in the assignment was leading up to a major discussion, which never came, I was forced to write a conclusion in two lines, run downstairs and knock on Espen's door to borrow his bike, pedal like a maniac to the university and hand in my assignment on the dot of nine o'clock.

When the grades were pinned on the board outside the institute a few weeks later and I saw that once again I had a 2.4, I wasn't disappointed, I had expected worse, and it was still possible to blag your way up two tenths at the oral exam. That is, if I had done the reading. But I hadn't and was forced to improvise, in front of Kittang of all people. He was kind to me, whenever he noticed I was struggling he gave me a pointer, but not even he could extricate me from the mess I was in when he asked what Kittang wrote about this problem. There were several articles by him on the reading list, but I hadn't read them, and with him present in the room it wasn't possible to wriggle my way out, clear unambiguous answers were required, which I didn't have.

But it didn't matter. It had never been my intention to become an academic. I wanted to write, that was all I wanted, and I couldn't understand those who didn't, how they could be happy with an ordinary job, whatever it was, whether teacher, camera operator, bureaucrat, academic, farmer, TV host, journalist, designer, promoter, fisherman, lorry driver, gardener, nurse or astronomer. How could that be enough? I understood it was the norm, most people had ordinary jobs, some put all their energy into them, others didn't, but to me they seemed pointless. If I were to take such a job my life would feel meaningless however good I was at it and however high I rose. It would never be enough. I mentioned this to Gunvor a couple of times, and she was in total agreement, only in reverse: she understood how I felt but was unable to identify with it herself.

What was this feeling?

I didn't know. It was beyond investigation, beyond explanation or justification, there was no rationality in it at all, yet it was self-evident, all-eclipsing: anything other than writing was meaningless for me. Nothing else would be enough, would quench my thirst.

But thirst for what?

How could *it* be so strong? Writing a few words on paper? And yes, which wasn't a dissertation, research, a report or any of writing's inferior varieties but literary?

It was madness, for this was precisely what I couldn't do. I was good at academic assignments, and I was good at articles, reviews and interviews. But as soon as I sat down to write literature, which was the only way I wanted to spend my life, the sole occupation I perceived as meaningful *enough*, then I fell short.

I wrote letters, they just flowed, sentence after sentence, page after page. Often they consisted of stories about my life, what I had experienced and what I had thought. Had I only been able to transfer that feeling, that state of mind, that flow into literary prose, everything would have been fine. But I couldn't. I sat at my desk, wrote a line, then stopped. I wrote another line, stopped.

I wondered whether I should go to a hypnotist who could transport me into a state where sentences and words poured out of me, the same as when I wrote letters – that should work, I had heard about people who gave up smoking thanks to hypnosis, so why couldn't you be hypnotised into writing light, flowing Norwegian?

I looked up hypnotists in the Yellow Pages, this professional category wasn't there, and I didn't dare ask anyone, it would spread like wildfire, Yngve's brother wants to use hypnosis to become a writer, I dismissed the idea.

On the afternoon of New Year's Eve we carried our instruments and amplifiers up to the music venue, which was the top floor of Rick's. While the organisers were decorating and arranging the place we did our sound check. This wasn't going to be a proper concert, we had no PA, the drums weren't miked up and we had to perform on the floor, there was no stage, but I was still queasy with nerves.

Hans stood at the other end of the room and listened to us playing, he said it was good, we all went home to change.

Had I not been playing in the band, I would never have been invited to this. It was a fiftieth birthday party, in the sense that two twenty-fifth birthdays had been rolled into one, and everyone present had a connection with what I considered to be the Vestland mafia, students with links to the periodical *Syn og Segn*, the magazine *Dag og Tid*, *Mållaget*, an organisation to promote Nynorsk and the No to the EU organisation. Even though they were only a few years older than me they had already made it. Ragnar Hovland was also going to attend, it was rumoured, as the conclusive seal of approval, this is the place to be, these are the people to know.

I returned to Rick's alone, walked up the broad majestic stairs, entered the room, which was now full of young women in their party frocks and young men in dark suits, urbane and worldly and self-assured Vestlanders. The buzz of conversation, peals of laughter, the expectant atmosphere that only precedes a celebration. I stepped back and searched for Yngve.

Yngve, Yngve, where are you when I need you?

There was Hans anyway. But he was also one of them, urbane and worldly and self-assured, always with an ironic riposte on his tongue. I was proud of being in the same band as him, but not of being in the same band as Yngve, because everyone realised it was thanks to him that I had the chance to play and be here.

I slowly mingled in the crowd. Many of the faces were familiar, I had seen them at Høyden and Café Opera, Garage and Hulen, although I could put a name to less than a handful.

I caught sight of Ragnar Hovland and wondered whether to approach him. Being seen in conversation with him would do wonders for my status.

I moved towards him. He was talking to a woman in her mid-thirties and didn't see me until I was next to them.

'Hi,' he said. 'It's the man himself!'

'Yes,' I said. 'We're going to play later.'

'You're in a band! Well, I'm pleased to hear that.'

His eyes were smiling but also shifty.

'How's it going at the Academy?'

'It's good. We had to introduce compulsory attendance after you left. But they're behaving well.'

'I know Espen,' I said. 'He's a good friend of mine.'

'Is that right?' he said.

There was a silence. Both he and I scanned the room.

'Any books on the go?' I said at length.

'There's one I'm messing about with,' he said.

The natural response would have been to ask me how my writing was going, if I had any new books on the go, but he didn't. I could understand why, and I didn't blame him, but it still rankled with me.

'Right,' I said. 'Perhaps talk later. I'm just going for a walk.'

He smiled and turned back to the woman. I noticed Yngve arrive, moved towards the entrance area, where he was standing and looking around. I raised my hand and went over to him.

'Butterflies?' he said.

'Yes, terrible,' I said. 'And you?'

'Not so bad. They'll come soon enough.'

I lit a cigarette, we joined Hans, chatted for a bit until a girl clapped her hands and silence spread like a flock of pigeons startled into the air. She welcomed everyone. There was a dinner, there were speeches, there was entertainment and last of all a gig with Kafkatrakterne.

My stomach knotted so hard it hurt.

We went to the table, there were name cards, I found mine and sat down, a long way from Yngve and Hans unfortunately.

Each card bore a sentence about the bearer, a personal characteristic. Mine said *Twenty years on the outside, a thousand on the inside*.

Was that how they saw me? Was that how I was seen?

In the last year I had spoken less and less, become more and more reticent, that was probably what the card was alluding to.

The girl beside me, who was wearing a short black skirt with some net trimming at the bottom, dark stockings and red

high-heeled shoes, unfolded her serviette and laid it on her lap. I
followed suit.

She looked at me.

'Who do you know here? I mean, of those who organised the
party.'

'No one,' I said with a blush. 'I'm playing in the band.'

'Oh,' she said. 'What do you play?'

'The drums,' I said.

'Oh,' she said.

I looked the other way for a while and that was the end of her
questions.

I ate without saying a word to anyone, occasionally casting a
glance at Yngve or Hans, who were both chatting away with their
neighbours.

The dinner lasted an eternity.

There was a storm outside. The wind was so strong that dustbins were sent rolling through the streets, I could hear the clatter
below, and now and then windowpanes tinkled.

The moment the dinner was over I joined Yngve and Hans and
stayed at the front until we were due to play.

We were introduced, I could barely stand up straight, people
clapped, we went over to our instruments, I sat down on the little drum stool, put on the NFK cap which I had brought along as
a little gesture to the audience – NFK was an agricultural co-op,
they might be on their way to glittering academic success, but
they had grown up with tractors, combine harvesters and cans
of formic acid, the whole bunch of them – wiped my hands on a
towel, grabbed the sticks. People stood watching us. It was my job
to count, but I didn't dare in case Pål or Yngve weren't ready.

'Are you ready?' I said.

Yngve nodded.

'You ready, Pål?'

'Count, Karl Ove,' he said.

I hummed the first riff of 'Over My Head' sotto voce.

OK.

I counted and we started to play. To my horror, I discovered that the bass drum was sliding away from me with every beat. Not much, but enough for me to be sitting with my leg fully out-stretched by the end of the song, and as I had to hit the hi-hat and the snare drum at the same time I must have looked like some kind of elongated monster spider.

They clapped, I pulled the bass drum back, counted for the next song and slipped back into my spider pose. People started dancing, it was going well, Hans especially made sure of that, he was the showman, undaunted and, luckily, uncritical.

When I got home, after crossing the wind-blown deserted town in the early hours, I cried. For no reason, everything was great, the concert had been a success, at least as far as we could judge, but it didn't help, the moment my head touched the bed the tears came.

In the new year I was offered a regular weekend temporary post at the hospital, which I accepted. In addition, I put my name on the temping list and, so gradually that I hardly noticed, I found myself working there full time. I put my studies on hold and said yes to everything, I had an appetite for it, almost an urge, I wanted to work as much as possible and did so all the following year. Some days I did double shifts, started in one ward in the morning, transferred to another in the evening and in this way worked sixteen hours in succession. Some weeks I took shifts in the hardest ward, those who worked there were to a large degree bouncers, and I was ill at ease, in fact I was scared the whole time, a couple of the residents I considered extremely dangerous although the bouncers just laughed at them and sometimes even put them on their laps and patted them while they watched TV, as if they were cats.

One in particular was terrifying. His name was Knut, he was in his late thirties but had the physique of a teenager. Slim muscular body, an attractive shaven head. He had his head shaved because otherwise he would pull out his hair and eat it. He also ate dust balls if he found any, and one afternoon I saw him open the fridge and take out an onion. He sank his teeth in, tears began to roll, but he took another bite and another and soon he had eaten the whole onion, the outer layer and everything, still crying. He could be aggressive. More often than not he hurt himself, once he rammed his head against the wall so hard that he cracked his skull. What he liked best was walking. If no one had been there to stop him he would have walked to Siberia, he was like a machine, he just walked and walked and walked. When he came towards me in the ward with those dark eyes of his, which expressed exactly that, darkness, I was always afraid. Once I was supposed to shave him while he was in the bathtub, he must have sensed my fear because he grabbed my hand, I couldn't move it, and then he bit. I had to have a tetanus jab afterwards. They told me I could go home, but I went back to work, I was afraid of course but I didn't want anyone to know that.

I was often on suicide watch, many of these patients were more communicative than those in the difficult wards for chronic patients, many had drug problems, some of them were seriously psychotic or paranoid, others manic or depressed, most were young.

In the ward where I worked normally I got to know the other staff well and gradually began to go out with them. Some lived close by or next to Åsane Shopping Centre, there would often be pre-drinks on a Friday or Saturday night, I went, got drunk with all of them, these women, who were between twenty-five and forty, and later caught the bus into town to go out. Whereas students went to places south of the centre, near Høyden, the hospital crowd went to places in the north, around Bryggen, where students, at least the arts students, never set foot unless they were being ironic. There were piano bars, sing-a-long bars, Bergensians and Striler – people from the coastal region north of Bergen – of all shades and hues. They liked me, I didn't shirk on my shifts, and the fact that I didn't say much was interpreted charitably by them, from what I gathered. They were friendly and nice, and I was too when I drank, I met them halfway, once I carried one of them up the stairs to shouting and cheering and laughter, another time I expressed my admiration for them and said exactly what I thought, my eyes moist and shining with affection. I got on espe-cially well with one called Vibeke, she and I could sit and chat for a whole morning if the ward was quiet, and she often confided in me, for some reason she trusted me. Then there were others who were more challenging. Åge in particular was wearing. He was a student who had abandoned his studies and now worked at Sandviken full time. He tried to get close to me, clung to me like a rash, he got involved in countless arguments, now he wanted me, first, to listen to his complaints and backbiting and, second, to support him, and I nodded and said yes, you're right, to this, and, you don't say, oh really, to that, in a way that made him think he was actually my friend. We were often out with patients, when he moaned and groaned and stared at me with those insanely intense eyes of his, he was also bearded and pale, a wimp, a poor wretch, a loser, who in his own mind was a student, someone far better than the housewifely assistant nurses in the hospital or the superior psychiatric nurses, who were after him, always after him, and then all of a sudden he wanted me to visit him, we were supposed to go out together, and then, for the first time since I was a boy, I answered someone who wanted something from me with a clear and resounding no.

'No, I don't think so,' I said.

He withdrew and began to avoid me.

Then he turned and began to accuse me of betraying him.

What sort of a creep was this?

A terrible thought occurred to me as I was on my way home that night: was he actually me? Would I become like him? An ex-student drifting around for years taking shifts until it is too late, all the options are gone *and this becomes life*?

Would I be stuck there, forty years old, telling the young students who came and went on temping contracts, actually I was going to be a writer? Would you like to read a short story? It was rejected, but that's only because the publishers are so damned conventional and daren't take a chance on someone who takes risks. They wouldn't recognise a genius if they had one stuffed up their jacksies. Look, by pure chance, I happen to have a copy in my bag. Yes, it's about my life and you'll probably recognise the odd detail about the institution I describe, but it's not *this* one, actually. What was it you were studying again? Philosophy? Yes, I had a sniff at that too. But then I went for literature. I wrote about Joyce, you know. A bit about intertextuality and the like. I was told it was brilliant. But I don't know. Feels a bit dated in some ways, yet there's something universal about literature which . . . well, shines *through* its epoch. But take it and tell me what you think during the shift tomorrow. OK?

I wasn't forty but twenty-two, otherwise the image fitted pretty well. I was working there for money to live on, and I lived to write, which I couldn't do, I just talked about it. But if I couldn't write at least I could read. For that reason I took quite a few night shifts, then I could read until four, usually undisturbed, and then clean the ward for the two last hours when I was so sleepy anyway that it was hard to concentrate. I read Stig Larsson's *The Autists* and *The Comedy 1*, and admired the realism that was so natural, while there was always an underlying sense of menace. This menace was the capriciousness of futile existence. I read Flaubert, his *Three Tales*, they were by far the best thing I had read, the stories hit the bull's eye, they touched on the essential core, particularly the one about bloodlust, the hunter who slaughters all the animals that cross his path, I understood it, it resonated with something I felt inside and knew was important, but not in a way that could be explained in rational terms, for there was nothing to explain, the narrative was everything. I read his historical novel *Salammbô*, it failed totally, though in a creditable way, he had invested everything into that book, used all his skill and the whole gamut of his talent, but to no avail, there was no life in it, everything was dead, the characters were wooden, the setting felt theatrical, although this artifice also had an appeal, it also brought something, not only in the way that the time it portrayed was in fact dead for ever, but also in the way the novel in its own right, as an artefact, as an artistic product, made its mark. And then I read his novel about stupidity, *Bouvard and Pécuchet*, which was brilliant because he didn't find stupidity at the bottom of society, in the lower classes, but in the middle class, and showed it off in all its complacent splendour. I read Tor Ulven and relished every sentence he wrote, the unprecedented, almost inhuman, precision to them, the way he managed to make everything equally important. I talked a lot to Espen about it, about what it was that made Tor Ulven's prose so good, what actually made it tick. There was a kind of parity between material and man, where psychology had no place, and that meant the existential drama was being played out the whole time, not only during a crisis, such as people separating or losing their father or mother or falling in love or having children, but all the time, while they drank a glass of water or cycled with a flickering light along a road in the darkness, or you simply weren't even there, in the empty room he described with such mastery. And this wasn't something that was said or written, it didn't exist *in* the text, it *was* the text. The language brought it out, as we liked to say, through its modulation and figures of speech, not through direct expression but in its form. I read Jon Fosse, and it was as though a door had been opened into his books when *The Boat House* came out because of its simplicity, its dynamism. I read *The Georgics* by Claude Simon and,

with Espen, admired the complexity of his style and the absence
of any overriding perspective, everything was somehow at the
same level, and chaotic, echoing the confusion which the world
really was. But the best writing I read during this period was still
Borges, I was attracted by both the adventure in it, which I knew
from my childhood and didn't know I had been longing for until I
had read him, and the way the images, all simple, carried signifi-
cances almost endless in their complexity.

I wrote next to nothing. I played around with a story about a
man who was tied to a chair in a flat in Danmarksplass, he was
tortured and in the end shot through the head, and when that
happened I tried to slow time down to almost nothing, describe
how the bullet penetrated the skin and bone, cartilage and fluid,
into the brain and the various parts there because I loved the
Latin terms, they sounded like names in the countryside, valleys
and plains, but it was just nonsense, there was no point to any of
it and I deleted it. Two pages, six months' work. We went with the
band to Gjøvik and recorded a demo, two of the songs were played
on NRK, and we got a warm-up spot at Hulen during the Bergen
International Festival. It went well, *Studvest* wrote that even though
we weren't on the poster we were the hit of the evening and we
were given another gig there, this time a whole evening on our
own. It was packed, we were too nervous, little or nothing went
right, on our recording a voice from the crowd yelled, *This is bloody
awful!* But *Studvest* gave us a nice write-up again. This time I wasn't
as flattered on the band's behalf as before because the journalist
who wrote it came from the same place as Hans and had even
played in several bands with him. When we started talking about
taking on another guitarist, his name was suggested, no one had
any objections and so he turned up at a practice session, he was
withdrawn but not unassuming, and immediately got into the
songs. His name was Knut Olav, he had long reddish hair, an open
face, a clearly defined austere almost connoisseur-like taste in

music. He played the drums much better than me, probably the bass better than Pål and it wouldn't have surprised me if he sang better than Hans. With him in the band we made a little more progress and I had someone new to test my mettle on. He said very little about himself, would never have dreamed of describing himself in rosy terms, not even indirectly, in the way that everyone pushes themselves forward without wishing to give the impression that that is what they are doing. His face was open, his eyes were open, and although he wasn't considered introverted in social contexts, there was still something closed and secretive about him. He was one of the few who could drink through until day broke, one of those who would never go home if something was happening, a quality I shared with him, and so many was the time we were sitting in a flat somewhere in Bergen drinking coffee at eight o'clock in the morning, good and drunk, chatting about stuff we had both forgotten all about the next day. One of the conversations, however, did stick in my mind, I was rambling on about the universe, how it might open in the future, how we were getting to know more and more about it and hence about ourselves, we were made of stardust, I said, I was well into the shiny glittering festive mode the combination of alcohol and the sight of stars in the sky could transport me to when he said, it was quite the opposite, new discoveries would be inward, our future lay inwards. Nano-technology. Genetic engineering. Atomic power. All the power and all the explosiveness was to be found in the tiny, in the microscopic, not in the great, the macroscopic. I looked at him, of course he was right, we were on our way inwards. Inwards, that was the new outwards.

I wrote a short story about a man who died, I told it in the first-person singular, he was stretchered into the ambulance just below the underpass by Danmarksplass, his heart had stopped but his story went on, to the pathologist, in the coffin, in the cemetery, in the ground. Three months' work, two and a half pages, meaningless, deleted. One evening the police raided the flat next door, their kitchen window faced my wall, two metres away, the following day it was in *Bergensavisen*, they had found a stash of weapons and fifty thousand kroner in cash. I took the newspaper down to Espen, we laughed in shock; only a few nights ago we had come home drunk, gone into my kitchen to get a cup of coffee, shadows were moving behind the curtain on the other side, I opened the window and threw a liver-paste can in their direction, it hit the glass pane with a clatter, we shrank out of sight, nothing happened except that the curtain was pulled aside and a guy peered out. So they were bank robbers!

Mostly though I worked at Sandviken Hospital. Sometimes it felt as if my whole life was being lived there. The people I worked with were low status, I needed that. The money I earned, I needed. And perhaps doing something else, something practical, something outside the university, gave me a different self-image, which I needed to keep myself going: the real purpose of what I was doing was writing. Everything converged on that fact, or was supposed to.

One Saturday evening I was alone at work, Mary phoned not long before the night shift was about to begin.

'Hi,' I said. 'Did you forget something?'

'No,' she said. 'I'm here all alone and I thought you might like to pop by after work. We could share a bottle of wine or something.'

I could feel the heat rising. What was she saying?

'I don't think so,' I said. 'I'm afraid I have to go home.'

'I'll be frank with you, Karl Ove,' she said. 'I want to sleep with you. I know you have a girlfriend. But no one will find out. It's absolutely safe. I promise. Once. Then never again.'

'But I can't,' I said. 'It's no good. I'm sorry.'

'You're absolutely sure? This is absolutely definite?'

Oh, how I wanted to shout YES, PLEASE! and run down to her.

'Yes, I can't. It's no good.'

'I see,' she said. 'I hope you don't think I'm stupid for asking so directly. I don't want you to think I'm stupid.'

'No, no, no, are you crazy?' I said. 'That's the last thing I would think.'

'You promise me?'

'Yes.'

'See you tomorrow then. Bye.'

'Bye.'

The morning came, I was nervous about meeting her again, but there wasn't any indication in her behaviour that anything special had happened, she was exactly as she had always been, perhaps a touch more reserved towards me, that was all.

I thought about her offer every single day for several weeks. In a way I was glad I hadn't succumbed to temptation, I didn't want to cheat on Gunvor and, provided I was sober, that wasn't difficult. In another way, when I thought about it, I burned with regret, because if I had been totally free I would have taken her up on it. But I couldn't. Next year I would be moving to Iceland with Gunvor, she would take her history exam at the university there, I would write full time. Until then I worked as much as I could at Sandviken. Wiped excrement off the walls, restrained residents with psychotic fits, was hit in the face by one, went for endless walks inside the hospital grounds or just outside, unless we were driving around the district in one of their minibuses.

Hans, who had become the editor of *Studvest*, asked if I was interested in reviewing books for him. I was, and I did. I slaughtered Atle Næss's novel about Dante and wrote a whole page about *American Psycho*, which also had a connection with Dante in that the protagonist reads some graffiti on a wall travelling through town in a taxi: LASCIATE OGNI SPERANZA, VOI CH'ENTRATE. The gates of hell here, now, Jesus, that was good. What a novel it was. What a

novel. Hans asked if I would like to write a Christmas short story
for them. I said yes, but I didn't manage it, I got no further than a
few lines about a guy on his way home in a bus for Christmas. I had
been planning a kidnapping, someone being bound and tortured
on Christmas Eve, but it was just rubbish, like everything else I
did. I read Paul Auster, the New York trilogy, and thought, I could
never do that. I made pizza for the patients one Saturday evening,
it felt as though I was demeaning them as I did so. I went home to
mum's for Christmas, sorted out a tenant for my flat while I was
away in Iceland, one of Yngve's Arendal friends, went into Bergen
and packed two full suitcases, said bye to Espen, caught the plane
to Fornebu, then to Kastrup and from there to Keflavik, where
the plane landed in the late evening. The darkness was dense and
impenetrable, I saw nothing of the countryside I passed through
an hour later in the airport bus, and I got no impression of the
city I entered, which was Rekyavik. I jumped into a taxi, showed
the driver the note Gunvor had given me with the street name on,
Gardastræti, it was, we went past a lake, up a hill, the houses were
big, like monuments, we stopped in front of one of them.

So this was where we were going to live. In an elegant town-
house in the middle of the Atlantic Ocean.

I paid, he took out the cases and passed them to me, I walked
through the gates and up the path to the house. The door to the
basement flat opened, there was Gunvor, beaming. We embraced,
I could feel how I had missed her. She had been here a week and
showed me round our flat, it was large and impersonally furnished but it was ours, this is where we would live for the next
six months. We went to bed and afterwards we wanted to take a
shower, but the water smelled like rotten eggs, I couldn't stand
it, she said all the water smelled like this, it came from the vol-
canic sub-surface, the terrible smell was sulphur.

A few weeks later I loved the smell, as I loved everything about
Rekyavik and our life there. After she had gone to university in

the morning I had a long breakfast alone before either walking
into town and sitting in a café with my notebook or a novel, struck
every day by the beauty of the people there, the girls were unbelievably beautiful, I had never seen girls like them, or I took my
swimming things and walked up to the local outdoor pool, where
I swam a thousand metres under the open sky, in rain as well as
snow or sleet, before slowly lowering myself into a *heitapottur*, as
it was called, the Icelanders' small hot pools. Afterwards I went
home to write. In the evenings we watched TV, I loved that too, the
language was so similar to Norwegian, it was so close in tone and
sound, but completely incomprehensible. Gunvor made friends at
the university, mostly other foreign students, and she acquired an
Icelandic 'family' friend, Einar, who was not only at our service
twenty-four hours a day but also popped in at least four evenings
a week. He had big black bags under his eyes, an incipient paunch,
he worked and drank too much, but not so much that he didn't
have time to drop by and ask if there was anything he could do to
help. I never understood what he wanted, he never got anything
back for all his efforts, at least not as far as I could see, and I wasn't
too happy about that, he was like a leech, yet he was the only person I could drink with, beggars can't be choosers, I thought, and
hung out in Icelandic bars with him, drunk and silent.

Through one of Gunvor's foreign friends I got to know an American of my age, he was interested in music, said he penned his
own songs, was enthusiastic and naïve, we talked about forming a
band, he knew an Icelander who played, one evening we went out
to see him, he lived in a damp cellar, there was something nineteenth century about it, he coughed like a miner and was just as
thin, and his wife smoked and carried around a baby and shouted
at him, he just shrugged and took us into an even smaller room,
crammed with all sorts of useless junk, where we could play, but
first of all, he said in English, first we have to smoke. The joint did

the rounds, he took out his guitar, Eric, as my American friend was called, took out his and I was given a bucket to use as drums. It was a very ordinary bucket, red with a white handle, I turned it upside down, put it between my legs and started tapping and thumping on the bucket while the other two picked out a bluesy tune on their guitars and the baby screamed its lungs out next door.

Gunvor laughed so much she cried when I told her.

We visited the farm where she had worked, they received her warmly, were shy with me, they spoke very little English, they said, but later that evening, driving to the community centre to take part in a big do with all the others in the district, they thawed. I ate ram's testicles, buried shark and other oddities, all washed down with their schnapps, and their reticence and shyness, which I had found so liberating as I was the same myself, disappeared in a heartbeat, suddenly, on all sides, the atmosphere soared to the rafters, soon I was sitting there arm in arm with my neighbours swinging from side to side belting out something similar to what they were singing. Everyone was drunk, everyone was happy, it was like me a hundred times over, and when the party was over, in the early hours, everyone drove home drunk. In our case, the cows had to be seen to, so after a whisky in the kitchen with the farmer I followed him into the cowshed. While he staggered around with the muck rake groping for the cow fodder and straw bales he told me to clean their teeth, a suggestion he found so amusing that he had to sit down so as not to topple over with laughter.

The wind was blowing outside. In Iceland the wind always blew, it gusted off the sea day and night. Once I was on my way to Nordens Hus to read some Norwegian newspapers when I saw an old lady blown over. I wrote three short stories and filled a whole notebook with comments on them and what I wanted to achieve in my writing. At night I dreamed about dad, more frightened asleep than ever I was awake. Gunvor's girlfriends were boring, I avoided them as often as I could. A Swedish student, maybe ten years older than Gunvor and me, invited Einar and us to dinner, he was friendly, shy, had a big heart, lived in a fantastic flat and served a gourmet dinner he must have spent all day preparing. We invited him back to ours, I found a recipe for lamb which looked delicious, Gunvor's farm had given us a bag of lamb and a bag of horsemeat. They looked the same, I took a risk, I made a mistake, and I didn't even get close to the picture of the meal the recipe showed with the joint of meat elegantly arranged with mushrooms, onions and carrots, the meat slid off the bones, so what they got, our guests that Saturday evening, gathered around the table in our little kitchen, was horsemeat soup. Oh, it tasted absolutely dreadful, salty and horrible. But the Swede, Carl, nodded and smiled and said what I had made was very good. Einar, who was Icelandic enough to know this was horsemeat, said nothing, just smiled his inscrutable though not unfriendly smile. I began to get the picture, he had no friends. We were his friends.

We got drunk and went out. I had wondered about Carl all evening, there was something refined about him, even though he looked like a farmer, refined and perhaps a little feminine, and then there was the way he referred to his partner back home in Sweden, never by name, nevertheless something about the way he did this made me think the partner might have been a man.

I explained this to Gunvor and Einar, we were standing in a packed bar, the music was loud, I had to raise my voice to be heard.

'I think Carl might be a homo!' I shouted.

Einar stared at me with frenetic eyes. Then past me.

I turned. Oh my God, there was Carl.

He was crying.

And then he dashed out.

'Karl Ove,' Gunvor said. 'Run after him and apologise.'

I did as she said. Out into the street into the hellish wind, a look up, nothing, a look down, there was Carl hurrying home.

I ran after him and caught him up.

'Listen, Carl. I'm sorry,' I said. 'But that was what was on my mind and it just came out. I'm pretty drunk, you see. But I didn't mean to hurt you. I think you're a great guy anyway. I like you a lot. Gunvor also likes you a lot.'

He looked at me and sniffled.

'I wanted to keep it a secret here,' he said. 'I didn't want anyone to know.'

'But what does it matter!' I said. 'Come on, let's go back to the others. We won't ever need to talk about it again. Come on. Let's have another G and T!'

He dried his tears and joined me. This was the first gay man I had known. Afterwards he began to mention his partner by name, who some weeks later came to Rekyavik, they invited us to dinner and it turned out he was fully informed about us and our lives there. Carl had bigged us up, in his partner's eyes we were people of importance and I – so I understood – was a bit of an enigma. I had never said what I was doing in Iceland, not even when Einar or Carl had asked me directly. I lazed around, swam, read and at night, I had said once, I sat in front of the oven watching the bread I was baking slowly go golden brown and crispy. For me it was the other way around: for me Carl and his partner were the enigma, in their similarity, because how was it possible to look for the same? To want the same? To love the same?

For some reason, not long after, I ended up in a gay club. I had been boozing with Einar and, as so often, I wandered around town after we had said goodbye searching for places that were still open, wanting something to happen, anything actually, and that night I came across a cellar club, I went down, at first I didn't notice anything unusual, bought a drink and scanned the room, they were playing Bronski Beat, lots of people were dancing, I went to the toilet for a pee, and there, on the cubicle wall was a poster of an enormous dick. I was so drunk it felt as if I was in the middle of a dream, I went out, and yes, there were only men. Back on the street, my head bowed into the wind, someone called to me. I turned. A man of around thirty came running towards me.

'Sean!' he said. 'Is it really you?'

'My name's not Sean,' I said.

'Stop messing around,' he said. 'Where have you been? I never thought I'd see you again!'

'My name's Karl,' I said.

'Why do you say that?' he said.

'Look,' I said, taking my passport from my inside pocket. 'Karl. Do you see?'

'You're Sean,' he said. 'You're Sean. You're Sean.'

He took a few steps back as he scrutinised me, then turned on his heel and disappeared down a side street.

I shook my head, continued through the lifeless wind-blown streets, let myself in, got into bed beside Gunvor, who would soon have to get up, and crashed out as if I had been shot in the head.

From the first moment we decided to move to Iceland I had thought about writing articles there and selling them to newspapers. When it transpired that Einar knew Bragi, the bass player in the Sugar Cubes, I didn't hesitate, I managed to get an interview arranged and went to his house. He'd just had a child, whom he showed me, we sat down at the kitchen table, I asked my questions, he answered, and as they had just released a new record, which perhaps wasn't as good as their debut album, although better than the follow-up, and with an incredibly catchy song as the opener, 'Hit', there was no problem getting a newspaper to buy it. Bragi smiled when I told him which newspaper: *Klassekampen*. It must have sounded absolutely crazy to a foreigner's ears. As I was about to leave he said they were going to be playing in Rekyavik

soon and I absolutely had to come backstage and see them afterwards.

Gunvor was at the farm then, so I went alone, got so drunk
on schnapps that before the gig I was rocking to and fro on one
of the enormous lighting stands, it was highly dangerous, but I
didn't give it a thought. A guard ran over and told me to stop, yes,
sir, I said and left. If it had been Norway I would have been man-
handled and slung onto the street, but here people were used to
all sorts; because of an earlier ban on beer almost everyone drank
schnapps and when beer was finally introduced the habit was so
established that beer was almost exotic. What was more, half a
litre cost a small fortune. Schnapps was what they drank, so it
wasn't just me staggering around town. At night the lower part
of the main street was packed with young people. The first time
I saw it I wondered what on earth was going on, Gunvor told me
it was always like this here. They stood elbow to elbow and were
drunk. Iceland was full of such idiosyncrasies, which I saw but
didn't understand.

The band started. They were good and playing in front of their
home audience, the gig was amazing. After the performance I
went backstage. I was stopped, I said I was from the Norwegian
newspaper *Klassekampen* and in fact had arranged to meet Bragi
here. The guard came back, it was OK, I walked down the aisle,
entered a crowded room, everyone was excited and in high spirits,
the atmosphere was bordering on wild, Bragi was perched on
the edge of a chair and waved me over. He introduced me to the
drummer, said something to him in Icelandic, I heard the word
Klassekampen and they both burst into laughter.

I had nothing to say, nevertheless I was happy, Bragi handed me
a beer, I sat looking at the motley and outré selection of people
around me, particularly at Björk of course, it was hard to take your
eyes off her. The Sugar Cubes were one of the best bands in the
world at the moment, right now the room I was in constituted the

epicentre of rock music. I was already looking forward to telling Yngve.

Bragi got up.

'We're off to a party. Want to come?'

I nodded.

'Just stick with me,' he said.

I did. I stayed close to him amid the crowd of musicians and artists walking through the town down to the harbour, where Björk had her flat. It was on two floors with a broad staircase in the middle and was soon full. Björk herself sat on the floor by a ghetto blaster, surrounded by CDs, playing one song after the other. I was so tired that I could hardly stand. I slumped at the top of the staircase, leaned my head against the banisters and closed my eyes. But I didn't sleep, something was rising from within, from my stomach and up through my chest, soon it would be in my throat, I jumped to my feet, took the last steps to the first floor, ran to the bathroom, opened the door, bent over the toilet bowl and spewed up a magnificent yellow and orange cascade that splashed everywhere.

Some weeks later mum visited us, we went to Gullfoss and Geysir and Thingvellir with her one day, another down to the south coast, where the sand was black and there were immense solitary rocks standing in the sea.

We went to an art museum together, the walls and floor were completely white, and with the sun flooding in through large roof windows the light inside was almost aflame. Through the windows I could see the sea, blue with white crests of waves and breakers, a large white-clad mountain rose in the distance. In these surroundings, in this bright white room on the edge of the world, the art was lost.

Was art only an inner phenomenon? Something that moved within us and between us, all that which we couldn't see but

marked us, indeed, which *was us*? Was this the function of landscape painting, portraits, sculptures, to draw the external world,
so essentially alien to us, into our inner world?

When she went home I accompanied her to Keflavik Airport
and said my goodbyes there, on the way back I read *Stephen Hero* by
James Joyce, the first book I had bought by him and quite evidently
his weakest, it was also unfinished and not meant for publication,
but there was something to learn from it too, how he slowly transformed the autobiographical element, which was obvious here,
into something else in *Ulysses*. Stephen Dedalus was a strong young
character, summoned home to Dublin by his father's telegram,
'Mother dying come home,' but in the novel – *Ulysses,* that is – this
arrogant brilliant young man was perhaps first and foremost a
place where things happened. In *Stephen Hero* he was a person,
distinct from the world around him, in *Ulysses* the world flowed
through him and the story, Augustine, Thomas Aquinas, Dante,
Shakespeare, everything moved through him and the same was
true of the little Jew, Bloom, except that in him it wasn't the highest and the best that was in motion, that flowed, but rather the
town with its people and phenomena, advertising slogans and
newspaper articles, he thought about what everyone else thought
about, he was Everyman. There was, however, another level above
them, namely the place whence they were observed, which was
the language and all the insights and prejudices the various forms
of language embraced, almost in secret.

But in *Stephen Hero* there was none of this, there was just the
character, Stephen, in other words, Joyce, set apart from the world,
which was described but never integrated. This development cul-
minated, from what I could infer, in his final book, *Finnegans Wake*,
which I had bought but hadn't read, where the characters had
disappeared into the language, which lived its own everyman life.

I jumped off the bus at the stop between the university and the
landmark building Perlan and walked the last part home through

the embassy district. It was raining and misty, I felt empty, like a nobody, as a consequence of saying goodbye perhaps. In the flat Gunvor was huddled up in the armchair reading with a cup of tea on the table beside her.

I hung up my coat and went in.

'What are you reading?' I said.

'About the famine in Ireland,' she said. 'The Great Famine. Did she get off OK?'

'Yes.'

'It was nice having her here.'

'Yes, it was.'

'What are you going to do this evening?'

I shrugged.

She was wearing a shirt with nothing underneath and tracksuit bottoms. I wanted her and leaned over her. It had been a long time, it had bothered me, not for my part because I just wanted to have some peace, but for hers, she might have thought there was something wrong, that I didn't want her.

But there wasn't. I just wanted space around me, and I had that here, walking alone around an unfamiliar town during the day, swimming and sitting in cafés, and during the night writing at my desk while she slept in the bedroom, but even this space was too small, even there she came too close.

I was happy therefore my desire was so great that everything else was swept away. Then I couldn't understand why I had been abstaining, there was nothing I wanted more, and afterwards we were close again, as we had been when we first got together, then it had been only us two and not a word had to be said for it to be like this. Everything lay in the attraction and the pleasure, it looked after itself. But without it the distance had to be broken down or counteracted with words or actions, and if I didn't want to or didn't have enough strength to sustain my desire we were just two young people living together, sharing nothing more than age and culture.

She had never done anything bad to me. She had been good for me, always wanting the best for me. She had no defects, flaws or shortcomings. She wanted only good and she did good. The defects, flaws and shortcomings were all mine. I tried as hard as I could to hide them from her, and I was usually successful, but it was always there, inside me, a shadow I cast, and it gave me a bad conscience. I wanted to be out of this, I wanted to be alone, then it would disappear as it wouldn't affect anyone else, I would be left with it. But to be alone I would have to leave her, finish what she had invested so much in and where, in a way, I too had invested so much. She often told me she loved me, and I didn't want to hurt her, not for anything in the world, I didn't want to turn away from her, from someone who loved me so much.

Everything was good again this evening though. I had a shower, walked barefoot over the wall-to-wall carpeting, a feeling I liked very much, she watched TV, I sat down beside her, laid my legs across hers, she did simultaneous translation whenever I asked, but it didn't happen often, nearly all of the pictures on the Icelandic news programme were of fishing boats or fish auctions.

She went to bed, I switched on my computer and began to write. The telephone rang, I answered, there was silence at the other end.

'Who was that?' Gunvor shouted from the bedroom.

'No one,' I said. 'Weren't you going to sleep?'

'Yes, but the phone woke me up.'

Now and then there were voices at the other end when we picked up the phone although no one had called or dialled a number. It was strange, but there were embassies everywhere and right below us, over the road, was the Russian embassy, and it seemed to me the telephone cables in the district were under such heavy surveillance that the Icelandic authorities had lost sight of which were which. The country had a population of only 250,000 people, it was impossible for them to be up to date in all the fields a modern state requires.

I switched off the lamps in the hall and the sitting room, making the desk with the computer a little island of light in the darkness, put on my headset and started to write.

One short story was about a man in a swimming hall, the prosthesis again made an appearance, propped up against the changing-room wall, but I was unable to develop it from there into something that wasn't vacuous. The descriptions were good, I had spent several weeks on them, but they weren't enough. One and a half pages, one and a half months. I looked at it, put it to one side, looked at the next, a man with a camera walking around town taking photos, at the margin of one picture he sees someone he knows but hasn't seen in ten years or so and is reminded of the summer they had spent together when the man's girlfriend had drowned. She had swum a few metres from the quay, at the bottom of the sea there were bits of masonry and reinforced steel from work on the quay two years before, and she had dived down, perhaps three metres below the surface, and tied her hands to the metal. That was how they found her, with her hands bound, her hair drifting to and fro in the currents, all as a storm loomed over the island, with the sky black and vast.

Three pages, two months' work.

The problem with it was that I didn't believe it, a woman drowning herself, how could you make that seem realistic?

I put it aside and opened a new file, took out my notebook and flipped through the ideas I had jotted down, decided on the following: *man with a suitcase in a train compartment.*

The next morning I had finished it. Ten pages. I was happy, not because it was good but because it was finished and because there were so many pages. Over the last two years I had written in all somewhere between fifteen and twenty pages. To write ten pages in a night was amazing. Perhaps there might be enough for a collection of short stories by summer after all?

*

The next weekend we went to the Vestmanna archipelago, caught the bus down to the south coast and from there a boat over the sea. We went on deck and took pictures of each other, Gunvor with the hood of her blue raincoat over her head and raindrops on her glasses, me with one hand on the railing, the other pointing to the endless ocean like Leiv Eiriksson.

Then the islands appeared, they came out of nowhere and were a powerful sight, tall steep rocks, clad on one side with mist-shimmering grass, where sheep were grazing, up there they hung like little clouds, on the other, steep and without any vegetation, the rocks plunged vertically to the sea and birds were perched everywhere, on all the ledges and crags.

The ferry glided slowly between two of the rocks, inside a natural harbour opened and we went ashore, left our things at the guest house and walked around the island, which was tiny. The houses nestled just beneath the volcano, the top ones were covered with lava after an eruption in the early 1970s. We walked up to the top of the volcano, where the ash was still hot.

'I wouldn't mind living here,' I said as we strolled back down to the guest house. 'That would be fantastic.'

'What would you do?'

I shrugged. 'Just be here. On an island in the middle of the sea. What more could you ask for?'

She laughed. 'Quite a lot, basically.'

But I meant it. Renting a house here, in the middle of the sea, surrounded by shimmering grass, beneath a still-hot volcano. I could imagine that.

One evening Gunvor called Einar, he worked with computers, now we were having problems with ours, would he mind coming to have a look? He didn't waste any time, an hour later he was sitting in front of the computer in our sitting room and working. Gunvor took him some tea, I asked him what the prognosis was, he said it wasn't a big problem, he would soon have it cracked. He stayed a while, we chatted about this and that, he was interested in everything we did but never said much about himself. I knew he lived on his own, that he worked a lot, that he knew half of Rekyavik, at least judging by all the people he exchanged a few words with on a night out.

'When's your brother coming?' he said, standing in the hall and putting on his jacket.

'Next week,' I said. 'Perhaps you could take us out and show us the town?'

'Consider it done,' he said. 'I'll do it with pleasure. Just give me a ring.'

And then he was gone.

Yngve came with his friend Bendik and Åse, Bendik's girlfriend. I met them at the airport, happy that they were actually coming to visit me, happy they were going to stay with us, and horrified at the same time, I had nothing to contribute, nothing to say, and they were going to be here for close on a week.

I made dinner, Bendik said it was really good, I looked down and blushed, everyone noticed. They rented a car, we drove to the Geysir district, Bendik had brought some eggs with him, which he boiled in a tiny pool of hot water. The geyser itself was dead, there were no more eruptions, but jets of water could still burst forth, if you poured in enough green soap they would spout up as in the old days. But that was something you only did on special occasions, as I was informed, during state visits and the like, so we had to make do with its smaller brother, Strokkur, which erupted every fifteen minutes or so. After the eruption the water lay still, it looked like any water, a shiny surface reflecting the greyish sky, but not long afterwards the ground beneath us began to roar and soon the water rose, formed a dome, which then suddenly exploded into an enormous pillar of water. Steam and water everywhere in the air around us. Everywhere on the ground there were small simmering bubbling springs. The terrain was a vegetationless wasteland.

I could have watched Strokkur all day, but soon we were off again, searching for a pool where we could swim. The idea of it appealed to everyone, bathing in scalding-hot steaming water outdoors in the middle of a wilderness. We saw some steam a few kilometres away, drove towards it, there was a pool, we made do with that, me silent, serious, tormented by the thought that I was silent and serious. Especially together with Bendik, who chatted and laughed non-stop and was the type to say whatever came into his mind. You're so quiet, Karl Ove, what's up, have you filled your pants or what? They were like beings possessed when they discovered how good the shops in Rekyavik were, bought trainers, jeans, old tracksuit tops, jackets and CDs of Icelandic bands, which were the new big thing. They also liked the bars, we went out every night, to the first one with Einar, who was much more passive and reticent if Yngve, Bendik and Åse were there than he usually was with us, when he tended to take the initiative. After a few hours we were propping up some bar drinking schnapps and Einar said he would have to leave us, he had to meet someone, have a good time anyway, see you soon, he said to me and slipped into the night. I felt a little sorry for him, Gunvor and I were, it seemed, his arena, a place where he could be important, however I couldn't make this add up, he clearly knew lots of people in lots of places, how could he possibly need *us*? But a few minutes after he had gone I had forgotten all about him, the alcohol was having an effect, I was thawing, started to chat, I was getting higher and higher as the night wore on, but at a certain point it turned, I felt a need to destroy something, hit someone, I hated everything, myself and my whole damned life, but I said nothing, did nothing, just stood there drinking, more and more out of my skull, and when I arrived home I got it into my head that I should tell Gunvor what I had been thinking for the last year, I was completely

addle-brained, saw nothing of what I had around me, I was obsessed with one idea, suddenly and for no reason: to tell the truth.

She was asleep, I had been in the kitchen drinking, now I woke
her up and said what was on my mind, everything.

'You're drunk, Karl Ove,' she said. 'You don't mean what you're
saying. Please say you don't mean this.'

'I mean it,' I said. 'And now I'm going.'

I opened the window and jumped out. Walked down to the
road, under the light May sky, and on to the town, up and down
the streets, all dead and still, until I was so tired I started looking
for a place to sleep. After a few blocks I found a flat-roofed garage
beside a private house, clambered up, lay down and fell asleep.

I was insanely cold when I woke up, it had rained, I was soaked
through. Vaguely I remembered what had happened. But not
what I had said.

Was it all over now? Was everything ruined?

I sat on the roof, dazed, climbed down a second later so that I
wouldn't be found there and staggered homewards.

They were having breakfast when I arrived. Bendik smiled,
Yngve was serious, Gunvor wouldn't meet my eye and Åse acted
as if nothing had happened.

'I'm sorry,' I said, standing before them. 'I got too drunk last
night.'

'You can say that again,' Bendik said.

'Where have you been?' Gunvor said.

'I slept on a roof somewhere in town,' I said.

'You're going to have to stop drinking, Karl Ove,' Yngve said.
'We were actually frightened for you. Do you understand?'

'Yes,' I said. 'Sorry. But now I have to go to bed. I'm on the point
of collapse.'

Gunvor and I went out for a chat when I woke up. I said I hadn't
meant any of what I had said, I didn't know why I had said it,

I was two different people, one when I drank and one when I didn't drink, she knew that, but I love you, I do love you, I said, and although what I had said, which I didn't even know, never completely vanished but lay between us, we continued to stay together, what we had was precious, especially for me. I decided to cut down on my drinking, that was where the problem lay, but the very next day I was out again, it was the last night, the following day I would be flying back to Norway with Yngve, Bendik and Åse while Gunvor would stay on for a few more weeks, we had arranged that a long time ago, and it felt good, I had outgrown my life here, what had been wonderful before, the vast sky, the windy streets I walked alone, the swimming pools and cafés, the writing at night, our trips out of Rekyavik at the weekend, everything had become infected, in a way, become entangled with the darkness of my inner life, the inadequacy of my soul, and so Bergen, with the job at Sandviken Hospital and its implicit renunciation of responsibility for my own life, appeared attractive.

Gunvor and Åse went home early, and Yngve and Bendik wanted to go too, Yngve almost dragged me, but the bars were still open, it was ridiculous to leave now, you lot head on back, I'll follow you soon. What are you going to do out alone? Yngve said. I might meet someone I know, I said. Who knows what might happen?

And in fact I did. When I entered Filmbarin there was Einar at the bar. He waved and smiled when he saw me, I went over to him, we drank and chatted until the bar closed an hour later. He knew someone who was having a party, soon we were up in an attic flat somewhere with five or six others, each holding a glass of whisky in our hands.

I lit a cigarette, he leaned forward with a little smile on his lips.

'Nice short stories,' he said.

I stared at him.

'What are you talking about?' I said.

'The short stories you wrote. They're good. You've got talent.'

'How the hell would you know?' I said, getting up. 'Have you read them? How . . .?'

'I copied them when I was fixing your computer,' he said. 'You've never wanted to say what you were doing here. I was curious. So when I saw your file I copied it.'

'Bloody hell!' I said. 'You little shit!'

I turned and walked off, down the stairs, cigarette in one hand, glass in the other, outside into a backyard, where I was going to hurl the glass against the wall but changed my mind, I wasn't that drunk, instead I put it down on a small transformer, or whatever it was, a little box that hung on the wall, went into the street, down towards the tiny parliament building and uphill to our flat, where everyone was fast asleep.

After six months on the desolate treeless black island in the middle of the Atlantic Ocean the sight of trees below the plane seemed unreal, and when, a few hours later, we were walking through the warm crowded streets of Copenhagen, with lush green parks and avenues, there was a touch of paradise about everything, as though it was too good to be true for the world to be like this.

I had told Yngve the strange story about Einar, he just shook his head and said the little he had seen of him hadn't been very confidence-inspiring. The fact that he had read my short stories was, strictly speaking, of little importance, and I had rather regretted my reaction by the time I was leaving, perhaps I should have asked him a few questions and got a more comprehensive evaluation of the stories. But that wasn't the main issue, the main issue was the way he had acquired them and why he had done it.

Who copies other people's files? And why did he tell me about it?

What did he want with us?

Some problems are geographical, this was one of them. When we walked through the swing doors at Flesland Airport later that evening and emerged in the square where the bus waited, neither Einar nor Iceland was in my thoughts. Late May in Bergen, that was green mountainsides, light evenings, energised people a-quiver with life. We couldn't go home and sleep, we had to go out, the air was warm and bright, all the cafés and restaurants were full, and the first stars were twinkling in the gently darkening sky.

The next afternoon I knocked on Espen's door. I hadn't seen him for six months, it felt like a long time, before then we had generally spoken every single day.

I told him a bit about Iceland, he told me a bit about what had happened here: he had taken philosophy this year and done some writing.

'How's it going with the manuscript then?' I said.

'It's finished,' he said.

'Terrific!' I said. 'Have you sent it?'

He nodded.

'It's been accepted as well.'

'Accepted? Are you going to make your debut?'

Green with envy, I stared at him as I squeezed out a smile.

He nodded again.

'How fantastic!' I said.

He smiled, fidgeted with the lighter on the wooden board he used as a table.

'Which publisher?'

'Oktober. I've got a really good editor there. Torleiv Grue.'

'What's the title going to be?'

'*Slow Dance from a Burning House*, I think.'

'Good. That's a great title. When will it come out? In the autumn?'

'Yes, probably. There's still a bit of work to do.'

'Yes, I'm not at all surprised,' I said.

In the kitchen the espresso maker stopped hissing. Espen got up and went out, returning with two cups of steaming coffee.

'What about you?' he said. 'Did you get anything written in Iceland?'

'Bit. Some short stories. They're not that good, but . . . at least I was working.'

'*Vinduet* is going to have a debutant issue this autumn,' he said. 'I thought of you when I heard. Perhaps you could send one in? I've already sent one.'

'It can't hurt anyway,' I said. 'A rejection in the hand is worth ten publications in the bush.'

'Ha ha.'

My jealousy burned for an hour, in which time I felt little good-will, but then it passed, he had always been in a different place from me, had written brilliant things from the first moment I met him, and if there was anyone I knew who deserved this it was him.

He was twenty-one years old and was going to make his debut. It was fantastic. And he had opened up literature for me. He had been so selfless, he never kept anything to himself, he didn't carefully guard his writings, he didn't hold back any insights, Espen was never like that, he had always shared everything and it wasn't to be generous, to create a good impression, to do a good deed, but because he was like that, he bubbled over with enthusiasm he wanted to share with me.

Was I going to begrudge *him* his debut?

I wished it for him with the whole of my heart. If it rankled it was because it threw me and my life into such stark relief.

'How does your summer look?' he said.

'I'm working at Sandviken Hospital. Then I might go to Kristiansand and visit my dad. Yes, and I suppose I might spend a few weeks in Jølster. And you?'

'I'm definitely going to Oslo. And then I'll have to find myself somewhere to live.'

'Why?'

'Haven't you heard? We've been given notice. They're going to demolish the house.'

'What?'

'Yes, we've got to be out by the summer.'

'Oh shit. That is bad news.'

'Shall we look for a place together?'

'You mean share a flat?'

'Yes.'

'Why not?' I said.

I had been given a month's contracted work at Sandviken and they seemed to be pleased to see me on the ward – well, not the patients, they were as indifferent as ever, but those working there – and I slipped back into institutional life as though I had never been away. I printed the short story about the man with the suitcase and sent it to *Vinduet* without much optimism, and stopped writing because the job was taking too much of my energy and because I didn't feel like it. Gunvor was working in her village, so on my free evenings I mostly sat at home reading. I went on the town a few times with Yngve, we also had a couple of sessions with the band, but it was all half-hearted. In the two years we had been together we had played Hulen twice, Garage once, we had recorded a demo and performed one song in a proper studio, which appeared on a record of selected Bergen bands, and that was good, but if we wanted to go any further we had to invest more time – go all out – and no one really wanted to do that, it appeared.

One night I couldn't stay in, the summer weather was too overpowering, staying in and reading seemed unhealthy, so I went out, through the park and down to Café Opera. Yngve's friend Geir, whom I didn't know but who had rented my flat while I was in Iceland, was there, I bought myself a beer and joined him and his friends. It was a weekday, not very busy, but a couple of girls I half-knew from the first year at university came in, I chatted to them, one was blonde and good-looking, I'd had my eye on her before, she was one of those who gladdened my heart when I looked around the reading room, for no other reason than that she was lovely, so when Café Opera closed and I was in my most upbeat mood, I invited almost everyone there – Geir, one of his friends, the two girls and six Africans – to a party at my place, I still had some tax-free booze left. I didn't know the six, but I had spoken to them in the café and thought they might not know that many Norwegians, perhaps they hadn't really got into life here, and asked them if they would like to come to a party so that we could chat and drink some more. The one I spoke to nodded and smiled, yes, thank you, that's kind of you. As we drove through the warm light night, however, it wasn't the Africans who were on my mind but the blonde girl, and she, sitting on the other side of the rear seat, must have been thinking about me because when we entered, after I had paid for the three taxis, and sat down to drink – the crowd at Café Opera had seemed small, but they filled my flat, when had there last been eleven people here all at once? – she looked at me, asked me what I was doing now, how I was, what I really thought about the first year and about them.

'About you?'

'Yes? You seemed so arrogant.'

'Arrogant? Me?'

'Yes. You were the one who had read Dante and had been to the Writing Academy. One of the clever ones.'

'Clever? I knew nothing.'

She laughed, I laughed, we went into the kitchen, she leaned against the wall, I propped up the worktop, we chatted but I was hardly listening to what she said and a moment later I leaned over and kissed her. Went closer, held her, squeezed her to me, she was soft and good and not unwilling. I whispered that we could go to the room next door. It was Jone's, but he was in Stavanger, and we sank into his huge water bed. Oh, she was wonderful. I lay on top of her, she had her arms wrapped around me, then I heard a movement behind us and turned.

It was one of the Africans. He was watching us in the semi-darkness.

'You have to leave,' I said. 'We want to be left in peace.'

He didn't move.

'You can't stay here, as I'm sure you know,' I said. 'Will you please leave the room?'

He didn't move.

'Don't take any notice of him,' she said. 'Come here to me.'

I did, and it was soon over. When I rolled over onto my back the African was on his way out of the room.

'That was quick,' she said.

Was she being sarcastic?

No, she was smiling and stroked my cheek.

'I've wanted to do that for a long time,' she said. 'Shame it was so short. But I'll be off now. It's late. See you.'

She left, I fell asleep, and when I woke up, with a pounding headache, the flat was empty. The two bottles of schnapps were gone as well as the wallet I had left on the hat shelf.

That was all my money.

I sat down and rested my head in my hands.

Why had I done it? Why, why, why?

The guilt I felt was boundless. The shame burned in me from the moment I woke to the moment I fell asleep. The thought of what I had done didn't leave me. It was always there.

This was hell. Being torn into pieces by remorse, this was hell. And it was my own fault, it was me who had done it.

Why, why, why?

I didn't want this. I wanted to live a calm, quiet, warm and intimate life with Gunvor, that was what I wanted, and it ought to have been easy to achieve, it wasn't black magic, it was something everyone was capable of and always had been. Gunvor, was she unfaithful? Had she ever been?

No, of course not.

Had she ever thought of being unfaithful?

No, of course not.

She was decent, sincere, honest, kind, good.

She must never find out what had happened.

The blonde girl had said she would be working at a hotel in Hardanger that summer, I rang the next day and got through to her. I had dreaded this, it was degrading and humiliating, but I had to do it, there was no way round it.

She was happy to hear my voice.

'Hi!' she said. 'Thanks for last night!'

'That's why I'm ringing,' I said. 'I've got a girlfriend. She mustn't find out what happened. Can you promise me you won't tell anyone? Can you promise me it'll stay between us?'

She went quiet.

'Of course,' she said. 'Are you ringing to tell me that?'

'Yes.'

'OK,' she said.

'OK?'

'Bye.'

'Bye.'

I waited several hours before ringing Gunvor, I wanted the conversation with her to be as pure and uncontaminated by what had happened as possible.

Of course she was pleased to hear from me. Of course she missed me. Of course she was looking forward to us seeing each other again.

I had known I wasn't worthy of her. But I clung on. I lied, and the distance between us grew, although she was unaware of it. I hated myself, and I should have finished it, not for my sake but for hers, she deserved better.

Why didn't I do it?

I was on the verge, but I couldn't.

The next morning I caught the bus to Sandviken, and there was some comfort in that, even the smell of the institution, even the comfortless sight of people immured there provided some comfort. This was life, and what I had done was also life. I couldn't escape it, I had to accept it. What I had done, I had done. Yes, I was distraught now and would be for weeks, but time dims everything, even the worst horrors, it interposes itself, minute by minute, hour by hour, day by day, month by month, and it is so immense that ultimately what happens completely dissolves and is gone. It is there, but so much time, so many minutes, hours, days and months lie in between that it can no longer be felt. And it is feelings that count, not thoughts, not memories. And slowly I came out of it, all the while cleaving to the notion, the redeeming notion, that if she doesn't know, it doesn't exist.

It didn't exist, she came back to Bergen and at first my guilt flared up again, I was a liar and a traitor, a bad person, an evil person, for some weeks that was what I thought when I was with her, but then that too dulled and lay like a constant though manageable emotion slightly beyond my consciousness.

It hurt when she smiled, it hurt when she said she loved me and I was the best thing that had ever happened to her.

Then it didn't hurt any more.

Espen and I searched half-heartedly for a flat for some weeks, we went and had a look at a couple, however neither was suitable, instead we moved into separate accommodation: Espen to a flat out of town, me to Asbjørn's former bedsit in Nøstet.

One day I received a letter from *Vinduet*. I opened the envelope and read the contents at full throttle standing next to the post boxes in the hall. There had been more than one thousand five hundred stories sent in, thirty had been selected and they were happy to inform me that mine was one of them.

I couldn't take this in and reread it.

Yes, it really did say that. My story would be published in the debutant issue.

I walked down the steps into my new bedsit, sat on the chair with the letter in my hand and read it again.

There had to be a mistake. Or else the standard of the contributions had been exceptionally low. But one thousand five hundred texts? From five hundred writers? Could they all have been that bad?

That wasn't possible.

So they must have mixed me up with someone else. Kramsgård or Knutsgård or something.

I laughed.

I had been accepted!

A few days later I was called up to do my national service. I had to go to Hustad towards the end of autumn and then I would have a work placement somewhere for sixteen months. Basically that suited me fine, more than two years at Sandviken Hospital was probably enough, and I didn't want to study.

I continued working, I also continued writing book reviews for *Studvest* as well as doing interviews which Hans suggested, mostly with writers as that was my field, but with academics too and any other people a student newspaper might be interested in covering. I had nothing to do with the rest of the paper, I went in and picked up a tiny tape recorder, did the interview, wrote it up and delivered it, that was it. Hans liked what I did and he said many others did too.

Just before going to Hustad two copies of the debutant issue arrived in the post. I found my contribution, it was called *Déjà Vu*, beside the title there was a picture of me, a little passport photo they had blown up, and in the introduction below my name my date of birth and profession, which I had given as 'unemployed'. It looked good, no posing, no boasting, in fact, as near to nothing as you could get in a brief bio.

The issue was reviewed in all the big newspapers, not least because the previous one, which had come out in 1966, had contained stories by Øystein Lønn, Espen Haavardsholm, Knut Faldbakken, Kjersti Ericsson, Olav Angell and Tor Obrestad, so when *Vinduet* did the same twenty-six years later everyone had an eye on the possibility that an equally strong generation might be in the offing. The conclusion most papers drew was that this was not the case. In all the reviews names were bandied around as more promising than others; mine was not among them. That was understandable: my story belonged to the weakest contributions and perhaps should not have been there at all. By the time I caught the plane up to Molde and the bus from there to Hustadvika I had put all this to the back of my mind. I would soon be twenty-four and in the last few years my life had stood still, I hadn't developed in any direction, hadn't done anything new, I had only continued the pattern that had formed during the first few months in Bergen. When I looked around me now, I saw no openings anywhere, just more of the same everywhere. National service came heaven sent. It gave me sixteen months to defer decisions. Everything would be decided for me for more than a year, I wouldn't have any responsibility for my life, at least not that part to do with studies, work and career.

Early one morning one of the staff at Hustad came into my room and woke me. There was a telephone call for me. It was only six o'clock, I realised something had happened and hurried down to the phone booth at the end of the corridor, lifted the receiver to my ear.

'Hello?' I said.

'Hi, mum here.'

'Hi.'

'I'm afraid I've got some bad news, Karl Ove. It's grandad. He died last night.'

'Oh no.'

'He died on the way to the hospital. He rang Kjellaug in the evening, she rang for an ambulance and Jon Olav went over. He was there when grandad died. I don't think he suffered. It was quick.'

'That's good anyway,' I said.

'Yes,' mum said.

'He was old,' I said.

'Yes, in the end.'

The funeral was due to take place in a week's time, I applied for leave, was granted it, flew down to Bergen a few days later, caught the boat to Rysjedalsvika with Gunvor, mum picked us up, drove us through the rainy November countryside, across the small mountain district to Åfjorden, where grandad had lived his whole life. Born in 1908. To parents who lived in straitened circumstances. Everyone out here did. A mother who died while he was still small. A father who built houses and worked on trawlers. His father married again later in life and had a daughter. When he fell ill while fishing one winter in the early 1930s and died straight afterwards in Florø Hospital, grandad laid claim to the house where the new wife and the little daughter were living. There was a court case, grandad appealed to the Norwegian Supreme Court and won. His father's wife and his half-sister had to move out and grandad took over the house, where he had lived until now. He got married in 1940, to Kirsti Årdal, had four children between 1942 and 1954, ran the smallholding with her, worked as a driver, kept mink, bees, a few cows, a few chickens and cultivated soft fruit. All the children apart from the youngest moved away, grandad retired, his eldest daughter was an *ungdomskole* teacher, the next a nursing teacher and the youngest a psychologist, while his only son was a ship's pipefitter and a poet. That was how it was, that was how things turned out, now it was over.

We drove up the hill to the house, opened the doors and got out. It was raining, the heels of my shoes sank into the soft gravel as I opened the boot and took out the suit bag and little suitcase.

His blue overalls hung on the hook in the hall and his black cap with the short peak. His boots were on the floor.

Voices came from the sitting room, I put down the luggage and went in. Kjellaug, Ingunn, Mård and Kjartan were there, they hugged us and asked how Gunvor and I were getting on in Bergen. Ingunn enquired if we were hungry. There was a happiness in the room, there always was when they met. I thought, this is what he has left behind: Kjellaug, Sissel, Ingunn and Kjartan; their husbands: Magne, Kai Åge and Mård; their children: Ann Kristin, Jon Olav, Ingrid, Yngve, Karl Ove, Yngvild, Odin and Sølve. Tomorrow we would bury him. Now we would eat and talk.

The mist drifted in great sheets above the dense dark green bordering on black spruce trees on the hillside across the mere. It was nine o'clock, mum asked if I would mind scattering spruce sprigs over the road by the gate. This was an old custom. I went down in the rain, laid sprigs over the gravel, looked up at the house, the windows aglow in the grey morning. I cried. Not because of death and its coldness but for life and its warmth. I cried because of the goodness that existed. I cried because of the light in the mist, I cried because of the living people in the dead man's house and I thought, I can't waste my life.

Jon Olav was supposed to give a speech in church, he was crying so much he couldn't get out a word. He tried, failed, whenever he opened his mouth to speak another sob emerged. When the service was over we carried the coffin through the church out to the waiting hearse. We joined mum, drove slowly through the village, past the house, to the cemetery, which was situated on a hill above the fjord, where the grave stood open in readiness. We carried the coffin over. We sang, we sounded so strangely fragile in the enormous space. Beneath us lay the fjord, grey and heavy; on the opposite side the mountain plunged vertically into the sea, wrapped in mist and cloud. The priest threw earth onto the coffin. Earth to earth, ashes to ashes, dust to dust. For a moment mum stood alone in front of the open grave. She bowed her head, a fresh wave of sobs went through me, the last, for as we left to go to the community centre, where hot meat broth was being served, the mood lightened, it was over, now life would continue without him.

I travelled back to Hustad, started ringing around the places which employed conscientious objectors in Bergen, got an immediate nibble at Student Radio as I had two years' experience of local radio, and after a few days of Christmas holiday at home with mum in Jølster I went up to the Student Centre for my first day as a conchie. The door to the open-plan office on the first floor, where Student Radio, *Studvest* and many other student organisations were located, was locked, so I waited downstairs for the manager to arrive, paced back and forth, reading the notices, looking at books Studia had displayed, sat down and lit a cigarette, nearly an hour passed, what was this, had I got the wrong day?

An hour and a half after the time we had arranged he appeared. Was that *him*?

A fat long-haired guy with glasses approached. He was wearing a denim jacket, jeans and a pair of the ankle-high yellow and black football boots with rubber studs we wore when we were small, before football became organised and we had proper boots. One night three years ago I had been boozing and smoking hash in his bedsit. It felt as if the gates of hell had opened. How could *he* be the manager?

'Hi, hi,' he said.

'Hi,' I said. 'Are *you* the manager of Student Radio?'

'Yeah, baby.'

'I was at a party at yours, do you remember? Long time ago.'

'Yeah, you were well out of it, weren't you.'

'No, I wasn't. But you were!'

He laughed, a low chuckle. Laughter was an integral part of him, it seemed to flow around him, he laughed at nearly everything that was said.

Then he became serious again.

'Something happened that night. We realised we'd gone too far. I think we went out on the town a couple more nights and then packed it in. Per Roger travelled abroad, and when he came back he'd cleaned up his act. And me, well, you can see what I'm doing! Come on and I'll show you around,' he said, jangling a big bunch of keys.

We went up the stairs and into the offices. Student Radio's rooms were at the back. Three desks, a corner sofa, some cabinets separating their section from the next.

'Here's your desk,' he said, nodding to the closest. 'I sit over there. And the people working here share the last one. Most of the work takes place in the studio. Have you been there?'

I shook my head.

'That's where you'll be most of the time. Your main task is to put the record archives onto the computer.'

'Really?' I said.

He laughed.

'Archiving broadcasting schedules. The so-called TONO schedules. Archiving reels. Maybe playing them onto DAT if you've got time. Making coffee. Buying coffee. Let's see what else. Going to the Post Office. We get a hell of a lot of post. Ha ha ha! Any other tedious chores we have? Cleaning the studio. Hoovering. Copying flyers. Copying documentation for meetings. We're so happy to have a conchie it's not true. You're the lowest on the ladder. You'll be our dog! That's your job description. You'll be our dog and at my beck and call! I'm in charge here.'

He smiled, I smiled back.

'OK,' I said. 'Where shall I start?'

'Everything starts with coffee. Put a pot on, can you.'

I did, fetched water from the downstairs toilet, sprinkled coffee into the filter and switched on the machine while Gaute sat working in front of his computer. Apart from us two there wasn't a soul around. I sat down at my desk, opened the drawers to see what was in them, went for a walk to see what was on the shelves, looked out of the windows, up at the park, the black branches stretching towards the sky. When the coffee was ready I poured out two cups and put one on his desk.

'Thanks,' he said.

'What are you working on?' I said.

'Wolfenstein,' he said.

'Wolfenstein?'

'Yes. It all takes place in Hitler's bunker. The idea is to move up the floors. The old man's on the top floor. But it's not so easy because there are Nazis everywhere. The higher you go the harder it is.'

I stood behind him.

There was a machine-gun barrel at the bottom of the screen moving forward along an empty corridor. At the end there was a lift. Suddenly the door opened and some white-clad soldiers burst out.

'Oh dear,' Gaute said.

They saw 'him', there was an exchange of fire, they were around a corner, a couple of them fell to the ground, but then another lift-load of soldiers appeared, 'Gaute' was hit and the screen filled with blood.

It was creepy because you saw the corridors and soldiers as if through a pair of eyes, and when the blood came I thought, this is what it is like to die, your eyes filled with blood, game over.

'I've only played a couple of times,' he said. 'You've got the game on your computer as well. And Doom.'

He stretched.

'Shall we call it a day then?'

I looked at him.

'I'm supposed to work eight hours a day. They're very strict about that. I have to fill in forms and stuff, which you have to sign.'

'Who are "they"? I can't see any "they" here.'

'Fine by me,' I said. 'But perhaps we should drink up our coffee first, eh?'

It soon emerged that, as far as Gaute was concerned, appearances deceived. I thought he was a slacker, a skiver and a shirker, but this was not the case. He was ambitious, had ideas in all sorts of areas for how radio could be improved, and during the time I was on national service there he reorganised the whole radio and made it more professional, from the management side to the music profile, and updated the technical equipment so that all the tapes I edited during the first months I worked there, when all the programmes were analogue, had gone by the time I finished after sixteen months, and everything was digital. Wolf was only played after working hours, and then I became obsessed, often leaving the office at two in the morning, having played nonstop from four in the afternoon, sometimes I was still playing when the others came in to do the morning programme. We had a football-manager game as well, which was perhaps even more addictive, I spent all my free time buying and selling players and playing match after match until my team had won the European

Cup, which could take several weeks. After a twelve-hour stint my head was ice cold and utterly empty, this was systematised meaninglessness, but I couldn't stop myself, I was hooked.

Something else at Student Radio which I hadn't seen before was the Internet. This was also addictive. Moving from one page to the next, reading Canadian newspapers, looking at traffic reports in Los Angeles or centrefold models in *Playboy*, which were so endlessly slow to appear, first the lower part of the picture, which could be anything at all, then it rose gradually, the picture filled the frame like water in a glass, there were the thighs, there, oh, there was . . . shit, was she wearing *panties*? . . . before the breasts, shoulders, neck and face appeared on the computer screen in the empty Student Radio office at midnight. Rachel and me. Toni and me. Susy and me. *Hustler*, did they have their own website as well? Rilke, had anyone written about his *Duino Elegies*? Were there any pictures of Tromøya?

After Christmas the outgoing conscientious objector returned, and he went through all the jobs with me. He was amazed to discover that I didn't know how to edit, didn't know the first thing about a broadcast technician's work, in fact, didn't know anything. On the radio in Kristiansand I'd had my own technician, all I needed to do was speak into the microphone, either outside, when I was interviewing someone, or in the studio, when I had my programme. The technician took care of everything else. Here it was different. He was also amazed to see I wrote down everything I was going to say, even the simplest things like 'Hi, welcome to Student Radio,' and I didn't ad lib the way he and all the others working there did. But I learned fast. In the holidays the conscientious objector ran the programmes, then I had to be able to work solo, that is, switch on the transmitter, play the radio jingle, the programme jingle, introduce the programme if I decided to play a repeat or sit there and play records and chat, perhaps ring someone up and interview them on air, which I enjoyed more and more, it gave me a real kick to do live radio alone, and the more complicated the schedule the bigger the kick. But usually I didn't run programmes apart from a short student news bulletin that was broadcast every day, which I spent all morning collating, sifting through the newspapers to find anything student-related, writing and recording. In addition, I compiled items for the culture programmes, interviewed writers or taped book reviews, and every day I thanked my lucky stars I had washed up here and not, for example, at Sandviken or some other institution. Olav Angell had translated *Ulysses*, so I rang to ask him about his work. Fredrik Wandrup slated Ole Robert Sunde in a review, I rang Wandrup first, then Sunde, added some comments of my own and pieced it all together. Dag Solstad was in town, so I went down to his hotel and interviewed him. This was the first time I had worked on something I really liked. And I was not the only one who did, there was such an enthusiastic atmosphere, yet laid-back, this wasn't a place for students wanting to further their careers; on the contrary, up in the studio and down in the offices people hung around all day doing nothing special, drinking coffee, smoking, chatting, maybe flicking through the new CDs that had arrived or browsing through papers or magazines. I said nothing for the first few weeks, nodded to anyone who came, worked as hard as I could, if I had fifteen minutes free I would key in a few record titles on the computer, if I had to go to the Post Office I would run up and down the stairs. At the meetings between managers I wouldn't say a word, however, I wrote down everything they said. But gradually I began to recognise the various faces and even remember their names. As I was the only person sitting there the whole time, everyone knew who I was and gradually I began to exchange a few words with them, perhaps even crack a joke. During one meeting Gaute suddenly eyeballed me and asked, what do you think, Karl Ove? To my astonishment, I noticed that everyone was staring at me expectantly, as though they really believed I had something to say.

At the beginning of every semester new assistants were recruited. Gaute asked me to make a flyer, it was the first real task I had been given and I was concerned I wouldn't perform it well enough, worked all evening on just the title, which ended up as Free Studio Loan, and sacrificed my favourite picture in the Dante edition I had, with the Doré illustrations, cut out the last picture, where they see God, the last and the first light, and stuck it on a sheet of paper, which I copied two hundred times and for the whole of the next day I stood handing them out in the Student Centre concourse, which was swarming with new students. At the introductory meeting a few days later the room was jam-packed. Most sat or stood quietly listening to Gaute, but some also asked questions and among them I noticed a young guy with a shaven head and Adorno glasses, not least because he had a copy of Ole Robert Sunde's novel *Of Course She Had to Ring* on the desk in front of him. This was a statement and a signal, a code for the initiated, of whom there were not many, and therefore particularly significant. He read Sunde, he *had* to be a writer himself.

Some days after the meeting the interviews began. I sat alongside Gaute in a conference room asking successive candidates questions and jotting down brief notes. It was a peculiar role because I knew nothing, certainly no more than they did, yet they had to sit nicely and squirm in the chair and answer as well as they could, which no one demanded of me. Afterwards we went through the list of names, discussed our impressions, and that was strange too, how much I enjoyed picking and choosing. Three of the girls had been especially attractive, one sat looking at us through anxious blue eyes under black mascaraed eyelashes, with high cheekbones, long blonde hair, probably about twenty, she had to be in. Another had her dark hair collected in a long plait, kept moving her lips, perhaps the most beautiful mouth I had ever seen, sat with a straight back and her hands resting in her lap, elegant in every way, and when she said she played the drums, I was sold, she had to be in. Gaute laughed and added that she did in fact have experience of local radio as well and was an obvious choice anyway. The Sunde guy had to be in, the conventional Business School guy as well so that it wasn't just arts students, and definitely the girl who was so knowledgeable about classical music . . .

After a couple of weeks' training the various departments were in place. I was beginning to get to grips with the job and was no longer nervous as I set foot on the steps up to the offices. Now it was the opposite, I looked forward to going to work. Student Radio was the first time I had felt part of my own group in Bergen, hitherto everything in my life had gone through Yngve or Gunvor, that didn't happen here and I was pleased, although it also created problems. It felt as if something new had started in my life and it had done so outside Gunvor and me, outside our relationship, which was as before, we had been together for close on four years, we were best friends, we knew everything about each other apart from the terrible things I had done to her, which were still there, inside me, not in her, she knew nothing, she saw me as a good person. But when she came to visit me at Student Radio, it felt wrong, I was uncomfortable, it was as though I were cheating on her merely by being there. I realised it was over, but I was unable to finish it, I didn't want to hurt her, didn't want to disappoint her, didn't want to ruin something for her. Furthermore, our lives were interwoven in other ways, at home she was one of the family, especially for mum, who had become attached to her, and for Yngve, who was very fond of her, but also for those not so close, such as mum's brother and sisters, and the same was true on Gunvor's side. As if that weren't enough she had got to know Ingvild last year, the two of them were friends now, and Gunvor moved into the collective where Ingvild had lived, the one with precursors going right back to Fløgstad's Bergen period, the one which in recent years had been dominated by Arendalers, in other words, Yngve's friends.

Could I cut the bonds to all this?

No.

I was too weak.

So I lived a kind of double life, I erected a wall between the various parts and hoped everything would resolve itself.

The guy who had brought Ole Robert Sunde's novel to the first meeting was called Tore, he came from Stavanger and brought a wealth of ideas to department sessions. One morning when he was in the office we got into conversation. I asked him how it was going with Sunde, he said he had thrown it at the wall in frustration and was writing an essay about precisely that right now, which he would try to sell to a journal.

'Have you read it?' he said.

'Not that one. I only got through the first twenty pages. But I read the one about O, you know, his Odysseus-style novel. I don't remember what it was called.'

'*Contrapuntal*,' he said.

'Yes, that's the one. I did my first-year assignment on Joyce, though. So I'm interested in that tradition.'

'I'm more of a Beckett man myself.'

'You like the secretary better than the master?'

He smiled.

'Doesn't sound so good when you put it like that. But Beckett's bloody good.'

'Yes, he is.'

'In fact, I'm writing a sort of Beckett novel at the moment. Well, that may be overstating it. It has elements of the absurd anyway.'

'You're writing a novel?'

'Yes. I'm going to send it in this spring. Then I'll get the usual rejections. Interesting blah blah blah, but I regret to say blah blah blah. I've got sixteen of them at home.'

'*Sixteen* rejections?'

'Yes.'

'How old are you actually?'

'Twenty. And you?'

'Twenty-four. I've had only *one* rejection.'

'So you write too?'

'Yes . . . or no, not really.'

'Do you write or don't you?'

'It depends what you mean . . .'

'Mean? Surely, either you write or you don't? There's no half-way house, to my knowledge.'

'Then I do. But it's not very good.'

'Have you had anything published?'

'A short story. In *Vinduet*'s debutant issue. Have you?'

He shook his head.

'That's sixteen–nil to me in rejections, and one–nil to you in acceptances.'

'Well,' I said. 'The *Vinduet* acceptance might sound good, but the short story isn't.'

'We've spoken for three minutes and you've already told me twice something's not very good. I detect a pattern. A personality trait.'

'I'm telling you the truth. It's got nothing to do with my personality. It's an objective fact.'

'Right,' he said, looking at his watch. 'I've got a lecture now. But what about a beer afterwards? When do you finish?'

'Half past four.'

'Five at Café Opera?'

'OK, why not?' I said, and watched him go down the aisle between the partitions and disappear down the stairs.

He was sitting alone at a table on the ground floor when I went into Café Opera later that afternoon. I got myself a beer and joined him.

'I've read your short story. *Déjà Vu*,' he said with a smile. 'It's good.'

'You've read it. Today? Where did you get a copy?'

'It was in the university library. Influenced by Borges, wouldn't you say?'

'Yes. Or Cortàzar.'

I looked at him and smiled. He was the type who didn't leave a stone unturned. Would I have gone to the trouble of checking out the library for a short story written by a guy I didn't know before meeting him? Not on your life. But Tore did.

He was short of stature but possessed immense energy, on the one hand there was something open and receptive about him – he was the kind of guy who would look around when he laughed and drop comments all over the place, completely unconcerned by how he might be interpreted – and on the other there was something closed about him, which could manifest itself after immersing himself in one of his frequent bouts of sociability, then he might suddenly go absent, his eyes were totally vacant, and he heard nothing of what was being said, it lasted a few seconds, that was all, and wasn't very obvious, but I noticed it at our very first editorial session, and it sparked an interest.

'Have you lived here long?' he said, looking at me over the top of his beer glass, from which he took sips.

'Four and a half years,' I said. 'And you?'

'Only six months.'

'What are you studying?'

'Literature. I think I'll take philosophy afterwards. And you?'

'I've got a subsid in literature. But that's a long time ago. My life has stagnated for three years now. Nothing's happened.'

'I'm sure that's not true,' he said.

It was as though he didn't want to know that things could go badly. But I said nothing, drank and looked out of the window, at the streets, cold and grey, passers-by in coats and cloaks, the occasional puffy bubble jacket.

I looked at him again. He was smiling, and it was as though the smile and the ensuing laughter lifted him and pushed him forward.

'I played in a band in Stavanger,' he said. 'Everyone knows everyone there. One of the guys I met while I was at *gymnas* runs his own record company and has a little shop in Stavanger. His name's Jone. And he came to Bergen to study for a year. He told me he shared a flat with a total nutter. He played the drums and read books and was going to be a writer. That was all he did. His place was overflowing with books, he was completely possessed. You know, Dostoevsky novels in the kitchen cupboard and Sandemose's collected works in the toilet. And he played in a band. A student band.'

'What was it called?'

'Kafkatrakterne,' he said. 'Do you know them?'

I nodded.

'Yes, I played the drums with them.'

He jerked back in his chair and stared at me.

'Was that *you*? You lived with Jone?'

'Yes. I thought that was why you were telling me. You'd realised it was me.'

'No, no, not at all.'

He went quiet.

'What are the odds on that?' he said eventually. 'On the guy being you?'

'Pretty good,' I said. 'Bergen's a small town. You'll find out soon enough. But say hi to Jone and tell him not to exaggerate. Everything was very normal there. I did read, that's true, but the flat wasn't exactly overflowing with books. Though it might have seemed like that to Jone as he isn't a very literary person.'

'But it's true you had rats there?'

'Yes.'

I laughed. What sort of picture had Jone drawn? I could see him in his record shop encircled by *gymnas* students: *In Bergen, lads, it's the Wild West.*

But I hadn't even read much. Skimmed a few books, yes, but I hadn't read them in any depth, as Espen had, for example. I had rarely played the drums. And the rats . . . yes, there had been two. One I caught in a trap and one I poisoned which lay rotting in the wall behind the stairs.

'Do Kafkatrakterne still play then?' Tore said.

I shook my head.

'Do you?'

'No, not here.'

We sat in Café Opera for two hours. We liked the same sort of music, British pop and indie, except that his taste was more defined and categorical than mine. The Kinks were his big band. XTC, a close second. He also talked a lot about the Smiths and Japan, R.E.M., the Stone Roses, Bowie, Depeche Mode, Costello, Blur. Every time I mentioned a band he hadn't heard of I saw him make a mental note. Boo Radleys, I said, you absolutely have to check them out. And The Aller Værste!, you really don't know anything about them? Norway's greatest band!

Then we talked about literature. He was up to speed on everything that had been published. All the novels, all the poetry collections, everything.

'Do you know Espen Stueland?' I said after a while.

'*Slow Dance from a Burning House*?' Tore said.

'He's my best friend,' I said.

'Is that right?' he said. 'That's terrific! One of the best debut collections for ages. Do you *know* him?'

'Yes, we studied lit. together. And he lived in the flat beneath me for two years.'

'What's he like? A prodigy, eh?'

'Yes, not far off it. At any rate extremely dedicated. And he has incredible insight into everything he reads.'

Tore stared into the distance for a few seconds laughing quietly and mumbling. Then he sat up straight.

'Rune Christiansen. Have you read anything by him?' he said.

'I've heard of him. But I haven't read anything,' I said.

'Then I'll bring you his latest collection of poems. What about Øyvind Berg?'

'Heard of him. *Totschweigetaktikken* and *Et foranskutt lyn*. But I'm a poor poetry reader, just so that you know. Espen's a fan of Berg, by the way. And Ulven, of course.'

'Oh my God, he is *so* good,' Tore said.

We almost had tears in our eyes when we talked about how good Tor Ulven's books were. Tore also loved Jan Kjærstad and *Knife to the Throat* by Kjartan Fløgstad but not his other works, although I did. I guessed that had something to do with academia. Of Norwegian poets he put Eldrid Lunden at the pinnacle, he said.

'Haven't you read any Lunden? Bloody hell, Karl Ove, you've got to read her. This is important! *Mammy, Blue* is the best collection of Norwegian poetry ever. After Obstfelder, of course. Obstfelder, Lunden, Ulven. But I'll bring you a copy. And *Det omvendt avhengige*. You've *got* to read that!'

When I returned from lunch in the canteen next day there was a little pile of poetry books on my desk. And, on top, a note:

Karl Ove,
To be read,
from your friend Tore.

My friend?

I took the books home, skimmed through them as I usually did, to have an overview when he talked about them, the way I had done with Espen. He dropped by the next day, we had a coffee in the canteen, he wanted to know what I had got out of the books, especially *Mammy, Blue*, which I could see meant a lot to him. Now he wanted it to mean a lot to me.

What energy he had.

For the moment it was directed at me, and I liked that, in a way it was flattering, there was an element of him looking up to me, I was four years older, had done a course at the Writing Academy, I'd had a short story published in *Vinduet* and would soon start reviewing books for them. That had materialised a few weeks before, I had interviewed Merete Morken Andersen for *Studvest*, she was about to take over as the editor of *Vinduet*, and as a former Bergen student she was an obvious target for an interview. I met her at the Arts Faculty, we talked for an hour, when I had finished and had switched off the tape recorder she said she had been planning to bring in some new names on her appointment as editor, it was so easy to turn to the same old people, but she wanted some serious innovation in the journal and wondered if I could envisage writing for her.

I realised how this might seem through Tore's eyes. But it would only be like this for the few weeks it would take him to get to know me properly and suss out what was what, I was a wannabe who was actually unable to write because I had nothing to say, who wasn't honest enough with himself to draw the appropriate conclusions and was therefore trying to get a foot in the world of literature at any cost. Not as someone who created something himself, someone who wrote and was published, but as a parasite, as someone who wrote as others wrote, a second-rater.

I was a second-rater and that was why it pained me to see Tore's interest in me. But what should I do? Say no, back off, you're wrong?

He continued to pop his head in at Student Radio every so often, we would go to the canteen and chat, now and then he would join us when we went out after work, or on Fridays when those who wanted collected in the office and drank beer and went out afterwards or to one of the many private parties thrown by the staff. But his heart wasn't in radio, I sensed that immediately, he wasn't interested in any of what went on there, wasn't gripped by any of the intrigues, had no idea about the conflicts of personality that existed, couldn't care less who had been making out with whom, set up or split up with whom, and as far as the practical side of radio production was concerned he didn't know a thing and didn't want to. He performed his weekly spots and made a good job of them, such as the interview with Jon Fosse, which filled an entire programme, or the book and play reviews he wrote, but that was it. He belonged to one category of staff that Student Radio employed, those who joined to gain experience before moving on. The other category was those who stayed for many years, for whom radio was a kind of leisure club, a place where you could hang out and always find a drinking partner for the evening. Among them there were several nerds and losers who otherwise wouldn't have fitted in anywhere, just sat in their nerd and loser bedsits with their nerd and loser friends. Having them at Student Radio made it an immensely more pleasant place to be than, for example, *Studvest*, where everyone was out to learn and move on – however, their presence also made me nervous because I was just as addicted to the social life as they were, I had just as little outside it, and in reality I was like them, I sometimes thought in my darkest hours. But there weren't quite as many of them as before, the radio station was full of good people I got to know, not least those working in the culture section, such as editor Mathilde, a witty, cheeky and attractive Nordlander, or cheery Therese from Arendal, or Eirik, a tall strong Bergensian, as sharp as he was garrulous, or Ingrid from Trondheim, who didn't say a lot, Tore – he had noticed her too – and I called her Garbo. One evening I was sitting in the studio working after a programme, she was around, clearing up, and when she came into the room where I was I wrote a sentence on our new speech recognition programme, which one click later was read out by an automaton voice.

Ingrid is dead, the voice said.

Ingrid is dead.

Ingrid froze and looked at me with scared black eyes.

Ingrid is dead.

In the darkened room, where only she and I were, it sounded eerie. The voice seemed to come from beyond the grave.

'Switch it off,' she said. 'It's not funny. It's not funny.'

I laughed. Funny was precisely what it was. But it had spooked her, and I apologised. She left, I was alone, but I didn't want to go home so went up to the office and played Wolfenstein until three, when I walked down to the collective in Nygårdsgaten, let myself in and slipped into bed beside Gunvor, who without waking up put her arm around me and mumbled something incomprehensible.

The following evening I was going to dinner at Tore's. He had dropped by and invited me, I accepted and was happy to be asked, he had all his friends living in Bergen, as far as I knew, so it wasn't a foregone conclusion that he would include me. I bought a bottle of wine after work, had an hour's nap, took a shower and then walked across town and uphill to the Sandviken side, where he lived in one of the buildings at the very top. Once there I turned and gazed across Bergen, which sparkled and glittered in the sea of darkness between the mountains.

Tore's flat was on the first floor, the downstairs door was open, so I walked up the stairs, where it was so cold you could see your breath in the harsh light, along a narrow musty corridor to a door. A piece of paper above the doorbell said renberg/halvorsen. Renberg, that was Tore's name, wasn't it?

I rang the bell.

He opened the door and smiled at me.

'Come in, Karl Ove!' he said.

I took off my shoes, hung up my jacket and went into what turned out to be the sitting room. It was completely empty. Apart from three candles on the table, it was also completely dark.

'Am I the first to arrive?' I said.

'What do you mean?' Tore said. 'You're the only guest.'

'Am I?' I said, looking around apprehensively. The table was set with a cloth, two plates and two wine glasses, which reflected the flickering candlelight.

He continued to look at me with a smile.

He was wearing a black shirt and a pair of black trousers.

Was he a homo?

Was that what this was about?

'The food's ready,' he said. 'We can eat straight away if you like.'

I nodded.

'I brought you some red wine,' I said and passed him the bottle. 'Here you are.'

'Any musical requests?' he said.

I shook my head, glanced around discreetly to look for more signs.

'Is David Sylvian OK? *Secrets of the Beehive*?'

'That's a good one,' I said and walked over to the wall. A large framed poster of XTC hung there.

'It's signed, see?' Tore said from behind me. 'I went to Swindon one summer and rang the bell at Andy Partridge's house. He opened up and I said, hello, I'm from Norway and was wondering if you'd mind putting your signature on a few things.'

Tore laughed.

'He said it had been quite a few years since a fan had last rung the bell. I think he thought it was amusing.'

'Who's that then?' I said, pointing to a photograph of a beautiful blonde girl.

'Her? That's Inger, that is. My girlfriend.'

I was so relieved I laughed.

'Isn't she lovely?' he said.

'Yes, she is,' I said. 'Where is she now then?'

'Out with some friends. I had to clean the house for you, you know. But let's eat!'

We chatted all evening, presenting our lives to each other, the way you do when you are getting to know someone. We agreed we would make a series of programmes about the ten best pop albums of all time, one programme for each record, we would call the programme *Popkarusellen*, in the best spirit of the 60s, and try to spell out pop's ten rules while we were at it. And we agreed we would start a band. Tore would sing and write songs, he already had several new ones lying around, I would play the drums, we could get Yngve on guitar, so all we needed was a bass player.

He kept moving between his chair and the stereo, playing new singles by bands he liked and wanted me to hear, drawing my attention to particular details, the way a melody was phrased, for example, or to an especially good line in the lyrics. Oh, that's just great! he would say. Listen, oh shit, isn't that fantastic? There! Did you hear?

He told me the guy who lived below them was a nutter, he stood at his window in the morning, just staring at them as they passed, and howled and roared at night. He told me he had gone to *gymnas* with Inger, she irritated him then, she was one of the self-righteous Young Friends of the Earth girls, but he fell head over heels in love with her afterwards. He told me he had an older brother, his parents were divorced, his mother was a wonderful person and he worshipped his grandmother, but his father was an alcoholic and off the rails. He was a teacher. I said my parents were divorced too and that my father was also a teacher and an alcoholic. We talked about them at great length. It was as if we were brothers. I felt huge warmth for him.

He got up and went into the bedroom and returned with a manuscript in his hands.

'Here it is,' he said. 'The novel. I finished it yesterday. But I was wondering if you'd mind reading it before I send it in.'

'Not at all,' I said. 'I'd be more than happy to.'

He passed it to me. I glanced at the title page.

Takk's Cube
Novel
Tore Renberg

At that moment the door opened and the girl from the photo-graph walked in. Her cheeks were red from the cold or perhaps it was the steep incline that had produced the flush.

'Hi,' she said.

'Hi,' I said.

She came in and shook my hand, settled down in the chair be-side Tore and tucked her legs beneath her.

'So I've finally got to meet this Karl Ove!' she said. 'How tall you are!'

'It's us who are so short,' Tore said. 'We come from short stock, we two do.'

They laughed.

'Well,' she said. 'I'm hungry. Is there any food left?'

'There's a bit in the kitchen,' Tore said.

She stood up and went in.

'What's the time actually?' I said.

'Half past twelve,' Tore said.

'Then it's probably time I wended my way homewards,' I said and got up. 'Thanks for everything!'

'My pleasure,' Tore said, accompanying me to the hall. 'How long do you reckon it'll take you to read it?'

'I'll do it over the weekend. Drop by on Monday and we can talk about it.'

'Great!'

Inger came to the hall, I said goodbye, closed the door behind me and set off downhill towards the town.

His novel was almost completely without action, it had no plot, everything revolved around the main character, called Takk, and his lonely humdrum life in a flat. It wasn't bad but so influenced by Beckett that it seemed unoriginal. It had nothing to do with Tore, none of his charisma and temperament was evident in the manuscript. When we met to discuss his novel I said nothing of this directly, I didn't want to offend or hurt him, but I implied it and he wasn't unfamiliar with this reaction, it turned out. He still sent the manuscript in unchanged to the publisher and received positive feedback from the reader.

My first book review came out in *Vinduet* and not long after I was contacted by *Morgenbladet*, who asked if I would be interested in reviewing books for their newspaper. I was. This was not altogether positive, for the path this was indicating was that of a critic, not a writer, and I almost felt it would have been better to do something else because as a book reviewer I looked defeat in the face every time I wrote. I could write about literature, could see whether it was good or bad and describe in which ways, but I couldn't move beyond that. There was a wall of glass between me and literature: I saw it, but I was separate.

Kjartan came up to Student Radio a couple of times to ask if I fancied a coffee, and there was something so slow about his movements, he could barely drag himself forward, that the others in the office asked who on earth *that* was. They were all young, apart from perhaps the caretakers, so this grey-haired tousled man with such a slow gait stood out. He had an exam in May but couldn't study any more, he said. He was considering giving up. I said he mustn't, he just had to hold on, even if he didn't study he knew so much he would be fine. The exam was important, I said, and if he didn't take it the whole year would have been wasted. He looked at me and said I might be right. He asked me if I would like to visit him at his flat one afternoon, he had some poems I could have a look at if I wanted. Of course I would, I answered, and one Saturday afternoon I went there with Gunvor. Although he didn't live far from me I hadn't been there before. The flat was on the ground floor, but there was something cellar-like about it. The curtains were drawn, we sat drinking coffee in the semi-darkness, Gunvor kept the conversation going and I saw how much Kjartan liked her and somehow became lighter in her company. But not by much, the heaviness in him was still palpable. As we left I wondered if gravitational force had a stronger effect on him or whether the earth had a stronger pull, and that was why his movements were so slow, he had to tug his foot free from the ground, yank the hand holding his coffee cup from the table. Kjartan, the man who wrote so much about air and skies, light and suns, the man who lived in the weightless realm of the spirit.

A few weeks later he was readmitted.

At the end of April I went to Prague with Espen. His debut book had been well received and he had joined the editorial team at *Vagant* in Oslo. He discussed literature with Henning Hagerup and Bjørn Aagenæs, Arve Kleiva and Pål Nordheim, went with them for a beer after meetings and had got to know many authors, among them the novelist Jonny Berg and the poet Rune Christiansen. Even though Espen was Espen and I had known him for more than three years, I felt so inferior to him for the entire trip. He was a writer; I wasn't. If he looked left, I looked left, to see what he found so interesting. I was so puppy-like I was destroying our friendship. In Berlin we had a few hours free before the train left, Espen bought a newspaper and discovered that a Romanian poet was going to be at the Romanian embassy, his poems had just been translated into German. Although I knew no German, and a reading would therefore have been utterly meaningless to me, I didn't say no, can we do something else, as I didn't want to obstruct his need for poetry.

We found the embassy and went in. A waiter stood there wearing white gloves and holding a tray of aperitifs, men in suits and women in elegant costumes mingled. Espen and I, who were not sweet-scented after a night on the train and a day in the streets, nor especially spruce, to put it mildly, caused a stir when we appeared. People sent us sidelong glances, and I thought, thank God Espen is a poet, at least we could say that, if anyone were to enquire what we were doing here. A Norwegian poet, which would explain our clothes and the somewhat sharp odour we exuded.

We stood in the middle of the floor without saying a word to anyone.

'At least I can get a sense of the language,' I said. 'The tone and the timbre and the rhythm.'

'Yes,' Espen said.

The doors opened and we entered an auditorium full of chairs with a stage at one end, on which stood a table with three microphones.

Espen walked along the front row, I followed, we sat down in the middle, taking the best seats. The audience was small, numbering perhaps twenty. Three people, two men and a woman, took seats behind the microphones. The woman talked. People laughed and chuckled every now and then. I didn't understand a word. Then the man I assumed was the poet began to read, while the man next to him sat with his arms crossed and his eyes half-closed, listening.

The poet peered down at the book lying on the table and then he looked straight at me. Not just the once, though, no, he kept his eyes fixed on me. Accordingly I had to nod as if I were deriving enormous benefit from his reading, and to flash the occasional smile. Why he had picked on me was impossible to say, it might have been because of my central position, it might have been because we looked so different from the others.

To my horror, Espen let out a snore. I glanced at him. He was sitting with his arms crossed, his head at a slight angle and his eyes closed. His chest rose and sank at regular intervals.

I nudged him discreetly and he sat up with a start.

The reciter of the poem eyed us as one German word tumbled from his mouth after another.

I smiled and nodded.

Espen went back to sleep.

I nudged him again. This time he didn't move, just opened his eyes, blinked and was gone again.

So all the responsibility rested on me. If he was asleep I would have to appear doubly interested. I opened my eyes wide, studied the ceiling pensively, narrowed my eyes, *that* was interesting, nodded to myself, stared straight at the poet with a look of acknowledgement.

All to a stream of unintelligible words and sounds.

At last he stopped. The woman presenter thanked him, that much I understood, and added something, then everyone stood up. I looked at Espen, who was conscious now.

'What did she say?' I said.

'It's the interval,' Espen said. 'Let's go, shall we?'

'Yes,' I said and headed for the exit with a determined step because the poet looked like he was interested in a chat. I turned my head, nodded and hurried out. On the other side of the door the waiters were standing ready with their trays, which we nearly bumped into as at last we made our getaway.

I had lost all sense of proportion, that was what had happened, for the inferiority I felt became only stronger when we arrived in Prague and wandered around its beautiful streets. We didn't see the same things, we didn't even look for the same things, I was just your standard stupid guy who didn't notice anything and wasn't interested in anything. Espen wanted to see the Jewish cemetery; I didn't know there was one. We went there, strolled around, afterwards he asked me if I had seen all the slips of paper on the gravestones, I shook my head, I hadn't, how could you *not* have seen them? he riposted, I don't know, I answered. He wanted to see houses some famous architects had designed in the 1920s, we went there, I just saw houses. We went into a church, he looked left, I looked left, he looked right, I looked right. He sat down on a bench and bowed his head. Why did he bow his head? I wondered, panic-stricken. Is he meditating? Why is he meditating? Is it the atmosphere here? Can he feel the presence of something hallowed or sacred? Is there anything special about this church? Has Kafka been here perhaps? No, he was a Jew. It must be the atmosphere. The sanctity. Some existential force on this very spot.

After a while Espen looked up again and we left. On the way I asked, as casually as possible, what he had been doing inside the church.

'Were you meditating or what?'

'No, I was asleep. Obviously I haven't had enough sleep over the last few days.'

On our return to Oslo I stayed with him for two nights, we went out both times, on the second we went to Barbeint, I went with a girl back to her place, we made love in her bedsit, it was just sad, I came straight away, I wasn't there for much more than half an hour. The day afterwards I couldn't remember her name or what she looked like, only that she'd had a poetry book by Øyvind Berg on her bedside table. On the train the following afternoon I decided to finish it with Gunvor. It was no good any more, nothing was any good any more, I called her from a phone box at the train station, said I had done something I shouldn't have and we had to talk. I went to her place. Fortunately no one else was there. She made some tea, we went to the sitting room. I cried when I said we had grown apart, what we had belonged to the past, not the future. She cried too, four years of our lives were over. Afterwards we laughed. For the first time in ages we were open with each other and chatted for several hours. I felt guilty about my behaviour, as I was actually relieved the relationship was over and I was therefore crying crocodile tears. Yet they weren't, the situation itself, the intimacy of it, wasn't insincere, and that was what had made me cry. Gunvor couldn't have been aware of the distinction, couldn't have known the tears were masking something, and in her eyes it must have looked as if I really was sad it was over.

Late that night I got up to go. We embraced, stood in the hall holding each other tight, and then I went down the stairs, my eyes blind with tears. I had betrayed her, but now it was over and the guilt I felt was easier to bear as it only affected myself.

In the summer nothing much happened at Student Radio, there were very few students in town, and Yngve was in Arendal, so I was mostly alone, spending my time either at the radio station or at home, I tried to write, but it didn't amount to much, a short story entitled *Zoom* about a man who met a woman, she went back to his place, her poses became more and more pornographic, and that was it, she went home, he heard her footsteps fade in the street. Oh, it was nothing, an idea, a piece of stupidity. I showed it to Tore when he came back to Bergen, he said it was good, I had created a good character, but perhaps I should develop him further and also the plot? I couldn't, I had stretched myself to the limit, it wouldn't get any better. Every sentence was meticulously constructed, which meant every word was important but only within the internal system that constituted the story, because for the reader, in this case Tore, it didn't matter whether I wrote 'clutching claw-like fingers' or 'scratching cloaca finger movements' or any of the sentences I had shaped with such care.

In the autumn I slaughtered Stig Sæterbakken's novel *The New Testament* over a full-page spread in *Morgenbladet*, it was all the various styles and pastiches I didn't like, and when the main protagonist sits in a wing chair at a party and inwardly abuses all those present it was so like Thomas Bernhard that I couldn't see the novelty in it. It was a big novel, it had been many years since a young novelist had dared to invest such commitment, but sadly it hadn't

come off. I had sat up all night at the radio station, writing; when
Tore arrived in the morning I read it to him. I wrote that the novel
was like a giant dick, impressive at first sight but too big for the
blood to create a fully functional erection, it only got semi-stiff.
Tore screamed with laughter when I read it out.

'Are you going to write *that* in *Morgenbladet*? Ha ha ha! You *can't*
do that, Karl Ove! *No way!*'

'But it's an apt image. That's exactly what the novel is. Big and
ambitious, yes, but *too* big and ambitious.'

'All right, all right. It might be exactly like a giant dick, ha ha
ha, but that doesn't mean you can write that, you twonk!'

'Shall I delete it?'

'You have no choice.'

'But that's the most precise image of the novel.'

'Come on! Delete it and we'll go for a coffee.'

A few weeks later Alf van der Hagen from NRK's P2 rang, he
wondered if I would be willing to review a novel, the first in
Thomas Mann's four-part series *Joseph and His Brothers*, for the radio
programme *Kritikertorget*, I was enormously flattered, of course I
would. I caught the bus to Minde, where NRK had its base. I was
expected, my name was registered in the receptionist's book, the
very idea of it, Knausgård 1 pm, *Kritikertorget*, Studio 3. *Kritikertorget* was the most important literature programme in Norway by a
long chalk, all the good critics reviewed there, Hagerup as well as
Linneberg, now I had a foot in the door. They would ring again, I
would become a known voice, it would be heard every Saturday
afternoon, my name would be one to be reckoned with. Knausgård asserts his writing is overrated, do you agree? Knausgård has
chosen your novel as the pick of the crop this autumn, what do
you say to that? Naturally I'm flattered. The man knows what he
is talking about.

I was guided through the corridors in Minde by a woman, past
the editorial staff at work in an open-plan office, computer screens

shone, voices buzzed, and into a studio bigger and smarter and more open than ours, where I put on a headset and spoke directly to Alf van der Hagen. Just the name, aristocratic and noble, sent shivers down my spine. He was friendly and welcoming, said the manuscript was good, all I had to do was read it. He interrupted me on occasion, asked me to repeat, but that was the way it had to be. And there I sat, the radio critic van der Knausgård, the new voice, the new generation of critics, reading a manuscript about Thomas Mann. Reading aloud on radio was something I could do, I had been doing it every day now for close on a year, but van der Hagen was not satisfied, I had to read it again and again, and when we finally stopped I had the impression he didn't think my rendition was good enough, he was stopping because we couldn't keep on going ad infinitum without making any progress.

The review was broadcast, I got everyone I knew to listen, this was the real McCoy, this was NRK, not some poky local radio station in Sørland or Student Radio in Bergen. Everyone thought it was good, but the follow-up phone call never materialised, NRK never made a further approach, they didn't want anything to do with me, obviously it hadn't been good enough.

Nevertheless my name was doing the rounds, I received a request from *Kritikkjournalen* to review a novel by a Japanese writer by the name of Murakami, the book was about someone hunting special sheep, and I slated it, mainly because it was so Western. I slated several novels for *Vinduet*, did several interviews for *Studvest*, worked at Student Radio, went to Rica, Garage, Café Opera, the Football Pub and drank beer with the others from the radio station, sometimes I walked home alone, sometimes I walked home with a girl, for something had happened to me too, they no longer said no to me, perhaps because I no longer cared so much that I was rendered speechless, capable only of staring at them with those wild desperate eyes of mine, or perhaps because they knew who I was already. But I had no friends there, apart from Tore,

who had moved with Inger into a big flat below the university.
I often went there – trudged up with a bag of beers in my hand,
shall we drink them and then go for a walk – so often I had to
restrict my visits in case they began to form suspicions about me
and realise that actually I had nowhere else to go.

Inger considered it a bit too much, I could see that in her face,
she joked that Tore's personality had changed after he met me,
now he wanted to go drinking all the time, there was something
in that, and I knew it, both of them were rooted somewhere, they
had something, whereas I had no roots and I saw myself through
their eyes, a tall hapless guy with no friends, forcing himself on
Tore, who was *four* years younger.

In town, sitting at a table in Garage drinking and chatting, I
forgot about all this, then what we had was good. Every Saturday
morning we met and made a programme in our *Popkarusell* series.
So far we had done the Kinks, the Beatles, The Jam, the Smiths,
Blue and the Police. I recommended Tore to *Morgenbladet*, they were
interested, he started reviewing poetry books for them while still
writing himself, now he was working on short texts. He showed
me some of them, and they were good, really good. Suddenly he
had his own language. Green-eyed with jealousy, I read them with
him next to me, but I kept my feelings well hidden, Christ, Tore,
I said to him, this is really *good*. He shone like a little sun, put the
texts on top of his disturbingly high pile and said he was beginning to find his feet. After such sessions it was straight home to
the computer. I started a new short story, which I called *Blank*, it
was about a man who woke up in a park not knowing who he
was. Walked around town, recognised nothing. Someone waved
to him and called him Sean. Sean, was that me? he wondered. I
wrote three pages, polished every single sentence like a diamond,
yet they didn't sparkle. They were like sentences in a bad detective
novel or, even worse, in a school literature essay. There was *nothing*
of the personality Tore had managed to conjure up in his writing,

the unprecedented concentration of atmosphere he had achieved, which lay *not* in the descriptions, not in the space where the action took place, but in the *language*. In other words, he wrote like a poet. Not to mention Espen, who *was* a poet. This wasn't about atmospheres but bursts of language, sudden revelations, images that were so unexpected they opened new associations.

Espen had been there ever since I first met him, so I didn't feel any envy towards him, but with Tore it was different, especially the ignominy of him being four years younger than me. I ought to have been a kind of Nestor, an older experienced student who could cautiously lead him to where he wanted to go, an older-brother figure in his life, instead I found myself left behind after six months.

We kept shifting positions with respect to each other, immature or mature, experienced or inexperienced, it was all up in the air, one moment I saw his vulnerability, which normally he showed no one, it appeared when you were close to him, the next he was utterly superior to everyone else I knew. It was the same with Inger. Sometimes I saw them as children and felt like the oldest twenty-four-year-old in the world when I was with them, at others they laughed at me and my plastic bags and they were two independent academically gifted students on their way to the top while I was a dropout with a second-rate university qualification, three years old now, as my sole achievement.

Once when I went there they were in the process of frying a smoked mackerel for dinner.

Another time, sitting on the sofa, I happened to comment that I needed a haircut, Tore, never short of brainwaves, suggested Inger could do it. She cuts my hair, you know, he said. Or shaves my head with an electric razor.

'Hey, Inger. Can you cut Karl Ove's hair?'

She came out and tilted her head, a little embarrassed.

'Yes, I could do,' she said.

'There you are then!' Tore said. 'Now it's done!'

I was sceptical, but he was so determined that I got up and went with Inger to the bathroom. She pulled out a chair, I sat down, she wrapped a towel around my shoulders, ran a comb a couple of times through my hair.

Our eyes met in the mirror.

She smiled and looked down.

'How do you want it?' she said.

'Cut it all off,' I said.

'OK,' she said.

She placed a hand on my head and our eyes met again.

This time it was my turn to blush.

Slowly the shaver began to buzz its way across my head, from the back of my neck all the way over. She moved around me, leaned against my side with her thigh, stretched to complete the run of the shaver and pressed a breast against my shoulder. She tried to hide her embarrassment behind a closed professional expression, but an occasional flush flitted across her cheeks, and I could feel her enormous relief when she had finally finished and was able to take the towel off my shoulders.

'There we go,' she said. 'Is that OK for you?'

'It's great. Thank you very much!'

'I should produce a little mirror now so that you can see the back of your neck, but I'm afraid I haven't got one.'

'I'm sure there isn't any hair there anyway,' I said and got up, running my hand through my centimetre-short hair.

I had a feeling she would give Tore the benefit of her opinion as soon as I had gone, how could he have put her in such a difficult spot? Why on earth should she cut his friend's hair?

In the middle of September I met Gunvor for the first time since I had finished with her. We bumped into each other in Nøstet, very close to my bedsit, she was going to Verftet to meet someone in a café, it was Sunday morning, the weather was fantastic.

I asked her how things were, she said fine.

'How about you?' she said.

'Fine,' I said.

'That's good!' she said. 'We'll bump into each other again, I'm sure. Bye!'

'Bye,' I said and walked down the hill while she carried straight on. When I went into my room, pitch black after all the light outside, I cried. Lay down on the bed and tried to sleep, in vain, the fount of slumber had dried up. Hardly any wonder, the previous night I had slept fourteen hours. So I just had to lie there and read until it became possible again.

A few weeks later Tore and I began to play music together. Yngve had at last finished his studies and was looking for a job, he was on the dole and more than willing to come along. We got a room in a derelict factory, there was a ravaged drum kit, a PA system and some Peavey guitar amps, the corners were heaped with rubbish, the concrete walls were cracked and dark with damp, it was freezing there during the autumn – all this notwithstanding, we met once a week and did our best.

I visited Espen in Oslo, I tried to do that as often as possible, I could live for weeks off the train trip across the mountains, sitting in the restaurant car and alternately reading and gazing at the countryside, which was absolutely stunning in its autumn colours, and the stay itself, in his elegant spacious flat. When we talked I would sometimes say things I had never even thought before, galvanised by the situation and Espen's enthusiasm, suddenly something in the room burst into being, it became a focus, not for me and my self-absorption, my constant sensitivity to what others thought about me, no, what we talked about detached itself from all that, the *I* disappeared until the moment was over and we were back sitting on opposite sides of the table, which, as it were, became visible again. Travelling back home after these weekends, which were invariably eventful, whether we went out in the evening or he invited people for dinner, I usually had a rucksack full of books I had bought and which I read on the journey across the mountains. Once Thomas Bernhard's *Extinction* was among them, it was shocking, as cold as it was clear, constantly circling around death, the parents and sister of the protagonist die in a car accident, he goes home to bury them, filled with hatred, which all Bernhard's characters are, but in this book there was an objectivity which I hadn't seen before in him, it was as though the hard facts of life came to the fore, as though they were so overriding and powerful that they took over the angry hate-filled monologues, that death crushed even the greatest hatred and fury, in a way it took residence in him, and it was so cold and so hard and pitiless, though also beautiful, everything came into existence through the insistent elaborate rhythm of Bernhard's language, which flowed into me as I read and continued even when I had put the book aside and looked out of the window, at the snow that had just fallen on the heath, the wild stream that hurtled over the ravine, and I thought, I have to write like this, I can write like this, go for it, it is not an art, and I began to formulate the start of a novel in my head, in Bernhard's rhythm, and it went well, a new sentence came, and another, and the train jerked into movement again, and I thought up sentence upon sentence, which, when I sat down in front of the computer that afternoon, had completely disappeared. The sentences I'd had in my head were full of life and energy, those I saw on the screen were lifeless and hollow.

One day Yngve came up to the radio station to ask me if I wanted to go to Grillen with him for a cup of coffee. He still had no job and was bored, he was ready to move on as so many of his friends had done, but nothing was happening, he was still drawing unemployment benefit and living alone in a bedsit in Møhlenpris, no longer a student, nor anything else.

I said yes, of course, and walked beside him down the stairs.

'Who's the girl behind us?' he said. 'Don't turn round.'

I didn't need to, I had seen them as we left the office.

'That's Tonje and Therese,' I said.

'Who's the one on the left?'

'Left as we're walking or left if we turn round?'

'Left as we're walking.'

'That's Tonje.'

'She's unbelievably good-looking!'

'Yes, Tonje's nice.'

'What does she do?'

'Studies media. Works as a social correspondent.'

We went up the stairs on the other side and into Grillen.

'She'll probably be going to the media party before Christmas then,' he said.

'She probably will,' I said. 'But you won't.'

'I will. And so will you.'

'Me? What's that got to do with me?'

'You're playing the drums. I'm playing a few songs in a band with Dag and Tine, you see, and we need a drummer. I said you wouldn't mind. You don't, do you?'

'No, not at all. Provided we practise a bit first.'

'There are only six songs. And for your information, our name is Di Derrida-da.'

'OK.'

Tonje was one of the girls I had noticed during the interviews a year earlier. Her face was both open and secretive, she dressed elegantly, often braided her long hair into a thick plait, but it was also loose sometimes. Her mouth, which was what I had noticed first, was beautiful, though also a little lopsided, and her eyes were dark, though not in any sombre way, nor melancholic, there was something else, I didn't know quite what, but I noticed it. She had started working as a social correspondent, was serious and ambitious, but moved outside the circles I frequented, had her own friends in radio, Therese in particular seemed to be close, and my interest in her waned. My days were filled with work and little infatuations, a hand gesture here, a curvaceous thigh there, a dark eyebrow here or a turn of the body there. A girl with long blonde hair and black mascaraed eyes, tall and slim with full breasts, I stood talking with her at Landmark one evening, she was shy, I kept my distance, but then she got drunk and came back, wanting to provoke me, I accompanied her uphill to near the Student Centre, she pulled off the ring I wore in my ear, ran away with it in her hand, I caught her up and put my arms around her, we kissed, she lived nearby, when we arrived at her place she put Motorpsycho on full blast, cleared everything off the table with a sweep of her arm while I stood by the wall watching, she really was stunningly beautiful, and I was drawn to her, but she only wanted to smash things and cry, there would only be a little smooching then I had to go, she said, but I also had to promise to return, tomorrow at five, everything would be fine again, but of course it wasn't, when I rang the doorbell the next day after work, as horny as a billy goat, no one answered, and the next time I met her she was drunk again and claimed she had been at home but hadn't dared to open the door. If I called again she would. OK, I said, she went onto the dance floor, I was at the bar, immediately afterwards the band stopped playing, someone had thrown beer at the synth, I had seen it all, it was her.

There was another girl who sometimes came to see me in the evenings, but she had started to fall in love with me, so on the last occasion I didn't answer the door. Then there were a couple of others I had something with, I was incredibly attracted by one of them and had opened myself up to her, and taken her home once, but she made it very clear that this was a mistake, she wasn't interested in the slightest, in fact she even went so far as to ask me not to tell anyone. At the radio station there were phone calls for her in the evening, I knew who was ringing her and was out of my mind with jealousy, not that I had any right to be, I didn't even know her.

Tonje was outside all of this. I exchanged a few words with her when the opportunity arose, if, for example, she came into the studio when I was working there or she needed a technician for some news item or something, but I knew nothing about who she was or what she did.

She was incredibly good-looking, as Yngve had said, but she was nothing to me.

In the first week of December I had my twenty-fifth birthday. It was an important event, a milestone, I should have had a party, but I didn't know enough people for that to be a possibility, so when I went to the radio station no one knew what a big day it was for me, which in itself I liked, it was fitting for the person I had become, someone who kept a low profile and did not attract unnecessary attention, someone who didn't boast and knew his place.

I arrived early, the office was empty and I cleared the table by the corner sofa, put on some coffee, began to scan the newspapers for any student-related news items I could cut out. Outside, the snow had settled, a faint shimmer extended into the darkness by the windows, that was all it took to change the whole office atmosphere.

The door by the stairs opened and I glanced over.

Ingvild!

She smiled and waved and walked up to me.

'Long time, no see,' I said and gave her a hug. 'What are you doing here?'

'Happy birthday,' she said.

'Thank you,' I said. 'How did you know?'

'I've got a memory like an elephant.'

'Would you like some coffee?' I said.

'Please,' she said. 'I have to be going soon though.'

She perched on the edge of the sofa. I took the jug from the machine and quickly poured two cups while the filter trickled and dripped onto the hotplate.

'What's it like being twenty-five then?' she said. 'Does it feel good?'

'I can't notice any difference. Did you?'

'No, other than it's good not to be twenty any more.'

'Tell me about it,' I said.

'I've got something for you,' she said, producing a parcel from a bag and passing it to me. 'Here you are.'

'Have you bought me a present as well?'

'Naturally,' she said as she looked away, a little flustered.

I unwrapped it. It was a grey lambswool sweater from Benetton.

I looked at her, then at the sweater.

'Don't you like it?' she said.

'Yes, I do, it's great,' I said. 'But a sweater? Why did you buy me a sweater?'

'I thought you needed one,' she said. 'But if you don't like it you can change it.'

She sat with her hands in her lap, watching me.

'Thank you very much,' I said.

I realised that she interpreted my reaction as meaning I didn't like it, and there was an awkward silence until I realised I should try on the sweater. But that just made the situation even more awkward because what confused me was the sweater. Why buy me a sweater? It cost several hundred kroner. And, in a way, it was personal. A record, a book or a flower, if she was going to give me anything at all. But a sweater?

She stood up.

'I have to go now. My lecture's at a quarter past. But enjoy the rest of your birthday!'

She disappeared down the stairs and I went on reading the papers with a pair of scissors in my hand.

Yngve came by late in the afternoon, he just wanted to say happy birthday and that unfortunately he had no money for a present but better times were around the corner and then he would buy me something really nice.

That was all that happened that day. I went home as usual, read and played records as usual, talked to mum, who told me what had happened on this day twenty-five years ago. Dad didn't ring, he never did, I wondered if he didn't actually know when we, Yngve and I, had been born or he knew but didn't care, but I was used to this, it didn't matter, he lived his life, I lived mine.

The following week was the media party. It was being held in Uglen, Bergen's infamous watering hole, where the most desperate and ravaged individuals hung out, typical of the humorists in media studies, who put Madonna on the same level as Mahler. I went there early, we were going to do a sound check and run through the songs, which we had hardly practised, for a final time. The snow had settled, it was cold in Bergen now, and for the first time in the five years I had lived there you sensed a Christmas atmosphere in the streets.

We played five songs, among them '*Forelska i Lærer'n*' and 'Material Girl', as well as an original which Yngve had written the music for and Marit, the vocalist, the words.

Afterwards we stood by a table making a start on the beers we had been given for performing. Yngve knew a lot of people, it was only six months since he had finished his studies; for me most of the people were new faces, apart from Tonje, who came over and said hi after we had played.

'Are you here too?' she said.

'Yes,' I said. 'I get hired to play the drums all over town. It's especially busy at Christmas.'

She smiled.

'Aren't you going to introduce us?' Yngve said.

'Tonje, this is Yngve, my brother. Yngve, this is Tonje from Student Radio.'

They shook hands, Yngve smiled and looked her in the eye as he asked her if she was in her first year.

They chatted for a while, had more in common than she and I had, and I looked around as I knocked back the cold beer and enjoyed the taste, perhaps not so much its slight bitterness as the promise of eventful nights and the mounting pleasure that came with it.

Tonje rejoined her friends, Yngve took a long swig, put his glass down on the table and said she was so good-looking, that Tonje was.

'Ye-ah.'

I glanced over, she was talking to a guy but looked up at once, met my gaze and smiled.

I returned her smile.

Yngve talked about the various jobs he had applied for and how difficult it was to get in anywhere if you didn't have any contacts, perhaps he had made a mistake focusing on finishing his studies instead of working on the side.

'That's what you did,' he said. 'And now you're writing for *Morgenbladet* and freelancing for NRK. You've had a lot more opportunities than if you'd just kept studying.'

'Maybe,' I said. 'But writing book reviews isn't exactly lucrative.'

I met Tonje's eye again. She smiled across the room and I smiled back. Yngve was oblivious.

'Not book reviews, no,' he said. 'But if you stick at it you'll soon have a name. Then everything'll get much easier. If you have something concrete to show. I've got just the subject and the grade.'

'It'll all come out in the wash,' I said with a smile, feeling light-headed. Whenever I looked at her I got a tingle in my stomach. She seemed to possess a sixth sense because however deep in conversation she was she always looked up when I glanced over. The people she was with noticed nothing. Yngve noticed nothing. It was as though we were sharing a secret. Whenever she smiled, she was smiling at herself.

Hey, it's us two, isn't it? Her smile seemed to say.

Us two? said my smile. Are you joking?

No.

No?

Come here and let's see what happens.

You look terrific.

You too.

Us two?

Yes.

Yes?

Come on. Then you'll see.

'What are you smiling at?' Yngve said.

'Nothing special,' I said. 'I'm just in a good mood. It all went well with the band and so on.'

'Yes, it did. It was fun.'

We drank a bit more, Yngve went for a walk around the room, I was alone and she came over.

'Hi,' she said.

'I'm glad you've come over,' I said. 'I don't know anyone here.'

'I was surprised to see you here. But that question was soon answered.'

She looked down and pursed her lips for an instant, then looked up and smiled.

'I was hoping you would be here,' I said.

'Were you?' she said. 'Did you know I was in media?'

'Yes, but that's all I know about you.'

'Sounds like I have you at a disadvantage,' she said. 'I know quite a lot about you, you see.'

Yngve came back.

'You're so like Karl Ove,' Tonje said. 'I guessed you were his brother as soon as I saw you.'

She stayed with us for a while, Yngve did most of the talking, as on the first occasion, but all the tension was between us two.

'You're not going soon, are you?' she said, looking at me as she went to rejoin her friends again.

'No,' I said.

I watched her go. Her back was straight, her neck long and elegant, half-covered by hair, which was collected in a plait. At the radio station she would often hide in big clothes, as many girls do, wear a military jacket, thick jumper and black boots, but this evening she was wearing a plain black dress which clung to her slim waist and gave her quite a different allure.

'Hm. You're a dark horse,' Yngve said.

'Eh?' I said.

'You didn't say there was anything between you when I asked you who she was.'

'There wasn't. We'd just exchanged a few words.'

'What's going on now then?'

'You know as much as I do.' I smiled.

Every time our eyes met that evening it was as though everything else was blanked out: Yngve, all the students and lecturers who were there, all the chairs and tables, and not only that, everything in my life, everything that I carried with me, which could be such a burden, was gone. All that existed as we gazed across the room was her and me.

It was odd.

Even odder was that I was completely relaxed. There was nothing to fear, nothing to worry about, I didn't have to perform, do anything, be someone. I didn't even have to say anything.

But I did.

We sought each other that evening, she moved around, we exchanged a few words off and on, then we were suddenly standing there alone and chatting, utterly immersed in each other, I saw nothing except her, she shone with such a strong radiance that everything else vanished.

All evening men had made passes at her, the way they do at parties like that, when you have seen one another for a whole semester, in reading rooms and lectures, in the canteen and library, and then you meet, dressed up and primed with drink, ready to grab your opportunity. I saw all of those who wanted to talk to her, but what did she do? She looked up and smiled at me.

When at last it was only us two, Sverre Knudsen came over to our table. He had played in The Aller Værste! and was one of my old heroes, but of course he wasn't interested in that or me, it was Tonje he had his eye on. He talked and talked in a manic frenzy, he wanted to know all about her, he said, she hesitated, he said he knew who had shot William Nygaard, the CEO of Aschehoug and publisher of Salman Rushdie, he was going to Oslo early tomorrow morning and would reveal the truth, she had to read *Dagbladet* in two days' time, it would be there. He said he feared for his own life, he had been followed for several days now because he knew what he knew, but he was too smart for them, he was two steps ahead, he knew Bergen like the back of his hand.

Yngve came over, he wanted to leave. I looked around, he wasn't the only one, the party was drawing to an end.

Sverre Knudsen wanted to stay longer with Tonje, she laughed and looked at me, it was time to go, would I walk her back?

It was snowing when we got outside.

'Where do you live?' I said.

'I'm living with my mum at the moment,' she said. 'Next to Støletorget. Do you know where that is?'

'Yes. I lived not far from there once.'

We walked down towards Hotel Norge, she was wearing a long black coat, I was wearing my old hairy coat. Hands in my pockets, a couple of metres from her, the mountainside high above us gleaming in the darkness.

'Do you live at home?' I said. 'How old are you actually?'

'I'm moving out after Christmas. I've got a room by the bus station. Behind there,' she said, pointing.

We walked along by the hotel and into Torgalmenningen, which was deserted and covered with a thin layer of white snow.

'They're going to Africa after Christmas. So I have to move.'

'Africa?'

'Yes, Mozambique. Mum, her husband and my sister. She's only ten. It's going to be tough for her. But she's looking forward to it.'

'What about your father? Does he live in Bergen as well?'

'No, he lives in Molde. I'm going there for Christmas.'

'Have you got any more brothers and sisters?'

'Three brothers.'

'Three brothers?'

'Yes, anything wrong with that?'

'Wrong? No-o. It's just a lot of brothers. And when you say it like that, three brothers, well, I got the feeling they were the kind that look after their sister. That they're skulking around here somewhere, waiting for us this minute.'

'Perhaps they are,' she said. 'But if so, I'll tell them you have only good intentions.'

She looked at me and smiled.

'I *do*!' I said.

'I know,' she said.

We continued without speaking. Snow was falling. The streets around us were perfectly still. We looked at each other and smiled.

Crossed Fisketorget, with the sea beside us, all black. I was happier than I had ever been. Nothing had happened, we had only chatted and now we were walking here, I was two metres from her, with my hands in my coat pockets, that was all. Nonetheless, this was bliss. The snow, the darkness, the light from the Fløybane sign. Tonje walking beside me.

What had happened?

Nothing had happened.

I was the same person. Bergen was the same town.

Yet everything was different.

Something had opened.

What had opened?

I walked beside her in the darkness, up the hill to the funicular railway, along the walls of the old school, up Steinkjellersmauet, and everything I saw, everything I thought, everything I did, even if it was only putting one foot in front of the other, was tinged with hope.

She stopped by the door of a narrow old white timber house.

'Here it is,' she said. 'As you've walked such a long way, you could come in, if you like?'

'OK,' I said.

'But we have to be quiet. They're still asleep.'

She opened the door and we were in a hall. I carefully took off my shoes, followed her up the cramped stairs. By the bend there was a kitchen, but she continued up another floor where there were two rooms, both with sloping ceilings. The rooms looked like they do in home design magazines.

'It's lovely here,' I said.

'That's mum's doing,' she said. 'She's got flair. Can you see that picture over there?'

She pointed to a picture made of fabrics, portraying a choir, with lots of small puppets, all with their own individual expressions.

'She's an artist. But she doesn't do much art any more.'

'It's great,' I said.

'It's quite funny,' she said. 'The pictures would go like hot cakes if she had a mind to sell them.'

I took off my jacket and sat down in a chair.

'Anything you'd like? Tea?'

'Tea would be perfect,' I said.

She went down to the floor below, I sat still until she returned five minutes later with a cup in each hand.

'Do you like jazz?' she said.

I shook my head. 'I'm afraid not. I'd be lying if I said I did. But you do, I can see.'

'Oh, yes. I love jazz.'

'Then play some.'

She got up and put a record on the old Bang & Olufsen stereo.

'What is it?'

'Bill Frisell. You have to hear it. It's fantastic.'

'I only hear sounds,' I said. 'Slightly strained sounds.'

'I work at the Molde Jazz Festival every year,' she said. 'Have done since I was sixteen.'

'What do you do?'

'I take care of the musicians. Pick them up from the airport and drive them around and try to entertain them the best I can. Last year I went fishing with them.'

I imagined her wearing a chauffeur's cap and uniform and laughed.

'What are you laughing at?' she said.

'Nothing,' I said. 'I just like you so much.'

She looked down and pursed her mouth for an instant, the way I had noticed she was wont to do, then she looked up at me and smiled.

'I hadn't anticipated I would be sitting here with Karl Ove at the crack of dawn when I left home last night,' she said.

'Do you see that as positive or negative?' I said.

'What do you think?' she said.

'It would be smug to say positive. So it has to be negative.'

'Do you really imagine I would have invited you up here then?'

'Who knows,' I said. 'I don't know you.'

'And I don't know you,' she said.

'No,' I said.

The sense of falling snow had stayed with me; as we sat there I imagined it swirling down from on high and landing soundlessly on the roof above us, flake by flake. We talked about Student Radio and the people there, we talked about music and about playing the drums, she wanted me to teach her, I explained to her that I wasn't really any good at it. She told me she had worked in local radio ever since she went to *ungdomskole* and for a long time she had worked at one of Bergen's most controversial stations, run by an anti-immigration MD, so controversial that even I had heard of him. She said he was a friendly though eccentric man, she didn't agree with his opinions, but freedom of speech was paramount and it was strange that so few people remembered that when they condemned him and his radio station. As she talked she became more and more heated and involved, I could see she was committed, committed to radio and free speech, and liked that, however unfamiliar this was to me, because it was fringe. The milieu she was describing was right on the fringe irrespective of how matter-of-fact her tone.

'I'm chattering away here,' she said at length. 'I don't usually do that.'

'I believe you,' I said.

Down below a door opened.

'They must be waking up now,' she said.

'Yes, I should go,' I said.

Up the stairs crept a little girl. As thin as a straight line, large brown eyes, wearing a white nightdress down to the floor.

'Hi, Ylva, are you out of bed?' Tonje said. 'This is Karl Ove. A friend of mine.'

'Hi,' she said, staring at me.

'Hi,' I said and stood up. 'I have to go now.'

I took my jacket from the arm of the chair.

'You're so tall,' she said. 'How tall are you?'

'One metre ninety-three,' I said. 'Would you like to try on my coat?'

She nodded. I held it out, she stuck first one arm in and then the other. Took a few steps, the lowest part hung like a train behind her. She laughed.

I was in a family house.

Tonje accompanied me to the door, we said goodbye and I walked downhill into town, which during the time I had been at Tonje's had totally changed character: big buses were driving through the streets now, people got on and off, hurried up and down the streets, most with umbrellas because the weather had turned milder and the snow that fell was wet and heavy. It was past seven o'clock, there was no point going home, so I headed for the Student Centre, let myself in and went up to the office.

Someone was sleeping on the floor of the conference room.

It was Sverre Knudsen.

Beside him was a kind of board, and I immediately recognised it, it was the same colour as the door. I stepped back and checked: spot on, the top piece, over the lintel, had been removed. So that was how he had got in. How he had circumvented the front doors, however, was a mystery.

I went into the room, crouched down beside him and placed my hand on his shoulder.

'You can't sleep here,' I said.

'Whazzat?' he said, sitting up.

'You can't sleep here,' I said. 'People'll be here soon.'

'You,' he said. 'I remember you. You were with that Tonje.'

I got up.

'Would you like a cup of coffee?' I said.

He nodded and went into the office with me, sat down on the sofa and rubbed his face with his hands. Then he jumped up, went over to the window and peered down at the road.

'You didn't notice a green Beetle when you arrived, did you?' he said.

'No,' I said.

'They're after me,' he said. 'But I don't think they know I'm here. Perhaps they're waiting for me in Oslo. I know who shot Nygaard.'

'So you said last night,' I said.

He didn't answer, sat down on the sofa.

'You probably think I'm paranoid,' he said.

'Not at all,' I said. 'But why did you sleep here?'

'That Tonje said she worked for Student Radio. I thought she might be here.'

'I've been a fan of The Aller Værste! ever since I was a little boy,' I said. 'It's great to meet you. I've also read one of your books. *Butterfly Petrol*.'

He waved his hand dismissively.

'Shall we do an interview now that you're here?' I said. 'About The Aller Værste! days?'

'All right,' he said.

I passed him a cup of coffee, drank mine standing beside the desk. On the stairs I saw Johannes coming up.

'Early start today?' he said.

'Yes,' I said.

'See you later,' he said and went down to the other end. He was doing his national service.

I put the radio on to hear what was being broadcast and who was there.

Sverre Knudsen studied me.

'This is going to be a sensation,' he said. 'Just wait.'

Half an hour later we went up to the studio. I put on a reel, flicked up a knob on the mixing console and went back to him. I was really exhausted and at the same time full to the brim with the events of the night, and found it difficult to concentrate, but that was nothing compared with Sverre Knudsen. Sweat was pouring down his face as he sat there trying to recall the events of fifteen years ago, which, even with the best will in the world, he was unable to summon any interest in now. After twenty minutes I said stop, he seemed relieved, I shook his hand, he stumbled down the steep stairs and hurried into town while I went back to the office and tried to kill time so that I could . . . well, could do what?

Be alone and think about Tonje.

All day flashes of happiness swept through me. Something fantastic had happened.

But what?

Nothing had happened. We had chatted a bit, that was all.

For a year she had worked here, for a year I had seen her going to and fro, and she had seen me. I had never felt any of what I felt now. Not once, not even close.

Then we had met at a party, smiled at each other – and that was that?

Yes, that was that.

How was it possible? How could it change everything?'

Because everything was changed, I knew that. My heart told me. And the heart is never wrong.

The heart is never ever wrong.

I went home, slept for a couple of hours, had a shower, sat down by the phone, had to ring her and thank her, ask if we could meet again. I hesitated, suddenly afraid to ruin anything. But I had to.

I forced myself to dial the number, stopped before the last digit, then dialled. A woman, it must have been her mother, answered.

'Karl Ove here,' I said. 'Is Tonje at home?'

'No, she isn't. She's out at the moment. Can I give her a message?'

'Please tell her I called. I'll try again later perhaps.'

I lay down on my bed, my whole body aching.

I stood by the window, looked down at the enormous aerials on the TV2 building, felt the allure of the darkness above them.

I dressed and went out. I ached. I walked towards Nordnes, a snowplough thundered past with flashing lights. I passed the aquarium and went on towards the park, reached the point of the headland, stood there with the wind blowing against me and watched the sea washing ashore below, the vast darkness where everything was at rest now.

I looked around. Not a soul.

OOOOOHHHH, I shouted.

Then I walked to the totem pole and examined it, thought of the continent where it originated, the Indians who had once lived there knowing nothing of us, us knowing nothing of them. It was such an incredible thought, the freedom of not knowing, just living, believing they were the only humans alive, their surroundings the only world.

I saw her in front of me and a wave of happiness and sorrow rose within me.

How was this going to turn out?

How was it going to turn out?

On my return I waited for another hour before ringing.

This time she answered.

'Hi!' she said. Her voice was warm and very near.

'Thank you for last night,' I said.

'Likewise,' she said. 'My sister has been talking about you all day. I've just been out with her now.'

'Say hello from me,' I said.

'Will do.'

Pause.

'When mummy told me you'd rung I had to lie down on the floor,' she said.

'On the floor?'

'Yes, I had such pains in my stomach.'

'Hm,' I said.

Pause.

'I was wondering . . . actually . . . well . . . if . . .' I said.

'What were you wondering?'

'If you . . . or we, erm . . . or, well, if you'd like to meet me again. And go out or something?'

'Yes.'

'Yes?'

'Yes.'

'Just a cup of coffee or something,' I said. 'But not at the radio station. Nor in the canteen, nor in Grillen. Nor in Café Opera.'

She laughed.

'Wessel?'

'OK, shall we say Wessel? Tomorrow?'

The following day there was a meeting in the Social Affairs section. I had forgotten about it, but of course she would have to go.

Her gaze brushed me as she arrived, no more than that, and she seemed to be smiling to herself, otherwise we didn't exchange a word, it was as if I didn't exist.

I looked through the window of the conference room, there they sat talking and gesturing without a sound. She looked up at me, flashed a quick smile, looked away.

What did that mean?

Tore came down the corridor.

'How's it going, Karl?' he said.

'I'm up to my bloody ears in love,' I said. 'My body hurts. My joints. My joints *ache*.'

He laughed.

'I saw you two days ago. You didn't say anything.'

'Course I didn't. It happened the day before yesterday.'

'This is like being at infants school,' he said. 'Have you asked her out?'

'No.'

'Tell me who it is and I can ask her.'

'It's Tonje.'

'Tonje? Student Radio Tonje?'

'Yes.'

'Her sitting in there?'

'Yes.'

'Does she know?'

I shook my head.

He laughed again.

'She probably has an inkling,' I said. 'We're meeting afterwards. I rang last night. Come on, let's go. Fancy a coffee in the canteen?'

I hadn't eaten all day, and I couldn't get anything down at home either, I wasn't interested and food didn't seem necessary. I was burning up.

For the two hours I had to wait before I could leave I wandered around, lay down on my bed, stared at the ceiling, got up and paced to and fro. It was terrible, I was so high that all I could possibly expect now was a fall.

What would I talk about?

It wouldn't work, I was somewhere else now, I would sit and fidget and blush and be a total idiot, I knew myself so well.

I didn't have a mirror in my flat, in that way I was able to avoid having to look at myself, but now it felt as if I urgently needed one, so after changing and putting gel in my hair, I turned over a CD and held it in front of me from several different angles.

I locked the door behind me and went out.

I had pains in my stomach.

This was no fun.

Just painful, all of it.

The snow shone in the streets around me as I walked up the gentle incline to the little kiosk beside the swimming pool, past the theatre and Café Opera, round the corner and into Wesselstuen.

She wasn't there, and I thanked the Lord, now I would have a few minutes to myself. I found a table and sat down, told the waiter who came over that I was waiting for someone.

She arrived ten minutes later. I trembled when I saw her. She was carrying lots of bags, leaned them against the wall and took off her coat, then sat down, somehow she had brought with her everything that existed out there, the street lamps and the shop windows, the crowds and the snow, it was all part of her aura, the same way a cat brings the forest and the darkness indoors when it comes into the house in the morning.

'I've been buying Christmas presents,' she said. 'Sorry I'm late.'

'No problem,' I said.

'Have you ordered?'

'No. What would you like?'

'A beer maybe.'

Soon after, we were sitting with our beers in front of us on the table. The room was full, there was a great atmosphere, the last Christmas dinners were being eaten, around us sat men in 1980s suits and women in dresses with broad shoulders and plunging necklines shouting *skål* and laughing. We were the only ones not saying anything.

I could have said she was a star, a shining light, my sun. I could have said I longed for her so much I was making myself ill. I could have said I had never experienced anything like this in my entire life, and I had experienced a lot. I could have said I wanted to be with her for ever.

But I didn't.

I looked at her and smiled gently. She smiled back, gently.

'You've got such unbelievably beautiful ears,' I said.

She smiled and looked down at the table.

'Do you think so?' she said. 'I've never heard that before!'

What had I said?

That she had beautiful ears?

It was true, her ears were unusually well formed, but so was her neck, and her lips, and her hands, small and pale, and her eyes. Complimenting a woman on her ears, that was crazy.

I blushed to the roots of my hair.

'I suddenly noticed,' I said. 'And so I said it. I know it sounds a bit strange. But it's true! You do have beautiful ears!'

The explanation just made things worse.

I took a long swig.

'You've got a nice sister anyway,' I said.

Anyway?

'I'll tell her you said that,' Tonje said. 'She thought it was very exciting having you there. She's at that age. She doesn't really know what *it* is, but maybe she thinks she does. And she absorbs everything she sees.'

She rotated her glass, pursed her lips, looked up at me with her head at an angle.

'Are you going to have a Christmas break? Or will you send your presents?'

'I'm going to my mother's on the twenty-third. I'll stay a week.'

'I'm heading north tomorrow,' she said. 'My brother's giving me a lift.'

'Does he live in Bergen?'

'Yes.'

Nothing was left of what we had between us on the first evening and night. Everything was inside me.

'When are you coming back?' I said.

'At the beginning of January.'

That was a long time. Anything could happen. She might meet someone up there, some guy she hadn't seen for ages, and she might get together with him.

The longer I sat next to her, the worse my chances were. She had to start understanding something.

We chatted about the radio, normal things, everyday life, as though we were just two Student Radio employees having a beer together.

She looked at her watch.

'I'm meeting my mother and sister soon,' she said. 'They're doing their Christmas shopping as well.'

'You go and do that then,' I said. 'I'll see you after Christmas!'

We left together, stopped in Torgalmenningen, she was going left, I was going right. She stood with her bags in her hands. I should have given her a hug, there was nothing wrong in that, it was absolutely natural, we'd just had a beer together, but I didn't dare.

'Happy Christmas,' I said, clumsily raising my hand in the air.

'Happy Christmas, Karl Ove,' she said.

Then we each went our own way, me up over Høyden and down to Møhlenpris, to Yngve's flat, which he shared with a girl he had studied with. Fortunately she wasn't at home.

'How's it going?' he said. 'Anything happen after the party?'

We were in the sitting room, he was playing 'My Bloody Valentine'.

'I went home with her. Nothing happened, we just chatted. I've met her again now, in Wesselstuen. I'm so in love I don't know what to do.'

'Is she?'

'I've no idea! I wasn't able to say a single sensible word to her. Do you know what I told her?'

He shook his head.

'I complimented her on her ears! Can you imagine that? What lovely ears you have! Of all the things I could have said, I chose that.'

He laughed.

'I'm not sure that was so stupid. It's original at any rate!'

'What shall I do?'

'Ring her again? Go out again? If something's meant to happen, it'll happen of its own accord.'

'So that's your opinion: it'll happen of its own accord?'

'Yes.'

'Anyway, she's going home for Christmas tomorrow. I won't see her until January. I was thinking of writing her a letter. What do you reckon?'

'You can do that, can't you?'

'And buying her a Christmas present. I want to surprise her. And I thought of buying something that would make an impression. Not a book or a record and so on, something else. Something personal. But I can't think what.'

'Ear warmers, of course,' Yngve said. 'Then you can write that you chose them so that she would take care of her beautiful ears.'

'Excellent!' I said. 'I'll do that. Could you come shopping with me tomorrow afternoon? Perhaps we can buy a present together for mum while we're at it.'

And that was what we did. I wandered around town with Yngve searching for ear warmers. They weren't exactly common, but in the end I found a pair. They were dreadful, covered in a kind of green fur, but it didn't matter. I had them gift-wrapped, spent the following evening writing a letter and sent everything up to Molde.

Mum noticed something had happened the moment I stepped inside her door.

'Have you met someone?' she said.

'Is it that obvious?' I said.

'Yes,' she said.

'It's nothing yet,' I said.

'I've got a Christmas card from Gunvor,' she said.

I looked at her.

'To be honest, that's over. You're welcome to stay in contact, but for me it's all over.'

'I know,' she said. 'I just thought it was nice she remembered me. What's the name of the girl you've met?'

'I'll tell you if it gets off the ground.'

Mum seemed tired, she was pale and didn't have the energy she usually had, I could see that, just setting and clearing the table was an effort.

On Christmas Eve she unwrapped Kjartan's present and her face went white.

'What have you got?' I said.

'A wreath,' she said. 'I'm sure he meant to give me a nice Christmas wreath, but he's sent me a funeral wreath. The type you give at burials.'

'There's nothing symbolic in it,' Yngve said. 'It doesn't mean anything. He's just made a mistake. It's typical of him.'

She didn't answer, but I could see it had affected her and she did think it had meaning.

After we had opened all our presents and had eaten biscuits and drunk coffee I went up to the study and called Tonje.

'Hi!' she said. 'Thank you for your present! That was really nice.'

'So it did arrive?'

'Yes, it came today. I was wondering if I dared open it with all the others there. After all, I didn't know what you had bought me. But I did anyway. They all had eyes like saucers. "Who's Karl Ove?" "Why has he given you ear warmers?"'

We chatted at length. All her friends had come home for Christmas, she said, they went out or they visited each other and were still close even though it was five years since they had left *gymnas*. She also told me they'd had lots of snow there and her three brothers had been clearing the roof all morning. I could visualise it all: the house, which was at the top of a hillside with a view of the whole town and the fjord beneath and the mountains behind, from what she said, and her three brothers, who in my imagination had taken on fairy-tale roles, they looked the same, stuck together and worshipped their little sister.

Going down to the sitting room afterwards, I missed her so much it was almost unbearable. I had never imagined that happiness could hurt so much.

Between Christmas and New Year I went back to Bergen to put together some programmes. Tonje returned at the beginning of January, I rang her and invited her to dinner at my place.

Yngve usually made spaghetti carbonara with bacon, leeks, blue cheese and cream, it was simple and good, I wanted to try to make it. I didn't have a dining table, so we would have to eat it on our laps on the sofa, that would have to do. If we met in town, we would just be sitting at a table and chatting, here it felt a bit freer, I could stand up and cook, serve her wine, play my music. There was room to move here.

Yngve suggested I put some white wine in the sauce. I followed his advice, but when I tasted it, only minutes before she was due to arrive, it was sweet and tasted horrible. I called him.

'What shall I do?'

'Pour in more wine. That helps.'

'Hang on a minute. Don't go away.'

I poured more wine into the sauce. Stirred it, tasted.

'Now it's even sweeter! Oh, hell, this is a disaster! She'll be here soon!'

'What sort of wine is that?'

I read him the name.

'Doesn't mean a thing to me. But it is dry, is it?'

'Dry?'

'Yes.'

I scrutinised the label.

'It says it's semi-dry. I thought it would be good if it wasn't very sweet.'

'No wonder the sauce is sweet. You'll have to pile on the salt and pepper and hope for the best. Good luck!'

He rang off, I sprinkled some salt and pepper on the sauce, tasted it with my little teaspoon again and again.

The bell rang.

I hung up my apron, made a dash for the door at the end of the stairs.

She was all hat and scarf, two big eyes and smiling mouth.

'Hi,' she said, bending forward to give me a hug.

It was the first time we had touched.

'Come in,' I said.

She followed me down the stairs and into the hallway, removed her outdoor clothes while she looked around. What was there to see? Brick walls, a few posters, a kitchen further along, brick walls there too, and the adjacent room, a bed, a bookcase, an armchair, a desk, some posters, a couple of rag rugs from Ikea.

And yes: three lit candles in a candelabra on the windowsill.

'How nice it is here,' she said. Glanced at the two pans. 'What are we going to eat?'

'Well, it's just a spaghetti dish.'

I spooned some spaghetti onto the two plates, added the sauce, got a small black stool and placed it in front of her so that at least she had something reminiscent of a table, put my plate on my lap and then we ate.

'Mm, that was good!' she said.

'Come on,' I said. 'It wasn't. I poured in some white wine, but it was too sweet.'

'It was a little sweet, yes,' she said with a smile.

I removed the plates, put on a record, *Siamese Dream* by the Smashing Pumpkins, we sat drinking sweet white wine, her in the yellow armchair, me on the bed. I didn't want her to think I only wanted to sleep with her and made no attempt to get close. We talked, that was all. For some reason the conversation turned to various Bergen bands. Completely out of the blue, she said the vocalist in the band we were discussing was bisexual. Our eyes happened to meet just as she said it and I blushed. I thought she might think I was bisexual. Even if she didn't, the fact that I blushed at the very moment the word was uttered would make her suspicious. I tried to find a different topic of conversation, but failed, and the ensuing silence was awkward and unpleasant.

This was no good. She would never be mine. How could I make her mine?

It would be so much easier to give up, to say a cold goodbye and not contact her again. All the problems, all the pain, all the defeats would finish there.

But I couldn't.

She stood up, it was late, time to go home. I accompanied her to the door, said bye, watched her go, she walked up the hill without turning.

When I went back down I put on *Siamese Dream* again, lay back on the bed and let my mind fill with thoughts of her.

The next time we met it was a little better, we ended up in a café just below Steinkjellersmauet, it was late and we were the only ones there. We sat by the window, snow covered all the surfaces outside, which seemed to break the fall the town found itself in when the rain deluged down in the autumn, then it was as though everything was sinking, the streets, the narrow passages, the houses, the parks. The snow held the town firm, and I loved it, loved the new light it cast all around, the moods it created. And I loved her. She talked about her family, there was a grandmother and a mother, there were brothers and a sister, a father and a father's twin brother, I said it sounded like a Bergman film. She smiled and said she was moving at the weekend, could I give her a hand? Of course I could. I appeared outside her flat between the bus terminal and the train station on Saturday afternoon, a white van was parked on the pavement, five people were already carrying furniture and boxes. Tonje brightened up when she saw me. I hurriedly shook hands with all the others, three boys, one of whom was her brother, and a girl, and grabbed a box. The stairway was run-down and draughty, the flat was on the third floor and big, it had two rooms but was in a state of disrepair, and the toilet, I discovered, was on the other side of a narrow open passageway, like a bridge, on the outside of the building.

'Even Fridtjof Nansen would think twice about going to the toilet in the morning,' I said. 'Imagine what it's like when it's raining. Or if it's snowing!'

'It does have its charms,' she said. 'Don't you think?'

'Yes. You can imagine it's the bridge on a ship or something like that in the worst storms.'

I placed the box on the worktop and went downstairs to get another, nodded briefly to the others as they came clumping up. My role in all this was a bit unclear. The others were obviously good friends. No one could maintain I was. So what was I?

Whatever I was, there was nowhere else I would rather have been. Carrying up her possessions to her flat. Catching a glimpse of a mixer. A glimpse of a shoe sole in another box – imagine, that's her shoe. Her saucepans, bowls, plates, cups, glasses, cutlery, frying pans, records, cassettes, books, clothes, shoes, stereo, TV, chairs, tables, bookcases, stools, bed, plants, her whole world, I was helping to carry the whole of her life up the stairs this Saturday afternoon.

The van did two trips, and after the last load had been deposited Tonje went out for some takeaway pizzas, which we ate in the middle of the chaos. I said nothing, I didn't want to occupy space, the others knew her better, I would fit in wherever.

This was great because, sitting there on the floor, my back to the wall with a slice of pizza in my hand, listening to the conversation, I knew she was mine. Occasionally she flashed me a little glance and a smile, sending shivers through me. The thought of her was light, it arched like a sky over everything, but the thought of approaching her was heavy. What if I was wrong? What if she said no? What if she laughed at me? What has got into you? Who do you think you are? Do you imagine I would go out with you? You're just a miserable wimp!

But tonight I would have to!

Tonight I had to.

Her brother said his goodbyes and left. One of the others did the same. I stayed where I was. When the last two stood up to go, I followed suit.

'Are you going too?' she said.

'I thought I would,' I said.

'Couldn't you stay and give me a hand with the unpacking? I have to assemble the bookcase. That's hard to do on your own.'

'Yes, no problem.'

We were alone.

I sat against the wall smoking and drinking Coke. She sat on a wooden box in the middle of the room swinging her legs.

I was burning up. She was making me burn up. If she looked at me my cheeks went hot.

'Are you the handyman type?' she said.

'Me? No,' I said.

'Guessed as much.'

'Are you?' I said.

'In fact I am. I like fixing things. My dream is to have an old house one day, do it up and design it exactly to my taste.'

'What else do you like doing?' I said.

'I like sewing. And cooking. I love cooking. And playing the drums.'

'Mm,' I said.

'And you? What do you like?'

'I don't like sewing. I don't like cooking.' *I like you. Say it now! Say it, say it!*

'I asked you what you liked doing. Not what you don't like doing!'

I like you, I like you!

'I like playing football,' I said. 'But I haven't played for years. And I like reading.'

'That's not my strong suit,' she said. 'I prefer to see films.'

'What films do you like?'

'Woody Allen. He's a favourite.' She got up. 'Shall we assemble the bookcase so that we can play some music?'

I nodded. When we had found all the bits I held it while she screwed the cross braces into position and slipped in the shelves. Then she started to put together the stereo.

'Isn't that the same one as at your mother's house?' I said.

'Yes. She said I could borrow it if I was careful with it.'

She put a speaker on either side of the room, opened a box of CDs and flicked through.

'Jazz?' I said.

'No,' she said. 'This is a song I want you to hear.'

'Who by?'

'The Smashing Pumpkins. It's on an album with various groups. I haven't seen it anywhere else. There it is!'

She flipped in the CD.

She stood watching me as the music flowed into the room. There was something dreamy and boundless about it, as though it embodied that which went on and on and never ended.

'Isn't that great?' she said.

'Yes,' I said. 'Really great.'

Something inside me told me it would be fine if I got up and held her in my arms. She would respond and all I dreamed of would become a reality.

But I didn't dare. I didn't move and the moment passed; she set about organising the boxes.

I helped her to carry some into the kitchen, where she opened them and started putting items in their place. I watched for a while, wondering what would happen if I leaped forward and put my hands round her waist and kissed her fantastic neck.

She leaned forward, put a pile of pans on the worktop and opened the cupboard below.

'I think I'll be off then,' I said.

'OK,' she said, straightening up. 'Thanks for the help!'

I put on my jacket and shoes, opened the door, she went with me, I stepped out into the cold harsh light of the corridor and turned to her.

'Bye then,' I said.

'Bye,' she said.

And, I thought, now, now I'm going to do it.

I leaned forward to kiss her. At that very moment she moved her head to the side, the movement coincided with mine, so instead of my lips meeting hers, they met her ear.

I turned and went down the stairs as fast as I could, ran for a few blocks to put as much distance between me and the fiasco as possible.

What must she be thinking now? I was behaving like a teenager. Not only that, I also felt like one.

Soon I wouldn't have many chances left. Not if I was going to continue like this. How was she supposed to react? What good was I to her?

I decided to return the following day, just pop by, hope she would invite me in, and then be determined and resolute. No more dithering, no more fumbling, no more flushed cheeks and stuttering.

If she said no, so be it.

I was at Yngve's all Sunday afternoon and went at about seven, rang the bell, stepped back into the street and looked up at the windows on the third floor.

No lights?

Oh no, don't say she's not in.

A window opened and she stuck out her head.

'Hi!' she said. 'I'll come down and open the door!'

I walked to the doorstep. My heart was pounding.

The door opened.

'Karl Ove . . .' she said. 'Come in.'

She said my name in such an affectionate way that I went weak. Up the stairs, which she managed with swift light strides, my legs were trembling.

What sort of hell was this?

I went into the kitchen, which was behind the door, took off my shoes and jacket, hat and gloves.

'Would you like some tea?' she said.

'Yes, please,' I said.

I went into the sitting room, which she had as good as finished. Sat down on the low chair, rolled a cigarette.

'Can you roll me one too?' she said.

'Sure,' I said.

I put all my concentration and expertise into it, as it would be hers, but still it was a bit hard in the middle and a touch fatter at one end than the other. She was in the kitchen, I tore it up and made a new one, which turned out better.

'Here you are,' I said, passing it to her.

She put it between her lips and lit up. Inhaled slowly, the smoke drifted between us for a second, then dissolved.

'Do you like the room now?' she said.

'Yes. Very much.'

'Actually you came just at the right moment,' she said. 'I want to move the bookcase over there. But I don't want to take it to pieces.'

'Shall we do it straight away?' I said.

'All right,' she said, putting the cigarette in the ashtray and getting up.

After we had finished she put on the same song she had played the previous evening. We looked at each other and she took a step towards me.

'You tried to kiss me yesterday,' she said with a smile.

'Yes,' I said. 'But you moved away.'

'Not intentionally, of course. Try again.'

We embraced.

We kissed.

I held her tight and whispered her name.

I would never let her go. Never ever.

I stayed at hers all night. We sought each other, were completely open with each other, everything was filled with light. I ached with happiness because I *had* her, she was *there*, all the time. All the time she was there, around me, and I ached with happiness, everything was filled with light.

Life can be so fantastic. Living can be so fantastic.

We played the same song again and again. We couldn't keep our hands off each other. At the break of dawn we slept a few hours, I had to work, but it was no good, I couldn't, not with her there, and we went outside to a telephone box. While I rang she waited outside, laughing, woollen gloves on her hands, hat on her head and a big scarf draped around her neck. No one had arrived yet, I spoke on the answer machine, said I was ill and couldn't come to work, rang off, went out, hugged her and walked beside her as close as it is possible to be.

'I've never skived before,' I said. 'Not once. I've got a bad conscience now.'

'Have you got regrets? You can go in and tell them you suddenly felt better.'

'Of course I haven't got any regrets!'

'Thought not!'

Of all the things to do, we went to the aquarium that day. It was January, not a soul was there, and we just ambled around, laughed when the penguins rushed towards us under the water, I took pictures of her with the camera I had rushed home to get, she talked at great length about what she would make for dinner, it had to be special, this was the first day we had been together. Because now we were together!

Wave after wave of happiness surged through me that day.

She made boeuf bourguignon, I stood watching, and she dipped a spoon in the saucepan, turned to me, put it in her mouth and rolled her eyes.

'Mmm! Fantastic!' she said.

'I love you,' I said.

She stiffened, glanced across at me, almost frightened. Turned, took the lid off the other saucepan and poked a little pin in a potato boiling in the bubbling water. The steam billowed out.

'Two more minutes,' she said.

I went over to her and wrapped my arms around her, kissed her neck. She turned her head and kissed me.

'I had a day like this when I was small,' she said. 'When everything was fantastic. Mum took me out. We were going to have a duck day. We saw Donald Duck in the cinema, we fed the ducks in the park, I got a Donald Duck comic and finally we went to a restaurant to eat duck.'

'Is that true? Wasn't that a rather barbaric end to the day?'

She laughed.

'I love duck. It's my favourite meal. And it was then too! But the best bit was that it was only mum and me. All day. I've thought about it many times today. I've been so happy.'

After we had eaten she discovered she hadn't got any coffee. She said she would just run down to the petrol station to buy a packet. I answered that she didn't need to, but she insisted and was off down the stairs at once.

I was uneasy. The day had been so endlessly happy. Now I was imagining she was going to die out there. I knew it was a delusion, that the chance of this happening was so minute it couldn't have been smaller, nonetheless I could see it in my mind's eye, the bus coming, not seeing her, the lorry driver glancing up at the sun visor for an instant, he had a packet of cigarettes wedged up there, and didn't see her as she ran across the road . . .

Ten minutes passed. Twenty minutes. Thirty.

Why wasn't she back?

Something *had* happened.

Oh no, please don't say it had. Don't say it had.

I was close to throwing up.

Then came the sound of footsteps on the stairs, then she came into the kitchen wearing her broadest smile and holding a red pack of Friele coffee in one hand.

'I met someone I hadn't seen for yonks,' she said, unwinding her scarf. 'Was I away long?'

'You won't get permission to be away from me so long again,' I said.

'Go with me next time then!'

When midnight approached we walked to my bedsit, Tonje had her things in her rucksack. From my door handle hung a plastic bag. I opened it and looked inside. A pack of coffee and a big bar of chocolate.

'Who gave you that?' Tonje said.

'No idea,' I said.

Most probably it was one of the girls at the radio station, but I couldn't say that. And I didn't know anyway.

'I can see lots of us are looking after you in Bergen,' she said.

'Looks like it,' I said.

We went in, she showered, came into the room with a towel swathed around her. In her hand she was holding a bottle of L'Oreal children's shampoo.

'Is that the shampoo you use?' I said, pulling her close.

'Yes, why? It's the best for my hair.'

'You're full of secrets,' I said.

'This is a rather small secret, isn't it?'

Yes, I'd been ill, I said at Student Radio three days later, it had been flu, a bit of a temperature, not so high but enough to stop me working. Tore dropped by in the morning and the mystery of the bag on the door handle was solved, it had been him.

'Heard you were ill, so I thought I would take you something to cheer you up.'

I didn't have the heart to tell him I hadn't been ill. But I told him about Tonje, I couldn't stop myself, I was so full of it.

That evening we went to the cinema and saw *True Romance*. Afterwards we were going to her place to make waffles, I had the waffle iron in a bag between my feet in the cinema, when we came out it struck me that I was the antithesis of what we had just seen. They had their bags full of weapons, I had a waffle iron. I couldn't stop laughing.

On Friday we went to Café Opera, it was the first time we had shown our faces to others, we crossed the street hand in hand, stood smooching in the queue as we waited to get in, there were lots of people from the radio station, I saw them talking about us, Tonje and Karl Ove are an item, and I didn't want to be there, I didn't want to drink, I just wanted to be with her. All the spaces we were in were transformed, they were enhanced with the most fantastic atmospheres, irrespective of their actual appearance, her flat, my bedsit, the small cafés we went to, the streets where we walked.

After two weeks I did something stupid. Yngve was going to a gig at Garage, he rang and wanted me to go with him, I said yes, I'll ask if Tonje wants to come too, is that OK?

It was OK. We walked there hand in hand, paid, had our hands stamped and went down to the cellar, Yngve was already there. I bought a round of beer for us, we sat at his table, made tentative conversation, they didn't know each other and for some reason I didn't have a lot to say.

The band began to play, we moved forward to see them, Yngve and Tonje chatted, he leaned over and spoke in her ear, she nodded and looked up at him, I was happy at first, they were the two most important people in my life, I bought another round, started feeling a bit drunk, squeezed Tonje's hand, she squeezed back but wasn't quite present, wasn't quite where she had been, and something in me turned, I became more and more upset, bought more beer, and when we sat down again I had nothing to say, all the happiness had left me, I drank and stared into the air, smiled at Tonje when she smiled at me, she didn't notice that anything had changed because Yngve was happy and chatty, and she was happy and chatty, one subject led to the next, they laughed and enjoyed each other's company.

They enjoyed each other's company. And why shouldn't they? Yngve was Yngve, charming, amusing, experienced, in all ways a better man than me.

She laughed at him. He laughed at her.

What was going on?

I felt heavy, I could barely move, I was all black inside. Every glance they exchanged was a stab in my chest.

He was better than me. She knew that now. Why should she have me when she could have him?

Yngve stood up to go to the toilet.

'What's the matter, Karl Ove?' she said.

'Nothing,' I said. 'Just thoughtful. So much has happened in the last few days.'

'It has,' she said. 'I'm so happy. You've got a nice brother.'

'Good,' I said.

But it wouldn't stop, it just carried on, they chatted as though I didn't exist, I drank and became more and more desperate. In the end, I thought, fuck all this living hell. To hell with all this fucking shite.

I got up and went upstairs to the toilet. I rested my head against the wall. I saw a smashed beer glass on the floor. I bent down, took a shard, looked at myself in the mirror. I ran the shard down my cheek. A red stripe appeared, some blood trickled off my chin. I wiped away the blood, no more came. I ran the shard down the other cheek, this time as hard as I could. I wiped the blood away with paper, threw it in the toilet, flushed, put the shard behind the waste bin on the floor, went out, sat down at their table.

For some insane reason it was as though what I had done gave me renewed energy. I bought another round of beer, Tonje held my hand and pressed it to her thigh as she kept on chatting, she may have sensed what was on my mind and wanted to comfort me. I drew her hand to me, drank half the bottle in one draught, suddenly I felt an urge to go to the toilet, suddenly all I wanted was to go there and I got up and went again, locked the cubicle door behind me, took the shard of glass and made two long cuts beside the previous ones, and then one across my chin, where the skin was softer and it hurt more. I wiped away the blood, a bit more came, I rinsed my face in cold water, dried it and went back to them.

I smiled at them and said I was so happy that they seemed to like each other. All three of us *skåled*.

'What's that on your cheek?' Yngve said. 'Did you have an accident shaving this morning or what?'

'Yes, something like that,' I said.

The room was dark, the place was heaving, and both Tonje and Yngve were drinking and preoccupied with each other, so neither of them saw what I was doing, apart from that once when Yngve made a comment. But he didn't have enough imagination to suppose that I was cutting myself. I did it for the whole of the rest of the evening, coldly and methodically, every part of my face was covered with cuts and stung more and more, in the end, sitting beside them and drinking, it hurt so much I could have screamed had it not been for the fact that, simultaneously, I enjoyed it. There was a joy in the pain, there was a joy in thinking that I could stand it, that I could stand everything, everything, everything.

'Let's go to Café Opera before they close, shall we?' Yngve said.

'Good idea,' Tonje said. I had already stood up, I put on my coat, wrapped the scarf around my neck ensuring that the lower part of my face was covered, pulled my hat over my forehead and went up the stairs ahead of them into Nygårdsgaten. The air was cold and good, it seemed to bite into the cuts as we walked. I was as drunk as I could be, but my gait was steady, my voice – if I could think of anything to say – absolutely as normal.

My mind was empty. Apart from the feeling of triumph at what I had done.

Tonje took my hand, Yngve slightly lowered his head as he walked, as always.

There was a queue in front of Café Opera. We joined it at the back.

Tonje looked at me.

She screamed.

'What's happened? What's happened? YOU'RE BLEEDING!' I walked across the street.

'What have you done, Karl Ove?' Yngve said, following me.

'I haven't done anything,' I said. 'Cut myself a little, that's all.'

Tonje caught up with us.

She was crying, she was hysterical.

'What have you done?' she said. 'What have you done?'

I started walking down the hill. Yngve followed me.

'I'm going home,' I said. 'Take care of Tonje for me.'

'Are you sure? You're not going to get up to anything else?'

'Leave me in peace, for Christ's sake. Take care of her.'

He stopped, I carried on without a backward glance, up the hill by the Pentecostal church, into Skottegaten and down to where my bedsit was. I unlocked the door, got into bed fully clothed, waiting for the doorbell to ring, she had to follow me, she had to, she had to leave Yngve and come down here, ring the bell, she had to, and I lay listening, and I heard nothing, and I fell into a deep sleep.

Even while I was asleep I knew I mustn't wake up, something awful was awaiting me, and for a long time I succeeded in staying there, in the zone beneath consciousness, until the well of sleep had run dry and I had to move on.

My face ached, I sat up, all that had happened returned. Now I have to take my life, I thought.

I had considered this option many times, but it was a game, I would never, not under any circumstances, do it, not even now.

Nevertheless, I hurt so much inside that this thought was my sole relief.

The pillow was bloodstained. I went into the hall, took down the CD I had hanging on a nail and studied my face.

I had ruined it. I looked like a monster.

If there were scars I would always look like this.

I showered. I lay down on the bed. I tried to imagine what it must have been like for Tonje. What she might be thinking now. Whether it was over or not.

This wasn't what she had anticipated when she got together with me.

I sat up and bowed my head.

Dear God, I said. Let this go well.

I went into the kitchen, looked down into the backyard.

I had to meet her.

Perhaps not today though.

Perhaps best to keep my distance today.

In the evening I was supposed to play with Yngve and Tore in the disused factory. I went down to Yngve's a few hours before.

'You look terrible,' he said when he saw me. 'Why did you do it?'

'I don't know. I just did. Got too drunk. Can I come in?'

'Course.'

We sat down in the sitting room. I couldn't meet his eyes, stared down like a dog.

'What were you thinking about?' he said. 'Not Tonje, that's for certain.'

'How was she?' I said. 'What happened?'

'I took her home.'

'What did she say?'

'Say? Nothing. She cried the whole way home. No, she did say she didn't understand anything. She said you'd both been so happy. She said she thought you'd been happy too.'

'That's true.'

'It didn't look like it, you know.'

'No.'

There was a silence.

'You've got to stop drinking. You *mustn't* drink any more.'

'No.'

Another silence.

'Do you think she'll leave me?'

'How should I know? And there's only one way to find out. You have to go and see her.'

'Not now. I can't.'

'But you have to.'

'Can you come with me? Well, not to see her, just walk with me. I don't want to be on my own.'

'OK. I need a walk anyway.'

Yngve talked about other things, normal things, as soon as we got outside. I said nothing, I was happy to let him talk, it helped. In case she wasn't at home I asked him to wait. I rang the bell, looked up, nothing, I went back to him. We went to the twenty-four-hour café that shift workers, lorry drivers and taxi drivers used, where the chance of bumping into anyone was minimal. When it started to get dark we picked up Yngve's guitar from home and went to meet Tore.

Tore stared at me, white-faced.

'What have you done?' he said. I had to look away; he was crying.

'It looks worse than it is,' I said. 'They're not deep. It's just a few scratches.'

'Jesus, Karl Ove,' he said.

'Come on, let's make some music,' I said.

After an hour in the freezing room, all wearing hats and scarves and thick jackets, the breath from our mouths like clouds, we left. Yngve had to go home, Tore and I chatted on the corner. He told me a good friend of his had once tried to commit suicide. He had gone into the forest and shot himself in the chest with a shotgun. He was found and he survived.

'I didn't know that,' I said.

'No, how could you?' he said. 'Don't you dare try anything like that.'

'But it wasn't anything like that, Tore. Not even close. I just got drunk and it seemed like a good idea.'

'Well, it wasn't.'

'No, in retrospect I can see that.'

We laughed and started to walk. Said goodbye at the corner by the Grieg Hall, he went uphill to his, I walked to Tonje's flat.

This time she opened the window. But she didn't come to the door, as she had done every time so far, instead she threw the key down to the street. I let myself in and went up. She had a visitor. Her best friend was there with her boyfriend.

I stopped in the doorway.

'I'm sorry,' I said. 'I look absolutely terrible. I got drunk and cut my face.'

Tonje couldn't look at me.

'We were just going,' the boyfriend said.

They got up, put on their coats and hats, said goodbye and left.

'I'm so sorry for what happened,' I said. 'Can you forgive me?'

'Yes,' she said. 'But I don't know if I can be in a relationship with you. I don't know if I want that.'

'No,' I said. 'I understand.'

'Have you ever done anything like this before?'

'No. Never. And I'll never do it again.'

'Why did you do it then?'

'I don't know. I have no idea. I just did it.'

I sat down on the chair, looked up at her, she was staring out of the window.

'Of course I want to be with you,' she said and turned. Tears were coursing down her cheeks.

One year later we moved in together. Right below the Science Building we found a two-room flat which we tried to fit out as best we could with the little furniture we had. The bedroom was at the back, it was as small as a cabin on a boat and we had no room for much more than the bed. Outside it was the sitting room, also small, and to make more room we partitioned it with a bookcase. On one side I had a little place to write; on the other we put the sofa, chairs and a table.

Here we had our first rows, this was the practical side of living together you had to get used to, but also our first real life together with each other, suddenly we shared everything. In this little flat we slept together, we ate together, listened to music or watched TV together, and I liked her always being there and always returning after she had been out. She was now a manager at Student Radio and worked long hours. I had started studying again, after a four-year break, I took history of art and was so ashamed at being much older than most of the other students that I never attempted any contact. When I wasn't attending lectures and studying slides of artworks I was poring over books in the reading room and devouring them like a maniac. After my national service had finished in March the year before I had joined Jon Olav and some of his friends in Vats, where a gigantic oil platform, Troll Oil, was being built, and they had got some work. I went along in the hope that more employees would be needed in due course, and after having slept on the sofa in an admin hut for three nights, of all the fortune hunters only Ben and I were left, and even though we, or at least I, had to be the worst qualified construction workers they had ever assessed, we got jobs in the end. I worked there for two and a half months, down one of the shafts, which when I started rose perhaps twenty metres above the sea, but by the time I finished were more than a hundred metres high. At the beginning I suffered from vertigo, but the shaft grew so slowly that I eventually became used to heights, and during my last days I moved around outside on scaffolding which consisted of three planks and an insubstantial rail a hundred metres above the water with a sense of pride and without feeling the slightest fear. I was a dreadful labourer, but the job was so simple that I still coped. We did twelve-hour shifts, either day or night, and walking around at night beneath the stars amid the drone of machinery, seeing the lights of the three other shafts in the middle of the fjord, surrounded by the vast darkness while the wind howled around our ears, was magical, it was as though we were alone in the universe, a little colony of humans on an illuminated vessel in the great nothing. Tonje was furious with me when I returned, not because I had left her for a job only a few weeks after we had got together, but because I hadn't called her once. I explained to her that in fact I had tried once, but she hadn't been at home and apart from that one attempt there hadn't been time. I slept, ate, worked, that was it. She didn't believe me, I realised, she thought this *meant* something, was a *sign* of something. Perhaps it was, I hadn't thought about her much, I had been fascinated by the fantastically exotic nature of the work, but what did that matter as long as I could look her in the eye and say I loved her and really *mean* it? Look her in the eye and say she was the only girl for me, now and for ever?

The money had poured into my account and I wanted more. The work at Troll Oil was finished for me, but I could carry on at Troll Gas, which they were building at Hanøytangen, just outside Bergen. I rang them, and when I said I had worked for Norwegian Contractors, the door was open. They were probably expecting an expert of some kind or other and must have been disappointed when they realised I was only a cack-handed academic, but I kept the job until the work was finished. It was heavy going and monotonous, but I liked it so much I started wondering about applying for other big projects, such as the new airport they were building in Østland that I had heard talk of in the breaks.

While I worked at Hanøytangen I had lived at home, and in my free weeks I was with Tonje all the time, down in my bedsit, where I woke up early every morning and dashed out to buy fresh shrimps, fresh bread, freshly ground coffee, fruit and juice for our breakfast, or up in her crooked windblown flat, which would be eternally illuminated by love's first glow.

One day I finally met Tonje's mother and her husband, who had been living in Africa for some months. Now they were back in their homeland for a few weeks, they had borrowed a house from some friends, we had dinner in the garden, I was nervous, but it all went fine, they were kind and curious to meet me, and as we were about to leave they said we should visit them in Africa, at Christmas perhaps. We accepted the invitation. We had the money and the time.

I tried to restart my writing, but it didn't flow, nothing came of it, nothing serious, at least not compared with what Kjartan or Espen wrote. I thought I would have to travel for a while, write full time, and as it was possible now to have unemployment benefit sent from Norway to EU countries I thought I might just as well live in one of them, such as England, and got in contact with Ole, an old student friend. He had married an English girl and lived in Norwich and said it would be a great town for me.

The morning I was due to leave I broke a mirror. Tonje said nothing, but I knew she was angry. In the taxi on the way to the boat I said I hadn't done it on purpose.

'It's not the mirror, you muppet,' she said, crying. 'It's the fact that you're leaving me.'

'Are you upset about that?'

'Didn't you know?'

'No. It's only for three months. And you're going to visit me. And then we're going to Africa afterwards, for Pete's sake. Besides I have to write something soon.'

'I know,' she said. 'I'm just going to miss you terribly. But I'll be fine. You don't have to feel sorry for me, if that's what you think.'

She smiled.

As I was going up the tubular gangway to the boat an hour later and turned and saw her standing there, and we waved to each other for a last time, I was thinking I loved her and wanted to marry her.

This was one of those thoughts that change everything. One of the thoughts that just appear and everything else slots into place. It was a thought with future and meaning. That was what I was missing and had missed for so long. A future and meaning.

Of course we could just live together and see what happened. Actually there was no less future and meaning in that. Tonje was Tonje whether we were married or living together. Nevertheless. No one else I knew, of my age, was married, marriage belonged to the generations before us, it was a nineteenth-century anachronism, created as a result of a rigid sexual morality and an equally rigid view of humanity, in which the woman was at home with the children and the man out at work, it was as antiquated as a top hat and a chamber pot, Esperanto and a paddleboat. The sensible option for modern men and women was not to marry, the sensible option for modern men and women was to live together, to respect each other for what we were, in ourselves, and not to be dependent on external institutions to live our lives. There was nothing to say we *had* to run around in jogging pants and watch videos in the evening, have a few kids, split up and have custody every second week. We could organise our lives in a dignified manner with the means our era had placed at our disposal. That was the sensible and appropriate option. But love wasn't sensible, love wasn't reasonable, love wasn't appropriate, it was more than that, had to be more than that, so for Christ's sake why not drag up marriage from the mists of time and impose its form on love again? Why not use the big words again? Why not solemnly state that we will love each other for ever? Why not insist on the profound solemnity it implied? Honour the lifelong obligation? Everything else we did was nonsense, irrespective of what we were doing, it was nonsense, no one believed in it, not really. No one I knew anyway. Life was a game, life was a pastime, and death, it didn't exist. We laughed at everything, even at death, and that wasn't completely wrong, laughter always had the last word, the skull's grin when one day we lay there with earth in our mouths.

But I wanted to believe, I did believe, I would believe.

I got my cabin key from reception, dropped off my suitcase and went up to the café. Everything lay open before me. I was going to a new country, to a town I had never seen, I had nowhere to live and no idea what was awaiting me.

I would be there for three months. Then we were going to Africa and there I would be free.

It was perfect.

The boat slid out. Tonje would probably be on her way home now, I thought and went up on deck to see if I could catch a glimpse of her. But we were already quite far away, it was impossible to identify any of the black figures walking along Bryggen from this distance.

The sky was grey, the water we steadily made our way through, black. I held the railing and gazed towards Sandviken. The old idea of leaving everything returned for a brief instant. The worst of it was that it would be all right. I had always known that I could turn my back on everything and just leave, with no regrets. I could also leave Tonje. I didn't miss her when she wasn't there. I didn't miss anyone and never had done. I never missed mum, I never missed Yngve. I never missed Espen, I never missed Tore. I hadn't missed Gunvor when we had been a couple, and I didn't miss Tonje now. I knew I would wander through the streets of Norwich, sit in lodgings somewhere writing, perhaps go out for a drink with Ole, and I wouldn't miss her. I would think about her now and then, with warmth but not with longing. This was a flaw in me, a shortcoming I had, a coldness in my heart. If I got close to people I could sense what they wanted and subordinate myself to that. If Gunvor had felt I was too distant from her I sensed that feeling and tried to meet it halfway. Not for my sake but for hers. If I said something Espen considered stupid I was ashamed and tried to make amends, his assessment of me was paramount. Couldn't I be distant and stand firm? Couldn't I be stupid and stand firm?

No, not there, not in front of them.

But when I was alone it meant nothing.

This coldness in my heart was terrible, sometimes I thought I wasn't human, I was a Dracula who lived off other people's emotions but had none myself. My love affairs, what else were they but a mirror? What else were they but my own feelings?

What I felt for Tonje was genuine, however, and since a genuine feeling was more precious to me than anything else, I had to commit everything to that.

But I didn't miss her.

All day and all evening I sat reading and jotting down ideas and thoughts in my notebook. It was now or never. I couldn't be someone who wrote but wasn't published for much longer, both for purely practical reasons – one, I already lagged several years behind those I had started studying with and, two, I had to make a living – and for reasons of dignity. A twenty-year-old writing full time to become a writer is simply charming; a twenty-five-year-old doing the same is a loser.

A short story like Joyce's The Dead, *I wrote in my notebook. A family gathering in which all the characters represent stages of life, childhood, adolescence, middle age, the declining years, but are at the same time themselves, idiosyncratic people, in the middle of life. Such a gathering, with all its conflicts, when the 1940s are present, the 1960s are present, like pockets in the here and now, the complexity, without any history, then the gathering disperses and the little nuclear family is on its way home. In the back of the car the two children, the elder one is asleep, the younger awake with closed eyes listening to his parents chatting about something dreadful. Either from the past, something important, or something that is going to happen. It is snowing. They arrive, the house is dark and still, they go in . . . and then? What's going to happen now? What is big enough to build on everything that has gone before?*

I closed my notebook and immersed myself in *Ulverton* by Adam Thorpe. It had been translated by Svein Jarvoll and was about a fictional place in rural England, every chapter recreated a different epoch, the first the 1600s, the last our century. The chapters were written in a variety of forms and dialects. Jarvoll had chosen the Skjåk dialect for one, and it was strange how well it fitted: the gates in the fences that were opened for riders to pass through, the fields and the trees, the low crumbling houses, it all fitted the Skjåk dialect. Perhaps in a way because dialects grew from the countryside around them, the style of speaking originated just there, in that particular valley, where the pronunciation of one word, for example, had come into existence with the great oak tree which was now almost a thousand years old, the pronunciation of another with the terrain being cleared and the ancient stone wall built. In other areas there were other words and other oak trees, fields and stone walls.

Time flowed through this novel, whirled through human lives. The appeal was enormous.

Perhaps I was attracted towards it so much because I had grown up in a place where there was only the present day and the past was in books?

I bought a beer, wrote *1600s* in my notebook, looked at my watch, it would soon be twelve, drank up and went to bed.

The cabin was deep in the bowels of the boat, just under the engine room. This made me think about grandad, he always used to book a cabin above the waterline. If he couldn't, he would sleep in a recliner. I wasn't bothered by such concerns, the ship could sink while I was asleep for all I cared.

I undressed, read a few pages of *Ulverton*, turned off the light and fell asleep. I awoke in the darkness a few hours later from the most fantastic dream I'd ever had.

I sat up and laughed to myself.

I had been walking down the road outside our house in Tybak-ken. Suddenly there was a roar from above the earth. The noise was deafening, I knew there had never been such a roar before, it rolled across the sky like thunder, though infinitely louder.

It was God's voice.

I stopped and looked at the sky.

And then I was raised up!

I was raised up to the sky!

What a feeling it was. The roar, the majesty of God's presence and then the incredible moment when I was raised up. It was a moment of peace and perfection, joy and happiness.

I lay down again.

OK, so it was only a dream. But the feeling, that was real. I had really felt it. What a shame I had been asleep when I felt it, but now I knew it existed anyway, I thought, closed my eyes and dived into sleep, hoping something even more fantastic was in store for me.

When I was seven we went to England on holiday, my memories of it were the best I had of my childhood, and they all returned when, next afternoon, I stood holding the railing and gazing at the strip of land that had appeared in the distance. It was England. We passed some fishing boats on our way in, seagulls circled in the air above them, before us the land seemed to sink as we approached, I saw more and more of it until we entered what was like a canal and actually found ourselves in its middle. Run-down warehouses and factory buildings on either side with large areas of rubbish-filled wasteland between them.

The grass was yellow, the sky grey, and if anything at all glowed it was the brickwork of the buildings, but it was with rust, the colour of perishability and decay. Oh, that filled my soul, this was England; the buildings we saw probably originated from the first period of industrialisation, I loved the empire that had declined but was still proud, and those who grew up in this dismal

greyness captivated us all, first the 60s generation, pop, the Beatles and the Kinks, then the 70s heavy rock, all the evil bands
from the metal-working towns in the Midlands, filthy rich in
their twenties, then punk in the mountains of uncollected rubbish in 1976, then post-punk and goth rock, the enormous seriousness they brought to their music, and then, now, Madchester,
raves, colours and beat. England, I loved England, everything
about England. The football, what more could you want than a
tired old stadium from the beginning of the twentieth century
filled with ten to twelve thousand grim-faced fiery working-class
men, the mist over the heavy muddy pitch and tackles so hard
they echoed between the advertising hoardings? The dark houses
with wall-to-wall carpets everywhere, even on the stairs and in
pubs.

When the boat docked I got on one of the double-decker buses
going to the town centre. The cries of newspaper vendors met me
first as I alighted. The air was noticeably much warmer than it
had been in Bergen, I was in another country again, everything
was slightly unfamiliar. I walked to the train station and bought a
ticket to Norwich, waited in a café there for a couple of hours and
boarded the train.

In Norwich I took a taxi to the University of East Anglia, Ole had
said they rented rooms there before term started, which was correct, I was allocated one, I dropped off my luggage and walked
down to the student bar I had noticed when I arrived. I sat alone
for a couple of hours drinking and watching the students and trying to pretend I belonged there. The following day I went into
town. It was small, surrounded by the remnants of a medieval
wall, full of small churches used now for a multitude of purposes,
in one I saw a pub and in another a sports shop. There were rivers with houseboats moored to the banks and there was a beautiful towering medieval cathedral. I bought a loaf of bread and

some salami slices and sat down in a field nearby. Some boys were playing rugby in front of me, schoolboys, I assumed. The sight of their kit and the exotic game evoked strange melancholy feelings in me, I was reminded of Victorian times, the empire, boarding schools, factories, the colonies, of which these young boys were a part. It was their history and could not be mine.

I bought two local newspapers and sat in a pub beside the river, ordered a cider and read through the accommodation ads, circled three which might be possibilities.

The first only rented to students, I was stupid enough to say I was unemployed and she just put down the phone. The second was more promising. She had a room in town, she said, but they lived somewhere else, could I go there?

Yes, I could. I jotted down the address, bought some chewing gum so I didn't smell of alcohol and got into a taxi.

A man in ragged clothes with a beard and earrings opened the door, shook my hand, said his name was Jim, called his wife, who came out and said hello. You come with me, he said, passing me a pisspot-type helmet. His motorbike was in the garden. It had a sidecar, which I was supposed to get into. The sidecar was a bathtub, which he had welded on. He pushed the vehicle forward, gestured, take a seat. I clambered in and reluctantly sat down. He started up and we moved into the road and headed for the city centre. People on the pavements and in cars stared at me. A Norwegian measuring almost two metres was sitting in a bathtub wearing a pisspot and weaving through the streets of Norwich.

The house was in a working-class district. A long row of identical brick buildings on either side up a gentle incline. He unlocked the door, I followed him in. First there was a staircase, carpeted, leading up to two rooms, of which I would have one. A bed, a wardrobe, a chair and a desk, that was it.

He asked me what I thought.

'It's brilliant,' I said. 'I'll take it.'

We went back down, into the sitting room. It was full of objects from floor to ceiling. All sorts of junk, from old car parts to stuffed birds. He said he was a collector.

This was not the only surprise. In a huge aquarium on the part of the floor that wasn't yet occupied was a boa constrictor.

He said that usually he would have let me hold it, but it was too hungry now.

I checked his expression to see if he was joking.

He was utterly serious.

Behind the sitting room there was a little kitchen, and behind that a little bathroom with a tub.

'It's brilliant,' I repeated, paid him two months' rent as a deposit, he showed me how the gas oven worked, said I could use anything there and he would pop by in the next few days to feed the snake.

Then he went, and I was left with the boa constrictor. It slowly coiled round the aquarium and nestled up to the glass. I was trembling as I watched and felt more and more nauseous. Even while I was unpacking upstairs in my room my body trembled with unease, the thought of it downstairs preoccupied my mind to the exclusion of everything else, also when I was asleep, I had nightmare after nightmare about snakes of all shapes and sizes.

Ole had written to say he would be in Norway when I arrived, so my immediate world during the first few days was the small carpeted room, which I left in the morning, to wander around town, and returned to in the afternoon. The noises outside were unfamiliar, children playing, shouting and screaming in English, and I never really got used to the long row of dirty terraced houses I faced, it was as though I was in an English TV series, meanwhile the snake downstairs was getting hungrier and hungrier. Sometimes it reared up and banged its head hard on the glass. A chill ran though me. But I was also fascinated, I would sit on the floor by the aquarium and closely scrutinise this outlandish creature with which I shared my house.

At the end of the week the landlord returned. He shouted for me to come, this I had to see.

He took out some mice he had in a freezer box. On the same shelf that I had put my sausages, I noticed. He warmed the mice lightly in the oven, lying on their backs with their legs sticking up. When finally they had thawed – meanwhile he had been sitting and smoking his pipe and showing me a Norwegian tobacco blend, Eventyr, from the 70s he had in his heap of junk, which my dad had smoked when I was a boy – he took one mouse by the tail, pushed the top of the aquarium to the side, tapped on the glass a few times to wake the sleeping snake and then dangled the mouse to and fro. The snake, sleepy and lethargic, slowly raised its head and then, so quickly I recoiled, launched itself at the mouse. It was given four mice. For the next four days it lay still in the aquarium with four large bulges in its otherwise slim body.

Once the world consisted of creatures like this one, deeply primitive, they slithered across the ground or thundered along on their huge-clawed feet. What was life like when that was all there was? When we knew that once there had been nothing else, and actually it was still like that? Just a body and food and light and death?

One thing I had learned when I was working at the first institution: life wasn't modern. All the variants, all the deformities, all the freaks of nature, all the mental disabilities, all the insanity, all the injuries, all the illnesses, they still existed, they were as present now as they had been in the Middle Ages, but we had hidden them, we had put them in enormous buildings in the forest, created special camps for them, consistently kept them out of sight so as to give the impression the world was hale and hearty, that that was how the world and life were, but they weren't, life was also grotesque and distorted, sick and crooked, undignified and humiliated. The human race was full of fools, idiots and freaks, either they were born like this or they became like this, but they were no longer on the streets, they no longer ran around frightening the wits out of people, they were in civilisation's shadow or night.

That was the truth.

The snake's life in the aquarium was another truth.

Once upon a time there were no creatures on earth with eyes. Then eyes developed.

After a few days in the house I realised I could forget about writing. I tried but to no avail, what could I write about? Who did I think I was, believing I could create something which would interest anyone apart from my mother and my girlfriend?

Instead I wrote letters. To Espen, to Tore, to Yngve, to mum, to Tonje. I described my days in detail, from the postman whistling the Internationale as he walked past in the morning, everything I saw on my many long walks through the town to the strange experiences I had at the Job Centre, all the poverty and misery revealed there, the seriousness of life that contrasted so starkly with my own, since nothing was at stake for me, the unemployment benefit I received was probably ten times higher than theirs, and actually just a nonsense, something I had applied for in order to create time to write. The welfare officer I was assigned to must have been suspicious, at any rate he raised his voice with me now and again and threatened to withdraw all payments if I couldn't provide evidence soon that I was actually looking for work in Norwich.

Ole returned from Norway, I visited him and his wife in their flat. It was tiny and she very English. Ole was exactly as I remembered him, self-effacingly nice yet intense. He was still studying his subjects but never took any exams, he was paralysed by fear; however much he knew, however brilliant he was, he couldn't make himself sit an exam. We did the rounds of all the second-hand bookshops, his favourite writer was Samuel Johnson, whom he occasionally translated on his own, for fun, and Boswell, and still Beckett, as five years ago.

I liked him a lot. But that didn't justify my stay here. I *had* to write. But what? Five days in succession could pass without me saying a word to anyone. Everything was unfamiliar, the houses, the people, the shops, the countryside, no one needed me, no one cared about me, and that was perfect, that was exactly how I wanted it, just walking around and looking, and looking at everything in existence without it looking back.

But to what end? And with what justification? What was the point of looking if you couldn't write about what you saw? What was the point of experiencing anything at all if you couldn't write about what you had experienced?

I got drunk with Ole a few times, he always went back home when the pubs closed, I didn't want to, and he would accompany me to one of the nightclubs, say bye outside, and I would go in and continue drinking on my own, without talking to a soul. At four I would stagger home and to bed. Sleep in the next day, full of angst, listen to Radio 1, read all the major newspapers, that took all day, and then I would go back to bed.

Supergrass's debut single was played around the clock. I bought it. Elastica were in Norwich, I went to see them, drunk and on my own. With the money I received from Norway I bought second-hand 70s tracksuit jackets, shoes, jeans, records and books. Caught the bus to London in the morning, trudged around the Tottenham Court Road area all day and came back in the evening.

After I had lived like this for two and a half months, Tonje came to visit me. We went to London, bought tickets to Johannesburg and Maputo and caught the plane home together to Bergen.

In Africa I asked her if she would marry me.

She said yes, I will.

*

Back in Bergen, in the new flat, I realised I couldn't go on like this any more. We were getting married in a few months and I couldn't let Tonje marry an idiot who thought he could be a writer, someone who was throwing his life away, I prized her too highly for that, so I went out and bought the most important art history books, borrowed the rest from the university library and set about reading them.

Tore, who was still studying literature, writing a dissertation about Proust and his name, told me that an editor in Oslo had rung him, he had read Tore's reviews in *Morgenbladet* and wondered whether he would like to work as a reader for him. Tore said he would, had also told him he was a writer, and the editor, whose name was Geir Gulliksen, wanted to read what he had done.

I had also written reviews in *Morgenbladet*. Indeed, it had been me who got Tore into *Morgenbladet*. So why hadn't Geir Gulliksen rung *me*?

But then something happened for me too. I received an invitation in the post to contribute to an anthology. The Writing Academy had some anniversary or other and they were looking for contributions from alumni. I sent them *Zoom*. It wasn't a competition, the anthology was open only to alumni and I hadn't even considered the possibility of a rejection. But I was rejected. They didn't want it.

I had reacted to every other rejection with composure, they were expected, all of them. But this one crushed me. I was completely demoralised for several weeks and this led to me taking the final decision to stop writing. It was simply too humiliating. I was twenty-six years old, I was getting married, I could no longer live with the dream.

Some weeks later I went up to Tore's, we were going to Verftet to practise with the new band. It consisted of Hans and Knut Olav from Kafkatrakterne plus Tore and me. Lemen, we were called, the hyperactive Norway lemming, after Tore, his shaven head and inexhaustible energy.

We walked downhill to the centre. It was the beginning of March, one o'clock in the afternoon, the streets were dry and filled with that delicate pale spring light that came gradually and imperceptibly after the winter's endless succession of damp grey dark days.

Tore looked at me.

'I've got some good news,' he said.

'Oh?' I said, fearing the worst.

'My manuscript has been accepted. It's coming out this autumn! I'm going to make my debut!'

'Is that true? But that's fantastic, Tore,' I said.

All the energy I had drained away. I walked beside him, black to the core inside. It was so unjust. It was so bloody unjust. Why should *he*, *four* years younger than me, have the talent and not me? I had long reconciled myself to the fact that Espen had the talent, his debut was no surprise, it made sense. But *Tore*? And so young?

Shit.

Tore was beaming like a sun.

'"This has to be published," Gulliksen said. 'I sat up all night thinking of titles. I've got a list of them here. Would you like to see?'

He took a folded sheet of paper from his inside pocket and passed it to me. I read as we walked.

Julian's Calendar
Once as Invisible as Nausea
Snowflake
Sleeping Tangle
A Liberated Blush
A Tangled Second
For Shame's Sake
Once and for All

'*Julian's Calendar*,' I said. 'Without any doubt.'

'I like *Sleeping Tangle*,' Tore said.

'No, it's too cryptic. What is a sleeping tangle?'

'It's a mood, a problem that exists but hasn't had any impact as yet. There's something passive about it. Or abandoned. Above all, though, it creates a mood.'

'*Julian's Calendar*,' I said, giving him the sheet of paper. He put it back in his inside pocket.

'We'll see,' he said. 'Actually I'll soon have finished. Only have to polish it now.'

'Would you like me to read it?' I said.

'Not yet. But if you wouldn't mind reading the final version.'

I had already read a lot of his work and this much I knew: I couldn't help him. It was much better than anything I had written. The most disturbing feature of it was that he hadn't just taken a narrative form and filled it with what he had learned it should be filled with, as one might be tempted to think would be the case with a debutant who was only twenty-two. He had taken a form, that was true, but the whole project, everything he wrote about, was in some unclear but obvious way connected with himself, his very essence, all the fascinations he had and was almost unaware of, and he could therefore write about with the unfettered joy of discovery.

'Congratulations,' I said. 'That's absolutely fantastic news.'

'Yes, it bloody is,' he said. 'At long last! Seventeen sodding rejections it took. But now I'm there.'

At that time we practised a lot, the band was going to play at the new Studentkvarteret in the spring and we hadn't been together that long, there was still a lot to work on. Tore, our singer, had written half of the songs, Knut Olav, who played the guitar, the other half, apart from one, which Hans, now the bass player, had written. Knut Olav was prodigiously talented, he played all the instruments and composed fantastic pop songs and could have gone far if he'd had better musicians around him. But he wouldn't hear of it. As a drummer, he was perhaps a thousand times better than me, but he put up with me slowing and accelerating the tempo of his songs, and when he arranged them all he had in his head was something unfussy. With Tore on vocals as well, utterly undaunted by his high profile as he was, brazen even, everything worked out fine.

There was nothing I liked more than playing with them and then going out afterwards. Maybe ringing Tonje and getting her to come along. All while the light was growing and the leaves were coming out on the trees.

May 19 was the day we were playing at Kvarteret. I turned up a few hours before the sound check, Tore met me at the door, I could see at once that something had happened.

'Have you heard?' he said.

'Heard what?'

'Tor Ulven's dead.'

'Dead? Is that true?'

'Yes. Geir Gulliksen rang to tell me.'

'But he was young.'

'Yes. And Norway's best writer.'

'Yes. Oh Jesus. How awful.'

We went into the café and discussed the news further. Both Tore and I considered Ulven quite different from and much better than the rest of Norwegian literature. I thought of Espen, it had been him who had introduced me to Ulven and he had read him more intensely than anyone I knew.

Hans and Knut Olav came, we drifted into the auditorium, did the sound check and gradually stage fright took over, half an hour before we went on I was on the point of throwing up, but as usual the fear vanished the moment we appeared and played the first bars.

Afterwards we sat backstage drinking beer and chatting about the performance – what were you actually doing there, I completely lost it there and had no idea where we were – and someone poked a head in and said the crown prince had been in the audience, we laughed, but Tore wasn't with us, he was in shock at

Ulven's sudden death, I could see it in his face, the brief moments of total absence that punctuated his otherwise sociable persona. If anyone had inspired him in the writing of his book it had been Ulven. Nonetheless, we moved on, went to Garage, and when it closed I walked home with Tonje, the night was still, the streets spring-light beneath the mountains and the sky with its twinkling stars.

We spent more and more time discussing the wedding and planning it. It would be at her home in Molde, she wanted it on the island of Hjertøya, and so it would be, I wanted it as small as possible, only the family, she agreed to that as long as we had a party afterwards with everyone we knew.

I rang dad and told him I was getting married. Still he had a hold over me, still not a day passed without my thinking about him, and I had long dreaded this conversation. He had separated from his wife and moved to Østland, but I managed to track him down at grandma's.

'I've got some good news, Dad,' I said.

'Oh yes,' he said.

'I'm getting married.'

'Uhuh. Bit young, aren't you?'

'No, I want this. You were only twenty when you got married.'

'Different times. I had to, you know.'

'We're getting married in Molde this summer. I'd like you to come of course.'

'I can do that. Grandma and I will drive up, I imagine. What's the name of the girl you're marrying?'

'Tonje.'

'Ah, so it's Tonje, is it. OK, that's good. But now I have to be off.'

'All right. Bye.'

'Bye, Karl Ove.'

*

The thought of him coming was a concern for me, not only because of his drinking but also the fact that I would see him with mum for the first time since I was sixteen. On the other hand, I wanted him to be present. I was getting married, he was my father, it was important. It was of less concern that Tonje's family would see the state he was in and he might cause a rumpus.

It was also important that Tonje should meet him. I had told her a lot, but meeting him was quite another matter. What I had told her would have a different meaning then.

A few days later Tore said he was moving to Oslo, he wanted to be there when the book came out, that was where it was all happening. Inger would go with him of course, otherwise he wouldn't have gone. Tore couldn't be alone.

'But what about the band?' I said. 'It's finally beginning to click. You don't need to move just because you're making your debut, surely!'

'We've lived in Bergen for so long now,' he said. 'It feels as if the town has nothing left to offer.'

'You don't say!' I said. 'I've lived here for seven bloody years!'

'Anyone would think you'd been forced to live here the way you're talking. Take Tonje and move to Oslo as well.'

'I'll never do that. You can say what you like about Bergen, and perhaps not a lot happens here, but at least it's not the centre.'

'No, because the centre's where it all happens!'

'Yes, and I don't want to be there.'

'Oh, so you'd rather sit on the margins as the unrecognised genius?'

'Genius? Do me a favour. You go. The cemetery's full of irreplaceable people, as Einar Førde once said.'

'What's up with you today?'

'I mean what I said. We've got something good going with Lemen.'

Tore threw up his arms.

'*C'est la vie*,' he said. 'I can't sit on my hands here just because you want me to.'

'No, basically you're right about that.'

He handed in his Proust dissertation, gave me his manuscript, which was theoretically ready to be published, I read it, made a few comments which he accepted with gratitude, albeit without acquiescing to them, and one day I saw them off, Tore and Inger, on their way to their new flat in Oslo. I often crossed the mountains to visit Espen, now I could visit Tore as well. My life was here, with Tonje, in Bergen.

Three weeks before the wedding, dad rang. He said he couldn't come after all. Grandma was poorly, he said, it was a long trip, he couldn't risk her health.

'So I can't make it, Karl Ove,' he said.

'But I'm getting *married*!'

'I can't make it, you have to understand that. Grandma's fragile and . . . Well, we can't drive all the way up to Molde now.'

'You're my father!' I said. 'I'm your son! I'm getting married. You *can't* say no.'

I started crying.

'Yes, I can,' he said. 'I'm not coming, and that's it.'

'Then you're just like your own parents,' I said. 'They didn't go to your wedding either. Not to your first, nor to your second. Are you going to do the same to me?'

'Well, I can't be bothered to listen to this,' he said and put down the phone.

I cried as I had never cried before, completely overcome by my feelings, I stood in the middle of the floor, bent double, as wave after wave of sobs racked my body. I couldn't understand it, I hadn't realised how important it was for me that he come to the wedding, I'd had no idea, but it certainly had been, I concluded, put on my sunglasses and went to town to walk it off. I cried all the way to the bus station, it was sunny and the streets were crowded with people, I felt excluded from them, I was deep inside myself, and when I had calmed down and was sitting in the café at Hotel Terminus, I understood nothing. Thinking coldly and calmly, I was glad he wouldn't be there. I had been worried about it actually, in my heart of hearts I hadn't wanted him there, neither at my wedding nor in my life. Then he said he wasn't coming to the wedding and I broke down.

Understand that if you can, I thought, worn down by all the crying, in the middle of that beautiful, spacious, almost empty, 1920s café, with a little pot of coffee on the table in front of me, from whose spout at that very moment a droplet fell onto the white cloth, which greedily absorbed it.

We went to Molde a few days later. Even if the wedding wasn't to be a big affair there was still a lot to be done. Boats to and from the island had to be arranged, the food had to be organised and all the practical details connected with it, I had to write a speech and teach myself to waltz, the two events I dreaded most. I wrapped my arms around a cushion and tried to practise the steps on the sitting-room floor after the others had gone to bed, to the music of Evert Taube, and I was reminded of grandad: it takes all sorts to make a world. Mum had bought my suit, one day we went out in Bergen and found one in olive green. Tonje's dress, which she loved, was a plain creamy yellow.

The day came, we went down to the function room where the ceremony would take place, I was nervous and thought I had everything under control, but when I met Mård and Ingunn outside and they congratulated me I realised this was not the case, I had nothing under control, because I suddenly started crying. I didn't understand why, but I summoned all the willpower at my disposal to suppress it.

When we said 'I do' to each other we both had tears in our eyes. Afterwards the whole company walked down to the harbour, where the boat was waiting. People snapped photos, the food was served, I made a speech, Yngve, who was my best man, made a speech, Tonje's father made a speech and mum made a speech. The sun shone, we danced on a terrace outside the reception room, I was both pleased and sad because Tonje was happy and I wasn't worthy of her.

We went for our honeymoon to England, I insisted on this, she had suggested a hotel by a beach in a hot country, where everything was easy. I wouldn't have that, so there we were on a bus from London to Cornwall, where I had been as a six-year-old, although I recognised nothing at all. For a week we hopped from village to village along the coast, living in small dirty hotel rooms, apart from one, which was magnificent and as romantic as Tonje had hoped, with a terrace and a view across the sea, champagne waiting for us when we arrived, walks along the wild cliffs, dinner in the restaurant, me in a suit, her in a dress, we were, after all, newly-weds, which the waiters knew, they were very attentive, and I sat blushing and squirming, uncomfortable with all the attention, uncomfortable in the suit, I looked like an idiot, unable to escape the little picture and rise to the bigger one. Tonje, cool and beautiful, didn't understand this side of me, but she would.

Back home, we moved into a new flat, in Sandviken, opposite the church, consisting of a long combined kitchen and sitting room, as well as a bedroom, and, unlike all the other bedsits and flats I had lived in over the last seven years, the building was in good condition. We couldn't afford it, but we rented it anyway. I was happy there, I especially liked the view of the church and the trees surrounding it.

At the end of August we went up to mum's, where Yngve and I painted the house. Kjartan dropped by, he had written something, he said, but didn't have much hope, he had been refused too often for that, he was going to send his manuscript to the publishing house Oktober, he reckoned. What did I think?

Send it, send it, it's excellent.

Kjartan was a writer. Espen was a writer. Tore was a writer. But I wasn't, I was a student, I had come to terms with that and I used every ounce of strength I had to study. I went up to the reading room early in the morning, followed the courses of lectures, sat in the reading room until late at night. I liked the subject, especially the lectures, since so many of them were spent viewing slides of the greatest buildings, sculptures and paintings in existence. All the material I had found difficult and impenetrable before, when as a twenty-year-old I had made a stab at hard-core theory, was now easily comprehensible, and this was strange as I hadn't tackled any theory since, however I didn't waste any time pondering this, I was there to read, and read I did.

Tore's book came out, it received good reviews, he was invited to join *Vagant*, where two of my friends worked now. Tonje continued at the radio station, at weekends we visited her mother or her brother's family, unless it was just us two, either at home in front of the TV or out with friends. Life had settled down, it was good and, provided that I could pass the two subjects I needed and make a start on my main course, everything to do with job and career would sort itself out. In addition, I was also making a last desperate attempt to write again. This was against my better judgement, I no longer believed I could do it, I was running on pure self-will. No more short stories, now it was to be a novel. It was about the slave ship *Fredensborg*, which had sunk off the island of Tromøya some time in the eighteenth century, and it was discovered when I was a boy, by the head teacher of my school among others. I had always carried this story within me, had always been fascinated by it, not least when I saw objects from the ship exhibited at the Aust-Agder Museum, the world and history coincided in a point near where

I grew up, and now I was going to write about it. Progress was slow, there was so much I didn't know, such as daily life on board a sailing vessel of almost three hundred years ago, I knew nothing about that, had no idea what they did or what tools they used or what they were called, only things like the sails and the masts, and that meant I had no freedom at all. I could describe the sea and the sky, but that wasn't much on which to base a novel. Their thoughts? Yes, but what did a sailor think in the eighteenth century?

I didn't give up, I fought on, borrowed books from the university library, wrote a sentence or two after I returned from the reading room in the evening and for a few hours on Sunday mornings, it wasn't good, but sooner or later it had to click for me too, as it had done for Kjartan: Oktober had accepted his collection of poetry, it would be published next autumn. After twenty years of writing poems he was finally where he wanted to be and I was ecstatic on his behalf because he had resigned from his job, he had been forced to stop his studies, so writing was all he had left.

Late that autumn I got a phone call from Yngve in Balestrand, Gunnar had rung him, dad had gone missing.

'Gone missing?'

'Yes. He's not at work, not in the flat, not with grandma or Erling.'

'Could he have caught a plane and headed south?'

'Doubtful. Something's probably happened to him. The police are searching for him. He's been reported missing.'

'Really? Do you think he's dead?'

'No.'

A few days later he rang again.

'Dad's been found.'

'Oh? Where?'

'In a hospital. He's paralysed. Can't walk.'

'You're joking. Are you telling me the truth?'

'Yes, that's what I've been told. But it's unlikely to be permanent. It's alcohol-related in some way or other.'

'What'll happen now?'

'He'll be admitted to a detox clinic.'

I rang mum and told her. She asked me for the name of the clinic, I said I didn't know, but Yngve probably did.

'What are you going to do?'

'I was thinking of sending him my love.'

The exam came, I wrote about Greek statues, it went well, at the oral they told me it didn't matter what I said, they couldn't give me a better grade than the one I already had. I continued with history of art and took philosophical aesthetics on the side, read Kant's *Critique of Pure Reason* all Easter, Tonje applied for a radio job in Volda, Tore rang to say he would be editing an anthology and wanted a text from me. But I haven't got anything, I said. Then you'll have to write something new, he said. You're doing this. I perused the little I had, there was nothing of any value apart perhaps from a passage in the novel, which was almost finished now. *Fredensborg* is sailing between the islands of Mærdø and Tromøya on this day in the eighteenth century, from Copenhagen bound for Africa to collect slaves, one of the crew stares over at the shore, there is a farm, a woman is drawing water from a well in a bucket, he looks at the house, which is derelict. Flies are buzzing around her. In the house a man lies in a coma, he is sleeping more and more hours in the day, everything is crumbling around him, until at last sleep encloses him, encapsulates him, and she, after fighting against everything, is set free. I turned the text into a short story, entitled it *Sleep* and sent it to him.

In late spring Eivind Røssaak phoned, he had been appointed the culture editor of *Klassekampen* and enquired whether I would like to review books for him. I said yes. The history of art exam came,

I wrote fifty pages about the concept of mimesis, a whole booklet, which I handed into the university porters before going home. The grades I was awarded were obscenely good and more and more I was reconciling myself to the idea that I was going to be an academic.

Tonje had been accepted in Volda and was going to move up there while I would stay in Bergen, start on my main course and join her for her last year. Tore had accepted my piece, the anthology had come out to a deafening silence, but it did do some good, Geir Gulliksen rang one day and asked if I would be in Oslo in the near future, if so, he would like me to drop in on him so that we could talk about me and my writing.

In fact I would be, I lied, and we arranged to meet.

In Oslo I stayed with Espen, as always. Now Tore was in Oslo too, the three of us met up, cycled over to see Vigeland's morbid chapel in the morning and in the evening met again to go for dinner. It was a *Vagant* dinner, everyone who worked on the journal was there, Kristine Næss, Ingvild Burkey, Henning Hagerup, Bjørn Aagenæs, Espen, Tore – and then me. They had asked me to interview Rune Christiansen, it was to take place the following day, so I was a kind of associate member of the editorial team for a weekend. The dinner was at Kristine Næss's place, we sat around a small table, it was all nice and intimate, my two best friends were there, I was inside the circle, I was where I wanted to be, but my respect for them was too great, I didn't dare say anything, I just listened. Henning Hagerup, the best critic of his generation, sat next to me and asked me one or two polite questions, and I *didn't answer*. I said nothing, just looked down and nodded, glanced up at him, he smiled at me and turned away. We ate, the conversation was lively, but I was mute. I didn't dare say anything. In a big room with a lot of people this wouldn't have mattered because no one would have noticed, but here, where there were so few of

us, it stood out. The longer I remained quiet, the more conspicuous it became, and the more conspicuous it became, the more
impossible it was to say anything. I cursed myself, tied myself in
knots inside, couldn't stop, listened to what was said, formulated
something I could say, but didn't, held back, held everything back.
An hour passed, two hours passed, three hours passed. We had
been sitting there for three hours and I hadn't said a single word.
The atmosphere was warming up, beer and wine and cognac were
on the table. Four hours passed, five hours passed, I hadn't said a
word. Then another problem presented itself. Soon I would have
to go, but how could I do that, after five hours I couldn't just get up
and say thank you for everything, it's been nice, I'm afraid I have
to go, that would be impossible. Nor could I leave without saying
anything. I was trapped, as I had been trapped all evening, naturally everyone had noticed and both Espen and Tore had watched me
initially with curiosity, then with concern, but in that gathering,
which consisted exclusively of writers and critics, I couldn't speak,
I had nothing to offer, I was an idiot, a blushing tongue-tied little
shit who came to Oslo from the provinces thinking that with his
savage reviews in *Klassekampen* and his glowing grades he at least
had *something* to offer, but I had nothing, I was a nobody, a zero,
indeed such a nonentity that I couldn't even get up from the table.
I couldn't speak and I couldn't leave. I was trapped.

Five and a half hours passed. Six hours passed.

Then I went to the toilet. Went into the corridor, put on my
shoes and jacket, poked my head round the door, they were still
sitting around the table, and I said, 'Got to be off. Thanks for
everything. It was nice.'

Everyone shouted bye and nice to meet you, I carefully closed
the door behind me, went down the stairs, and when I emerged
and the cold sharp autumn air hit my face I burst into a run. I
sprinted as fast as I could across the road and down the block, the
veins throbbing in my neck, my mouth gasping for air, and that

was why I did it, I assume, that was why I ran, I needed to feel that I was actually alive.

I had read Rune Christiansen's work for years, his visual, almost filmic, poetry had a strong appeal for me, and the moods it evoked or were aroused in me were a kind of constant in my life, which always informed the way I saw and felt but on which I never reflected. If the theme of transience appeared in his poetry it wasn't brutal, as it was with Tor Ulven, this osteal hardness which could occasionally split open into a death's-head grin, this bone-rattling merry dance, laughter as life's sole bulwark against the void, no, with Rune Christiansen transience was gentler, bathed in a light of reconciliation, it was rust, autumn, decay, hedgehogs shuffling through a pile of leaves, planes crossing the sky, romance in a hotel room, in a subway entrance, in a train clattering through a forest somewhere.

I met him in a Sunday-empty café in Lommedalen. In the forest outside the darkness fell as we talked with a Dictaphone on the table between us. Hardly any newspapers or journals wrote about poetry, and this was to be quite a big interview, so he had prepared well, keeping some densely written sheets of paper at his side, presumably containing everything he had considered bringing up. I was no poetry expert, but in some way or other the questions appeared to strike a chord with him or else he managed to twist everything towards the essence of what he was trying to say in his writing, because the interview was a success, we sat there for close on two hours, and when I left to catch the bus to town it felt as if everything was within my reach, I was on to something important, all I had to do was stretch out for it. This was a vague feeling, nothing on which you could build, but all the same I knew I had something there. In the mist, in the darkness of the forest, in the dewdrops on the spruce needles. In the whales that swam in the sea, in the heart beating in my breast. Mist, heart, blood, trees. Why were they so appealing? What was it that enticed me with such power? That filled me with such enormous desire? Mist, heart, blood, trees. Oh, if only I could write about *them*, no, not write *about* them but make my writing *be* them, then I would be happy. Then I would have peace of mind.

The following morning I had arranged to meet Geir Gulliksen. He worked for a publishing house called Tiden, they had an office in Operapassasjen, I stood outside the door and wiped my palms on my thighs, hardly able to believe this was happening, I had an appointment with an editor in Oslo. Tore had engineered it, this was true, I had nothing to show him, this was true too, but I *was* actually standing here, I *did* have an appointment, no one could take that from me.

I took the lift up and went into reception.

'I have an appointment with Geir Gulliksen,' I said.

At that moment he walked around the corner, thin, rangy, smiling, self-assured. I recognised him from the photos I had seen.

'Karl Ove?' he said.

'Yes.'

'Hi!'

We shook hands.

'We can go into my office,' he said.

Manuscripts lay there piled up, big envelopes that probably also contained manuscripts, and books stacked high.

We sat down.

'Well, you sent us a *damn* good short story,' he said. 'I'd just like to put that on record.'

'Thank you very much,' I said.

'Are you working on anything now? Or have you got anything else that's finished?'

I shook my head. 'No, but I've got a largish project in mind.'

'I'd be happy to read it.'

Then he started asking me all sorts of questions, what I had done, what I liked reading. I told him Stig Larsson.

'Hah, *all* the young writers say Stig Larsson now. Two years ago *no one* talked about him.'

'That's good, isn't it?' I said.

'Of course it's good,' he said. 'Anyone else you read?'

'Tor Ulven.'

'Right,' he said and laughed. Aligned the edges of a manuscript. Did that mean my time was up?

I rose to my feet.

'I'll send you something as soon as I have it.'

'Yes, you do that. It might take a *while* before you get an answer.'

'That's OK.'

He stood up and accompanied me out, raised a hand to wave goodbye, turned and went back in. He had lots of important manuscripts to read, I thought, lots of important writers to meet. I wasn't one of them, he had arranged the meeting because of Tore, but I had a foot in the door, now I wasn't just a name but also a face, and he had promised to read what I sent him.

We spent Christmas with Tonje's father in Molde. I liked being there, he had a big house with a view of the fjord and the mountains behind, there was a swimming pool on the ground floor, a wet room with a sauna and diving equipment in a corner, a large open sitting room on the first floor, above it a loft with a ping-pong table. It was always tidy there, everything worked, there was snow-shovelling in the early morning, skiing late morning, they had good lunches, cosy evenings and if there were any problems in the household, if there were any hidden secrets, I never came across them. We used to go down to the city centre in the mornings, often bump into her friends, with whom I never managed to behave naturally, I was always quiet and tormented, apart from when we went out and I drank of course or on New Year's Eve, when we ate at Tonje's father's place, with all her friends, and suddenly I could talk from the heart with them. Even the angst the following day was less there, in well-ordered surroundings, I felt less like an evil person than a young son-in-law letting his hair down on holiday.

At the beginning of January Tonje went back to Volda while I took my computer and headed for Kristiansand, where I had rented a room in an old manor house on the island of Andøya provided by the local council's arts department. The poet Terje Dragseth had been behind this. After living in Copenhagen for many years he had returned to his hometown, where he worked as a literary liaison officer on the local council. He was published by Tiden and was held to be one of the best poets of his generation, his poems were often described as hymnic, I hadn't read any of them myself. He was energetic and outgoing, his personality razor-sharp. He drove me to the manor house, which had once been situated a long way out of town, in the country, but now it found itself in the middle of a housing estate. He showed me round, said I only had to ring him if there was anything, worked for a while in his office at the other end of the building, which I could use any time I wanted, then he went back to town and I was alone. I took my computer from its cardboard box, connected everything, put the books I had brought with me in a pile next to it. Two volumes of *À la recherche du temps perdu*, *Avløsning* by Tor Ulven and Tore's debut novel, *Sleeping Tangle*.

The room was small, a bed, a desk, a kitchenette, but the building around it was enormous. From what I had gleaned, it had once belonged to the violinist and composer Ole Bull. In the evening I wandered around inside, the furniture and the wallpaper and everything was intact, like in a museum. I nosed around Dragseth's office, browsed through a few books, went back and sat down in front of my computer, but too much had happened that day for me to be able to work, so I rang Tonje and talked with her for an hour instead, then went to bed.

I woke up at eleven, had breakfast, switched on my computer and sat down.

What was I going to write?

I didn't have the foggiest.

I opened some files to see if there was anything I could work further on.

There is a time for everything. Now it is here, in this house, by this window with a precise segment of nature outside, resting in the dim May darkness; it cannot be other.

Footsteps across the soft grass, swish swish, in the rain. The rain falling on the field, the drops from the branches onto his neck as he stops to open the gate. It emits a gentle creak, thuds back against the post, is fastened with a wire loop. His hands are freezing cold. He shoves them into his pockets and walks on down the narrow muddy path.

The figure appears in the deep snow, running, head bowed into the wind. He notices the movement from the window, the figure becomes clearer, clearer against the heavy grey unchanging background; the eager flushed face of a boy with important news and a big responsibility. He knows what it is about, heard the shot himself some minutes ago. It filled him with such disquiet that to begin with he doubted what he had heard and speculated that it might have been thunder; instead of going out into the storm, up the hill, to investigate the matter, he chucked another log on the fire and sat down in the chair by the window, his head still muzzy with sleep. But now he had to go out, the boy was pounding on the door with his fists and shouting his name.

Every night the same. On scaffolding, high up, with an iron bar in my hand. The streets of the town so far below. A siren somewhere. The sudden clang of metal on brick. Someone shouting. I walk over to the railing. One of the cranes swings above the rooftop. The container hanging from the chains sways gently to and fro. Like prey, I think. I turn, smash the bar against the lock. What satisfaction. Grip the railing. Fingers in the glove, the coarse material against my skin. I know the metal is cold, I know I will feel it if I keep holding. But I duck underneath, walk along the planks on the scaffolding. Tip back my helmet, take off one glove, scratch my scalp. Feel the sudden cold on my sweaty forehead. Feels like the cold is coming from inside. One of the older workers is leaning against the railing and staring out. I walk over to him. He says nothing. We gaze across the town. The sun is almost white against the hard blue sky. It gives everything we see great definition, I muse. The sun makes the scattered patches of ice glint. I feel like saying something to him. The shadow of the housing block beneath us stretches across the pavement, making a sharp dividing line. The concrete bridge's gentle arch over the ice-bound lake. The smoke rising from the chimneys on the rooftops, almost invisible, just an undulating wave in the air, a darker hue. Heat. And the crane's leisurely hydraulic movements. I say nothing. I never say anything.

I could see no further than the hills twenty metres from the house, with the cluster of rowan trees and the rickety fence at the top which marked the boundary to the neighbouring farm. The countryside beyond, the fjord, and the steep mountain on the far side of it, were hazy in a heavy grey mist. I opened the window a fraction. The rush of the ever-rising stream became louder. The deep ruts from the tractor wheels in the field were filled with turbid greyish-brown rainwater. I thought about the ferocious noise. With every turn of the wheels the tractor had sunk deeper, the sound had intensified in volume, in aggressiveness and power; a sign of impatience, of further activity and the dogged belief that all problems can be solved. Then it was quiet. The neighbour jumped to the ground beside his vehicle in his thigh-length boots and yellow rain jacket, stood there studying it for a while, then returned in the ruts made by the tractor. He walked up the slope, across the field of redcurrant bushes, over the fence, which the tractor had ploughed through without ceremony, and for those of us standing at the window, watching, he disappeared from view. A little later we heard the sound of a second tractor, it swung up the gravel path and lumbered into the field; a neighbour was standing on the footplate holding on to the door frame, another neighbour was in the cab. Grandad stood at the window while they attached the chain between the tractors and started them both up, he saw the thick black smoke pouring from the exhaust pipes as the engines were put under strain, the tractor rocked back and forth until in a matter of minutes it was pulled onto firm ground and the second neighbour could drive away. He watched with a blank expression on his face, I couldn't read any of his thoughts and I couldn't ask. Two days before, on the first evening here, he had discreetly referred to Kjartan's plans for what he still called the bog land, what he had intended to do with it this year. After seeing him stare at all this activity outside his own window, in which we weren't involved – Why didn't the neighbour come in and ask us for help? Why didn't he use our phone? It was right here, in the hall. He could have used it to call, couldn't he? – I didn't consider his remarks to Kjartan about the running of the farm to be a sign of calculated malice, as I first thought, nor incipient senility, as though he had forgotten what it was like here, no, it was a loss so great that he couldn't take it in, he had to act as if nothing had changed, re-create what went on outside here every day, find an explanation he could accept. Are you

sure we can afford to hire all these people? he asked Kjartan
later that day, when we were in the sitting room eating waffles. He drank the lukewarm mixture of half cream and half
coffee, sucked a sugar cube, waited for an answer. I looked
at Kjartan. He made no attempt to answer, carried on eating,
but not in such a convincing way that I was unaware he was
repressing enormous irritation. This had been going on for
some time. But of course you've got another income on the
side, grandad said, and with that he calmed down. I didn't
know what to say, so we continued to eat in silence. There
was nothing to ask, nothing to discuss.

I took the lid off the saucepan. Circles of grease had floated to the top, a couple of sausages had already split. I pulled it
off the heat and took a pair of wooden tongs from the drawer.
The clock on the wall above the window showed it was nearly twelve. Even if the land was leased out and everything that
could be called farm work had ceased many years ago, they
still maintained the old mealtimes: breakfast at six, lunch at
twelve, tea at five and supper at nine. Habits that were tied to
farm work. This was how it had been around here for many
centuries. And it had been like this for a reason. The fury I
occasionally felt as they sat down to eat lunch at twelve sharp
was completely unjustified, it was unreasonable to get het up
about this. Yet, somehow, yes, it was reasonable: what sort
of life was it getting up at the crack of dawn to sit around all
morning, as she did, in a chair, or as in his case, to lie on the
sofa, with the radio on so loud that the voices were distorted,
what sort of a life was it, living day after day, as though they
were waiting for something and while they waited went into
the kitchen to eat, then returned to wait and so on and so on?
It was deeply entrenched inside them, almost an instinct, any
tiny deviation could cause tremors that spread and became,
or so it seemed, unbearable, perhaps even life-threatening.

I took the bread for the sausages out of the oven, turned off the stove and put the sausages in a dish, then I went into the sitting room to get them. Grandad was lying on the sofa, as was his wont, wearing a black suit, a tie, a somewhat stained, not-quite-white shirt. I glanced at the television and the picture of drenched bedraggled children walking in line down a road somewhere in Norway shouting sporadic and half-hearted hurrahs, switched it off with the remote control and bent down by grandma's chair. She was also in her finery, a blue dress with white embroidery, a brooch fastened to her chest. A strip of kitchen roll hung from the neckband.

This is what I had. Two years' work. I knew the sentences off by heart. The slog it had been was unbelievable. And the happiness at finding a phrase: *head bowed into the wind, swish, swish in the rain.* But this wasn't something I could take any further, everything in these sentences stopped there.

What should I write about?

I switched off the computer, got dressed, went out to the bus stop by the main road and caught the bus to town. It was smaller than I remembered and closer to the countryside, especially the sea beyond the streets, heavy, brooding. I walked up and down Markens a few times, there weren't many people out and about, but the atmosphere felt congenial, people greeted one another or stopped and chatted. The sky was grey, and what I saw, I thought, was everyday Kristiansand, one of an endless number of days that came and went. The people walking past were in the middle of their lives, in the middle of the depth of their existence. It was as though I was on the outside, I didn't belong here, for me this was just a place and my relationship to it a mystery. What was belonging, really? It wasn't the place itself, for that was only houses and a few rocks by a sea, rather it was what they had made the place, the meaning they had infused into it.

Everything is woven into memories, everything coloured by the mind. Then time flows through the cocoon that is our life. Once we were seventeen, once we were thirty-five, once we were fifty-four. Did we remember that day? 9 January 1997, when we went into REMA 1000 to do our shopping and came out again with a bag in each hand and walked down to the car, put the bags on the ground and unlocked the door, placed the bags on the back seat and got in? Beneath the darkening sky, by the sea, the forest behind, black and bare?

I bought a few CDs and a whole stack of books which were on offer and I thought I might need for my writing.

I ought to go and visit grandma, I couldn't stay in the town without doing that, I might bump into Gunnar at any moment, for example, and he would think it was strange and perhaps also impolite to be here without telling them.

But it could wait a few days, I was here to work primarily, they would understand that. Instead, I went to the library café, bought myself a cup of coffee and sat flicking through the books with an occasional glance through the window. I recognised the girl working behind the counter from *ungdomskole*, but I didn't know her well enough to say hello and she evinced no signs of recognition. The town was full of such faces which once had formed the context of my life but no longer meant anything except for precisely this.

A girl parked her bike outside, performed all the necessary movements with consummate ease, in with the wheel, out with the lock, click it into position, straighten up, look around, head for the door and remove the hood of her rain jacket.

She greeted a girl at the table behind mine, ordered a cup of tea, sat down and started chatting. She talked about Jesus Christ, she'd had a religious experience.

I wrote down exactly what she said.

This is where the novel should start. Right here, in this town by the sea, in this library café, with this conversation about Jesus Christ.

Excited, I made notes. A young man arrives in his hometown, Kristiansand, overhears a conversation in the library café, meets an old *gymnas* friend, Kent, and is transported back in time.

In my room a few hours later I began to write. At around ten in the evening I rang Tonje and read her what I had written. She said it was good. I continued through the night. Whenever I dried up or I thought it wasn't good enough I leafed through one of the books I had with me, particularly Proust, and, invigorated by the atmospheres of that fantastic world and the clear language, I went on. There was no plot, I wanted to entwine the internal with the external, the neural pathways in the brain with the fishing smacks in the harbour, and so that the protagonist should not be me I made the language conservative, I no longer used the Norwegian 'a' endings, I rewrote everything, it came to half a page, and I went to bed.

By the weekend I had eight pages.

I rang grandma. Is that you? she said. I told her I was in Kristiansand, would it be convenient if I dropped round? She replied that dad was there and it would be nice if I did.

I hadn't seen dad for almost two years. I had no wish to see him either, but now he knew I was here so I couldn't not go.

I walked all the way from the bus station, over Lund Bridge and the final kilometre up to the house, nervous and tense the whole while, frightened for brief instants as well, he was going to haul me over the coals, why hadn't I kept in touch?

I rang the bell, minutes passed, grandma opened the door.

She had changed. She was thin, her dress was stained and in a mess. But her eyes were the same. Radiant one moment, distant the next.

'He's upstairs,' she said. 'It's good you've come.'

I followed her up the stairs.

He was in the sitting room watching TV. He turned his head when I entered the room. His face was damp with sweat.

'I'm going to die,' he said. 'I've got cancer.'

I looked down. He lied about everything, even this, but I couldn't show I knew, I had to pretend I believed him.

'How awful,' I said, glancing at him.

'I've just been to the hospital. They cut my back open. You can see the scars if you want.'

I said nothing. He looked at me.

'Your father's going to die,' he said.

'Right,' I said. 'But it could turn out OK, couldn't it?'

'No,' he said. 'That's out of the question.'

He watched TV, I sat down on the footstool. Grandma came in and sat on the other chair, which faced the TV. We watched for a while.

'Everything going well here, Grandma?' I said.

'Yes, it certainly is,' she said. A cloud of smoke hovered above her head. Dad struggled to his feet, lumbered across the floor to the kitchen, returned with a bottle of beer.

They were sitting in what had once been the parlour, used only on special occasions.

'I'm in Andøya Manor, writing,' I said.

'That's good, Karl Ove,' he said.

'Yes,' I said.

All three of us watched the big TV. A girl was playing the flute.

'They say Erling's youngest girl is very musical,' grandma said.

Dad looked at her.

'Why are you always talking about her?' he said. 'I'm also very musical.'

I went cold inside. He had claimed that in all seriousness.

After half an hour in front of the television I got up and said I had to be off.

'Let's go to the restaurant one night while you're here,' dad said. 'My treat.'

'OK,' I said. 'I'll ring. Take care.'

No one went down with me. Distraught, I left, caught the bus to Andøya, where the mist lay thick and heavy between the houses on the estate, unlocked the door and went in, fried myself three eggs, put them on three pieces of bread, ate them standing by the window, sat down and began to write again.

Back in Bergen three months later, I had sixty pages, which I posted to Geir Gulliksen. In the two weeks that passed before he phoned me, I was beset by dreadful bouts of shame and terror. At first I tried to repress what I had written, pretend it didn't exist, but to no avail, and so to gain control over these overwhelming feelings of humiliation I sat down one morning and tried to read my text through his eyes. I switched on the computer, opened the file and the title page shone up at me.

A TIME FOR ALL

Novel, 1997

By Karl Ove Knausgård

FIRST PART

TIME'S PIONEER

The town is there, a place in the world, with its houses and shops, its streets, its harbour, its uplands. Geography, architecture, materiality. A place. Now and then I think about this town just before I fall asleep, follow one of the streets downwards, pass house after house, block after block, I might stop in front of a façade and allow my eyes to wander over a myriad details. The sun always shines on the dirty white wall, glints on a half-open veranda door, in front of it a terracotta flower box, two empty bottles, a plastic bag the wind has wrapped around the bars of the balcony balustrades. A hand grips the door, a face is glimpsed for a few seconds, the door slides shut. There is someone inside, I think, in this dark room, and that is how it is all over this town. An elderly woman draws the curtain to the side and stares out, her attention attracted by a sound. It is the neighbour opening his garage door; as so often before she watches him getting into the car, reversing down the drive, and she lets go of the curtain and lowers her head to concentrate on the crossword on the worktop in front of her. Sometimes she lights one of the many half-smoked cigarettes in the ashtray, pencils in a word. A student sits gaping at the television, exhausted, with the sound off and the picture unclear in the glare from the morning sun. A woman bends her head and strokes her neck, a boy, ill in bed, watches the car he is operating race around the track again and again, another is in front of a computer shooting at anything that moves. There is no one to see them and they act without thinking; she crosses the kitchen floor to open a cupboard while the onions sizzle in the pan on the stove and the radio blares. A cat wakes up and stretches before slinking over to see if there is any food in the dish, a baby screams. This is how it is around me, I think, and see the shadow of the squat row of houses casting a sharp dividing line roughly where the patches of ice and remnants of snow lie between the pavement and the street. The traffic lights emit their shrill squeals to help blind pedestrians cross the road. Cars idle waiting, shiny, beautiful; it is cold and I inhale a mixture of chill air and mild car fumes as I walk across the road to go down Dronningens gate, today with the sun shining on me, as I have done so often before, the streets of this town I sometimes traverse in my mind's eye. In the bedroom of my flat in Bergen, in the guest room of my grandparents' farm

in Sogn, even in a hotel room one night at the southern end
of Africa, in the Transvaal, I can visualise them, the streets,
even as I walk along the stunning Cromer beach it hits me:
the light, the sea; I have it in me, I carry it inside me, in the
darkness of my brain.

The clear blue sky, the low sun on the tall hotel, the
crowds. You go there to get the best possible view, squeeze
between people behind the provisional barriers and the rope
to keep them at a safe distance. Bodies push against you, all
with heads back, tilted to one side, eyes trained on the top
of the building. Bluish-black smoke seeps out and rises, follows the unpredictable currents of wind, disappears. More
and more black smoke is belched out into the clear air. A fire
engine ladder glides upwards, you can hear the faint hum
mixed with the crowd's murmured expressions of awe. One
of the hotel occupants had jumped. The rime frost on the tarmac in front of you and the blue sky. It is clean, it is clinical,
the world is precise. But the smoke continues to belch out,
thick and black. You can't see any flames, only smoke. This
disaster is soundless in the same way that pain is soundless.
Behind you people are shoving. Another ambulance weaves
its way in, two men get out, lean against the side of the vehicle and stare up as well. The hotel is empty now. Only fire-
men with breathing apparatus and astronaut costumes move
through the corridors and search the rooms in case there are
any more guests who hadn't managed to get out before being
suffocated and lie in heaps where they fell, their bodies unable to absorb any more smoke. It must be like drowning, you
think, but much worse because there is plenty of air nearby,
they have hope, they die in hope. This is your death day. You
eat in the hotel restaurant, have an early night, flick through
the TV channels, maybe find an old film, you fall asleep. A
few hours later you wake up, snow on the screen, a blind

channel, you switch off the television, get undressed, crawl under the duvet and go back to sleep. When you wake up now it is for the last time. To screams and slamming doors, to the roar of flames, this is how you will die, in the smoke seeping into and filling your room, visibility is zero, you are disorientated out of your wits, and so you die, sitting on the bathroom floor with a wet cloth over your face. And now it's over, you think, the dead are carried out, the survivors are evacuated. But the fire rages on. The flames switch directions blindly, frighteningly, spring up in more and more places, it is out of control.

'Hi, Henrik.'

You turn when you hear your name and see Kent waving, he comes towards you wearing his long grey coat and carrying a white helmet in one hand.

'You're skiving too, eh?'

'Heard the news early this morning. Seems to be over though.'

'It's still burning,' he says, looking up.

'But they got everyone out, they said.'

'It's terrible,' Kent says, smiling.

'The worst is all the people who come here to rubberneck. That's terrible,' you say and smile as well because you feel a sudden happiness standing here and talking to Kent, as only a seventeen-year-old can. The sudden happiness a seventeen-year-old can feel at even the most mundane humdrum things, such as talking about everyday matters with someone his own age, a happiness that, if it continues, threatens to take control, his voice can fill with emotion or laughter, he can laugh and laugh at trivia, he becomes intoxicated by it, it grows until he is so overcome that he has to start avoiding these situations. He has to look down instead of into people's eyes, withhold a comment instead of blurting it out to all-round hilarity and acknowledgement. You can't trust yourself any more, you think, something is happening to you. There is also the opposite, this sudden urge to cry that comes over you in the strangest situations, your eyes go moist, you can't cope and have to look down, hold back. Like now, in front of the hotel, you can feel the happiness bubbling away, but you force yourself to focus on the smoke as if you are extremely interested in it and what it attests: a hotel fire. Later that evening footage of the conflagration is broadcast around the world, Germans sit in front of the screen and see pictures of the hotel, this is where it happened, Swedes, the British and the French, in this town, Danes and the Swiss, in this hotel.

Fourteen people lost their lives.

From there the text moves to Bergen, where the main protagonist lives, an incident describing him sleeping outdoors, and when he crosses Torgalmenningen on his way home, I had a ridiculous idea, he stops at a telephone box, dials the number his family had during his childhood, and he himself is at the other end, ten years of age, talking about how he is right now.

What would Geir Gulliksen think?

He had got himself involved with an immature person who not only unabashedly sent him the most hair-raisingly stupid stories, but also imagined, in all seriousness, they would be published and someone apart from himself would be interested in reading them.

How was that possible?

How could I be so crass?

So conceited?

The telephone call came.

'Hi, Geir Gulliksen here.'

'Hi.'

'Hi! What a fantastic piece of writing!'

'Do you think so?'

'I certainly do. It's very, very good. Especially the bit where the protagonist rings himself, you know . . . He's crossing the square. Do you know which bit I mean?'

'Yes.'

'You've really got something there.'

'Oh, yes.'

'You have to continue. Write more. This is going to be good, you know. I mean *really* good. If you want me to read anything along the way, just send it. I can also read the whole book when you've finished if that suits you better.'

'Oh, yes,' I said.

'There was one tiny thing I was wondering. At the end of the sequence, you write, in the world, out of the world, in the world, out of the world. Do you remember?'

'Yes.'

'That's fantastic. I was thinking, is there a title in that? A potential title? *Out of the World*. Give it some thought anyway.'

Tremendously encouraged, I wrote two hundred more pages, also a long passage about dad, and I cried as I wrote it, I could scarcely see the screen for tears, and I knew it was good, it was quite different from anything I had done before.

That spring there was a family gathering in Kristiansand, one of Gunnar's sons was being confirmed. I travelled down again and arrived at grandma's house in the early morning. Dad was sitting in the kitchen, fat and heavy, his hands trembling and his face shiny with sweat. He was wearing a suit, shirt, tie. In the sitting room behind us were his brother Erling and his family, with grandma.

For the first time in my life I felt stronger than him, for the first time in my life I didn't feel a trace of fear in me when I was in the same room as him.

He was harmless.

I asked him whether he was still with the woman he had met, whose name I didn't even know.

'No, I'm not,' he said. 'She told me where to put my shoes. That's no good.'

'No,' I said.

'Can you decide where you put your shoes?'

'Yes, I think so.'

'That's good. You mustn't lose your freedom. You must never do that, Karl Ove!'

'No,' I said.

He looked down at the newspaper on the table in front of him. He was heavy and slow, but his manner wasn't – that was nervous and jumpy.

'You'll have to help me with my tie before we go,' I said. 'I still haven't learned how to do it.'

'Who does it then?'

'Usually Yngve.'

'Does he know how to do it?'

'Yes.'

He struggled to his feet.

'Let's do it straight away. Where's your tie?'

'Here,' I said, taking it from my jacket pocket.

He put it around my neck. His breathing was laboured. He crossed the ends, folded over and through, watching carefully as he did so, then tightened.

'There we are,' he said.

Our eyes met, mine were moist, he turned and sat down. Erling came in the door, holding a bunch of keys.

'Let's go, shall we?' he said. 'We don't want to be late for church, do we.'

'Doesn't Karl Ove look smart today?' dad said.

He actually said that.

'Yes, he does,' Erling said with a smile. 'But let's go now.'

*

The priest talked about prayer in his sermon. He said that God wasn't like a Coke machine; you put money in and out came a bottle. I couldn't believe my ears. He had six years of theology studies behind him and close on thirty years of experience, judging by his appearance, and he spoke about divinity in that way.

When the service was over I met an old acquaintance outside. I hadn't seen her for many years. She gave me a hug, we chatted, she said she had fetched up in Kristiansand again somewhat apologetically, as though she had ceded control to greater powers than her own. While we stood there I watched dad make his way to the car. Perhaps it was because of all the people, perhaps because of our surroundings, where I wasn't used to seeing him, but suddenly I could see him as he was now. All that usually drew my eyes in his direction, for the whole of our lives together, everything he had done, been and said, that which in total was 'dad' and was immanent in him or in my view of him whatever his appearance, all that was suddenly gone. He looked like a drunk who had put on a suit. He looked like an alcoholic his family had collected, smartened up and taken along.

In the car the conversation was about the best route to Gunnar's. Dad maintained we should turn right. No one listened to him, he got angry, talked non-stop about the road to the right, said he knew and they would see. I watched him, chilled to the soul. His regression was massive. He was like a child. All the way to Gunnar's house he sat whingeing that we should have gone the way he said. When we arrived he stepped out carefully onto the gravel and shambled to the door. During lunch he was on his own, completely outside the conversation; now and then, however, he did make a comment, which was always out of place. He was sweating profusely and his hand shook when he raised a glass of cider to his mouth. After the meal the children ran around and played, and soon they discovered a new game, namely yelling dad's name, running over to him and touching him while shouting his name and laughing. He did nothing, reacted with surprise and stared at them. Erling had to tell them to stop. The rest of the time we were outside I had the children's jeers ringing in my ears.

This was a man who had once had the strength and magnetism of a king.

There was nothing left of him.

And now, now everything was over, he turned to me. Only now could he say I looked smart. But I was twenty-eight, not eight, I no longer needed this and I no longer needed him.

We went back in two smaller cars, Erling's family and grandma in one, dad and I on the rear seat of the other. I was in a hurry, I had a plane to catch and my bag containing my everyday clothes was in the hallway. Dad stood on the steps fumbling with the keys. He eventually found the right one and opened the door. The burglar alarm went off quietly. Dad stared at it.

'Tap in the code,' I said.

'Yes,' he said. 'But I don't know it.'

'I've got to have my bag now,' I said. 'It's just inside. Do you think I can nip in and get it? Double quick?'

'Go on then,' he said.

I dashed in. The alarm immediately emitted a shrill penetrating howl. I grabbed my bag and ran back out. I was sure he would read me the Riot Act, but he just stood there eyeing the code panel and fiddling with the keys. Grandma came walking up the hill.

'Have you managed to set off the burglar alarm again!' she shouted. 'How many times do I have to tell you? You have to tap in the code before you go indoors!'

She walked past him, tapped in a number.

'I couldn't remember the code,' he said.

'But it's so simple!' grandma said in a loud voice. 'You're absolutely impossible! You can't do anything!'

She glared up at dad with fury in her eyes. Dad stood with his arms at his sides, looking down the hill.

In Bergen I continued to work on my novel. By the middle of May it had grown to roughly three hundred pages, which I sent to Geir Gulliksen. He asked me to drop by so that we could talk about it properly, I went to Oslo, stayed with Espen, when I went into his office, my manuscript lay on his desk.

He spoke about it for perhaps ten minutes.

Then he said, 'Would you like to sign a contract now? We can do that, you know. Or would you rather wait until you have a final version? If we hurry we could publish it in late autumn.'

'Publish it?' I said. I hadn't even considered the possibility.

'Yes,' he said. 'It's as good as finished. If you were run over by a tram on your way out we'd have enough to publish.'

He laughed.

In the white spring light I threaded my way through the pedestrians on the pavement as if in a trance. What he had said reverberated in my brain; everything around me seemed to be so far away. A tram clattered past, a fat man got out of a taxi, two buses went up the hill one after the other. I couldn't believe it was true, so I repeated it to myself again and again. I'm going to make my debut. My novel has been accepted. I am a writer. I seemed to be staggering under the weight of my elation. I was going to make my debut. The novel has been accepted. I am a writer.

Espen answered when I rang the doorbell, turned and went into the room at once, he was in the middle of something. I used his phone and rang Tonje. Of course she wasn't at home. Then I rang Yngve at his office. I told him the novel had been accepted.

'Oh yes,' he said.

I couldn't understand the lack of interest in his intonation.

'Isn't it fantastic?' I said.

'Yep,' he said. 'But you must have known it was going to happen, didn't you? I mean, you've been in contact with a publishing house for a long time.'

'I didn't know at all. In fact, I thought it was never going to happen.'

'Yeah, yeah,' he said. 'Have you been out yet in Oslo?'

After we had rung off I sat on the sofa waiting for Espen to finish so that I could tell him. But he didn't show much enthusiasm either.

'I heard you say on the phone,' he said. 'Congratulations.'

For him this might have been a matter of course, I thought. Nearly everyone he knew was a writer.

'Did you believe I would make it? I said. 'That I would ever make my debut?'

'Yes, I did. But perhaps not in literature. I suppose I thought it would be a collection of essays or something.'

At the beginning of the summer we emptied our flat and put everything in storage outside town, where it would stay until the end of August, when we would move up to Volda. Tonje had applied for a summer job in NRK Hordaland, which she didn't get, so to earn some money she was going to work at her father's surgery in Molde. We went up to mum's place in Jølster, where the plan was that I would finish the novel. While we were there Tonje rang NRK Sogn og Fjordane and, miraculously, was offered a job, she cancelled her secretarial work, and we stayed there all summer. She drove to NRK in the morning, I wrote, she buzzed around the county of Sogn og Fjordane in her white NRK car while I sweated in a room so full of light that I could barely see the letters on the screen in front of me, she came home in the afternoon, we went swimming or we had a barbecue in the garden or we watched TV. I wasn't making any headway with the novel, I was stuck and becoming more and more desperate,

I started working every hour there was, also at night. It was all I thought about. To publish it as it was now would have been a terrible mistake; the storyline lacked a motivating force. A young man returns to his hometown, rents a room, meets some old friends and his whole life takes a turn for the better, a series of protracted memories, in itself absolutely fine, but why tell them? There was no narrative engine. I had to make one. But how? Obviously he must have come from somewhere, and in that place something must have happened that was harrowing enough, severe enough, for him to flee and simultaneously cause him to relive his life, to search for a reason, to search for some coherence, to try and understand himself.

There was no space inside me for anything else. I kept everything else at arm's length. One night Tonje shouted at me in her frustration.

'I don't want this! I'm only twenty-six! I want to live, Karl Ove! Do you understand?'

I tried to calm her down, this had nothing to do with her, I had to write, and I didn't have any space for anything else, but it would soon be over and I loved her, I always would. It helped to talk, above all it helped her, she poured her heart out that night, we became closer to each other, it was as though we were starting anew.

Some days later I wrote a passage about northern Norway, with Henrik Møller-Stray, the name of the main character, working there as a teacher. I had him sitting in the staffroom, talking to the other teachers, then going into the classroom with the pupils, he was their form teacher, and in that instant I knew I had the solution to all my problems.

He fell in love with one of the pupils, slept with her in the end, she was only thirteen, he had to flee and had nowhere else to go but Kristiansand.

It fitted perfectly, but I couldn't do it, couldn't have him falling in love with a thirteen-year-old and definitely couldn't have him sleeping with her. That was immoral, and it would be exploitative because the justification for using it was novelistic technique. I needed a plot with the most powerful fulcrum I could find. He could kill someone, but I wasn't interested in that kind of conflict. Steal something? No, no. It had to be a positive force that drove him, something fine and beautiful, falling in love, nothing else fitted.

But I couldn't do that.

If I did, that is what would be discussed, the morality of the novel, and I wasn't in the slightest bit interested in that.

Another consideration was the unease I would feel if I wrote myself into the novel, for some of this was indeed true, which no one should ever find out, and if I wrote it, it would exist in the world, not only inside me, however much of it was fictional.

Tonje went to Molde, I stayed to meet Tore, we were going to one of the mountain cabins my family owned to finish writing a film manuscript. It was about an apartment block, several stories were played out there, the most important of which concerned a woman who heard strange noises in the ventilation shaft. Towards the end of the manuscript, after many misfortunes, it emerges these noises come from an apartment belonging to two brothers, where they are holding their father prisoner and abusing him.

One night, after we had finished working, I explained my dilemma to him.

'Do it, for Christ's sake, don't even think about it. Go for it! It'll go down a bomb!'

We were there for four days, several times I expressed my doubts and uncertainties, he remained rock-solid, go for it, do it. We strolled down the narrow gravel path through the forest to the lake, where we went into the little shop, I took him to see Borghild, who laughed at us and our shaven heads, you two look like convicts, you do. She made us coffee and I asked her about her childhood, she told me she'd had TB and spent many

months in a sanatorium high above a fjord, the cure had been
to get as much sun as possible, so the women had sat in chairs
on the first-floor veranda, and the men on the ground-floor veranda, because we were topless, as they say today, she said with
a laugh, then she went on to tell us what it was like when she
returned home, there was a stigma attached to the illness and
the tan you got at sanatoriums. Tore was fascinated by her and
she liked Tore. Everyone liked Tore. We went back up and carried
on with our work, a horse stuck its muzzle through the window
while we were sitting there, we gave it some sugar cubes and an
apple, in the evening we sat outside drinking beer and smoking
surrounded by the roar of the waterfall from the forest, with the
snow on the mountain tops on the other side shining in the glow
from the setting sun.

In the middle of August I travelled up to Volda. Tonje met me at
the bus stop, we walked uphill to the house where we would rent
the whole of the first floor, it was old and not in great shape, but
there were three rooms and it was only us two living there. She
had shared it with another student all last year, now it was ours.
We were husband and wife, the thought of this still sent tingling
sensations through me. We were going to share our lives together,
and now we were here, in a little village full of students between
the mountains.

From the room I used as a study there was a view of the fjord
and the ferry that plied to and fro almost round the clock, glittering in the night darkness, and the instant I put my computer on
the desk I knew I was going to be able to work here.

Tonje was enjoying her course, she had a lot of friends on it,
sometimes they came back to see us, but usually she met them
away from home. I joined her now and then but not so often. I
was there to write, this was my last chance, in only two years I
would be thirty, I had to give it everything I had. Unlike in all the

other places I had stayed, I had almost no relationship with Volda at all. I got up in the evening, wrote through the night, went to bed in the morning, longing for the evening when I could write again. Occasionally I would cycle down to the little town centre to buy CDs or books, but even the short time that took felt like a huge sacrifice, something I really shouldn't allow myself. What I discovered during these months was the great power of routine and repetition. I did exactly the same every day so that I didn't have to waste any energy and could put it all into my writing. Which also derived energy from the same source, three pages in one day became three hundred pages in a hundred days, and in a year more than a thousand. From the cigarettes I rolled in the course of a night, twenty or so, I always spilt some of the tobacco, which after six months built up into quite a pile beside the chair leg. The letters on the keyboard slowly became worn according to a system that remained a secret to me, some shone bright and intact after six months, others were as good as erased. But the routine had a further function: it protected me from seeing what I wrote from the outside. Routine had the effect of keeping me inside my writing day after day. If I upset the pattern – visited someone or perhaps had a few beers out with Tonje – everything was dislocated, I lost my rhythm, saw the routines and what I wrote, which was ridiculously poor, what was I thinking, that anyone would have any interest in my childish immature thoughts? Then this idea found reinforcement and the stronger it became the more difficult it was to get back into routine's exclusion and tranquillity. As soon I was back in the groove, I decided not to make the same mistake again, not to meet anyone, not to go out drinking with Tonje. Then the decision also vanished, because that was how it was inside writing, everything on the outside vanished. During working hours I often stood by the hot radiator on the bathroom wall staring out of the window, not dissimilar to a cat, I would watch everything that moved outside, would stand there for half an hour, an hour, then went back in and carried on working. It was a way of having a break and resting without losing my rhythm.

The feeling I had was fantastic. I had spent ten years writing without achieving anything, and then all of a sudden, out of nowhere, it was just flowing. And what I wrote was of such quality, compared with what I had produced earlier, that I was surprised every evening when I read through what I had written the night before. It was like having a head rush or walking in your sleep, a state in which you are out of yourself, and what was curious about this particular experience was that it continued unabated.

Tonje knew it was important for me, and she was independent, lived her own life, had her own ambitions, but sometimes I noticed she wanted more of me, of us, that this wasn't enough for her, and then I tried to give it to her, not for my sake, I needed no more than I already had, but for hers.

Once she asked if she could use my computer, only for half an hour, there was something she had to write and going all the way up to the school was a hassle. I was extremely annoyed but I said nothing, of course she could use my computer for half an hour, and so that she would understand what a sacrifice it was for me I sat on a chair in the corridor, outside the door, waiting, seething with impatience.

She often referred to the opinion one of her friends had expressed about our life together, how strange it was that I worked all the time and never showed my face outside with her, of course she told me this because she thought the same, deep down I was angry, what we did with our lives was none of his business.

One evening in spring she got terrible abdominal pains. She had to go to the out-of-hours doctor, she said, I asked if I should go with her, no, she said, you write, it'll be fine, and then from the sitting-room window I saw her walking up the hill stooped over and I thought it was generous of her to let me write instead of accompanying her to the doctor. Personally, I had no objection to doing this kind of thing on my own, I was unsentimental in this regard, and I was happy she felt the same.

Two or three hours later she phoned, they had admitted her to hospital, they didn't know what was wrong and were going to perform a little procedure to find out.

'Shall I come?'

'Yes, could you?'

She was lying in bed when I arrived, her smile gentle and apologetic, the pain had gone, it was probably nothing.

The next day I went back up, they hadn't found anything, it was a mystery. I was going to Oslo for a final discussion of the manuscript, the plane tickets had been booked ages ago, so she would have to make her own way home, it wasn't a problem, and she had lots of friends who could go shopping for her, if need be.

In May I revised the manuscript for the last time, everything that had to be done had to be done now, so when 17 May came, Constitution Day, Tonje asked if I could be with her that day, first to have breakfast with some friends, then to walk to the town to watch the procession and afterwards to have a few drinks in a pub, but I couldn't, work was at a crucial point, I couldn't lose a whole day, anyway you know lots of people there!

She went in her sailor's jacket, she looked a dream, I watched her from the window and that was what I thought, then I sat down in the sun on the veranda and began to plough through the manuscript with pen in hand. After a while I went in and had a bite to eat, continued to read, until the telephone rang. It was Tonje.

'I miss you so much,' she said. 'Can't you come on down? Just for a little walk? I'm having a great time, but it would be even better if you were here. And the others are asking me if there's something wrong. As you're not here.'

'Look,' I said. 'You know I have to work. I can't. You understand, don't you?'

Yes, she did, perfectly.

We rang off.

I stood scanning the fjord.

What on earth was I doing?

Was I a complete cretin?

Was she supposed to sit all on her own in her sailor's jacket on 17 May?

I threw on my jacket, jumped into my shoes and hurried up the hill. As soon as I reached the top and started to walk I saw Tonje. She was ambling along with her head bowed.

Was she crying?

Yes, she was.

Oh Tonje.

I ran over to her and held her in my arms.

'Don't take any notice of me,' she said. 'I don't know what's come over me.'

As she said this, she smiled.

We walked back down to the centre, into the bar where her friends were sitting and then to the pub, where we got drunk, as is right and proper on Constitution Day. While we were sitting there I said my novel would be on the front page of *Dagbladet* when it came out. Tonje eyed me. 'Want a bet?' I said. Yes, she said. A trip to Paris. If you win you take me. If I win I take you.

We walked home that night with our arms entwined. She told me how the way we lived had worn her down, I said it would soon be over, there was only one more month, then everything would be different.

'The worst is I believe you,' she said.

The night England played Argentina in the World Cup a removal van collected all our things. We flew to Bergen and waited outside our new flat the following day for the van. We had answered a box number advert, Tonje had written a letter explaining who we were, and we got the flat, an old lady owned it and wanted very little for it, although it was big, at least by our standards.

My phone rang, it was the van driver, he was at the bottom of the hill and couldn't get any further. We ran down to meet him.

'It's no good,' he said, scratching his cheek. 'I'll have to unload your things here.'

'Here? In the street?' I said.

He nodded.

'But you can't do that!' I shouted. 'We've paid for the move. You'll obviously have to carry the stuff to the flat!'

'But I can't get up the hill,' he said. 'You can borrow a handcart if you promise to bring it back.'

I gave up and helped him to move all the furniture and boxes off the van. The pile was the height of a man. He drove off, I rang Eirik, the only person I knew who was in town right now, but he was busy, so it was a case of rolling up my sleeves.

People walking past stared at the household goods. There was something completely wrong about it, I thought, putting three boxes onto the handcart and pushing it uphill. It looked obscene, naked, unprotected. A divan in the road. Our bed in the road. A sofa, a chair, a lamp. Pictures. A desk. All shining in the sunshine against the dry grey tarmac.

Over the following days we painted the flat, and once we had finally decided how to arrange the furniture we were happy. It felt like our first decent flat, we were no longer students, the future started here. Tonje had a job with NRK Hordaland, my novel was finished, all that was left was the proofreading. And the cover. I went down to see Yngve in Stavanger for some help with that. I had photos of Zeppelins with me, I had thought from the beginning that a Zeppelin would be right for the atmosphere I was seeking in the novel, the overwhelming feeling of everything that had been lost, all the time and all the eras, there was little that expressed this better than the German airship, this whale of the air, this Moby Dick of progress, so beautiful and alien it hurt. As an alternative I had a book I had once been given by dad, it was about space, no photographs, just drawings. Early 1950s, space travel didn't exist yet, but there was speculation, there were designs of space outfits, this is how the first space traveller would be dressed. There were designs of rockets, houses on deserted planets, moon vehicles. All in the style that was so typical of the 1950s, American advertising optimism. A father with his child pointing to the starry sky. The future, adventure, the entire universe at man's feet. The covers Yngve and Asbjørn designed, with Zeppelins and 50s drawings, were good but not precise enough for the novel. They tried more and more variations, and I was beginning to reconcile myself to their suggestions when Asbjørn came up with some photos by Jock Sturges, an American photographer, in a magazine. One of them showed a girl, perhaps twelve years old, perhaps thirteen, she was naked and stood with her back to the camera, and when we saw it the search was over. This was actually what the novel was about. Not time that was lost but the main character's desire for a thirteen-year-old girl.

Back home again, I spent my days reading newspapers and watching TV, sitting in Verftet and drinking coffee with a book in my hands while Tonje worked, I was in limbo, a routine no longer did anything for me, it was just a routine, the days in it were empty. Yngve and Asbjørn lived in Stavanger, Espen and Tore lived in Oslo, Hans and nearly all of the others had also moved there. Only a handful of friends remained in Bergen. Ole was in town, I knew, he had got divorced and moved back, I rang him, we went out for a beer. Eirik, whom I had first got to know in Student Radio, was doing a doctoral thesis in literature, I cycled up to his office and had a coffee with him in the canteen.

When I returned mum rang, Borghild was dead. She had passed away, she hadn't been ill, hadn't had any pain, she died in her sleep. It was a year since I had last seen her, I had cycled up to hers from mum's, sat on her veranda and asked her questions about farm life in the old days. I wrote down what she said in a notebook; what were memories for her was history for me. It was incomprehensible how different that world was from this. Borghild belonged in both, but now she was dead, and I could hear how upset mum was. We arranged that I would go to the funeral. Tonje was working and couldn't make it, but I packed my suitcase the night before, had breakfast and was about to go down to the bus station when the telephone rang. It was Yngve. He said dad was dead.

Four days later I left the chapel in Kristiansand after seeing dad, or what had once been him and was now a corpse with his features, for the second time. The sky was bright but hazy. A stream of vehicles drove past on the road in front of me. Seeing him had been terrible, especially as in the days that had passed since I first saw him he had changed. His skin had gone yellower, it seemed more sunken. He was on his way to the earth, something was drawing him there, with great force. I went over the pedestrian bridge, beneath me cars swept past, the drone of engines seemed to resound inside me, I lit a cigarette and looked up at the tops of the houses in front of me. They said something, just by the way they stood there, what they said wasn't human, it wasn't living, but it was a statement. The house across the road, which might have been from the 1930s, said something else, and so it was with the houses all over town, in all towns. A blank expression beneath the sky, people entering and leaving.

Where the hell had all the blood come from?

When we went to see him for the first time the undertaker warned us – there had been a lot of blood, he had said, it might be a bit distressing. Naturally they had washed him, but they hadn't managed to remove it all, the blood seemed to have sunk into his pores. And his nose had been broken. However, in the sitting room where he had been found there had been no blood. Had the pain been so great that he had risen, fallen against the wall by the fire, for example, broken his nose, dragged himself up into the chair, died and been found there? Or had he broken his nose the day before, on a walk into town? Or had the fracture and the blood been what had caused his heart to stop?

But where was the blood?

I would have to ring the doctor tomorrow and ask him what had actually happened the day he was found.

Grandma was sitting at the kitchen table when I returned. She brightened up for an instant, she didn't want to be alone, not for one second: whenever Yngve and I left the house she followed us.

I put on a jug of coffee, went into the sitting room and phoned Yngve, after closing the kitchen door first.

'Have you spoken to the doctor?' he said.

'No, not yet. I was planning to do it tomorrow.'

'Good,' he said. 'How's it going down there in Kristiansand?'

'I've cut almost all the grass in the garden today. Or hay or whatever you like to call it. I was thinking of cleaning tomorrow.'

'The priest?'

'Oh, yes, that's right! I'll sort that out. I'll ring him after this. But I think the undertakers have contacted him.'

'Yes, they have. But you have to go through the ceremony with him. He'll probably say a few words about dad as well, so you'll have to put him in the picture.'

'What should I tell him?'

'Well, just give him an idea of his life. Teacher on Tromøya, active in local politics, philately. Two children from first marriage, one from second. Interested in . . . erm, what was he actually interested in?'

I let out a soundless sob.

'Fishing,' I said. 'He liked that.'

There was a pause.

'But . . . do you think I should say something about the end?' I said. 'His last years?'

'Perhaps not in so many words.'

'Say it had been difficult for him?'

'Yes, that'll do.'

'I'd like it to be dignified.'

'I know. Me too.'

'When are you coming down?'

'The day of the funeral, I expect. Or the night before.'

'OK. I'll ring you tomorrow whatever happens.'

'OK.'

'Bye.'

'Bye.'

In the evening the clouds opened and the low sun cast its orange light across the town as dusk slowly settled over the fields and soon it would begin to rise and fill the space all the way up to the sky, which was light's last bastion, it hung there, deep and blue, and then, almost imperceptibly, the light from a star came into view, as fragile as a newborn child, but it grew stronger, was surrounded by other stars, and soon the still-light summer sky was full of them.

While grandma sat in the sitting room watching TV, I stood on the veranda alternately studying the sky and gazing across the town and the sea. I thought about the 1950s book dad had given me. He had read it here. Dreamed about space the way children do, wondered what the future might bring in terms of rockets and robots, inventions and discoveries. What would that have been like for him?

How had he felt?

The summer he met mum, when they had been seventeen years old, that is in 1961, he had told her he had testicular cancer and might not be able to have children.

It was a lie, of course, as it had been a lie when he told me he had cancer and was going to die.

But it wasn't a lie that he was going to die.

Perhaps it wasn't a lie that he couldn't have children either? In the sense that he didn't want them, he knew it wasn't a good idea.

Good God, they had been twenty then. If they had been as immature as I was when I was twenty, it was quite a feat they had pulled off.

I stubbed out my cigarette and went into the house.

The telephone rang.

'You answer it,' grandma said without looking at me. Again it was as though she was talking to someone else, using a different tone, and this other person could have been no one else but dad.

I went into the dining room and lifted the receiver.

'Hi, Gunnar here. How are you two doing?'

'Not bad under the circumstances,' I said.

'Yes, this is an awful business, Karl Ove,' he said. 'But we were thinking of taking you to the mountain cabin tomorrow. So you get a change of air. The forecast is good. What do you say?'

'Sounds brilliant.'

'So let's do it. We'll be round early tomorrow morning to pick you up. Make sure you're ready! It's best to leave early so we get something from the day, don't you agree?'

'Yes,' I said. 'That's best.'

We went to bed at the same time, I followed her down the stairs, she turned in the hall and said goodnight and disappeared into her room, I opened the door to my room, sat down on the bed, put my face in my hands and cried for a long time. Actually I had wanted to go to sleep fully clothed, but Gunnar was coming

tomorrow and I didn't want to give him the impression I was
scruffy or untidy, so I summoned the last strength I had, went
into the bathroom and cleaned my teeth, washed my face, folded
my clothes and placed them on a chair before going to bed. I had
dreaded this, the worst moment was when I closed my eyes and
lay there without being able to see anything in the house, it was
as if all my terrible thoughts, finally liberated, launched themselves at me, tonight as well, as I sank slowly, dangled as it were,
into sleep, not unlike a hook on the end of a line, I caught myself
thinking, which the weight drags down, then darkness fell at a
stroke and I disappeared from the world.

When I woke at eight grandma was already up. She was wearing
the same filthy dress she'd had on every day so far, she smelled
and was sunk deep inside herself.

She should have a bath, she should put on clean clothes. Her
mattress should be thrown away, she should have a nice new one
with nice new bed linen. She should have food, good hot food, and
she should be allowed to rest.

I could give her none of this.

'They'll be here soon,' I said.

'Who?' she said, looking up at me, a curl of cigarette smoke rising between her fingers.

'Gunnar and Tove,' I said. 'They're taking us to the cabin today,
remember?'

'That's right,' she said. 'That'll be nice.'

'Yes,' I said.

At a little past nine their car drew up outside. Grandma peered
out of the window in exactly the same way she had when I was a
child, turned to me and flicked her hair up from her neck.

'It's Gunnar,' she said.

'Shall we go down then?' I said.

'You don't think they'll come up?' she said.

'They're taking us to the cabin,' I said.

'That's true,' she said.

I followed her down the stairs. Gunnar stood in the hallway waiting. Tanned, blond, tall and slim. He regarded me with affection in his eyes.

'How are you getting on?' he said.

'Quite well,' I said with moist eyes. 'It'll be nice to get out for a bit.'

Grandma put on a coat, grabbed a bag, which she carried on her forearm as we went down the steps to the car. Tove, squinting into the sun, welcomed us, took grandma's arm and helped her into the car. I walked round to the other side and got in.

The cabin was about twenty miles east of Kristiansand, in the skerries. It was many years since I had been there. When I was growing up we used to go there perhaps once a year. There were many rituals connected with the journey there at that time and it was all an adventure. Just the car park, which was a little field in the forest with each place marked with a car registration number painted on a rock or a piece of wood. Grandad drove into their spot by a stone wall, beneath the flickering shade from the branches of a large oak tree, I opened the door and got out, the air there, smelling of earth and grass and trees and flowers, was so hot it felt as if I was stepping into it. Apart from birdsong and perhaps some scattered voices or an outboard motor from the little harbour where we were going, all was quiet.

Parking the car on grass!

The big square cooler bag grandma lifted out of the boot. The dry moss in the cracks of the stone wall, all the smells there, some of them very dark and mouldy, if you lifted a stone, it could be damp underneath and tiny insects would dart in all directions. The same was true of the stiff grass, it smelled dry and hot, but beneath it, if you dug down a little, there were quite different smells with more presence and depth, akin to decay.

The bees buzzing around the rose hips on the other side of the stone wall. The air above the path, where the sun had been all morning, sections of it were like bunkers of heat, rooms you stepped in and out of. The salty tang of sea became stronger, and of rotten seaweed. The screams of gulls.

We were always taken over to the island by the same elderly boatman. Grandma and grandad stood on the quay and passed him whatever we were taking with us, he placed it at the bottom of the boat, then we climbed on board and sat down. Grandma, an elegant woman in her early sixties who, when the wind ruffled her hair, always fought against it and kept patting it in position; grandad, an affluent man a few years younger with black combed-back hair and sensitive lips. The old boatman, wearing boots and a black peaked cap, one hand around the throttle handle of the outboard motor, the other resting in his lap. Slowly we made our way out, crossed the sound, went ashore on the jetty at the other side, below the simple white cabin. Both Yngve and I used to long to come here. Where wild cherries and apples grew. You could swim by the smooth rocks beside the cabin. From the jetty we could fish for crabs. There was a little red Pioner dinghy we could row. But best of all we liked playing football on the little field behind the cabin, especially when the adults joined in: grandad, Gunnar and sometimes dad.

All this was in my gaze this morning. The car park was no longer grass but tarmac. The long walk through the forest was not long but covered in a matter of minutes. No boatman was waiting for us, he had probably died ages ago and the atmosphere of industry in and around the harbour during those days had completely gone, now it was one of small boats and cabin life.

Nonetheless. The forest was the same, the sounds and smells were the same and the sea with its islets and islands was the same.

Gunnar pulled the boat to the quay, Tove helped grandma in, soon we were heading across the sound beneath the high blue sky. Grandma sat motionless, eyes cast down as though the surroundings, the open space and the light that met us, hadn't reached her. Her pale lean bird-like face was even more painful to see here than at home. Because here there was bronzed skin after long days in the sun, salt in your hair after a refreshing swim, laughter and smiles, happy flirtatious eyes, evenings with shrimps and crabs and lobsters.

Tove laid her hand on my shoulder and sent me a consoling smile.

I started to cry.

Ooooh. Ooooh. Ooooh.

I turned away, stared at the sea. The sound was full of boats, this was a main thoroughfare for tourists in the summer. The small waves beat against the hull, showering us with saltwater spray.

While Tove was helping grandma ashore and Gunnar was mooring the boat, he turned to me.

'Did grandma have anything to drink yesterday?' he said.

My cheeks flushed, I looked down.

'I think she had a little,' I said.

'Thought I could smell it,' he said. 'That's not good.'

'No,' I said.

'She can't look after herself any more.'

'No,' I said. 'That's obvious.'

'We've helped them for so many years,' he said. 'Both your father and Erling moved away, so we had to pitch up.'

'It's incredible you've had the energy,' I said.

'It's got nothing to do with energy,' he said. 'It was something we had to do. She is my mother, you know.'

'Yes,' I said.

'Go and get yourself a cup of coffee!' he said.

I went up to the cabin, my eyes wet with tears. I was in a state. A little smile, a friendly hand, that was all it took, the dam burst.

Grandma was his mother. Dad had been my father. I knew how he felt, I knew he wanted to die. I hadn't lifted a finger. I could have travelled down, talked to him, told him he had to go to a detox clinic. Yngve could have accompanied me, we could have stayed there, his two sons, and taken responsibility for him.

The thought was as alien as it was impossible. I was capable of doing many things, I was able to force myself to do almost anything if it was necessary, but I could not have done that. Not ever.

Should I have been able to say to him, you come to Bergen, you can stay with Tonje and me for the time being, then we'll sort out a flat for you nearby?

Ha ha.

Ha ha ha.

'Sit down, Karl Ove, and relax,' Tove said. 'You've been through a lot. You can enjoy some space out here. You'll both have to go back soon enough.'

I sobbed and covered my eyes with one hand.

Grandma sat smoking and glanced down at the quay as Gunnar walked up.

An hour later he took me on a walk through the island. At first we said nothing, just walked side by side along the path, surrounded by trees, tall dry grass, scrub and bushes, bright flowers here and there, bare ridges, all grey with patches of multicoloured lichen, the odd hollow with wispy stalks of grass swaying in the breeze, and then everything opened into a rectangular clearing, some houses shone white with orange roofs and red pennants fluttered on the flagpoles.

'Do you recognise this?' Gunnar said.

'I do,' I said.

'I can remember being here when I was small,' he said. 'Your father was a young man then. He was studying in Oslo. I looked up to him in the way that only a younger brother can.'

'Mhm,' I said.

'There was something special about him. He wasn't like the rest of us. I remember he used to sit up late at night. No one else did that.'

'Uhuh,' I said.

'He was so much older than me that we didn't grow up together,' he said. 'When I was ten he already had a son of his own. He already had his own life.'

'Oh,' I said.

'He didn't have it easy at the end. It was sad that things turned out as they did. But when it comes down to it, perhaps it was for the best. Do you know what I mean?'

'Yes, I think so.'

'There's a little restaurant here in the summer now,' he said, motioning with his head to a house we passed.

'Looks nice,' I said.

As we were walking I cried a soundless stream of tears. I no longer knew why I was crying, I no longer knew what I felt or where all this came from.

We stopped by the old skerry harbour, where all the sailors' houses had been renovated and everything sparkled with affluence and prosperity. The horizon in the distance was razor-sharp. Blue sky, blue sea. White sails, laughter from somewhere, footsteps on a gravel path. A woman was watering a flower bed with a large green can. The drops from the rose on the spout glinted in the sunlight.

When Gunnar parked his car outside the house in town it was five o'clock and all the trees were rustling in the breeze wafting in off the sea.

'We'll pop by tomorrow,' Gunnar said. 'Then we can give you a hand here. I suppose there'll still be a bit left to be done.'

He smiled.

I nodded, we went indoors. After all the light and air outside, the state of decline in the house, which in a way I had become used to, was evident again. As soon as we were upstairs I carried on cleaning. This time I turned my attention to the two sitting rooms beyond the kitchen. The bench, the dining-room table, the chairs, all in 1930s style with vaguely Viking carvings, the coffee table, the white wall panel that had been installed in the 80s, the windowsill, the veranda door, the staircase. Both rooms had wall-to-wall carpets on the floors and I hoovered them, but it didn't make a great deal of difference; tomorrow I would have to buy detergent for them, I reflected, poured away the water and rang Tonje.

She had bought a plane ticket so she could join me and two for us to go back. I updated her on what was going on, I would be meeting the priest tomorrow, and there was so much left to do, but I would manage. I said I missed her and wished she were here. The former was true, the latter wasn't. I had to be alone here or with Yngve. The funeral was another matter entirely, she had to be here. She said she thought about me all the time and she loved me.

After we had rung off I called Yngve. He wasn't going to come to Kristiansand until the funeral, it was too complicated with his children, but he would do what he could from there. Phone relatives and invite them, keep in touch with the undertaker, all the things I found difficult.

Gunnar and Tove came the next day. Tove helped grandma take a bath, found her clean clothes and cooked while Gunnar and I washed and scrubbed and threw things out, me in as minor a role as I could manage, after all he had grown up in this house, grandma was his mother, I was the son of the man who had ruined everything. For grandma the spruce-up worked wonders, she seemed to come out of herself, suddenly I saw her going downstairs with a bowl of water in her hands and a cigarette in the corner of her mouth. Tove, who was cleaning the coat room, laughed and winked at me. She looked like a brewery worker, she said.

At two I went to the church office in Lund. Entered a long corridor, peeped through an open door, a woman was sitting behind a desk, she stood up and asked what I wanted, I told her, she showed me to the right door, I knocked and went in.

The priest, a middle-aged man with kind eyes, shook my hand and we sat down. I didn't have much confidence in Norwegian priests, I remembered the Coke machine analogy from last spring, and the sole reason I wanted dad buried in a churchyard was tradition, the dignity of it. He was damn well going to have God's words read to him. It was therefore with some scepticism that I started speaking to this priest. I wanted a traditional ceremony with psalms, a sermon, soil thrown on the coffin, as few personal details as possible, as much distance as possible. I wanted dad's life to be seen in that perspective, not the close-up, not the man children feared and who later drank himself to death, but the broad view, a human who was born on earth, pure and innocent, as all are at birth, and who lived a life as all humans do and died his death.

But it didn't go like that. After we had discussed the practicalities, we started talking about what the priest should include in his commemorative speech.

'Who was your father?' he said.

I said he had studied in Oslo, worked for many years as a qualified teacher at an *ungdomskole* in Arendal, married Sissel, had two children, Yngve and Karl Ove, divorced and remarried, lived and worked for some years in northern Norway, had a daughter, moved back down south and died, fifty-five years old.

'Who was your father to you, Karl Ove?' he said.

I didn't like his attempt to achieve intimacy with the use of my name, yet I longed to succumb. It was a terrible technique, I knew that of course, because he didn't know me from Adam, I met his gaze though, and in it I saw he was not an idiot, not a redeemed ignoramus, I saw warmth and understanding. He was no stranger to people drinking themselves to death, I recognised that, nor was he a stranger to people being bad, and he was no stranger to the notion that this was not the end of the world, actually it was the world.

'I was afraid of him,' I said. 'I was always so bloody frightened of him. Well, in fact I'm frightened of him now too. I've seen him twice this week and I'm still not convinced he's really dead, if you see what I mean. I'm frightened he's going to come and . . . erm lose his temper with me. It's as simple as that. He had a hold over me and he has never let go. I'm glad he's dead. Actually that is what I feel. It's a huge relief. And this weighs terribly on my conscience. He didn't *mean* to do this or be like this.'

I looked at him.

'What was your brother's relationship with him like? Is it the same for him?'

'I don't know. I don't think so. I think Yngve hates him. I don't. But I don't know. He was always much worse to Yngve. He could reach out to me, try to make amends, but Yngve didn't want to know about that. He rejected him.'

'You say he didn't mean to do this. Why do you think he did it then?'

'He was tormented. He was a tormented soul. I can see that now. He didn't want to live the life we lived. He forced himself. Then he got divorced and wanted to do what he really wanted, and it was even worse, he started drinking and at some point he lost his grip. He simply didn't give a damn then. At the end he was living with his mother. That was where he died. He drank. Actually it was suicide. He wanted to die, of that I'm sure.'

I started to cry. I didn't care if it was in front of a stranger. I was beyond all such considerations. I cried and cried and I poured my heart out, and he listened. For an hour I sat there crying and talking about dad. When I was about to leave, he shook my hand and thanked me, looked at me with his gentle eyes, and I cried again and said it was me who should thank him, and as I left the place, along the corridor and down the stairs, through the housing estate to the main road, it was as though something had let go, as though I was no longer carrying this, what I had been carrying, myself. We had only talked about dad and me, but the fact that he had been there and listened, as he had to be there and listen to countless people who unburdened themselves to him, from the depths of their difficult lives, meant that it hadn't only been dad and me we had talked about but life: this was how this life had turned out. Dad's life, it had turned out like this.

Tonje arrived, I hugged her tight, we rocked back and forth, arms wrapped around each other.

'It's good you're here,' I said.

'I've missed you so much,' she said.

The house had been cleaned, it was still run-down, but as clean as it could be. I had washed all the plates, cutlery and glass, I had set the table and there were flowers everywhere. Yngve, Kari Anne, Ylva and little Torje had come. Dad's brother Erling and his wife and three children were there. Grandma sat on a chair at the dining table, which we had moved into the parlour. She was going to bury her eldest son today, I couldn't look at her, those vacant staring eyes. But an hour earlier there had been a glint in them when Yngve showed her Ylva, and she had tousled his hair.

I looked at Tonje.

'Could you do my tie?'

She nodded, we went into the kitchen, she put it round my neck and – ta-dah – there it was, all done. It was the same tie I had worn at our wedding.

She took a step back and studied me.

'Does it look OK?'

'It looks very good,' she said.

We rejoined the others, I made eye contact with Yngve.

'Shall we go then?'

He nodded, a few minutes later we were off. The sky was white, the air was warm, we closed the car doors and walked towards the chapel. One of the undertakers came over to us and gave us the programme. Yngve glanced at it.

'The name's wrong,' he said.

The undertaker stared at him.

'I'm extremely sorry,' he said. 'But, regrettably, there's no time to change it now.'

'It doesn't matter,' Yngve said, catching my eye. 'What do you reckon?'

'I agree,' I said. 'These things can happen.'

Nevertheless we both had our own opinions about the name we didn't bear ourselves. He had invented it, as his grandmother had invented ours.

Gunnar and his family arrived. Alf's daughter came with Alf, who hadn't changed and must have been eighty-odd now. He was senile, she led him with a kind but determined hand towards the entrance.

I took Tonje's hand and we went in.

The first thing I saw was the white coffin.

Are you in there, Dad? I said under my breath. Is that where you are, Dad?

We sat down. Tears were streaming down my cheeks. Tonje squeezed my hand hard a couple of times. Apart from the family, which was tiny, there were three other people present.

I dreaded it, I knew what was awaiting us.

Behind me came a sound from Erling's son. A pure high note. The note continued and concluded with a sudden plummet, and I realised he was crying, because then it came again, he was sobbing, and it was heart-rending, his little soul had seen the coffin, and it was enough, now he was crying for all he was worth.

The service commenced. The precentor we had hired was old, his voice was cracked and the cello sonata he played was not exactly a virtuoso performance, but it was apt, life was not perfect, only death is, and this was life watching death, the boy crying over the coffin.

The priest spoke. He talked about dad's life and about those who were present today to take their leave of him. He said it was vital to have a focus. If you don't, you fall by the wayside. It was vital to focus on your children, on your nearest and dearest, on what is important in our lives. If you don't do that, you lose sight of everything and then you have nothing. No man is an island.

Yngve cried, and when I saw that, him sitting there and shaking, his face distorted into grimaces, him raising it to the ceiling and opening his mouth for air, I sobbed aloud with sorrow and joy, sorrow and joy, sorrow and joy.

We stood up and each laid a wreath on the coffin.

Stood in total silence before him with our heads bowed.

Fare well, Dad, I thought.

When we sat down and the cellist played Bach in his rusty, creaky way I cried so much I thought I was going to split in half, my jaw hung open, wave upon wave of the very deepest emotions, those which only appear when all else has gone, washed through me.

After it was all finished Yngve hugged me, we stood crying on each other's shoulders and then, walking across the gravel, watching cars pass in the distance, an old couple walking through the cemetery, a gull sailing through the air above us, it was over. At long last it was over. I took several deep breaths and there were no more sobs.

The couple I didn't know came over to us. They introduced themselves as the parents of Rolf, Ann Kristin's husband. They said dad had been such a fantastic teacher and Rolf had talked about him with such enthusiasm. We thanked them for coming and they walked over to their car.

'Who's that?' Yngve said, nodding discreetly in the direction of a woman. She wore a hat with a veil which concealed her face.

'No idea,' I said. 'But all self-respecting funerals have a woman no one recognises.'

We laughed.

'Well, the danger's over now,' Yngve said, and we both laughed again.

Close family returned to grandma's house, *smørbrød* were served, no speeches were given or commemorative words said, I wished it had been otherwise, sitting between Yngve and Tonje, but that would have meant doing it myself, and it would have gone badly, I couldn't have done it. Afterwards we sat outside on the veranda, Alf said there was a man on the roof and I realised he was back in time, long long ago, when he had been here and there *had* been a man on the roof. That was good. It was a day when both dad and his father had been alive.

The novel had been out for a few weeks, nothing had happened, when one morning the telephone rang. Tonje, who was having breakfast, picked it up, I was in bed though not sleeping, and I heard her say she would see if I was awake.

I went into the sitting room, put the phone to my ear.

'Hello, Karl Ove here.'

'This is Mads from Tiden. Have you read *Dagbladet* today?'

'No, I was asleep.'

'Then I think you should go out and buy it at once.'

'Is there a review?'

'Yes, you could say that. I won't say any more. Go out and we'll talk later!'

I replaced the receiver and turned to Tonje, who was standing beside the table and finishing off her tea. She ran her hand over her beautiful lips and smiled.

'There's a review in *Dagbladet* today,' I said. 'I'll run up and get it.'

'Did he say what was in it?'

'No. He was being secretive. But I would guess it's good.'

She put on her jacket in the hall while I got dressed in the bedroom. When I came out she was hanging over the handlebars of her bike.

We kissed fleetingly and she cycled down the hill while I walked up, beneath the heavy trees, continued along the road and up the slope to the hospital. A sallow-looking man was checking the magazine shelf, a fat woman sat in a wheelchair by the cash till with a purse in her lap, she wanted *Hjemmet*.

I stopped by the *Verdens Gang* and *Dagbladet* stand.

At the top, to the right of the logo, there was a little picture of me. Sensational debut, it said.

Well, that was good. At least I had won the bet with Tonje.

I took a newspaper, paid and went towards the entrance, opened it at the culture section. The review was a two-page spread. Rottem had written it. He compared me with Hamsun, Mykle and Nabokov.

Well, that was good. Could hardly have been better in fact.

I shoved the newspaper under my arm and walked back home, made myself a cup of tea, sat down at the table and lit a cigarette. Then I rang Tonje. She had just seen it and was deliriously happy for me. Personally, I wasn't especially happy. In some strange way I had expected it.

Later that morning a journalist from *Dagbladet* rang, he wanted to interview me as a follow-up to the review. We agreed to meet at Hotel Terminus at two.

It was raining, I decided to catch the bus instead of cycling to town and then walked up to my hairdresser, whom I had originally chosen because the salon couldn't have been less hip and because the guy who owned it, a young energetic guy, was so nice.

'Hi,' he said as I walked in.

'Any chance of an appointment? Like now?'

'In ten minutes,' he said. 'Take a seat in the meantime.'

Was that all there was to it?

Outside the window people passed by clutching at swaying umbrellas. The hairdresser finished the customer, an elderly man, he pronounced himself pleased, on the floor lay his dead white hair. When the door shut with a jangle I sat down in the chair, the cape was whirled around me, I said I wanted it short, as usual, and he began to cut.

'I've got an interview afterwards,' I said. 'So I have to look as smart as possible.'

'What have you done now?' he said.

'I've had a novel published. It's received good reviews, so now they want to talk to me.'

'Is there any money in it? How many copies have you sold?'

'I don't know. It's just come out.'

'What's it about then?'

'Bit of all sorts.'

'Any murders?'

'No.'

'Love?'

'Yes, actually there is some.'

'No good for me then. Wife's just moved out.'

'Has she?'

'Yes.'

There was a silence. His scissors snipped away above my head.

'You want it over your ears, do you? Shall I shave your neck?'

'Perfect.'

It was only after I had paid that I started feeling nervous about the interview. I had done one already, on the day of the press conference, *Dagsnytt 18* had rung me and asked if I would go on the programme. It had been live, sitting on the sofa outside the studio I was so nervous I could barely swallow the coffee I was passed. Tomm Kristensen, who was the TV host, had come out and said that unfortunately he hadn't read my book.

'So I'm going to ask you questions about what it's like to make your debut and so on,' he said. 'In the blurb it says the book's about male shame. Could you say a few words about that, do you think?'

'I didn't write the blurb,' I said. 'I didn't know it was about shame until I saw it.'

'We'll find something else to talk about then,' he said. 'It'll be fine.'

Straight afterwards I was shown in. Kristensen sat with his headset on, scribbling on a piece of paper in front of him, I put on the headset in front of me, I could hear the item before mine.

Then he introduced me.

'There's a big paedophilia case in Belgium at the moment,' he said. 'You've written a novel about a teacher who has a sexual relationship with a girl of thirteen. Would you say you've jumped on a bandwagon?'

I eyed him with horror. What was he actually saying?

'No,' I said. 'I wouldn't. This has nothing to do with Belgium.'

I noticed that I could in fact speak and my nerves vanished.

'You're making your debut now. How has this process been? Do you feel your publishing house has failed to take you into account, by deciding on the blurb and things like that?'

'No, I don't feel that. I chose the picture for the front cover, for example.'

'Yes, it's a photo of a naked girl. Why did you choose that? Is it meant to be provocative?'

'No, no. It's relevant to what the book's about, actually.'

I was bathed in sweat after the interview was over, and also a little indignant, all I had done was write a novel, you would have thought I had killed someone judging by his questions.

The present interview, however, wasn't live, and it would probably be slanted towards the book's good review, so I had nothing to fear. Nevertheless I was nervous, and on my way there, through the rain-glistening streets, with all the car lights diffused in the grey daylight, I considered what I was going to say. Inside the café someone stood up, I guessed he had to be the journalist, his name was Stang, we chatted for more than an hour and it went fantastically well, I talked and talked about literature, Norwegian and international, about my own book, what my aim was, well, it was to escape from the minimalistic, into the maximalistic, something bold and striking, baroque, *Moby Dick*, but not in an epic way, what I had tried to do was take the little novel, about one person, where there is not much external action, it is all internal, and extend it into an epic format, do you understand what I mean?

He nodded and wrote, wrote and nodded.

I was excited when I bought *Dagbladet* next day.

But the interview was short, it said I was proud of and pleased with the newspaper review, and that I had read *Dagbladet* ever since I was twelve years old.

I cycled up to the university and knocked on the door of Eirik's office.

'You've read *Dagbladet* ever since you were twelve, I see,' he said and laughed. 'And that's something to *boast* about!'

I sat down on a chair and he could see I was actually pretty shattered by the interview, I came across as an idiot, a completely deranged numpty, 'proud and pleased', my God, I was so ashamed that I didn't know where to look.

'Probably doesn't make the slightest bit of difference,' he said.

'No, maybe not,' I said. 'But everyone will read it. What a bloody fool I am!'

'You aren't a fool though, of course,' Eirik said. 'Take it easy now.'

'I'm beginning to wonder,' I said. 'I did *say* what he's written in the review.'

'Bit more subtlety required for interviews, that's all,' Eirik said. 'Then it'll be fine.'

Eirik was the type who had something to say about everything. Not in any vague or ungrounded way, he was well read about everything between heaven and earth, and for me he was a boon during these months, in the same way that Espen and Tore had been before, because he had read the novel and I used what he said about it shamelessly, such as it was an 'auto-geography', in all my interviews, of which there were now more and more. I sat down in Hotel Terminus and talked or I invited them home and sat at the sitting-room table and talked, and when Tonje came home I talked about everything I had talked about. Reading these same interviews, I burned with shame. I lay awake at night squirming at the thought of what an idiot I was. If nothing happened for a few weeks it felt like a complete void. I wanted more, and when more came it was always terrible. At the same time I was also being invited to a variety of events. I went to Kristiansand for a reading with someone called Bjarte Breiteig and someone called Pål Gitmark Eriksen, they had also made their debuts that autumn and held Tor Ulven in the very highest esteem, it turned out after a few minutes' conversation. They were so enthusiastic and in tune with each other that I saw them as literature's answer to Joe and Frank Hardy. As we were about to set foot on stage there were four people in the audience. I knew one, he was one of my old *gymnas* teachers, but when I went up to him afterwards he said he was there because he was good friends with the family of one of the other writers. I did a reading at Hotel Terminus, everyone I knew in Bergen had come, the room was packed, but I had to perform without a microphone and without a stage. I stood in the middle of the floor, it was like reading to people in your sitting room at home, and when I did there was a passage in which the main protagonist, Henrik, sees someone mimicking him. I began to blush because I imagined everyone would be thinking I was Henrik and the description of the mimicry was a description of me while I was reading. I blushed, lost my rhythm, squirmed like a worm on a hook, and this with friends present, they must have thought I was an even bigger loser than they had ever imagined because this was public, this was where I really had to sparkle, and all I could think of was that the mimicry was becoming a mimicry of me now and I read faster and faster to finish.

After the reading someone in the audience put up his hand. This was a so-called literary salon, this was normal practice.

'Now Knausgård may not be the world's greatest reader,' he said, 'but I have to tell those of you who haven't read this novel yet: it is really good.'

He had round spectacles and big old-style radical hair and wanted to help me. But the reading comment smarted because I had been hoping all my thoughts had been confined to my own head.

Afterwards he came up to me. He had an idea for a film and was wondering if I would write the manuscript for it. He explained what the idea was, producing lots of documents and pictures, I said it was extremely interesting and very topical while inwardly I consigned him to hell, never to show his face again.

I also did a reading at a Sunday event in Bergen, the town's leading lights were gathered, the stage acts were a potpourri, among them was a revue artist who directed traffic off a ferry to music, people were screaming with laughter. There was one number with semi-naked women dancing with top hats and sticks. Then there was me. I had bought myself a nice new Hugo Boss suit. Tonje had told me categorically to say a few words before I began reading. I stepped onto the stage.

'I'm going to read a text about death,' I said.

Some people in the audience started giggling. They didn't stop, not even when I was reading, and it spread. Death, ha ha ha. I could understand them, I was a self-important pretentious young writer who thought he knew something about the big issues in life.

I attended what was termed a book-bath in one of the Vestfold towns, with a crime writer who had also made his debut that year.

I puffed myself up and spoke as if I were Dante to the twelve or thirteen people who had turned out. Afterwards the crime writer refused to exchange books with me.

What was the point of all this? Flying all over Norway to read for ten minutes to four people? Talking smugly about literature to twelve people? Saying stupid things in the newspapers and burning with shame the day after?

Had I been able to write then this might not have mattered. But I couldn't, I wrote and deleted, wrote and deleted. At the weekend we often used to visit Tonje's mother or brother, go to Café Opera, Garage or Kvarteret, unless we went to the cinema or rented videos. The social scene was different now from when we had been students. A lot of people had moved away, and those who remained worked or were not as flexible as they had been. They had started treating me differently now I was someone, and I hated this. The meaning of everything had disappeared, that was what had happened.

In March my novel won the Critics' Prize. When they rang up and told me, I had just got myself entangled in a minor email nightmare, at first I had written something stupid, then I had tried to repair the damage, and then it had become even more stupid and impossible to repair, a third email was out of the question. This was all I could take in. Tonje told me to pull myself together, this was a big prize, imagine if I had been told this two years ago, and I agreed, but it didn't help, what would he think when he received the second email?

I invited Yngve and Tonje to the award ceremony, they were sitting at a table at the back when I stepped up to receive the prize. The little storm of camera clicks that met me was fantastic. Geir Gulliksen said a few words, I was touched and didn't know where to look. Afterwards we went to Theatercafé with the publishing house people, initially I was ill at ease and said next to nothing, but luckily I warmed to the occasion. At the Savoy I met Kjartan

Fløgstad, he had been nominated for the prize, my first inclination was to apologise to him for winning. Instead I asked him if he remembered me interviewing him. No, he didn't, he said with a smile, had I? He suggested we exchange books and then he rejoined his friends. By the time we got to Lorry I was well gone and when I spotted Ole Robert Sunde at a table I immediately went over and sat down. He was with a woman. They were also good and drunk. Suddenly she leaned over to me, took my face between her hands and gave me a lingering kiss. Ole Robert Sunde said nothing, just averted his eyes. I stood up horrified and returned to our table.

In May, at the literature festival in Lillehammer, where I was attending a seminar with other debut authors, I met Ole Robert Sunde again. He was sitting at a table in the festival hall on the final evening. On seeing me, he shouted in a loud voice, 'There's our Knausgård! He's good-looking, but he can't fucking write!'

My primary reaction was confusion. What was this? An insult and not a petty one. The tone may have been jocular, but this was obviously something he had on his mind. At any rate, he shouted out the same thing on several occasions that evening. And, the second time, as I passed a few metres from his table on my way to the toilet, he shouted, 'Knausgård's writing is so po-oor! But he is good-looking!' I didn't do anything then either. Quite the contrary, when he beckoned to me on my return, I went over to his table. There were two women standing beside him. 'Here's our Knausgård,' he said. Then, to the women, 'Isn't he good-looking? Look.' And he grabbed my hands. 'Look at his hands! So big. And you know what that means, don't you?' The next moment he grabbed my crotch. I could feel his fingers on my dick and balls. 'There's something else which is big!' He laughed. Even then I did nothing. Mumbled some comment or other, extricated myself and left. The incident was unpleasant while it lasted because he came so close to me in a purely physical sense – actually he is the first and still the only man to grope me – but it didn't bother me, the only impact it had was surprise. I knew some people considered me good-looking so that wasn't a revelation, and as for my writing being poor . . . well, that was possible, but it can't have been *that* bad, after all the novel had been accepted by a publishing house and it had been published. The only new element, apart from the intimidation, was the underlying implication that there was an *essential difference* in the literature I produced and what Ole Robert Sunde wrote. At that time I no longer read his books, but that didn't mean I wasn't aware of his intellectual stature. My literary identity when *Out of the World* was published was high modernism, under the umbrella of which came such Norwegian writers as Ole Robert Sunde, Svein Jarvoll, Jon Fosse, Tor Ulven and early Jan Kjærstad. But in Lillehammer six months had passed, my book was selling well, I had given one fatuous interview to newspapers after another, said asinine things on the radio, been on TV, performed in libraries and bookshops, and slowly I was beginning to realise that the image I had of myself as a writer might not match the image others had. Stig Sæterbakken had, for example, called Tore Renberg and me Faldbakken & Faldbakken in a readers' column in *Dagbladet*, Liv Lundberg had hissed with contempt at us when we went to Tromsø for a reading and afterwards we sat together at a party; everything we said during the night angered her and in the end she even went so far as to spit at us. And then there were Ole Robert Sunde's shouted insults in Lillehammer, which of course everyone heard. That really took the wind out of my sails. I went to Kristiansand to write, it had worked once before, now I would try again. The same area, the same atmosphere, a continuation of the same novel. I managed one page, emailed it to Nora, who had read *Out of the World* before it was published and had been enthusiastic and who also had a collection of powerful poetry to her name, *Slaktarmøte*. She emailed me back and said that unfortunately she didn't think it was so good, especially the image I had worked on for so long, of a water sprinkler that waved like a hand, which she considered particularly weak.

I wondered if Hanne might still be living in Kristiansand and, if so, whether to call her. I decided not to. I contacted Jan Vidar, it was a long time since I had seen him, we went out, a stunningly beautiful girl, perhaps twenty-five, blonde, came over to me and asked if I was Karl Ove Knausgård. I said yes and I went home with her, she lived not very far from where I'd had a bedsit as a sixteen-year-old, in a basement flat under her parents' house. She was curvy and lovely, but as I stood there in the middle of the night, well drunk, fortunately I realised what was about to happen and halted my advances, she made tea, I kept my distance and talked about dad's death, of all things. As I left I felt like the idiot I was, but I was also happy, it had been a close shave. I loved Tonje, I didn't want to ruin our relationship, it was the only blessing I had.

In the winter I went to the archipelago of Bulandet, I had rented a house on a little island where I would stay to write for three months. The island was so small that I could walk from end to end in ten minutes. The sea lay straight ahead, the winter storms were as wonderful as they were terrible. Five other people lived on the island, one died while I was there, I saw the ambulance take him one morning, it was snowing, four figures stood on the quay as the paramedics carried the stretcher on board.

I wrote nothing of any use. I went fishing every day, I read for a couple of hours, then I worked all evening and night. The results were worthless, but at some point surely it would have to flow, wouldn't it? Or was I a one-book writer? Had I shot my bolt?

Geir Gulliksen rang me on my mobile, he said my novel had been bought by an English publisher. I imagined English journalists coming out here to interview me, their photos of me standing with my fishing rod by the stormy sea in the *Guardian*, *The Times*, the *Independent* and the *Daily Telegraph*.

I went up to northern Norway and rented a run-down shack in Lofoten so that I could write. Nothing.

Then something freed up. John Erik Riley rang me and asked if I had anything for *Vinduet*. I said I would see and get back to him. I probably had four or five hundred pages' worth of openings to novels, I read through them, found one that might be usable and worked on it as a short text, not a novel.

It was published on their website a few days later.

FIRE

Fire belongs to the group of phenomena that has never undergone any evolution. Change is therefore alien to its form, it will not be moved in any direction by the many fluctuations of its settings, it rests in its own completeness. Fire is perfect. But fire's unique feature, that which sets it apart from many of the other unchanging phenomena that exist, is that it has managed to detach itself from the tyranny of time and place. While water is doomed to be situated in a particular place for ever, in some form or other, as air and mountains also are, fire has this remarkable ability to cease existing, quite simply – not only to disappear from view, to go into hiding, but indeed to allow itself to be extinguished – only to reappear exactly as before, in a new place, in a new time. For us, this makes fire difficult to understand, used as we are to regarding the world as a coherent system of continuous events, which at countless different speeds – from the tree's endlessly slow growth to the rapid fall of raindrops – progress temporally. Fire stands outside this system and that must have been why in the Old Testament the Divine revealed itself to man in the form of a flame: the form of revelation and fire are the same. The Divine also has this ability to reveal itself suddenly, in its complete form, only then to disappear. The Divine also has this mysterious alien and merciless nature, which causes us to both fear and admire it. Anyone who has witnessed a house burning will know what I mean. Fire moves through the rooms and consumes everything in its path, the eerie roar of the flames, the blind will that only hours ago was non-existent, but which has suddenly returned and wreaks havoc in front of our eyes with such abandon you would have thought it was happening for the very first time.

But now, in this, our world of fire alarms, sprinkler systems, fire engines with ladders, breathing equipment, hydrants, hose pipes and powder extinguishers, no one fears fire any longer. It has been brought under control and takes its place in the world in much the same way that wild animals in zoos do, something we look at when we are relaxing, such as a fire in the hearth or a flame on a candle; states in which its former abandon is only seen as a residue: the crackle of wood, the swirl of flames in a draught, the shower of sparks against the wall as we push the logs closer together. And the Divine? Who talks about the Divine nowadays? You can't. It is impossible to talk about the Divine without feeling ridiculous. There is now a sense of shame attached to talking about the Divine. And as shame is based on a disparity between two entities – most often the person you are to yourself in relation to the person you are to others – it would not be unreasonable to assume that the Divine's somewhat comical status is due to the fact that it is out of sync with the era we live in and thus joins the succession of past customs and objects that time has left behind, such as airships, top hats, polite forms of address, the chamber pot and the electric typewriter. Things disappear, new things appear, the world slowly changes. Then we wake up one day, we rub the sleep from our eyes, draw the curtain aside and look out: clear air, bright sunshine, sparkling snow. We amble into the kitchen, switch on the radio, start the coffee machine, butter some bread, eat, drink, take a shower, dress, go to the hall, put on a hat and coat, lock the door and set off in this Østland dormitory town towards the station, which every morning is crowded with commuters. They stand on the platform with rolled-up newspapers under their arms and bags in their hands, strolling up and down in the cold, yawning, staring at the clock, peering down the railway line. Then, when the train thunders into the station, they form small queues in front of the doors, board a carriage, find a seat, fold up their coats, place them on the luggage rack and sit down again. Oh, the tiny pleasures of commuting! Take out a ticket, place it on the armrest, unfold a newspaper and start reading as the train slowly glides out of the station. Occasionally raise your eyes to look out: the blue sky, flashes of sun on the bonnets of cars driving along the road across the river, the smoke from farmhouses in the valley, snow-capped mountains. The sudden noise as the door is opened, the bang as it is closed again, the conductor's voice approaching your seat. You give him your ticket, he scribbles his mark, you carry on reading. The next time you look out you have entered a forest. Dark green spruce trees huddle together on both sides of the track. Their branches exclude the light, but you think it is the opposite, they are preventing the darkness from rising, as if remnants of the night are still here, along the snow-covered ground beneath the trees in the forest you are speeding through. Sometimes the forest extends into small copses, you see fences, glistening wires, small piles of timber. Then, as you turn your head back and look down at the newspaper on your knees, the train crashes. The carriage where you are sitting folds like paper, you find yourself pinned up against the seat in front and lose consciousness. When you come to a few minutes later you can't move. Diesel from the locomotive has sprayed into the carriage, you can hear the roar of the flames, passengers screaming, you try to free yourself but to no avail. In the snow beneath the rails passengers from the rear carriages file past. You can hear the flames approaching your seat, you are trapped and can only wait until the fire reaches you. Outside, flakes of ash settle on the snow. Soon the first ambulances arrive. You can smell melting plastic, you can smell burning diesel. You sit there unable to move, in the escalating heat, until it becomes unbearable and in your helplessness you pray to your God, the Almighty, the Creator of Heaven and Earth, whom you have never been closer to than at this moment, for this is how He reveals himself to us now, in his purest and most beautiful form: a blazing train in the forest.

So should I be writing short texts?
For lack of anything better, I started there.
I wrote one about dad. Yes, almost everything I did was about him, in one form or another, countless were the variants I had of two brothers, Klaus and Henrik, who travelled back to their hometown to bury him and went around cleaning the dreadful house where he had died. But this one came to nothing. I didn't believe in it.

Days passed, months passed, it was two years since I had made my debut, I had produced nothing, one night I was in the sitting room, drunk, and decided to fly to Kristiansand as soon as it was morning, I had received some emails from a girl who lived in the skerries off Kristiansand, in one she had written that she wasn't wearing anything, when I was drunk that was enough for me, and I *was* capable of this kind of stunt, even if I was broke, you just paid with a credit card. But the closer the morning came, the more sober I became, it was a crazy idea, typical of how I thought when I was drunk and I went to bed, where Tonje had been asleep all this time while I had been going la-la in the sitting room.

Darkness descended.

I had everything I wanted. I was a writer and lived off writing, at least until my stipend ran out, I was married to a beautiful woman whom I loved and who let me do as I pleased. She didn't object when I said I was going to be away for two months, she said nothing when I went out at night and came home plastered at five in the morning, and she never threatened to leave me even though I had been depressed for two years and obviously hated myself.

How could that be?

It wasn't the whole picture. I was good for her too, she needed me, and we had a good life together in Bergen, both when we were alone and when we were together with others, the circle of family and friends around us, so if I was filled with inner despair it had nothing to do with life as it unfolded around me, with the trivial incidents that make up all lives and can suddenly shine bright in the dusk of meaninglessness: the door goes, she comes home, bends over and takes off her shoes, looks at me and smiles, her face is magical and childlike. She pours paint from a five-litre can into a small receptacle, clambers up on a chair and starts painting the moulding over the window wearing a workman's overalls stained with paint. She snuggles up to me on the sofa, we watch a film, tears run down her cheeks, I laugh at her and she laughs through her tears. There are thousands of such moments, lost the second they occur yet still present because they are what form a relationship, the particular way *we* stayed together, which was the same as everyone's, though different, it was her and me, no one else, it was us, we dealt with everything that came at us as well as we could, but the darkness in me thickened, the joy in me evaporated, I no longer knew what I wanted or what to do, only that I was standing still, I was stuck, this was how it felt, as though I wasn't formed on the inside, I was only a mould shaped by everything on the outside. I walked around like a kind of imprint, a multitude of incidents and activities pressed tight against a mould, completely hollow on the inside. At night, when I was out, the longing for something else was all that existed, I could do anything and in the end I did. I was at Café Opera, there were lots of people I knew, there was a party afterwards, I drank steadily and was completely out of it, but it helped to drink, I got into the mood, sat chatting with Tomas, whom I had met some years earlier and immediately liked but didn't often chat with, we just exchanged the odd word every once in a while in one of Bergen's bars. At five we decided o take a taxi to his and carry on drinking there, him, a friend and me. While I was waiting for the taxi a woman from the party came down to the front door, she must have been in her mid-thirties, she had looked at me several times during the course of the evening, I had been evasive, I hadn't looked at her, hadn't spoken to her, but now this was different, I went over and asked if she would like to come too, she said yes, the taxi arrived, we got in, she sat close to me, I had my hand on her thigh but sat still otherwise, the other two didn't notice what was going on, in the town centre we tumbled out of the taxi and went up to Tomas's flat, at the top of a large block, I had been there several times, always at night, always drunk. There was a balcony outside where once, with many others, we had watched two people fucking in the backyard, she had been lying over the bonnet of a car, he had stoked away from behind, I had gone in to chat with someone, had a bit more to drink, gone back, they were still at it. When at last they finished we applauded. He had bowed to us while she had grabbed her clothes and sped off. Tomas was a writer, his face was handsome and sensitive and very distinctive, as soon as you saw him you realised he wasn't like anyone else, he was an exception, boundlessly generous and kind, deeply serious and passionate about what he was doing, independent in that rare way, you only find a handful of such people in every generation. He had done some boxing and fencing, he surrounded himself with women in an enthusiastic boyish fashion, and he was the only person apart from Tore I knew who had read *À la recherche du temps perdu*. His style was elegant, he sought perfection and beauty, and in that, as in almost everything else, he was my antithesis. He led tonight, he opened the door and let us in, put on music, produced some whisky, we were going to discuss Proust, and I did but not for long, I was beyond everything, all I had in my head was her, who was also there, sitting on a chair, some distance away, I wanted her, so I went over to her, she sat on my lap, we smooched, my hands were all over her, I didn't care that all this was going on in front of Tomas and his friend, this was everything now, she was everything, I lifted her and stood up, took her hand and went into the bedroom, Tomas's bedroom, I closed the door and tore off her clothes, pulled the two sides of her jacket apart without bothering about the buttons, kissed her, undid her skirt and flung it off, pulled down her tights, she was nearly naked now, I unbuttoned my trousers and let them fall, threw myself on top of her, out of my mind with desire, without a thought for anything else, no, somewhere I was thinking I want this and I'm doing it, this is me who wants it, why shouldn't I do it? She groaned and I shouted, I came, I got up to go, she lay there watching me and said I mustn't go, she wanted more, I thought OK, lay down on her again, but it was no good and I got dressed, went into the sitting room without a second look, grabbed my jacket and went down into the street, flagged a taxi, gave our address, paid him five minutes later, unlocked the door, let myself in, undressed and got into bed beside Tonje.

When I woke I was in hell. It was completely dark outside. Tonje was in the sitting room watching TV, I could hear it. My clothes, which lay in a pile beside the bed, smelled of perfume. I smelled of sex. The thought of what I had done, the guilt and the shame and the angst, were so great there was nothing else. It was bottomless. I was paralysed, I couldn't move, I lay there in the darkness knowing the only way out of this was death. I hadn't moved since I woke up, it was as though the darkness was pressing down on me, it hurt so much I wanted to scream, but I lay there, motionless, perfectly still, from the sitting room came the sound of the TV, and then she walked through and stopped in the open doorway.

I lay with my eyes closed, breathing heavily.

'You still asleep?' she said. 'It's almost six. Can't you get up so we can enjoy *some* of the day?'

'I'm very worried,' I said. 'I was so drunk.'

'Poor you,' she said. 'But let's walk down and rent a film, shall we? I can make pizza.'

'OK,' I said.

'Good!' she said.

She left, I sat up in bed, still drunk. I took my clothes with me into the bathroom, put them in the washing machine with some other clothes and switched it on. Then I had a shower. I was in hell, this was hell. But I would cope. If I could get through today, and the next day and the one after, I would be fine.

I should go in and tell her, I thought. This was too much for me to bear. Her feelings were genuine and pure, she was honest in what she did, and then she was with me, who was so bad and did the worst things. If I told her what I had done she would leave me. I couldn't risk that. Better to lie for all eternity. Lying was something I was really bad at, but now I would have to. I would have to lie every single day for the rest of my life, but I would cope, I would.

It was good we were going out, the telephone was here, and it was conceivable that both Tomas and the woman might ring.

We set off downhill to Danmarksplass, where the big video shop was.

'Was it fun last night?' she said.

I shook my head.

'No, not really. Pretty run-of-the-mill. But there were lots of people I knew there.'

She asked who and I told her.

'You didn't get involved in anything, did you?' she said.

I flushed with shame and horror, my face was scarlet, but I forced myself to continue walking at my usual speed and held my head still, it was dark, she couldn't see.

'No, no,' I said.

'But why did you come back so late? It was eight when you came in.'

'I went back to Tomas's place after the party, me and a friend of his. We drank whisky and discussed literature. That, in fact, was pretty good.'

We rented two films and bought the ingredients for a pizza. When we returned the light on the answerphone was flashing. I hadn't considered that. It was worse because it would be played through the speakers, into the room, so if the message was about what happened she would hear.

She went into the kitchen, organised things, started frying the minced meat, and I pressed the button on the answerphone, hoping she would be too busy to notice.

It was Tomas. He said nothing specific, only that we could talk if I wanted.

'Who was it?' Tonje said, standing in the doorway with the spatula in her hand.

'Tomas,' I said. 'He just wanted to catch up.'

I deleted the message and went in and sat down on the sofa.

The next day she went to work as usual. I rang Ole, I had to talk to someone, I couldn't deal with this on my own. We arranged to go to the film club at Verftet, where they were showing a David Lean film.

Most of our friends in Bergen were shared, I couldn't tell any of them about this. But Ole, who had got divorced and moved back from Norwich, was outside the circle. Yes, he knew Tonje, they liked each other, but primarily his relationship was with me. He was still translating Samuel Johnson, mostly for his own and for interest's sake, he had dropped out of university and was training as a nurse instead. Once he had taken me down through all the subterranean corridors beneath the hospital, I was going to write about them, and I was far more fascinated by them than I anticipated. It was its own little world down there under the ground. Ole and I went to see the Lean film. It was about infidelity, I sat in my seat in agony, I was in hell. Afterwards we went for a beer at Wesselstuen and I told him everything. What I wanted to know, what I needed his advice about, was whether I should confess and tell and trust she would forgive me or keep mum, pretend everything was hunky-dory and let it pass of its own accord, I hoped it would.

'Don't even think about saying anything,' Ole said. 'What purpose would it serve? Then she would have the burden as well. You would be putting the responsibility on her. But it's yours. You did it. You can't undo anything, *you* did it. In this sense, it doesn't matter whether she knows or not.'

'But then I would be deceiving her. I would be lying to her.'

'You *have* deceived her. Words and actions are not the same thing.'

'No, you're right,' I said. 'But this is just the worst experience of my life. I have never hurt so much. It's absolutely indescribable. It's so painful it feels as if it would be better to shoot myself.'

'Have you got a gun then?'

'Ha ha. It's all I can think about. It's always there, from the moment I wake up till the moment I go to sleep. There's nothing in my head except what I did. And then Tonje . . .'

'It'll go. It sounds cynical, but it will go.'

'I hope so,' I said.

But it didn't. Whenever the telephone rang, fear flared up in me. I took out the plug as often as I could without arousing suspicion, at least in that way I could have some kind of peace, knowing no one could ring. When we chose films in the video shop I always read the blurb to see whether there was anything about infidelity, if there was, I made up some excuse for not wanting to see it. I carefully scrutinised the TV listings so I knew what I could see and what I couldn't. If there was any infidelity I watched something else. But despite this sometimes the topic cropped up, people were talking about it, and then my head burned with shame and I tried to distract attention by changing the subject. I was stiff and unnatural, it was strange she didn't notice, but I presumed the idea that I might do something like this was so far from her perceptual world that it never occurred to her. My bad conscience was a constant, my sense of guilt towards her a constant, whatever we did I was false and a liar, a cheat, a bad person, and the more affectionate she was to me, the closer she came, the worse I felt. I acted cool, but everything had been destroyed, everything had become a game.

We bought some property. Someone at Tonje's workplace wanted to sell, we got it cheap, it was in Minde, near NRK. It was a three-storey detached house built in the early 1900s, we bought the top two floors, one measuring a hundred and ten square metres, where we lived, and a smaller flat in the loft, which we rented out. I polished the floors and oiled them; Tonje painted and wallpapered. We took the doors off their hinges and stripped them, we started to get quotes for the bathroom, which we wanted renovated. Afterwards we would tackle the kitchen. We liked the flat, it was a bargain. I had a spacious office, there were also two sitting rooms and a bedroom, a balcony and a large garden. Life was normal, the future was ours, we began to talk about children. I couldn't write, four years had now gone by since my debut, I had nothing to show for them and probably never would have. But I carried on trying, lowered my head and typed away. Every time the telephone rang a chill went through me. It would never disappear. Whenever I laid eyes on Tonje or she smiled at me I was overcome by pangs of conscience. But they passed, I coped, days passed, perhaps in the end they would go. Hans and Sigrid had come back to Bergen, we spent a lot of time with them, took a flight to London together, had meals at each other's places, and with their friends, this was a social circle, this was a life. Hans and Sigrid moved into a house high above Sandviken, I went there one day to give Hans a hand with painting, it was September, the sky was clear and blue, in the fjord a lifeboat was practising a manoeuvre, an enormous shower of spray shot up skywards and glistened in the sun. It was one of those days when everything was open and the town lies there, in the middle of the world, beneath a vast sky, and you think life is worth living. Suddenly Tonje rang, she said we had to turn on the radio, there had been an attack on the World Trade Center, a plane had flown into one tower. We did, we stood there painting in the sunshine as reporters tried to describe what was happening and what had happened. I couldn't visualise anything, it was all so un-clear, Hans said it was probably bin Laden, which was the first time I had heard his name. I went home, Tonje sat watching TV, they showed images of the plane flying into the tower again and again and then the building collapsed. We watched all evening. The next day we flew to Paros, where we would be for a week. We buzzed around on a moped, Tonje on the pillion with her arms around me, we swam and read, made love and ate out in the evenings, wan-dered around the wonderful streets, one day we went to Antiparos, where I had been thirteen years before and I remembered every-thing and laughed. On that island out there I had sat writing a novel on my pad, I read Ulf Lundell and had ambitions of being a writer. All on my own out there, and when I went for a swim I was overcome by a sudden fear of sharks. Here, in the Mediterranean!

Oh, it was great. But at home things continued as always, autumn passed, I couldn't write, Tonje worked, I gave a start whenever the telephone rang, expecting only nastiness. Several times someone had rung without speaking, that kind of thing goes on of course, but it was impossible for me not to connect it with what had happened almost a year ago.

Then, in February, I had a dream. I dreamed that I was standing in front of a bull, it was buried in the sand and struggling to get out. I had a sword in my hand. I slashed at the bull's neck. Its head fell off, but the bull kept fighting, it tore its way out of the sand and I woke up.

Something terrible was going to happen. I knew it was. The dream had told me.

But what?

My first thought was the woman who lived above us, she was young and had a permanent job, so we didn't see much of her, but as she was in the house I thought the attack might come from her, she would report me for molestation or something because she had become unstable and was fixated on me. I'd had this obsession for a while, it was totally without justification, rooted in my own bad conscience and mangled self-image, but with the dream as well I could imagine it happening.

The whole day passed. I worked in my study, Tonje came home, we ate, I went to my study to read, I had an armchair there, a little table with an ashtray and a cup of coffee, bookshelves circled the walls, one of my greatest pleasures was to sit looking at all the books, taking them out, browsing. Now I was reading Burton's *The Anatomy of Melancholy*. It was just after eleven, the house was silent, the streets outside still. I put a CD on the mini-stereo I had bought, Tortoise, I lit a cigarette, poured some coffee.

From the sitting room came the sound of the phone ringing, I just heard it, as if from a distance.

I switched off the stereo.

If someone was calling so late, it meant something had happened. Someone must have died. But who?

Tonje opened the door.

'Phone for you,' she said.

'Who is it?'

'He didn't say. Some friend or other I haven't met because he made a joke.'

'A joke?'

'Yes.'

I got up, went into the sitting room and picked up the phone. Tonje followed.

'Hello?' I said.

'Is that the rapist Karl Ove Knausgård?'

'What are you talking about?' I said. 'Who is it?'

Tonje had stopped, she was standing by the wall and looking at me.

'You know bloody well what I'm talking about. You raped my girlfriend a year ago.'

'No, I did not.'

'But you know what I'm referring to?'

'Yes, but it wasn't rape.'

As I said that I glanced across at Tonje. Her face was white. She was staring at me with large eyes. She almost stumbled back against the wall.

'Yes, it fucking was. And unless you admit it we'll be round your place right now. If you don't open the door, we'll smash it in. If you don't admit it then, we'll smash you in. We'll beat your face to pulp. Now, writer, do you admit it?'

'No. It wasn't rape. We went to bed together, I'll admit that. But it wasn't rape.'

Tonje's eyes stared and stared at me.

'It bloody was. She woke up with her clothes torn. How do you explain that? She's right here.'

'It wasn't rape. Whatever you say and whatever she's told you.'

'Then we're on our way up.'

'Let me talk to her.'

'If you admit you raped her.'

'It wasn't rape.'

'Well, then you can hear it from her own mouth.'

Seconds passed. I looked up. Tonje had left the room.

'Hello,' she said from the other end.

'Your boyfriend says it was rape,' I said. 'How can you say that? You were up for it as much as I was.'

'I don't remember anything. I woke up with all my clothes torn. I don't know what happened. It might not have been rape. But this has been terrible. So I told him and he wanted to drive up and get you. I managed to stop that. But they're off their heads.'

'They?' I said.

'Yes,' she said.

Apparently there were two of them, one was her ex-boyfriend, the other a writer I didn't know but had met many times.

'He says you aren't as good as everyone makes out,' she said.

'What's he got to do with this?'

'He's a friend.'

'OK,' I said. 'I can't have it said about me that I've raped someone. It wasn't rape. Tell them it wasn't rape.'

'It wasn't.'

'Are they still coming up here?'

'I don't know what they think now.'

'The best thing would be if we met,' I said. 'You, your boyfriend and me. So that we can talk about it.'

'Yes,' she said.

'What about tomorrow? Two o'clock in the café by the decorative art museum?'

'Yes, that's fine. I want to talk too. I've rung you several times, but your wife has always picked up.'

'See you,' I said and rang off.

At that moment Tonje came into the room, she must have been waiting. She glared at me.

'We need to talk,' I said.

We sat in my office. It was as though I had stepped into a zone, the light was all white, nothing existed beyond it. We talked about what had happened. I told her about the night in detail. Why didn't you say anything? Tonje kept saying. Why didn't you say anything? Why didn't you say anything? I apologised, I said I hadn't meant it, I asked for her forgiveness, but we were both in a completely different place, this wasn't about forgiveness, this was about what we had together, which had been so wonderful that it was ruined. The way all of this had come out, the brutal and uncontrolled manner of it, had given her a shock, she was in shock, her face was still ashen, but she wasn't crying, she was just attempting to grasp the significance of it. I was also in shock, the white light seared out everything else, all that was left was the terrible deed. I told her it wasn't rape. Of course, she said, I know, that's not what this is about. For me though it was also what this was about, anything could happen, she could go to the police, they might come here and arrest me. No one in the world would believe me, I would be convicted as a rapist, the worst thing that could befall me, the greatest ignominy, for all the future, for the rest of my life. What was more, I was in the public eye, if the press got hold of it I would be hung out to dry on every single front page in the whole country. I didn't give that any thought then though as we sat talking in my study, it was what I had done to Tonje that counted. She didn't cry, but she had withdrawn, she was deep inside herself, shaken to the very bottom of her soul.

The next day I walked into town, which had totally disappeared, it had been erased, the thought of what I had done was all that existed.

They weren't in the café. I waited for an hour, they didn't come.

I rang Tomas and brought him up to date. He was furious. He said he knew Arild, which was his name, her ex, he was a criminal, a drug addict, he was nothing to be afraid of, but if you like, Karl Ove, I can go and pay him a visit and frighten him so much he'll never contact you again. I'll knock him senseless if necessary. Shall I? Let's wait a bit, I said, and see what happens. If he contacts me again you could perhaps have a word with him. I'll do that. You can rely on me. That kind of person is just evil.

When I returned, the flat wonderfully illuminated by the glow of the winter sun, I heard Tonje running water into the bath. I didn't want to disturb her, I went into the sitting room and looked up at the mountain opposite.

The sound of running water stopped.

A long drawn-out heart-rending sob came from her.

The despair in her sobs was so great I cried.

But I couldn't console her, couldn't help her. They never rang again. I never heard any more from them. But our relationship was ruined anyway, and perhaps it had been from the night I did what I did, nevertheless we decided I should go away for some time. I rang the people I had rented the house from on Bulandet the year before, it was empty, I could move in straight away, and I did, caught the boat to Askvoll, then to Bulandet, the westernmost point in the country, far into the sea, that was where I was going to be.

I didn't write, I fished, slept and read. I was distraught, not temporarily but deeply, that was how it felt, it didn't get better, it didn't change, every day I woke to bottomless despair. It was purely a matter of endurance. That was all I focused on. I had to endure. I read Olav H. Hauge's diaries and that was an enormous solace, I had no idea why, but they were, for the few hours I read them I had peace. Every time the ferry docked I stood by the window and watched to see if anyone got off – perhaps Tonje will come, I thought. We hadn't arranged anything, all we had agreed on that we needed time to ourselves, each in our own place, and I came here. I didn't know if our relationship was over, if she wanted to separate or if she was yearning for me and wanted us to carry on. I bore all the guilt, I didn't want to burden her, I kept away, she would have to work out what she wanted to do herself. I watched the ferry and hoped. But she didn't come. Once I was convinced it was her getting off, I jumped into my boots and dashed over to meet her, but I immediately saw it wasn't and walked back.

Espen rang, he was going to Bergen, I longed for someone to talk to, caught the ferry, met him, we had a few beers, I slept in his hotel room. While we were out we met one of Tonje's friends. She looked as if she had seen a ghost when she spotted me. The following day I returned, and in a strange way it felt like home, this tiny little island far out in the sea, the yellow 1950s house on the promontory where I was staying. I loved the sky there, it was so vast and dramatic, and I loved the few days when there was sun and tranquillity. I loved standing on the quay and looking down into the compelling fresh clear green water, where long strips of seaweed stood vertically and fish swam past and crabs moved sideways. Starfish, mussels, the whole rich sub-aquatic world. A plastic bag could drift out, deep in the water. I also loved to gaze at the quay, the small warehouses, all the equipment, all the yarn and all the buckets and boxes and cans. But most of all I loved the sky, the way the clouds slid through the darkness at night, like ships on their way to land or towered up before a storm, which always came from the west and made the entire house shake and quiver and gasp and throb.

On all my fishing trips I saw things, once an otter that was resident in the vicinity; it had made a little slide in the snow and would dive down it every so often. Sometimes I saw it swimming towards me, a little black head just above the surface of the water.

One night it ran at full speed across the veranda outside my house. I liked the otter, I was happy when I saw it, it was like a friend.

One morning the whole island was covered with birds. They made an unparalleled commotion. Then they took off, there were several hundred of them, a cloud rising into the air, they circled the island a few times then slowly landed, like a carpet. At night they stood still in the darkness. I thought about them before I went to sleep, the silence of the living is quite different from the silence of the dead, and woke to their din early next morning.

Winter turned to spring. I didn't have a television, didn't have any newspapers, ate nothing but fish, crackers and oranges, and all I thought about, when I wasn't thinking about Tonje, was that I had to be a good person. I had to be a good person. I had to do everything I could to be a good person. I mustn't be a coward any more, I mustn't be evasive and vague, I had to be honest, upright, clear, sincere. I had to look people in the eye, I had to stand up for who I was, what I thought and what I did. I had to treat Tonje better, if we were still together. I mustn't be grumpy, mustn't be ironic, mustn't be sarcastic, but rise above it and always keep the bigger picture in mind. She was an exceptional person, absolutely unique, and I mustn't take her for granted.

Most of all I wanted action. To do something. But what?

I considered committing suicide, simply swimming off into the sea, it gave me a fine tingling feeling, it had an appeal, but I would never do it, giving up wasn't in my nature. I was the kind to endure. No one had said you couldn't become a better person through endurance.

I wrote letters to Tonje but didn't send them. I didn't receive any, didn't hear anything and in the end I returned.

We hadn't seen each other for three months. I rang her from the hill below the house.

'Karl Ove, have you come back?' she said in that voice of hers which was so intimate.

'Yes,' I said. 'I'm outside.'

'Are you here?'

I unlocked the door, went up the stairs, she came into the hall, behind her was a colleague. Oh, fucking hell, I thought, has he moved in? Are they an item?

They weren't. He had come by to fix the sliding door in the bathroom for her. She was thin and seemed sad. I was also thin, and there was no joy to be found in me.

We talked for days. She wanted to carry on, I wanted to carry on, and we carried on. House, friends, family, Bergen. I wrote during the day, she worked for NRK. Everything was as before. The summer came and went, Christmas came and went, we talked about having children but didn't take the final step. One evening I received a phone call from a stranger. He said he had been married to the woman I had been unfaithful with. They had children together. Now he wanted sole responsibility for the children. There was going to be a lawsuit. He wondered whether I would like to testify. He said that she and her boyfriend had done the same to a priest: she'd had sex with him, he had rung the family and told them about it. The priest had been forced to resign, this man said, I didn't know what to believe, at first I thought it was some kind of trap, someone was recording the conversation, but he seemed genuine. In the end I said I couldn't help him. When I told Tonje about this she said it would have come out straight away, all the media checked events in the courts, if I had said yes, as I had considered doing, the papers would have run the headline FAMOUS NORWEGIAN WRITER (32) ACCUSED OF RAPE with enough information for readers to know who was meant.

I clung to my writing, sat in my study from morning till night, nothing. Journalists had stopped calling ages ago, on the rare occasion one did, it was to ask whether I would be interested in contributing to an article about writers' block or one-book writers. But in

February 2002 something happened. I had started another short text, located it in the nineteenth century but let everything that exists now exist then, and the scene was Tromøya yet it wasn't, a completely different story emerged, and in this parallel world, which resembled ours but wasn't, I had Yngve, dad and me taking a boat to Torungen one summer's night. I described the night as I remembered it with one exception: the seagull dad shone his torch on had a pair of small thin arm-like growths beneath its wings. They had once been angels, I had him say, and then I knew: this is a novel. Finally, a novel.

I was so excited. Suddenly I had bags of energy, went shopping and made food and chatted about everything under the sun, full of initiative with regard to Tonje: we could go there, do this, everything was possible again.

Tonje went to a seminar in Kristiansand, I had the whole day and night to write in, she came home three days later, wanted to go straight to a party, her band, made up of NRK staff, was going to play, she asked if I wanted to go with her, but I had to write, she went alone. After an hour I regretted my decision and went anyway, saw her playing the drums, I was moved for some reason, but when I went over to her afterwards and she was packing up the kit she was evasive, wouldn't look me in the eye and wouldn't talk. I knew that side of her, something was bothering her.

She carried the cymbal stands along the corridor, I had the snare drum in my hands, and I asked her to tell me what was up. I know there's something, so tell me what it is. I can see something's eating you.

'I wasn't going to tell you,' she said. 'But since you ask I will. I've been unfaithful.'

'In Kristiansand? Just now?'

'Yes.'

I looked at her. She looked at me.

I was angry. The thought that she had given herself to another man was terrible, but I was relieved too, now it wasn't only me at fault.

When we got home we sat in my office as we had done a year earlier. I was no longer in a state of shock, since what had happened, what she had done, was no more than an extension of what I had done, but it was as terrible.

'Why did you do it?' I said. 'I was so drunk I didn't know what I was doing. But you never do anything on impulse. You knew what you were doing.'

'I don't know. I think it's because you were suddenly so happy. Suddenly you were walking around beaming with happiness. You've been depressed for four years, ever since the autumn your father died and you made your debut, and it's been so hard, so little fun. I've tried, I've tried everything. And then you start writing and you're happy again! That was just so immensely provocative. It feels as if I have nothing to do with your life. It feels as if I'm on the outside. That was the last straw and, I thought, well, what the hell. And then I did it.'

I put my face in my hands.

I looked at her.

'What do we do now?' I said.

'I don't know.'

We went to bed, early next morning I packed a suitcase and travelled up to Yngve's, he had moved to Voss. I was there for two days, talked to him, he thought I should stay with her. We were quits. Tonje was a fantastic person, I shouldn't leave her.

I caught the train back to Tonje, we talked all night, I had decided to leave. I wanted to get away from everything. We kept everything open, it wasn't finished, nothing was definitive, but we both knew it was over, at least I did.

She accompanied me to the railway station.

She embraced me.

She cried.

I didn't cry, I put my arms around her and told her to take care of herself. We kissed, I got on board and as the train eased out of the station I watched Tonje walking down the platform and into the town alone.

I was on the night train to Oslo, everything I did on the journey was to avoid thinking. I read one newspaper after another, afterwards I read a novel by Ian Rankin, the first crime novel I had read for twenty years, until I was so tired I would fall asleep the instant I closed my eyes. In Oslo I bought another Rankin novel, changed trains, destination Stockholm this time, boarded and started to read.

That was how I left Bergen.